Praise for John Francome's previous novels:

'A taut and twisting plot gallops along all the way to the finish line' *Daily Express*

'The natural successor to Dick Francis' *Irish Times*

'Mr Francome is a natural storyteller' *New York Times*

'Thrills, twists and turns on and off the racecourse' *Irish Independent*

'Francome has produced his best thriller by far. An action-packed storyline that gallops to a thrilling end . . . Likely to get the thumbs-up from Dick Francis' *Racing Post*

'Look out, Dick Francis, here's Francome riding another winner' *Peterborough Evening Telegraph*

'Mr Francome adeptly teases to the very end and cleverly keeps a few twists up his sleeve until the closing chapters' *Country Life*

'Pacy racing and racy pacing . . . Francome has found his stride as a solo novelist' *Horse and Hound*

'Authentic, thrilling and compulsive' *Bookseller*

'Move over Dick Francis, here's competition' *Me* magazine

Stud Poker

John Francome

headline

First published in 1991
by HEADLINE BOOK PUBLISHING

First published in paperback in 1992
by HEADLINE BOOK PUBLISHING

This edition published in paperback in 2006
by HEADLINE BOOK PUBLISHING

A HEADLINE paperback

1

ISBN 0 7472 3754 9

Printed and bound in Great Britain by Clays Ltd, St Ives plc

Headline's policy is to use papers that are natural, renewable and
recyclable products and made from wood grown in sustainable
products. The logging and manufacturing processes are expected to
conform to the environmental regulations of the country of origin.

HEADLINE BOOK PUBLISHING
A division of Hodder Headline
338 Euston Road
London NW1 3BH

www.headline.co.uk
www.hodderheadline.com

ACKNOWLEDGEMENTS

The author is grateful to Terence Blacker for his help in the preparation of this manuscript.

Inspiration and information for the poker scenes in *Stud Poker* came from Anthony Holden's superb *Big Deal*, (Bantam Books, 1991).

Chapter 1

Like most jockeys' valets, Jim Wilson could read race-course rumour like a professional gambler could read a racecard. He knew what was true and what was bullshit. He knew the young jockeys who would still be in the weighing-room in ten years' time and those who would fade into obscurity after a season or two – or, as in most cases, a ride or two. He knew who was drinking, who was fighting a losing battle with the scales, who was in the pocket of the bookmakers. And, of course, he knew whose nerve had gone. There was something in the eyes of a jockey in those moments after he had weighed out for a novice chase and was waiting to be called to the paddock.

So when Jim Wilson, on a cold wet November morning, trudged through the car park at Plumpton racecourse carrying a suitcase full of breeches and saw Alex Drew sitting alone in his Audi Convertible with what appeared to be a fur coat on his lap, staring palely into space, he added the information to his vast storehouse of unofficial racing knowledge.

'Morning, Lex,' he called out, but Alex had seemed not to hear.

Jim glanced at his watch. Eleven-thirty. He was surprised to see Alex at the racecourse so early. His first ride was not until the fourth race and, until recently, he'd been one of the cool ones, turning up as late as possible in his flash car, exuding all the confidence of the young and talented.

Until recently. Wilson looked back at the Audi, parked in the far corner of the jockeys' car park. This season, something had happened to Alex. Two years ago, he had been no more than just another claiming jockey, an amateur with ambition. Last year, he had turned professional and a combination of luck – Ron Charlesworth's stable jockey had broken his leg in the first month of the season – and talent had marked him out as a possible future champion jockey. He had ridden over fifty winners, including a breathtaking success in the Champion Two Mile Chase at the National Hunt Festival on a horse of reckless brilliance called Spurgloss. Few, if any, of the top jockeys would have won on him.

But now something was wrong in the life of Alex Drew. Muttering to himself, the valet walked on to the racecourse, dismissing thoughts of Alex from his mind. Jockeys came, jockeys went. Promise turned to failure. It was life.

'He's gone.' Alex pulled back the mink coat and touched the blonde head that was resting on his lap.

'I was just beginning to enjoy it down there,' said Zena Wentworth, sitting up and checking her hair in the rear view mirror.

'Sorry.' Alex smiled palely. 'Jim's a bit of an old gossip. It's best to be careful.'

'Don't tell me jockeys aren't meant to be seen with girls before a race.' Zena put a well-manicured hand on Alex's thigh.

'Don't be daft.' Alex allowed a hint of irritation to enter his voice. Girls. That was a laugh. Zena Wentworth had stopped being a girl some time ago. In fact, even when she was a girl, to judge by some of the stories she had told him, she was doing wild, womanly things. 'It's just that talking to an owner's wife in the corner of the car park – people might misunderstand.'

'Spare rides?'

'Something like that.' A car drove by and parked some way in front of them. Two jockeys emerged, took their bags from the boot and walked briskly towards the racecourse entrance. 'Perhaps you had better tell me the message you've been asked to give me.'

'That won't take long,' she said. 'Just make sure that Dig For Glory doesn't win the handicap hurdle.'

'They've told me that already.'

'Something about keeping him on the inner, would that be it?'

Alex nodded. 'No problem. Paul always stays glued to the rails and I'll be on his outside making sure he

3

can't squeeze his way through.'

'Make certain he comes unstuck.'

'Easy,' Alex said sarcastically. Of all the people in the world, Paul Raven was the one he wanted least to cut up on the rails – he was Alex's best friend. 'Piece of cake.'

Zena ran a hand up his thigh. 'It's only one race,' she said softly. 'No need to look so miserable.'

'I've been wasting,' Alex said. 'I have to do ten two in the last.'

'Ten to what?' said Zena, a coquettish smile playing on her lips as her hand came to rest. She raised a well-plucked eyebrow. 'You seem to be a bit over-weight there, Alex,' she said, slipping down in the seat and pulling her mink coat over her head.

'Not . . . now.' But what he had intended as a protest came out as a sigh. Life had been saying 'Not now' to Zena for several years but, even at the age of forty-three, with the evidence of too many good times written clearly on her face, she had refused to listen. She wanted it now, she had never been good at waiting. While other women faced middle age with careers or children, Zena extended her competence exclusively in the area that she understood. Pleasure, taken and given. That – Alex looked down as the fur coat undulated like an animal stirring after a long sleep – yes, that she understood all too well.

A mere twelve months ago, he would have laughed at the idea of a secret assignation with an owner's wife in a car park at Plumpton. The idea of submitting

4

to the eager caresses of Zena Wentworth would have been absurd, but not as crazy as the notion that he would stop Paul winning a race. Closing his eyes and gasping, Alex tried to forget his lost innocence, to think of this afternoon's last race, which he would win. The fur came to rest.

'That should help your weight problem,' said Zena, sitting up, daintily dabbing at the corners of her mouth with a long finger.

'I'd better go.'

'Fine.'

She checked her face in the mirror, saying, 'Do I look like a woman who's just had sex in the car park?'

Alex glanced at her. Zena Wentworth always looked like a woman who had just had sex in the car park. 'You look the perfect owner's wife,' he said.

'Thank you, jockey.' Zena opened the door and got out. 'I'll see you in the paddock.'

'Old Lex is here a bit early today, isn't he?'

Jim Wilson, limping slightly from the back injury that, twenty years ago, had ended an unpromising career as a jockey, laid out breeches, boots and colours in the weighing-room.

'Lex?' Paul Raven smiled. He was glad that he had Jim for a valet. Not only was he reliable, but he was a purveyor of the latest, twenty-two carat gossip – rarely malicious, but often useful. His only irritating habit, that of using the one nickname you didn't like, Paul found almost endearing.

'Yeah, Sexy Lexy. Sitting in his motor in the car park like he's in a fucking trance. Bit early, isn't he?'

Paul shrugged, recognizing the gentle probe of a professional gossip. 'Maybe he's got a spare ride in the first.' He sipped at the half-cup of sweet tea which, however light he had to ride that day, he would drink about an hour before his first race. He was worried about Alex – normally they travelled to the races together but today he had made some excuse and driven from Lambourn alone – but he was not about to discuss it all with Jim.

He looked up at the weighing-room clock. It was time to change. Unlike Alex, who took a cavalier attitude to routine, Paul liked order in his life, particularly on race days. He would arrive well on time, walk onto the course to check the going, have his cup of tea and stay in the weighing-room until it was time to weigh out for his first ride. It wasn't that he felt superior to the drifters and hangers-on who liked to pass the time with jockeys, simply that he preferred to concentrate on the job ahead.

He was riding Tidy Item in the second race, a novice hurdle. The horse had a chance if it remembered that it wasn't running on the flat any more and that there were eight hurdles to negotiate. He'd ride Dig For Glory in the handicap hurdle, a dream ride but a little lacking in speed. The guv'nor, Ron Charlesworth, was confident, in that gloomy, monosyllabic way of his, although Alex's mount, Freeze Frame, was also in with a chance. Then, in the last, all being well, he was due to ride a novice chaser trained by a permit holder who, after it had fallen twice under its regular jockey, had decided to use Paul. The joker in the pack. Still, there was a touch of class about the horse and there was nothing else of note in the race. If he could get it round safely it ought to win. Maybe he'd ride a treble.

That perhaps was Paul's secret. Every time he received a leg-up on to a horse in the paddock, whatever its form, whatever the competition, he believed it would win. This steely confidence, which older, more battered jockeys would call crazy optimism, helped earn him a growing reputation among trainers, and thirty-three winners last season. While others would accept less promising rides – the dodgy jumper in the last, for example – thinking only of the fee and survival, Paul saw each as another potential winner.

A tall man entered the weighing-room, his expensive tweed suit, the bag he was carrying and his general air of unease marking him out as an amateur. You could always tell the guys who were doing it for fun. Big and soft-skinned, it was as if they belonged to different species from the wiry, weather-beaten, professionals. Their gear was new; they fussed about with their silks and made frequent trips to the lavatory.

At first, Paul had assumed Alex Drew would be like that – a privileged, public school wally with a foppish hairstyle that came straight out of *Brideshead Revisited*. Paul remembered the first time he had seen

him. It had been an early season meeting at Fontwell
and Alex, who was riding in an amateur race, had
behaved as if he had been walking in and out of
weighing-rooms for years, joking with the valets,
chatting with the older jockeys with an easy, dis-
respectful charm. Paul had taken an instant dislike to
him, had even permitted himself a smile when Alex's
horse turned over at the last when challenging for the
lead. Alex walked away, cursing, but back in the
weighing-room, bruised and mud-spattered, he was
soon back on song, as if he couldn't wait for his next
ride.

There was something else that had been different
about Alex Drew; the way he rode. He was better
than any amateur Paul had ever seen. On form, his
horse – Paul couldn't remember the name – had no
chance, and the cocky little bastard had taken him
along easily at the back of the field, keeping the
more fancied horses in his sights, unflustered by the
ridiculous early pace, making his move with all the
coolness of an experienced professional. At the last
fence, he had been upsides but struggling, so he'd
taken a gamble, asking his horse to stand off outside
the wings and win rather than fiddle the fence and
take second place. It hadn't paid off and Alex had
taken a bone-crunching fall. But Paul was impressed.
Judgement and nerve – it was rare to find those in a
young amateur.

'Morning, Mr Wenty,' Jim Wilson called out to the
tall man who had sat down and seemed uncertain

what to do next. He smiled thinly at the valet. 'Clay, please, Jim,' he said.

'Right, Cleggy,' said Jim, bringing Paul his breeches and winking. 'How many rides have we got today?'

'Just the one. Skinflint in the fourth.'

Now Paul knew who he was. Mr Clay Wentworth, claiming seven pounds, successful property developer, unsuccessful amateur jockey, son of Sir Denis Wentworth who had bought Skinflint as a present for his son – a touching family gesture that had landed one of the best chasers in the country with one of the worst jockeys. It was a waste but, in racing as in life, money talked.

Paul drained his cup of tea. It was time to get changed. As he checked his weight on the weighing-room scales, he became aware that Clay Wentworth was watching him.

'Nice horse, that Dig For Glory.' To Paul, the son of a brickie in Wigan, Wentworth's voice jarred. Nasal and authoritative, it belonged in the paddock or the members' bar, not here among the professionals.

'He's not bad,' he said, returning to where his clothes were. To his annoyance, Clay Wentworth followed him. The last thing he needed before a race was small talk, particularly with a man he didn't know.

'Fancy your chances?'

It was the apparently innocent question which all jockeys are asked. He shrugged. 'We've got as much chance as anyone,' he said.

'Thought of buying him once.' Wentworth opened a silver cigarette case which he waved, with a seigneurial gesture, in Paul's direction. Paul shook his head. 'We weren't sure he stayed the trip.'

'Oh yeah?'

'Needs holding up, they say.'

'Do they?' Paul smiled coldly. 'Thanks for the advice.'

As a general rule, cocaine and Plumpton Racecourse do not go together. Champagne at the bar: of course. Benzedrine in the weighing-room: perhaps. But a line of pure white powder inhaled through a rolled-up fifty pound note in the ladies' lavatory: no, not at Plumpton.

It was unusual, but then the presence of a moneyed pleasure-seeker like Zena Wentworth at a damp and modest National Hunt racecourse was in itself unusual. Zena needed something to help get her through an afternoon spent out of doors in the company of rat-faced men, large women with too much make-up, and horses. She was, by nature and inclination, a high-flyer and sometimes she needed help to fly as high as she liked to be.

Brisk and bright-eyed, Zena re-entered the bar, where a group of her friends were drinking champagne.

'Better, darling?' Lol Calloway, a former pop star who, even now that he was bald and pot-bellied, was occasionally recognized on the street by an ageing fan, gave her a knowing leer. 'Powder your nose all right, did you?'

His wife, Suzie, giggled.

'I just felt a little bit woozy,' Zena explained to a woman in a sheepskin coat who was sitting uneasily with them. The woman smiled politely. Owners were the worst part of training, Ginnie Matthews had decided some time ago, but since Clay Wentworth had brought something of a fan club with him, it had seemed ungracious to refuse the offer of a glass of champagne before the first race.

'D'you get nervous when Clay is riding?' she asked Zena.

'Not on Skinflint. He's as safe as houses, isn't he?'

'Almost.' Ginnie smiled, thinking that Clay Wentworth was capable of wrestling any horse to the ground, however safe.

'Zena's just a bit highly strung, aren't you?' A woman in her thirties with dark, cascading hair smiled at Zena. 'She has a lot on her mind, don't you, darling?' Alice Markwick smiled discreetly. She liked Zena, her sense of fun, the sparkle she brought even to a grey afternoon at a God-forsaken racetrack; the way, when she was in a really good mood, she let Alice sleep with her. Yes, she was fun.

'Look,' Zena trilled, pointing out of the window as the runners for the first race filed out of the paddock. 'Horses!'

'Did you have to get wired?' Clay Wentworth muttered as, a dark blue coat over his silks, he sat down with the group. 'Couldn't you stay straight for one afternoon?'

'I was nervous. There's so much riding on this.'

'Did you see Drew?'

'Yup.' Zena smiled at her husband, her eyes sparkling. 'He knows exactly what he has to do.'

'A winner for me, a loser for Paul Raven.' Wentworth lit a cigarette and inhaled deeply. 'Just what the doctor ordered.'

Racing journalists had taken to describing Paul Raven as 'cool', 'dispassionate', and 'machine-like' and it was true that, beside the sport's more extrovert characters, he might have seemed taciturn, possibly even dull. If you dressed him up in a suit and put him on the 8.20 from Surbiton to Waterloo, he would pass for a young, good-looking articled clerk on his way to work in the City.

Paul didn't care. To him, riding horses was a job, a way to escape the harsh poverty of his family background. As the other lads at Ron Charlesworth's yard could testify, he had a quiet, wry sense of humour and, unlike other jockeys on the brink of success, he was prepared to help the newer lads in the yard, giving them advice, intervening on their behalf when they were on the receiving end of Ron Charlesworth's icy disapproval.

He knew what it was like to be an outsider, to be starting on the lowest rung of the ladder in one of the harshest sports in the world. Like any large stable yard, Ron Charlesworth's had its hierarchy, its harsh traditions. Charlesworth himself, a tall, trim man with the cold, blue eyes of an executioner, was pitilessly ambitious – his horses and the men he paid to ride them were no more than part of a career plan.

His head lad, Jimmy Summers, a wiry Scotsman with a legendary temper, understood his boss as well as anyone. In racing, there was no gain without pain and Jimmy was an expert at ensuring that the lads under his care – particularly the teenagers stupid enough to think that shovelling horse-shit and riding out in sub-zero temperatures was the road to stardom – understood all about pain.

Watched by a handful of racegoers including the Wentworth party in the Members' Bar, Paul rode Tidy Item onto the racecourse.

'He's in great form; you could win this, you know, Paul.' Bill, one of the older lads, chattered away as he led the horse out. 'Just need to give him a view of the hurdles, hold him up, he's got the speed and . . .'

Paul turned out, as Bill told him yet again what he already knew. Tidy Item, a lightly-framed bay four-year-old, already had a great future behind him. In his first season as a two-year-old, he had won a decent race at Goodwood. The following year, his Timeform rating had plummeted and, by the end of the season, he had won only a moderate handicap over a mile and a half at Nottingham. As if aware that appearing in a novice hurdle at Plumpton, a gelding, was hardly what was expected of a horse of his breeding, Tidy Item had a listless look about him, his coat was stary and dull. For the first time today, he was wearing blinkers.

'Cheers, Bill.' As the lad released him Paul turned and cantered down to the start.

Tidy Item had a long, rangy stride which made him an easy ride on the flat. It was the hurdles which bothered him. The first couple of times Paul had schooled him at home, he hadn't had a clue what to do, hurling himself at them in panic. These days, he took the marginally safer course of galloping straight through them, often losing lengths in a race, shattering the hurdles as he went. Getting in close and fiddling a hurdle was something Tidy Item knew nothing of.

But he could win. 'Try jumping them this time, fella,' Paul muttered as he showed the horse the first flight, patting him on the neck. His seven years riding racehorses had convinced him that the best way of getting winners was the quiet way: settle them, relax, let the other jockeys scream and swear. Riding Tidy Item over hurdles might be like surviving eight earthquakes but, when he wasn't kicking bits of timber into the air, he was a good ride. Yes, he would win. Paul was confident.

The race followed the pattern Paul had anticipated. A couple of horses set a smart pace which had several runners, bred less aristocratically than Tidy Item, off the bit from the start.

Paul allowed Tidy Item to dawdle near the back of the field tight on the inside rail, a position which gave him little view of the hurdles but since even if the horse had the entire racetrack to himself he would crash through every flight, taking him the shortest way made sense.

Despite destroying six flights of hurdles, Tidy Item entered the straight at the back of the leading group still on the bridle. Paul let the leaders run off the bend and then let him run through smartly on the inner. He was going so easily it was almost embarrassing. As if sensing that the unpleasant experience of smashing timber at speed was soon to be over, Tidy Item lengthened his stride approaching the last hurdle and, by his standards, jumped the last well, diving through it a foot above the turf, and actually made ground doing it. Paul didn't even have to ride him out, as he won pulling the proverbial cart.

'Cocky bastard,' Dave Cartwright, who had ridden the second horse, called out as they trotted back having pulled up. No one, even at Plumpton, likes another jockey to get up their inside. 'You could have won that by ten lengths.'

'Somebody's got to ride them.' Paul trotted on. He didn't care what other jockeys, or journalists, or lads or even Ron Charlesworth said to him.

He had won it; and that was what mattered.

The bastard was cool. Clay Wentworth sipped the one bucks fizz he allowed himself on days when he was riding and watched a TV screen on which, in silent slow motion, Tidy Item was once again being gathered up after his mistake at the last hurdle.

'So *cheeky*.' Zena's voice, like a distant mocking soundtrack, penetrated Clay's thoughts. 'Why don't you try and win like that, darling?'

He smiled wanly without taking his eyes from the screen. For a moment, he had managed to forget that, in a little over an hour, he would be riding Skinflint. 'Maybe I will,' he said.

Where did it come from, the coolness, the poise, that converted the will to win into the ability to win? Nobody wanted to win races more than Clay Wentworth did but his determination was panicky and ineffective. Whereas jockeys like Paul Raven looked in a finish as if they were part of the horse, its powerhouse, he flapped about like a duck landing on ice with a broken wing. Occasionally his horse won a race but it was always in spite of his efforts, not because of them.

'Clay's psyching himself up,' Lol Calloway was saying to Zena and to Alice Markwick. 'It's like a big gig at Madison Square Garden. I'd get the band together and say "Guys, we're gonna fuckin' blow them away tonight, right?" They'd go, like punch the air, and say "Yeah, right, Lol!" Then, after I'd done a line and fucked a groupie, we'd go on like well psyched.'

At a nearby table, a local doctor and his wife, who liked an afternoon at the races, muttered poisonously

16

to one another before draining their drinks and moving away.

He hated it, that was the truth. Clay Wentworth, never one for deep self-analysis, knew this at least. He hated the weighing-room where suddenly he was no longer the boss but some sort of junior. He hated the walk out to the paddock, the cold, the wet, the pervasive smell of horse shit and cigar smoke. He hated the moment he was given a leg-up, when he was left all by himself with the horse to canter down to the start. He hated circling round at the start, hearing the starters' roll-call – 'Mr Wentworth,' 'Sir.' He hated, Christ he hated, the moment when the field jumped off and there was no escape and the first fence, getting bigger and bigger, loomed up before him, the kick, the lurch, the shouts and curses all around him. After the first, it got better, particularly if he were riding Skinflint, but he never liked it, not until he was back among the racegoers, preferably in the winners' enclosure. There was nothing like the feel of the ground beneath his feet when he dismounted.

Clay took another sip of his drink. No, he sighed quietly to himself, he was not a natural.

That was what made Alex Drew the perfect patsy. The moment he had joined the Circle, playing poker like he rode horses – with style and bravado – Clay had known what had to be done. They needed someone who rode as a professional, competent enough to stop another horse, straight enough to keep himself

17

out of the stewards' room, weak enough to bend under pressure.

Alex discovered that poker is not like racing, but he discovered too late. Nerve and skill are not enough. You have to know how to bluff, how to cheat, your every move must be informed by rat-like cunning and deception. That cheerful openness, which served him so well on the racecourse, had betrayed him at the table.

Zena had worried. What if someone got hurt? What if Alex's career was destroyed? Clay had frowned as if considering the moral options. There was no reason for things to go wrong. The risks were as low as the stakes were high.

He smiled. It was a lie, of course – as big a bluff as he had ever played at the table. If someone's career hit the rocks, he was certain it would be Alex's. If someone's body paid the price of Clay's ambition, there was no better body than Alex's.

'Everything all right, Clay?' As usual, it was Alice who understood better than anyone what was going through his head. Her dark, smoky voice carried concern but Clay was aware that there was nothing personal there. Alice's concern was always financial.

'He's thinking about his race, ain't you, Clay?' said Lol Calloway. 'Trying to decide whether to sneak up on the rails like the last winner or to take it easy and win by ten lengths.'

'Of course,' said Alice. 'It's a big day, isn't it?'

Clay Wentworth nodded. 'Yes, it's a big day.'

* * *

Paul Raven had never known Alex like this. In the early days, he had distrusted Alex's high spirits, his ability to make a joke even when things were going badly. Alex was an amateur when they had first met and it was as if the years of money and privilege had come bubbling to the surface in an excess of optimism and good humour.

Three years later, he knew better. Joking had been Alex's way of dealing with stress. Once he was in the saddle and the flag went down, he was a different person. It seemed odd now that it was Paul who was doing the talking before the fourth race, as Alex sat, pale and distracted, like a man facing a death sentence.

'That Tidy Item's going to bury me one day,' Paul said. 'When they send him chasing, the ride is yours.'

Alex didn't reply. He wanted it to be over, or at least to explain to Paul before it was too late and explanations were superfluous.

It was unusual for them both to be riding for Ron Charlesworth in the same race. Ron was good at placing his horses and, unless he was giving one of them an easy ride, or a fancied runner needed a pacemaker, he avoided sending out two runners to compete for one prize. This two-and-a-half-mile handicap hurdle had been intended for Freeze Frame, Alex's ride. It was only when the weights had been announced, allotting Dig For Glory an absurdly generous ten stone three, that Dig For Glory had been included. He needed the race to be fully fit but his owner Lady Faircroft had been anxious to see him run. Reluctantly, Ron had agreed.

The two jockeys sat together, having weighed out, the brickie's son and the former amateur, one dark and wiry, the other with the cherubic, long-haired look of an overgrown schoolboy. They were an unlikely couple.

'What's the problem then, Alex?' Paul asked. 'Anybody would think you were nervous or something.'

'You must be joking.' Alex tried a smile, but it was an unconvincing effort. 'I'm fine.'

With anyone else, Paul might have suspected normal jockey problems – money, weight, an unhealthily close association with bookmakers – but he knew Alex, for all his wild talk, was too sensible for that.

'Just tell me if I can help, that's all.'

Alex looked at him oddly. 'Thanks, Paul,' he said.

The bell sounded for jockeys out.

'Paddock, jockeys.' A bowler-hatted official stood at the door and the riders for the fourth race at Plumpton filed out to make their way to the paddock.

'Good luck, boys,' said Jim Wilson.

'Cheers, Jim,' said Paul.

Alex said nothing.

Chapter 2

Peter Zametsky had thought he was getting used to the English way of doing things. He had sat in pubs where Londoners gathered to complain about life. He had travelled by underground where they stared ahead of them, not acknowledging the existence of other human beings despite being pressed up against them in a position of forced intimacy. He had been to a football match where they stood up and swore at one another. He had visited a church on Christmas morning where they had seemed ill at ease except when booming out tuneless versions of the carols.

But nothing had prepared him for a betting shop.

There was a reverence here which had not been evident in the church. Through the pall of cigarette smoke, under the bright strip lighting, men – and just a few women – were staring, staring upwards as if praying for a miracle. Some held slips of paper in their hands; others were seated in front of newspapers. Around the room were television screens which were showing some sort of dog race. The murmur of a commentary could be heard, but Peter understood little of what was being said, although certain numbers seemed to be repeated like a mantra.

'Go, on, number three.' A tall West Indian, standing in front of Peter, was muttering. 'Go on, my son.'

'Excuse me, sir.' Peter was unsure of the procedure on these occasions, but his three years in England had taught him that no one helped you unless you asked first. 'To place a bet?'

The man seemed to be suffering from some kind of attack. 'Yes,' he said, occasionally looking away from the television screen as if the mystery unfolding there was too much for him to take. 'Yes, my son. *Here* he comes.'

As Peter waited patiently for an answer, the man gave a sort of moan and then, with intense loathing, balled the piece of paper he had been holding and threw it onto the floor in a gesture of terminal despair. 'Bastard,' he said.

'Where to place a bet, please?'

As if coming out of a trance, the man turned his bloodshot, tear-stained eyes in Peter's direction and burped. Peter, a small bespectacled man in his thirties, with thinning hair and a dreary suit, moved through the crowd of punters.

'To bet?' he asked an elderly woman who was staring into space. She nodded over her shoulder. 'Over there,' she said.

Peter made his way to a counter at the back of the shop.

'In the two-thirty at Plumpton,' he said nervously to a plump girl behind the counter. 'I'm wanting...'

'Slip,' said the girl. As Peter frowned helplessly, she pushed a piece of paper across the counter. 'Fill it in,' she said loudly. 'Comprende?'

Peter found an empty corner in the betting-shop and sat down on a stool. There was a small, slightly chewed biro on the ledge in front of him which he looked at, as if it were a specimen in the lab, before picking it up. 'How is it, Peter,' his wife used to say, 'that in some things you are so brilliant, in others so completely foolish with your frown and so innocent eyes?' Klima was right: at work, Peter was almost masterful, as he sat at his bench, crouched over a microscope or tapping easily at his computer. It was real life that caused him problems.

He looked up at a screen. Four to one. He was not by nature a gambler but he had confidence in his work. Carefully, he wrote on the betting slip. 'FREEZE FRAME – £100 (win), Plumpton, 2.30', adding as an afterthought, 'Ridden by A. Drew'.

Once you're in the saddle, it's just another job of work. From his earliest days as an amateur, Alex had learnt to exclude the personal from his race-riding. Cheerful and outgoing before the race, the chat and the jokes were put on hold as soon as he was in the paddock. As for the other jockeys, they were no longer friends or enemies but simply part of the job. It was the two-ride-a-week merchants that were the trouble. Most of them were all over the place in a race, just like weekend drivers. It was beyond some of them to ride in a straight line, which when you're doing fifty miles an hour towards a fence doesn't make life easy, especially when the horse you're riding doesn't jump very well. As for the bends, well, if you were foolish enough to be on the girth of one of them there, then you deserved whatever happened.

Those were relevant considerations; character – friendship, in particular – needed to be forgotten until after the race.

And yet. Cantering down to the start, Alex watched the orange and black colours of Lady Faircraft, worn by Paul on Dig For Glory some five lengths in front of him. And other images of Paul flashed before his eyes – the quiet lad at Charlesworth's yard taken for granted by everyone, the workaholic, the jockey glancing across at him as they raced knee to knee on the Lambourn downs, helping him to polish up his riding, the friend who was always the first to say well done when he rode a winner and most important, the one who always came to make sure he was all right after a fall. On paper, there was little to separate Freeze Frame and Dig For Glory although, given the choice, Alex would have chosen Paul's horse, a big five-year-old whose inconsistent form last season due to weakness had ensured that he was well down in the weights. Dig For Glory had developed over the summer months and, even though the ground had been firmer than he liked, he had run promisingly in a two-mile handicap hurdle at Leicester. The soft ground and the extra half-mile at Plumpton would suit him. Under normal circumstances, Alex would have fancied Paul's chances.

They pulled up at the start and Paul glanced across at Freeze Frame, who was sweating up slightly. 'He looks well,' he said quietly.

Alex smiled, patting Freeze Frame. The horse was small and a brilliant jumper but he lacked finishing speed. Ron Charlesworth's instructions had been to lie up with the leaders and make the best of his way home from three flights out but – Alex felt a wave of nausea as he remembered the task before him – today he had other priorities.

'Where are you going?' he asked.

Paul looked at him, surprised. If there was anyone in the world who knew that he always rode his races from the inside, hugging the rails, it was Alex.

'Guess,' he said.

'There are some bad jumpers in the field.' Alex tried to sound casual. 'I'd keep him out of trouble on the outside.'

Paul grinned. 'Nice try, Alex,' he said. It was at that moment, as the jockeys circled around the starter, that Paul realized that, for some reason, this race was not like all the others. He couldn't put his finger on it, but something wasn't right. Everything seemed the same as normal – the other jockeys chatting, the sound in the distance of the racecourse loudspeaker, but something was different.

'Smith.' The starter's voice was briskly military.

'Sir.'

'Drew.'

'Sir.'

It was Alex, that's what was different. He had sensed it on the gallops, in the yard – that look of a man haunted by something stronger than ambition or friendship, but it had never happened on a racecourse before.

'Raven.'

Keep him out of trouble. What had Alex meant, what was he trying to say?

'*Raven*.'

'Sir.'

'Wake up, we haven't got all day.'

The starter, still grumbling, mounted the steps and brought them under orders. Paul took up a position directly behind Happy Fella, who usually made the running. As the tape rose and one or two of the jockeys slapped their horses down the shoulder, helping them into their stride, Paul banished all thoughts of Alex from his mind and concentrated on the race before him.

The race was a good one, considering the state of the ground, and, by the time the field streamed past the stands with two circuits to go there were one or two struggling to lay up. Dig For Glory was going easily in sixth place, some eight lengths behind the leaders. Paul looked at the horses ahead of him and noticed with some surprise that Freeze Frame was not among them. As they turned away from the stands, Alex loomed up beside him, on a tight rein.

Paul looked over. 'They're not hanging about. I hope I'm going this well next time around.'

'So do I.'

By the time they'd completed another circuit, the pace had slowed considerably, Paul had Dig For Glory precisely where he wanted him, in fifth place on the rails with the leaders, including Freeze Frame, well within striking distance and that was where he stayed as they raced down the hill on the far side for the last time. A good jump at the third last took Dig For Glory even closer. All four jockeys in front of him were now pushing hard for home, and Paul began to niggle at Dig For Glory. The ground and the pace were taking their toll and Paul wasn't certain Dig For Glory's stamina would see him home. As they rounded the bend and turned towards the finish, Alex and Freeze Frame looked beaten and Paul called to his stable companion to lay over and leave him the inner. Alex immediately pulled Freeze Frame to his right as Paul urged Dig For Glory through the gap. They were within two strides of taking off for the second last when Alex suddenly shut the door. Dig For Glory, whose heart was bigger than himself, was suddenly faced with a large, solid wood wing and instead of slamming on the brakes made a vain attempt to jump it. There was a sickening sound of splintering wood as horse and jockey went crashing through to the ground, where both now lay motionless.

'Dig For Glory, a faller at the second last.' The commentary from Plumpton to betting-shops throughout the land laconically recorded the facts without dwelling on the human drama behind them. 'Over the last it's Happy Fella and Sweet Charity with Freeze Frame getting into it. It's going to be close, they're all tired, but it looks like Freeze Frame's going to do it there at the line. Freeze Frame the winner. Happy Fella second. Sweet Charity third.'

Peter Zametsky stared at the slip of paper in his hand. It had worked. The one gamble in his life had paid off. He would buy Klima new shoes, perhaps a fridge, clothes for the baby. Yes, it had worked. Peter felt sick.

In a trance, he walked to the counter and passed the betting-slip to the teller.

'Not weighed in yet,' she said.

Peter frowned. 'Weighed in?'

The woman sighed. 'You wait five minutes. Then we give money and you go and don't come back, okay.' She turned to the young man sitting beside her at the counter. 'E's won £500 and doesn't even know what weighed in is.'

'Please,' Peter ignored the man standing behind him who was muttering impatiently. 'What happened to the jockey?'

28

'*Jockey*?' The woman leaned forward as if talking to a child. 'I expect he's very happy now. Celebrating, you know.'

'No, not him. Can we see the television again?' Peter pointed to a nearby screen on which, once again, greyhounds were racing. 'The other jockey. The one who fell. Is he all right?'

'What's he talking about?' the woman asked her colleague. 'Only races here, mate. Just winners and losers and odds, d'you understand?' She looked over his shoulder to the man behind him. 'Next.'

Only the ignorant or those greedy to collect their winnings hurried away from the grandstand after the two-thirty at Plumpton. The binoculars of most regular racegoers were trained on the second last flight where Dig For Glory and his jockey Paul Raven still lay motionless.

Alex was not the praying type. At a Christmas carol service, he might pray for a hat-trick on Boxing Day; the next day, perhaps he might pray that his modest turkey dinner wouldn't show up as overweight when he sat on the scales, but these were light-hearted, insurance prayers intended for any Superior Being who happened to be tuned in to him.

But he prayed now. 'Let him be all right,' he whispered as he trotted Freeze Frame past the stands, standing in his stirrups in an attempt to see what was happening down the course. 'Just let him be okay.'

An older jockey, Dermot O'Brien, who had finished way down the field, cantered up to him.

'Nice one, Alex,' he said, pulling down his goggles.

'Cheers, Dermot.' Alex smiled thinly. O'Brien was one of the old school, a tough Irishman who had broken every bone in his body and had little time for small talk or sentiment.

'Sure, I couldn't have done him better myself,' he added with a trace of admiration in his voice.

There was a subdued welcome at the winners' enclosure where, to Alex's surprise, he was met by Liz Charlesworth, the plump and apologetic wife of his trainer.

'Where's the guv'nor?' Alex asked, dismounting.

'On the course.' Even by her standards, Liz seemed distracted and unhappy. 'It doesn't look good.'

Bad news reaches the weighing-room fast. By the time Alex had weighed in and returned with his saddle, the word was out. An uneasy silence greeted him as he walked in.

Jim Wilson took his saddle, unusually avoiding his eyes.

'How's Paul?' asked Alex nervously.

The valet looked up at him accusingly. 'If he hasn't broken anything it'll be a miracle.'

'It was an accident,' Alex said quietly. 'He went for a gap that wasn't there.'

Dave Smart, whose horse Sweet Charity had finished third, stood in front of Alex. 'The gap was there. I was a couple of lengths behind him. You did him.'

Alex shook his head in weary denial.

'Some fucking friend,' Smart muttered, wiping the mud from his face with a towel.

Five long minutes later, one of the jockeys told Alex that his trainer needed to see him outside the weighing-room.

Ron Charlesworth was not an emotional man – love, regret, sadness and humour played an insignificant part in his life – but on the rare occasions when he was angry, it was plain for all to see. Although his voice remained as dry and precise as that of a solicitor reading out the details of a particularly unfavourable will, two vivid blotches of colour appeared high on his cheekbones, remaining there until the rage had subsided.

So, although he smiled at Alex as, with an arm around his shoulder, he led him to a corner away from the scales and the ever-alert ears of racing's gossipmongers, Alex knew that he was in deep trouble.

'I should give you the fucking sack,' Charlesworth said quietly. 'You don't deserve a job in racing.'

'I've just ridden you a winner.'

'You've just killed one of my best horses.'

Alex looked at Charlesworth, expecting news of Paul from him.

'What were you playing at? Did you two have some sort of lovers' tiff? What the fuck's going on?'

Running a hand through his thick hair, Alex closed his eyes. 'How's Paul?' he asked.

'You're damned lucky they've got lenient stewards here. They're having an enquiry and it isn't going to look good and I ought to let you take what you deserve for this.' The trainer made no attempt to conceal the disapproval in his voice. He paused for a moment. 'Trouble is I'll lose the race if I tell them what I think, so I'll just say that the horse has a tendency to duck to his left and we'll stick to that.'

'It was an accident,' pleaded Alex, trying to convince himself more than Ron.

Charlesworth looked at him coldly. The normal pallor was slowly returning to his cheeks. 'I hope so – for your sake.'

'How's Paul?'

'Hospital.' Charlesworth shrugged as if another injured jockey was the least of his problems. 'You'd better get ready for the fourth. You're lucky I'm not jocking you off.'

Lucky. Alex felt the unluckiest man alive. As he returned to the weighing-room, the jockeys for the amateur race were being called out to the paddock.

The tall figure of Clay Wentworth loomed up before him. 'Well-ridden, Alex.' Although the voice was neutral, there was mockery in his expression.

Alex looked away, apparently muttering to himself. Only Clay Wentworth was close enough to hear the words, 'Debt repaid.'

Alex was just pulling on a new set of colours when he was called to the enquiry. As he watched the head-on of what he'd done to his best friend he felt sick.

A jury could have found him guilty of attempted murder. The stewards took no action.

It was cold. It was wet. Something rather disgusting seemed to have become attached to the sole of her Gucci shoe. The noise in the Members' Bar was like feeding time at the zoo. The company at her table was neither intelligent nor attractive enough to be remotely interesting. She hated horses.

All in all, Alice Markwick had decided, National Hunt racing was not for her. She glanced at her watch. One more race – Clay's big moment – and she would be off. There was work to do back home. Then, later tonight, she would slip down to Heaven, her favourite club, to pick up someone soft and understanding. God knows, she deserved it.

Beside her, Zena was conducting a coke-fuelled monologue that had already covered a variety of topics including the excitement of the last race, except for what happened to that poor jockey who fell off, how she loved to go racing when Clay was riding, why she needed to buy some more clothes, a woozy reference to a night she had once spent with Alice, a discussion of how cocaine and champagne worked together, a scurrilous commentary on a group of men standing at the bar, her husband's obsession with work, a brief attack on that cold, sinister bastard her father-in-law, and some rather sordid story involving a jockey in the car park before the races.

Alice smiled at Zena, her thoughts miles away.

The great advantage of substance abuse was that it required no effort from the other person. A woman on coke was her own best company, entirely self-sufficient. In her thirty-five years, Alice had learned that to make love to someone so wired that she was on another planet was a ghastly, monotonous, exhausting experience but, when it came to conversation, the stuff had its uses. Red-eyed, her chin working overtime, Zena would dribble on like a running tap until it wore off and she returned to the civilized world.

'There he goes,' Zena trilled, pointing to the racecourse where her husband was cantering down to the start on Skinflint. 'He's in the lead, Alice!'

'I don't think they've started yet.' Alice sighed. She was no expert but even she realized that, with one horse walking and another trotting, these were mere preliminaries.

'Haven't they?' Zena laughed girlishly, then covered her mouth. 'Where's Lol gone?'

Alice sighed. Even the short-term memory was going now. 'They've gone to watch the race from the course,' she said. 'Remember?'

'Aha, yup, right. *God...*' Zena looked wildly around the bar. 'They're so serious in here, why aren't they excited? *I'm* excited, and sort of nervous at the same time –'

It was a long way from Prague, Alice thought to herself, as Zena resumed her monologue. Yet even this, a grey afternoon at Plumpton, represented a new start. Alice was not nostalgic – she rarely looked back to the days when, as simple Alzbeta Flaishman, she had arrived from Czechoslovakia to make her life in London. After all, there were a few good memories, apart from the day when, by some act of an ever-merciful God, her husband had suffered a heart attack and died, leaving her a legacy that only now, over fifteen years later, was coming to fruition.

Alice thought of the humiliations that she had suffered to reach this point, of the freedom and riches that lay ahead of her. What a strange place this was for your life to change. She must have drifted off into a distant world of moneyed fantasy for it seemed only seconds later that she became aware of Zena gripping her hand and bouncing up and down in her seat. And there, down on the racecourse, she saw men on horses galloping past the finishing post. Ahead of them, by some ten lengths, also bouncing up and down, was Clay Wentworth. Even to Alice's untutored eye, Clay looked absurd, more like a drunk trying to direct traffic than a jockey riding a finish.

'He won!' Zena's eyes sparkled. 'He *won* the race, Alice.'

'Isn't that just great?' Alice smiled. 'Today, everyone's a winner.'

More than once, as Alex sat in the reception area of Lewes Hospital, he was asked if he needed Casualty. He had the look of a patient – deadly white and apparently in shock.

'No,' he shook his head. 'I'm waiting for a friend.'

It was early evening and he had been at the hospital for over an hour. On his way out to ride an undistinguished young horse in the novice 'chase, the second last race of the day, a reporter had walked beside him and asked him for his version of the incident involving Dig For Glory and Paul Raven.

Alex had walked on, declining to comment.

'They say he's pretty smashed up,' the journalist had said, adding quickly, 'there's been a press release. No limbs broken but badly shaken.'

Alex looked at the reporter. He might have been making it up but that phrase 'badly shaken' had the ring of truth to it. If some of the racecourse officials had been 'badly shaken' in the way that jockeys had been, in that phrase they used so easily, they would be on the way to the mortuary.

'D'you know anything more?' Alex asked.

'One of the press boys claims that he was still unconscious when they took him off to hospital.'

Alex closed his eyes for a moment. Then, remembering he had a race to ride, he walked towards the paddock, wondering whether Ron or Liz Charlesworth knew anything more. Knowing the guv'nor, he would be driving home by now. Alex touched the peak of his cap as Eddie Marwood, a small West Country trainer whose horses he sometimes rode, gave him his instructions.

Within moments of finishing well down the field in the novice 'chase, he was back in the weighing-room, giving Jim Wilson his mud-spattered gear before changing and hurrying out to the car park.

'He's not going to be able to see you tonight.' A young nurse stood before Alex.

'I'll wait,' he said.

'He's really not very well.' The girl was slim, with her short blonde hair tied back severely. She seemed too young to endure the daily sadness of a hospital. At any other time and in any other place, Alex would have been thinking of ways to get her telephone number.

'Is he conscious?'

'Yes,' she said quietly. 'He's conscious, but we're keeping him in intensive care for the time being.'

Alex rubbed his eyes wearily. To his surprise, the nurse sat down beside him.

'What about you?' she asked. 'You don't look so good yourself.'

'I'm all right.'

'You're a friend of his?'

Alex nodded, reflecting with a wry smile on the kind of friend he had been that afternoon.

'Go home,' the nurse said. 'Perhaps you could call his family to reassure them. Ring in tomorrow morning. He might be able to see you then.'

'No,' said Alex. 'I'll wait here.'

Dr Michael Evans had had a bad day. He estimated that he had worked a daily twelve hours for the past six days and he was on a late shift again tonight. He had had enough sick people to last him a lifetime.

And now even the healthy were giving him grief. When Nurse O'Keefe had asked him to speak to some idiot jockey in reception, he could hardly believe it. If Dr Evans had his way, little men with bandy legs who cluttered up the hospital every time there was racing at Plumpton would be sent to a special clinic for racing fools.

'There's absolutely no point in your staying here,' Dr Evans said loudly as he walked into reception.

Alex looked up at the man with tired eyes and a white, unbuttoned coat.

'I'd just like to see him,' he said.

'Impossible. Even if you were his long-lost brother, we couldn't let you in.'

'But he's conscious now, is he?'

Dr Evans sighed. 'Yes of course he's conscious. He just had a bang on the head.'

'So, if he hasn't broken anything and he hasn't serious head injuries, he might be out of here soon?'

'He won't be out of anywhere soon,' said the doctor impatiently. 'At least, not under his own steam. It looks like he's broken his back.'

Chapter 3

Life had been hard on Ginnie Matthews. Born some forty-seven years ago into a racing family, she had never known her mother who, when Ginnie was three years old, had run off with a travelling salesman to live in Scotland. From the age of five, it seemed to her now, she had looked after her father whose unpromising career as a trainer near Malton in Yorkshire had been seriously impeded by an ever-increasing dependence on whisky. Ginnie remembered him as a kind, weak man, awash with whisky and self-pity.

By the age of sixteen, she had learned the art of lying to owners, a talent that would stand her in good stead later in life. Daddy was a bit tied up at present. Daddy was out at the stables. Daddy was seeing another owner. Her best efforts were finally in vain. When she went racing, people smiled at her politely but their eyes said it all: Daddy was a loser, a piss-artist heading hell-for-leather for the gutter. Daddy was finished.

Owners deserted him. Horses were taken away. Lads sought other employment. Eventually, Ginnie left, too. At the age of seventeen, she came south and worked in a yard near Lambourn.

She was slim in those days and had a certain chirpy competence that men – particularly weak, mother-fixated men – found attractive. Four years after she had left home, she married Harry Matthews, who was assistant to the legendary Arthur Williamson, by general consent the most successful trainer of his day.

It was early morning, two days after Skinflint had won at Plumpton. Ginnie stood by her Range Rover, watching the string making its way through the early morning mist towards her and thinking about the only man she had ever slept with.

On the face of it, Harry Matthews had been quite a catch. A charming, good-humoured man, whose ten years in the army had left him with an easy manner with employees and a faintly ludicrous moustache which suited his healthy, high-coloured face. Harry was a card, a character; he was good company, always popular on the dinner-party circuit. Despite their age difference – he was forty when they married – she fell for his charms, ignoring the rumours that he had something of a weakness for fun and fast ladies.

'Charm,' Ginnie muttered as she stepped forward, standing in the centre of a circle formed by her horses like a ringmaster at a circus. 'Down with charm.'

She ran an expert eye over the horses, noting which were carrying too much weight, which needed building up. Ginnie prided herself on turning out horses that not only won races but that looked well too.

'How is he?' she called to the lad riding Skinflint.

Pete, a quiet lad who had worked for Ginnie five years now, smoothed Skinflint's coat behind the saddle. 'I don't think he knew he was in a race.'

Ginnie smiled. 'I'm not sure he was,' she said.

It was Wednesday, the day when most of the string were given half-speed work over a mile. Today Rock Steady, a four-year-old hurdler belonging to Clay Wentworth, was being schooled over hurdles. Mr Wentworth was not an amateur jockey who was prepared to tack his horse up and ride him out with the rest of the lads. He liked all that to be done for him so that he could drive to the gallops, work his horse, then return to London. Today, as usual, he was late.

As the horses cantered away from her to the end of the gallops, Ginnie found herself wondering why, at this of all times, she had been ambushed by reminiscences of the past. Under normal circumstances, she rarely looked back – the past, as far as she was concerned, was not just another country, but an alien, distant land hardly worth considering.

It was the thought of a visit from Clay Wentworth that had done it. He was the sort of owner her former husband had cultivated for social as well as financial reasons. Beefy, empty-faced officers, flabby City men, the occasional farmer made good – they had flocked to Harry Matthews when he established his own yard in Lambourn. He had loved it, spending night after night with these idiot amateur jockeys, flirting, getting drunk, frequently returning the following day, leaving Ginnie to look after first and second lots. He called it a sales drive and, for a while, she had believed him.

But Harry's amateur friends let him down. The officers were late paying their bills. Every time the economy dipped, the City men sold their horses – almost always out of the yard.

In the distance, Ginnie saw Clay Wentworth's Mercedes making its way up the lane by the gallops. Harry would have liked Clay. Doubtless he would have joined the famous Wentworth poker circle, if he were still in charge of the yard, if his charm hadn't let him down in the end.

After ten years of marriage, Ginnie had concluded that, perhaps through some odd psychological need, she had managed to find a husband who, in his way, was as big a loser as her father had been. The other women she could just about understand – her infertility was the excuse he used for his philandering; the booze she could live with. It was the lying and incompetent dishonesty that she hated.

Harry lost owners. Like many other trainers, he tried to escape financial ruin by setting up gambling coups. Even that, he screwed up. Horses that were meant to lose, won; good things turned out to be bad

things. The Jockey Club took an increasingly close
interest in his affairs and, after a particularly transparent act of fraud, took away his licence for two
years.

At that moment, Ginnie had decided she was
through with charm. She filed for divorce, borrowed
enough money to buy him out of the yard, and began
to rebuild.

Now, seventeen years later, she was one of the
most successful trainers in the country, and her only
use for men was as employees. She had learned the
hard way.

'Ginnie, the top of the morning to you.' Clay Wentworth emerged languidly from his car. To Ginnie's
surprise, he was wearing a pin-striped suit.

'Are you schooling like that?' she asked.

'Bit stiff after Plumpton.' Clay arched his back,
wincing slightly. 'Thought I'd let one of the lads have
a go.'

Ginnie nodded. She had often wondered why Clay
put himself through this. His nerve was bad and he
lacked any natural ability or understanding of horses.
There was something apologetic about his tall, slightly
stooped figure, particularly when his father was present. She glanced in the direction of the Mercedes
and there, sure enough, was Sir Denis, sitting stonily
immobile in the passenger seat.

'Morning, Sir Denis,' she called out.

The old man nodded curtly.

'My father was wondering why you were working

Skinflint.' Clay smiled weakly. 'I mean, hasn't he done enough this week?'

Ginnie looked away towards the string as it came up the gallops. She couldn't stand owners who thought they knew better than she did. 'He thrives on work,' she said eventually. 'A half-speed will relax him.'

'That's what I told Dad,' said Clay.

'I've entered him in a couple of decent handicap 'chases in the New Year,' she said. 'If he's well in at the weights, we might consider giving him a crack at the big guns.'

'Excellent,' said Clay, adding as an afterthought, 'We don't want too light a weight, of course.'

She said nothing.

'I'm a bit strapped to do anything under twelve stone, to tell the truth.'

As she watched the horses trot back towards them, having pulled up at the end of the gallops, Ginnie swore silently. An owner for whom money and the pleasure of having a top-class horse in his name were enough, would have understood what she was saying. There comes a time when the owner should step down and make way for a professional jockey. Skinflint had the ability to beat the best in the country over three miles but, under the dead, uneven weight of Clay Wentworth, he was nothing special.

Unfortunately Clay and his ill-tempered old father were not interested in prizes or the pleasure of owner-ship; they wanted to see a Wentworth riding into the winners' enclosure, whatever the cost in money and wasted opportunity.

Clay patted Skinflint, who was hardly blowing after his exertions. 'Good boy,' he said. 'We're going to win lots more races together, aren't we?'

'Pete, can you get on Rock Steady and pop him over a couple of hurdles with old Home Boy?'

While the lads exchanged mounts, Clay muttered, 'You do understand why I want to ride him, don't you?'

'He could be a Gold Cup horse.'

Clay smiled. 'Maybe next year. This year it's the Kim Muir. A big amateur race at Cheltenham – it's not bad, is it?'

'No.' Ginnie smiled wearily. 'It's not bad.'

Some horses are lucky with owners – the great Arkle was owned by the Duchess of Westminster throughout his racing career. Others are less fortunate. As a four-year-old hurdler, Skinflint had been sold out of a yard in Newmarket to a Colonel Gilbert, an old enthusiast who kept a few horses with Ginnie.

By the time the Colonel died two years later, Skinflint was a top novice 'chaser with the temperament, toughness and turn of foot to become a Cheltenham Gold Cup prospect. When Mrs Gilbert, who had always resented her husband's interest in racing, put all his horses on the market, Ginnie had worked hard to find a new owner who would keep him in training with her. Clay Wentworth, who had just sent her a young hurdler called Rock Steady, had seemed ideal.

But Ginnie had underestimated Clay's – or rather, his father's – ambition.

'Will Sir Denis want to come over to the schooling ground?' she asked.

'He'll watch from here,' said Clay. 'He just likes to feel involved.'

Together, they walked to the schooling ground, an area of about twenty-five acres with lines of hurdles and fences of varying heights. They watched Rock Steady canter down to the far end of the gallop with Home Boy. Both horses were shown the first flight of hurdles.

'Do we know who are going to be our two main rivals in the Kim Muir?' Clay asked.

'Not officially, but I could take a pretty good guess.'

'You couldn't be terribly kind and jot them down for me, could you?'

'Jot them down?' Ginnie looked at Clay with some surprise. 'Can't I just tell you?'

'No, put them down – with owners and trainers. On a piece of paper. Know your enemy and all that. Besides, with my memory I'd forget them.'

She shrugged, as the two horses turned towards the first hurdle and set off at smart gallop.

'Here they come,' she said.

The more they talked of miracles around Paul's bed at Lewes Hospital, the more depressed he became about the future. It had been a miracle, Dr Evans had told him, that the impact of a racehorse falling at racing speed on top of him had not been fatal. It was a miracle that he had recovered consciousness so quickly. It was a miracle the way his body was responding to treatment so that now, five days after his fall, he was out of intensive care and back in a ward.

Then, subtly, the emphasis began to change. It would be a miracle if he were out of hospital within six months, and – the one that went through his mind a thousand times a day – it would be a miracle if he ever walked again. Three days after he had been brought into hospital, Paul had asked Dr Evans when he would recover the movement in his legs. 'Tell me what's going to happen,' he asked. 'Without the miracles.'

And the doctor, normally so direct, had been evasive, explaining with the help of X-rays he extracted from the folder he was carrying that the problem was a series of crushed vertebrae at the base of the spine. 'If the damage had been two inches lower,' he said, 'the risk of fundamental damage would have been less. As it is, we have to wait for your body to recover from the shock of the fall and for the swelling to subside, before we can conduct an exploratory operation. Only then will we know what the future holds for you.'

'Fundamental damage.' Through a haze of morphine Paul sensed the reason for Dr Evans' uneasiness. 'Does that mean I'm out for the season – or for ever?'

Dr Evans gestured to Nurse O'Keefe, who was standing at the foot of the bed. The nurse drew the curtains around the bed.

'Listen, let's take one step at a time.'

'What about walking?'

'I honestly don't know, only time will tell.' The doctor paused.

Paul had closed his eyes as the doctor had explained, as dispassionately as a science master, the medical advances in the field of spine damage.

'We find that attitude's important.' Dr Evans tried a smile but there was something chilling about his bedside manner, as if somehow Paul had brought this on himself.

Attitude. Paul understood that. After Dr Evans had left to continue on his rounds, he stared ahead of him at the plastic curtains which the nurse had left closed, thinking of the path which had led him to this hospital bed.

His family had laughed when he had told them his ambition. They had been having tea as usual, after his father had returned from work at the building site and the mood had been jovial, it being the end of the week and times in the building trade being good. His two older brothers, both in their teens, had been unenthusiastic about the idea of work but had grumpily given the impression that, like their father, they would work in construction. Mary, Paul's sister, wanted to be a nurse.

48

'I'm going to be a jockey,' Paul had said. He was five at the time.

But, to the Raven family's amazement, Paul's obsession with horses had grown stronger as he grew up. He watched racing on the television, discussing form with his father from the age of seven. There was a riding-school on the outskirts of Wigan and, ignoring the taunts of his schoolfriends, he worked there during the school holidays. He was even allowed to compete in the local shows and, although the ponies he rode were less well-fed and schooled than those ridden by the sons and daughters of local farmers, he won his fair share of show-jumping classes.

It took attitude to overcome the opposition of his father, who wanted him to serve an apprenticeship on the site like his brothers, and his teachers, who claimed he was too bright to leave school at the age of sixteen, and to come south, looking for a job in racing.

He had rung three trainers for work and luckily it was the fourth, Ron Charlesworth, who had agreed to take him on. Surly and mean, Charlesworth believed in bringing on his own lads, and that had been the making of Paul Raven.

Maybe he should have stayed in Wigan, he thought. His father and his two brothers were on the dole now; his sister was married with two children; but at least none of them faced a future in a wheelchair.

'How are you feeling?'

Nurse O'Keefe stood at the foot of his bed. Paul was grateful that she wasn't wearing the hospital smile, an expression of phoney sympathy that he found increasingly irritating.

'Numb,' he said. 'I can't take it in. I keep thinking that the drugs have got to me and I'll snap out of it.'

The nurse walked around to the side of the bed. As she was tucking in his sheet, she said quietly, 'If you need someone to talk to, just say the word.' She smiled at Paul in a way that verged on the unprofessional. Then, as if the sister had just walked into the ward, she said more loudly, 'That's what we're here for.'

'Thank you, nurse.'

'Angie.'

'Thank you, Angie.' Paul watched the slim, pale figure as she made her way down the ward to see another patient. 'Angie,' he said, and for the first time for five days, he smiled.

That night, Angie O'Keefe had agreed to go out for a meal with some of the other girls but, when they knocked on her door in the nurses' hostel, she told them she was tired, she had a headache. Eventually, she agreed to meet them later at the restaurant. Now she sat on her neatly-made bed, thinking of the quiet, dark jockey who, Dr Evans said, could be paralysed for life.

Angie's small room was a credit to the convent in Berkshire where she had been educated: neat, well-dusted and decorated only with photographs of her parents and two younger sisters. Unlike many of her contemporaries, she had never reacted against the discipline of her education by running wild in her late teens. Now twenty-one, she had avoided drinking to excess, swore only occasionally and she was a virgin. Not that sexual purity was something to boast about – Angie felt almost jealous when she heard tales of heart-thumping promiscuity from the other girls – she simply preferred to wait for the right man.

She saw the dark, even features of Paul Raven in her mind's eye and shook her head firmly. On every count, he was Mr Wrong. First of all, he was a patient and it was a golden rule among the nurses not to make a difficult job worse by falling in love, or even flirting, with one of the customers.

Then he was a jockey. Angie smiled as she remembered the scandal of one of the old girls who was said to be dating a bookmaker. Fast men who made a questionable living out of fast horses: nothing could be more dangerous for the purity of a girl's soul.

His connections hardly inspired confidence. Two days after Paul had been admitted, his mother, a short angry woman who seemed ill at ease away from the north, had appeared in the ward. Mrs Raven had not exactly told Paul to pull himself together and stop moping about like a big girl's blouse, but she was hardly sympathetic, implying to her son – and, indeed, to the rest of the ward – that, if he were daft enough to ride horses for a living, what else did he expect but to end up in hospital? Like the majority of people, she had no perception of the word paralysed.

The same day a Mrs Charlesworth, the wife of Paul's trainer, had shuffled in. Ron was away racing, she said. Ron needed him back as soon as possible. Ron had been in a filthy mood ever since the race at Plumpton. Without enquiring into Paul's state of health, she had eaten the grapes she had brought, then scurried out of the ward, leaving it smelling faintly of the stables.

Slowly, Angie unbuttoned her nurse's uniform. She walked across the small room to a basin in the corner above which there was a mirror. Angie had never been vain – she had never understood why men looked at her the way they did – but now she stood before the mirror, taking in the pale skin, the athletic figure, the shadows of tiredness under her eyes, the practical, no-nonsense haircut. She ran her hands over her hips as if smoothing down an invisible skirt.

Above all, there was the third reason why Paul Raven should be erased from her thoughts as soon as possible. Angie was a good nurse, but she was no Florence Nightingale. When she gave herself to a man – and she hoped it would be soon – she was old-fashioned enough to hope that he would sweep her off her feet, take control. There was little chance of Paul being able to do that. Caring and convalescence belonged at work, not at home.

Yesterday the other jockey, Alex – the one several of the nurses were talking about in the staff room –

had visited Paul once again. There was something wild and distracted about the man; his conversation was too loud and cheerful to be entirely natural. While they were talking, Angie had called by to check that Paul's drip was still working and, as she walked away, she had sensed that they were discussing her. Paul said something quietly, and she had heard the clipped tones of Alex Drew, saying, 'You know what they say, Paul. There are only two certainties in life – death and nurses.'

She had been unable to resist glancing back. To her relief, Paul wasn't laughing.

That evening, after Alex had left, the customary calm had descended on the ward as the patients watched early-evening soaps on the television. For the nurses, this was about the only time during the day when they could relax, confident that, for a few minutes, the sun-drenched domestic dramas of Australian suburban life would distract the patients' minds from their own troubles.

Angie noticed that Paul never bothered with these programmes. Tonight he seemed quiet, more distant than usual, as if the visit from his friend had unsettled him. Most of the lights in the ward had been switched off, the curtains drawn, so that, briefly, it was lit only by the light from the television.

'So you're not an addict.' Angie smiled, sitting on the chair which Alex had left beside the bed.

'Can't follow the plot.'

She laughed softly. 'How are you feeling?'

'Alex is taking this badly. He keeps going over the race, talking about it. He knows I can't remember anything about the fall but it's as if he wants me to blame him. I've seen the video of the race and there's no doubt he stopped me deliberately. What happened was a chance in a million, but it's eating him up. He looks terrible.'

Angie remembered his remark about nurses, the confident tone of the young middle-class male. 'He seemed all right to me,' she said.

'You don't know him.'

Paul was staring sightlessly in the direction of the television. In the gloom, he reminded Angie of some wounded hero of an old black-and-white film, his dark troubled features against the white of the pillow, his eyes catching the light and seeming to sparkle feverishly. A dying member of the French Resistance, perhaps, even a consumptive poet. Raven – he was well named.

'Tell me something, Angie,' he said. 'Not as a nurse but as a friend. Assuming the worst – that I'll never walk again – ' He paused then plunged on. 'Does that mean that I'm finished as a man too?'

'No. It doesn't.'

He had turned to look at her, surprised by the confidence of her reply.

'You understand what I'm asking?'

'You're all right,' she said. 'If you had no feeling in your legs, there would be a problem. As it is, your – ' Angie hesitated. 'The rest of it will be unimpaired.'

'You're sure about that?'

'I'm sure.' In the semi-darkness, she lay a hand softly on his. 'I asked the doctor myself.'

Back in her room, as the warm water filled the basin before her, Angie remembered the conversation with Paul. She rubbed her hands on the soap, then carefully washed her face. Once she had prided herself on being in control of her life. Too many of her friends had fallen in love with the wrong men at the wrong time and in the wrong way. Not her, she had always vowed. Now she wasn't so sure.

She rinsed her face. Perhaps, after all, she would join her friends at the restaurant. She felt like company.

'Fifty to come in.'

Clay Wentworth pushed a small pile of plastic chips into the middle of the table and allowed his large, fleshy features to assume the expression of relaxed inscrutability he felt was appropriate for these occasions. He stared at the suit – king and five – he held in his hands, as four of the other players – Lol Calloway, Alice Markwick, Digby Welcome and Harry Biddulph – came in.

Clay felt lucky. They were playing his favourite form of poker, Texas Hold 'Em, and already he was seven hundred quid up on the night, thanks to a combination of good hands and cool play. The dealer for the game, Perry Smythe, rolled two more kings and another five and laid them in the middle of the table. Yes, it was his night. When Clay bet £250, the maximum allowed on Thursday Poker Night, Alice, Digby and Biddulph folded. With his usual confident smile, Lol raised it to five hundred.

Lol couldn't handle poker politics. Never had and never would. Clay glanced across and for a moment he was fixed by Calloway's hooded eyes. There was something impressively sinister about him, his bald pate and long, lank hair giving him the look of a bank robber rather than a former rock star, but he was no card-player.

It was time for a spot of Wentworth bluff. Clay glanced down at his hand, frowning as if his best plan was going horribly wrong. He chewed his bottom lip for a moment like a man whose every instinct told him to cut his losses and fold.

Lol Calloway had never been able to read a bluff. Clay looked to him for a 'tell', some small tic that would betray the strength of weakness of Lol's hand, and found it. When the God of poker was smiling on him, Lol would purse his lips, draw the cards together, then re-open them. This, Clay had learned over the two years in which he had been doing poker nights with Lol, was a sure sign that he held a good hand. Despite appearing in cameo roles in the occasional TV detective series, the man was no actor.

He drew his cards together, shook his head, and looked at them again.

A certain etiquette had evolved on Thursday Poker Nights. A player who had folded, or who was sitting out the game, was not meant to comment on proceedings, however light-heartedly. Now Alice, Digby Welcome and Harry Biddulph sat at the table, silent and straight-faced, as Clay called Lol's five hundred and re-raised him another six hundred.

Two cards remained to be shown. Clay judged that Lol must hold the last king and possibly an ace. To match Clay's full house, he needed an ace from one of the next two communal cards. Smythe the dealer dealt the top card, laying it aside face down – an entirely unnecessary touch of melodrama since no one, on Thursday Poker Nights, had been known to cheat – then rolled the top card. It was a four. Lol closed his eyes briefly then nodded. Smythe dealt again. A jack.

'Fuck.' Lol threw down his cards, revealing a king and a nine, and with a passable show of nonchalance wandered over to an open fire on the far side of the room near which there was a drinks trolley. He poured himself a large whisky. 'A whole day's fucking PR receipts. You are one lucky bastard.'

Clay smiled as he raked in his chips, estimating over a grand of clear profit on the game. Sure, he was lucky – not so much with the cards he was dealt but with his poker partners. Over the past two years,

a small but significant percentage of Lol's massive
earnings had found its way into his pocket and those
of the other Thursday regulars. It was as if Lol were
punishing himself for making so much money so
effortlessly. Three good years as a guitar hero in the
early seventies, some clever management of his dim-
inishing assets and the new obsession of advertisers
for revising old tunes had yielded a salary that hit the
half million mark – on a bad year.

'It's called skill,' Clay said amiably, leaving the
game and placing his chips on a side table. That was
the great thing about the Thursday game. From Lol
Calloway, for whom losing fifteen thousand pounds
in ten minutes was mildly irritating but soon forgotten, to Digby Welcome, for whom an equivalent
crash-out would be three hundred or a week's drinking money, the regulars knew how far to take it.
Maybe that was why they were regulars – the guys
who lost it, who went 'on tilt' as they say in gambling
circles, desperately throwing good money after bad,
tended not to last long.

'We need new blood in the school,' Lol muttered,
as if reading Clay's thoughts. 'Another fuckin' Alex
Drew. Otherwise it's always going to be me that's
turned over.' Clay sat in the armchair opposite Lol
and crossed his long legs.

'Couldn't you tell I was looking at a full house?
You were crazy to follow me up.'

Lol stared gloomily into the fire. 'You looked so
fuckin' depressed,' he said. 'I was thinking, it's got

to be bullshit. No way has Clay got a king in the hole
and a five. No one can get that lucky. Oh well – ' he
slurped noisily at his drink. 'Can't win 'em all.'

'No, you can't.'

'Heard from Alex, have you?'

'Had a couple of calls.' Clay noticed that, even
though Digby, Harry Biddulph, Alice and a couple
of the newer members of the group had begun
another game, the focus of attention in the room had
shifted from the poker table to the conversation.
'He's not a happy boy. In fact, he's rather upset about
what happened.'

'Too right,' said Lol. 'A broken back's a fuckin'
bummer in any language.'

'As I understand it,' said Digby Welcome, without
taking his eyes off the two cards in his hand, 'the boy
Raven has crushed vertebrae. Not what I'd call a
broken back.'

A silence descended on the room. It was odd, Clay
thought, that Digby, the one Thursday night regular
who claimed to understand racing, to have it in the
blood, was the person least concerned by what had
happened. Even Alice, in her glacial way, had noted
that there had been what she called 'an unscheduled
casualty'.

He didn't like Welcome, but then few people did.
For a moment Clay watched the stout figure, whose
comical little legs hardly reached the floor, as he
played his normal tight, careful game of poker. If it
was true that in every fat man a thin man was trying

to get out, the inner Digby was a sour, ungenerous bastard strangely at odds with the roly-poly exterior and the flushed round cheeks.

'I fold.' As was his custom, Digby decided that discretion was the better part of valour and left the game at an early stage. The man was a dull poker player, meanly backing good hands while taking few chances. Every Thursday, he gained between £100 and £200 – but then again he probably wasn't there for the money.

No one knew the truth about Digby Welcome. He claimed to be an old Etonian but this, like so much of his personal history, might have been a fraud. By guile and cultivating the right contacts, he had, it was said, established himself as a National Hunt trainer and had a fairly successful yard in Sussex during the 1960s. More surprising still, he had married the reasonably attractive daughter of one of his owners.

It went wrong, but not in the usual way of racing failures – Digby's was not a gambling yard. His innate meanness found him out. The horses were underfed, the lads underpaid. As the winners dried up, owners deserted him and so, amid rumours of unseemly marital demands in the Welcome bedroom, did his wife. Digby gave up his habit of paying bills late, opting instead for not paying them at all. The withdrawal of his trainer's licence was followed, within a month, by bankruptcy.

These days, Digby Welcome represented a small

and somewhat shady manufacturer of horse tonics, travelling in his Volvo Estate from stable to stable. He still went racing, but had more enemies than friends and was frequently to be seen drinking alone at the members' bar.

Having left the game, he placed himself in front of the fire, his short, tubby figure shielding Clay and Lol from the warmth.

'That's racing,' he said, almost sitting in the fire in an attempt to warm his over-generous behind. 'I always used to warn my jockeys about coming up on the inner. Raven's been around long enough to know the dangers.'

'Do me a fuckin' favour, Digby.' This was too much, even for Lol Calloway. 'We all know there was more to it than that.'

Clay darted a warning glance in the direction of the table where the two new members of the Thursday Night school were still playing with rapt concentration. 'Not all of us know that,' he said quietly.

'Well, I feel bad about it,' Lol muttered.

Briefly Clay looked troubled. 'There's nothing we can do now,' he said.

They were on their last game for the night when the call came through. It was almost four o'clock, and Clay was back at the table, taking some money – off Perry Smythe and one of the stockbrokers who had recently joined the school. Alice was just about breaking even and Digby had made his almost statutory two hundred pounds. Only Lol was by the fire, moodily nursing a large glass of whisky.

He looked at his watch without any particular surprise as the telephone continued to ring.

'Must be the fuckin' Coast,' he murmured as he made his way unsteadily across the room. In Lol's world, the only time it was inconsiderate to call was during daytime working hours when he was normally asleep.

''Ullo.' He swayed backwards and forwards like a sailor in a storm. 'Who the fuck is this?' he asked. The answer appeared to take some time. 'Oh, it's you. Why didn't you fuckin' say so? He's in the middle of a game right now.' Lol winced and held the telephone away from his ear. 'All right, all right, keep yer 'air on.' He turned towards the table where the game was taking its course. 'It's for you, Clay. Alex. Says it's important.'

Clay frowned, laid down his cards and walked over to the telephone.

'Alex,' he said silkily. 'Where are you? We were expecting you.'

The call took ten minutes and when he put down the receiver, Clay's good humour had faded. He returned to the table, looking pale and weary.

'Alex Drew wants to talk,' he said.

Digby looked up from his cards. 'He should have come round this evening. A touch of poker therapy would have done him the power of good.'

'To the authorities, I mean.' Clay sat down slowly, still deep in thought. 'I think I dissuaded him.'

'There's not much to talk about.' Alice looked only mildly concerned. 'Nothing can be proved.'

For a moment, there was silence in the room, and from outside the first early twitterings of birdsong could be heard.

'Fuckin' dawn chorus,' muttered Lol.

Clay threw his cards into the middle of the table. 'I'm out,' he said.

From his chair by the fireside, Lol gave a little, drunken laugh. 'Alex was well gone. That little bastard was feeling no pain.'

Clay stared into the dying embers of the fire. 'If only that were true,' he said.

Alex Drew sat on the side of his bed, pressing the mobile telephone to his forehead as if it were a poultice. He didn't cry – he was past all that – but he muttered to himself, again and again. 'No going back. No going back now.'

In his twenty-three years, Alex had experienced his share of good times. He had been to all-night parties. He had lived hard and wildly, drinking and making love. He was no stranger to the more fashionable of recreational drugs – cocaine, amphetamines, even, on a couple of occasions, heroin had assailed his senses. It was life – at least, it was life if you were young, good-looking and from a family where money was never going to be a problem.

And yet he had retained the smooth-faced innocent look of a grown-up choirboy. One day maybe his body would protest, fast-lane wrinkles would appear on his face. Then again, maybe not.

Carefully, Alex switched off the telephone and laid it on the bed. Anguish and guilt had marked his face in a way that too many parties never had. There were rings under his eyes, the once-smooth cheeks were unshaven, the hair, which he wore longer than most other jockeys, was lank and dull.

Like a man preparing for an execution, he stood up, took off his jeans and slipped into his riding-out clothes – jodhpurs, boots, a dark polo-neck sweater. He took a trim jacket from the wardrobe, picked up his car keys from the dressing-table and left.

It was light now. Within an hour the lads would be arriving at Charlesworth's yard to prepare for first lot. Alex unlocked his Audi and, driving with a care that was unusual for him, set off towards Lambourn.

A horse-box was already in the yard, and Alex cursed softly. Having told the guv'nor that he was ill, he hadn't ridden out for three days. Presumably one or two of the horses were running at a distant race-meeting today and needed to set off early.

'Och aye, he's back at last.' Jimmy Summers, the head lad, was putting a couple of hay-nets in the horse-box. 'Better, are you?'

Alex kept walking. 'Much better,' he said.

'You look fuckin' terrible,' said Jimmy cheerfully.

Behind the stables were some farm buildings. He needed to get there and back to the car without arousing Jimmy's suspicions.

'Who's running today then?' he asked.

'Och, it's the big time,' Jimmy smiled. 'We're taking Smile Please and Pretty Marie up to Fakenham. Fuckin' waste of petrol if you ask me.'

The head lad disappeared into the horse box and Alex continued on his way across the yard.

'No going back now,' he said, as memories, unwelcome memories, flashed through his mind.

Someone, somewhere had said to him, as if revealing one of life's eternal verities, that those who play must pay. It had stuck in Alex's mind as being as stupid a cliché as he had ever heard.

The girl – yes, it was a friend of his older sister who, during her brief and otherwise forgettable affair with Alex had allowed herself to get pregnant – had really believed it. She had actually held out her hand and, for a moment, he had failed to understand the precise nature of the payment she was looking for. She was more specific. The cost of the abortion was down to him. He had given her £300 in cash, which was the cost of the operation plus £50 for her trouble – an uncharacteristically spiteful touch, but then he had only been eighteen at the time.

If that was how those who played paid – with a trip to the bank – Alex was unconcerned. Life had given him a blank cheque. The world was his plaything.

By the time he had first met Paul Raven, Alex had decided that there was only one activity about which he would be wholly serious. When he rode horses, the nonsense, the laughter ended. He had ridden his first winner under rules, an amateur hurdle at Devon and Exeter, when he was eighteen. The following year, he was champion amateur and, to the dismay of his father, a wealthy and shrewd Scottish land-owner, he had decided on a career in racing.

The idea of becoming a professional jockey – of riding for money – had come later. Until he was twenty, Alex had assumed that he would work among the ranks of racing's tweed-suited elite – an assistant trainer perhaps or something in bloodstock. His father, a generous man who believed that youth should have its fling, paid for Alex's year at Ron Charlesworth's yard, confident that, by the time he reached his twenty-first birthday, his son would be ready to embark on a serious career.

It had been Paul who changed all that. At Alex's request, he was treated like a normal stable lad at the Charlesworth yard, living in the chilly hostel and spending long, harsh hours mucking out stables and cleaning tack. It was a far tougher baptism than Alex had expected, for his accent, his clothes and, above all, his sports car set him apart from the other lads and made him an obvious target for persecution. Only Paul, the quiet northerner who had already ridden several winners for Charlesworth and other trainers, recognised that behind the soft-skinned facade of a privileged amateur, beyond the playboy image, there was a steely determination.

They should have been enemies. Their backgrounds, their characters, the growing competition for spare rides from the stable seemed sure to set them on a collision course. But, as they rode work together, discussed the horses in the yard, the qualities of the top jockeys they both admired, a mutual respect developed between them.

'Leave him be,' Paul would say with quiet authority. 'Just 'cause he doesn't talk like you, it doesn't mean he can't do the job.'

Gradually the jibes subsided, Alex established his position at the yard and the professional regard between him and Paul developed into friendship.

'How come that leery bastard runs for you when he won't do a tap for me?' Paul had asked half-jokingly after they had worked a couple of three-year-olds over a mile and a half.

'I talk to him nicely.'

'Typical.' Paul had smiled. 'Even the horses are snobs round here.'

Thanks to Paul, Alex had the confidence to join the ranks of professional jockeys and, thanks to him, he had the strength to withstand the storm of disapproval that broke over his head when he told his parents. In a way, he owed Paul everything.

Larks were singing in the pale morning sunlight over the downs as the Audi made its way up the lane beside the gallops. It stopped at a point where there was a hedge beside the track, on the far side of which was Ron Charlesworth's schooling ground.

Moving more deliberately than was his habit, Alex got out and lowered the roof of the convertible. He reached on to the back seat, picking up the rope that he had picked up in Charlesworth's farm building. He glanced up the gallops to ensure that no early morning joggers or dogwalkers were watching and briefly he heard the thunder of hooves as the string made its way up the slight slope towards where he stood. Then, shaking his head as if to rid himself of memories, he took the rope and adeptly formed a loop at one end, smiling to think how the knowledge of knots he had acquired when sailing as a boy was being put to belated use. Laying the coiled rope on the back seat of the car, he took its other end and attached it to the trunk of a stout oak that formed part of the hedgerow. He tugged at it twice then walked slowly back to the car and sat in the driver's seat.

For a moment, it was as if he had drifted off into a trance. Then he reached behind him, took the end of the rope and, as carefully as a woman trying on a hat in a shop, he placed the noose around his neck, tightening it so that the knot rested against the back of his neck.

He glanced at the coils lying on the back seat, then fastened his safety belt. Twenty yards, and in a car with powerful acceleration. It would do.

Alex switched on the engine, gunned the car, priming it as if it were a sprinter in the stalls. He slipped it into first gear, saying quietly, 'Those who play must pay.' This, at least, was true payment.

Taking the handbrake off, he closed his eyes and pressed the accelerator to the floor, drowning out the singing of larks for ever.

Chapter 4

'The VART man?'

There were times when the deep and husky voice of Alice Markwick became aristocratic in its disdain, when a stranger might be forgiven for assuming that she was the daughter of a White Russian countess rather than of a factory worker in Prague.

'The VAT man, yes.' Norman Little, her secretary, stood in the door to her office. A neat, unambitious man in his late twenties, Norman was used to Mrs Markwick's ever-changing moods and had learned to ignore them. 'He claims he has an appointment.'

Alice looked at the leather diary on her desk. 'He is wrong. Tell him to come back next week. Say it's a bad moment.'

Norman touched his temple with thumb and forefinger, like a man sensing the first twinge of a migraine. 'I think that would be unwise, Mrs Markwick. They can make life very awkward, these VAT people.'

'V.A.T. spelt G.O.D. This country's bureaucracy gets more Eastern European every day. Ask Simon to show him the books. He wants the finance director, not me.'

'He insisted that he should see you.'

'Hell and damnation. Get me the books and the last company accounts. And show him into my office – after a quarter of an hour or so.' Alice grimaced as her secretary shook his head disapprovingly. 'All right, five minutes.'

'Yes, Mrs Markwick.'

'And give him a cup of tea – or whatever VART men drink.'

Norman smiled. 'Already done,' he said, retiring from the office like a well-trained butler.

'Bloody VAT.' Alone in her office, Alice closed the desk diary and lit a cigarette. She had nothing to hide from any government money snoop and, if there was one thing you learned from being brought up in Czechoslovakia, it was how to deal with bureaucrats. All the same – Alice stood up and walked to the window – it was bad timing. She felt uneasy, as if some small part of her carefully laid plans had gone wrong, but she didn't know how.

Perhaps it was the jockey. Just over three weeks ago, Alex Drew had committed suicide. There had been an absurd amount of fuss – Alice had never understood the seriousness with which violent death was taken in this country – and the press had pored over his last days in a way which briefly had unnerved her.

'Another casualty,' the fool Wentworth had said when he had rung her with the news. Barely keeping hysteria at bay, he had described how a torso had been found in Alex's car by the lads riding out for Charlesworth. His head had later been discovered in a hedgerow, near a noose.

'How frightfully macabre.' She had tried unsuccessfully for a lightness of tone. 'There were no notes or anything, I hope.'

'I don't think so.'

And there hadn't been. Alex may have been as flashy in death as he had been in life but at least he had been discreet. His death changed nothing, in Alice's view. He had served his purpose.

'You know how your saying goes,' she had said to Clay. 'The one about making omelettes, breaking eggs.'

'Yes.' Clay seemed to be pulling himself together now.

'You're right, of course.'

'Remember. It's some omelette we've got cooking.'

Alice looked down at the laboratory, across a yard from her office. It was a modest set-up, a complex of ill-designed modern buildings, entirely in keeping with the other small businesses run, mostly by Asians, in this particular part of Willesden. Only the discreet but highly sophisticated security system suggested that Markwick Instruments plc was anything out of the ordinary.

The door opened behind her.

'Mr Birtwhistle,' said Norman. 'From the local VAT office.'

'Ah, good.' Alice turned, smiling, even shaking her dark curls with a hint of coquettishness. This, after all, was an occasion for charm. 'So sorry to have kept you waiting, Mr Birtwhistle.'

After two decades in England, Alice could still be surprised. The young man standing before her eyes was not at all her idea of a Mr Birtwhistle from the VAT office. With thick dark hair slicked straight back, a raffish moustache, and smooth, even features, he looked a successful City man, a broker or commodity man with a mobile phone, a Porsche and a string of girlfriends. Even his dark, pin-striped suit seemed rather too well-tailored for a VAT inspector in Willesden.

'The apologies are mine,' he said, a suggestion of a south London twang in his soft voice. 'I was thirty minutes late myself. I had a bit of bother with the address.'

'It's a warren round here.' Alice sat behind her desk, gesturing in the direction of the guest chair nearby. 'People can get lost for days.'

Birtwhistle sat down, laying his shiny black briefcase on his knees. 'I'm still a bit of a stranger to the area,' he said.

'When did you arrange the appointment, exactly?'

'Must have been last Monday.' The VAT man had opened his briefcase and had taken out a form. 'The lady I spoke to assured me this morning was clear for you. Now I needn't detain you long. My department is involved in a background briefing exercise involving businesses in the area whose turnover exceeds half a million pounds and which . . .'

Alice nodded politely as the young man recited his well-rehearsed lines. He was sounding more as she had expected now. Perhaps his manner and style of dressing were merely a sign of the times – these days, even VAT inspectors were upwardly mobile.

He had been talking for about a minute when Norman entered the office, bearing a number of files which, with an apologetic smile, he hid on the desk with a muttered 'The books, Mrs Markwick.'

Birtwhistle paused until Norman had left. 'Sorry,' he said mildly. 'I should have explained. I don't need the figures today – just a few details from you.'

'Details?'

'As I've explained – it's for our local firm profile operation.'

'Ah, yes.' Alice glanced at her watch. 'Well, my late husband set up the firm in 1964. He was a physicist, specialising in optics, in particular early research into lasers. By the time he died we were selling optical instruments to a number of medical establishments and engineering firms throughout the United Kingdom.'

Birtwhistle looked up from the form on which he

was making notes. 'He died when, precisely?'

'1972. Heart attack.'

'And you were . . .'

'We had married in 1969. I had been his secretary.'

'It must have been a great shock.'

'Yes.' Alice quickly closed down that line of questioning which had nothing to do with anybody but her. 'He was only forty-three. But – ' she smiled bravely ' – he left the firm in good shape, with some excellent researchers.'

'Local people, I imagine?'

'They came from all over. Some from England, some from my native country. If they knew about lasers, I didn't care where they were born.'

'And you continued to run the firm.'

'I have a good team. Our turnover topped five million last year.'

'D'you take on defence work?' Birtwhistle asked casually. 'Lasers can be used as a weapon, as I understand.'

Alice smiled. 'Not our type of lasers. We work to make people better, not to kill them.'

'I see.' Birtwhistle took some time to note it down. 'Perhaps you could show me round – when we've finished.' His smile was boyish, almost mischievous.

'Of course,' Alice said. 'I have a meeting in fifteen minutes. Until then – ' she returned his smile with a hint of professional flirtatiousness ' – I'm all yours.'

'One more step.'

Angie O'Keefe stood behind Paul, a hand on each of his hips, ready to catch him should he fall backwards from the walking frame on which he was leaning.

'Jesus.' Paul gritted his teeth as, with effort which seemed to wrack his whole body, he willed his right foot forward. 'Whoever said nursing was one of the caring professions?'

Angie laughed. 'Cruel to be kind,' she said. 'Go on, Paul. One more – for me.'

It wasn't really a step. It was a desperate, unsteady, old man's shuffle which covered barely six inches of the shiny floor in the Physiotherapy Room – but for Paul it felt more important than his first winner. As time had passed and the swelling reduced, relieving the pressure on his spinal cord, so the feeling in his legs had gradually returned. There was no paralysis, but the injury to the bone was quite extensive.

'Enough,' he gasped, as Angie placed his wheelchair behind him. He swayed as she took away the walking frame and stood in front of him. He placed his arms around her neck, saying with a weary smile, 'We can't go on meeting like this.'

She lowered him gently onto the wheelchair.

'I'm exhausted just looking at you,' she said.

Paul smiled. Love and rage were a potent combination, motivating him to push himself faster than ever the doctors wanted.

Thanks to a contribution from the Injured Jockeys' Fund, he had been transferred to the Croydon

Rehabilitation Centre where he devoted his every
waking hour to walking once again.

Angie had taken to visiting him on her days off
work, talking through his despair, helping him to look
to the future, always encouraging him.

'Thanks, nurse,' he said. 'I don't know what I'd do
without you.'

Angie stood in front of the wheelchair smiling, her
arms crossed. 'All part of the service,' she said.

Paul looked away. 'Don't feel you have to visit
me,' he said. 'You should be going out – this must
be just like work for you.'

'I'm not a health visitor,' she said leaning forward
and touching his cheek briefly with her hand. Then,
as if she had suddenly made some rather important
decision, she kissed him – at first tentatively, then
with a firm, deep insistence.

When she stood up, there was colour in her normally pale cheeks.

Paul smiled. 'What do I get after walking six steps
then?' he asked.

'I've never kissed a man like that before,' Angie
said distantly.. 'I mean – it's not like me to make the
first move.'

Paul looked into her clear blue eyes, so close to
him as she stood, one hand on each arm of the chair.
Her face, framed by the short blonde hair, seemed
younger, more vulnerable than when he had first seen
her in the hospital. 'If you hadn't, we might have had
a long wait on our hands,' he said.

Slowly, she pushed the wheelchair down the corridor and back to his small room. Only when she had closed the door behind them did Paul finally speak.

'I need your help,' he said hesitantly. 'I've no right to ask you and I'll understand if you refuse.'

'Don't be . . .'

Paul held up a hand. 'I'm not talking about . . . all this.' He paused. 'I've got to know what happened to Alex.'

Angie turned away to a desk on which there lay some newspaper cuttings. A headline – 'JOCKEY IN SHOCK SUICIDE MYSTERY' – caught her eye. Paul had reacted with incredulity to news of Alex's death but, in time, grief had turned to anger. Although he had been unable to speak of his friend until now, she had noticed the look of quiet determination, almost of anger, that crossed his face when the memories returned.

'What can we do?' She laid a hand on Paul's shoulder. 'Alex is dead. You saw how he was after your fall. He was obsessed with guilt about what had happened.'

'I'm not saying he didn't kill himself. Just that – he was involved in something before the race at Plumpton. I think – I know – that if my fall was just an accident, he would never have killed himself. He was too strong for that. He was a survivor.'

'How long had you been friends?'

'Three years. When he first came to work for Charlesworth, I couldn't stand him – he was so jaunty, so confident. The lads took against him – the way he talked, his good looks, his car. And of course he was an amateur.'

'That matters?'

'It matters. A few years ago, trainers used to put amateurs up on their horses to save the cost of a jockey's fee. These days, they have to pay the Jockey Club so that amateurs and professionals are competing on level terms but the idea that somehow they're taking bread out of the mouths of lads who have worked their way up the hard way lives on.'

'I can understand that. If it weren't for his father's money, Alex would never have made it as an amateur. Compared to someone like you, he had it easy.'

'Didn't matter to me. It wasn't his fault that his parents were rich. But it was never his background that made him different from the lads – it was the fact that he rode better than them. I knew he'd turn professional that first time I rode work with him. It was the only thing he really wanted to do – ride horses and win races.'

'You encouraged him.'

'Of course. We were a bit guarded, at first, but soon we got on well.

'Although we were different, in many ways we were in the same situation – more than lads, once we started getting rides, yet not fully-fledged jockeys. That brought us together. And we trusted one another – in racing, that counts for something.'

Angie sat down at the desk and picked up one of

the cuttings. For the week following his death, there had been lurid speculation about why a young jockey, on the brink of a successful career, should commit suicide. There were rumours of gambling debts, problems with a girlfriend, a rift with his father and mother. A couple of reporters had even tried to talk to Paul but he had refused to comment.

'A few days after Plumpton,' Paul said, 'a reporter from the *Guardian* wrote to me in hospital. It was before it had been announced how badly I was hurt. He had seen a video of the race. He knew nothing about horses, he said, but he was surprised that there was no investigation.'

'Why?'

'He seemed to think Alex put me through the wing deliberately. He wanted my view.'

'What did you say to him?'

'I said he stopped me getting up his innèr, which he is entitled to do, and that there was no way he could have known Dig For Glory would take on the wing. Anyway the article he was writing didn't interest me at the time – he was an anti. Believed racing should be banned. He seemed to be more interested in poor old Dig For Glory than he was in me.'

For a moment, there was silence in the room. Outside, a number of patients in wheelchairs were making slow progress down the drive. It was like a procession of war veterans.

'I read the piece,' Angie said eventually. 'It

mentioned your race. I thought – ' she hesitated ' –
I thought he had a point. Over two hundred horses
were killed last year – it seems a lot for a sport.'

Paul glanced at her, surprised. 'Don't tell me you're
an anti too.'

'I have an open mind.' Briefly, she had the look of
a sixth former asked to defend her position in front
of the class. 'Perhaps now's not the best time to discuss this.'

'I kept the article.' Paul wheeled himself to the
desk and leafed through the cuttings until he found
it. 'I was wondering if this man – ' he glanced at the
byline ' – Gavin Holmes – knew anything. If he's
right – and Alex wanted to stop me in that race for
some other reason – it would explain a lot. Why he
was so distracted that day. Why he was so concerned
about how I was going to ride the race.'

'Why he killed himself.'

'Could be.'

Angie took the cutting and, folding it carefully, put
it in the back pocket of her jeans. 'As your nurse,'
she said, 'my advice would be to look to the future,
not the past.'

'But you're not my nurse any more.'

'No.' She smiled and kissed Paul lightly on the lips.
'I'm not your nurse any more.'

One day, Clay Wentworth thought, he would live in
Ireland. He liked the pace of life, the sense that
nothing – not jobs, not politics nor your home life –

was quite as important as horse-racing. One day, when his father died – if his father died, he was tempted to say – he would sell up, buy some land in County Limerick, and breed horses for the rest of his life.

Leaning on the rails at Leopardstown racecourse, Clay felt at ease with the world. He was more of a countryman than his father had ever been. On the rare occasions Sir Denis Wentworth gazed at a green field, his only thoughts would be of the number of houses it could accommodate and what percentage profit the development would earn.

'Silly old fool,' Clay muttered, as the runners for the Dunraven Handicap Chase cantered past him on their way to the start. Clay was never happier than when a stretch of deep blue seawater stood between him and his father.

He respected Sir Denis, of course. He was immensely grateful for what he would give him one day. The son of a Luton warehouseman, his father had trained as an accountant, then during the 1950s he had become interested in buying and selling property. Thirteen years later, thanks to energy, enterprise and a winning way with corruptible local councillors, he had become a millionaire, one of a new generation of tough industrialists. A knighthood followed and soon, all talk of corruption and ruthlessness forgotten, Sir Denis Wentworth was a pillar of the establishment. Leaning languidly on the rails at Leopardstown, his only son could hardly resent that

– nor the considerable fortune to which he was heir.

Clay made his way from the rails to the grandstand. This was the race he had come to see and he had no intention of being jostled by over-excited Irishmen during its closing stages.

Ballina Lady was the last to go down and, taking his position, Clay followed her progress with binoculars. The publicity surrounding the mare had not been exaggerated – she was impressive-looking, a good seventeen hands and powerful with it. Although she was only six and this was her first season over fences after a successful career as a hurdler, there was an intelligence, an authority to her which suggested real class. There was a stir of interest from the crowd as she cantered down, ridden by the top Irish amateur, Tim Heaney.

It was occasions like these that made Clay aware that he was happier in a warm tweed suit, standing in the grandstand, than out on the course, the reins in his hands and half a ton of horseflesh beneath him.

Clay had been unable to resist a small bet of a hundred pounds on the second favourite. Although he knew little of its form, the prohibitive price on Ballina Lady – three to one on at the bookmaker Clay had used – had pushed out the odds of the other eight runners. On paper, the mare would have little trouble recording her fifth successive win of the season – her jumping was impeccable, the going was as she liked it and, even with a penalty from her last win, she was well handicapped.

There was a buzz of anticipation as the racecourse commentator announced that the field for the Dunraven Handicap 'chase was under orders. As the starter let them go, Clay felt the same clammy-handed expectancy that he had experienced before the race at Plumpton – only now he could enjoy it in the knowledge that today he wasn't riding in a later race.

It was clear why Ballina Lady demanded such a following from racegoers. Ears pricked, she made the running, taking lengths off the other runners at every fence. As the field passed the stand, led by some five lengths by the favourite, one or two racegoers were unable to resist applauding her as she went.

She jumped from fence to fence and seemed to take one stride for everyone else's two. At the end of the back straight for the last time, with three quarters of a mile to run, the race had become a procession, with Tim Heaney hunting the mare along easily, now some fifteen lengths to the good of her nearest contender who was fading.

As Ballina Lady rounded the final bend, with two fences to go, Clay raised the binoculars to his eyes.

Later, they said the roar of the crowd had distracted her. Others claimed that, in the split second before she took the fence, the mare had suffered a massive heart attack. She had met the fence right, Heaney riding her as strongly and confidently as ever. But then she seemed to falter, to lose her way at the last crucial moment. Instead of taking off for the fence, she crashed through it, cartwheeling before

landing awkwardly on her neck on the far side.
Heaney, thrown clear by the fall, lay still as the rest
of the field galloped past him, then sat up on the
damp ground.

Ten yards from him, the best horse he had ever
ridden was not so lucky. It took one look to see that
the mare would never race again. Ballina Lady had
broken her neck.

Clay Wentworth lowered his binoculars. The horse
he had backed had jumped the last fence well clear
but Clay had forgotten about the race. He reached
into the inside pocket of his jacket and took out a
handwritten list. Carefully, with his gold-plated biro,
he crossed out one of the names on it.

'Fucking horses.' Gavin Holmes sat slumped in front
of his screen on the vast open-plan floor at the *Guardian*'s Farringdon Road office. He was tired, he needed
a drink and the editor had wanted yet another update
on his racing story. Yesterday, at some poxy racecourse in Ireland, another nag – apparently a good
one too – had gone belly-up. There were rumours
that a member of the RSPCA Executive was about
to launch a campaign to ban steeplechasing. One of
his stringers was trying to find out how many horses
were killed in training every year.

Gavin looked at his watch. It was six o'clock and
his piece was complete and on-screen. In the unlikely
event of his date for the night coming up with something tasty, he could always phone it in.

Gavin, who was thirty-five but had the muscle tone and liver of a man ten years older, stood up, hitched his jeans over the beginnings of a paunch and slipped on the leather jacket that had been draped over the back of the chair. His reputation as a ladies' man surprised some of the younger journalists – he had the jowly, pallid look of a man allergic to any kind of healthy living, he dressed like a slob and he was distinctly light on romantic charm, 'Are we going to do it or what?' being one of his more subtle approaches.

He made his way to a corner office in which his news editor sat, checking copy, a cigarette dangling from his mouth.

'Checking out a lead, Harry,' he said, standing at the door. 'I'll ring in any changes to the racing piece.'

'Hope she's worth it,' said the news editor without looking up.

Gavin took the lift to the ground floor. Once upon a time, he'd enjoyed his reputation for wildness but now he was discovering that today's tearaway is tomorrow's randy old drunk. Once he had been discussed as a future foreign correspondent; of all his contemporaries, Gavin Holmes was thought most likely to land his own column – witty, informed, knowing. Instead he was still on home news and his only claim to fame was that he had bedded a healthy percentage of his young female colleagues. 'Better than nothing,' he muttered, stumbling out of the lift.

Standing outside the *Guardian* building, the

journalist patted his pockets. He had his cigarettes, he had his tape machine and, the eternal optimist, he had in his wallet a packet of condoms. Gavin smiled as he hailed a taxi. Maybe it was true what they said about girls and horses. Maybe tonight, he would get lucky.

'I don't ride horses myself. I – my boyfriend does.'

Angie felt uneasy as she sat across from the overweight, chain-smoking journalist at a corner table in a city bar. All around her, there was noise and laughter, punctuated by the occasional pop of a champagne cork. Somehow she had found herself backed against the wall, her knees unavoidably touching those of Gavin Holmes. If she tried to move them, she had no doubt that he would misread her body language as some kind of response and move in closer.

'Tell me about him. Your lover.'

Gavin filled the two glasses in front of them with champagne, drained his glass, and refilled it. In the ten minutes since they had met, he had smoked two cigarettes, made light work of a bottle of Möet et Chandon and casually dropped the names of several politicians and actors with whom he appeared to be on first-name terms.

'He comes from the north,' Angie said. 'He's a jockey. He's brave.' Angie was unhappy at the way the discussion was going.

'Will he ride again?'

'Probably not. He can't really walk yet.'

'Poor bastard.' Gavin waved at the barman and, ignoring Angie's protests, ordered another bottle of champagne. 'Where do I come into this?' he asked.

'In your article, you mentioned a video – taken head-on at Plumpton.'

'Right. I used a contact on the racecourse staff. He gave it to me.'

A waiter brought the second bottle of champagne to the table, filled Gavin's glass and poured a polite drop into Angie's which was already full.

'I thought your friend would have wanted to see it. What does he think?' Gavin asked. 'It looked deliberate to me.'

'He thinks – ' Angie checked herself, her head was aching now from the smoke and champagne. 'He thinks there's more to it than just one jockey stopping another.'

Gavin looked at Angie with his best knowing smile. This girl was cute – very cute. Young of course, and a bit shy, but he liked that.

'So it's a favour he's asking,' he said.

'A small favour.'

Angie closed her eyes, as the journalist moved his knee up and down against hers. She decided, for Paul, to give it one more try, then to leave.

'There may be a story in this,' she said. 'A big story. Paul would give you first shot at it.'

Suppressing a belch, Gavin muttered, 'Stories – who needs fucking stories? I've got stories up to where my hair used to be. They're the last thing I

89

need – particularly if they're anything to do with sodding horses.'

'Fine.' Angie picked her bag off the floor. 'It was just a thought.'

'On the other hand,' Gavin said quickly. 'You never know. Why don't we talk about this over dinner? Maybe we could – ' the hint of a leer entered his voice ' – work something out.'

'I have a train to catch.'

The journalist muttered, 'How about a quickie then?' Misunderstanding, Angie smiled politely. 'No, I've drunk too much already. I really ought to go.'

'I'll get you a taxi later. The paper'll pay.'

Angie tried to stand up but found her way barred.

'I think I might be able to help you with that favour,' Gavin was saying. 'Maybe two favours.'

Angie pushed back the table and, trying to ignore the hand that touched her thigh as she passed, paused briefly. 'Two favours?'

The journalist smiled. 'He can't walk, you say, your lover. Disabled. It must be tough on you. No nooky.'

Ignoring Angie's angry look, Gavin added quietly, 'I'll get you back in the morning. You and me, eh?'

She turned and walked quickly out of the bar.

The photographer sat in his BMW, some thirty yards away from the entrance to Markwick Instruments plc. He was a heavy man but the watchful look in his eyes and the slightly tanned face suggested that, should he ever be required to, he could defend himself in a tight corner. He had risen early that morning and now, at ten thirty in the evening, he looked unshaven and tired.

Peter Zametsky emerged from the front door of the office building, looked quickly left, then right, and walked towards the car. As he approached, the photographer got out, handed him the keys. The two men spoke briefly and quickly in their own language. Then the photographer crossed the road, unlocked an old Jaguar and drove off at no particular speed.

Peter sat in the BMW and spoke into the car telephone. When he had finished he drove the car towards the office building. As he approached, the metal gates that led to the office yard opened, allowing the car through.

After they had closed, a man watching from the darkness of a nearby alley walked away quickly down the gloomy side street towards the lights of Willesden.

Chapter 5

Racing likes its heroes dead and dignified, or alive
and winning. It has no place for the halt and the
lame. If Paul had been killed by Dig For Glory's fall
at Plumpton, his tragically brief career would have
been commemorated by an annual race at the course
– the Paul Raven Memorial Hurdle or something simi-
lar. If he had walked away unharmed, the calls from
trainers would have continued to come in. As it was,
he was no more than a distant memory. In the harsh,
enclosed world of racing, there's no place for fellow
travellers.

It was a month after his discharge from the Home
in Croydon and, on the face of it, he had much for
which to be thankful. With the help of two walking
sticks and occasional pain-killers, he could walk,
albeit slowly and uncertainly. The doctors, whose
experience had taught them to be pessimistic about
back injuries, had found themselves revising their
prognoses as, step by painful step, Paul proved them

wrong. Those who once confidently predicted that he would never be free of his wheelchair admitted that a few, shuffled paces a day would be a possibility. When Paul walked twenty, then thirty, then fifty yards, they admitted they may have over-estimated the damage to his vertebrae. On the day he discharged himself from the Home, they warned him of the consequences but, among themselves, they were pleased to see him go. He was a difficult patient. Bloody-minded. He had never done what he had been told.

Yes, he was thankful to be away from the men in white coats, thankful to be walking slowly, still with two walking-sticks but more confidently now, down Lambourn High Street. He was home and, although he could do nothing to help in the yard, he had been allowed to stay in the small flat rented by Ron Charlesworth for his more favoured staff. This, by Charlesworth's standards, was an act of almost unprecedented generosity.

It was too early to say what he would do with his life. Angie, who visited him on her days off, believed he should get out of racing altogether, but Paul knew he couldn't. Not yet at least.

He turned into a newsagent where an elderly man handed him a *Sporting Life* with a cheery 'What do you know, Paul?'

'Not much, Bill.' Paul smiled. Like several of his friends in Lambourn, Bill Preston overcame the embarrassment of his disability by refusing to admit it existed. Every day, he was as eager for tips from Paul as if he were on his way to the races, at the centre of things, as he had been in the old days.

He took the paper and glanced at the headlines, the tips and whispers about the day's runners. No, Angie was wrong – racing was in his blood. Until he knew what had happened to Alex, it would stay there.

Paul was greeted by a couple of stable lads from Charlesworth's yard but resisted the temptation to ask them of any news. Although the trainer was making use of freelances, it could only be a matter of time before he signed up a new stable jockey. For their part, the lads seemed uneasy, hurrying on after exchanging a few pleasantries with Paul, as if his bad luck could be catching.

A dirty yellow Rolls Royce cruised down the High Street. It passed Paul, then stopped some twenty yards ahead of him. The driver had made no attempt to park, leaving the car some two feet from the kerb. A woman, blonde and in her late thirties or early forties, emerged and half walked, half ran, a fur coat billowing behind her, tripping on high heels towards where Paul stood. To his surprise, she held out an elegant hand.

'Mr Raven?'

'That's right.'

The woman smiled, perfect capped teeth gleaming behind the lipstick.

'Zena Wentworth. We haven't met.'

Guardedly, Paul hooked the walking-stick over his

arm and shook her hand. The woman's breezy confidence and cut-glass tones were not endearing. 'How can I help you?' he asked.

'It's about Alex Drew,' she said. 'I was a friend of his.' Behind her, several drivers, held up by the badly parked Rolls, were sounding their horns. 'Dickheads,' she said conversationally.

'How did you know Alex?' Paul asked.

Zena flashed another smile and glanced over her shoulder. 'The natives appear to be getting restless,' she said. 'Let me give you lunch.'

Paul thought for a moment, then nodded. 'All right,' he said. 'Let's go to a pub.'

Zena Wentworth wasn't used to pubs. Three had been rejected on the grounds of being too smoky, too common and too full of darts players before they found a hotel on the outskirts of Wantage which she found acceptable. A fast driver, she had kept up a monologue, rarely interrupted by Paul.

Half listening, while gripping the side of his seat, Paul had discovered that Zena was married to Clay Wentworth, that she had not the slightest interest in racing and that she appeared to be on first name terms with most of the well-bred wallies whose faces Paul had seen in gossip columns and glossy magazines.

It was only when they were sitting in the dining-room of the Bell Tavern, Wantage that Zena mentioned Alex Drew. Already, she had made it clear that the quiet, unpretentious atmosphere was not what she was used to, bewildering the young waitress by asking for a tequila before settling sulkily for a large vodka and tonic. When the waitress brought them the menu in a plastic folder, she had opened it, placed a hand over the typed contents and said, 'Let me guess. Steak and chips. Gammon and chips. Plaice and chips.' And she was right, of course.

After the waitress had taken their order, she lit a cigarette. 'God, I hate the countryside,' she said cheerfully. 'This is the sort of place Alex used to take me to.'

Paul watched her as the cigarette smoke caught the winter sun shining into the half empty dining-room. There was something odd about Zena Wentworth, a tension which suggested that her sophistication and worldliness were a disguise, a cover.

'How did you know Alex?' he asked again, quietly.

'Met him at a party in London,' she said vaguely. 'Usual thing. Boy meets girl. We – ' she gave him a knowing smile ' – clicked.'

'Are you telling me – ' Realising that his incredulity might be taken for rudeness, Paul hesitated. 'But he had a girlfriend.'

'Everybody has a girlfriend. And everybody cheats.'

The waitress brought the drinks. Zena raised her glass before drinking deeply. Paul sipped at his tomato juice, thinking about Alex. That his friend had been unfaithful to Joanna was hardly a surprise. But Zena Wentworth? She could have been his mother.

'What's this got to do with me?' he asked.

Zena seemed more relaxed now that she had a glass in her hand. 'I heard – a little birdy told me – that you wanted to know more about Alex's death.'

Paul nodded. For all her apparent lack of interest in racing, Zena Wentworth seemed well-informed. Over the past month, he had been ringing around his contacts, people who knew or had worked with Alex. The story had always been the same. Until the beginning of this season, Alex had been fine. Since then, as Paul had noticed himself, he had become less reliable, turning up late for work, struggling to make weights that last season would have been easy. Like Paul, no one seemed to know what his problem was. But there was something outside racing that had been distracting him. Paul had spoken to Joanna but she had seemed embarrassed by the call, as if Paul's interest was no more than a morbid obsession with the past.

'I want to know why he killed himself,' he said. 'I haven't been able to do much – I only started driving last week – but I'm convinced he was involved in something.'

'There's a little man I know who's become rather interested in Alex's story. A somewhat unsavoury journalist called Gavin Holmes. I believe you know him.'

'I know the name,' Paul said carefully. 'I wouldn't have thought he was on your circuit.'

Zena gave a contemptuous little laugh. 'He isn't, thank God. A couple of years ago he developed an interest in the scandalous use of drugs in society. Some little prig gave him my name. We developed what you might call a working relationship.' She paused, as if expecting a question. 'Like most journalists, the man's infinitely corruptible. I hadn't heard from him for a while until he called the other day. It appears that he's taking an interest in Alex. He told me that a little friend of yours had seen him.'

'Yes. He wasn't helpful.'

'Tell me why you're so interested.'

'I need to be convinced that it was an accident.'

'Did you know Alex gambled?' Zena asked suddenly.

'He didn't gamble. I'd know if he was in the pocket of the bookmakers. Stewards may not be able to tell the triers from the non-triers, but one jockey can't fool another, and believe me, he always did his best.'

'Not bookmakers. Cards. He fancied himself at stud poker, poor boy.'

'I know. He used to play with the other jockeys in the weighing room. He was quite good. How did you know he played cards?'

Picking unenthusiastically at her microwaved plaice and chips, Zena told him about the Thursday poker nights – how Alex, at first an occasional player, had over the months before his death become a regular. When Paul shook his head incredulously, she said, 'He wanted to be a grown-up, poor boy. He wanted to be one of the big guys.'

'Did he win?'

Zena shrugged. 'You should understand that, in my marriage, communication is limited to the practical. Clay would no more tell me about his poker nights than I would tell him about my... private business. I understood from Alex that he was in some difficulty. He didn't like talking about it.'

'What sort of people go to these poker nights?'

'They're either rich and bored, or on the make. The only regulars that I know of are Lol Calloway, the clapped-out rock star, and a man called Digby Welcome. I can try to get more names, if you want.' She smiled, lighting up another cigarette although Paul was still eating. 'Maybe we could work together on this.'

'The names would be useful, although I still don't see the connection between Alex's gambling and what happened at Plumpton.'

'Nor me.' Zena picked up the leather bag that she had laid beside her chair. 'I must be going. I'll see if I can find out any more for you.'

'How?'

Zena Wentworth gave a histrionic little shudder. 'I don't even want to *think* about it,' she said.

Later, driving back to London, Zena thought about Paul Raven. She had, of course, told him only part of what she knew, but the information would revive his faltering attempts to discover what had happened to Alex Drew.

She was coming down, the couple of pills she had

taken that morning to get her through the day had been nullified by the vodka. Zena accelerated, pushing the Rolls up to a hundred and ten as she fumbled in her bag. Expertly, she removed another pill from a small bottle and tossed it back into her mouth.

She smiled at the thought of Paul Raven's expression when she had left. For a man who rode horses, he was no fool. He realised what she meant. He was so young, so innocent. For him, the most simple of sexual transactions had a deep significance. Zena tried to remember what that purity had been like, but failed. It was all so long ago.

She thought of Alex, of how she and Clay, in different ways, had corrupted him and felt a fleeting pang of guilt. Yes, what she was doing was right. Paul Raven was a bonus. On the racecourse at Plumpton, he had seemed just another scrawny jockey but weeks of inaction had filled out his face. Pain and anger had made it interesting.

'Just once,' she said. 'Once is all I want.'

In America, Alice Markwick had always thought, they organized things better. If her first stop from Prague had been New York rather than London, she wouldn't have found herself dealing with bungling, weak amateurs, with the astonishing complexities of Britain's subtle class system, with the obstacles placed in her way by interfering government bureaucrats.

Behind Alice's large desk, a cold winter dusk was settling sullenly on the streets of Willesden. The workers from the factory below were making their way home, doubtless cursing her name and dreaming of a time when their futures would not be bound up with that of Markwick Instruments plc.

She didn't give a damn. Dispensing human happiness had never figured among her priorities. Once, three or four years ago, she had employed a Personnel Officer but he had disagreed with her on a matter of basic policy – as to whether to treat personnel like human beings or expendable units – and she had fired him within the month. Her firm was no place for tenderhearts.

She pulled a small white telephone on her desk, her personal line, and stabbed out a number. It was time to put a call through to the man who made even her short-lived Personnel Officer seem like a tower of strength.

'Clay,' she said. 'Alice. I hear we're in business again.'

At the other end of the telephone, Clay laughed nervously. 'Went like a dream,' he said.

'No problems at all?'

'There are one or two comments in the racing press but everyone puts it down to bad luck.'

'It's a funny old game,' said Alice flatly.

'D'you have the *Sporting Life*?'

'I'm not a regular reader, I'm afraid, Clay.'

'Let me read you their report.' There was the sound of rustling paper and Alice imagined Clay in his large office, the huge photograph behind him showing Mr

C Wentworth as he jumped the water at Kempton on Skinflint. She sighed. A captain of industry. God help England.

'Here we are,' he said finally. ' "JINX HITS CHELTENHAM HOPE . . . . The extraordinary run of bad luck that has befallen the season's contenders for the top amateur prizes continued yesterday at Huntingdon when the highly fancied Brut Force failed to finish after a bizarre accident in the Valentine Hunter Chase. The experienced nine-year-old, who started at eleven to four on, appeared to be making light work of the field of six when, after jumping superbly throughout, he entered the final turn with a ten-length lead only to fail to negotiate the bend, crashing through the stand side rails in a horrific fall. His young amateur rider Jamie Saunders, who was miraculously uninjured, was mystified by the normally reliable Brut Force's lapse. 'Until then, he hadn't put a foot wrong,' Saunders told me. 'But, as we came out of the bend, he seemed to panic and I couldn't steer him.'

' "Trainer Charlie Dixon had been mystified as to what went wrong and added that the horse appeared to have injured his back and had lacerations to his hindquarters.

' " ' Brut Force won't run again this season,' he said, 'but we hope to patch him up for next year.'

' "Brut Force is the latest of a series of horses fancied for one of the major amateur races at the

National Hunt Festival which have been forced to withdraw, after the tragic deaths over the last month of the Irish mare Ballina Lady and the crack northern 'chaser Whataparty." '

'Accidents will happen,' said Alice. 'Perhaps we should leave it there. We don't want to stretch coincidence too far.'

'One more,' Clay said briskly. 'Thursday, Wincanton. As we agreed.'

Alice sighed. 'At least there's no danger of a post mortem this time,' she said.

'Right,' said Clay. 'Are you coming to play poker this week?'

'I hope so.'

After she had hung up, Alice sat at her desk, deep in thought. True, Clay was a bungling amateur, but he was a useful bungling amateur, and expendable. After all – she glanced at the photograph of a frail-looking man that was given pride of place in the office – bungling amateurs had served her well.

Not that the late Dr Eric Markwick was an amateur in every way. As a scientist, he had been years ahead of his time. It was real life that caused him problems.

As Alice's ambitions had begun to seem realizable at last, she found herself thinking more and more of Eric. Doubtless he would have thought her plans dangerous, immoral even. His risks and gambles rarely extended beyond the theoretical and scientific; his weakness was not for money or power, but simply for Alzbeta Flaishman, an innocent little Czechoslovak girl trying to find her way in a wicked western metropolis.

Alice smiled. She must have been innocent once, when she was Alzbeta, but she really couldn't remember when. Prague during the 'fifties and 'sixties was no place for childish illusion. Her father worked in a munitions factory, spending what little he earned on vodka, occasionally venting his rage against a grey, unjust world on Alzbeta, her older brother Tomas and, above all, on her mother. Partly to earn extra money and partly to escape from the bellows and the flailing of her husband, Alzbeta's mother Irina had taken a job, cleaning government offices in the evening and late into the night.

She was beautiful. No misery could extinguish the sparkle of those dark eyes, the long dark curls, the frail but womanly body.

Their life changed. Mr Flaishman was given promotion and an honorary post in the local party. The family was able to move to a larger flat in a better part of town. Maybe, when she was seven or eight, Alzbeta might have believed that this was the way life was – you worked, you were rewarded – but there was something in her mother's eyes that told her differently, that spoke of corruption and compromise.

There was one moment that changed it all. One night – Alzbeta was just ten – word came from the local bar that old Flaishman had hurt himself, having become involved in a brawl. A neighbour had seen the fight and ran to tell Alzbeta and her brother that their father had been taken unconscious to the local hospital. Tomas had gone to the hospital while Alzbeta went through the dark streets of Prague to the Central Party offices where her mother was working.

It was ten-thirty when she arrived in the vast building. Frantically she had asked a couple of crones sweeping a downstairs corridor where she could find Mrs Flaishman. Her question had caused much hilarity, but eventually they had directed her to the top floor.

The building was five floors high, there was no lift and by the time she reached the top, she was breathless and tearful. She tried office after office, nervously opening each door in the brightly-lit warren of corridors. It seemed a lifetime but it must have been five minutes at the most when she pushed open the large door to a corner office.

The man was large and wearing the grey uniform of a senior officer in the army. His face was red and transfixed by an ugly smile, or perhaps a grimace. His fat hand, like that of a priest conferring a blessing on a communicant, lay on her mother's head as, kneeling – crouched under the pendulous bulk of the man's paunch – she worked on him, nodding like a doll with a broken neck. As Alzbeta stood there, the man tightened his grip on her mother's head, not allowing her to turn towards the door. 'Welcome, little one,' he said thickly. 'Have you come to join the party?'

She stood there for twenty seconds, perhaps thirty. Then, without a word, she had turned, rushing blindly down the corridor, almost falling down the stairs and into the icy cold night where she had run, tears streaming down her face, back to the flat.

Because everyday existence in Prague was full of such humiliations and sleazy compromises, nothing much changed among the Flaishmans after that night. Alzbeta's father recovered but, whenever the mood was upon him, would blame Irina for not visiting him in hospital that night. But then little Alzbeta had failed to find her. While old man Flaishman grumbled and Tomas mocked Alzbeta for her ineffectiveness, the two women of the family had caught one another's eye and each had looked away quickly, unwilling to acknowledge the guilty secret they shared.

When she grew up, she came to think of her mother as a heroine, abasing herself night after night, an unofficial whore, so that her family could survive. But then, with the clear, unforgiving eyes of childhood, she felt nothing but a deep sense of betrayal – of her father, of the family, above all, of her. A coldness entered the home as little Alzbeta extinguished the warmth and laughter she had once brought to it.

Seeing her mother kneeling before the soldier changed Alzbeta's life for ever. She knew, even at ten years old, that she had to get away from the family, possibly even from the country. Never political, she spent her teens begging her parents to be sent to the west to study, professing a deep interest in the ways of capitalism. An exit visa, of course, was impossible; the Flaishman family had little enough money without the expense of sending a daughter abroad.

And here was the ultimate compromise. Alzbeta knew the way things worked in Czechoslovakia. She understood that her mother could win her escape only one way, yet she asked for it. While treating her mother with cold disapproval, she accepted the rewards of whatever Irina did at the government offices into the early hours of the morning. On her eighteenth birthday, Alzbeta was given an exit visa and one hundred pounds in English money. When she cried, her father and Tomas assumed it was out of gratitude. Only Irina knew the truth.

Something else changed that night when old Flaishman got drunk and was taken to hospital. As the girl became a woman, as beautiful as her mother, with the same dark curls and slender waist, Alzbeta knew with a deep certainty that, whatever else she did, she would never make love to a man. She would lose her virginity, of course, she would use her beauty, but in submitting to men, she would be the exploiter, not the exploited. She might smile, flirt, feign desire but it would be done with a clear-eyed coolness that had nothing to do with love. The idea of being penetrated was loathsome to her; it was a foul invasion, for which she would demand, and receive, the highest price.

The heating in the offices of Markwick Instruments had been turned off, and Alice shuddered. 'Poor Eric,' she said quietly, as she tidied the papers on her desk. Poor Eric had only discovered that too late.

Turning off the lights in her office, she made her way downstairs, across the yard to the laboratory. Zametsky would be there, of course. Despite the young wife and baby whom he worshipped, Peter usually worked late, so absorbed in his work that he would hardly have noticed that the sun had set, that his colleagues had gone home. Sometimes he worked until nine or ten at night, the light in his corner cubicle shining like the beacon of pure research into the grubby gloom of Willesden.

Pure research. Alice Markwick smiled as she entered the laboratory.

'What about that poor wife of yours, Peter?' she called out as she made her way down one side of the lab, switching off work-lamps.

There was a distracted grunt from the direction of Peter Zametsky's desk. Sometimes, when she had interrupted him as he worked on a problem, stabbing at the keyboard of his computer, making swift, feverish notes on a lined pad on the desk, he had seemed in a different world, had turned to her with a look of fierce concentration, the light in his eyes fading slowly as he turned back into the dull world of reality. He should have been at a university where such intensity was regarded as normal but there again no university could give Peter Zametsky what she could offer.

Alice was about to leave the genius in his laboratory, working for the good of human knowledge and Markwick Instruments – though not necessarily in that order – when she noticed through the frosted glass of his corner office, that he appeared not to be sitting on his chair. Then she saw a foot, trembling slightly, obtruding from the office.

He was lying on his back, his legs awry and his hands palm downwards on the floor, clawing at it. His shirt appeared to have burnt around the chest and neck but Peter's head was hidden behind the desk. As Alice stepped, his body shook epileptically. Then she saw his face – or, at least, what remained of his face under the bubbling, suppurating purple surface that had once been his flesh. The eyes were gone, the nose was no more than a white bone extending from a featureless mass. His hair, like the carpet beneath his head, had been burnt away, but the mouth – a lipless, gaping cavern – was open in a silent scream of pain.

Alice stepped back. She took a deep breath, swaying slightly. Then she walked quickly to a nearby telephone, stabbing three digits quickly. Her voice, when it came, had only the hint of a tremor.

'Ambulance,' she said.

Digby Welcome was asleep in his deep and comfortable single bed when the call came through. He had had a busy day – a full five hours work on the daytime job, followed by a late evening trawl among his Kensington contacts, and he was tired. As his head touched the pillow, he was off, enjoying the profound, untroubled sleep of a man with no conscience.

'Is it a bad moment?' The voice at the other end

of the telephone was Clay Wentworth's. He sounded more than usually rattled.

Digby looked at the leather-cased alarm clock by his bed. 'Two thirty in the morning is always a bad moment, dear boy.' He sat up in his bed and switched on the light. In his well-cut flannel pyjamas covering his globe-like stomach, he looked almost cuddly. 'But I'm not fucking anyone, if that's what you mean.'

'We have a problem. Alice's senior boffin appears to have been attacked. She's spitting – thinks there's been some sort of security leak.'

'Bloody fool. Why does she think that has anything to do with us?'

'It appears she's had her suspicions for some time. She rang me a few days ago about some taxman snooping around. She had managed to convince herself that he was part of the opposition. Just turned up out of the blue, claiming to have made an appointment through a female secretary.'

'I thought she only employed male secretaries.'

'Precisely. Then this chap Zametsky had told her that he thought the offices were being watched – cars parked across the road and so on. Next thing she knows the guy's had some sort of acid splashed over him.'

'Oh shit.' It was an utterance of vague annoyance, like that of a man finding he hasn't a clean shirt in the morning.

'She's managed to keep the police out of it. Luckily the acid came from the Markwick stores so she managed to persuade the doctors that it was an accident. Anyway, I promised her I'd ring round. You haven't been talking have you, Digby?'

'Don't be absurd. I may not be good for much but my discretion's phenomenal. Have you tried Lol?'

'He said the same thing.'

'Zena? No one could be less discreet than your wife when she's on the stuff.'

Clay Wentworth gave a humourless laugh. 'She knows nothing about this.'

'Well then.' Digby yawned, running a hand over his large stomach. 'No problem. Probably Alice getting the jitters. You know how she is. What about her chap – the one with the acid? Has he said anything?'

'He's in intensive care. Alice seems to think that he won't make it.'

'Poor bastard,' said Digby cheerily, promising to see Clay at Wincanton.

'Yes, poor bastard,' he muttered after Clay had hung up, but he was thinking of himself now. He was awake, his fat frame full of an unmistakeable restlessness for which there was only one known cure. He reached into a drawer in the bedside table, taking out a small black book. He found a number and dialled.

Chapter 6

It was a long, painful walk from the car park at Wincanton to the weighing-room. Even now that he had graduated from two walking-sticks to one, Paul could shuffle only slowly, and with many rests. Then there was the pain: in spite of Angie's protests, he had weaned himself off painkillers, determined, in an obscure, unmedical way, to fight his handicap on his own terms.

There was another kind of pain. It was Paul's first return to a racecourse after his fall at Plumpton and he had to endure the sympathy and covert, sideways looks of those who had known him when he was fit and on the way up. A few pretended not to notice him and hurried by, but most of them – particularly the trainers and jockeys – paused to talk to him, their voices unusually loud and hearty, their eyes betraying embarrassment, fear and, worst of all, pity.

Angie helped. She walked beside him slowly, with the easy amble of one who's happy to take her time.

She asked him questions about racing – innocent daft questions that, had they been asked by anyone else, Paul would have found irritating. It was the first time she had been racing and her clothes – a light girlish dress, a beret on her head, a bright green scarf wrapped around her neck – gave her away. Paul glanced at her and smiled. She looked sexy, fashionable, and desirable. On the whole, people who came racing at Wincanton in February were none of these things.

'You look good,' he said quietly, as they made their way onto the course.

'I'm not sure I approve of all this. I might stage an anti-racing demo in the paddock.'

Paul laughed. 'That would be the end of a beautiful friendship,' he said.

'Bloody hell, I thought you were crook, Raven.' The unmistakeable, booming tones of Ginnie Matthews interrupted their conversation.

Paul stopped, leaning briefly on his walking-stick, as the trainer sized him up, as if he were one of her charges after a spot of work. 'Not finished yet, Mrs Matthews.'

Ginnie glanced at Angie. 'So I see,' she said, introducing herself to Angie with a smile. 'Better go and see my fella at the stables. How about a drink later? Catch up on the news.'

'That would be good.' Paul smiled. For all her bluff heartiness, Ginnie Matthews was one of the few trainers who wouldn't make him feel uneasy. 'Just the one runner today?'

'Skinflint. We should win the amateur race.'

'Tanglewood's useful.' Ginnie dropped her voice to what she assumed was an undertone but still made nearby heads turn. 'Which is more than could be said for our jockey.'

'Who's the jockey?' Angie asked, after Ginnie had left.

'A man called Clay Wentworth,' said Paul. 'It was his wife who came to see me.'

'Small world.'

'Yes. Everybody knows everybody else's secrets.'

'Which should make it easier to find out what happened to Alex.'

'Let's hope so.'

Paul took Angie to the bar where he bought her a drink and found her a quiet table. 'I'm going to the weighing-room,' he said. 'I need to talk to someone. I'll be back in a few minutes.' Then, seeing the look of uneasiness that crossed Angie's face, he added, 'Don't worry. It's one of life's golden rules – no one gets picked up at Wincanton.'

Angie looked around the bar, where men and women were earnestly discussing the day's racing. Apart from the occasional, distracted glance in her direction she might have been invisible. 'Don't be long,' she said.

It was strange re-entering the weighing-room, leaning on a stick, a bystander to the day's action. Already, Paul felt an outsider. Although the official at the door, who was only supposed to admit jockeys riding that day, had nodded him through, there was a hint of sympathy to his smile; there was no mistaking the warmth of the greetings given to him by his fellow jockeys and by the valets but here, for the first time, in the smell of cigarette smoke, linament and saddle soap, he became aware of the void that would be left in his life now that he was unable to ride any more. Suddenly he was an outsider, a hanger-on, a has-been.

'You look better than ever, Pauly.' Jim Wilson sat down beside him during the brief lull that followed the jockeys for the first race trooping out of the weighing-room. 'If it weren't for that stick, I'd be laying out your gear as if nothing had happened.'

Paul smiled. 'And I'd be getting into it. I can't get used to this spectator lark.'

'When will you be back? End of the season?'

'They don't know.' Paul looked away. He wasn't in the mood to discuss his future. 'Tell me what the lads have been saying about Alex.'

'Lex.' The valet wiped his hands with the cloth he was carrying. It was an odd, uncharacteristic action and he suddenly seemed older and more fragile than his years. Alex, Paul remembered, had been one of Jim's favourite jockeys. 'Now there's a thing for you.'

'Someone must have an idea what made him do it.'

'He was in a bad way. We all knew that. Even before – ' Jim hesitated ' – even before Plumpton, he had been acting strange. But you know how he was, he'd keep on joking, never letting on what was really happening.'

'Bookies?'

'No. I asked around. He didn't bet – at least no more than any of the lads did. I have a feeling it was something to do with his life outside racing.'

'I saw the head-on of our race at Plumpton,' Paul said quietly. 'There's no doubt that he was up to something.'

'You mean he put you through the wing.'

'Let's just say he could have given me more room.'

'I can't understand it. He was your mate.'

'Nor can I. But if he did put me through the wing and then thought that I'd never walk again, it could explain why . . .' Ambushed by obscene imaginings of his best friend, Paul stared ahead in silence.

'I saw him alone in the car park that day. Then one of the lads said he was talking to Digby Welcome near the Members' Bar.'

'Welcome?' Paul was incredulous. 'That bastard offered me two grand to stop a horse at Lingfield once. What would Alex want with him?'

For a moment, the two men sat in silence, thinking of Alex Drew. Then Jim stood up. 'Is it a good idea, this?' he asked. 'Maybe you should be thinking about your own future, rather than digging around in the past.'

'I'll have plenty of time for that.'

'Better get on, Pauly.'

'Let us know if you hear anything, right?'

Jim nodded. 'I'll do some asking round,' he said.

Angie had always considered herself an easygoing, gregarious sort of person who could adapt to most social environments. A couple of years ago, her father had taken her to Henley where she had smiled her way through a tiresome afternoon of straw hats and champagne without too much difficulty. One of her first boyfriends had been obsessed by grand prix racing – hours at Silverstone spent jostled by men in sheepskin coats with their willowy girlfriends against a background of screaming engines had posed no problem. A passing-out parade at Sandhurst, a *thé dansant* at the Savoy, a fashion show in aid of Africa's starving millions, an acid house party in a disused hangar off the M25 – Angie had endured them all with the same sweet tolerance.

But National Hunt racing on a Thursday, particularly now that Paul had left her on her own while he visited old friends, was proving to be a trial. Wherever, she went, she felt eyes following her, as if no one young and well-dressed had ever been seen here before.

In the bar, she had been ignored until two men in officer issue overcoats had, after a languid enquiry in her direction which she had failed to understand, sat down at her table to conduct a hearty conversation about breeding and bloodstock. Occasionally one of the men had glanced at her with undisguised suspicion so that eventually, feeling like a spy, she had left the table and stood at the bar to wait for Paul.

There was only one group of racegoers, Angie decided, that belonged to a world that she recognized or understood. Some ten yards away from her was a table already laden with champagne bottles. Two women – one dark and with her back to her, the other a jaded blonde who was doing most of the talking – sat across the table from a long-haired man, whose face seemed vaguely familiar to Angie, and a red-faced, pot-bellied character whose glittering little eyes darted around the bar-room as if looking for someone he recognized.

It occurred to Angie that, despite the ease with which they were working their way through the champagne, these people, like her, were outsiders.

'Hullo, darling. Come 'ere often, do you?'

Angie turned, her social defences at the ready, to see Paul, smiling.

'Thank God you're back,' she said, laughing uneasily.

'What happened to your table?'

'I was joined by two middle-aged men who started talking about sex.'

'Sex? At Wincanton?'

'Between horses.'

Paul laughed. 'That's all right then.' He told her about the conversation with Jim Wilson. 'I need to see one or two people. Then we'll have that drink with Ginnie Matthews and be off.'

Angie looked away. 'I don't like being the little

woman, Paul,' she said quietly but firmly. 'It's not my style.'

'Give me until after the second race. Why not get away from these idiots and go onto the racecourse. Stand by a fence. You can find out whether racing's as cruel as you think.'

Reluctantly, she agreed. Sometimes these days she wondered about Paul Raven. The icy, almost obsessive determination that had helped him out of the wheelchair onto his feet was praiseworthy enough, but he could be cold. Nothing would stand in the way of his need to find out what happened to Alex. The desire for revenge was there, at the centre of Paul's life; perhaps, Angie thought now, not for the first time, it excluded the potential for love.

'Talk of the devil.' Paul was looking across the room to the party of two men and two women that Angie had noticed.

'Which devil is that?' she asked quietly.

'A man called Digby Welcome. Sitting with Zena Wentworth, the blonde woman on his left.'

'Wasn't she the one who came to see you?'

'Aye.' Paul smiled as Zena looked in his direction but she pointedly ignored him. 'But it seems she's forgotten me already.'

So, with a reluctance that she hoped was obvious even to Paul, Angie agreed to watch a race by herself and made her way to join a small crowd of spectators and photographers standing in the centre of the course by the last fence. She looked at her racecard.

Twelve horses were running, including Skinflint, the horse Paul had discussed with the hearty woman trainer. Its owner-rider was Mr Clay Wentworth.

Angie shivered slightly in her light overcoat. At least she had an interest in one of the runners.

It's not easy to follow a man when you can hardly walk, and Digby Welcome, despite his bulk, moved with the sprightly gait of the school fat boy heading for the tuck shop. Briefly Paul had considered asking Angie to tail him but he knew that was impossible. Besides he had something to tell Welcome in person.

After he had seen Angie making her way onto the course, he returned to the bar, just in time to see Digby pushing back his chair. 'Time for a little punt,' he said, patting Zena Wentworth on the shoulder, and scuttling off.

Slowly, Paul followed in the direction that he had gone, watching the broad back as it was engulfed by the crowd of racegoers who were making their way to the Silver Ring to put on their bets before the second race. Although he couldn't stay with him, Paul noted the name of the bookmaker, Bert Lomax, at whose stand Digby placed a bet. Then he turned and made his way back to the bar.

Paul played his own small gamble. Digby had consumed a fair amount of champagne. Even that fat gut would need relief sometime. Pushing his way through a door marked 'Gents', Paul selected a cubicle and waited.

There was no mistaking the approach of Digby Welcome. He wheezed like a tired steam engine approaching a station. Paul heard the sound of a zip being undone and a heavy sigh, before silently drawing back the bolt.

It was perfect. There was no one else there but Digby, his little legs apart, humming to himself, enjoying the moment of relief.

Paul turned his walking stick upside down, swung it back in an easy golf swing, and brought the heavy curved handle up sharply between Digby's legs.

It wasn't a scream of pain, or a gasp – it was the surprised yelp of a brutalized puppy. Digby collapsed, his face sliding down the urinal before he lay on the ground clutching at himself, his normally flushed face drained of colour.

Recovering his balance Paul took the handle of his walking-stick, placed its point on the side of Digby's neck and leaned forward, pinning him to the ground.

'Not me,' Digby managed to say, his eyes squeezed shut with pain and fear.

'Get in the toilet,' Paul said with quiet urgency.

'Wha – ? Wha – ?'

'Get your fat arse off the ground and into the cubicle.'

'Can't . . . move.'

Paul jabbed the end of his stick and Digby gave another little yelp as he dragged himself towards the cubicle.

There was wetness down the front of his trousers.

122

'For fuck's sake, put yourself away,' Paul muttered following him. 'Sit on the seat.'

Digby opened his eyes now and shook his head as he scrambled miserably onto the seat of the lavatory. 'There's been some mistake,' he whispered.

Outside, there was the sound of voices approaching. Paul closed the door of the cubicle, holding up a warning finger to Digby. They heard voices outside, two men discussing the amateur race. By the time they had left, a mottled unhealthy colour had returned to Digby's cheeks and he was breathing more easily.

'Would you care to explain why you've assaulted me, Mr Raven?' he said with a feeble attempt to retain his dignity.

'No.' Paul held his stick to Digby's neck, pushing him back against a pipe behind him. 'Tell me what you know about Alex Drew.'

'Racing. I used to see him racing.'

Paul jabbed the walking-stick. 'Friends, were you?'

The normal look of evasive cunning had returned to Digby's eyes. He was no hero but, now that the throbbing pain in his groin was receding, he could see that a man with a walking-stick – a man who had difficulty walking – was hardly in a strong position.

'We met occasionally,' he said. 'And unless you let me out of here, I'll report you to the stewards.'

Paul laughed. 'Get me warned off, will you? Excessive use of the walking-stick?' He lowered his voice.

'I know things about you that would destroy you. I just need information.'

'Alex wasn't the saint you seem to think he was.'

'Go on.'

'He couldn't keep his hands off women. He was addicted to it.'

Paul shrugged. 'People don't kill themselves for getting too much sex. Was he stopping horses for you?'

'Not his own. He was too ambitious for that.' Digby took the point of the walking-stick and, with an ironic wince, pushed it slightly aside.

Slowly lowering the stick, Paul asked, 'So he gambled, right?'

Digby Welcome nodded, as he attempted fussily to adjust his clothing.

'I don't understand why having the occasional punt on a horse should have destroyed him.'

Checking in his top pocket, Digby took out a betting-slip as if to reassure himself it was still there, then returned it to the pocket. 'Punt?' he managed a pained smile. 'It wasn't horses. It was poker – stud poker.'

Paul reached into Digby's top pocket and examined the betting-slip. 'Got a good thing for the next race, have we?'

The fat man swallowed hard. 'Steal that,' he said quietly, 'and you won't have heard the last of it.'

'Mmm.' Paul examined the slip. 'Sounds like a very good thing – but I'll resist the temptation. Jockeys aren't allowed to bet.' He pulled back the bolt behind him and backed out of the cubicle. Holding the betting-slip before him, he tore it up, throwing the pieces into the next-door toilet and flushing it away.

Hearing the rushing water, Digby darted into the cubicle in a doomed attempt to retrieve the slip. His hands wet he turned red-faced to where Paul was standing. 'You don't know what you've started, Raven,' he said.

Paul smiled coldly. 'I'd tidy yourself up before you go back to the Members' Bar,' he said. 'You've got piss in your hair.'

The crowd was thinning as Paul made his way down to the Silver Ring. Glancing down the course, he could see the runners and riders, circling around the starter in the last moments before the 'off'.

Although unlike many jockeys, Paul had always considered betting too risky a way of supplementing his income to justify breaking the rules of racing, he had a nodding acquaintance with the bookmakers whose pitches were frequently on courses where he was riding.

Bert Lomax was one of the old school. A small hunched man with the lined, expressive face of a lugubrious music-hall comedian, he rarely smiled and, when he did, it was while the rest of the world was cursing. An odds-on favourite that broke its leg, a housewife's choice going arse over tit at the first fence in the Grand National – these were moments when there would be the faintest trace of facial movement around the fat cigar Bert invariably smoked. 'Lovely job,' he would say before his features settled back, into impassivity, like mud disturbed by a passing gumboot.

'Wounded hero, is it?' Bert Lomax glanced at Paul as he approached. 'When you going to start riding again, Paul? We need a few more beaten favourites.'

'Thanks, Bert,' Paul smiled. 'I knew I could count on you for a few encouraging words.'

Bert puffed at his cigar without removing it from his lips. 'Bloody shame it was,' he said. 'Bloody diabolical.'

Paul looked at the bookmaker's board. In the field of eight for The Gentleman Jim Handicap 'chase for Amateur Riders, two horses – Skinflint and Tanglewood – were joint favourites at six to four. Punters had seemed to give the other runners little chance, the next most fancied horse being Drago's Pet at six to one.

'Busy?' Paul asked.

'Not bad for a bumper,' Bert said. 'Lot of late money for Tanglewood.'

'Nice horse,' Paul said. 'I rode it once in a novice hurdle. I always thought it would make a chaser.'

There was a scurry of activity as the racecourse commentator announced that the field was under orders. As Bert had said, most of the money seemed to be going on Tanglewood. 'They're off.' Bert wiped the chalked prices off his board and stepped down from the small ladder on which he had been standing.

'Did Digby Welcome have a bet with you?'

'Yeah, the fat bastard.' All the bookmakers knew Digby and most disliked him. 'Had to lay it off too. He had three grand on that Skinflint and a couple of ton on Drago's Pet. He must be flush. Tight bastard usually. Fancy Tanglewood, do you?'

'Don't know about that.' Paul smiled at the bookmaker. 'They've all got a chance until the tapes go up.'

He made his way slowly back to the grandstand. If he had been a betting man, he would have ventured a few bob on Tanglewood, the big bay he saw bobbing along the outside of the field as they jumped the fence in front of the stand. Although he was held on form by Skinflint, he had two great advantages over him: a pull of eight pounds in the handicap, and the fact that he wasn't being ridden by Clay Wentworth.

With mild interest, Paul watched the runners as they wheeled right-handed into the country. Wentworth was easy to spot – he was the one standing up in the stirrups like a policeman directing children across the road. Even two hundred yards away the man exuded incompetence.

There were even more people at Wincanton than usual, local racegoers having been tempted by the bright, wintry weather and the prospect of seeing several fancied candidates for the big prizes at Cheltenham running for the last time before the National Hunt festival. Paul trained his binoculars on the second last fence where Angie stood in a small group of spectators, a splash of colour against the grey and brown.

Maybe she would learn to like racing, discover that there was more to it than small men lacerating horses with their whips, more than broken bones and heartbreak. Paul smiled. She had been nervous about coming. She'd embarrass him, she had said – use the wrong terms, say the wrong things, she would be an outsider. As if that mattered.

The field was strung out on the far side of the course. As happened so often with amateurs, the early pace had been too fast, and already the horses or jockeys who needed the race were losing touch. With a mile to go, one of the outsiders, thirty lengths behind the field, tumbled wearily over a fence, unseating its jockey as if protesting against the whole absurd business. Tanglewood had moved closer to the leaders but was still a couple of lengths behind Skinflint who, in spite of Wentworth's worst efforts, was gaining ground with every fence.

At least, Paul thought, the face that Angie saw at close quarters from the racecourse was unlikely to reveal the sport's harsher face. There was a gentility about the way amateurs rode: most of them lacked the killer instinct that caused crashing falls over the final fences, and excessive use of the whip was beyond their area of capability. Amateurs of the type Alex Drew had been were rare. Of those riding in this race, only Bill Scott, the young farmer's son who was on Tanglewood, had any hope of turning professional.

Of course, Jim Wilson was right. The obsession with Alex's death, with the past, could lead him nowhere. A sensible man would weigh his assets – youth, a passable brain, a loyal girlfriend – against his liabilities – the small matter of a broken body – and look to the future. Acting the avenging angel, he risked losing more than he had already lost.

Four horses were left in it with a chance. Snow Leopard, a big grey who had made all the running and whose lead had been narrowed to a couple of lengths, Drago's Pet who was being tracked by Tanglewood and Skinflint. Distracted by thoughts of Alex, Paul trained his binoculars on the leading group as they took the turn into the straight.

It was one of the favourites' race, that was for sure. Although Skinflint was going the easier, Clay Wentworth seemed intent on making the cardinal error of riding against one horse in particular. Glancing across at Bill Scott on Tanglewood, he pushed Skinflint half a length up so that he was challenging Drago's Pet. The grey was now falling back as if he had decided that two and three quarter miles was quite far enough to gallop at racing speed.

As they entered the straight, Paul found himself watching Clay Wentworth. Every few strides, he glanced back, taking Skinflint wider and wider of the bend, as if inviting Bill Scott to challenge him on the inner. Sensibly, Scott had followed Skinflint so that, as they approached the third last fence, the two favourites were on the stand side, leaving Drago's Pet to approach the fence on the inner. The crowd in the grandstand stirred in surprise and some amusement. There was no reason for jockeys to take the long way home – the going was good on both sides of the course – and for the leaders to be dividing, leaving ten yards of course between them, was inexplicable.

'Prats,' Paul muttered to himself as he watched Clay bump uneasily over the second last fence. There was no doubt in his mind that, barring accidents, Bill Scott had his race won – Tanglewood had a fair turn of foot while Skinflint's jockey would be nothing but a handicap in a tight finish. He was watching the two favourites so closely that at first when he heard the gasp from the stands, he thought something had happened to one of the backmarkers. Then he trained his binoculars down the fence. Drago's Pet lay motionless on the landing side; his jockey had rolled under the rails but at least he was conscious.

Paul lowered the binoculars. The spectators by the fence had backed away but he could see the slash of green that was Angie.

He had started shuffling towards the fence by the time Tanglewood and Skinflint passed the post. It had been a closer race than Paul had anticipated, Skinflint having put in a stupendous leap at the last, but on the run-in the wild efforts of Clay Wentworth, which defied all laws of rhythm and gravity, had pulled the horse back and Tanglewood, ridden coolly with hands and heels by Bill Scott, had stolen the race. Even pulling up, Clay conspired to look inept, looking over his shoulder as if to see how and where he had managed to lose the race he should have won.

Angie stood before him, having run across the course towards the grandstand. She looked pale and was breathing heavily. Paul wanted to say something, to explain that falls as heavy as that of Drago's Pet were unusual in racing but words seemed inadequate.

'Can we go?' she said quietly.

Peter was lost in a nightmare of pain and darkness.

He knew little beyond the fact that he was in hospital, that his skin was on fire and that he was afraid. The morphine they gave him induced wild, technicolour dreams but slowly the memory of how he came to be here became clearer, like a ship of death, looming through the fog.

Twice they had changed the bandages on his face and his hands, and the black before his eyes had changed to a dark and muddy yellow but, beyond that, he had no sense of time. At least, they had left gaps in the bandages so that he could hear the sound of the hospital – the muttered consultations of the doctors, the chatter of the nurses, the soothing tones who had visited him three times, the cries of fear of the baby which gave the only clue to how he looked.

No policemen. That surprised him.

Once he had tried to communicate with Klima to tell her what happened but his words come out as a rattle, behind an eerie monotone. He had moved his chin but felt only pain where his lips should have been.

'Another visitor, Peter,' the sing-song voice of one of the nurses interrupted his thoughts. 'You're popular today.'

He turned his head slowly in the direction of the voice. Klima had just left. The Markwick woman was unlikely to call. The police – it had to be the police at last.

'It's your brother,' said the nurse. 'Come to see how you're getting on.'

'Poor old Peter. You look like an Egyptian mummy.'

'Not too long,' warned the nurse. 'He's still very weak.'

Peter raised an arm feebly, as the nurse with a cheery 'I'll leave you lads together, then,' left the room. He heard the squeak of her rubber soles as they receded down the corridor.

'So how are we, Bruv?'

Breathing heavily, Peter let his head fall back against the pillow. He was beyond fear, yet his heart thumped painfully in his chest. Helpless, he listened to the voice of a stranger.

'As it happens, we didn't want this,' the man said. 'When I asked a friend of mine to lend me a spot of acid, I thought he'd give me the stuff they put in car batteries.'

The man paused, as if expecting Peter to interrupt.

'I had no idea that it would take your whole fucking face off.'

Peter struggled to remember where he had heard that voice before. It was villainous, plausible and would have suited a new-style City broker as easily as it would a bank robber.

'Still, look on the bright side, eh? At least this way we know where we stand. You've got what we want and you're going to tell us how to get it. We want to deal with you, not Alice. She can be so unreasonable.'

There was the slightest pull on the drip leading into his arm. The man, he was sure now, was trying to cut the supply of morphine which kept the waves of pain at bay.

'So you get well soon, eh? I'll be back as soon as you're talking.'

'Don't touch the drip, please.' The nurse's voice, as she returned, was brisk.

'I thought it wasn't working,' the stranger said. 'I can't bear to think of my brother in pain.'

The nurse dropped her voice. 'I think you'd better go,' she said. 'He gets very tired.'

'Right.' The man stood up. 'I'll be off, Bruv.' Then from the direction of the door. 'I'll give Klima your love. I plan to visit her soon. Family's got to stick together, hasn't it?'

After the man had gone, the nurse turned to the bed. Peter seem disturbed, upset. He kept making that odd, keening sound though his lipless mouth, almost as if he were trying to tell her something.

133

She checked his drip once more and straightened his sheets. Poor man. He would be unrecognizable when the bandages came off, but he would never be able to see that horror his featureless face would cause in others. Sad because, if he had been anything like his brother, he must have been a good-looking man before the accident.

Still, at least he had a family to look after him.

It had not been a successful day. Paul had hoped that Angie would be won over by the atmosphere and excitement of a Saturday's racing. Instead, her worst prejudices had been confirmed by a horse turning over at speed only yards from where she had been standing.

They drove back to Lambourn in silence. Angie was still distracted by what she had seen and Paul's back ached from the hours spent standing up. Doubtless the tussle with Digby Welcome had hardly helped.

He parked the car beside her Mini on the street outside his flat. Remembering that she was working on the early shift at the hospital, he asked, 'D'you want to go home?'

'Not yet.'

'I can offer you supper. Frozen chicken pie à la Raven.'

She smiled and he saw that she was sad, not angry. 'My favourite,' she said.

There was a tension between them that evening.

134

They talked little, like a married couple who had fought and were carefully choosing topics of conversation in which there was no risk of renewed hostilities.

After they had eaten in the kitchen, they sat on each side of the open fire, Paul nursing a whisky while Angie, who had seen too many road crash victims to risk a drink when she was driving later, sipped a cup of coffee.

'I spoke to Digby Welcome today,' Paul said eventually. 'A friend of mine had told me that Alex had some connection with him.'

'What's he? A jockey?'

Paul smiled. 'Hardly. He's the sort of character you find on the fringe of racing. Part fixer, part crook. A hanger-on.'

'Doesn't seem Alex's type.'

'Alex was a good jockey, but he was no angel. He wanted to be in the fast set – parties, girls, his face in the gossip columns. Whenever he had a spare moment, he would be into his car and up to London. He wanted me to come but I couldn't live like that.'

'And that's how he knew this Welcome man.'

'Everybody knows Digby Welcome. If you're sensible, you keep your distance. There's a corruption about him that's catching.'

Angie found herself thinking of Gavin Holmes, the journalist. 'I know that type,' she said.

'I asked him whether Alex was in trouble with the bookmakers. He said something strange – something about stud poker. That Wentworth woman mentioned poker too. When I asked if he had stopped horses, he said, "Not his own." '

'Which would confirm your suspicions about your race. You think he had been told to stop you.'

Paul stared into the fire. 'I don't understand it. When a jockey's been got at, there's gambling involved. Yet at Plumpton, there was nothing unusual in the betting pattern; I checked with the Betting Officer – no late support for Freeze Frame, Alex's horse. More importantly, Dig For Glory's price never drifted. It seemed that everybody thought I'd win.'

For a moment, Angie watched as he poked at the fire, the glow lighting up his dark eyes. She wanted to go to him, to hold him and tell him that nothing could come of this obsession with his friend's death, but something held her back. 'You're really hooked now, aren't you?' she said.

Without a word, Paul stood up and, with some difficulty made his way to the telephone. He dialled a number.

'Mrs Matthews,' he said. 'Paul Raven. Sorry I couldn't make that drink. My... back was playing up a bit . . . Yes, some other time. Sorry about Skinflint. Thought you were a bit unlucky there.' He laughed quietly. 'He's no Lester Piggot in a finish that's for sure.' Angie heard the raised tones of Ginnie Matthews as she enlarged, with a string of obscenities, on the performance of Clay Wentworth as a jockey. 'Somebody told me he was a bit of a poker player,'

Paul added casually. 'They asked me if I wanted to join some sort of gambling party.' He listened for a minute or so before saying, 'Aye, perhaps you're right, Mrs Matthews. Bit out of my league.'

After he had hung up, Paul turned to Angie. 'Wentworth has a poker evening once a week. High stakes. You need to be invited.'

'What's that got to do with Alex?'

'A couple of times I've seen Welcome with Clay Wentworth. It would explain how Alex knew Zena. If I could get into the poker circle, maybe I could find out what was going on.'

'School. It's a poker school.'

Paul smiled. 'Don't tell me you're an expert.'

'I know a bit.' Angie gave a self-mocking woman-of-the-world smile. As she looked up at him, Paul noticed that the top button of her blue dress, so wrong for Wincanton and so right for now, had come undone revealing a pale throat, the shadow of a breast. 'It was about all I learned at school.'

'Will you teach me?'

'While you were making that telephone call in the middle of our conversation – ' smiling, she held up a hand to stop his interruption ' – I reached two decisions. The first was that I'm leaving the hospital. If you're serious about finding out what happened to Alex, you're going to need help. I'll do agency work – it's better paid and I can work the hours I want.'

Paul looked at her in amazement. 'Angie, that's crazy. You don't have to do that for me.'

'It's not for you, it's for me.'

'And the second decision?'

'Ah, that.' Angie looked away and Paul thought he could see a heightened colour in her cheeks. 'For the second decision I'll need a drink.'

'But you're driving. What about – ?'

'That's the second decision.' Angie turned to him solemnly, her lips slightly parted. 'Tonight I'm not driving anywhere.'

It wasn't how she had imagined it. In her fantasies, she had imagined a powerful man, his heavy weight on her. She had expected fear and pain with the pleasure.

Instead, when she came to Paul's bed, her athletic body caught by the lamplight from the street outside, his body dark and taut against the white sheets, she was the seducer, the conqueror.

'You realise you're going to have to do this,' Paul said quietly.

'That's what nurses are for,' she said, and she knew as she caressed his body with her hands and her lips that this, all along, was how she had wanted it. Her fears of doing the wrong thing, the last vestige of shyness, disappeared as she made love to him, gasping more with pleasure than pain, when she lowered herself onto him, sighing with relief, and gentle aching desire, her days of waiting for the right man, for Mr Right, over at last. The girls had never told her that at the end, she would cry with happiness.

Afterwards they lay together for several minutes.
'Where did you learn all that?' Paul asked at last.
'I learned that at school too.'
And, in the semi-darkness, they both laughed.

Chapter 7

There were some virtues left within the soul of Gavin Holmes; not honesty, or industry, or fidelity – which he had outgrown within his first year on Fleet Street – but he still had one quality in which he took a certain amount of pride. He never bore a grudge against a woman who had refused to sleep with him.

In this, he was unusual. Most of his male colleagues would express their frustration and guilt by spreading unpleasant rumours about the woman who failed to be attracted by them. Not Gavin – he almost admired someone who had the spirit to reject him. From that moment on, she moved out of the sexual arena to become something else – a friend, a rival, a person. Oddly enough, he had more difficulty with the ones he *had* slept with, who either wanted to do it again when he would rather forget the whole thing, or if he did happen to fancy a spot of auld lang syne, pretended nothing had ever happened. That was another point in his favour – he never forgot the face of someone he had taken to bed, however drunk he had been at the time, however messy and unfortunate the subsequent experience.

'In fact, I'm full of fucking virtues,' Gavin muttered to himself, sitting in the wine bar where his blundering attempt to seduce the O'Keefe girl had gone so wrong. Yet here he was, waiting for her again – only this time she was bringing her boyfriend.

A story, she had said. Gavin drank deeply at the glass of wine in front of him. They always had a story.

'Not more gee-gees, please,' he had said, when little Angie O'Keefe had rung him at the office.

'We think we have something which could interest you. About the death of a jockey. It's confused but we think Clay Wentworth's involved.'

He had asked a few more questions, the answers to which had faintly quickened his interest. Money seemed to be involved. Maybe even sex. The equestrian element had seemed to be mercifully small.

Angie had asked him about a man called Digby Welcome and, after an hour of punching up a selection of old stories from the information service database, he had become more confident. Yes, it was distinctly possible there was a story here.

'Gavin, this is Paul.'

The journalist looked up from his drink, and there was Angie, her hand resting gently on the arm of a dark, good-looking man carrying a walking-stick.

'Hi, Paul.' Gavin extended a hand, nodding curtly in the direction of his legs. 'How's it coming on?'

'Not bad,' Angie laughed as she drew up a chair for Paul.

'According to the doctors, he should still be in a wheelchair.'

She was hardly recognizable as the pale, edgy girl whom Gavin remembered. There was an openness about her, a warmth in the eyes that seemed entirely new. 'What's his secret cure?' he asked, a hint of irony in his voice. Nothing made Gavin more nervous than young love. It made him feel his years. Angie blushed, looking at Paul as if the question were absurd.

After a waitress had brought two more glasses, and Gavin had poured, he said 'Okay then, what's the story?'

Paul looked across the table with an unnervingly direct gaze.

'First,' he said, 'tell us what you know about Digby Welcome.'

It took a lot to rattle him. Over the years, after more tumbles and setbacks than most men were forced to endure in a lifetime, Digby had learned to roll with the punches.

Some five miles west of the bar where his chequered career was being discussed, he sat in a restaurant at his usual table, eating his usual meal and wondered how best to discourage Paul Raven. Contacts, of course – Digby had plenty of those. Violence, almost certainly. He shifted his bulk uncomfortably, wincing with pain as he did so. Yes, the jockey had certainly done enough to be damaged a little bit more than he was already.

A dark girl in the tight white tee-shirt that the waitresses were required to wear when working at the restaurant hurried by, pointedly not looking in Digby's direction. Languidly, he held up the empty wine bottle on his table, letting it swing between two fingers. On her return, the waitress hesitated nervously and took the bottle. Digby held onto the neck and looked up, his greedy little eyes taking their time to work their way up her body.

'Everything all right at home, is it, Diana?'

The girl took the bottle and said in a heavy East European accent 'Is good, Mr Welcome, thank you. Another bottle wine?'

Digby nodded slowly. These girls, he sighed. The trouble they caused him.

'It's as if he's had several incarnations.' Gavin was interested enough in the case of Digby Welcome to slow down his drinking for a while. 'I kept reading these Digby Welcome stories from the archives to find a different character popping up each time.'

'I would never have thought that he was that interesting,' Paul said.

'First of all, he was at Eton – his name keeps cropping up whenever some nobby businessman or cabinet minister is asked about his schooldays. Apparently he was something of a card – a practical joker, smart but lazy. They say he was good-looking then.'

'Bloody hell,' Paul muttered.

'He was expelled for some prank. Joined the army. Appeared to be something of a high-flyer until he left under a cloud when he was in his mid twenties.'

'More pranks?'

'No, the army can handle that. Something more serious – money or sex, I suspect.'

'Then he got into racing.'

'Yes. Again it all looked very promising. He got a yard on the Sussex Downs when he was quite young, trained a few winners, seemed to be going places. The next thing the cuttings reveal is that he was banned from all racecourses for two years. Something about not paying bills.'

'Right.' Paul nodded. 'That's the part I know about. He was a tight bastard – not unusual in racing, but he didn't pay wages, his cheques bounced. He underfed the horses. In the end, even his friends at the Jockey Club couldn't ignore it.'

'So there he was – fat, nearly forty and famous for all the wrong things. He had a marriage that had gone wrong – his wife divorced him for mental cruelty. He ended up in a part-time job selling horse tonic.'

'It doesn't make sense,' Paul said. 'Clay Wentworth only hangs out with people who are useful to him. And another thing. If Welcome was so chronically mean, what was he doing putting three grand on a horse in an amateur race?'

Gavin shrugged. 'Maybe he was doing it for

someone else. Clay, for example.'

'There's no rule against amateurs betting. Clay would have an account with a bookmaker.'

'Unless Digby has yet another incarnation.' Gavin filled his glass. 'Another source of income.'

'Something mucky, I imagine,' Paul said.

Gavin smiled. 'Could be very mucky. I asked one of my colleagues about Digby. He had heard some nasty rumours. Apparently our friend's popular on the coke and champagne circuit. They say he's an ace supplier.'

'Dope?' Angie laughed at the idea of the tubby buffoon in tweeds as dealer in narcotics to the fast set.

'Not drugs.' Gavin sipped at his wine, enjoying the drama of the moment. 'Girls. Wives.'

Zena Wentworth wandered from room to room like a restless and unhappy ghost in the large house in Harley Gardens. She felt empty and alone, trapped by a gloom so deep that not even a trip to the medicine cupboard where she kept all kinds of mood-changing pills seemed worth the effort. A couple of those brightly-coloured items might pick her up, propel her out of the door to a place where there were lights and music only to slam her back down to earth in the desolate early hours of the morning. These days, the pleasure of going up hardly seemed worth the pain of coming down.

Barefoot, in a dark red kimono, she ran a finger

along the mantelpiece in the high-ceilinged sitting-room. Her eyes scanned the invitations, some for Mr Clay Wentworth, some for Mr and Mrs Clay Wentworth, none for Mrs Zena Wentworth. She hooked a finger around the bronze figure of a horse and jockey driving for the line.

'Whoops,' she said, pulled it slowly over the edge so that it fell with a clatter on the marble fireplace below. 'Favourite's down.'

Zena picked up the bronze, noting without much interest that the jockey's head had been bent to one side, giving him a comical look as if he were wondering what all the fuss and effort were about. She ran a long finger down his bronze back, around the back of his bronze thighs, thinking vaguely of Paul Raven.

'Horses,' she said, looking at the painting on the wall, the ornaments on tables. 'Nothing but bloody horses.'

The house was unusually quiet. Emilio and Maria, the Spanish couple who lived in the basement and looked after the Wentworths, had gone out to some obscure spot in the suburbs where Spaniards met on their nights off. When Clay and Zena had moved into this house, shortly after their marriage, the idea had been that it would be filled with children. Now, ten years later, the quest for a family was over, giving Clay and that creepy old father of his yet more reasons to despise her.

Slowly Zena crossed the hall, ruffling her faded blonde hair like someone who had just awoken from a long sleep. She entered a small room which smelt of stale cigars – her husband's study, his little retreat. She sat on the leather chair, leaning back and placing her bare feet on the desk so that the kimono fell back, revealing her long slender legs. Yes – Zena ran a hand over one smooth thigh, and then the other – at least she still had good legs. Not that anyone cared.

There were two photographs on Clay's desk. One showed her husband on Skinflint, taking a water-jump. Zena smiled – it had taken quite a search to find a shot that made Clay look like a real jockey and even this one showed him with his mouth open like a goldfish – but it was good enough to be blown up and featured above his desk at the office. Poor, foolish Clay.

The other photograph was an old portrait of Sir Denis, taken shortly after he had received his knighthood. Against the background of what seemed to be a setting sun, he stared out at her with his cold tycoon eyes.

Creepy. Zena pointed a toe like a ballerina and pushed the framed photograph off the desk.

He had always hated her. He had distrusted her looks, the way she exuded pleasure in the good things of life. Even in the early days, when she had acted the proper daughter-in-law, he had shown her little respect, hardly bothering to talk to her, introducing her to his important friends with an apologetic mumble. Then, as it became obvious that she was unable to fulfil her most important function – to provide an heir for the Wentworth millions – he had ceased even to acknowledge her existence, drawing his son into the business and away from her.

Clay, as was his habit, took the line of least resistance. Torn between father and wife, he returned to the cold bosom of the family. He spent evenings with Sir Denis, still the little boy desperate to please Daddy.

Languidly, Zena pulled open the top drawer of the desk and took out her husband's Filofax. She flicked through the pages, forlornly hoping to find signs that Clay was more than a cypher in his father's plans. There were notes about race meetings, business addresses but – unless Clay had shown an intelligence and cunning uncharacteristic of him – not the slightest hint of adulterous behaviour. Zena sighed. Her husband had always regarded sex as yet another chore life had burdened him with.

A small scrap of paper fell onto her lap. It had been folded many times and contained a list of names, written in an unfamiliar hand. The first three items on the list had been deleted with a line. The last, 'Tanglewood', had been circled heavily with blue biro.

It took a few seconds for Zena to remember where she had heard the name Tanglewood. Of course – that had been the horse that had beaten Clay in his last race.

She looked more closely at the list and noticed, written faintly in a corner, in pencil by her husband, the words 'Dig For Glory'. They too had a line through them.

Zena put the Filofax back in the drawer, which she closed. She stood up and, fanning her face with the slip of paper, made her way out of the study and up the stairs to her bedroom. In her handbag was a small notebook, which she flicked through until she found what she was looking for. She dialled a number on a telephone beside the bed, then drummed the long fingers of her right hand as she waited. 'Bloody machine,' she muttered.

'Paul, this is Zena Wentworth,' she said. 'I think I have something which might be of interest.' She paused. 'It's to do with Alex. Perhaps you could call me as soon as possible.' She gave her number and hung up.

Smiling, she folded the piece of paper and put it in her bag. Maybe she was being disloyal to her husband. Perhaps the list meant something.

At least she'd be able to see Paul again.

It was a tremendous game – the best game Digby Welcome had ever played. The fat man puffed out his cheeks as he cupped his hands around a brandy glass, gazing into it as if he could read his future there.

It was almost eleven thirty. The kitchens were closing, customers were being turned away at the door. Soon the waitresses – including Diana and Juljana, both of them his girls – would be dividing up the evening's tips and going home to lives of sweet, if not entirely simple, domesticity. At about the same time, Roberto the manager would amble over to his table, sit down and spend a few minutes chatting with him. Business might be discussed – girls who needed Digby's help.

Other games – at school, in the army, on the turf – had tended to end in tears, those in authority frequently failing to share his sense of humour. But in this game, he was in control. He called the shots.

It had been so easy, such an obvious development of Digby's personal interests – money, food and, of course, people. In the early 1970s, after his career as a trainer had been terminated, Digby had taken to dining out in restaurants in the Kensington and Chelsea area. His easy charm and teddy-bear looks had encouraged the girls to chat to him. One – he forgot her name now – had, late one night, opened her heart to him. Her student permit had expired, the immigration people were after her, yet she would rather die than return to the grey and cold of Warsaw. She needed a husband within a week – she could pay £2,000.

Digby helped her. He knew plenty of Englishmen happy to lose their bachelor status for the three years required in return for instant cash. The girl had a friend with the same problem, which Digby also solved.

His strength was that he never asked too many questions. Where the money came from, for example, or whether the husbands he provided – some of whom were frankly rather dubious characters – demanded more of their new wives than mere cash.

Since then, he had become a familiar figure around the restaurants of London. It turned out that Eastern Europe was full of families who had sent their girls to make their way in the West, and London, of course, was not short of husbands.

Digby's unofficial marriage bureau had flourished and – even allowing for kickbacks to managers like Roberto – he had flourished too. The only disadvantage to this part-time job was that some evenings he was obliged to eat two or even three dinners and that, for Digby Welcome, was no great hardship.

He looked across the restaurant to where Diana was talking to the manager. She was a nice little thing – dark, slim, with a look in her eyes that promised much in the way of diversion – but these days Digby resisted the temptation to combine business with pleasure. Once he used to demand a non-fiscal bonus with some of his more attractive girls, but it hadn't been a success: the demands he made of them had been rather too sophisticated – too much of a culture shock – to be acceptable. After one tearful scene too many, he had decided not to jeopardize the business. There were experienced business girls he could call – girls who took him for what he was, warped and all.

The door opened behind where Roberto and Diana were standing, and a slight girl with short blonde hair entered. Digby was trying to remember where he had seen her before when he noticed, standing behind her, the face of a man he knew all too well.

Roberto was telling the girl that the restaurant was closed, but Paul Raven had seen him, and the manager smiled and gave a nod as if to say that any friends of Mr Welcome were friends of his.

The couple approached, the girl waiting for Paul to make his way slowly past the tables.

'Digby,' said Paul. 'Here you are. We heard this was one of your watering-holes.'

Digby scowled as the girl pulled back a chair for Paul, then sat down herself.

'This is my friend Angie,' Paul said conversationally. 'Angie, this is Digby Welcome. We met one another briefly at Wincanton the other day.'

'What do you want?' Digby avoided Paul's eyes. 'I was just going.'

'We know all about you,' Paul said quietly. 'Your little business looks like it will be getting some belated publicity in the press.'

'Business?'

'Your work as Agony Uncle.'

'I don't know what you're talking about.' Digby swirled the brandy around in his glass before drinking it back in one gulp.

'Invite me to one of your poker evenings,' said Paul. 'And we might be able to keep your nasty little secret quiet.'

An ingratiating little smile played on Digby's lips,

as if he couldn't believe his luck. 'They're not my poker evenings. They're Clay's.'

'Well, get me invited.'

Digby took a calling-card from his top pocket and scribbled an address on it. 'Next Thursday,' he said. 'I'll tell Clay you're my guest.'

Paul took the card and, glancing at it, gave it to Angie. Leaning heavily on his walking-stick, he stood up. He looked at the stick as if suddenly remembering something.

'How are they by the way? Still sore?'

Digby's face turned a darker shade of red. 'Very amusing,' he said.

After Paul and Angie had left, Roberto came over to the table. 'Nice girl,' he said easily. 'One of yours, was she?'

With a distracted stroke to his head, Digby muttered, 'No – just old friends, you know.'

'Can we talk business?'

But Digby was staring at the door of the restaurant like a man who knew his gravy train had just left the rails. 'No business tonight, Roberto,' he said.

'Puttana!'

The tall, thin man stabbed the table with a knife, leaving it quivering like an arrow until a passing waitress removed it with a muttered *'Idiota'*. The man watched her walk away. He was only young and his chiselled good looks had caused many a female customer of his small pizza parlour to return in hope and lust, but his cold green eyes gave him a harsh, forbidding maturity.

He was sitting with two other men, one in his sixties who was examining his carefully manicured nails with a look of intense concentration, the other in his late twenties with a dark moustache, good-looking but with a pale, apologetic smile on his face. 'Giorgio,' he said quietly, 'we've only just begun.'

The young man, Giorgio, darted a look around the room. The last customers in the small cellar, a popular haunt among the young and upwardly mobile of Wandsworth, had gone home, leaving the three Italians alone, except for one waitress who was cleaning the tables. 'Every time she tricks us,' he said.

'We know where it is,' said the man with a moustache soothingly. 'Our little Polish friend has not responded well to his acid bath.'

'What about his wife?'

'We know where she lives. I could – '

'No.' The older man spoke for the first time. 'There's no point in that.'

'We're losing time, papa,' Giorgio said quietly.

'Salvatore has done well, Giorgio.' The grey-haired man picked at one of his nails with a fork. 'You know the layout of the factory, right?'

The man with a moustache nodded. 'But I can't be a VAT man again. She was suspicious last time.'

'Hurting the Polak's wife would be counter-productive. Perhaps we should turn our attention to other members of the syndicate. The man Wentworth. Or

Calloway. We know we can reach Welcome.'

'Time, papa!' There was anger in Giorgio's voice, and a hint of panic.

'We have three weeks.'

'There's another problem,' said Salvatore. 'I have heard that someone else is interested, is snooping about.' He reached into the inside pocket of the jacket of his dark suit and took out a photograph torn from a newspaper. He unfolded it, laying it in the centre of the table.

'Who's he acting for?' the older man asked.

Salvatore shrugged. 'He's some kind of jockey.'

'Jockey?' Giorgio said softly. 'What's a jockey got to do with this?'

'We had better discourage him,' his father said mildly.

Salvatore reached for the photograph. 'I'll ask if anyone has heard – '

'No!' Giorgio spoke sharply. 'There's no time for that.'

The waitress marched across the room and, with a reproachful look in the direction of the manager, began to clean the table. As if it were contaminated, she picked up the photograph, glancing as she did so at the dark features of Paul Raven.

'Mmm,' she muttered. *'Che bel tipo.'*

'Not for long,' said Giorgio. 'Not for long.'

Chapter 8

It wasn't the first time she had returned to Czechoslovakia since the day she had left to find her future in the West but, every time that she alighted from the plane into the greyness of Prague airport, a touch of claustrophobia, of a deep, psychic anxiety, gripped her.

Whatever the changes – to her, to the motherland, to the world – the dark, crumbling buildings and the weary, watchful eyes of the Czech officials always meant the same to her. It was a trap. This time she would not escape. The sins of her past – those deeply capitalist sins of greed, lust and selfishness – would come back to haunt her.

With the other passengers, she was herded into an airport bus, which smelt faintly of cheap, stale cigarettes and disinfectant. The engine sounded unhealthy and the driver drove with contemptuous speed towards the main terminal as if, whatever the politicians might say, the old disapproval of the soft, decadent ways of the West still endured. Around her, the other passengers seemed uneasy – perhaps the bus with its crazed driver would head out of the airport, take them without a word to another, more sinister destination. A middle-aged businessman tried a joke about local driving standards, but no one smiled and his words died on his lips.

Sitting on one of the few benches on the bus, Alice noticed, were two teenage girls, one of whom – with dark, cropped hair and fine features – she might, under other circumstances and in another country, have tried with a smile. Not here: it was strange how even her most natural instincts went into retreat in her cold, forbidding homeland.

In the main building, there were queues. The English thought they understood patience – they boasted about their queues – but they were amateurs compared to her countrymen. Here you stood in a line for everything: sometimes you queued for a permit to join another queue and, by the time you reached the front of it, you'd forgotten what you had wanted in the first place. Alice shivered – she hated coming back – and gathered her fur coat more closely around her.

On this occasion, she was met by a government functionary, a middle-aged man with shifty eyes and a coat too thin for the climate. 'Miss Flaishman?' he said, as she walked towards the queue.

'Markwick,' she said.

The man nodded. 'Please follow me,' he said.

It was better. Every time she returned, she was treated with more respect. Twenty years ago, the man would have called her by her surname, holding her eyes with the stare of a man with power over her, perhaps even allowing himself a speculative glance at her legs. Now she was in charge; he avoided looking at her. Conversation would be minimal.

The man nodded to passport control officials as he took Alice past the queue through the hall of the terminal and into a large car that was waiting at the entrance. Sensitive to the essential signs of social and political importance in Czechoslovakia, she noticed that the car was not quite the most luxurious available. Those had been reserved for the party officials and were now used by the new brand of politician scrambling for power under the free, post-communist constitution.

New. Free. Settling back in the adequate comfort of the car, Alice smiled. They were just words. Nothing had really changed.

On the way to the Ministry of Defence, the car drove past the huge government building where, all those years ago, Alice's mother had once worked. There was something desolate about it now as if its power to terrify had gone for ever. Alice stared at it without feeling any of the old dread and disgust. That ghost, at least, was dead.

Josef Petrin, her contact, was waiting in his large, chilly office when she was shown in by the official. He smiled, extending his arms in a phoney gesture of welcome which, when he saw the icy disapproval in Alice's eyes, became a brisk handshake. They exchanged pleasantries about the journey, as he escorted her to a chair in front of an ancient gas fire, which had been installed in the ornate fireplace.

'Now, Mrs Markwick,' Petrin smiled ingratiatingly. 'You cannot keep us waiting any longer. Tell me when we take possession.'

'Quite soon.' Alice spoke slowly as she placed her briefcase on a table in front of her and fiddled with the security lock.

'How soon?'

The question contained an undertone of impatience, perhaps even threat. Petrin was the new breed of official but, while his suit came from Savile Row, his shiny black shoes from Rome, and his slick smile owed much to Madison Avenue, he was not that different from his predecessors, only younger – in his late thirties – and marginally more plausible. Briefly Alice wondered whether he demanded intimate overtime from office cleaners. No, the modern way was a hunting-lodge, complete with young mistress, in the forest nearby – such was progress.

Alice took a folder out of her briefcase and gave Petrin a videotape. 'The tape I promised,' she said, choosing to ignore his questions. 'You have the machine?'

Petrin nodded and, taking the tape, crossed the room to a table on which there was a television and a video machine. He stood in front of the machine as a sequence of films was shown. Occasionally he gasped and laughed, like a little boy watching a circus.

'Excellent,' he said, after the television screen had turned to grey. 'You use peculiar clinical models but that is your choice.'

'We had our reasons.'

'And afterwards? Any problems with the post-mortems?'

'Nothing.'

'Of course, we need a human test. As you promised.'

'Humans talk.'

'We have humans that don't – or won't, if we ask nicely.'

'No. Leave it to us. We'll manage something.'

'Fine.' Petrin smiled once more like a barrister addressing a hostile witness. 'When?'

'You'll have your evidence in a week. If you're still happy, we deliver at the end of March.'

'Not before?'

'There's still work to be done.'

'And we're exclusive? That's what we're paying for. My colleagues will be very unhappy to hear of models going elsewhere. We're depending on you for this.'

Alice closed her briefcase with a click. 'Trust me,' she said. 'Remember I'm a Czech.'

'That's what worries me,' said Petrin, and they both laughed guardedly as he showed her the door.

There were three hours before her plane left for

London, but Alice had only one call to make. She told the driver to take her to the west side of the city, a square mile where the houses were painted and had heating that worked even in the winter when, as if by tradition, the power in the big housing blocks used to fail, sometimes for days at a time. This was where the foreign diplomats lived, and senior civil servants and politicians. There were few shops and no bars for the poor to gather and drink vodka and talk of future freedom. It was the acceptable face of the new Czechoslovakia.

At first, Alice's mother had objected when, as a condition of dealing with the government, her daughter had secured her a two-bedroom house in the suburbs. Since her husband had died some seven years previously, she had lived alone, depending on neighbours and the occasional visit from Tomas, her son, for company. The new house might be comfortable, she argued, but she would be lonely. But Tomas had a car these days and, aware that one day he might inherit the house, he had promised to bring his family to see her every weekend.

The car drew up outside the house and Alice told the driver to wait for one hour.

'Alzbeta.' The old woman opened the door and embraced her daughter, then held her at arms' length, stroking Alice's fur coat. 'My daughter.'

The two women sat in the kitchen drinking tea while Alice gave her mother a sanitized version of her work in London. Her mother, as usual, became tearful and asked her when she would be coming home for ever.

'One day,' Alice said, 'when I've made my fortune.'

'Money.' Her mother looked away, ashamed by the memories that swarmed in. 'It's always money in our family, isn't it?'

And, with the faintest shiver of repulsion, Alice agreed. Yes, it was always money.

At first, when Ginnie Matthews had written to Paul suggesting he ride out for her, he had assumed it was her idea of a joke. Although the doctors were pleased with his progress, he could still only walk slowly and his legs felt as unsteady and weak as those of a new-born foal.

Then, when Paul had rung her, Ginnie had explained that she had an old hunter in the yard called Monty who needed exercising. He was dead quiet and Paul would be able to sit on him and go where he wanted. He could even come up to the gallop and watch her horses working. To his surprise, the specialist raised no objections. Nor, less surprisingly, did Ron Charlesworth. Still he hesitated.

'Try it once,' Ginnie had said. 'What's the problem?'

At that moment, Paul knew what the problem was.

'I'll be there,' he said quietly. 'What time d'you need me?'

Under other circumstances, it would have been comical. Paul Raven, the ice-cool jockey, afraid of the idea of mounting a fat and ancient hunter. Yet as, early the following morning, Monty was pulled out and led by one of the lads to a mounting-block in the corner of the yard, Paul felt sick with fear. He climbed the steps of the block slowly, like a man going to his execution.

'Hold him up for the first couple of miles, then give one behind the saddle,' joked the lad. 'He's got a great turn of speed.'

As Paul hesitated on the block, the reins in his hand, Ginnie walked towards him. 'Step one of Raven's comeback,' she said loudly. 'Don't hang about, Paul – you're not at Charlesworth's now.'

Paul lowered himself across the saddle and slowly pulled his right leg over. Ginnie helped him adjust the stirrups. 'All right?' she asked.

Paul nodded, his face pale.

And it was. Although he felt weak, he followed the string out in the cold morning mist and, even when the horse in front of him had shied violently, causing his lad to curse at him, the old hunter had hardly turned a hair. As the string worked at half-speed over six furlongs, Ginnie had watched with interest, noting how they had all gone, and it crossed his mind that if he couldn't race again, then, despite all the problems, maybe he would try training. Cheltenham was now two weeks away and Ginnie had three fancied contenders for the big prizes – The Smiler for the Trafalgar House Hurdle, Harry's Champ for the National Hunt 'Chase and Skinflint for the Kim Muir.

Looking down the hill to the all-weather gallop, Paul noticed Skinflint, pulling hard, at the back of the string. 'He must have a decent chance,' he said.

'Yes.' Ginnie narrowed her eyes as if not entirely comfortable with the subject. 'The race has cut up badly.'

There seemed to be an easiness about the lads who worked for Ginnie Matthews. Behind the jokes about 'the missus' and her booming voice, there was none of the edgy competitiveness that Paul remembered from Charlesworth's yard. As the string made its way back, the sun showed through the mist and one or two of the lads had lit up cigarettes. The talk was of racing and horses and women. Paul smiled and patted Monty's neck. It was good to be back.

These days, although Alex's death was still at the front of his mind, so was his own future. His mother had taken to sending him letters advising him to find a desk job while there were still vacancies – she didn't actually spell out that soon Paul and his racing successes would be forgotten and he would be just another applicant, but she didn't need to. He had thrown away the pages from the local paper with jobs circled without even looking at them. Maybe one day he would become a tea-boy or an office clerk, but not yet.

Strangely enough, it had been Angie who had convinced him that only when he had settled his mind about what had happened to Alex would he be able to start a new life. She was working out her notice period at the hospital but, since the night Gavin Holmes had told them about Digby Welcome, she had become quieter, more subdued.

He thought of the message from Zena Wentworth on his answering-machine. It had been two days since he had heard from her but something – perhaps a wariness about her motives – had prevented him calling her back. Whatever Zena could tell him, Paul was convinced he could find out more by attending one of her husband's poker evenings.

On returning to the yard, his back was aching but he insisted on unsaddling Monty himself. The old hunter had done him more good than all the doctors put together, and for the first time Paul began to feel more like he had before the accident.

Zena Wentworth was bad at waiting at the best of times and now wasn't the best of times. The previous night Clay had stayed out late, having dined with his father and Lord Wallingford, another bent peer with property interests, at one of their dull gentlemen's clubs. On his return, Clay had been more monosyllabic than usual. She had even accused him of cheating on her. Clay's face had been such a picture of astonishment that she had had to laugh. Clay Wentworth an adulterer – there was certainly something comic in that.

Two days she had waited for Raven to respond to her bait but there had been nothing, not a nibble. After Clay had gone to bed, she had taken a pill and stayed up all night watching television. At six, she had had a bath, washed her hair, put her face on. By eight o'clock, she was in the Rolls heading down the M4.

She had been surprised to find that he was out, but her patience had paid off when, twenty minutes after she had parked outside his door, Paul had drawn up behind her in his car. Zena watched in her rearview mirror as he lifted one leg and then the other onto the pavement, before pulling himself out. She checked her face one more time, then opened the door.

'Riding again?' she asked breezily.

Paul looked surprised, and less than pleased, to see her.

She smiled and walked lazily towards him. 'You look good in your... togs.'

'Thanks.' Paul walked slowly to his door and Zena followed him.

'I drove down from London to see you,' she said.

'Why?'

'You didn't answer my call. I wanted to help you.'

Paul unlocked the door and hesitated as he opened it. 'Help me?'

'I admire you,' she said brightly. 'There aren't many wounded heroes where I come from. Can I come in?'

'All right.' Paul sighed. 'I have to be going soon, though.'

'Pity,' said Zena quietly.

As Paul put on the kettle, she sat at the kitchen table, crossed her legs and glanced into the sitting-room next door. 'Cosy.'

'It does. Why don't you tell me what you're here for.'

'Two reasons.' Zena opened her crocodile skin bag and took out a small folded piece of paper, which she laid on the table. 'What horse were you riding at Plumpton?'

'Dig For Glory.'

'I found this in my husband's desk. Why d'you think he's written the name of your horse on it?'

Paul turned and looked at the list of names. 'Did your husband write this?' he asked.

'No. That's a woman's writing. Apart from Dig For Glory, what are the other names?'

Paul looked more closely at the list and frowned. It was strange. 'Just horses,' he said quietly.

'Wasn't Tanglewood the horse that beat Clay at Wincanton?'

'That's right.'

'And it's the only one that's not been crossed out.'

'So it seems.'

Either Zena knew more than she was letting on or – and this seemed more likely – she was too stupid or uninterested in racing to see the connections between all the horses whose names had been deleted from the list. All had died in racing accidents over the past two months. As he gave Zena a cup of tea, he glanced at her, catching her eyes on his legs.

'They suit you, those jockey trousers,' she said.

'They're called jodhpurs – I never thought of them as a fashion accessory. What was the second thing?'

'Mmm?' she smiled, parting her painted lips.

'The second reason you came down here.'

In reply, Zena leaned forward and extended a hand across the table, placing it on Paul's hand.

'You know the answer to that,' she said.

He tried to withdraw his hand but found that her grip was surprisingly strong. 'I'm very good, Paul,' she said. 'Alex could have told you that.'

'Aye.' Paul wrenched his hand back. 'And look what happened to him.'

'I'm serious.'

'And so am I. Drink up your tea, Mrs Wentworth. I have things to do.'

'Mrs Wentworth.' Zena spoke coldly. She took a sip of tea then stood up, smoothing the front of her skirt down her thighs. She brushed his cheek with her long fingers. 'Mrs Wentworth wants you, Paul. And what Mrs Wentworth wants, she gets.'

Paul watched Zena as she strolled to the door, with a lazy swing of the hips, and let herself out without a backward glance. Outside, there was an angry purr and a squeal of tyres as the Rolls set off back to London.

What was her game? Paul was used to fending off the attention of libidinous older women but there was a dangerous, driven quality to Zena that worried him. He reached for the slip of paper, which lay on the

169

kitchen table. After a moment, he picked it up and walked slowly through to the sitting-room. At his desk, there was a copy of Chaseform, a small plastic-bound book whose weekly supplements recorded every race in the calendar.

Apart from Dig For Glory, whose fate Paul knew all too well, there were four names on the list – Ballina Lady, Whataparty, Brut Force and, undeleted and with a heavy circle around it, Tanglewood. Paul flicked through the pages to find Ballina Lady's last race, the Philip Cornes Handicap 'Chase at Leopardstown. The summary beside her name was succinct. '*Always going well. Fell second last. Destroyed.*'

Whataparty had run on Boxing Day at Haydock Park and he too had failed to finish. His final entry read, '*Settled early, improved rapidly at half way. Led third last clear and going easily when fell last. Destroyed.*'

Paul recalled Brut Force's last race – his accident at Huntingdon had made the headlines in the sporting press. Once again Chaseform's summary was brief and laconic: '*Always with the leaders. Left in front at the third last. Ducked out at last bend. Destroyed.*'

There was no need to look up Tanglewood's form. Paul remembered the race well, Bill Scott tracking Clay Wentworth until they approached the last fence, then riding his horse out with hands and heels while, behind him, Clay did his imitation of a drunken bandmaster wielding the baton with impotent fury. Another image flashed across his mind – Angie, staring with undisguised horror as the other horse in contention, Drago's Pet, lay motionless a few yards beyond the second last fence. He too had been destroyed. Even in a sport where equine casualties are the norm, it seemed too much of a coincidence.

Paul reached for the telephone and dialled. He hadn't warmed to Gavin Holmes – there was something seedy and unhealthy about the man – but, for the moment, they had a shared interest. The woman who answered his extension laughed incredulously at the idea that Gavin should be at work at ten. She'd try to get him to call back when he made his customary late-morning pit-stop at the office before wandering off to lunch.

Hanging up, Paul looked once more at the piece of paper Zena had left him. The writing seemed somehow familiar. He shuffled among the papers on his desk before finding what he was looking for.

He put the letter he had received last week beside the shopping-list of ill-fated horses. There could be no mistaking the bold, round strokes, the way the cross on each 'T' floated oddly above the perpendicular, the confident 'F' on the name Brut Force.

Few village gossips were as effective, as ruthless professionally, as Joe Taylor. While others might happen upon an interesting titbit which was broadcast, suitably embellished, to anyone who cared to listen, Joe hoovered up the gossip at Lambourn and passed it on to one or more of his contacts. And, because horse chat can often be converted into money, Joe made a good living.

The word about Paul Raven riding again was hardly vintage material – no one was going to get rich on a broken-backed jockey – but it had a bit of colour to it, brought a smile in a grim and grey month, so, as soon as he heard about it, within a matter of hours of Paul alighting carefully from Monty's back, he rang one of his journalist contacts. It was a soft story but it would make a paragraph in the morning's gossip column and provide Joe Taylor with a handy £25, so all things considered, Paul Raven's return to the saddle was good news for everyone.

A profound restlessness assailed the heart of Digby Welcome. It was nine in the evening and, instead of working, he had spent most of the day worrying about developments in his life. On a normal night, he would be out there on his territory, bringing a harsh and chilly relief to Dianas and Juljanas all over West London, setting up marital deals that would keep them one step ahead of Immigration. There was work to be done – just because the authorities in Eastern Europe were happier to export the young and ambitious than they had once been, it didn't mean their counterparts in England would ease control on human imports – but tonight Digby hadn't the strength to engage in his own peculiar form of social work.

He sat in front of a fake coal fire warming his neat

and chubby hands on the gas flame. Already he had tried different forms of distraction – a brandy and ginger ale, a quiz show on television, a few minutes on the crossword puzzle – but his mind kept returning to the mess of grimy deals and petty corruption that was his life.

If only his business and personal affairs were as ordered as the neat bachelor flat off the Old Brompton Road where he lived. Digby sat back in his armchair and closed his eyes to it all. With those glittering little points of greed extinguished, he appeared almost amiable, a red-faced, roly-poly character in an expensive tweed suit, the sort of man you might see asleep in a corner of one of London's better clubs – a card, a joker, a gentleman.

Digby drummed the short, well-manicured fingers of his right hand. Wearily he opened his eyes and reached for a telephone on the table beside him, placed it on his knees. He dialled Clay's private number – the number to which crazy Zena had no access – and waited.

'Clay,' he said eventually. 'Can you talk?'

There was a brisk and not entirely friendly reply from the other end of the telephone. Whatever else he was, Clay was no gossip. Besides, few people spent more time chatting to Digby Welcome than was strictly necessary.

'Ran into that chap Paul Raven the other day. Mmm. Met him at the sports.' On occasions like these, Digby's voice became plummy and distracted.

'No, didn't say a word about poor little Alex. He seemed to have heard about our Thursday nights. I said he could come along, try his luck.' He winced comically as Clay, with a certain impatience, presented his objections. 'I don't know, old boy. Felt sorry for him, I suppose. His back and all that kit. Perhaps a spot of gambling would take his mind off it.' An effete and deeply insincere chuckle shook Digby's frame. 'I don't know where he gets his money,' he said. 'Maybe the Injured Jockeys' Fund is more generous than we thought. That's his problem. Hmm. My guest, of course. I hear what you're saying, old boy, but I can't believe that one night can do any harm. Well done, good kit, see you on Thursday.' Digby hung up. 'Fucking bastard,' he drawled with quiet vehemence.

What he had never understood was how men like Clay – or indeed women like Alice Markwick – managed to get through life without the disastrous, crippling setbacks that seemed to afflict him. While his career could be seen as a juddering switchback ride, theirs was a straight line, an inexorable upward graph. He was brighter than they were – brighter, at least, than Clay – yet there was something about him that invited distrust and, after distrust, disaster.

He reached into a drawer and took out a box of expensive cigars which he kept hidden in case one of his rare guests at the flat expected to be offered one. He lit up, puffing at the cigar restlessly as if, within moments of indulging himself, he wanted it to be gone.

He thought of school, army, his racing stables. The pattern was always the same. Up, then down. Boom, then crash. Order, then confusion. The business in which he had been engaged over the past decade or so had been good to him but now – Digby knew to the core of his substantial frame – it was all about to go wrong.

He was sensitive in that way, with the crook's instinct for the job that he shouldn't do, but always will.

Briefly, Digby considered ringing Alice Markwick. He didn't like the woman but if his other business interests were about to hit the rocks, it was important that his investment in Markwick Instruments paid the spectacular dividends that he expected. 'Alzbeta,' he said quietly. How she had changed over the years.

Laying the cigar in an ashtray, Digby pulled himself out of the armchair and walked slowly towards the bedroom.

Something bad was coming. He just knew it.

The organization had many divisions, each of them catering in a highly efficient way for different forms of human weakness. Drugs, ranging from the recreational and mind-expanding to the more serious and death-dealing, was an ever-buoyant area. Fraud, funny money games played with neat, hi-tech sophistication, was demanding more and more attention.

And, of course, there was sex – there was always sex.

Maria Curatullo checked her make-up in the mirror of a Maida Vale flat, then looked, with a brisk professionalism, in the leather carrier bag on the floor beside her. Seven days she had been waiting in this grey city where the men watched you with dirty-little-boy stares and the women scurried home from work as if they had sand in their knickers.

Maria had worked most of the cities in Europe. She liked Paris, which was like a flighty and expensive mistress; she was always happy to return to Frankfurt, a sharp and ambitious teenage whore of a town, ready for anything at the right price. Rome, of course, was like her – a big, generous woman of the world who understood pleasure. But London? She was a sour old widow, shrivelled up with repressed and twisted desire. Only for very special cases did Maria come to London.

The dark Rover that waited for Maria Curatullo outside her flat might have belonged to a senior sales director of an international firm, just as the young man in suit and tie who sat in the driver's seat might have been a professional chauffeur. The organization liked to look after its executives.

There was no need to give the driver the address to which he was taking her. The words '*Al lavoro*' were good enough. The waiting was over, the time-killing expeditions to shops or cinemas were behind them. The young man, an apprentice in the organization, risked a glance at his passenger in the rearview mirror. Despite the night outside, the signorina was wearing dark glasses.

Behind the shades, Maria's face showed no interest in the streets of London as they sped by. Once, when the Rover stopped at a red traffic light, two men in a nearby car stared across, laughing uneasily at her menacing sexuality. Maria ignored them. With the self-knowledge of a true professional, she knew that her eyes were most effective when hidden. Without dark glasses, she was no more than a handsome woman with a knowing look, a wife even; with them, she was forbidden and dangerous.

From the early days, when she was recruited as a teenager to work for the organization, she had fallen into the habit of giving her punters nicknames. It made the work easier, these private labels. The job tonight was on 'Il Grassone', the fat one.

Maria pulled the leather hold-all closer to her at the thought of the task ahead. Once she had needed no more than her own body but, as the years went by and she became known for experience and skill rather than youth and beauty, she needed props, a bag of tricks. Some of the older women she saw stepping into limousines in Mayfair, or Les Halles or on the Via Veneto, were practically carrying suitcases. In that sense, Maria considered that she was lucky. Sex was no longer her exclusive area of expertise – she had diversified, made herself useful to the organization in another way.

The car pulled up and Maria told the driver that

she would be an hour, maybe slightly more. Relaxing at last, he watched the signorina as she walked up the steps towards the block of flats. She still had good legs – the man smiled – despite the miles on the clock.

Maria pressed a button on the intercom at the entrance. 'Mr Welcome,' she said, 'Ees me.'

There was a pause of some seconds before the door clicked open.

By the time the lift had taken her to the third floor, Il Grassone had left the door to his flat a little ajar. With a slight sense of foreboding – you never lost the smallest frisson of fear the first time with a new man – Maria pushed the door and entered a small, dimly lit hall.

'I was expecting Nicola.'

Il Grassone was standing at the entrance to the sitting-room, his hair slicked down, wearing a maroon silk dressing-gown – an English client of the traditional variety.

Maria slipped off her coat and threw it over a chair. 'Nicola ees eell. You got Maria,' she said huskily. 'I go away?'

He stood there taking in the statuesque body in the black Armani dress. She was too big. Too old. Too much of a woman.

'Did you talk to Nicola? About me?'

'Yes, Deegby. I talk. I know.' She stepped closer to him. They never changed their minds – once they had made the call, slipped the leash from their sick and feverish desires, there was no going back.

178

'So you know how you are required to oblige me?'

Il Grassone had stepped back, as if afraid of being touched. She knew nothing of this Nicola, except that, just this once, she had been taken off the case; but experience told her what the man needed.

'Oblige me? What means this?' she asked.

'Bloody hell, they've sent me someone who doesn't even speak English.'

Maria glanced at her watch. 'You want conversazione, I fetch someone else,' she said.

'No.' Il Grassone's pleading, glittering little eyes told their own story. Anger was precisely what he wanted.

'Maria.' He seemed to cower slightly. 'I've been a very naughty boy.'

'To bedroom,' she said like a school matron. 'Get ready for Maria.'

Il Grassone ran a nervous tongue over his lips, then turned towards the bedroom.

'*Fai presto!*' she hissed, reached for her leather bag. *Dio*, these Englishmen were all alike.

Her right arm ached. She was getting bored. For twenty minutes she had been working on Il Grassone who lay face down on his bed, the acres of white flesh now striped with red marks from the whip. As he whimpered, it wobbled like some disgusting English summer pudding.

He had had his fun. He was relaxed. It was time for business. 'Turn over, you fat peeeg,' she said.

Nervously, painfully, he lay on his back, exposing his vast belly and pitiful manhood to Maria's scornful gaze. His eyes, wet with tears, widened as she took two pairs of velvet-lined handcuffs out of her bag. 'That was antipasto,' she said, clicking them onto his wrists. Roughly, she wrenched the cuffs upwards and attached them to the bedhead. 'Now is time for main course.'

Caught between fear and pleasure, Digby whispered, 'Sorry, Maria.'

Briskly, she reached into the bag, this time bringing out a small cassette recorder which she placed on the bedside table, then an electric lead, a plug on one end, two naked wires on the other. With genuine alarm, Digby tugged helplessly at the handcuffs.

'*Allora*'. Maria switched on the cassette and, as loud disco music filled the room, plugged the lead into a nearby socket. Humming softly to herself, she looked into the hold-all once more and took out a piece of paper which she unfolded. 'I have to ask you some questions, Deegby.' She ran the hand holding the live wires across his hairless chest and down over his stomach. 'Ees true what you say. You were a vairy naughty boy.'

She turned the disco music up louder.

At the pizza house in Wandsworth, three men sat at the corner table. Conversation was flowing less easily tonight, as if all three of them sensed that what, they had assumed, would be a simple task, had proved to be a problem.

When the telephone rang at two-fifteen, it was Giorgio who walked to the bar, picked it up and listened. 'No,' he said eventually. '*Si*.' He hung up wearily.

'*Niente*,' he said, returning to the table. '*Assolutamente niente*.'

The three men sat in silence for a moment, before Salvatore asked a question, a casual afterthought.

Giorgio shrugged. '*Naturalmente*,' he said.

Personally, Maria had nothing against Il Grassone. He had been an easy patient, succumbing to electricity with only slightly more noise than he had made under the whip. And it was hardly his fault that he had been unable to give her the information the organization needed on the whereabouts of the Markwick machine, whatever it was.

Personally, she would have left it there but Giorgio had insisted and, above all, she prided herself on her professionalism.

Maria shifted slightly on Il Grassone's face. Luckily he was tired and, when she had settled on him, placing one foot each side of his great white stomach, he had writhed only for a few moments. She glanced at her watch. In half an hour's time she would be at the airport hotel for four hours' sleep before she left to catch her flight home. It would be good to get away from this odd, depressing country.

Il Grassone trembled once more and was still. Maria sighed. Sometimes she felt she was growing too old for the game. Once sitting on a man's face had meant pleasure, not death.

Neither the sex nor the killing came as easy to her as it used to.

For a few more seconds, she sat there heavily, lost in thought, like a middle-aged washerwoman astride a log. Then with a quiet, 'Bye-bye, Deegby,' she lifted herself off the dead man and prepared to leave for the airport.

Chapter 9

It wasn't Watergate, but it was interesting.

Eyes closed, Gavin Holmes braced himself as another wave of nausea broke over him – but it took more than a Force Nine hangover to deflect him from a story once it started to buzz. 'Touch of 'flu, is it, Gav?' Shirley, one of the younger reporters, called out as she walked briskly past his desk.

'There's a lot of it about,' he muttered, carefully placing a third finger and thumb on his eyelids, as if to check the eyeballs were still in place. He opened his eyes to gaze blearily at Shirley's legs as she walked away. Maybe her turn would come.

He heaved himself back in front of the word-processor to look once more at his notes. On the screen, he read

DEAD NAGS

Five names on list given to Paul, all but one dead.

Except for Dig For Glory, all ridden by amateurs.

All fell towards end of race, three at a fence, one on the flat.

Postmortem: only two taken to Newmarket Veterinary College. Contact there – Heather O'Connell – claims neither horse, Whataparty or Brut Force, showed signs of substance in the bloodstream. Heart and lungs appeared to be entirely healthy.

Quote: 'It's a dangerous game and the majority of serious falls occur over the last half mile. Our conclusion was that these fatalities were the sort of thing that happen in National Hunt racing, no more, no less.'

Gavin sat back and massaged his eyes once more. It was just the sort of remark which, a week ago, he would have used but since then his area of interest had changed. 'The sort of things that happen in National Hunt racing.' That was yesterday's scandal. He punched some keys on the word-processor and more notes appeared on the screen.

Linked characters??

Clay Wentworth. Background – see Who's Who 1991. Chairman of Wentworth Properties and amateur jockey. Riding on the day Dig For Glory killed (not in same race). Also in race won by Tanglewood, the only surviving horse on the hit list. Ambitious?

List found in his possession?

Raven claims that Alex Drew used to play poker with him.

Strange (strained) relationship with wife Zena.

It wasn't much to go on. Gavin was as prepared as anyone to doorstep the great, the good and the guilty in pursuit of a story but the connection with Alex Drew's death seemed tenuous, even – Gavin remembered seeing photographs of Wentworth on financial pages – unlikely. He tapped in one more word onto the computer report.

Weak?

Gavin's notes on Zena Wentworth and Digby Welcome took him no further on the case. Zena, a former model, was said to have had a drink problem which developed into a fidelity problem – there was nothing new or unusual there.

Digby, 'the late Digby, was more interesting. According to Gavin's police contacts, the murder of Digby Welcome was being treated as a sex and robbery case. The flat had been turned over, a few items and possibly some cash had apparently been removed. The received opinion at Chelsea Police Station was that a business girl had got greedy and had graduated from prostitution to murder. Not even the fact that Digby was handcuffed to the bed, that his poor, abused frame showed signs of a beating and electrocution to sensitive erogenous zones, had aroused particular interest. The world was full of punishment freaks. The velvet-lined handcuffs, it was said, were made in Italy.

Gavin sat back and closed his eyes. The thought of Digby Welcome writhing around in pleasure as some hard-eyed tart goosed him with electric wires did nothing for his hangover. But it wasn't Digby's death, which he put down to the journalistic version of Sod's law – your best lead always dies – that interested him, but the connection with Clay Wentworth. On the face of it, they were ill-matched characters with no more in common than an interest in racing and, from what Gavin had heard, Digby was not one to spend time on normal social relationships. For him, friendship was always a means to an end.

There was another oddity. Paul Raven had discovered that Digby had put £3,000 on Skinflint to win, yet he was said to be funny about cash – after all, it had been chronic meanness that had finished his career as a trainer. Gavin didn't know much about racing but you had to be blind not to see that putting three grand on a horse ridden by Clay Wentworth in an amateur race was high-risk gambling bordering on lunacy.

Unless Digby had known that Tanglewood couldn't win, that after that race, the horse would be dead or injured and its name would be removed from Clay's list. As it was, Tanglewood won, although Raven had mentioned that there had been another casualty in the race.

He dialled Paul's number, but the boy wonder was out or busy with cute little Angie, because Gavin found himself listening to his soft northern tones on an answering machine. He decided to leave a message.

'These nags that bought it,' he said, as if they were in the middle of a conversation. 'What did they have in common which Tanglewood didn't? I was wondering if there was anything odd about the Wincanton race. The boffins at Newmarket are fucking useless, by the way. Give that darling girlfriend of yours a kiss or something from me . . .'

He hung up. Gavin preferred the company of women to that of men but he couldn't help admiring a man whose body had been broken but who was already walking, who was obsessively searching out the person behind his friend Drew's death and who, despite several disabilities – a lack of significant movement in the legs, a career in ruins, a family that came from north of Watford – had still managed to pull Angie O'Keefe. Gavin respected the man; in a world where words were cheap, his quiet determination was unusual.

He punched up more of his notes onto the screen.

OTHERS POSSIBLY INVOLVED

Ginnie Matthews (trainer)

Lol Calloway (rock star)

Alice Markwick (businesswoman)

With a grunt of effort and pain, Gavin stood up. He wandered across the large open-plan offices of the *Guardian* until he reached a group of desks where the staff covering the business pages worked. 'Sorry to wake you up, Peter,' he said to a man who sat, his feet on the desk before him, staring indifferently at the Teletext on the screen before him with the unmistakeable smugness of a journalist who has already filed his copy.

'I'm thinking,' said Pete Morrow, assistant business editor.

Gavin sat on the edge of the desk. 'What d'you know about Alice Markwick?' he said.

Kevin Smiley had once loved racing, but now he hated it. Fourteen years ago, he had left school with a dream in his heart of becoming a successful jockey. He had worked in a small yard near Leicestershire before trying his luck in Newmarket. He grew too heavy to get rides even in apprentice races, so he moved on yet again to a jumping stable outside Royston.

He was twenty-five before he began to realise that the dream was never going to come true. At first, he had thought it was his weight. Then he had convinced himself that the Head Lad disliked him. After that, he blamed himself – he was moody, sometimes giving the Guv'nor of the moment a piece of his mind.

Now that he was thirty, Kevin had discovered the truth that others had known for years. His problem was not on the scales, or in his character or attitude, but in the saddle. He wasn't exactly useless – sometimes he could look quite neat as he rode work – but he would never wear silks. He hadn't the judgement, or the balance, or the brains to ride competitively. His past, his present and his future were as a lad, not a jockey.

At first, he took his dissatisfaction out on the horses, prodding them with a pitchfork as he mucked out, jabbing them in the mouth as he rode them in the string. He became unpopular with the other lads, making trouble for them, bullying the younger apprentices, particularly if they showed a talent that he would never have.

Kevin was bent before he had come to work for Ginnie Matthews, supplying information, helping out when a certain runner needed to be slipped a certain untraceable substance with its morning feed. The fact that the Matthews stable was straight and the Missus trusted her staff implicitly changed nothing.

Kevin was part of racing's secret and corrupt network. He was a sleeper waiting to act on behalf of vaguely criminal elements. In return, he would receive money and, more importantly, experience the simple pleasure of doing someone harm.

'Morning, Kevin.' Paul Raven made his way slowly

across the yard on his way towards the Missus' house. 'Riding out second lot?'

'Nah.' Kevin looked away. 'You?'

Paul smiled. 'I'm giving Monty a half-speed over six furlongs,' he said.

'Right,' said Kevin, watching as Paul rang the bell at the Missus' front door.

Slo-Mo, he called him to the younger lads who were too afraid of him not to laugh. 'Here comes old Slo-Mo,' he'd say as Paul pulled himself out of the car before second lot.

He walked round to the tack room and reached for a bucket. Glancing around to check that no one was coming, he took some powder from his pocket and carefully poured it into the bucket which he half-filled with water.

He hadn't understood his instructions but he was confident that, somewhere along the line, he would be helping to cause a fair degree of pain and disappointment to some bastard who had it coming. Kevin smiled – it was good to feel wanted.

'How's Skinflint going?'

Breakfast with Ginnie Matthews was not a social affair – conversation tended to be minimal or non-existent – but there were two reasons why Paul had accepted the casual invitation, muttered the last time he had ridden out. The mixed grill cooked by the Irish maid was astonishing and Paul needed to resolve a question in his mind.

'Fine.' Ginnie hardly bothered to look up from her *Sporting Post*, tucking into the heaped plate before her as if she hadn't eaten for days. Manners had never played a great part in her life and, ever since she had lived alone, her breakfast behaviour had gone into a sharp decline. Through a mouth full of food, she added 'He'll win at Cheltenham if the jockey doesn't make a balls up.'

'The race has cut up badly.'

Ginnie nodded, as if to say that Paul had exhausted her supply of early morning conversation.

Paul persisted. 'Extraordinary how many of the fancied horses have gone wrong.' He looked away as the trainer did something mildly disgusting with a fried egg before shovelling it into her mouth. 'Died in fact.'

Ginnie glanced up and, below the thick make-up on her face, there appeared the hint of a blush. She finished her mouthful, reached for a napkin and wiped, not entirely successfully, the traces of egg from the sides of her mouth. 'Yes, I've noticed.'

Paul reached into the pocket of his jodhpurs and passed a slip of paper across the table.

'Who gave you this?' Ginnie asked eventually. She seemed more surprised than guilty.

'It doesn't matter. The writing's yours, isn't it?'

'Looks like it.' Ginnie pushed the paper back to Paul and busied herself spreading a thick layer of butter on some toast.

'The horses whose names are crossed out have all

been destroyed,' said Paul.

'Bloody hell,' Ginnie boomed. 'I may be keen on getting winners but I don't go around killing horses.' There was an edgy, unconvincing humour in her voice. 'The list is mine,' she added, 'but I didn't cross the names out.'

'What was it for?'

'An owner needed it.'

'Clay Wentworth?'

Ginnie nodded as she chewed on her toast. 'Some time back, Clay wanted to know the main contenders for the Kim Muir. I jotted them down for him.'

'Why Dig For Glory?'

'God knows. If you look at your piece of paper there, you'll see that name's in different writing. Anyway I wrote the list after your fall.' She glanced at her watch. 'Time for second lot. Or are you too busy playing detective to exercise poor old Monty for me?'

Paul stood up. 'How did he do it?' he said, almost to himself.

'It seems a bit efficient for Clay,' said Ginnie. 'I've always thought he lived like he rode – weak and ineffective.'

Paul smiled. 'He must have help.'

Ginnie walked briskly out of the door. Either she was a better actor than he would ever have believed or she was entirely innocent.

There were few advantages in being a part-time jockey on the mend, Paul reflected as he made his way out of the house towards the yard, but at least he was spared the drilling discomfort of riding out in the gloom and cold of first lot at seven o'clock. Now, as the lads pulled out the second string, a wintry sun was taking the bite out of the morning. There was another small privilege – Monty was tacked up for him by one of the younger lads.

As Paul approached Monty's box, a figure scurried out, carrying a bucket and sponge, whistling cheerily as he made his way back to the tackroom. Paul opened the stable door and, looking at Monty, noticed a dark stain on his chestnut hindquarters under the tail. Nothing unusual there – the Missus took a robust, old fashioned view of turn-out and had an eagle eye for dried sweatmarks behind the girth or a trace of muck on the hindquarters. The only surprise was that it was Kevin Smiley, not normally a perfectionist, who was attending to Monty.

The string had made its way past the farm buildings and neighbouring houses that backed onto the yard when Monty first swished his tail and lifted his hindquarters.

At first, Paul laughed. 'Who's been feeding up this old bugger?' he called out. 'He's trying to drop me.'

Pat, the Head Lad, who was riding in front of Paul in the string, looked around. 'You all right?' he asked.

Paul nodded. The old horse was jigging about like a two-year-old and, for the first time since he had resumed riding, Paul was nervously aware of his insecurity in the saddle. He laid a calming hand on Monty's neck and was surprised to find that, despite the cold, he was beginning to sweat.

There was a matter of seconds between Paul's realization that there was something wrong and the moment when it was too late to do anything about it. As the string turned right up a side road towards the gallops, Monty started to dance sideways, his eyes fearful, his mouth flecked with foam.

'Get off him, Paul,' Jamie called out. 'He must have something under his saddle.'

Paul kicked his feet out of the irons. The horse grunted, kicked the air and, before Paul could dismount, Monty had set off, first at a trot, then, snorting with pain, at a gallop away from the string. Like a clown on a circus horse, Paul clung to the mane, unable to grip enough with his legs to control the horse.

Pat set off in pursuit but pain had given Monty a surprising turn of speed and, before Paul could reach him, he had rounded a bend and was making for the main road.

Paul knew there was no choice. As pain wrenched his back, the wind whistling past his ears, he saw, drawing ever closer, the cars and lorries speeding along the road before him. Closing his eyes and doing his best to ball himself up as he fell, he dived to the left, hitting the ground a matter of yards before the main road.

Seconds later, Pat pulled up, alighting from the

saddle. He crouched down beside Paul, gently turning him over.

From the near distance, there was the sound of the blaring of car-horns followed by the unmistakeable sound of metal impact at speed.

Pat glanced towards the road, then back at Paul, registering the flickering of consciousness in his eyelids.

'Lie still,' he said. 'Don't move a muscle.'

Those who knew Alice Markwick well, a small and exclusive group, rarely guessed her true weakness. Although she had a deep and sincere affection for money, it wasn't financial greed. As for the trips to Heaven in search of someone young, firm and dressed in a leather skirt, that was controllable: her libido, while powerful and slightly odd, was not allowed to dominate her life.

The flaw in Alice's personal armoury was simple – she wanted to belong. All her life, she had been an outsider. Now, after two decades of work and discreet corruption, she felt it was time she became part of the inner circle where your place of birth was no more than an exotic extra, where the way you had made your money was irrelevant. Others slipped easily into Britain's legendary class system: why couldn't she?

She could have married again, of course, but that was an unacceptable option. For three years she had endured the demeaning reality of heterosexual sex. The day that she had stood by the coffin of Dr Eric

Markwick, she had promised herself that never again
would she allow her flesh to be invaded by a repulsive
male presence. Sex with Eric had been like submitting
to a herd of eager slugs, one of whom was carrying
an absurd and disgusting prong. No, never again –
not even as a means to acquire the respectability she
so longed for.

Alice sat in a deep armchair in her spacious and
tastefully decorated Islington flat, flicking restlessly
through a glossy magazine. It was about ten thirty;
normally she would have been at the office for two
hours by now but today, she deserved a morning off.
Today she would take one step nearer society, *le tout
Londres*.

She found herself thinking of Clay's father, Sir
Denis Wentworth, whom she had met a couple of
times. Like her, he had been an outsider, although
he lacked her sophistication and looks. And, despite
the fact that he was no more than a hard and humourless businessman, he had entered the magic circle
with apparent ease. Why? Because he was rich?
Because he was English? Because he was a man?
Certainly charm had had nothing to do with it.

The bell rang. Checking her appearance before a
large mirror, Alice walked to the intercom. 'Who is
it?' she asked.

'Gavin Holmes. *Mail on Sunday*.'

Alice pressed another button. 'Top floor,' she said.

It had only been a matter of time. With her looks
and contacts and professional success, fashionable

exposure in the right places had to come. When the man from the *Mail on Sunday* had rung her at the office and asked whether she would contribute to a series of profiles called 'Me and My Roots', she had jumped at the chance. A Sunday magazine, complete with colour photograph – it was too good to be true.

'Mrs Markwick?' the man at her door had the unhealthy pallor that she associated with journalists. He extended a hand. 'Gavin Holmes. So kind of you to spare the time for our little feature.'

'What about the photographer?' Alice asked.

Gavin shrugged apologetically. 'He'll call you later to arrange a time for the pictures,' he said, entering the flat and making his way into the sitting-room. 'We'd only have been in each other's way if he'd come this morning.'

The man talked. As Alice gave him coffee, hoping that he would note that it was the best Italian blend served in softly hand-painted porcelain manufactured in Longchamps, she listened to him explaining at length the rationale behind the piece. It wasn't muck-raking, he said, more lifestyle, a positive, life-affirming, upbeat story full of human touches, surprising, intimate, that would reach –

'Why don't you just ask me the questions and we'll take it from there?' Alice smiled, settling back into her seat like a charming English hostess. Noticing the flicker of sexual interest in the journalist's eyes as she leaned forward, she took off her shoes and curled her legs under her, affording him a better view of them.

She smiled. A ladies' man; this was going to be easy.

Gavin took out a notebook. 'Perhaps you could tell me about your childhood in Prague,' he asked.

'Ah, Prague.' Alice allowed a shadow of unease, suggesting painful memories, to cross her face. 'I was born into a poor working family. My father worked in a factory. My mother, a beautiful woman, was an office-cleaner. It was a hard life...'

She spoke eloquently, her husky, slightly accented voice presenting the vivid picture of her youth which she had perfected over the two decades in which she had been in England.

The journalist jotted notes onto his pad. 'So you came to London. What sort of work did you do?' he asked without looking up.

'Au pair. Washing-up. Translation.' Alice smiled. 'The usual things.'

For a few minutes, Gavin asked questions about London in the sixties. It was wild, wasn't it, something of a party? Alice was evasive. Not in her circles, it wasn't. As if talking to himself, Gavin spoke of the fascination the old permissiveness held for *Mail on Sunday* readers. The music, the drugs, the laughter.

'You're asking if I had lots of boyfriends? The answer is no,' Alice said more coolly.

'Did you know Digby Welcome?' The question came out of the blue, attended by an innocent smile.

Alice frowned. 'The name seems somewhat familiar,' she said eventually. 'Have I read something about him?'

'He was murdered recently. I read somewhere that he had introduced you to your future husband.'

Alice felt the colour draining from her cheeks. She leaned forward and took the journalist's cup. 'More coffee?' she asked. 'I'm rather pleased with this blend. Rozzo di Palermo. Bought it in Harrods Food Hall.'

Gavin smiled, but made no note on his pad.

'I thought this was a lifestyle piece,' she said lightly.

'Colour. A little mention of Welcome would give the piece what we call "contemporaneity". The feature editor likes that. So you knew him?'

'I worked in a restaurant. I think Welcome might have invited me to the party where I met Eric. It was a long time ago.'

'And you kept in touch?'

'Good Lord, no. The man gives me the creeps.'

Gavin frowned, allowing a moment of silence before speaking again. It was clear that Alice Markwick had nothing more to say on the subject of Welcome.

'So,' he said. 'Tell me about your husband.'

'Ah, Eric.' Alice relaxed, a distant look in her eyes. 'A sweet, brilliant man.'

It was another half hour before Gavin Holmes left the flat. Although Alice knew little of journalism – she rarely bothered to read beyond the financial pages of *The Times* – the interview had surprised her. She had been expecting something rather gentler, a light-hearted tour of the flat, some harmless chat about her past, her work methods, where she shopped. Instead Holmes had asked prying, insistent questions about the work carried out by Markwick Instruments. He had been alarmingly well-briefed.

Then there was Digby Welcome. How on earth had he known about that?

There were certain memories which Alice had tried over the years to erase from her mind – useless, negative memories of events which, even these many years later, made her feel sick to the stomach.

Staring out of the window, she heard once more the smug and sinister tones of Digby Welcome – 'your guardian angel, my dearest', he used to call himself in the early days. And, of course, he was right. If Digby hadn't been there to rescue her from the smoky Knightsbridge restaurant where she was working, she would never have reached where she was today. Marriage wasn't a problem; but Eric, by some freak of chance, had been perfect. He was brilliant, he was gullible, he fell in love easily and – the best kept until last – died at an early age, leaving his firm to Alice.

Once Digby had something on you, he never let go. At first, it had been easy – Alice shuddered as she thought of Digby's skin netted with the red lash marks from her whip – but, as if he had understood that hitting a man was a positive pleasure for her, he had given that up, taking instead some share options in the firm. The fact that, because of his mysterious demise, Digby Welcome would not be picking up his

share of the big pay-off caused Alice no disappointment whatsoever.

Her instinct told her that there was something not
quite right about Gavin Holmes. She picked up the
telephone book and, having leafed through its pages,
walked to the hall telephone and dialled.

'Features editor,' she said.

At the other end, the phone rang for some time
before a woman picked it up. The features editor was
in conference at present, she said.

'My name's Mrs Markwick, I'm sure you could help
me.' Alice put on her most ingratiating voice. 'Your
man Gavin Holmes has just been interviewing me for
your "Me and My Roots" feature. He told me I'd be
visited by a photographer. I really need to know when
he's coming round.'

'Holmes?' The woman at the other end seemed
confused. 'I think he's on the *Guardian*. He doesn't
work for us. Anyway we wound up that feature last
month. Who did – '

Alice hung up. It wasn't often that she was taken
in by a man and she didn't like it. She dialled another
number.

'I think I've found Petrin's guinea pig,' she said.

Clay Wentworth put down the receiver as if it were
a piece of rare china, and tapped his rolled gold biro
on the desk. He didn't like Alice Markwick and he
certainly didn't like depending on her. There was no
point of contact – not class, not sex, not humour. All

that bound them together was the project on which they both, in different ways, depended. She was too cold, too hard – she seemed to relish the danger of their plan, the pain it caused to others. He thought of her luckless employee, Zametsky. Alice had known that there was some connection between what had happened to him and her own dubious plans, yet she had insisted it had been an accident. Zametsky had, for some reason, seemed too afraid to tell the truth. In the end, it had been Clay who had sent his wife £1,000 in cash. The money was nothing when your face was missing but it made him feel slightly better.

'Lunch.' His father stood at the door of the office, leaning on his walking-stick. As usual, his short frame and glittering blue eyes emanated wordless disapproval.

Father and son went through to the boardroom of Wentworth Properties plc, where a plump and nervous girl, the daughter of a shareholder, served them with a beef casserole taken from some Cordon Bleu cookbook for executive lunches. As usual, Sir Denis's portion was microscopic and, after the girl had gone, he looked at his meal with distaste before poking at a piece of meat and fastidiously putting it in his mouth. His old jaws worked slowly.

Sometimes, during these meals, Clay would look down the length of the long mahogany table and think, 'Die, you stupid old bastard, choke on it.' Then he would think again. Not yet. Not quite yet.

'Who was she?' Sir Denis spoke little these days so that, when he did, his words came out in a slow guttural rasp, like the voice of a Dickensian villain.

'Who, father?'

'On the phone. In the office.'

'Just business.'

For a moment, the boardroom was silent except for the sound of silver on china.

'Business.' Sir Denis pushed a bit of meat around his plate. He understood Clay well enough to know that no mere matter of profit or loss would preoccupy him for long. His son had never understood the importance of money. 'You're poking, I suppose,' he said.

'No, father. I'm not poking, as you call it.'

Chewing slowly, Sir Denis looked at his son with chilly contempt. 'I don't suppose you are.' An odd, birdlike sound, somewhere between a laugh and a death rattle, came from him. 'Never much of a poker, were you?'

A flush of anger appeared on Clay's cheeks. He could just about take his father when he was lecturing him about company matters; when he moved into the personal area, he was impossible. Ever since Lady Wentworth, a quiet, blameless woman, had died in the early 1970s, Sir Denis had lived in a flat in Knightsbridge alone apart from the butler who looked after him. The spartan simplicity of his life had allowed him to comment, almost always unfavourably, on Clay's domestic arrangements.

'Ditch the bitch,' Sir Denis said as if reading Clay's thoughts. 'New young wife. Children. That's what you want.' A drop of dark gravy hung on his lower lip. '*She's* poking, you know.'

'Told you that, has she, father?' Clay pushed away his plate. 'You talk about poking with my wife?'

'Ditch her. You'd make an old man very happy.'

Maybe, when this was all over, he would. Living with a crazed, pill-happy, middle-aged woman was almost as depressing as working with his cold and sinister father.

He watched as Sir Denis toyed with his meal. It would be another fifteen minutes before Clay was free to return to his office.

'Maybe I will,' he said, thinking of freedom, a new start in life. It wouldn't be long now.

This story had led to some of the worst places – a cold stableyard, the backstreets of Willesden, and now the casualty ward of a run-down rural hospital. It wasn't what he'd become a journalist to do.

Gavin walked down the ward to a bed beside which sat Angie, a ray of beauty in a grim, off-white world.

'Gavin,' she said, smiling. 'Kind of you to visit.'

'My pleasure,' he lied. Reluctantly, he turned to the bed where Paul lay. 'You prat,' he said. 'What is it with you and horses?'

It had been twenty-four hours since Paul had been admitted. His face was decorated by vivid bruises and his right arm and shoulder were bandaged up. 'It wasn't an accident, Gavin,' he said quietly.

The journalist pulled up a chair and slumped into it. 'What do the docs say?' he asked.

'That he was a bloody fool to be riding in the first place,' said Angie.

Paul smiled weakly. 'It could be worse,' he said. 'Light concussion, fractured collar-bone. The back's shaken up a bit. I fell in the right way.'

'You seem to have lots of practice.' Gavin produced a packet of cigarettes and was just about to light up when he remembered where he was. Swearing softly, he put them away again. 'While you've been trying to kill yourself, I've been making myself useful.'

'A trainer called Ginnie Matthews made that list,' Paul interrupted. 'She gave it to Clay Wentworth.'

'You think she's involved?'

Paul shook his head, wincing slightly. 'She suspected something was going on but I'm sure she wasn't involved.'

'Yet it was at her yard that you had your accident,' said Angie. 'It seems a bit of a coincidence.'

'No, maybe Paul's right,' Gavin said. 'There seems to have been very little gambling involved in these races. I think the people behind it are outside racing.'

He told them of his visit to Alice Markwick, pointing out the connection between her and Digby Welcome.

'Markwick and Welcome used to go to Wentworth's poker evenings,' said Paul. 'But why were they involved in killing horses?'

'To help Clay win races?' Angie remembered the tall man she had seen in the bar at Wincanton. He had hardly seemed the ruthless type.

'And how?' Paul asked.

Gavin smiled triumphantly. 'As part of my profile, I asked Alice about the research being done by Markwick Instruments. It's into the use of lasers in surgery – particularly in eye surgery. She was evasive, claiming that she was a businesswoman who knew little about the technical side.'

'Eyes,' said Paul quietly. 'That's how they did it. They blinded the horse they were after as it approached the fence.'

'No, I checked with Newmarket,' said Gavin. 'According to the lab, there was nothing irregular about the horses' sight.'

'How do they do it then?' Angie asked. 'And what's their next target?'

'I've got to get to that poker school,' Paul muttered.

Gavin smiled. 'I wish I could help but both Alice and Clay would recognise me.'

'No,' Paul said. 'I'll go.'

'We need to get to Alice Markwick. Find out how they're blinding the horses – I'm sure that must be what they're doing.' Gavin sounded evasive, as if he had an idea which slightly embarrassed him.

'But how?' Angie asked.

'There is one way.' The journalist was looking at

her in an odd and slightly alarming way. 'But it's ever
so slightly tacky.'

'Surprise us,' said Paul.

There were times when Kevin Smiley cursed the day
his father took him racing. He had been thirteen at
the time and it had changed his life. The action, the
atmosphere, the smell of courage and money – even
though it was Haydock on a chilly Saturday, it had
been enough to infect little Kevin. 'I know what I
want to be,' he had said to his father, driving home
that night. 'I'm going to be a jockey.'

And, sure enough, he wasn't.

As Kevin packed his few belongings into a suitcase,
he thought of the cold mornings and casual humiliations that were the sum total of his racing career.
'You're fucking useless, Smiley,' one of the older
jockeys had told him when he was still in his teens.
'You haven't got it.'

The bastard had been right. Whatever the 'it' was
– that magic ingredient that turned boys into jockeys
– he didn't have it. Kevin glanced at his watch and
looked his last at the bedsit that had been home for
the last couple of years. He was thirty. It wasn't too
late to start again. He'd go to London, find a job.
He'd tell his parents later.

Kevin felt an uncharacteristic pang of guilt. It was
true that he had let a few people down. His mum and
dad, who had always believed in him, Mrs Matthews,
who had turned a deaf ear to those who had told her

that Smiley was a wrong 'un and taken him on all the same.

He thought of the last time he had seen his employer. She had been talking to the vet the day after the business with Paul Raven. Later, as he cleaned tack, one of the lads told him the rumour going round the yard.

'Weren't no accident, were it?' he had said. 'Fuckin' vet only found acid on poor old Monty's hindquarters. No wonder 'e went fuckin' apeshit. Burnin' into 'is flesh, weren't it?'

'Acid?' Kevin had acted as casually as he was able.

'Slow acting. Reacted with horse's body sweat, is what I heard. The more he sweated, the more it fuckin' ate into him.'

'So someone did it on purpose?'

'You're fuckin' quick, ain't you?' the lad had said. 'The Missus'll find him, that's for sure. Can't have her darlin' Paul buried like that, can we?'

It was hardly a glorious note on which to end his career but, if he had learned nothing else in a life of ducking and diving, Kevin knew when to cut and run. He clicked the suitcase shut and, leaving the light on and closing the door, he made his way down the stairs.

His car, a Ford Granada, drew up within seconds of Kevin appearing at the front door of the hostel.

'Minicab?' Kevin asked, as the driver opened the passenger door.

'For Mr Smiley,' said the driver.

'That's the one.' Kevin put the suitcase on the back seat and climbed in. 'Swindon station please, mate.' He sat back and closed his eyes, relaxing at last. It was good to get away.

It took a minute or two for him to realize that the car was heading the wrong way.

'Sorry, mate,' Kevin said uneasily. 'I said Swindon.'

In reply, the driver accelerated, flicking an electric lock on his door.

'What's up mate? What are you up to?'

'Child lock,' said the driver, his handsome dark eyes watching Kevin in the rearview mirror. 'Child lock for a very bad boy,' he said.

For a moment, Kevin was confused. Then he sat back and asked quietly, 'What exactly d'you want from me?'

'Nothing,' said the driver. 'Assolutamente niente.'

Chapter Ten

The photographer sat in his rabbit-filled bunker, thinking about the future. It was a small room, brightly lit by strip lighting, with a workbench in one corner and, occupying most of the floor space, the animals' play area.

He had enjoyed designing their little assault course. It had reminded him of when he was a small boy in Warsaw, of the toys he would make in the small back room of his mother's apartment, except here the toys were alive and, for a while at least, warm.

Of course, the rabbits were predictable in the stupid, panic-stricken way that they responded to scientific stimuli.

'Want to play, Fi-Fi?' The photographer spoke in the well-bred undertone of a man who had spent much of his life in university libraries and laboratories. He took a white and brown rabbit from a cage, placed it carefully into a corner of the play area enclosed by wire and turned to a control board on his desk. Humming softly, he pressed a couple of switches.

The prod flashed red, then green, then white as it approached Fi-Fi, causing her to cower against the wire. As it touched her white fur, the shock of an electric current jolted the rabbit's body. The prod withdrew before, flashing brightly once more, it advanced again. Fi-Fi was relatively intelligent and soon the first bright flash induced her to leap backwards against the wire in the knowledge that where there was light, pain would follow soon afterwards.

The photographer opened a small door, allowing her to escape into the rest of the cage. For a minute or so, he watched as she dashed backwards and forwards in her new-found freedom. He liked Fi-Fi – her rabbitty will to survive made her a good target. He reached for the camera on his desk.

It was too heavy, in his opinion. Zametsky had developed the prototype and had been indifferent to the photographer's complaint that, while it looked like a camera, a security guard or customs official merely needed to hold it to be suspicious. These people were trained to look for bombs and, although the camera was far more dangerous than mere explosives, its weight was a serious design flaw. Zametsky had smiled. Cosmetics, he had said, could come later.

Fi-Fi's efforts were tiring her. With a soft 'tut' of impatience, the photographer activated two more prods, one of which caught her, enlivening her performance. He weighed the camera in his hand, then took aim and shot.

The noise was good. The click and whirr was just like a real camera. Fi-Fi kept running, only this time she hurled herself against the wire. The photographer activated the flashing lights on the two electric prods. Frantic as she was, the rabbit made no effort to avoid them, running blindly into the first one and then the other. In a relatively short time, she lay in a corner, her sides heaving with exhaustion. The photographer moved the prod slowly towards her. It flashed red, green and white, but Fi-Fi no longer reacted.

Perfect. The photographer left the prod flashing before the rabbit's unseeing eyes and checked his watch. Four minutes. Fi-Fi would come round within the next sixty seconds.

At first, he hadn't believed that there was no trace, that the beam of Zametsky's gismo could penetrate the corneal cortex and freeze the iris without long-term damage. It was a miracle of technology, a laser that incapacitated yet was untraceable. The photographer felt proud to be a part of it, privileged.

There was a scrabbling from the cage as the life came back to Fi-Fi's eyes and she saw the flashing horror before her.

The photographer smiled at the rabbit's clownish double-take. Throwing the switches on the control board, he said, 'Good girl,' and opened the run and picked Fi-Fi up. Her eyes, if anything, seemed brighter than they had been before the experiment.

Smoothing down her ears, he put the rabbit back in her cage.

It was good. He was ready for the next job. The photographer hoped it would be on something more interesting than a horse.

It had been a long time since Zena Wentworth had been needed. Now and then, she might get a call from one of her part-time lovers who, in that presumptuous way that men had these days, told her that he needed her now, right now – but that wasn't need, it was boredom, like you needed a gin and tonic, or a holiday in the sun.

Paul Raven wasn't like that. When he rung her and explained that he needed her help, she was almost down the stairs, in the Rolls and on her way before he had explained the precise nature of his need. When he did, she had hesitated, briefly unsure, assailed by a certain illogical loyalty to her husband.

Then she agreed. Bloody hell, she had needs too.

Paul had seemed surprised that she intended to visit him. She could phone him, he said.

She had insisted. She had something to give him.

Zena parked the Rolls down the street from the flat and walked briskly, her mink coat hanging off her shoulders, towards the flat. She rang the bell, tapping her foot impatiently as she waited.

After what seemed an age, the door opened and Paul stood in a dressing-gown, his right arm in a sling, and leaning heavily on a walking-stick.

'Sorry,' he said. 'I've got a bit slower since I last saw you.'

'Your poor face.' Zena made to reach out for him, then, remembering that Paul was uneasy with flirtation, stopped herself.

'Better than it was.' He turned slowly back into the flat. 'Only been out of hospital a couple of days.' He made his way through a small, comfortable sitting-room. 'I'll have to talk to you in the bedroom. Doctors have told me not to move about for a while.'

'Who looks after you?' Zena picked up a framed photograph on the table. It showed Paul upsides over a hurdle at Cheltenham. The other jockey she recognized as Alex Drew.

'Angie comes by after work.' Paul made his way into the bedroom and, with some difficulty, eased himself into bed. 'I feel bloody daft,' he said. 'Make yourself a coffee if you like.'

'I won't bother.' Zena took off her fur coat, threw it across a chair and sat on the end of the bed. 'The next meeting of the poker school is at this address.' She opened her bag and handed him a piece of paper. 'I suggest you ring Clay and explain that Digby invited you before his... accident.'

'You won't be there yourself?'

'I'm not welcome. My husband says I talk too much. Don't take it seriously like I should.' She smiled. 'Our marriage isn't close.' She looked at Paul, who had his dressing-gown wrapped around him to his throat, and smiled.

'What was the other thing then?' he asked, eager to break the moment.

'Apart from an invitation, there's one requirement for joining Clay's poker school. You have to have a minimum of a thousand pounds in stake money.'

'I'll borrow it,' Paul said.

Zena took an envelope from her bag. '*Voilà*,' she said. 'Your entrance ticket. Two thousand pounds.'

Illogically, Paul felt a surge of anger within him. 'It's your husband's money.'

'Don't be so ridiculously old-fashioned. We're married. We share. He goes to work, I look after the domestic side – send Christmas cards, book restaurants, that sort of thing.'

'He earned it.'

Zena laughed harshly. 'My husband has earned nothing in his life. He's waiting for his darling daddy to topple off the perch. The money comes from the highly dubious enterprises of Sir Denis Wentworth.'

Paul felt uneasy at the woman's casual intimacy, the way she was half-lying now at the end of his bed, pinning down the blankets so that he was unable to move his legs. 'I couldn't gamble with your husband's money,' he said.

'Why are you going to Clay's poker school?' Zena asked, casually kicking off her shoes.

'Because I want to know what happened to Alex. I have a feeling your husband was involved.'

'What scruples you have. You think he might have been involved in finishing your racing career and

216

causing your best friend's death and you can't bring yourself to use his money against him.'

'You're very bitter.' Paul tried to move his legs but, now that Zena was kneeling at the end of the bed, he felt powerless. His shoulder was aching and suddenly he wanted to be alone.

'Use Clay's money. Nothing would give me more pleasure.' There was a sparkle in Zena's eyes as she leaned forward, proffering the brown envelope with her left hand. As he took the envelope, she shifted quickly, trapping his free hand beneath her. Paul gasped. Zena reached under the blankets and, before he could do anything about it, slender, knowing fingers were working their way up his bare thigh under his dressing-gown. 'Or almost nothing would give me more pleasure,' she added.

'Don't.' Paul looked at her coldly, then shuddered as her hand darted upward and found him. Zena closed her eyes ecstatically. He said, more threateningly, 'Get your hand off me.'

'Don't be like that,' she said, with a catch in her voice. 'I like you very much, Paul. You won't have to move.'

Paul swallowed hard. Trying to move his hand merely caused a searing pain in the other shoulder. To his horror, he felt his body responding.

'Everything else in working order, I see,' she purred. 'I'd really like to get your bit between my teeth.'

As she leaned forward, Paul gritted his teeth

and jerked his left hand free, brushing her off the bed. 'I'm not interested in being raped,' he muttered.

Zena stood by the bed, barefoot and contrite. 'Not even... ?' She gave an eloquently suggestive pout, her tongue across her upper lip.

'Bugger off out of it,' said Paul. 'And take your money.'

She put on her shoes and slipped into her mink coat. She walked over to a mirror and, checking and making some minor repairs to her make-up, she seemed cooler now, philosophical, as if such things happened to her every day.

'I'll leave the money,' she said lightly. 'You'll need it.' Without looking back, she swayed out of the bedroom.

Paul relaxed at last and closed his eyes with relief that she had gone. He glanced at the envelope still in his hand before becoming aware that Zena was back, standing at the door.

'Let me know if you change your mind,' she said. 'I have a feeling that we could be *very* good.'

The squire of Lenbrook Hall was out shooting on his estate. So far that afternoon he had zapped three rabbits, a couple of hares, five pheasants and a couple of smaller brown birds which he hadn't ever shot before. 'Not zapped, Lol,' the squire muttered to himself as he approached a cottage. 'Bagged.' He banged on the door with the butt of his shotgun like a sheriff making a house call, 'Ere, John,' he called out.

An old man wearing moleskin leggings and slippers opened the door. 'Mr Calloway,' he said. 'How did you get on?'

Lol thrust a black dustbin liner forward. 'That's what I bagged, John. Not a bad bit of bagging, eh?'

With a hint of a sigh, the old man opened the dustbin liner. 'Very good, Mr Calloway.'

''Ere, what's 'em little brown fellas, John? Grouse, are they?'

The gamekeeper held up a small bird. 'They would be mistle thrush, Mr Calloway.'

'Get away.'

'Tricky devils to shoot, sir.'

The squire looked disappointed. 'On the bird-table, weren't they,' he said sulkily. 'You can keep them. The old lady gets heavy about bodies in the kitchen.'

'Thank you, Mr Calloway.'

'Cheers, John.'

To tell the truth. Lol wasn't sure about that old bastard. There was something leery about him, like he was laughing up his sleeve all the time. He was good at his job, ensuring that the animals on the estate were plump, docile and slow, but he had an attitude problem: no respect. If the squire of Lenbrook Hall didn't deserve respect, who did?

Lol broke his twelve bore, took out the two cartridges and put them in the pocket of his Barbour, as he slouched across the lawn towards the house.

Although the owner of what the papers called a 'luxury Elizabethan mansion', he still didn't feel entirely at home there. Still, what with the leisure complex at the back and the conversion of the library into an indoor swimming-pool with jacuzzi en suite, it was getting there. He opened the french windows into the sitting-room and, leaning the twelve bore against the television, kicked off his green Hunter boots and trudged towards the kitchen.

'Cooee, darlin', I'm home,' he called out in the hall. There was no reply. 'Out playing Lady Fuckin' Bountiful, down the village, I suppose,' he grumbled.

Back in the seventies, Suzie had been the hottest groupie around. She was class, could do things that that geezer Kama Sutra had never dreamed of, and nice with it. You didn't mind waking up beside Suzie which, in Lol's extensive experience, was rare in a groupie.

But, ever since they had moved to the hall, she had been different. The middle-class background she had once been so ashamed of had re-established itself. Village fetes, the fucking Women's Institute, sending the kids off to nobby private schools. She had even objected when he changed the name of the house from Chevenham Grange to Lenbrook Hall, after his bassist Len Brook who had tragically died inhaling his own vomit back in 1969. Worse than all that, Suzie had become sniffy about the better things in life, like mind-expanding drugs. Lol laughed quietly. Now the only thing that was expanding was her bum.

Lol paused in front of the large oak mirror, which Lady Muck had bought for an arm and a leg the previous year. He pushed the deer-stalker to the back of his head and, as if to compensate for his bald pate, fluffed out the big brown locks around his collar. Whistling a song from the sixties, Lol pushed the door to the basement where he had built a games room. A touch of snooker, that's what he felt like; maybe a spot of indoor croquet.

It was as Lol was pouring himself a whisky at the customized cocktail bar in the corner that he became aware that he was not alone. Beyond the glass case containing his guitar collection, across the stretch of purple astroturf with yellow croquet hoops, there was a rocking-chair he'd bought in San Diego. It was rocking.

Stealthily, Lol backed towards the billiard table, keeping his eye on the chair. The door clicked shut behind him. 'Mr Calloway?' The voice was mellow and relaxed, like the voice-over for a coffee advert. There was a slight accent there. Lol turned slowly. From behind the door, a man in his early thirties stepped forward – his dark, even features, carefully tended moustache and well-cut suit suggested respectability, but the man's build, his broad and muscular hands, were not those of an office worker.

'Who the fuck are you?' Lol asked.

In reply the man stepped forward, picked up the billiard cue that was lying near Lol's right hand and broke it across his knee. Casually he threw the two bits onto the astroturf. 'I don't like snooker,' he said.

'How did you get in? The gate's locked. There's security.'

'Why so shy?' The man in the dark suit sat on the edge of the billiard table. 'You need security?'

'Fans. Autograph hunters.'

The man laughed humourlessly. 'There didn't seem to be many when I climbed over. Maybe the gate's too high for their bath chairs and walking-frames.'

'You didn't tell me who you are.'

'Call me Signor Salvo. I'm here to get your support for a good cause.'

'My wife – '

'Shut the fuck up and listen.' The man paused, as if slightly taken aback by his own outburst. 'I haven't got all day,' he said more quietly. Placing both hands on the side of the table, he lifted himself up like a gymnast on the parallel bars, landing on his toes. He walked over to Lol's guitar collection.

'All you got to do is give me some information,' he said. 'Then I'll leave you alone.'

Lol glanced towards the door. He might make it – a dash upstairs to the old twelve bore in the sitting-room – but then again he might not. With Signor Psycho here, it was no time for heroics.

'I believe you belong to a business syndicate.' Salvatore's hands were in his pockets now. 'You have an interest in a certain product being developed by Markwick Instruments.'

Lol shrugged.

222

'Right. My employers want your product. We want it exclusively and we want it very, very soon – before it gets into the wrong hands. And you're going to help, right.'

Lol was no stranger to violence – he had been yards away when his bouncers had clubbed an over-enthusiastic Hell's Angel to death during the 1970 tour of the States – but he didn't like it at first-hand, one to one. Suddenly he felt old and afraid.

'I have a lot of business interests,' he said. 'Maybe I am involved with Markwick. Why don't I talk to my people...' He hesitated as Salvatore ambled over to the purple croquet lawn and picked up the heavy end of the broken snooker cue '...and get back to you.'

Salvatore tapped on the glass in front of the guitars. It was like the window of a music shop, with no less than ten gleaming instruments on their stands. 'Are you going to open this or am I going to smash it?' he asked. 'I'm interested in music.'

'They're of purely historic interest, but – '

A sharp crack, followed by a tinkle of falling glass interrupted him. Salvatore put the snooker cue down and kicked in the rest of the glass. He reached into the display and took out a large red guitar, with the vulgar, extravagant curve of an old American car. Lol took a step forward, like a mother anxious about her child, but paused, as Salvatore froze him with a look. 'I've always hated rock and roll,' he said conversationally, picking clumsily at the strings.

'Different strokes for different folks, eh?'

'Jazz, that's what I like.' Salvatore turned the guitar over and tapped its shiny back. 'You know who the last decent guitarist was?'

Lol frowned, desperately trying to think of jazz guitarists. 'Pat Metheny? The blind Canadian geezer?'

'Django Rheinhart, dickhead.' Salvatore was holding the 1955 Gretsch by the neck as if it were a baseball bat.

'Ah,' Lol smiled. 'The gypsy.'

'*Not a gypsy*!' The guitar was held aloft a brief second before it fell like an axe, shattering on the side of the billiard table.

'Cool it, Luigi!' Lol had seen a few smashed guitars in his time – in fact, he'd stomped on a few himself as part of his stage act, but this was different. 'Jesus, man,' he sobbed, 'Scotty Moore played that axe.'

'Not a gypsy.' Salvatore turned the wrecked instrument over with his toe. 'A romany.' He seemed calmer now. 'And my name's not Luigi.' He glanced at the display case, as if choosing which guitar to destroy next. 'You feel like talking now?'

'I'm an investor in Markwick, that's all,' Lol said quietly. 'I don't know what's going on. There's this thing called Opteeka B – sort of camera-type gismo that their boffins have been working on.'

'We know all. What's the timing?'

'They've got a prototype they've been testing. They're going to sell it to some Czech geezer. Alice

Markwick's information was that the Ministry of Defence here and the Pentagon were a bit iffy about a weapon that blinded people.'

'When's it being handed over?'

'Soon.' Sorrowfully, Lol picked up the remains of the old Gretsch. There was a guy in Ealing who reconstructed guitars but, apart from the neck and the chrome machine-heads, this one was a goner. 'I'm just the money,' he said. 'They don't tell me nothing.'

Just the money. As Lol examined the mess of wire and wood, turning it over in his hands, memories of his ill-fated investments of the past crowded in on him. The independent record company. The rock magazine. The film company. All he had wanted was a safe home for his royalties, a bit of financial security, yet every time it went wrong. Opteeka B had seemed too good to be true, too easy. 'I'll help you if I can get my money back.'

'We might give you some compensation,' Salvatore said, 'when we take possession.'

Lol nodded wearily.

'You tell us where to find it, okay? I'll call you in a week's time. If you speak to the others – Markwick, Wentworth, Raven – it won't be your Gretsch that's destroyed. Remember what happened to your friend Digby.'

'Raven? Who's Raven?'

'The jockey – he isn't with you?'

Lol shook his head. 'Never heard of him.'

'One week.' Salvatore walked to the door. 'You're with us now, Lol.'

'Right.'

'By the way, what are those tests?'

'I dunno. Horses, mostly.'

'*Horses*?' Salvatore laughed. This was going to be like taking a toy from a baby. 'Be in touch, Mr Rock and Roll.'

'Sure, man.'

With a final look of contemptuous pity, Salvatore turned on his heel and left.

The place was going downhill and no mistake. Goods in the shops seemed shabbier and more expensive, the assistants less respectful. You held up your hand on a corner in Regent Street and taxis swept by as if a better class of passenger, with a bigger tip, awaited them around the corner. The locals had an edgy, defeated look to them as they went to work. In the evenings, the restaurants were virtually deserted, and the windows of the residential flats were illuminated by the glow of a million television screens. Outside there were beggars – disgusting, black-toothed creatures, toting some dog or baby, as they extended a grimy hand from their cardboard shelter in the entrances to shops. Policemen walked in twos, with surly expressions on their faces. The traffic moved with the speed of a glacier. Public transport was a joke in exceedingly poor taste.

'Two months ago.' Josef Petrin drummed his fingers on the counter of a gentleman's tailor in Savile Row. 'Surely to goodness you people can manage to put together a tweed suit in such a time.'

A grey-haired man with apologetic eyes, hunched by a lifetime of measuring inside legs, explained that there had been 'flu among their employees, and layoffs. If Mr Petrin could give them another fort-night –

'Heavens above, man. I could be anywhere in two weeks' time. I really can't build my schedule around the health of your staff.'

The tailor simpered some more. Maybe ten days was possible, quality was so important, it was vital not to hurry the final work on the suit.

With some difficulty, Petrin extracted a date from the man and left the shop exuding righteous indig-nation. There was no doubt about it – London was in terminal decline.

By some miracle, a black taxi deigned to stop for him. 'The Ritz,' he said.

The taxi-driver, a youth with the cropped hair of a football hooligan, nodded moodily. Whatever hap-pened to the cockney, Petrin wondered as he settled back in the cab – the cheery red-faced character full of vulgar working-class charm, the bloke who addressed you as 'Guv'? Nothing was simple any more.

The tea-room at the Ritz was full of Arabs and ancient women but, after a five minute wait, Petrin was shown to a table. Without waiting for Green, who would inevitably be late, he ordered tea.

He was on his second scone before Bernard Green, an overweight producer of what they called 'Talks' at the BBC, flapped into view and, with much huffing and puffing, slumped into the chair opposite Petrin.

'Bloody meetings,' he explained.

Petrin decided not to give Green the benefit of a smile but poured him a cup of tea. The producer eyed the scones like Bunter, the famous English schoolboy whose adventures Petrin had read while at university. 'Help yourself,' he said drily.

'So.' Green took a scone onto which he heaped a mess of butter and raspberry jam. 'How goes life in Prague now that you're liberated from the embrace of the Bear?'

It was always like this – the paunchy Englishman pretending, perhaps to himself, that they were meeting on BBC business. Petrin smiled at last. He enjoyed the irony of playing host to this unhealthy-looking fool, so old for his forty-odd years, wearing the cheap ill-fitting suit. Mao had been wrong – power does not grow out of the barrel of a gun but out of carefully maintained political contacts. 'Less has changed than you might think, Bernard,' he said. 'You'll be glad to hear.'

A look of unease crossed the Englishman's face. On Petrin's last trip to London, Bernard had casually suggested that *perestroika* had swept away the need for secret alliances. Petrin had dismissed Bernard's pathetic attempt to resign his commission with an airy wave of the hand. Astonishing as it was, he was quite a big wheel in the BBC, his radical past now no more than a distant memory – distant, but not forgotten. 'There's always room for unofficial diplomacy,' he said, adding more firmly, 'We still need you.'

Bernard was building up his cholesterol level, shovelling back scones and cakes with the determination of a man who'd like to be struck down by a heart attack before tea was over. 'What do we want to know?' he asked.

'There's a woman called Alice Markwick who runs a company specializing in lasers. She has a rather ingenious device which we covet.'

'A device of aggressive intent?'

'If you mean a weapon, yes. We're due to take possession within the next few weeks. I have a suspicion that Mrs Markwick might be contacted by someone else.'

'Like who?'

'As I say, it's an ingenious piece of technology. There might be interest from the Americans, or the French, or even some branch of private enterprise.'

Bernard winced. 'Weapons,' he said heavily. 'Haven't we outgrown weapons yet?'

'Maybe at your Television Centre they value your inquisitive spirit, your charmingly ineffective liberalism,' Petrin said more sharply. 'We just want you to do what you're told. The weapon, as it happens, has considerable political credibility. It's not in the least bit messy.'

229

'What do you – ' Bernard hesitated. 'What do we need to know?'

'Who the opposition is. Can we trust the Markwick woman? Is this thing any bloody good? Perhaps you could discover these things without alerting ten camera crews and the national press.'

Bernard nodded.

'I'm here for a few days.' Petrin stood up. Lowering his voice slightly he said, 'Let's not have one of your legendary British cock-ups this time, eh?'

Bernard ran a broad finger across his plate and licked the crumbs off it.

Not telling Angie about his visit from Zena Wentworth was the easiest decision Paul had ever had to make. Since his fall, she had been trying to persuade him that to risk future injury trying to discover what had happened to Alex Drew was putting death before life, the past before the future. Gavin's sleazy scheme to entrap Alice Markwick had alarmed her further. The news that Zena Wentworth had attempted to rape Paul on his bed of pain might have been the final straw.

'Welcome to the evil empire of Crazy Mary.' Angie held open the door of her Mini as Paul, whose arm was still in a sling, heaved his legs round and out of the car. He looked up at a discreet sign reading 'The Empire Club'. There was a burly uniformed doorman standing by the entrance of the club, stamping his feet in the cold.

'Looks respectable enough to me,' Paul said.

Angie smiled and slipped a hand through his free arm. 'Wait 'til you meet Mary,' she said.

It had been her idea to come up to London the night before the poker game. It would get Paul away from the flat, she said, tune him into the ways of the metropolis. They were staying in the Putney flat of an old school friend, whose work as an air stewardess took her away much of the time. Then there was the briefing session with Crazy Mary.

'We're here to see Mary Chivers,' Angie told the doorman. 'The croupier.'

The doorman showed them down the stairs, into a large room full of roulette and backgammon tables. Apart from a few cleaners, the place was deserted. The smell of the previous night's cigars hung heavily in the air.

The short, dark girl who walked towards them in a navy blue suit and flat shoes might have been a stockbroker.

'Hi, Chiv,' Angie said. The two girls brushed cheeks in greeting. 'This is Paul.'

'Hullo, Mary.' Paul extended his left hand.

'It's a bit grim at the moment.' Mary glanced around the brightly-lit room. 'We're only closed for three hours out of twenty-four. The punters will be back this afternoon.'

They went to a small office where, over coffee, the two girls talked of friends from school. As far as Paul could gather, most of them had gone wrong: one

worked for a discreet and exclusive escort agency,
another had run away to Spain with an ageing bank
robber, a couple had hurried into marriage and out
the other side.

'What was this, a reform school you went to?' Paul
interrupted at one point.

Mary shrugged. 'Convent girls,' she said, as if no
other explanation was necessary. 'You wait – you'll
discover Angie's hidden vices in the end.'

'I've discovered a few already.'

Angie blushed, but smiled with pleasure. 'It's Mary
here who's the fast one. Don't be taken in by the
respectable suit.'

'Croupiers have to be above suspicion,' Mary said.
'One hint of a relationship with a punter and you're
out.'

'That's why they call her Crazy Mary.'

The croupier frowned, as if surprised by the nickname. 'You become a bit of a control freak working
in a casino. Once every few months, I take time off
with some of the other girls to work on transatlantic
cruises.' She shrugged. 'I seemed to have acquired
something of a reputation.'

'She'll try anything once,' said Angie.

Paul smiled nervously. He felt ill at ease with this
casual talk of misbehaviour.

As if she sensed that now was not the moment
for confessional reminiscence, Mary opened the top
drawer of the desk and took out a new, unopened
pack of cards, which she unwrapped. 'Right,' she

said, shuffling the cards like a magician. 'Crazy Mary's crash course in stud poker.'

Chapter 11

There were times when Ginnie Matthew's love affair with racing went through a rocky patch, when she envied those friends of hers whose children were growing and whose husbands, becoming balder and duller by the minute, at least provided a stolid kind of security.

It was four o'clock on a chilly afternoon in late February. The racegoers at Lingfield Park were drifting home after a day's racing which had provided the Matthews yard with a disappointing third in the novice hurdle and a faller in the two mile 'chase. She walked briskly towards the stables where Skinflint and a decent five-year-old called Above Par were being saddled up for some post-race work. There had been two spare places in the horse-box and, once the Lingfield authorities had given her permission to gallop two of her horses on the track after the last race, she decided that Skinflint – and, more significantly, his jockey Clay Wentworth – would benefit from one last outing before Cheltenham.

'Looks well, don't he?' Pat, the Head Lad, stood beside her as Clay led Skinflint out of his stable.

Ginnie stepped forward and patted the horse, running a hand down his shoulder and his front legs. 'Could be worse,' she smiled, knowing Skinflint had never been in better condition. The Kim Muir had come just at the right time for him – but the same could be said of the Cheltenham Gold Cup, which was to be run the day after. The greed of owners, the vanity of amateur jockeys – Ginnie sighed, as she watched Clay Wentworth hold up a leg so that Pat could give him a leg-up into the saddle. He looked soft, slightly overweight and nervous; not for the first time, Ginnie found the comparison between Skinflint and his jockey painful to contemplate. At last she had a top class horse in the yard – and it was doomed to be ridden by Clay Wentworth.

From the next door box, Dave Smart led Above Par, checked his girths and hopped into the saddle. Dave wasn't the greatest jockey of all time but he was a good professional, honest and tough. He deserved the ride on Above Par in the Ritz Trophy at Cheltenham.

'See you in front of the stands,' she said.

Watching them as the two horses made their way onto the race-course, Ginnie found herself reflecting that although Skinflint was her favourite horse in the yard, she would have mixed feelings if he won at Cheltenham. There was something tainted about his success this season. It was as if his progress was inextricably linked with the misery of others – horses that were destroyed, the suicide of Alex Drew, the ending of Paul's career.

'Wish I'd entered that horse in the Gold Cup,' she said to Pat, who was walking beside her.

'With Mr Wentworth on board?'

'No,' Ginnie sighed. 'He'd need a jockey.'

It was never the professionals who caused her problems. It was when outsiders became involved, dabbling in racing for their own peculiar reasons, that it became confusing, demoralizing. Bent jockeys, corrupted stable lads – there was inevitably the hand of someone outside racing working them, misguided, greedy amateurs.

'I heard from Kevin Smiley's parents yesterday,' she said. 'They seemed to think what happened to him was our fault.'

'It wasn't suicide, that's for sure.'

The trainer and her Head Lad walked on, each thinking of the inexplicable death of Kevin Smiley. It was clear, even to the police who had seemed reluctant to treat his drowning as murder, that it was Kevin who had put acid on Monty's hind legs that morning. Possibly he knew the gravity of what he was doing; more probably, he took the money without asking questions.

A local mini-cab company had confirmed that he was due to be taken to the station that evening, but when the car turned up, there had been no sign of him. Next morning his body was found floating in the River Kennet, some eight miles away. A post-mortem had revealed alcohol in the blood and bruising to the side of the head consistent with a heavy blow.

'Who was he working for, that's the question?' Pat said.

Ginnie looked down to the racecourse, where Clay and Dave Smart were walking in a circle, waiting for her. 'Whoever it was seemed to be after Paul,' she said. 'And if they could do that to him, bumping off poor little Kevin was hardly going to worry them.'

'But why Paul?'

'Why indeed?' Ginnie thought of the note she had written for Clay, of Paul's determination to find the person behind Alex's death. Yes, sometimes she wished she had never set foot in a racing yard.

She glanced back to the grandstand, where a group of race-goers was lingering, watching her two horses through binoculars as the crowds thinned. A few would-be journalists and professional gamblers, but the majority would be the clueless addicts of racing whose dreams of a great gambling coup would never be realized.

'No shortage of spies, I see,' she said.

It was true. Ginnie never gave her horses trials. The punter and journos doing overtime at Lingfield would discover no more than what the more knowledgeable of them already knew – that the Matthews yard never sent a runner out for one of the big prizes who wasn't jumping out of its skin with health and fitness.

Sitting by the rails, hunched on a shooting-stick like an ogling vulture, sat Sir Denis Wentworth.

'I see Daddy's here,' Pat muttered.

Ginnie laughed. 'All teeth and smiles, as usual,' she said. The relationship between Clay and his father was a mystery. Neither particularly liked the other but, wherever the son went, the father seemed to follow. Yet Clay never objected. A generous interpretation would be that a cold, undemonstrative kind of family love was at work but there was no hint of affection in Sir Denis's pale watery eyes as he watched his son.

Ginnie stood beside the old man. 'Looks well, doesn't he?' she said.

Sir Denis moved his jaws as if he had been given something unpleasant to take. 'Very,' he said eventually.

'Hack on round to the two-and-a-half-mile start. Pull them up and let them get a breather and then carry on the rest of the way round.' She called out to Dave Smart and Clay. 'You can let them stride out the last couple of furlongs but don't go mad.'

As the two jockeys cantered their horses to the far side of the course Ginnie heard a guttural mumble emanating from Sir Denis. He might have been clearing his throat, or maybe making some comment to himself. The words sounded suspiciously like, 'Bloody fool, he is.'

She decided to ignore him. Ginnie had more important matters to worry about than Wentworth family relationships.

It was his first visit to a British racecourse and Gavin Holmes wasn't impressed. The afternoon had seemed to consist of a lot of standing around punctuated occasionally by equestrian events of highly questionable entertainment value. A large majority of the racegoers were the type of Englishman, goofy and over-confident, that he had until now thought were an endangered species. They honked, they drank, they talked about horses, they honked some more.

'Get on with it, you stupid *bastards*,' he muttered to himself, stamping his feet on the ground to keep the circulation going. Clay Wentworth and the other jockey seemed to be taking an age to do whatever they intended to do.

A ferret-faced little man, an ex-jockey, perhaps, looked up at him in slight surprise. Gavin smiled apologetically.

The only way he had managed to survive the afternoon was by putting away a bit at the bar. Bucks Fizz, during those brief early moments when he had felt he should behave himself; champagne to celebrate the completion of the first race; brandy and ginger ale, followed by brandy. It was one way to spend an afternoon at the races – in fact, it was the only way.

As the two horses had pulled up on the far side

of the race-course, Gavin put the binoculars he had borrowed from a colleague at the office to his eyes. He had difficulty focussing them, or maybe it was his eyes that couldn't focus any more.

To work while terminally pissed was a basic journalistic requirement. Over the years, Gavin had taken this skill one step further so that now he could only work while pissed. During the afternoon he had chatted easily with barfly racegoers, concentrating on the career and character of Ginnie Matthews. Was she ambitious? Was she ruthless? Was she bent?

The general consensus, gleaned from an in-depth survey at the Lingfield Park bar, was that Mrs Matthews was marvellous, bloody *marvellous*. Troubles in the past, of course, with that shit of a husband of hers, but good old Ginnie hadn't let that hold her back. Bent? Good God, no – she was straight as a die.

'Here they go,' said the ferret beside him in the grandstand. Gavin managed to focus his binoculars accurately enough to follow the two horses as they galloped down the back straight. Maybe, to the cognoscenti, the way the animals were moving had deep significance, but to him they looked like any other horses doing the sort of thing that horses do.

Gavin let the binoculars drop, and looked down to the rails where, broad-backed in her sheepskin coat, Ginnie stood between one of her employees and an old man Gavin guessed was Sir Denis Wentworth.

After the fourth race, he had ventured out of the

warmth of the bar down to the sort of clubhouse from where the jockeys appeared. One of Ginnie's horses had taken third place in the race which had just finished and he managed to talk to her briefly outside the winners' enclosure.

'Mrs Matthews,' he had said. 'Gavin Holmes, *Guardian*. D'you have a moment?'

'Holmes? Are you new on the racing page?'

'It's a general feature. We want to profile your owner, Clay Wentworth. A half-page on a business-man at play, that sort of thing.'

Ginnie Matthews had frowned. 'Businessman at play? Doesn't sound very *Guardian* to me.'

'It's a departure,' he said, noting that she was more perceptive than most of the people he had met racing. 'How is Mr Wentworth preparing for his big race at Cheltenham?'

'You'd better ask him that.'

'I have a meeting with him later. He suggested I watch him ride here, then we could talk afterwards. But you could tell me if, say, he goes to watch the horses he'll be racing against.'

'For example?' Ginnie seemed more interested now.

'Brut Force, was it?' It was lucky he had done his homework. 'Ballina Lady. Whataparty.'

The trainer looked away, then said more quietly, 'The businessman at play, eh?' There was nothing evasive about the way she had looked at him. 'Why don't you ring me this evening and we can talk about this at more length?'

It had not been the remark of a guilty woman.

'Look at that fucker go.' The ferret standing beside him in the grandstand muttered to himself. The two horses, Gavin saw, had just entered the home straight but, while Dave Smart was niggling at Above Par, Clay seemed to be having difficulty holding Skinflint. By the time they passed the stands, Skinflint was eight lengths to the good and still pulling.

'What a flying machine, eh.' Watching Skinflint go through his paces seemed to have cheered the man standing beside Gavin. 'He's got a wally on board, he's giving the other horse a stone and a half and he still trots up. Talk about a good thing for Cheltenham.'

'Right.' Gavin glanced at his watch. It was time to ask the wally a few pertinent questions.

As the taxi moved slowly through the streets south of the River Thames, caught up in the late afternoon traffic, Josef Petrin stared out gloomily onto the damp streets outside. Ant-like, the workers scurried into the underground stations, grabbing evening papers, ignoring one another in their feverish need to get home to television, a drink and some ghastly English meal. 'Don't hold your breath,' the taxi-driver had said. 'Bad time of day to be heading out of the centre of London. Early rush hour.'

243

Petrin smiled wanly. Did they really call this crawl a 'rush-hour'? Not for the first time, he found himself wondering whether his country's relentless move towards capitalism was such a good idea. There may have been queues and shortages in Prague, free speech might have been somewhat curtailed, but at least there was a kind of security in hopelessness. Here in London, no one was satisfied with his lot – jealousy, greed and resentment seemed to seep from the very brickwork.

The cab jerked forward as his driver neatly headed off a car trying to filter onto the main road in front of him. 'English – very bad drivers,' he said over his shoulder. 'Very dozy, right?'

'Right,' said Petrin.

'You wanna watch yourself down where you're going, mate,' the driver said.

'Yes?'

'Bandit country. Walk down the street in that overcoat, in those shoes, carrying that briefcase, and you'll be in dead schtuck, mate. Brixton, Stockwell – mugging's like the local industry down there. Everybody's at it.'

Petrin looked at his slim, expensive black briefcase. Perhaps it had been rather naive to venture out of central London with it.

'They have mugging where you come from, have they?'

'No,' said Petrin in a tone he hoped would discourage further conversation. 'Not yet.'

He wasn't nervous as he noted, as he neared his destination, the increase in litter on the streets – paper, tin cans, not to mention debris of the human kind – just mildly concerned. It was not that he was incapable of looking after himself – you didn't work your way up from the factory floor to the senior reaches of government in Prague, as he had, without learning about self-preservation, but he disliked fuss. Over here, the press was not as accommodating as it was back home.

'How long you going to be?' asked the cab-driver.

'Ten minutes maybe.'

'Tell you what. Pay me for the trip and I'll wait outside for you.'

'That would be most kind,' said Petrin.

The street in Brixton where the Zametskys lived was pleasingly grimy. The old communist in Petrin – part of him that he rarely mentioned these days – took satisfaction in reflecting that it was for this that the man Peter had fled his motherland – this was his precious freedom. The taxi drew up outside a forbidding two-storey house with dustbins tipped over by the front door and a window boarded up.

'Sure you've got the right address?' asked the driver.

'Yes.' Petrin stepped out. This was home sweet home for Mr and Mrs Zametsky.

As soon as he stepped into the cold, high-ceilinged room with its peeling wallpaper and yellowing posters, he knew it was going to be a depressing experience.

'Peter.' The plump Polish girl with the peasant eyes spoke softly. 'We have a visitor.'

He had never been a squeamish man when he was young, yet these days Petrin found he avoided visiting friends in hospital. Driving by an accident just outside Prague and seeing the body of a lorry-driver laid out beside the road had made him feel really quite nauseous. He put it down to middle age.

So he hesitated when he first saw the thing on the bed. It was particularly unfortunate that, while the parts concealed by a suspiciously off-colour blanket had presumably been unaffected by the accident, his hands and, more disgustingly, his face, were horrifically disfigured.

Hairless, wearing dark glasses, his flayed skin red and shiny on the cheekbones, Peter Zametsky was making an odd sound through the lipless void that was his mouth.

'Hullo, Mr Zametsky,' Petrin said, drawing up a chair some way from the bed. 'My name is Josef Petrin. We've not met.'

Klima, his wife, sat on the bed and laid a soothing hand on the scarred right hand. 'He wants me to stay,' she said. 'He's been very nervous of strangers since the accident.'

An angry sound came from the figure on the bed.

'Sorry, darling.' Klima smiled apologetically as she turned to Petrin. 'My husband believes it was no accident. You aren't the police, I suppose?'

In a way, thought Petrin. 'No,' he said.

'Somebody did this to my husband.' The woman's pale and placid features showed signs of animation. 'He was visited in hospital by a man, threatening to do worse. Even though the nurse gave them a description, the police have put it down to the effects of the acid.'

Peter made another incomprehensible noise.

'Yes,' said his wife. 'They think he's mad.'

Briefly, Petrin considered confiding his disappointment with the state of Britain, perhaps comparing it to the new vitality of Eastern Europe, but he restrained himself. It would seem like crowing; another time perhaps.

'I'm an acquaintance of Mrs Markwick,' he said. 'I'm here to offer some help.' Laying his briefcase on his lap, Petrin opened it and took a sealed white envelope which he gave to Klima. 'Please open it,' he said.

The woman blushed as she saw the £50 notes, as though she had already done something mildly immoral to earn it. 'It's money, Peter,' she said. 'This gentleman's giving us money.'

'A thousand pounds.' Petrin smiled. 'Not much, but a start perhaps. It's a sort of insurance payment.'

Peter stretched out a hand. His wife gave him the envelope. He said something, then hurled the money across the room.

'The money doesn't come from Mrs Markwick,'

Petrin explained smoothly. 'It's not compensation or guilt money.' From a distant room, he heard a baby cry. 'I'd keep it if I were you.'

Klima walked across the room where the £50 notes had spilled out of their envelope onto the bare boards of the floor. 'What do we need to do?' she asked.

'Alice and I are old friends. For some time now, we have been discussing the acquisition of her secret project, the development – ' he nodded in the direction of the shape in the bed ' – thanks to Dr Zametsky, of Opteeka B.'

There was a question from Peter, which his wife interpreted. 'He's asking how you know about Opteeka B,' she said.

'I am Alice's client. As you probably know, she has been talking to the Czechoslovak government. Once Opteeka B has completed its tests, I take possession of the prototype and the design plans. My problem is that I very much fear that there are others who may sabotage my agreement.'

'The people who did this to Peter.' Klima was holding the money as if, at any moment, she would have to hand it back.

'Precisely. They're remarkably unpleasant people. Civilians, I suspect. Whereas we would mass-produce Opteeka B for entirely legitimate military use, these people are nothing less than criminals. I dread to think what they have in mind.' The sound of the child crying was beginning to irritate Petrin. 'D'you want to fetch the baby?' he asked. 'I'm in no hurry.'

Klima hurried out of the room, returning moments later with a child, red-faced from its wailing. Without a word, she unbuttoned the front of her dress. Petrin looked away queasily but not before he had caught sight of a billowing, blue-veined breast.

'So.' As Klima looked from her baby to Petrin, her face became edgy and mistrustful. 'What do we have to do for the money?'

'It's yours.' Petrin smiled, forcing himself to look at the baby. 'It was the least we could do. You could – ' he hesitated, as if a thought had suddenly occurred to him ' – maybe earn a little bit more.'

For a moment, the room was silent but for the sound of the baby as it sucked noisily. Petrin swallowed as his sensitive nostrils were assailed by the sweet, sickly smell of mother's milk.

'Yes,' he said. 'If you were able to tell me how Opteeka B is going to be tested, and where. That would help me forestall any last-minute hitch in the arrangement with Markwick Instruments.'

'What about Mrs Markwick?' Klima asked. 'Why don't you ask her?'

'It's complicated. She denies there's a problem of security.' Petrin opened the briefcase and took out another envelope which he weighed in his hand thoughtfully.

'He's got some more money, Peter.'

There was an odd moaning sound from the bed. Peter Zametsky took off his dark glasses and, with the red stubs of his fingers, wiped a tear from his light grey, sightless eyes. He repeated the sound more loudly.

'Paper.' Klima stood up, holding her baby to her. 'Yes, that's right. You'll need some paper.'

It was twenty minutes, not ten, before Josef Petrin closed the heavy door behind him and, with just one glance down the street, stepped into the taxi.

'Sorry,' he said. 'My business took a bit longer than expected.'

'All right, squire.' The taxi-driver put down his evening paper and started the engine. 'The meter was running so I wasn't worried.'

'Of course.'

'Where can I take you then?'

'The Ritz.' Petrin had seen enough of Brixton to last him a lifetime. 'As quick as possible.'

On this story, Gavin had given himself so many false identities that he had almost forgotten who he was. Deception was part of the job, of course – it went with the territory – but he preferred distorting a few facts on the page to inventing aliases for himself. Written lies were somehow easier to live with.

Gavin poured champagne into the glasses of Clay and Sir Denis Wentworth, then filled his own, fighting back his need for a brandy. 'Cheerio,' he said raising his glass. 'Here's to Skinflint at Cheltenham.'

Lifestyle expert he had been with Alice Markwick; now he was a human interest journalist, contributing to the business pages. Gavin took out his spiral-bound notebook and smiled. What he did for his art.

'Fire away.' Clay Wentworth sipped at his drink with the air of a man who has better things to do than be interviewed by the press. 'Which area d'you want to major on?'

'Your hobbies. Horseback riding, for example.' Gavin smiled as Clay looked pained.

'It's rather more than a hobby,' he said. 'And we call it racing.'

The man wasn't bright, Gavin decided as he asked a few routine questions, noting down Clay's highly predictable answers, and there was something oddly immature about the way he occasionally glanced at the old curmudgeon, his father, before he spoke. It was almost as if he were a schoolboy rather than a grown man approaching middle age and the chairman of a company.

'You've had a spot of luck with the opposition,' Gavin said, 'A racing friend of mine said the Kim Muir was going to be easier to win than many expected.'

'I'd prefer to win on the racecourse against the best opposition.'

'So you'll be hoping this – ' Gavin referred to his notes ' – this Tanglewood doesn't suffer any untoward accidents?'

For a moment, Clay looked up sharply, as if he were about to depart from a carefully prepared script, but then the look of urbane boredom settled back on his face. 'Ron Charlesworth looks after his horses,' he said, 'I'm sure there will be no problem.'

The bar was empty now, and the barman was making enough noise as he washed up the glasses to suggest that he was planning to close up soon.

'Why d'you do it, Clay?' Gavin asked easily. 'I mean you've got everything – you run a company, you're not a teenager any more. It's *dangerous* riding those things, isn't it?'

Clay Wentworth looked out at the racecourse on which darkness was now falling.

'In a way, it's like business,' he said. 'You have to have the right product, your horse, if possible with a unique selling point that will cut it in the market-place. Speed, stamina, courage. Then you've got to gather the right team about you – from Ginnie Matthews, who I see as a sort of Technical Director, down to Joe, the lad who does my two horses. Without the right executive team – the "boardroom mix", I call it – the product has no position in the market-place.'

With a thoughtful frown, Gavin made a note in his notebook. It read 'Bollocks'.

'Then there's the personal challenge. The preparation for the launch of your product, the race. You have to be ready, fit. You have to know about the opposition. And on the day, it's all about concentration, skill – and, of course, keeping your nerve.' Clay looked pleased with his little speech. 'Then it's all down to luck.'

Gavin smiled. 'And there was I thinking you rode horses for fun,' he said.

'There's that as well, of course,' Clay said coldly.

More out of politeness than through some journalistic hunch, Gavin turned to Clay's father, who was sipping impassively at his champagne. 'What about you, Sir Denis?' he asked, raising his voice slightly. 'What do you think of your son's love of racing?'

The old man turned to look at Gavin with cool distaste. 'Whatever gives my son pleasure, gives me pleasure,' he said.

'Right.' Gavin made another careful note on his pad.

'Daddy?' he wrote. 'Check out Daddy.'

Although the walls in the Victorian row of houses were solid, Peter Zametsky could hear the thud of reggae music from the people next door. It was still early evening; by two in the morning the wall would shake.

Not that Peter minded. At least he could still hear things. The sound of other people's partying reminded him that he was alive.

He could feel, too. Right now, he felt the weight of two inprints on the bed, only one of which was familiar.

'He's asleep,' Klima said. She seemed to be fussing around with a blanket. 'He loves to sleep on your bed.'

He felt her touch the other weight, which was much

lighter than the baby, and heard a rustle of paper. Money. Klima was counting the money again.

'It seems too easy, *moje kochanie*. I'm frightened. I think we should tell the police.'

Peter made a sound in his throat which a stranger might have taken for a cough.

'Don't laugh, Peter,' said his wife. 'There's something wrong. If this man was dealing with Mrs Markwick, why did he come to you? And whoever heard of a Czech paying out £5,000? Not even in vouchers – in cash.'

Peter extended a hand and ran it through the notes as if they were a pool of warm water. Of course, Klima was right. The deal stunk. But what more could be done to him? The Italian who had taken away his face must know that he could give him no more information. As for the Markwick woman, her behaviour hardly merited loyalty. Not a single visit while he was in hospital and no mention of compensation above his salary.

'Someone's going to get hurt,' said Klima.

Peter made a sound, both anguished and angry. It meant, 'So long as it's not us, I don't care.'

'*Kochanie*.' Klima touched his hand. 'I hope you're right.'

Alcohol was brainfood for Gavin. The same substances that would render another man comatose – indeed, rendered Gavin comatose when he wasn't working – propelled him forward when he was working on a story. Admittedly, the propulsion often took him by a strange, indirect route, full of odd and inexplicable stop-ins, but that was good. Booze made him an instinctive reporter, who relied on an unsteady sixth sense that took him to destinations that mere logic would never find.

After the ordeal of passing twenty minutes with the Wentworth father and son team, feigning interest in Clay's banal, non-committal replies, he had needed a top-up before he went home.

'Give us a real drink, my friend,' he muttered to the barman, after saying his goodbyes to Clay and Sir Denis.

'We're closed, sir.'

Gavin held up a £10 note. 'If you've cashed up, no need to give me the change.'

The barman took the money and, with remarkably little grace for a man who had just received a tip, said, 'I'm locking up in two minutes.'

There was something odd about Clay Wentworth. Gavin had met a few sportsmen, professional and amateur, in his time; invariably, they came alive when talking about their sport. With Clay, it seemed forced, almost rehearsed. If riding nags at speed over bits of wood gave him no pleasure, then why did he do it? And the father seemed utterly uninterested in racing. Gavin gave a little shudder of satisfaction as the cognac burnt its way down his throat.

Maybe it was social. Yet the jokey questions Gavin had posed about the high-profile entourage of spectators Clay brought to watch him race – Lol Calloway, Alice Markwick, the late Digby Welcome – had been received with glazed indifference. 'They're friends,' he had said. 'They like a day at the races.'

It didn't wash. Gavin thought of Alice Markwick and of what he had heard or read about Welcome and Calloway. None of them were the types to spend afternoons at chilly racecourses for the sake of friendship. Money – that was what interested them all. Yet there seemed to be no gambling factor at work here.

Draining his glass under the hostile glare of the barman, Gavin slipped off the barstool and swayed palely for a moment. He extended a queasy hand to the bar to steady himself.

'Think I might have overdone it.' He smiled apologetically at the barman.

'You've had a heavy afternoon.'

'Too right, mate.' Gavin buttoned his bomber jacket.

'I trust you're not driving.' The barman polished a glass self-righteously. 'Drink and drive, you know.'

'It's not the drink that's the problem,' Gavin said. 'It's the fresh air. An afternoon of that's enough to make anyone feel woozy.' He shook his head like a man trying to shift some unpleasant thought from his mind, then made his way out of the bar, bumping against a couple of tables.

The racecourse was deserted now although there was the sound of voices coming from the Press Room, which was thoughtfully located close to the bar.

'Poor bastards,' Gavin muttered, thinking of the journalists urgently filing copy about how one nag ran faster than another. 'What a way to earn a living.'

At the bottom of the stairs, he looked onto the course where a tractor was already harrowing the turf between the fences. It took a moment of concentrated effort to remember where the car park was but then, seeing a couple of cameramen lugging their equipment behind the grandstand, he followed them. The car must be somewhere in that direction.

'Better call Raven,' Gavin said to himself. Paul had mentioned that Zena Wentworth had managed to get him an invitation to one of Wentworth's poker evenings. The boy was smart enough to extract information as effectively as the regulars would extract money from him.

Gavin was wondering vaguely at what price to Paul's innocence Zena's cooperation had been obtained as he tottered into the car park. There were only a few cars there and his car was near a van into which the two cameramen were already loading their equipment.

'And so we bid farewell to picturesque Lingfield Park,' he sang out softly as he fumbled in his jacket for his car keys. He wouldn't be going racing again in a hurry, that was for sure. Too many horses. Too much standing up. Above all too much fresh air.

'Mr Holmes?'

At first, Gavin thought that the words had sounded

within the alcohol-drenched recesses of his brain. He hesitated by his car.

'Do you have a moment?'

He turned, swaying slightly. The two men by the van appeared to be filming him – one, a small man wearing jeans, was training a video on him, the other was raising a large stills camera to his eye.

'Hullo, what's this then?' Gavin straightened his tie in a humorous way. 'Profile of Gavin Holmes, investigative journalist at work? Fame at – '

The camera held by the second man made a sound like a toy car being started, high-pitched and comical. Gavin looked into the lens then he felt himself thrown back against his car.

'What? *What*?' he heard himself saying feebly. At first, he thought the blackness came from a blow on the back of the head, yet the force had come from the front, hurling him backwards. 'What?' His arms felt behind him for the roof of the car and he sagged, his head lolling forward, like a boxer on the ropes. It wasn't a pain in his eyes, it was an ache, an anaesthetic tingling. Gavin rubbed them, as if to take away the darkness. Then he felt the knife against his throat.

A voice said, 'Move.'

Gavin pressed back against the car, 'What d'you want from me?' he whispered.

'Get away from the car.'

In the blackness all around him, Gavin moved forward. 'I can't see,' he sobbed. 'What the fuck have you done?' He needed to get away. Perhaps back on the course there would be someone who could help him. Arms outstretched like a sleepwalker, he took what he thought was the direction of the car park.

The blade of the knife touched him on the base of the throat, more gently this time. 'Turn,' said the same voice, with its odd foreign accent, 'Go the other way.'

Gavin turned back towards the car but, in his blindness, he must have wandered to its left because his hands felt the high brick wall against which the car was parked. He felt his way along the wall to the left. Maybe he would reach the road. There were no more orders from the men. Gavin sobbed with relief as he heard the engine of the van being started somewhere behind him. They were leaving him, thank God – sightless but alive. He fell against another car. Turning, he made his way back along the wall. If he could reach his car, maybe he could let himself in and lock the door until help arrived.

The van was driving away, yet seemed to hesitate, as if it were manoeuvring itself out of the car park. 'Don't let them come back,' Gavin sobbed. To his right, the van revved louder.

For perhaps two seconds, he realized what was going to happen. The van was coming towards him, reversing, it sounded like. Gavin broke into a run but it was too late. His last scream was drowned by the sound of the engine and the crash of metal against human flesh and brick.

* * *

The photographer jumped out of the van and, without a glance at the body by the wall, wiped some traces of blood from the back of the van with the damp cloth he was carrying. There was no need to arouse unnecessary suspicion.

'Off we go,' he said as he jumped back into the passenger seat.

The van left the car park at speed.

Stroking the Opteeka B, the photographer found that it was still warm. Carefully, he put it back into its aluminium case and locked it, pocketing the key.

'That's some machine,' said the driver, turning down a side road. Within two minutes, the van would be dumped and he and the crazed professor here would be making their way back to London in separate cars.

'Video?' said the photographer.

'It's all there.' The driver nodded to a hold-all on the floor of the van. 'I think you'll find my camera work is more than adequate.'

The photographer didn't answer. He was not a sadist, and being a party to the loss of life gave him little pleasure but, right now, he was exulting.

He hadn't seen a thing, the poor bastard. Fi-Fi was good, but this was better. It had been the perfect experiment.

Chapter 12

It was the entrance of a loser, a lamb to the slaughter, a patsy – but that suited Paul fine.

'Mr Raven.' Clay Wentworth was the first to react as Paul stood at the door, having been shown in by a butler. He had been sitting in a deep armchair but got to his feet like a public schoolboy whose housemaster has just walked into the room. 'What a surprise.'

Paul smiled. 'I meant to ring,' he said. 'Poor old Digby Welcome invited me some weeks back. I meant to be here last week but I had an accident.'

The arm had only come out of its sling yesterday and a stab of pain darted through his shoulder as Clay shook his hand with a muttered, 'Never knew you played.'

'I have a lot of time on my hands.'

Clay glanced at Paul's walking-stick and, for a brief moment, seemed embarrassed. 'You know we have a no-railbird rule.'

'Sorry?'

'We don't allow railbirds – kibitzers.' The smile on
Clay's face lost some of its friendliness. 'Non-playing
spectators,' he explained.

Paul grinned goofily. He had been warned by Mary
that he would be tried out with some recondite poker
slang. Her advice had been to play the innocent. 'No,
I'm here to play,' he said, patting the side of his
jacket. 'I've got enough for the, er . . .'

'Pot?'

'Pot.'

'How exactly did you know where we were
playing?'

'Zena,' said Paul significantly. 'We're friends.'

There was a tension in the room that was not
entirely explained by his presence. As Paul was introduced to the four other guests, he noted that they
seemed wary, like people forced together who have
little in common but their habit. Alice Markwick he
recognized. Then there was a stockbroker, a barrister
with florid skin and a loud voice and a man called
David who said he worked in a bank.

'A bank?' Paul acted surprised.

'Not that kind of bank,' said Clay coldly. 'Drink?'

Most of the gamblers seemed to have Perrier or
wine. 'A whisky would be nice,' said Paul.

'We're just waiting for our last player,' Clay said,
handing him an over-generous whisky. Uneasy small
talk had been resumed among the other guests.

'I was a friend of one of your regulars.' Paul

lowered himself carefully into a hardback chair. 'Alex Drew.'

'Alex.' Clay shook his head. 'Terrible business.'

It was another five minutes, during which Paul sat, contributing only occasionally to the stilted conversation, before Lol Calloway appeared, complaining about the traffic into London.

'Lol, you know everyone except Paul,' said Clay. 'Paul Raven.'

The balding rock'n roller winked, clicked his tongue and made an oddly old-fashioned six-shooter gesture with both hands. 'How ya doing, man?' he said.

'I'm doing well,' said Paul.

With a palpable sense of relief, the party moved to a table in the corner, and ceased to be an ill-assorted social gathering. The Wentworth poker school was in progress.

'We normally play Texas Hold 'Em,' Clay said, pulling up an extra chair at the table for Paul. 'That all right with you?'

Paul furrowed his brow. 'Just run it through for me, will you?' he said.

'Standard seven card stud. Each player's dealt two cards – five communal cards are revealed. You bet after the deal, the flop, the turn and Fifth Street.'

'Flop? Fifth?' Paul allowed a look of panic to cross his face. 'I'm sure I'll pick it up as I go along.'

Let them think you haven't a clue, Crazy Mary had said. Every poker school needs a supply of pigeons, plump and clueless. Play two or three games like an amateur and they'll be falling over to get at you. Then you hit them.

Ignoring his instinct to take the early games slowly, fold early and get a sense of how the others played, Paul laid £50 on the first game, despite being dealt a phenomenally poor hand. The flop gave him a low pair – two sevens – and when Alice, unable to keep the sparkle of triumph from her eyes, turned over a triple queen, Paul gasped in astonishment, revealing his pathetic hand with a wimpish 'Whoops!'

After two more games like this, played with transparent ineptness, Paul sensed a stir of interest around the table. It had been some time since fresh money had been introduced to the school. Even if the new man lacked big funds, his participation in the game would help the pot. Even Lol Calloway had a chance to stay in play that much longer.

'Tonight doesn't seem to be my night,' Paul said, as Clay Wentworth won another hand in which Paul should have folded but had stupidly insisted on playing.

He had lost £350 of his £2,000 when, with the banker, he retired to the other side of the room to sit out a couple of hands. Feigning a mood of deep gloom, he managed to discourage conversation as they sat by the fire.

So this was what had set Alex on his way to destruction. It seemed inconceivable, absurd. Paul had read somewhere that the serious gambler, the addict, is acting on a deep psychological need to punish himself – that, however much he wins, he'll return to the table for the throw which will finish him. Certainly there was more to Alex than his loud and cheerful manner revealed. Yet he never gambled on horses. All Paul's sources – Jim Wilson, the valet, the other jockeys, Ginnie Matthews – had agreed that he had no contact with bookmakers. And in racing, there was no jockey who placed illegal bets regularly without at least some of his colleagues knowing.

'Seems to be my lucky night,' Clay Wentworth muttered from the table as, with a languid hand, he pulled in the pot for another game.

'You're not a regular then?' the banker interrupted Paul's thoughts.

'No. I'm having a bit of difficulty with this Texas Hold 'Em thing.'

'Goes in runs, like everything.' The man stared gloomily at the fire. 'How much are you in for?'

Paul resisted the bait. 'Enough,' he said.

'Are you lads in or out?' Lol Calloway called from the table. The banker threw his cigarette into the fire and wandered back to the game.

'Next one and I'm in,' Paul said.

Crazy Mary hardly lived up to her nickname when it came to poker tuition. No one could have been saner or cooler. She knew Clay – he was a regular at most of the gaming clubs and a better than adequate social player. He liked seven card stud, and Mary had guessed correctly that Texas Hold 'Em would be the favoured game at his poker evenings.

'It's one of the easiest games to play,' she had said. 'But to make money at it, you have to be good.'

Paul had learned the moves – how to make like a high roller while playing tight, how to watch for 'tells' in other players, the jargon and in-talk. Mary had laughed when he had told her that, unbeknownst to Clay, he would be playing against his own money. The fact that, win or lose, Wentworth would be out of pocket, thanks to his wife's contribution, gave Paul a confidence that the other players lacked.

'But play as if it was your money,' Mary had advised. 'Too much confidence and you can go on tilt.'

It was almost one before Paul began to play seriously, by which time he was down to £700. The few games he had won, he made seem like fluke victories and celebrated them with excessive good spirits. By now, the banker had lost interest and, muttering something about throwing good money after bad, he pocketed his remaining cash and bid the school farewell. Clay's look of disapproval at this early departure suggested that he wouldn't be invited in the future. Calloway had lost more heavily than Paul and seemed to be what Mary had called 'steaming' – playing with wild lack of judgement. The barrister was making money but Miles, the stockbroker, had descended into something of a sulk.

Paul glanced across the table. Alice Markwick had seemed distracted and was marginally down on the evening. The biggest winner, of course, was Clay.

'I hope those aren't your life savings you're blowing there,' he said amiably to Paul as Miles dealt them in for another round.

Paul thought of Wentworth's wife and her long, prying fingers. 'No, but I earned it the hard way,' he said.

'Let's hope you don't lose it the easy way.'

It was strange. Clay must have been £2,000 up on the evening, yet there was something restless and unhappy about him. Paul sensed that it had something to do with his presence.

Clay glanced at his cards and, without a moment's hesitation, pushed out £700. Alice, Lol and the barrister folded but Paul, following his instinct, called, matching Clay's bet. To his left, Miles glanced at him with some surprise before folding.

The man made an unconvincing bully, Paul thought as, for a moment, he held Clay's stare. All his life he had been surrounded by solid, strong men – his father, his business rivals. He had seen the look on their faces as they closed the deal, turned the knife on some poor sap. But when he had to tough it out, like now, the merest hint of uncertainty, of a deep inner weakness in his soul, betrayed him and spoilt it all. As he went all-in, trying to break Paul, he was like a bad actor playing Macbeth.

Paul held two eights in the hole. The flop had brought an ace of diamonds, a jack of spades and an eight of spades.

Somewhere, in the poker textbooks, Clay must
have read that once you've earned the respect of your
opponents, you can frighten them into folding even
if your hand is weak. The other players had reacted
according to the book. Paul hadn't.

Impassively, Clay turned over his cards, revealing
that he was holding an ace, jack, queen and king,
inferior to Paul's trip of three eights. Abandoning the
dewy-eyed amateur act, Paul pulled in the pot with
the smallest of smiles. To his surprise, Clay left the
table, as did Alice Markwick.

The idea had never been to make his fortune and
Paul played the next two games tightly, folding early
as he tried to catch the conversation from where Clay
and Alice sat by the fire, but they were talking too
quietly.

It was almost three in the morning before Paul was
able to take his moment, by which time Lol Calloway
had bowed out with his normal string of obscenities.
Miles was playing well, but Alice had lost interest,
limping in late and low in those games where she
didn't fold. Clay was down by a few hundred but
appeared to have unlimited funds backing him.

The buck was with Paul, and by chance, he dealt
himself the sweetest hand imaginable – two kings,
followed by a flop of a king, a five and a four. After
Alice and Miles had folded, Clay chewed his bottom
lip in a pathetic attempt at a bluff, then pushed £1,000
into the centre of the table.

Paul hesitated for a minute or so. Then he raised

with all the money he had before him, confident that, even if Clay had aces wired in the hole – two aces – he was on a loser. The last two cards to be turned, a nine and a queen, sealed his fate.

Clay went for the full bluff, raising Paul by another £2,000 with a triumphant little smile. 'We work on the basis of IOUs in this school,' he said. 'Two weeks to pay.'

For a moment, there was silence in the room. Lol ambled over from the fire where he was sitting. 'You are one hard bastard, Clay,' he said quietly.

Paul looked at the two kings in his hand like a man reading his own death sentence. 'IOU?' he said. 'I hadn't realized I could run up debts.' Suddenly he found himself thinking of Alex. It was this easy to be caught in the gin-trap of indebtedness. The harder you pulled, the tighter you were held.

'You're with the big boys now, Paul,' Clay said. 'This isn't a social event.'

At poker, as in racing, there are amateurs and there are professionals. Paul swallowed, playing for time, allowing the tension around the table to build up. And professionalism was more than a question of skill and knowledge; it was a state of mind. Although Paul's experience of poker was limited to a few light-hearted games with the other jockeys and a two-hour lesson with Crazy Mary, he thought like a winner. Clay Wentworth was an amateur to the marrow of his bones.

'Perhaps,' Paul said, reaching into the inside pocket

of his jacket, 'I could bring this into play.' He threw a scuffed and faded piece of paper onto the pile of money. 'It's worth £2,000 of anybody's money.'

Clay leaned forward and picked up the piece of paper, a list of horses' names, most of which had been deleted. At last, there was panic. 'Where did you get this?' he asked, quietly.

'Win the hand and it's yours.'

Paul glanced around the table. Alice had looked away but seemed disturbed by the turn of events.

'What on earth's going on?' Miles asked. 'Is that an IOU?'

'Of a sort,' Paul said. He stared hard at Clay. 'Accepted?'

Clay nodded. 'Tricky little bastard, aren't you?' he said, turning over his two cards to reveal two jacks.

Paul flipped over the two kings. As he reached out for the pot, taking the piece of paper first of all and returning it to his inside pocket, he said, 'It's been copied, Clay – and two people know I'm here.'

'We need to talk about this – privately,' Clay said. 'The game's over.'

'That game's over,' said Paul. 'The other is just beginning.'

They should have stopped shooting. Alice Markwick stood on the steps of Clay's house in the early hours of the morning, and felt lost. The night had passed in a dream of poker hands, low birds and bantering conversation. Had she lost money? Did Paul Raven know about Opteeka B? Was Clay at this very moment revealing secrets that could destroy him and her? She didn't care.

They should have stopped shooting.

Alice wasn't aware of the whine of a milk float, approaching her from down the road. It stopped ten yards away and, with quite unnecessary jauntiness, a young man in his early twenties jumped out of the cab, took two pints from a crate and, whistling, walked towards the entrance to Clay's house. ''Ullo,' he appraised the dark, slender woman standing on the doorstep with a cheeky up-and-down look. 'Heavy night, darlin'?'

Alice looked at him slowly. 'They should have stopped shooting,' she said.

There was a roar in her ears. Alice wasn't drunk, although she had tried during the evening to dull the pain with the occasional vodka tonic. With a huge effort of concentration, she remembered where she had parked the car and, as the milk float moved away, she walked slowly down the street, feeling for the car keys in her handbag as she went.

Sometimes it felt lonely on the small, deserted island that she had chosen to inhabit. She wasn't made for relationships, for confidences, for the ghastly domestic messiness of cohabitation, so after the death of Eric, she had kept the world away from her little island. At times like this, she regretted it. She wanted to talk to someone. There were girlfriends, of course, but they belonged to another world – a world of music, laughter and easy gratification. If she rang them, they would misunderstand what she wanted.

Alice unlocked the door of her Aston Martin and drove carefully back to the flat in Islington.

She knew what she had to do when she arrived. Without even checking her answering machine, she walked into the sitting-room in which all the lights had been left blazing. Behind a mediocre nineteenth-century landscape painting there was a safe which, tapping out a number on its security board, she opened. The videotape lay there, like an unexploded bomb.

She had to see it just once more.

Alice poured herself another vodka tonic from a cocktail tray in the corner. Her television and video were designed into a bookcase and, having inserted the tape, she sat on the sofa and, curling her legs underneath her, watched the recorded last moments of Gavin Holmes one more time.

Despite inept camera-work, it was clear that Opteeka B had passed this, its most important test, with full marks. One moment he was standing there, unsteady but in control, in front of his car, the next he was as blind and helpless as a newborn kitten.

Alice gripped the glass. This was what she wanted, she told herself. It would provide a future free of the insecurity which had haunted her since she was a little girl in Prague. She would never have to suffer in the way that her mother had suffered. Freedom came with a price-tag attached.

On the screen, Gavin was feeling his way towards the exit of the car park. Then, with the knife at his throat, he was turned back to the wall.

The violence she didn't like. Even while Opteeka B was being developed, she would sometimes wake at night, ambushed by visions of how her brain-child would be used. If she could have won a lifetime of security with a device to save a child's eyesight, or assist in major operations, nothing would have made her happier, but of course that was impossible. Life paid badly; it was with death that you made a killing.

Tears filled Alice's eyes. She wiped them away angrily, forced herself to watch the screen.

Like a rabbit blinded by a searchlight, the man blundered along the wall, then turned back. The speeding van filled the screen, but the roar of its engine was not loud enough to obliterate entirely Gavin's last scream of terror. The experiment was proved, there was no need to keep filming. As the van moved forward, the camera trained on the journalist's twitching, bloodied body.

Dry-eyed now, Alice stared ahead of her. Petrin had his evidence. It would soon be over.

'They should have stopped shooting,' she said quietly.

'Perhaps I ought to tell you that my wife and I have no secrets.' Clay Wentworth sat at the mahogany desk in his small study and puffed at a large cigar he had just taken from a silver box. 'We tell each other everything.'

Paul looked up at him from a deep armchair. Clay had recovered his composure somewhat since the final game in the night's poker school. He had bid farewell to the other guests with cool courtesy and before ushering Paul downstairs to his small room with the weary disapproval of a schoolmaster.

'So it came as no surprise that you were in possession of that particular piece of paper,' Clay continued.

'You accepted it as a bet. You must want it back.'

'What a pathetic thing to do.' A look of irritation crossed Clay's face. 'Your little moment of melodrama. Yes, of course I'd like it back.'

'You can have it.'

'But you've got a copy.'

'The photocopy of a scrap of paper is hardly going to serve as evidence.'

Clay leaned back in his absurd leather executive chair, like a bad actor in a soap opera. He was probably an amateur at business too, Paul reflected. The layout of his dark womb-like little study suggested a deep insecurity. The guest chair was lower than Clay's so that Paul had to look up at him. The desk lamp was positioned to dazzle him. Doubtless a psychiatrist might say something about the big cigar Clay was toying with as he spoke. Despite his position and his money – or perhaps because of them – the man was a loser.

'You have a deal in mind, I suppose,' Clay said. 'Some sort of cheap blackmail.'

'You'll have the list back, once you've told me what happened to Alex Drew.'

'Alex?' Clay looked surprised, as if he had forgotten that the man had ever existed. 'I really didn't know him well.'

'He came to your little evenings.'

'Bloody awful gambler, your friend. Ran up debts of fifty big ones.'

'And committed suicide.'

'It's happened before.' Clay puffed at his cigar and waved away the smoke as if, with it, he could make memories of Alex fade. 'You knew the boy, Paul,' he said reasonably. 'He lived for racing, but he had his weaknesses – women, the need to be seen in the right places. I liked him. He begged me to let him join us on Thursday nights; I thought I was doing him a favour.'

It was almost four in the morning and, as he listened to Clay Wentworth trying to lie his way out of trouble, Paul felt a profound weariness. 'I'm not interested in this bullshit,' he said, 'Tell me – '

Clay held up a hand. 'I covered his debts, that's how much I liked him. He owed me around thirty – the rest was to other members of the school. I asked him to go to his parents but he was too proud. Tragic. I wish I'd been able to talk to him.'

Outside the window, a blackbird with a faulty body clock had started singing in the darkness. For a brief moment, Paul thought of his friend – Alex, joking as the string pulled out at Charlesworth's yard; Alex, talking to Jim Wilson in the weighing-room; Alex, his face a mask of pale determination as they circled around the starter before a race.

Misunderstanding his silence, Clay added, 'It was a terrible shock to all of us.'

With the clarity of vision that comes with the grave-yard shift, Paul saw that it wasn't greed for money or social acceptance that had led Alex to his death. It was weakness – the weakness of Clay Wentworth that somehow infected all around him.

'I'll tell you what I'm going to do,' Paul said softly. 'I'm washing my hands of this whole business. I'm going to hand this small piece of evidence – ' he patted his jacket pocket ' – to the Jockey Club. Just in case they reach an opinion that no respected amateur could possibly be guilty of driving a professional jockey to his death, I'll also tell the police everything I know. What happened to me. What happened to Alex. And what happened to the horses on the list. Then, just to make sure, I'll give the story to a journalist friend. Between them, they'll discover the truth about Mr Clay Wentworth and his friends.'

'Journalist?' Oddly, Clay seemed most alarmed by the least potent threat in Paul's armoury.

'Nobody you know,' Paul said. 'I've found out enough about Alex's death.'

'You know less than you think,' Clay muttered flatly.

There was a soft knock at the door. Before either man could react, it had been pushed open and a dishevelled figure in a white silk nightgown and a dressing-gown half hanging off a slender shoulder, stood at the entrance.

'Zena, what a nice surprise,' said Clay coldly.

'How did it go, Paul?' Zena asked woozily. 'Make lots of money, did you? Spend my investment wisely?'

'Yes.' The interruption was doubly annoying. Clay had seemed on the point of cracking. His wife's determination to reveal that he had been gambling against his own money was an unwelcome diversion. 'We were talking about Alex.'

'Oh, Alex.' Zena entered the room, running a hand through her hair. Whatever she was on, pills or booze, had done little for feminine allure, and the make-up around her eyes seemed to have smudged or run earlier in the night. 'One of our first victims, wasn't he, darling?' She smiled in the general direction of her husband as she sat on the edge of his desk, affording Paul an unavoidable view of her thighs.

'You're drunk. It's late. We're busy,' Clay said. There was a tightness in his voice that Paul had not heard before.

'I screw 'em, you kill 'em, isn't that right?'

'Alex committed suicide.' Clay glared at his wife but, behind the threat, there was something shifty and defensive. 'There's no need to bother Mr Raven with this.'

'I'm sure Mr Raven –' Zena smiled crookedly at

Paul and waggled a bare foot in his direction ' – would love to know this.'

Paul waited.

'Did you know a man called Gavin Holmes, darling?' Zena said suddenly. 'Journalist on the *Guardian*, nice man, bit of a lush – ' she paused ' – good lover, though. Killed today. Accident at the races. On the news it was. They say he was pissed, but we know better than that, don't we, darling?'

'Is this a joke?' Paul asked. 'Is Holmes dead?'

'Crushed against a wall. Went to Lingfield Park. Weren't you at Lingfield today, darling?'

With a sudden movement, Clay stood up and, taking Zena roughly by the arm, propelled her, drunkenly protesting, out of the door. Paul heard snatches of angry conversation in the hall. Eventually, Clay returned, closing the door behind him.

'Sorry,' he said. 'She gets rather emotional sometimes.'

'Is she right?'

'I heard an item on the news about this man.' Clay returned to his desk. 'It's the first time I've even heard his name.' He smiled wearily. 'It's all history,' he said. 'I'll tell you about the list you have, and you can do what you like with it.'

'History?'

'Yes.' Clay seemed haggard, broken by the events of the evening. 'I wish I had never become involved.'

The tape on the answering-machine turned slowly.

The voice of Clay Wentworth, weary but not defeated, sounded in Alice Markwick's flat.

'... an executive decision, no more or less. I've thrown him off the track. He has discovered why Drew died, which is all he really wanted to know. I managed to persuade him that the journalist's death was some sort of weird accident. He's finished his little quest. He'll leave us alone now . . . '

Alice sat on the sofa, an empty glass hanging loosely from her hand, the blank grey television screen before her.

' . . . the unfortunate fuss this evening about my shopping-list,' the voice from the tape continued. 'I even managed to persuade him to leave that with me so it's a question of hanging on until Wednesday. After that, we're free of . . . '

As if awakening from a dream, she put the glass on the floor, stood up and turned the television off. She pressed a button, removing the videotape and locking it once more in the safe.

Clay was still talking as Alice switched off the light and walked slowly to the bedroom.

Chapter 13

It wasn't like they show on the silver screen, the gathering of wrongdoers at a small terraced house in Perivale on the outskirts of London. The picture of the Virgin and child above the mantelpiece was good, so was the way one of the young men, the one with a moustache, cracked his knuckles occasionally, but the rest, three Italians sitting in cheap chairs by a gas fire, was too light, too domestic, too English – more *EastEnders* than the Godfather.

'So,' Tino, the older man, smiled with satisfaction. '*Il Cavallo di Troia* is doing his work.'

'*Cavallo? Troia*? What you talking about, papa?' The grey-haired man's son Giorgio looked mystified, as did Salvatore who, for a moment, was distracted from his knuckle work.

'*Dio*, do they teach you nothing in English schools. *Il Cavallo di Troia*? The Trojan Horse?'

'What's this, some kind of racehorse, is it?' Giorgio asked.

The older man laughed, but he felt sad. Even in Naples, where he had been raised, children understood the rudiments of classical education. Here, it seemed, school provided a foundation course in getting into girls' knickers and listening to loud music but little else. Occasionally he looked at Salvo and his friends and wondered whether the problem was not more with them than with the system but he quickly dispelled the thought. No, there was something rotten in the heart of this country. 'It's a reference to Greek mythology but it doesn't matter,' he said. 'I meant Calloway.'

'Ah, Johnny Geetar,' said Giorgio. 'He rang me. He does his work well.'

'It's impossible to get the *machina* from the factory, papa,' said Salvatore. 'Calloway says it's kept in some kind of bunker, guarded by the guy who uses it. Short of getting hold of the Markwick woman, there's no way we can find out where it is.'

'So?' Tino looked surprised. 'What's the problem? You get her.'

'That's just it,' said Giorgio. 'We don't have to. Our Trojan whatsit has told us where it's going to be used next.'

'Cheltenham, Tuesday,' Salvatore interrupted eagerly. 'There's a big race meeting and, in one of the races, a horse called Tanglewood's running. They're using the machine to stop it.'

'Where?' Tino sat still, waiting for the boys to understand.

'Cheltenham, papa. We told you.'

'Start, finish. First fence, last fence, bend. It could be anywhere.' Exasperation entered Tino's voice. 'We don't even know what the fucking thing looks like.'

For a moment, there was silence in the room, apart from the sound of Salvo's mother washing the dishes, humming to herself, from the kitchen across the hall.

Tino sighed. '*Cazzo*, you're useless, you two. You're not going to make it by knowing how to use a knife, how to make a man talk, how – ' he glared at Salvatore ' – how to smash up guitars.' He tapped the side of his head. 'Think,' he said more quietly. 'If you want to survive outside the law, you have to use this, you know.'

Giorgio and Salvatore looked at the floor, resentful yet slightly afraid, like two errant schoolboys who know that a lecture is on the way but don't have the nerve to interrupt.

'This is our big break,' Tino continued. 'We can go on working our little patch in London, running the girls, pushing the dope, carrying out the occasional bank job. But England is small, you want to get away. *Dio*, I want to get away. West Coast of America, or Chicago, or maybe New Orleans. They understand there. And, with this, they respect us.'

'We've got large parts of London tied up,' Giorgio muttered sulkily. 'Isn't that enough?'

'Not for these guys. They are big time, the true brotherhood.' For a moment there was silence in the room, and the unspoken word 'Mafia' hung in the air. Apart from a few Sicilian connections, Tino's London network was no more than an unofficial mafia and mention of the word was regarded as boastful, or even bad form. After this, they would be able to embrace the name with pride. 'They need a passport, a ticket of entry,' Tino continued. 'If I can go to Signor Guiseppi Vercelloni in New York and present him with the perfect weapon – a camera which blinds temporarily – our links with America will be assured.'

'Where?' said Salvatore eventually. 'We need to know where the photographer will be.'

'I'll call Calloway,' said Salvatore. 'I'm sure he'll be pleased to hear from me again.'

'This Cheltenham thing – it's big?' Tino asked. 'Lots of people?'

Giorgio nodded. 'They say it's a big deal for English racing.'

'Excellent,' said Tino.

Occasionally Zena Wentworth suffered from serious regrets and right now, as she lay naked on pine boards while her back was massaged by a beautiful and muscular Turkish homosexual at an exclusive health club in Chelsea, she found there was no escaping them.

She regretted the abortions when she was a teenager that later prevented her having children. That was normal. She regretted her dependence on alcohol and recreational drugs. There was nothing new there. She regretted the day that she had met Clay

Wentworth, and even more the day that she married him. That regret was with her at every waking moment. She regretted not telling Paul Raven everything she knew about Clay and Alice Markwick. This was new, a fresh psychic wound that had opened a few hours ago.

She winced. 'You're a sadist, Adnan,' she gasped as the fingers of the Paradise Health Club's most popular masseur seemed almost to reach into her flesh and touch the backbone.

A light laugh. 'Mmm. You're close, Mrs Wentworth,' the Turk said coquettishly.

In her life, she had done so little that was good. She gave her mother and her father Christmas presents, she went to church on the occasions when it was expected of her but, apart from that, she and common decency had parted company years ago. No one asked Zena Wentworth to be a godmother to their children.

Now was her chance, the time for a single act of blazing charity that would signal a turning-point in her life.

She thought of the conversation between her husband and Paul Raven which she had listened to, sitting on the stairs, after Clay had told her to go to bed. By his standards, he had been almost honest. He had told Paul about the small clique of investors who had put money into Alice Markwick's firm. He had explained precisely why Opteeka B was such a valuable scientific breakthrough. He had even confessed to the on-site racecourse experiments. But that was where his honesty had ended.

'What about the future?' Paul had asked.

'It's finished. The Ministry of Defence took possession of it this week. Our little investment has paid off.'

Only fear and weariness had stopped her going back into the study and confronting Clay with his lie.

Paul had asked about Gavin Holmes.

We knew nothing of that, Clay had said. There are undesirable elements interested in Opteeka B. He very much feared that Holmes had become involved with them and had paid the price.

She hadn't been surprised when Paul appeared to believe the line that Clay had sold him. Alex's death was explained. He had his own life to think of. The world of secret weapons was nothing to him.

'Turn?' the masseur asked.

Her back and shoulders tingling, Zena rolled over. It was a moment that even she found slightly disconcerting as she lay naked, her flesh glowing with sweat, beneath the entirely indifferent gaze of an oriental god. 'Are you absolutely sure that you're 100% gay, Adnan?' she smiled.

The man's eyes flickered down her pale, slack body, as if to confirm the rightness of his sexual orientation. 'Correction,' he said, starting to work on her left calf and thigh. '110%.'

After she had left the Paradise Health Club, Zena drove at speed back to the house. Ever since she had been a teenager, she had driven fast through London but there was a precision and determination to the way she took the streets now. Adnan always had that effect on her, as if his powerful hands had the power to cleanse her of poisonous thoughts, to make her as fresh and clean as the skin of her body. The good resolutions rarely lasted longer than the effects of the massage but her few hours of virtue convinced Zena that she was not entirely lost.

She ran up the steps, the keys of the house in her hand. Letting herself in, she took the stairs to the bedroom and sat on the side of the bed. Breathlessly, she dialled Paul's number. He deserved better than to be deceived by her husband.

'Paul,' she said, leaning forward, her hand on her forehead like a Victorian morality painting called The Ashamed Mistress or A Confession. 'It's Zena. No, wait, don't hang up – ' She hesitated. 'There are two things you should know,' she said. 'You should go to Cheltenham on Tuesday. Clay's little game isn't over yet. They're going to stop Tanglewood.'

At the other end, Paul asked a question but, before she could reply, a finger had broken the connection. Zena looked up to see her husband standing before her.

When he spoke, his voice was gentle, just like it was in the old days, although there was no tenderness there now. 'And the second thing?'

Clay replaced the telephone and lifted her face towards him like a man raising a pistol.

'The second thing, my sweet deceitful darling?'

* * *

The BBC was not generous with its offices. Producers, even tubby, self-important producers like Bernard Green, tended to be given a quality of work station which, in any other business, a junior secretary would find unacceptable.

Bernard was gazing at the wall-chart in front of his desk wondering, not for the first time that day, how he was going to bring in a programme on Northern Ireland on time, under budget and in a form that would not offend BBC governors, their wives or dinner-party friends, when the dull green phone beside him gave an uneven wheeze of a ring.

'BBC Psychiatric Intensive Care Unit,' he said laconically. It was one of his favourite jokes. 'Mr Joseph? For me?' Then, with a double-take that shook his ample frame in the tight off-white shirt he was wearing, he sat up straighter in his chair. 'Ah yes, Mr Joseph. Send him up.'

He put down the telephone with a muttered, 'Sodding hell.' Standing up, he reached for a corduroy jacket that had been left on top of an old grey cabinet. He put his head out of the office door and said, 'Be a love, Irene, and fetch us two cups of tea. Unexpected guest. Yugoslavian journalist called Joseph.'

A tall woman with glasses and the forbidding look of a senior librarian glanced unaffectionately in his direction, but, like the overweight ornament on a cuckoo clock, Bernard had ducked back into his office.

'Hot, steaming piles of *shit*,' he muttered to himself. 'How dare he come to see me *here*?'

As usual, Petrin seemed entirely at home when he was shown into the office, charming Irene and even accepting the grey, weak tea in a styrofoam cup with a modicum of grace. As the door closed, Petrin looked around the tiny office. 'How cosy,' he smiled.

'I frankly find your pitching up like this at my place of work, unannounced, beyond – '

'Shut up.' Petrin allowed his smile to disappear like the winter sun behind grey clouds. 'I have no problem with my security. If you're on some sort of list of suspects here, then you only have yourself to blame. Can we talk?'

Sulkily, Bernard said, 'We don't bug people at the BBC.'

'Next Tuesday, you will have a camera crew at Cheltenham. You will be obliged to attend yourself.'

Bernard shifted himself in his chair and gave a hopeless little laugh. 'My schedule's ridiculously tight but I just might be able to move a few things around.'

'How co-operative of you.'

'The camera crew's out of the question.'

Petrin looked at him coldly.

'We have such things as unions over here,' Bernard continued. 'I can't just send a crew off to some race-course. There'd be questions. We're meant to be cutting back on – '

'I didn't expect this sort of attitude from you of all people, Bernard. Particularly given your years of service for us. Years – ' he paused significantly ' – of which I have extensive notes and tapes.'

'I deserve better than this,' Bernard said weakly. 'It could finish my career if it got out that I'd been working for you.'

'The alternative certainly will. The choice is yours.'

'What do you want these men for anyway? They're very difficult, technicians. Ask them to do something that's not in their contract and you've got a strike on your hands.'

'Men? What men?'

Bernard was paler than usual, and his face was greasy with sweat. The unpleasant smell of human stress filled the airless office.

'The camera crew.'

'Ah, I failed to make myself clear. I don't need your technicians. I want to borrow some equipment for the afternoon. And, of course, we'll need a pass.'

'We?'

'You and me, Bernard. We are the technicians.' The stink in the office was becoming really quite unbearable.

'It's not possible. There are all sorts of regulations to bear in mind.'

Pausing with his hand on the door-handle, Petrin said, 'Do it, Bernard, or the Director-General gets your personal file.' He opened the door and switched on a smile. 'Thanks so much for the restorative cuppa,' he said, winking suavely at Irene.

Sleep had never been easy since the attack in the

laboratory but, ever since he had accepted money from the man called Josef, Peter had found himself waking in the middle of the night, drenched in sweat. He dreamed of himself alone in a barren snowscape but when he touched the snow, it burnt his flesh like battery acid, and Klima was before him melting, her mouth wide in a soundless scream, her eyes uncomprehending as she disappeared and he was unable, despite everything, to make a sound, while he cowered from a hand pressing him into the evil, death-dealing snow and a child was screaming, his son –

'Peter, Peter, calm.' His wife held him down on the bed and, as the sobbing subsided, Peter Zametsky knew with utter certainty that he had to act.

'Let's go to bed.'

Angie looked up from the floor where she had been sitting when the phone rang, bringing the news about Gavin Holmes' notes, and saw that Paul was lost to her.

'Mmm?' he frowned.

'Make love, remember? Act like a normal couple for a while.'

Paul leaned forward and ran a hand slowly over her fine blonde hair across her cheek, tracing the line of her lips. 'I've got to warn Bill Scott.'

'Who?'

'He's riding Tanglewood at Cheltenham. He must know that they're trying to stop him.'

Angie laughed briefly. 'You always were a romantic, Paul,' she said. 'I offer you my body and you prefer to go and chat to another jockey.'

'It's not a chat.' A flush of anger suffused Paul's cheeks. 'Christ, you should know what can happen to a jockey in a bad fall.'

She looked away. Every time she believed that she and Paul were going to be able to live a life of some normality, he was dragged back into the murky side of racing. 'It will never leave us, the ghost of Alex Drew, will it?' she said.

'This is no longer about Alex. He was weak. Some unscrupulous bastards put pressure on him to put me through the rails. He couldn't live with his guilt. But there are the other horses.'

'Why not just hand all the evidence over to the Jockey Club or whatever it's called?'

'What evidence? A bit of paper. A late-night conversation after a game of poker. And, remember, this is Mr Clay Wentworth we're talking about.' Paul smiled bitterly. 'The respected businessman.'

'It will never end,' Angie said bleakly. She thought of the day she had realized, back at the hospital, that this was the man she wanted. Since then she had given up her career for him. She had become involved in a sport she had once believed was inhuman. She had given him – a small thing but her own – her virginity.

'A few more days,' he said, as if reading her thoughts. 'Then it will end one way or another.'

Wearily, she nodded. 'So we collect Gavin Holmes' notes, then what?'

Paul looked at her almost impassively. 'You collect the notes, I go to see Bill. Time's against us now.'

Angie stood up and reached for a light green shoulder bag she had left on a chair nearby. 'This is how they do things up your way, is it?' she asked. She let her arms swing ape-like before her and said in a Neanderthal voice, 'Me macho man, you little woman run around for me, right?'

Paul looked into her angry, hurt eyes. 'This is important,' he said quietly but, as she turned away towards the door, it occurred to him that maybe nothing was as important as to hold her lithe and slender body close to his. 'There'll be time for love later,' he added.

But she was gone.

The photographer had been surprised to get a late commission only two days before the final experiment, and not entirely pleased. He was a professional; he needed to prepare himself for the pay-off, not run about the country doing last-minute errands for her ladyship.

'I wouldn't have asked you,' she had said. 'But I need someone I can trust.'

That was fair enough. When it came to tact, keeping schtum while all around him were shooting their mouths off or asking stupid questions, the photographer had few equals.

293

'You won't need any assistance, will you?' she had asked sweetly. 'After all, our man isn't exactly going to run away.'

So he had agreed to keep it simple, keep it in the family.

Mrs Markwick had been curiously distracted, confiding secrets which normally she would have kept to herself. There was a small hitch, she had said, Raven was taking an unhealthily close interest. He needed to be de-activated for a few days.

De-activated? What the hell did that mean?

Mrs Markwick had explained. He was to be brought back to the bunker beneath the office, and kept with Fi-Fi for a while. Mrs Markwick would find someone to guard him. The price of his freedom would be carefully explained to him – one word to the authorities and immobility would be the least of his problems.

A bit elaborate, wasn't it? Surely it would be simpler to –

But no. Something had happened to Mrs Markwick. Ever since the last, highly successful experiment, she had a look in her eyes the photographer had never seen before. Distant, almost wistful. She wanted no more killing. We fulfil our agreement with Wentworth, then it was farewell to Opteeka B and good riddance.

He didn't like it. Kidnapping was messy. It could go wrong.

The photographer sat in the driver's seat of an

old, battered Citroen parked outside the Blue Boar Tavern, Leatherhead. This was G and T country and, although it was Monday, the pub car park was full of company cars whose occupants were doing business the English way over steak and chips and an agreeable glass of Chateau Plonk. It wasn't going to be easy, breezing off with an unwilling individual, even one with wonky legs.

He's a boy, Mrs Markwick had said, an innocent and, as if to prove it, she had given the photographer Raven's number and told him to ring him. He was to be a friend of Gavin Holmes, a fellow journalist. He had some of Gavin's notes which the *Guardian* refused to touch. He owed it to Gavin to get them into the right hands. Could we meet? Say, the Blue Boar, Leatherhead. The car park, for security reasons. One o'clock, Monday, fine.

Candy from a baby.

The photographer lit a cigarette. It was five past one, and he was beginning to worry. The only person in the car park was a young girl with short blonde hair, wearing jeans and a light blue jacket. She seemed lost.

Then she saw his car and started walking towards it.

Until today, Paul's acquaintance with the young amateur Bill Scott had been restricted to occasional weighing room banter, but now, as he talked to him in his cottage near Wantage, he found that Bill reminded him of Alex Drew a couple of years back – the same enthusiasm for racing, the same diamond-hard will to win behind his easy manner.

'Let me get this right,' Bill said, sitting in towelling dressing-gown outside his sauna. 'You're saying that if I hadn't tracked Skinflint onto stands side at Wincanton, I'd have been brought down by some weird weapon that blinded my horse?'

Paul smiled. Described in Bill's broad West Country accent, the idea sounded even more absurd than it was.

'That's why Drago's Pet fell on the inner. They got the wrong horse.'

'Not very competent, were they?'

Sweat was still running down Bill Scott's face, the result of a final wasting session of the day. Although his weight on Tanglewood in the Kim Muir posed no problem, he had another ride earlier in the afternoon for which he would have to do ten stone two. 'The only reason I was tracking Skinflint was that my horse doesn't like to be left alone. Drago's Pet was fading so it made sense to go with Wentworth, even if he was taking the longest way round.'

'Not that competent,' Paul said, 'but ruthless. Three other horses fancied for the Kim Muir have been taken out. They claim that they've proved what they needed to prove, and that nothing will happen at Cheltenham, but I don't trust them.'

'You think they'd try something? At the National Hunt Festival?'

'The bigger the crowd, the easier the job.' Paul shrugged. 'I hope I'm wrong but the fact is, with Tanglewood out of the way, Skinflint's a certainty.'

'So what do I do? Watch out for a missile-launcher by the second last and duck?'

'How d'you normally ride Tanglewood?'

'Hunt him along for the first couple of miles, then start improving. He's a clever sort so jumping's no problem – I can place him anywhere. As I say, the only problem is that he goes to sleep where he hits the front.'

'That's perfect. If you can keep him covered up as long as possible, they'll have to get at you over the last couple of fences. Stay in the middle of the course to make yourself a more difficult target.'

Bill looked doubtful. 'It's a three mile 'chase at Cheltenham. If Skinflint's ten lengths up at the third last, you're not going to get me holding him up to avoid getting zapped.'

'You're right.' Paul stood up. Like any serious jockey, Bill Scott understood that danger went with the territory. Missing the chance of a winner at the biggest race meeting of the year because of the obscure threat of some secret weapon was hardly likely to appeal to him. 'Do me one favour, though. Try to stay on the stands side coming up the straight. I'll cover the inner.'

'I'll try,' Bill said, although the look on his face suggested that he had more doubts about Paul's sanity than his own safety.

'You're going to beat Skinflint tomorrow,' Paul said, hesitating by the front door. 'Do it for Alex, okay?'

Bill smiled indulgently. 'You just watch me,' he said.

The man in the Citroen had long grey hair and there was a high colour to his big rounded features. He looked like a film director who had once been big in the sixties, or a moderately successful second-hand car dealer or – yes, or a journalist. He opened the window to the car as Angie approached.

'Mr Davison?' she asked.

The man seemed suspicious of her. 'I was expecting Paul Raven,' he said.

'I'm Paul's friend,' she said. 'He's had to go somewhere and asked me to collect the material.'

'Wasn't the arrangement. I told him I wanted to see him personally.' The man glanced towards the girl's car, a Mini. There was no one else with her.

'You can trust me,' she said, a hint of desperation in her voice.

The man hesitated. 'Get in,' he said reluctantly, nodding in the direction of the passenger seat on which there was an orange file.

'Can't you just give it to me?'

'Forget it.' He started the car.

'No.' Angie walked round, opened the door and, as she stepped in, the man picked up the file to make room for her.

With the engine still running, he said, 'I need to explain this stuff to you.' Opening the file, he took out a small pistol. 'Sorry,' he said. 'I wanted your boyfriend but you'll have to do.' Pointing the gun at her, he leaned across and, with his left hand, locked the passenger door. 'We've got to make a little trip,' he said. 'All right?'

Angie sat back in the seat and closed her eyes. 'Thanks, Paul,' she said quietly.

Before – long before – he heard from them, Paul knew something had gone wrong. He cursed himself for not checking the journalist who had called with the *Guardian*. Not only had he failed to see the trap, but he had sent Angie into danger instead of him. As darkness fell, he recalled their last conversation, her sad, defeated words. 'It will never end.'

And why had he exposed her to Christ knew what risk? In order to warn an amateur jockey that some-one was going to stop him winning a horse-race – an amateur who, it turned out, suspected him of being deluded.

He called Angie's flat. There was no reply. Her friend in Putney hadn't seen her. Crazy Mary was working on the early evening shift. Finally, he con-tacted the manager of the Blue Boar. No, he had seen nothing strange, the man replied impatiently.

'A friend of mine was meeting someone in your car park,' Paul explained. 'She seems to have disap-peared.'

'Oh yeah?'

'She was in a Mini, registration A663 BLB. Is the car there?'

Sighing, the man put down the telephone. 'It's here,' he said when he returned. 'But no sign of your friend.'

Paul put down the phone. He should call the police. And say what? My girlfriend was meeting a stranger and hasn't been seen for a couple of hours? The world was full of disappearing girlfriends.

He was reaching for the telephone when the doorbell rang. He hobbled across the room and flung open the door.

The first thing he noticed was that the man was wearing dark glasses despite the fact that night had fallen. Then the face – or what was left of it. The man made an eerie gurgling sound.

A woman stepped forward out of the shadows. 'My husband says we have to talk,' she said.

Chapter 14

Stress affected her in a strange way. She knew other people who became tetchy and ill-tempered, or who resorted to intense alcohol therapy, or who simply slept. Right now, Alice wished she was like them.

But she wasn't.

Her heart was beating like that of a teenager going out on her first date as she drove across London from the flat in Islington to the office. The chain of events over the last twenty-four hours had filled her with dread – to lose the deal at this late stage because of some interfering little jockey seemed absurd. Yet the word from Clay was unambiguous. His silly bitch of a wife had tipped Raven off. He had to be stopped.

The hitch, followed by the solution.

He wasn't that smart, falling easily for the lie about Gavin Holmes and his notes. She had no worries about sending the photographer. After all, Raven's legs were still weak. The photographer was strong. He was also armed.

The hitch, followed by the solution, followed by the fuck-up.

Alice gripped the steering-wheel with anger as she thought of the call summoning her to the office.

'She's here.'

'She?'

'Raven sent his girlfriend.'

She had cursed. Then it all became clear. So the jockey has sent his lover into the lion's den. Very heroic. Perhaps it wasn't so bad. In fact, perhaps it was better.

'What shall I do with her, Mrs Markwick?'

'I'm on my way,' she had said.

She parked the car in the forecourt, uneasily aware that tomorrow's last experiment was no longer uppermost in her mind, that her hands were clammy. She checked her face in the rearview mirror, then stepped out of the car and walked briskly towards the darkened offices.

May she be fat, she said to herself as she unlocked the door and ran up the steps towards her office. May she look like a horse. She walked into the executive bathroom and unlocked what appeared to be a cupboard. May she have cropped, greasy hair. She descended a dark spiral staircase and pushed open a heavy metal door. At first the bright strip lighting blinded her after the darkness, then she saw the photographer at his desk, the gun on the blotter before him. He glanced across the room. May she have unfortunate skin.

The girl was tied to a chair, her arms bound at the wrists, each of her feet tied to the legs of the chair. She was small and slender and, when Alice first looked at her, a curtain of fine blonde hair concealed her face. Then she looked up, fear and anger in her light blue eyes.

Damn. It was as Alice had feared. The girl was perfection.

She really wished that stress didn't affect her this way.

As soon as Angie saw the woman standing at the door, smiling at her in that peculiar way, she knew she was in trouble. At first, she hadn't understood. The man with the gun and killer's eyes, the trip to London, her legs tied together with rope, the brightly-lit room that smelt of rabbits – none of it made sense. But now she began to see it all.

'Mrs Markwick,' she said. 'Would you mind explaining what all this is about?'

Alice ambled forward, picked up the ugly, black pistol that was lying on the desk, ran a finger down the silencer that was on the barrel and put it back carefully as if it were a piece of antique china. She dressed well and expensively, Angie noticed, and the long dark curls which might have seemed ridiculous on a woman of her age gave her a sort of cold stylishness. 'How d'you know my name?' she asked in a low voice, in which a foreign accent was just detectable.

'I've seen you at the races with your friend Clay Wentworth.'

'He's not my friend.'

'You haven't answered,' said Angie. 'Why are you doing this?'

Alice pulled up a wooden chair which she placed in front of Angie. 'You're hardly in a position to be asking me questions,' she said, as she sat down. Angie shrunk back from her. There was something faintly alarming about this woman, the way she sat too close so that Angie could smell the expensive scent on her. There was a rustle of silk as she crossed her legs. 'You don't look very comfortable,' Alice said, a hint of mockery in her voice.

Angie's shoulders ached and the back of the chair was biting into the flesh of her upper arms, but she said nothing.

'As it happens, this matter can be easily resolved,' Alice said. 'I would like you to make one call to Mr Paul Raven. Then you can relax, we'll take off the rope and let you go – maybe tomorrow night.'

'What am I supposed to say?'

'I don't want him to go racing tomorrow. I have a little project which, I'm told, interests him. There will now be … an alternative attraction.' Alice lingered over the word then, as if returning to more practical matters, she said, 'At four o'clock, he will receive a call at his house. It will tell him where in London he will find you.' She smiled. 'That's all. No money. No information. He'll just have to miss the races.'

'He'll tell the police.'

'Not if he likes his little girl, he won't. If anything

304

goes wrong at Cheltenham, your friend will not be getting you back in the condition he last saw you.' Alice hesitated. 'Personally, I had hoped Gavin Holmes would be our last casualty.'

Angie looked away. There was an unsettling intimacy in Alice Markwick's smile.

'One call?' Alice gave a girlish pout. Without taking her eyes off Angie, she added, 'Maybe you need a little encouragement. Maybe you'd like to see our performing rabbits.'

Behind her, the photographer reached for his camera. 'Fi-Fi?' he asked.

'Yes,' said Alice. 'Fi-Fi.'

It took a long time to get the truth out of Peter Zametsky. The strain of the past few months and the fact that he was unable to enunciate in a way that was comprehensible to anyone but his wife meant that his account of the development of Opteeka B, the deadly experiments demanded by the Markwick Instruments' main investor Clay Wentworth, and the deal with Czechoslovak Intelligence was halting and unclear. But gradually, through the translation of his wife Klima, the truth unfolded.

In the end, Paul knew everything except what he needed to know most. Who was holding Angie.

'My husband says he has not the address of Clay Wentworth,' Klima said.

Paul shook his head. 'They wouldn't keep her there. It's too obvious.'

They listened as, for almost a minute, Peter gasped and gurgled, what was left of his face showing increasing animation.

When at last he finished, there was silence, as if Klima was reluctant to convey what Peter had told her.

'The people who did this to my husband,' she said eventually, 'they too want Opteeka B. Is possible, he's thinking, that they find you as rivals. Perhaps they have your girlfriend.'

Paul reached for the telephone and dialled a number. 'Ginnie,' he said. 'Angie's disappeared. I think it's something to do with the race tomorrow. Give me Wentworth's number.' He jotted down the number on a pad, promising to keep her in touch with what was happening. When he dialled Wentworth, there was an answering machine.

'Wentworth, this is Paul Raven.' He spoke quietly and firmly. 'My girlfriend was meant to be meeting a journalist today. She's gone missing. If this has anything to do with you – *anything* – you should know that the police have been informed. You have my number. Ring me when you get in, whatever time it is.' He put down the telephone and pushed it away. 'We'd better wait,' he said. 'Maybe she's trying to contact me.'

It was the scream he heard first.

They must have been holding the telephone close to her mouth because, as Paul picked it up, the receiver reverberated in his hand. At first it seemed an alien, unrecognizable sound but as the scream subsided into sobs, he knew it was Angie.

'Mr Raven?' A man's voice came onto the line. 'We have your girlfriend. She will be released tomorrow afternoon if you do what we require.'

'Yes?'

'You should wait by your telephone tomorrow. At precisely four o'clock, you will receive a call from us which will tell you where you can find her. Go to Cheltenham or talk to the police and your friend will pay the price.'

'I'll do it,' Paul said quickly.

'Maybe you would like to talk to her – in case you think we're not serious.'

Angie seemed quieter now, almost sleepy. She whispered something which at first Paul couldn't catch. Then she repeated it. 'I...can't see,' she said. 'I...can't see.'

The phone went dead.

For a moment, Paul stood, the telephone in his hand. Then he put it down slowly. 'They've done something to her eyes,' he said.

With an odd croak of excitement, Peter Zametsky stood up, speaking quickly and incomprehensibly to his wife.

'We have to go,' Klima said finally. 'My husband knows where they are keeping her.'

It was like waking from a dream. Angie moved her

legs slowly then gently touched her eyes. There was a distant roar within her head and an ache behind the eyes but, when she opened them, she was dazzled by the light. Someone was touching her wrist. A woman with a distant, soothing voice.

She assumed that she had fainted. Memories of the night's events seemed as though they had happened somewhere else, and to someone else. She remembered the gun, being tied to a chair, the sinister dark-haired woman with the Eastern European accent. Then there was the rabbit, at one moment able to avoid the vicious electric pole wielded by the man, the next unseeing and panic-stricken. Its body had seemed to shudder when it had run blindly into the prod before collapsing. What had the man said as it lay, twitching in its death throes. 'Fi-Fi's last experiment,' he had said, almost sadly.

The low moaning sound that Angie heard as her head cleared seemed close. Then she realised it came from her.

'It's all right,' the voice said. 'You're all right now.'

For some reason, she was afraid to open her eyes, as if the blinding machine, the fake camera, was still directed at her. It had been like a blow to the head and, after the shock had receded, the true horror had begun.

'Open your eyes, my sweet.' The voice was almost a whisper now. 'You're safe.'

Through half-closed eyelids, Angie saw a hand, its long index finger stroking the dark red weal on her left wrist where the ropes had been, as if to smooth away the pain. She raised her head slowly, and opened her eyes.

'All over.' Alice Markwick's face was close to hers. Her sight restored, Angie saw in cruel detail its every contour – the tributaries of wrinkles leading into her wide eyes, the flecks of dark on the cold grey of the irises, the covering of down on her upper lip, the maze of tiny red veins at the base of her nostrils, the dark red tongue moving between the thin, glistening, grooved lips as she spoke.

'He's gone now. I've sent him away, Angie. I've untied you now that the business part's over.' The cold hand tightened on Angie's wrist. 'It's just you and me now. The night is young.'

Angie leaned back, pressing against the chair, but was too weak to escape Alice's insistent grip. 'What do you want from me?' she asked.

'Company. Girl talk. The usual things.'

The woman was mad. That much was certain. Since her hit-man, the man who had captured her, had gone and Paul had been set up for the following day, she had changed beyond recognition from professional woman to husky-voiced vamp. 'I want to hear all about you,' Alice was saying. 'Every little thing.' Angie thought she preferred the professional woman.

Over Alice's shoulder, she saw a hypodermic needle lying on the desk.

'Yes,' Alice said, following her eyes. 'I gave you a little jab while you were unconscious. It's a relaxant, nothing alarming. Now – ' She walked behind Angie's chair ' – if you'll excuse me a moment.'

Closing her eyes wearily, Angie said nothing. Fear had given way to a desperate need to sleep. Her head fell forward. Somewhere distant, she thought she heard a rustle, like the sound of falling clothes.

'Angie.' A hand cupped her chin and raised her head. She must have lost consciousness again. 'How do I look?'

Alice Markwick turned girlishly in front of her. Instead of a business suit, she was wearing a sheer black velcro dress over black tights. Her dark make-up was absurdly over-dramatic.

'You look like a witch,' Angie sighed.

Alice laughed and opened a small black handbag that was hooked over her arm. 'A devil more like.' A pair of handcuffs dangled from her hand. 'And you're my disciple.'

'What are you talking about?'

Alice stepped forward and touched Angie's face with the handcuffs.

'It's party time, my little one,' she said. 'I'm going to take you out on the town. We're going to celebrate in style.'

Like her husband, Klima Zametsky was seeing nothing, but that was because, as Paul's Saab hurtled through the streets of London, her eyes were tight shut. The country roads at eighty and ninety miles an hour she could take; Paul's town driving was another matter. She had gone beyond fear and nausea into a state in which she merely waited for the sickening crunch of metal, the searing pain and blackness of the inevitable crash.

'We're approaching a large roundabout with signs to Wembley and Willesden,' Paul said urgently. 'Which way?'

Peter made a sound which he interpreted as 'Left'.

As the car took the corner with a squeal of tyres, Peter added another instruction.

'The turning right after the Blue Turk pub,' Klima said faintly. 'Second right into the industrial estate.'

When they arrived, driving slowly past the offices of Markwick Instruments plc, there were no cars parked outside and no lights from the inside of the building.

'Now what?' Paul stopped the car around the corner and hesitated for a moment. He was hardly in a position to climb in through a window, and, of his passengers, one was blind, the other frozen with fear. 'Is there a back entrance?' He turned to look at Peter who was in the back seat.

Before his hairless, unseeing face, Peter held two keys.

It was a version of hell, Angie thought, as she stood unsteadily at the entrance to a large, dark room whose strategically placed lighting revealed murals of spectacular obscenity. In the centre of the room was a small, brightly lit swimming-pool surrounded by fake pillars and marble steps. The place was noisy and crowded and occasionally wild laughter could be heard above the pulsating music.

'Welcome to Slaves,' Alice said to her. 'London's wildest club. You'll love this, little one.' She stepped forward, tugging the handcuffs which connected her left wrist with Angie's right.

Angie stumbled forward. Her head was clearing but this felt like a dream – the Greek, neo-classical decadence, the noise, the pungent smell of marijuana. A tall black woman with a shaven head wandered past them, trailing a dog lead at the end of which, held by a black leather studded collar around the neck, was a subdued, slightly plump woman in her thirties. Both mistress and slave glanced at Angie appraisingly.

They found a table near the swimming-pool and a young waitress in a revealing toga took their order.

'I don't see any men,' Angie said quietly.

'Butch, fem, mistress, slave – they're all here,' Alice said, her eyes sparkling with pleasure. 'This is the first time I've been able to come with a partner.'

Angie looked at a trim, short-haired couple, one in a leather shirt, the other in a denim suit, and wondered vaguely who was meant to be dominating whom.

'You're crazy,' she said.

Fleetingly, as the three of them stood in Alice Markwick's office, Paul wondered what kind of woman it was who developed a bizarre secret weapon, planning to sell it back to the country from which she had fled, and who, for inexplicable reasons of her own, had become involved with Clay Wentworth.

Then he heard a sound from the adjoining executive bathroom.

'My husband wants you to follow him,' whispered Klima.

Feeling his way along the wall, Peter led them through a hidden door and down a steep spiral wooden stairway. The three of them paused before a heavy metal door, beyond which no sound or light came. Paul took the key and silently turned it in the lock. He pushed open the door and stepped inside.

Behind him, Peter groped for a switch that turned on the harsh strip lighting.

The first thing that Paul saw was a dead white rabbit lying in a run on the far side of the room. Then, near the desk, two wooden chairs sat facing one another. Beside one of them, there lay two coils of rope.

Peter said something as his hands ran over the open door of a wall safe by the desk, then groped inside its dark interior.

'The Opteeka B camera is gone,' Klima translated.

Near the ropes a small pile of women's clothes lay in a heap on the floor. Paul picked up a dark blue jacket, then let it fall over the chair.

'Angie's?' asked Klima.

Paul shook his head.

A dreary monotone emanated from across the

room where Peter stood. Klima seemed embarrassed, briefly lost for words.

'What's he saying?' Paul asked.

Klima blushed. 'This woman,' she said. 'My husband thinks that she likes girls.'

It was a strange paradox, to feel free at Slaves, but that was how it was with Alice. She had been here before but never with a partner and Slaves was not a place for meeting new friends. Most of the few loners there liked to watch and Alice had never been a watcher.

She noticed the covert glances in their direction, the way the other women looked at them. She smiled at Angie who was staring ahead of her. They made a good couple, one of them dark, tall and dominant, the other young, blonde and adorably submissive. 'Happy?' she asked.

'Take this absurd thing off my hand,' Angie said. 'I feel ridiculous.'

'Why should I trust you?' Alice asked, a flirtatious trill in the voice.

There was no alternative. For the first time that evening, Angie looked her full in the eye. 'You can trust me,' she said softly.

'You like it here?'

'Very much.'

Alice looked at her suspiciously. Was it possible that this sense of freedom had clouded her judgement – that the knowledge that, within twenty-four hours, her future would be secure had allowed her to relax her guard?

Angie seemed to have moved closer, so that her face was inches away from Alice's. Moments ago, she was pale and unsteady; now the colour had returned to her cheeks.

Slaves had that effect on a girl. 'Unlock me,' she said, 'and maybe we can get away from this noise.'

Alice ran a hand gently down Angie's forearm, toying briefly with the handcuff around her wrist. 'D'you like champagne breakfasts?' she asked.

'My favourite.'

'Then a quiet day at the flat, watching television?'

'The races?'

Alice laughed softly. 'Of course, the races. The Kim Muir Steeplechase. Then it's back to your little friend.'

'Please.' The girl's blonde hair was almost touching her face now. Alice imagined she could feel the warmth of her flesh. 'Unlock me.'

Alice looked at her sideways. 'I'm not sure about you.'

'I – ' Angie went through a pantomime of girlish embarrassment. 'I went to a girls' boarding-school, you know.'

'What happens there?'

'It makes this – ' Angie nodded confidingly in the direction of the throng of chain and leather gathered across the swimming-pool ' – seem like the fancy-dress at a church fete.'

315

Alice sipped her glass of wine thoughtfully. She had always prided herself on the erotic instinct that alerted her to girls who were broad-minded in every sense. As soon as she had seen Angie, tied so heart-breakingly to the chair in the office basement, she felt an affinity that was more than the mere tug of attraction. At first she had put it down to the stress of the moment but now, as she filled her glass yet again, she was sure she was right. 'How strange,' she said, looking deep into Angie's eyes, 'that something so bad could lead to something so good.'

'So bad?'

'I didn't want it, not all the nastiness and violence and lying. I just wanted to make enough from my husband's firm to retire, and live the life I was meant to lead. But – ' Alice waved the free hand which held her glass, spilling wine on the table ' – there's no money in lasers. You think there is, but there isn't. Not peaceful, friendly lasers. So when Zametsky, out of some weird scientific curiosity, began researching into optics, I encouraged him. It needed extra invest-ment so I brought in Wentworth and Calloway.'

Angie listened patiently to the older woman's ram-bling account. Doubtless Paul would be expecting her to be taking notes but right now Angie had only one thought on her mind – to get away from this drunk, and very possibly insane, lesbian. 'What about Digby Welcome?' she asked, more from a need to keep the conversation going than out of genuine curiosity.

'That was something different, a sort of long-term

blackmail. He introduced me to my husband when I first came to London. Welcome knew rather more about my past than was good for him.'

For a moment, the two of them sat in silence, Alice lost in the fog of memory, Angie deciding when best to raise once again the question of unlocking the handcuffs.

'All over tomorrow,' Alice said suddenly. 'One last obstacle – one last little death – before I hand over the whole thing to someone else. Or rather – ' she smiled crookedly ' – three last obstacles.'

'Maybe we could celebrate together?' Angie whispered.

'Would you?' Alice seemed almost tearful. 'You'd stay? After the race?'

Angie raised the wrist held by the hand-cuffs. Frowning, Alice reached for her bag and produced a small key. Fumbling drunkenly, she released the lock.

'Thank you,' said Angie, rubbing her wrist.

'Poor you.' Alice lowered her head to kiss the deep red mark, closing her eyes as if to shut out the noise and vulgarity all around them.

She never saw the wine bottle raised above her like an executioner's axe, catching the light as it fell, shattering with implacable fury on the back of her skull.

Angie ran through the dark streets of Islington. Freedom was a taxi-ride – a ten-minute drive to Mary's flat. Monday was an early night for her and, even if she were entertaining a man friend, she would normally be at home.

Her head was quite clear now but she was trembling from shock. If the need to escape from Slaves hadn't been so pressing, she might have fainted herself as Alice slumped forward, blood pouring from the back of her head. Luckily the regulars at the club regarded violence between partners as normal. By the time they had realised that this was rather more than an advanced love game, she had slipped away.

She turned onto a main street and, seeing three men walking on the far pavement, she slowed to a walk. In London vulnerability could attract the wrong kind of attention. Images from the evening crowded in on her. The death throes of a rabbit in a brightly lit basement. The impact of the camera, throwing her backwards. The slender finger, tracing the rope mark on her wrist. The crazed dark eyes, unfocused by desire and alcohol, staring at her longingly in the club. Snatches of conversation – nastiness and violence and lying, all over tomorrow, one little death, celebrate together –

As Angie shuddered with revulsion, a black taxi, its light shining like a beacon, turned a corner towards her. She held up her arm and it pulled up beside her. She gave the driver Mary's address and settled into the back seat, still breathing heavily.

One little death. Now what did that mean?

Chapter 15

Of the approximately forty thousand assembled at Cheltenham racecourse on the afternoon of Tuesday 12 March for the first day of the National Hunt Festival, slightly under half were there because of an abiding interest in racehorses. The rest were in attendance for professional, social or ritual reasons. For the pickpocket or the society hostess or the Irish clergyman, Cheltenham covered three red-letter days in the diary. To miss it would be unthinkable.

Tino Marchesi liked seeing the English at play – in fact, as he strutted across the grass in front of the grandstand in his green checked suit and trilby, a new pair of binoculars around his neck, he felt almost English himself. He wondered vaguely whether in America, where he was about to become a leading member of the brotherhood, such occasions as the National Hunt Festival existed. He hoped so. They reminded him of the good things in life – friends, sportsmanship, nice clothes, money.

Behind Tino, his son Giorgio slouched moodily with his friend Salvatore. The older man glanced back and smiled. Sometimes he despaired of the younger generation. Both wore bulky long leather coats and dark glasses and looked around them as if at any moment they could be jumped by some hit-man among Cheltenham's army of tweed and cavalry twill. If they had been wearing signs reading 'Hoodlum' and 'Gangster' around their necks, they could hardly have made their backgrounds more obvious.

'Relax,' said Tino. 'You're frightening the race-goers.'

The three men found a bar but, to Giorgio's disgust, they had to fight their way through a crowd of loud and happy middle-aged men and women before being served. It was a strange and unwelcome sensation to be one of a crowd. In London, they were given space at the bar and were served almost before they had ordered.

'So.' A glass of champagne in his hand at last, Tino looked at the racecard. 'Ours is the last race. Will our guitar-playing friend Mr Calloway be here?'

Salvatore smiled broadly, displaying a vulpine set of white teeth. 'He had to rehearse, he said. "Gonna give it, like, a miss, man." '

'But he's told us everything we need to know.'

'One of the last three fences. We take one each. After they make their move, we grab the machine and disappear,' said Tino. 'No macho stuff, okay? No violence.'

'Sure.' Salvatore nodded, while Giorgio looked disappointed.

Tino sighed. Today was not going to be easy.

'Ey!' Salvatore said angrily as a tall woman swathed in mink pushed past him, carrying two glasses before her like a mother in a parents' day egg and spoon race.

'Sorry, darling.' Zena Wentworth looked over her shoulder at the dark young man in a black leather coat.

'The noise, my dear,' she muttered to herself as she progressed through the crowd. 'The *people*.'

This was definitely the last race meeting she was ever going to attend. Apart from its few advantages – being able to wear mink without getting dirty looks and the chance to chat with friends from London, for example – Cheltenham was every bit as depressing as Plumpton or Wincanton.

With some difficulty, she fought her way through to a corner where Sir Denis Wentworth sat, staring at the throng around him with evident disapproval.

'Here we are,' she said, placing a whisky and soda before him and sitting down. 'Whoever said the middle classes knew how to behave in public had never been to Cheltenham on Champion Hurdle day.'

Sir Denis looked at her, his face a picture of apathy.

'It's like a rugger scrum back there,' Zena added, nodding in the direction of the bar.

The old man sighed, then raised his glass. 'Chin-chin,' he said quietly.

'Here's to Clay's last race,' Zena smiled.

'Hmm?' Momentarily Sir Denis seemed interested.

'He told me this morning. Win or lose, he's hanging up his boots. I don't think his heart is in it, to tell the truth.' She sipped at her drink, an orange juice, and grimaced. 'Clay gives up racing, I go on the wagon – it's quite a day.'

'You give up booze?' Sir Denis sniffed. 'Fat chance.'

'No booze, no substance abuse. I'll be a new woman.'

Zena smiled brightly but her father-in-law looked away as if to confirm that whatever she did, however she reformed, his view of her would remain the same. Christ, she needed a drink – an afternoon spent with Sir Denis Wentworth would have a methodist reaching for the vodka. Not for the first time she wished that Lol and Suzie Calloway were there – even Alice, who had behaved so oddly recently, would have broken the monotony. It was a puzzle why Clay's little fan club had deserted him at what could be his finest hour.

'There's something else I'm giving up,' she said.

Sir Denis glanced across the table with a weary *now*-what expression.

'Yes,' said Zena. 'I'm giving up Clay. I've decided to leave him.'

For a moment, there was silence between them. Sir Denis took another sip of his whisky, swilled it around his mouth, and swallowed it as if it were cough medicine. Then he smacked his lips and, for the first time that Zena could remember, he smiled, revealing yellow teeth and pale gums.

'Excellent,' he said.

'It's no good,' Angie said, as she walked slowly beside Paul up the slight incline towards the weighing-room. 'I've tried to like all this –' she looked at the race-goers hurrying past them to see the first three horses in the Champion Hurdle enter the winners' enclosure '– but I guess I'm just not a racing person.'

Paul laughed. 'You've hardly had the best introduction,' he said.

'I still feel sorry for the horses.'

She was paler than usual after last night, Paul decided, but otherwise she seemed to have survived her ordeal at the hands of Alice Markwick without ill effects. She had been tearful when she arrived at Crazy Mary's flat to find Paul was waiting there too. After visiting the Markwick offices, he had sent the Zametskys home and then, on a hunch, had rung Mary, who had suggested he should stay at her flat. After an hour or so, Angie had arrived at the door, upset but unharmed.

'There's only one horse I'm worried about today,' Paul said, 'and that's Tanglewood. I've got to have a word with Bill Scott in the weighing-room.' He squeezed her arm. 'Stay here. I'll be out in a minute.'

He felt bad leaving her alone after what she had been through, but it had been her decision to come to Cheltenham and it was important to reach Bill with the information Angie had gleaned from Alice last night. One last obstacle, she had said – rather, three last obstacles. It made sense.

Jim Wilson was the first to see him. 'Can't keep you away from this place, can they?' he said. 'How's the back coming on?'

Paul waved his walking-stick. 'I'll be throwing this away soon,' he said.

'Good on yer, Pauly.'

Bill Scott was chatting to Dave Smart, a cup of tea in his hand. His ride in the first race had finished well down the field, but most of the tipsters in the morning papers had suggested that, if Tanglewood could beat Skinflint, the Kim Muir would be his.

'Hullo, it's Hopalong Sherlock,' Bill said as Paul approached. 'Any news?'

Paul smiled. He didn't blame Bill for being sceptical – foul play was part of racing and, if you worried about who was trying to stop you winning, you'd never get into the saddle. Sensing that he wasn't wanted, Dave Smart wandered off, leaving Bill and Paul alone.

'It's happening,' Paul said. 'We know for sure.'

'So I keep him covered up as long as possible.'

'They're going for you at the third last, the down-hill fence.'

'How d'you know?'

'It doesn't matter. Stay in the centre of the course,

324

covered up if possible, and leave the rest to me.'

Bill shrugged. 'No problem,' he said. 'I wouldn't have hit the front by the third last anyway.'

Wishing him luck, Paul was about to return to Angie when he saw Clay sitting alone in a corner.

Never had the man looked less like a jockey. He was too big, the colour on his fleshy cheeks was too pale, the expression on his face suggested that he would rather be anywhere than riding one of the favourites at Cheltenham.

Paul was standing in front of him for a moment before Clay came out of his daydreams.

'Ah, the poker expert,' he said, aiming unsuccessfully for a jocular, patronizing tone. 'What a surprise to see you here.'

'You told me it was all over. I don't believe you,' Paul said quietly. 'If your people try to stop Tanglewood today, the world's going to know about it.'

'I told you after our little game of poker,' Clay said. 'I'm finished with all that.'

'Is your friend Alice Markwick here?' Paul asked very suddenly.

'I haven't seen her. I have better things to do than worry about who's here to see me.'

'Seems ungrateful under the circumstances.' Paul made as if to move away, then added, as an afterthought, 'I believe she had a small accident last night. You might pay her a visit – ' he smiled ' – after you've ridden your winner.'

325

Outside the jockeys' changing-room Paul saw Ginnie Matthews waiting near the scales for Clay to weigh out.

'Is that bloody jockey of mine in here?' she asked Paul.

'He seems to have a lot on his mind,' Paul said. He hesitated, wondering whether to tell Ginnie that he was convinced friends of her owners were out to ensure that Skinflint won, but then thought better of it. Either way, she wasn't involved.

'Paul,' she said. 'We need to talk.'

'About Clay?' Paul asked wearily.

'No, about you.' Ginnie frowned. 'I need an assistant trainer and was wondering whether you would be interested.'

Paul's first thought was of Angie. She was not exactly in love with racing and the idea of more chilly days waiting outside weighing-rooms was unlikely to appeal to her. 'I'd need to think about it,' he said.

'No hurry.' Ginnie saw Clay walking gloomily towards the scales with the saddle under his arm. 'Here we go,' she said.

'Good luck, Mrs Matthews,' Paul said, touching her lightly on the arm.

At first he didn't recognize the couple as they walked towards the entrance to the paddock – the old man seemed too old, the woman more elegant and calm than he remembered. Then, as if she sensed his presence, Zena Wentworth turned and stared at them for a moment. Her father-in-law tottered on, ignoring her.

'That's Zena Wentworth, isn't it?' Angie asked.

'Aye,' said Paul, remembering the cold knowing hand as it edged up his thigh. 'Let's get down to the racecourse.'

But it was too late. Hands sunk deep in the pockets of her mink coat, Zena walked slowly towards Paul and Angie. 'I wanted to tell you the second thing,' she said simply.

'Second thing?'

'What I was about to tell you the other day on the telephone before I was interrupted.'

'You told me enough.' Paul made to move away, but Angie caught his arm.

'No,' she said. 'It might be important.' She turned to Zena. 'Go on, Mrs Wentworth.'

'*Cherchez le père*,' said Zena. Then, as if regretting what she had said, she turned and walked quickly towards the paddock.

'What on earth was that about?' Paul asked.

'The father,' said Angie. 'She's telling us Sir Denis is involved too.'

The decision to make the hit at the third fence from home was not stupid, Paul reflected as he made his way down the course with Angie. Although, as Bill Scott had pointed out, there was the risk of Tangle-wood still being covered up by other horses, there was a good chance at the end of three miles that the field would be strung out. It was a downhill fence that often caused grief as jockeys kicked on for home, so that there would be few awkward questions in the event of a crashing fall. The fact that the crowd around the fence was thinner than at the last two fences would make Tanglewood an easier target.

'Anyone you recognize?' Paul asked as they crossed the course to the inside rail where a group of photographers had gathered. Angie scanned the men as they chatted easily to one another and shook her head.

'I hope Alice Markwick was right about it being the third last,' she said quietly.

Across the course, the crowd were now hurrying away from the paddock to place bets or to take up a favoured vantage point in the stands. As the field of fifteen made its way down to parade in front of the grandstand, Paul glanced at his racecard.

Under normal conditions, it was a race of limited interest to him. Tanglewood was no more than a good handicapper but had the advantage of being ridden by one of the best amateurs around. Skinflint, the class horse of the race, was carrying two distinct drawbacks – top weight and Mr Clay Wentworth. Beyond them, there was a young Irish horse called Fiddlers Three whose best form had been over two and a half miles, a grey mare from the north called Busy Lizzie and, also in with a chance of a place, a big plain six-year-old called The Killjoy who was trained by a successful permit holder down in the West Country.

As he headed the parade, Skinflint looked about him like a horse for whom Cheltenham, with all its excitement and drama, was his natural home. Ginnie had him looking superb and, briefly, Paul felt a pang of envy for Clay, who had done so little to deserve a horse of his calibre.

Angie laid her hand on his as he leaned on his walking-stick. 'You're out there, aren't you?' she said quietly. 'Whatever happens, you've got racing in the blood.'

'Yes.' Paul thought of his brief conversation with Ginnie Matthews, and knew that he wanted to accept her offer. 'I'd rather be up there than down here.'

Like any good professional, the photographer had walked the course. Now he stood some hundred years away from the jockey and his girlfriend across the course on the stands side, and made his final plans.

Something had gone wrong last night, as he had known it would. The moment Mrs Markwick had looked at the girl, there was trouble in the air. That brisk, cruel competence had softened to something almost vulnerable. The photographer had protested when she had told him that she would guard Raven's girlfriend until the following day, but it was no good – Mrs Markwick had that look in her eyes and, as usual, she got her way.

He took the machine with him, though. There was no way that he was going to risk leaving that with her.

When he had called in the morning, there was no reply, and here was the girl, free and with her boyfriend. The photographer ran a hand tenderly over the heavy black machine that hung around his neck. It didn't matter. They couldn't stop him now.

His instructions were laughably simple.

In a darkened flat in Islington, Alice Markwick watched the field for the Kim Muir Steeplechase at Cheltenham parading before the stands. Her head was bandaged. She hated herself for last night. But she was confident. Not even Raven or his vicious little bitch of a girlfriend could stop the photographer now.

Freedom, at last.

'Good luck, Clay,' she said, and laughed.

None of the photographers at the third last fence had the look of a killer, Paul decided. Several of them he recognized as regulars at race meetings, freelances and agency men. A few of the racegoers had small cameras but nothing that answered the description of Opteeka B that Peter Zametsky had given him.

'I think we may be on the wrong side of the fence,' said Paul, glancing up the hill to the bend some hundred yards before it. 'You get a clearer view of the field as it's approaching the third last from the stand side.'

'Shall I stay here?' Angie asked quietly. 'Just in case you're wrong.'

The field were turning in front of the stand to canter down to the start. 'No, this time we stick together.'

It was as they were crossing the course that Paul saw the dark young man in a long leather coat pushing his way through the crowd on the stands side. Although he was hardly the typical Cheltenham spectator, the man had no camera. Languidly, he walked on the course, staring straight ahead of him.

A racecourse official nearby shouted, 'Horses coming!' and the leather-coated man, abandoning his dignity, scurried over to Angie's side of the course.

Paul looked across and smiled. A small-time spiv. There was nothing to worry about there.

Cazzo, he hated horses. Salvatore looked around him in the hope that no one had seen his moment of panic. A slim blonde girl glanced at him briefly, then turned away. She was just his type. Salvatore sighed – the sooner this business was over and he could return to his life of minor crime and major pleasure, the happier he would be.

Looking up the racecourse, he could see Giorgio in place at the second last fence. Doubtless Tino was covering the last. The waiting was over.

The man in the black leather coat had seemed absurd as Clay had cantered past him, leaning against Skinflint, who seemed to be pulling harder than usual today. That was one of the few points in favour of riding in races; it gave you a chance to look down at the people, mere spectators, who had come to see you.

Yes, this would be his last race, whatever happened. Briefly, he envisaged himself at some future National Hunt Festival, a solid comfortable figure in the paddock watching as some wretched little jockey was given a leg-up onto one of his horses. By then everybody would be happy – Ginnie, because Skinflint could be ridden by a professional; his father, because he was no longer obliged to come racing; and, above all, Clay himself because he was grounded, his feet on *terra firma* for the entire afternoon.

He cantered past the starter's rostrum, turned and trotted back to the first fence. 'Clear round, eh?' he said quietly, patting Skinflint in front of the fence.

'Are you going on?' Bill Scott asked him.

'We'll be up there,' Clay said, smiling palely. Normally he disliked this habit jockeys had of asking what kind of race you intended to ride – it was like a business rival casually asking for details of your development plans – but he had no worries with Scott or Tanglewood.

Briefly he wondered why Bill Scott had bothered to ask him whether Skinflint would be among the front-runners. He was the sort of jockey who did his homework and would know how Skinflint was ridden. Of course, when Clay hit the front at the top of the hill, rather than making his run later, Scott would be surprised – but then Tanglewood would be pulled from the rest of the field like a thread from a skein of wool, into the sights of Opteeka B. Clay was confident that he could outstay the rest of the field up the Cheltenham hill.

The starter stepped forward and, as the field circled around him, began to call out the names of the jockeys.

Petrin felt comfortable in his new Savile Row suit. Perhaps, when this little stunt was over, he could consider staying in Britain. Across the course, the field was lining up. No, better stick to his plan; America was better. 'They're off,' said the racecourse commentator.

'For Christ's sake, pretend to shoot some film!' Petrin nudged the overweight figure before him. With a resentful sigh, Bernard Green looked into the eyepiece. 'Who'd have thought, when I joined the Party at Cambridge, that I'd end up as a fake cameraman at a race meeting?' he muttered.

'You do it beautifully,' said Petrin, raising an expensive pair of binoculars to his eyes.

After the first mile, Clay found himself wondering whether the plan to stop Tanglewood had been necessary. Skinflint loved Cheltenham and seemed to respond to the atmosphere of a big crowd. At every fence, he outjumped the horses around him, gaining so much in the air that Clay had difficult preventing him from hitting the front.

As the field passed the stands, he was going easily

in third place behind the grey Busy Lizzie who had set a good pace, and the Irish horse Fiddlers Three. Four or five lengths behind the leading group, the rest of the field was bunched up and, as they turned into the country, Clay looked over his shoulder. There was no sign of Tanglewood.

The pace quickened down the back straight and, when Busy Lizzie made a mistake at the waterjump, Clay had no alternative but to move up on the outside of Fiddlers Three, whose jockey was already niggling at him. Behind him, the leaders of the following group were moving closer but, from the sound of the cracking whips and jockeys' curses, none of them was going as easily as Skinflint.

'Give him a breather going up the little hill before the open ditch,' Ginnie had said. 'Stay with them until the third last, then make the best of your way home.' Clay kicked Skinflint into the open ditch. The horse stood off outside the wings and landed two lengths in front of Fiddlers Three.

'Here we go,' muttered Clay. This was where he disobeyed his trainer's instructions. Bill Scott was too experienced a jockey to allow himself to be given the slip. As he set off in pursuit, he would provide a perfect unimpeded target for Clay's unofficial helper among the photographers.

Clay was five lengths clear as he gathered Skinflint for the downhill fence. He glanced at the crowd on the far side and, as if some distinct, instinctive part of his brain were tuned into the fatal laser of Opteeka

B, he sat up straight in the saddle.

'No,' he screamed.

But it was too late.

It took Paul the briefest of moments to realize two things. The first was that the man operating Opteeka B was not standing by the fence but some fifty yards back. The second was that his target wasn't Tanglewood at all.

Simultaneously with Clay's scream, Skinflint faltered, his gallop becoming an unstoppable, drunken stagger into the base of the fence. Almost balletically, the horse's hindquarters formed an arc over the fence while miraculously, and fatally, Clay stayed in the saddle, his eyes dilated with horror as the earth hurtled towards him.

There was an unmistakeable crack as horse and jockey hit the ground together.

Beside him, Angie gasped. She had looked away from Skinflint up the hill. 'Look!' she said suddenly. 'It's – ' but already she was running.

'Angie!'

The photographer glanced back and, sensing trouble, he put the heavy camera under his arm and jogged, casually at first, up the hill.

'Bastard!' Angie kicked viciously at his trailing leg and as the man sprawled on his face, sending Opteeka B flying, she fell on him. By the time he had recovered from the shock, Paul stood over them, his walking-stick raised.

'It's him,' Angie said, breathing heavily as she stood over him. 'He's the man who kidnapped me last night.'

Behind them, the field was streaming up the hill to the Cheltenham roar, but already a small crowd was gathering around Paul, Angie and the photographer.

'My camera,' the man said weakly.

'Fetch the police,' Paul said to a young man in a dark leather coat who had just run up. Briefly the man looked alarmed, then muttering 'Yeah, sure,' he walked off quickly towards the stands.

Paul looked back to the fence, where Skinflint still lay on his side. A few yards away, two ambulancemen were crouched over the inert form of Clay Wentworth.

'Why Wentworth?' he asked the man cowering on the floor.

The photographer muttered, 'Orders from the top. Give me back my camera and I'll explain everything to you.'

'Camera?' Paul glanced at Angie, who shook her head. 'What camera?'

It didn't feel like triumph, merely the satisfaction of a job done well. Tonight, when the photographer returned, she would contact Petrin for the exchange – Opteeka B for financial security and freedom. Alice looked at the silent television screen on which presenters of a children's television show were dancing about in mute inanity. Perhaps, if Clay's race had not been the last to be televised, she would have been treated to a few more shots of her business partner, prostrate on the ground where he belonged.

She imagined that he was not badly injured, simply shaken up enough to understand that no man exploited Alice Markwick and emerged a winner.

There was a price for everything.

The machine was still warm. That was odd. Josef Petrin ran a hand over the dark metal of Opteeka B which lay on the passenger seat of his hired car. It had been so simple, so painless, so casual a victory, that he felt almost tenderly towards this country in which crime was as easy as picking up an object from the ground and merging into the crowd. Bernard had squawked when Petrin had told him to take the train back to London, but that had been an easy decision. The fat Englishman belonged to the past, to the days of grim ideology and patriotic duty; he wouldn't understand that times were different now, that it was every man for himself. Doubtless, Petrin's motherland could use a device like Opteeka B, but he was going private. This time tomorrow he would be in New York. The CIA maybe? There was too much risk there. He had been told the Mafia paid well for the right product. He even had a contact, a man called Guiseppi Vercelloni.

Petrin smiled. A new suit. A new toy. A new future. It had been a useful trip.

* * *

They stood in a gloomy little group outside the Treatment Room, as the last few racegoers made their way home, their conversation desultory and weary.

'How's the horse?' Paul asked.

Ginnie shrugged. 'Tough little bugger. He'll be a bit sore in the morning but the vet says nothing's broken.'

Again, Paul saw Skinflint turning, as if in slow-motion, the look of paralysed fear on Clay's face, the crack which, he now knew, was of a human bone not a horse's.

'They say our friend is co-operating with the police,' he said. 'Alice Markwick will be receiving a call at any moment.'

'There's no evidence,' Angie said quietly. 'What can they do without the laser?'

'Apparently the whole thing is documented at Markwick Instruments. The police had received a tip-off from Lol Calloway and picked up three Italians after the last race. They didn't have the camera but seemed to know something about it.'

The moment they saw Zena standing at the door-way to the Treatment Room, it was clear that questions were unnecessary.

'He's dead,' she said flatly. 'Broken neck. Multiple head injuries. He never regained consciousness.'

Angie stepped forward and took Zena by the arm.

'It was Alice Markwick,' said Paul. 'She wanted him out of the way.'

'No.' Sir Denis Wentworth appeared at the door-way and stood, staring across the racecourse. He seemed older, a diminished and pathetic figure. 'No,' he said. 'It was me.'

'He always was Daddy's boy,' Zena said with a trace of bitterness in her voice.

Sir Denis spoke as if in a trance. 'You want to ride horses, I told him, you ride to win. Prove yourself like I proved myself. Get yourself the best horse and win the best race. Then I'll know you're man enough to take over from me.' Tears filled his eyes at last. 'Of course, he couldn't do it the straight way, he had to cheat.'

'You old fool,' Zena turned on him savagely. 'He may have been weak but he was braver than you'll ever be. And more honest.'

'He was giving that horse a good ride,' Paul said. 'If it hadn't been for the Markwick woman – '

But Sir Denis had turned and was walking with silent dignity towards the car park, as if he knew his son better than anyone and that, whatever had happened, he had been right, that he had done it the Wentworth way. They watched him as he made his way out of the racecourse without once looking back, an old man, alone.

Chapter 16

It was high summer and, although he received the occasional call from journalists raking over the ashes of what had become known as 'The Wentworth Scandal', Paul had allowed his life to slip into the routine of an assistant trainer.

Sometimes, when leading the string out on a quiet old 'chaser called Slavedriver, he found himself thinking about Alex, about Clay Wentworth and the nightmarish events of last season, but the moment would pass. He had an unspoken agreement with Ginnie Matthews that nothing from the past should distract them from planning for the forthcoming season. Once, when they were walking past the field in which Skinflint had been roughed off for the summer, Ginnie had muttered, 'If only he knew,' and Paul had smiled but said nothing.

In September, he would be required to appear in court as a witness in the case of the Crown vs Alice Markwick in which the principal charge was one of

341

aggravated manslaughter. Although the prototype for Opteeka B had disappeared, the evidence of the photographer had been enough to build a substantial case against her. A number of further charges relating to the way she ran her business were said to be under active consideration.

Paul avoided taking breakfast with Ginnie, preferring to spend the time with Angie who had moved in with him, working as a freelance nurse in the Lambourn area.

So she was there when Paul received the letter from Sir Denis Wentworth and was leaning over his shoulder as she read it, with growing astonishment, at the breakfast table.

Dear Mr Raven

I write to you regarding the death of my son Mr Clay Wentworth.

It is now almost four months since the unfortunate events at Cheltenham and I have had much time in which to consider them. As you may be aware, I hold you in no way responsible for Clay's accident although I find it regrettable that you did not think fit to inform the police of your suspicions of Mrs Markwick.

The blame, I accept, is hers, for her financial greed, and mine, for the unreasonable expectations I had of my son. To demand that he should 'prove himself' in a way that was independent of my influence was, I now see, an

impossible burden for him to have carried. I
regret this.

I have spoken briefly to my former daughter-in-
law Zena Wentworth who believes that some
sort of compensation is due to you for the accident which ended your career. Although my
legal advisers tell me that you have no case in
law against me, I have decided to make a one-
off gesture of goodwill towards you.

As you may be aware, my son left his racehorses
to me. I have resolved to sell all of them except
for Skinflint. That horse is now legally yours.

I trust this meets with your approval. A formal
letter follows. Mrs Matthews has been informed
of my decision.

Please note that this action is taken without
prejudice and is in no sense an admission of
guilt.

Confirmation of receipt of this letter would be
appreciated.

Yours sincerely

Sir Denis Wentworth

For a moment, there was silence as Paul read the
letter again.

'His normal charming self, I see,' Angie said.

'Poor old bastard,' Paul said. 'It's probably as near
to being generous as he's ever been.'

'What will you do?' asked Angie. 'We can't afford training fees.'

'If Ginnie comes in as a partner, I can.' Paul smiled. 'You can come racing again – you know how you like that.'

Standing behind him, Angie put both arms around him and kissed his ear. 'The humane, politically correct thing to do would be to retire him.'

'All right. After he's won his third Gold Cup.'

Angie laughed. 'You're a cruel bastard, Paul Raven,' she said, allowing her hand to slip inside his shirt.

Deep in thought, Paul took the hand, kissed it and stood up. He walked slowly towards the bedroom, then turned, smiling at the door. 'How about a celebration?' he asked.

'What about your career? Your horse? What about racing?' There was a hint of mockery in Angie's voice as she walked slowly towards him.

Paul put his arm round her.

'Racing can wait,' he said.

10
18

12, AVENUE D'ITALIE. PARIS XIIIe

Sur l'auteur

Peter Tremayne, de son vrai nom Peter Berresford Ellis, est né le 10 mars 1943 à Coventry, en Angleterre. Ses origines familiales – à la fois bretonnes, irlandaises, écossaises et galloises – expliquent sans nul doute sa passion pour la culture celte. Après un premier livre sur le combat pour l'indépendance du pays de Galles en 1968, il devient écrivain à plein temps à partir de 1975.

Peter Tremayne est l'auteur de très nombreux pamphlets, nouvelles, biographies et essais. Il est aussi connu pour ses récits fantastiques fondés sur les mythes et légendes celtiques. Son recueil de nouvelles intitulé *Aisling and Other Irish Tales of Terror* lui a valu d'être comparé aux plus grands maîtres irlandais tels que Sheridan Le Fanu ou Bram Stoker. Il a reçu en 1988 l'Irish Post Award en reconnaissance de ses apports importants à l'étude de l'histoire irlandaise. Entre 1983 et 1993, il écrit huit thrillers sous le nom de Peter MacAlan, puis se lance dans la rédaction des mystères de sœur Fidelma, série qui compte aujourd'hui quinze titres.

Peter Tremayne est membre de la Society of Authors ainsi que de la Crime Writers Society.

PETER TREMAYNE

LE SECRET
DE MÓEN

Traduit de l'anglais
par Hélène PROUTEAU

INÉDIT

10
18

« Grands Détectives »
dirigé par Jean-Claude Zylberstein

Titre original :
The Spider's Web

© Peter Tremayne, 1997.
© Éditions 10/18, Département d'Univers Poche,
2005, pour la traduction française.
ISBN 2-264-03980-9

À mon excellent ami Terence,
The Mac Carthy Mór,
prince de Desmond,
qui représente la 51ᵉ génération
en ligne directe par les hommes
et les femmes du roi Eoghan Mór de Cashel
(mort en 192 apr. J.-C.), et qui compte maintenant
sœur Fidelma dans les ancêtres de sa famille !

« Les lois sont comme une toile d'araignée : les petits s'y font prendre et les grands la déchirent. »

SOLON d'ATHÈNES
(640-561 av. J.-C.)

NOTE HISTORIQUE

Les événements de cette histoire se déroulent au mois que les Irlandais du VIIe siècle appelaient Cét-Soman, qui deviendra Beltaine, puis mai. Cela correspond pour eux au début de l'été. Nous sommes en l'an 666 après J.-C.

Les lecteurs qui ont déjà suivi les aventures de sœur Fidelma connaissent maintenant les différences entre l'Église de Rome et l'Église irlandaise du VIIe siècle, connue sous le nom d'Église celtique. Leurs liturgies et leurs philosophies différaient sur plus d'un point mais, en ce qui concerne le concept du célibat des religieux, il n'était guère populaire ni dans l'une ni dans l'autre. Il faut se rappeler qu'au pays de Fidelma, de nombreux monastères abritaient des religieux des deux sexes qui se mariaient souvent et élevaient leurs enfants au service de la foi. Cela valait aussi pour les abbés et les évêques. Il convient de garder cela à l'esprit pour bien comprendre le monde de Fidelma.

Une carte du royaume de Muman permettra aux lecteurs de se repérer dans cette ancienne géographie. J'ai conservé l'appellation de « Muman » plutôt que « Munster », qui au IXe siècle après J.-C. a été forgé à partir du nom irlandais Muman et du terme nordique *stadr* (lieu), pour finalement donner Munster en anglais.

J'attire également l'attention du lecteur sur le fait que le *cumal*, l'unité monétaire, équivalait à trois vaches laitières. Utilisé comme unité de mesure de la terre, le *cumal* valait 13,85 hectares.

Fidelma évolue dans l'ancienne organisation irlandaise avec son système juridique, les lois de Fénechus, plus connues sous le nom de « lois des brehons » (de *breaitheamh* : juge). Elle est avocate des cours de justice, une position qui n'avait rien d'extraordinaire pour les Irlandaises de l'époque.

PERSONNAGES PRINCIPAUX

Sœur Fidelma de Kildare, *dálaigh* ou avocate des cours de justice du VIIᵉ siècle en Irlande

Frère Eadulf de Seaxmund's Ham, moine saxon des terres du South Folk

Cathal, abbé de Lios Mhór

Frère Donnán, un *scriptor*

Colgú de Cashel, roi de Muman et frère de Fidelma

Beccan, chef brehon, ou juge, de Corco Loígde

Bressal, un hôtelier

Morna, le frère de Bressal

Eber, chef d'Araglin

Cranat, femme d'Eber

Crón, fille d'Eber et sa *tanist*, héritière présomptive

Teafa, sœur d'Eber

Móen, un sourd-muet aveugle

Dubán, commandant de la garde d'Eber

Crítán, un jeune guerrier

Menma, chef des troupeaux au *rath* d'Araglin

Dignait, une servante

Grella, une servante

Père Gormán de Cill Uird

Archú, un jeune fermier d'Araglin

Scoth, sa fiancée

Muadnat du Black Marsh, son cousin

Agdae, neveu de Muadnat et le chef de ses troupeaux

Gadra, un ermite

Clídna, une tenancière de bordel

Le monde de Fidelma
Muman (Munster), VIIᵉ siècle après J.-C.

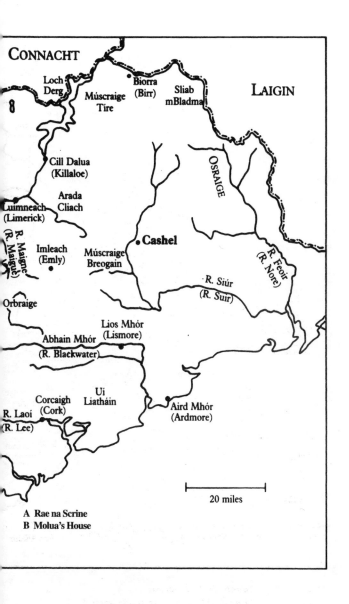

CONNACHT

LAIGIN

Loch Derg

Biorra (Birr)

Múscraige Tíre

Sliab mBladma

Cill Dalua (Killaloe)

OSRAIGE

Arada Cliach

Luimneach (Limerick)

R. Maigne (R. Maigue)

Imleach (Emly)

Múscraige Breogain

Cashel

R. Feoir (R. Nore)

R. Siúr (R. Suir)

Orbraige

Lios Mhór (Lismore)

Abhain Mhór (R. Blackwater)

Uí Liatháin

Corcaigh (Cork)

Aird Mhór (Ardmore)

R. Laoí (R. Lee)

20 miles

A Rae na Scrine
B Molua's House

CHAPITRE PREMIER

Le tonnerre grondait dans le massif aux sommets dénudés des Maoldomhnach, qui dans des temps immémoriaux s'étaient soulevés autour de Maoldomhnach's Hill. De temps à autre, les formes lourdes de celui-ci surgissaient dans la nuit, révélées par un éclair de feu, et des ombres couraient dans les collines, au nord de la vallée d'Araglin. Les nuages roulaient et s'amoncelaient dans le ciel, comme chassés par le souffle puissant des anciens dieux.

Dans les hauts pâturages, les vaches se serraient frileusement les unes contre les autres, meuglant pour se réconforter à l'annonce de la tempête ou pour donner l'alarme quand leur parvenait l'odeur des loups affamés et voraces, rôdant non loin de là dans les bois obscurs. À l'orée de la forêt, un cerf majestueux se tenait en sentinelle, veillant sur des biches et leurs faons. Naseaux frémissants, il tendait vers les nuées sa tête surmontée d'une imposante ramure. Malgré l'horizon d'un noir d'encre, il pressentait l'approche de l'aube, là-bas vers l'est, au-delà des montagnes.

Dans la vallée, un village se blottissait auprès d'une rivière bouillonnante qui serpentait dans la campagne. Les chiens sommeillaient et les coqs annonceraient bientôt l'approche du jour, relayés par le chœur matinal des oiseaux nichés dans les arbres des environs.

Mais à cette heure où le monde semblait inanimé, un être humain émergeait de sa torpeur.

Menma, le responsable des troupeaux d'Eber, chef d'Araglin, un homme grand et lourd avec une barbe rousse en broussaille, cligna des yeux et rejeta la peau de mouton de sa paillasse. Parfois, un éclair illuminait sa chaumière. Menma grogna et secoua la tête pour chasser les vapeurs entêtantes de la beuverie de la veille. De ses mains tremblantes, il tâtonna sur la table, trouva le silex et l'amadou et alluma la chandelle. Puis il étira ses membres endoloris. Sa tendance à abuser de la boisson ne diminuait en rien sa faculté innée à se repérer dans le temps. Peu importait l'heure à laquelle il s'était effondré sur son lit, il se levait toujours avant l'aube.

Pour saluer l'apparition imminente du soleil, cet homme massif accomplit alors son rituel immuable qui consistait à maudire copieusement la création. Menma adorait jurer. Certains commençaient la journée par une prière, d'autres en accomplissant leurs ablutions matinales, et Menma d'Araglin en insultant le chef Eber, auquel il souhaitait des morts ignominieuses par étouffement, étranglement, convulsion, mutilation, dysenterie, poison, noyade et tout ce que son imagination fertile en la matière pouvait lui souffler. Après quoi Menma se vouait lui-même aux gémonies, lui et ses parents, ni riches ni puissants, de simples fermiers qu'il accusait d'être la cause de sa condition misérable.

Ses parents, des journaliers sur les terres de leurs riches cousins, n'avaient pas réussi dans la vie et Menma, jaloux et amer, leur faisait porter le poids de ses échecs.

Il s'habilla sans prendre la peine de se laver ni de peigner les poils de sa barbe et la crinière cuivrée qui lui tombait jusqu'aux épaules. Puis, en guise de toilette, il avala une gorgée de mauvais *corma*, de l'hydromel, à même le pichet près de son lit. Il s'était fait de la propreté une ennemie irréconciliable et dégageait une odeur nauséabonde.

D'un pas traînant, il alla ouvrir la porte de sa hutte et cligna des yeux devant le ciel noir. Le tonnerre grondait toujours mais il savait instinctivement que la pluie s'était éloignée. La tempête faisait rage de l'autre côté des montagnes et se dirigeait vers l'ouest, sur une ligne parallèle à la vallée d'Araglin, épargnant les montagnes au nord. La journée s'annonçait sèche, froide et nuageuse. Il ne voyait pas les étoiles qui lui auraient permis de préciser l'heure, mais il devina la pâle lueur au-delà des monts.

Le *rath* du chef d'Araglin était toujours plongé dans l'obscurité. Bien qu'il ne s'abritât point derrière des murailles, on gratifiait toujours la résidence d'un chef du terme de *rath* ou forteresse.

Sur le seuil de sa porte, Menma, premier levé dans la nuit, avait maintenant entrepris de maudire le jour. Il enchaîna sur le bourg qu'il haïssait et commença à se répéter, car il avait atteint la limite de son répertoire d'imprécations.

Il retourna dans sa chaumière et souffla la chandelle avant de s'engager sur le sentier qui passait entre les maisons silencieuses pour rejoindre les étables. Ses pieds connaissaient par cœur le moindre accident du terrain. Sa première tâche consisterait à mener les chevaux aux prés et à nourrir la meute des chiens de chasse. Ensuite, il surveillerait la traite des vaches. C'était le travail des femmes et Menma ne s'abaissait jamais à toucher le pis d'un animal, mais on avait récemment volé du bétail dans la vallée et Eber lui avait ordonné de vérifier le nombre de têtes avant chaque traite. Qu'on ait osé soustraire des bêtes à Eber était une atteinte à son honneur. En apprenant que des brigands menaçaient la tranquillité des terres du clan, il avait piqué une formidable colère. Ses guerriers avaient en vain parcouru la campagne pour tenter de retrouver les coupables.

Menma approchait de la bâtisse ronde du siège de l'assemblée, un des rares édifices en pierre du vieux *rath* avec la chapelle du père Gormán, juste à côté. Les écuries étaient situées devant l'hôtellerie des invités. Pour y parvenir, le vacher devait emprunter un chemin circulaire qui passait devant les bâtiments en bois abritant les appartements du chef et de sa famille, à côté du siège de l'assemblée. Menma y jeta un coup d'œil envieux. Eber ronflait tranquillement dans son lit et ne se réveillerait que bien après le lever du soleil.

Menma se demanda avec un sourire lubrique qui, cette nuit-là, avait partagé la couche d'Eber. Puis il s'assombrit. Pourquoi Eber ? Pourquoi pas lui ? Qu'avait-il donc de si particulier pour posséder les richesses et le pouvoir qui lui permettaient d'attirer les femmes dans son lit ? Et quel destin l'avait condamné, lui, à n'être qu'un garçon d'écurie ?

Soudain, il s'immobilisa et tendit l'oreille.

Le *rath* était toujours plongé dans une profonde torpeur. Au loin, dans les collines, le hurlement d'un loup brisa le silence, mais ce n'était pas là le bruit qui avait attiré son attention.

Sans doute avait-il rêvé, souvent le vent qui soufflait dans les branches échauffait l'imagination. Il se remit en marche et puis cela recommença.

Un gémissement imperceptible.

Menma leva la tête vers la cime des arbres, plia le genou et se signa. Que Dieu lui serve de bouclier contre le mal ! Les petits habitants des collines, les esprits du *sídh*, s'étaient-ils mis en quête d'âmes chrétiennes à emporter dans leurs sombres cavernes ?

Soudain, un cri retentit, aigu et étouffé. Menma sursauta et les battements de son cœur s'accélérèrent. Le gémissement reprit, plus fort et plus soutenu.

Menma regarda autour de lui. Il était seul. En s'efforçant de repérer l'origine des plaintes, il comprit qu'elles venaient des appartements d'Eber et sortaient à coup sûr de la bouche d'un être humain. Menma poussa un soupir de soulagement. Tout plutôt que d'affronter les habitants du *sídh* quand ils partaient en chasse pour subtiliser des âmes. Eber était-il malade ? Il fronça les sourcils, indécis. Eber était son chef. Il avait des devoirs envers lui que rien, pas même son amertume, ne le dissuaderait d'accomplir.

Il s'approcha de la maison d'Eber et frappa doucement à la porte.

— Eber ? Êtes-vous malade ?

Il frappa plus fort, puis, n'obtenant aucune réponse, il prit son courage à deux mains et souleva la clenche du loquet. La porte s'ouvrit, personne ne se barricadait la nuit dans le *rath*. Le vacher se glissa à l'intérieur et se retrouva dans la « pièce de la conversation », la salle de réception privée du chef qui y recevait discrètement ses invités, loin du siège de l'assemblée. Ne percevant aucune présence, Menma se tourna vers la chambre voisine.

Un rai de lumière brillait sous la porte. Brusquement, le gémissement reprit.

— Eber ! Que se passe-t-il ? C'est Menma, le vacher.

Aucune réponse tandis que la plainte se prolongeait.

Il traversa la pièce, frappa du poing sur le battant en bois, hésita un instant puis entra.

Sur une petite table brillait la flamme d'une lampe. Menma cligna des yeux puis il distingua une personne qui geignait, accroupie près du lit, tout en se balançant d'avant en arrière. Des taches sombres maculaient ses vêtements. Des taches de sang ! Et elle tenait entre ses mains un objet luisant par intermittence à la lumière de la lampe. Un poignard à longue lame.

Menma se figea, et, s'arrachant à ce spectacle terrifiant, porta ses regards vers l'occupant du lit.

Eber, le chef d'Araglin, gisait nu au milieu des couvertures en désordre, un bras négligemment replié sous la tête. La lumière vacillante de la lampe prêtait une vie factice à ses yeux grands ouverts mais sa poitrine, où le couteau avait été plongé avec frénésie, n'était plus qu'un trou sanglant.

Déjà Menma s'apprêtait à joindre les mains et à faire une génuflexion quand il se ravisa.

— Il est mort ? demanda-t-il à l'ombre qui continuait de se balancer en gémissant.

N'obtenant aucune réponse, Menma s'avança, mit un genou en terre et posa deux doigts sur le cou du chef. Le sang ne battait plus, le corps était déjà froid et les yeux semblaient fixes et vitreux.

Il se redressa, fixa le cadavre avec dégoût et, après une brève hésitation, enfonça avec réticence le bout de sa botte dans la chair inerte avant de lui envoyer un grand coup de pied. Là, ses derniers doutes se dissipèrent : Eber n'était plus de ce monde.

Devant la silhouette qui émettait des sons plaintifs, cramponnée à son couteau, Menma le vacher fut bientôt secoué d'un rire rauque, car il allait devenir riche et puissant. À l'image des cousins qu'il avait enviés toute sa vie.

Il gloussait encore quand il sortit des appartements du chef pour se mettre en quête de Dubán, le commandant de la garde d'Eber.

CHAPITRE II

Le bourdonnement grave de la cloche donna le signal de la reprise de l'audience. En ce début d'après-midi, dans la petite chapelle de l'abbaye qui servait de tribunal, il faisait froid car les épais murs de granit ne laissaient pas pénétrer la chaleur. Sur les bancs de bois, là où la veille encore se pressaient les parties engagées dans un litige, les accusés et les témoins, il ne restait plus que quelques personnes car, à cette heure, la plupart des affaires en cours avaient déjà été jugées.

Quand le brehon fit son entrée, les participants à ce dernier procès se levèrent. Le juge était une jeune femme élancée, au visage avenant, qui n'avait pas atteint la trentaine et portait la robe d'une religieuse. Ses cheveux roux, qui s'échappaient de sa coiffe, tombaient en cascade sur ses épaules et la couleur de ses yeux, où s'allumait parfois un feu étrange, tirait sur le bleu ou le vert, au gré de la lumière et de ses humeurs. Sa jeunesse s'accordait mal à l'idée qu'on se faisait d'un juge érudit et expérimenté mais, au cours de ces derniers jours, alors qu'elle compulsait les documents et menait les débats, elle avait impressionné l'auditoire par sa bienveillance, l'étendue de ses connaissances et la rigueur de sa logique.

Il avait été octroyé à sœur Fidelma le titre de *dálaigh*, d'avocate des tribunaux des cinq royaumes[1] d'Éireann. Puis ses compétences l'avaient élevée à la qualification d'*anruth*, ce qui signifiait qu'elle était autorisée à plaider mais aussi, quand on l'en priait, à procéder à des auditions et statuer sur les différends qui ne nécessitaient pas la présence d'un juge de haut rang. C'est en cette qualité que Fidelma rendait aujourd'hui la justice à l'abbaye de Lios Mhór. L'abbaye se tenait à l'extérieur de « la grande fortification » dont elle tirait son nom, sur la rive du fleuve Abhainn Mór, « la grande rivière », au sud de Cashel, dans le royaume de Muman.

Tandis que Fidelma et les personnes présentes s'asseyaient, le *scriptor* de l'abbaye, qui tenait le rôle de greffier de la cour et consignait les débats, resta debout. Sa voix mélancolique rappelait à Fidelma les pleureurs aux enterrements.

— La séance est ouverte. Archú, fils de Suanach, contre Muadnat du Black Marsh. Suite des doléances d'Archú.

Il s'assit à son tour et tourna ses regards vers Fidelma, le style levé, prêt à coucher les actes sur ses tablettes d'argile humide, montées dans un châssis en bois. À la fin du procès, ce texte serait retranscrit dans un livre en vélin.

Fidelma, qui siégeait derrière une table en chêne abondamment sculptée, se pencha vers les deux hommes qui attendaient sur le banc en face d'elle.

— Archú et Muadnat, avancez-vous, je vous prie.

Le jeune homme se leva en hâte. Son comportement empressé rappelait celui d'un chien réclamant les faveurs d'un maître, songea Fidelma tandis qu'il

1. L'Ulster, le North Leinster, le South Leinster, le Munster (Muman) et le Connaught, avec respectivement pour capitale Emain, Tara, Dinn Rig, Temuir Erann et Gruachain. (*N.d.T.*)

se précipitait vers elle. L'autre avait l'âge d'être le père du premier et il arborait un visage sombre et austère.

— Après avoir entendu les dépositions présentées devant cette cour, dit Fidelma en les fixant à tour de rôle, je vais maintenant tenter de résumer les faits avec impartialité. Vous, Archú, venez d'atteindre l'âge du choix.

Le jeune garçon hocha la tête. D'après la loi, à dix-sept ans, il était devenu un adulte responsable de ses actes.

— Vous êtes le fils unique de Suanach, fille de l'oncle de Muadnat, décédée il y a un an.

— Elle était bien la fille unique du frère de mon père, acquiesça Muadnat d'un ton neutre.

— Donc vous êtes cousins.

Aucune réponse. Ces deux-là entretenaient des relations où l'amour tenait peu de place.

— Des parents aussi proches ne devraient pas recourir à la loi pour arbitrer leurs différends, les admonesta Fidelma. Vous obstinez-vous à solliciter le jugement de cette cour ?

Muadnat renifla d'un air belliqueux.

— Je n'avais aucun désir de me présenter ici.

— Moi non plus, répliqua le jeune homme en s'empourprant. J'aurais préféré que mon cousin se comporte comme la morale et le bon sens l'exigent, sans en venir à cette extrémité.

— Je suis dans mon droit, lança Muadnat d'un ton cassant. Cette terre m'appartient.

Sœur Fidelma haussa un sourcil moqueur.

— C'est à la cour, il me semble, de trancher sur le bien-fondé de vos revendications. Puisque vous l'avez sollicitée, elle rendra une sentence que vous devrez tous deux respecter.

Elle se renversa sur son siège, croisa les mains sur ses genoux et contempla d'un air pensif les deux visages courroucés qui lui faisaient face.

— Suanach a donc hérité des terres de son père. Puis elle a épousé un homme d'au-delà des mers, un Breton du nom d'Artgal, qui en tant qu'étranger n'était pas autorisé à posséder des terres du clan en son nom propre.

— Un inconnu nécessiteux, grommela Muadnat.

— Nous ne sommes pas ici pour exprimer des opinions sur la personnalité d'Artgal, le coupa Fidelma. Il épousa donc Suanach...

— Contre la volonté de sa famille, intervint à nouveau Muadnat.

— Ces circonstances ne concernent pas la cour. À la mort d'Artgal, Suanach continua de cultiver ses champs et d'élever son fils, Archú. Puis elle mourut il y a un an environ.

— C'est alors que mon cousin est arrivé en affirmant que la propriété était sienne ! s'exclama Archú.

— À la mort de Suanach, lâcha Muadnat d'un ton sentencieux, elle revenait de droit à sa famille et j'étais son plus proche parent.

— Il a tout pris, se plaignit l'autre avec amertume.

— Je suis entré en possession de mon bien. Et tu n'avais pas atteint l'âge du choix.

Fidelma s'interposa.

— Il suffit. Archú, au cours de l'année qui vient de s'écouler, Muadnat a donc été votre tuteur.

— Mon tuteur ? Mon maître, oui. J'ai été obligé de travailler sur ma propre terre comme un esclave en ne recevant que de la nourriture en échange. La famille de ma mère m'a traité plus mal que ceux qu'elle emploie pour les labours. On m'a contraint à manger et dormir dans l'étable.

— Je vous remercie de me rappeler ces faits dont j'ai déjà eu connaissance, soupira Fidelma.

— Nous n'avions aucune obligation légale envers ce garçon, grommela Muadnat. Il devrait nous être reconnaissant de ne pas l'avoir jeté dehors.

— Modérez vos propos, je vous prie. En résumé, si Archú vous a amené à comparaître ici, c'est qu'il estime avoir droit à une part d'héritage.

— Les biens de sa mère reviennent à sa famille. Lui ne peut hériter que de ce qui appartenait à son père, or il ne lui a rien laissé. S'il veut de la terre, il n'a qu'à se rendre en Bretagne.

Des yeux mi-clos de la *dálaigh* filtra une lueur vite éteinte.

— Quand un *óc-aire*, un modeste fermier, meurt, un septième de ce qu'il possède est prélevé comme impôt à l'intention du chef du clan pour les frais d'entretien du territoire dont il a la garde.

— Cela a été fait, déclara le *scriptor*. Ce document que le chef d'Araglin nous a fait parvenir le confirme.

— Très bien.

Fidelma se tourna vers Archú.

— Votre mère, en tant qu'héritière directe, avait la jouissance de la propriété de feu son père qu'en principe elle ne pouvait transmettre à son mari ou à ses enfants, puisqu'elle revenait de droit au parent le plus proche de sa propre lignée.

Les traits de Muadnat se détendirent et il jeta un regard triomphant à son jeune cousin.

— Cependant, reprit Fidelma en haussant le ton, son époux, en tant qu'étranger, se retrouvait dans l'impossibilité de transmettre du bien à son fils et dans ces circonstances, l'usage veut que l'on se réfère à l'arrêt de notre grand brehon Bríg Briugaid, qui sert maintenant de référence sur cette question. Son arbitrage stipule que, dans le cas présent, la mère est autorisée à transmettre de la terre à son fils à condition qu'elle n'excède pas sept *cumals*, une mesure censée représenter une propriété suffisamment étendue pour qu'un *óc-aire* puisse en tirer sa subsistance.

Il y eut un silence tandis que le plaignant et le défendeur s'efforçaient de saisir les implications de la sentence. Sœur Fidelma eut pitié d'eux.

— Le jugement a été prononcé en votre faveur, Archú, dit-elle en souriant au jeune garçon. Maintenant que vous avez atteint l'âge du choix, votre cousin devra vous céder sept *cumals* de sa terre.

Muadnat la fixait sans en croire ses oreilles.

— Mais… la propriété les couvre à peine. Autant dire qu'il ne me reste rien.

— D'après l'ancienne loi du *Críth Gablach*, reprit patiemment Fidelma, un fermier ne peut accéder au titre d'*óc-aire* à moins de posséder un minimum de sept *cumals* de terrain, ce qui correspond à la surface qu'Archú est en droit d'exiger. D'autre part, pour avoir agi en violation de la loi, ce qui a contraint Archú à présenter ses doléances devant moi, vous êtes condamné à payer une amende d'un *cumal* à cette cour.

Muadnat avait pâli et son visage exprimait une rage qu'il contenait à grand-peine.

— C'est une injustice ! articula-t-il d'une voix éraillée.

— Votre indignation est assez malvenue, Muadnat. À la mort de votre tante, il était de votre devoir de nourrir et de protéger votre cousin. Or vous l'avez exploité en lui refusant une juste rémunération pour son travail, et vous avez tenté de le dépouiller de son bien. Considérez qu'en m'abstenant de vous faire payer des compensations à Archú, j'ai tempéré la loi par la commisération.

L'homme cligna des yeux et avala sa salive avec difficulté.

— J'en référerai à mon chef, Eber d'Araglin, qui ne manquera pas de contester cette décision ! gronda-t-il.

— Les demandes d'appel ne peuvent être adressées qu'au chef brehon du roi de Cashel, l'interrompit le *scriptor* qui terminait de consigner le jugement. D'autre part, l'usage commande que vous vous absteniez de critiquer la décision du brehon ici présent.

Dans l'éventualité où vous solliciteriez un nouvel arbitrage, vous devrez suivre la procédure. En attendant un éventuel recours, vous êtes prié de vous retirer des terres qui reviennent à votre cousin Archú, dont vous serez physiquement expulsé d'ici neuf jours si vous n'avez pas obéi à nos injonctions. D'autre part, le délai qui vous est imparti pour payer votre amende court jusqu'à la pleine lune.

Muadnat sortit sans un mot de la chapelle. Un petit homme frêle à la crinière châtaine se leva et lui emboîta le pas d'un air penaud.

Quant à Archú, son visage disait clairement qu'il avait peine à croire à sa bonne fortune. Il prit la main de Fidelma qu'il secoua avec énergie.

— Dieu vous garde, ma sœur, vous m'avez sauvé la vie.

Fidelma lui retira sa main avec un petit sourire distant.

— Ne me remerciez pas, je n'ai fait qu'appliquer la loi.

Mais le jeune homme, illuminé par la gratitude, semblait ne pas l'avoir entendue. Toujours souriant, il alla retrouver une jeune fille dans l'allée qui se jeta dans ses bras. Fidelma, cachant son attendrissement, les regarda se parler à mi-voix, penchés l'un vers l'autre.

Puis elle se tourna vers le *scriptor*.

— Vous n'avez plus besoin de moi, frère Donnán ?

— Non ma sœur. Ce soir, j'aurai terminé de reporter vos jugements dans mon livre. Ensuite, je veillerai à ce qu'ils soient annoncés de la manière qui convient.

Il marqua une pause et s'éclaircit la voix.

— Il semblerait que l'abbé, qui se tient près de la porte, veuille s'entretenir avec vous.

Fidelma repéra aussitôt la silhouette aux larges épaules de l'abbé Cathal. Il avait l'air préoccupé. Elle se leva d'un geste vif et se dirigea vers lui.

— Vous me cherchiez, père abbé ?

Le moine était un homme d'un certain âge, taillé en force, qui avait gardé une allure martiale remontant à l'époque où il était guerrier. Originaire de la région, il avait rapidement abandonné la carrière des armes pour suivre à Lios Mhór l'enseignement du bienheureux Cáthach, qui en avait fait un abbé et un enseignant des plus accomplis. Fils d'un grand chef de guerre, Cathal avait distribué toutes ses richesses aux pauvres de son clan et vivait dans la simplicité commandée par son ordre. Sa franchise et ses manières sans détour lui avaient valu beaucoup d'ennemis. Un chef local, Maelochtrid, l'avait même emprisonné sous le prétexte, inventé de toutes pièces, qu'il pratiquait la sorcellerie. Pourtant, à sa libération, Cathal lui avait pardonné sa mauvaise action. Telle était la nature de cet homme.

Fidelma aimait la douceur de Cathal et son absence totale de vanité, contrastant avec l'arrogance assez répandue chez ceux qui occupaient sa position. C'était un des rares religieux qu'en son cœur elle jugeait un « saint homme ».

— Oui, je vous cherchais, sœur Fidelma, répondit l'abbé avec un bref sourire qui illumina ses traits. En avez-vous fini avec vos délibérations ?

Sa voix aux modulations feutrées ne trahissait aucune émotion, mais pour qu'il la vienne quérir dans la chapelle, Fidelma se doutait bien qu'il s'était produit quelque événement inhabituel.

— Je viens de juger la dernière affaire, père abbé.

Cathal hocha la tête d'un air distrait.

— Deux cavaliers, dont un étranger, viennent d'arriver tout droit de Cashel. Ils ont demandé à vous voir.

— Mon frère va-t-il bien ? s'enquit Fidelma, étreinte par une peur irraisonnée.

Colgú venait de monter sur le trône de Muman, le plus grand des cinq royaumes d'Éireann, et sa situation n'était pas encore bien assurée.

— Oui, oui. Votre frère le roi se porte comme un charme ! se récria aussitôt Cathal. Excusez ma maladresse. Et, maintenant, rejoignons mes appartements où vous êtes attendue.

Fidelma, piquée par la curiosité, pressa le pas dans les couloirs de la grande abbaye pour rester à la hauteur de l'abbé qui marchait à grandes enjambées.

Lios Mhór, la « grande maison », un lieu reculé, était devenue célèbre quand Cáthach de Rathan, Dieu bénisse son nom, y avait emménagé pour fonder une nouvelle communauté religieuse. Cela ne remontait qu'à une génération. Avec une incroyable rapidité, Lios Mhór était devenue un des centres d'enseignement les plus célèbres, où accouraient les étudiants de contrées lointaines. Comme pour la plupart des abbayes d'Irlande, il s'agissait d'une maison double, un *conhospitae*, où vivaient des religieux des deux sexes qui travaillaient et élevaient leurs enfants au service du Christ.

Alors qu'ils progressaient dans les cloîtres de l'abbaye, les étudiants et les religieux s'écartaient respectueusement devant eux, la tête baissée en signe de déférence. Les étudiants, filles et garçons, venaient de nombreux pays pour parfaire leur éducation dans les cinq royaumes.

Tandis que l'abbé Cathal, escorté de Fidelma, pénétrait dans ses appartements, le beau vieillard qui se tenait près d'une table massive se retourna avec un large sourire. Malgré son grand âge et ses cheveux argentés, il rayonnait d'énergie. Une chaîne d'or marquant son rang brillait sur sa cape.

— Beccan ! s'écria Fidelma. Quelle joie de vous revoir !

Le chef brehon sourit en lui prenant les mains.

— Retrouver une jeune personne objet de toutes les affections et que les membres de sa profession tiennent en haute estime sera toujours un plaisir pour moi, ma chère Fidelma.

Cet accueil cordial ne devait rien au protocole et tout à une sympathie sincère.

À cet instant, quelqu'un toussa derrière Fidelma, un frère dont les mains étaient dissimulées dans les manches de sa longue robe de bure. Sa tonsure romaine le distinguait des moines des cinq royaumes d'Éireann, qui arboraient la tonsure en demi-couronne des adeptes du bienheureux Jean, sur le devant de la tête. Le frère montrait un visage solennel mais, quand il s'inclina pour saluer Fidelma, ses yeux bruns brillaient d'une lueur amusée.

— Frère Eadulf, balbutia Fidelma. Je croyais que Rome vous avait assigné à la cour de mon frère[1] ?

— Certes, mais je me retrouvais un peu désœuvré à Cashel et quand j'ai appris que Beccan partait à votre recherche, j'ai offert de l'accompagner.

— Mais que se passe-t-il ? demanda-t-elle, ramenée à la réalité par le visage inquiet de l'abbé qui alla s'asseoir derrière sa table.

— Nous sommes porteurs de nouvelles inquiétantes, déclara Beccan sur un ton grave.

Puis il sourit.

— Mais j'aurais dû commencer par vous transmettre les chaleureuses salutations de votre frère qui est en bonne santé et affronte avec vaillance les difficultés de sa charge.

— Mais alors, quelle est cette nouvelle qui semble vous bouleverser ?

— Eh bien… figurez-vous qu'hier après-midi est arrivé à Cashel un messager du clan d'Eber d'Araglin.

Où Fidelma avait-elle déjà entendu ce nom ? Mais il y avait à peine un instant, car Eber était le chef de la région dont Archú et son cousin étaient originaires.

---

1. Voir *La Ruse du serpent*, 10/18, n° 3788.

— Poursuivez, dit-elle, car Beccan avait marqué une pause en constatant que ses pensées étaient ailleurs.

— Ce messager nous a annoncé qu'Eber avait été assassiné en même temps qu'une de ses parentes. Quelqu'un a été surpris sur la scène du crime.

— En quoi cela me concerne-t-il ? s'étonna Fidelma.

Beccan eut un geste d'excuse.

— Je suis appelé à Ros Ailithir pour des affaires urgentes, et je n'aurai pas le temps de mener une enquête approfondie en Araglin. Or le roi tient à un procès équitable. Eber d'Araglin était un fidèle ami de Cashel et Sa Majesté a pensé que vous étiez la mieux placée pour…

Fidelma devina la suite.

— … prendre en charge les investigations, soupira-t-elle. Ma tâche étant ici terminée, j'avais prévu de retourner demain à Cashel, mais rien ne m'empêche de retarder mon voyage de quelques jours. Cependant, si le coupable a déjà été arrêté, êtes-vous certain que ma présence soit nécessaire ? Entretiendrait-on quelque doute quant à sa culpabilité ?

— Pas que je sache. L'assassin a été surpris un poignard à la main, ses vêtements étaient tachés de sang et il se tenait près du corps d'Eber. Mais votre frère…

Fidelma leva les yeux au ciel.

— Je comprends. Eber était un ami de Cashel et la justice doit être rendue avec la plus grande rigueur.

— Aucun brehon n'est attaché à Araglin, intervint l'abbé Cathal. Il s'agit surtout de s'assurer que rien n'a été laissé au hasard.

— Existe-t-il des incertitudes quant aux circonstances du crime ?

L'abbé Cathal ouvrit les mains d'un air perplexe.

— Eber était un chef très populaire, aimable et généreux, les membres de son clan l'appréciaient, et nous craignons une justice expéditive qui verrait le coupable puni sans que l'on prenne le temps de respecter les procédures.

Fidelma comprit qu'il était troublé. Or Cathal connaissait bien cette région montagneuse pour la bonne raison qu'elle l'avait vu naître. Elle hocha la tête.

— Tout à l'heure, alors que je siégeais dans la chapelle, j'ai eu un bon exemple du peu de respect qu'inspiraient les lois à l'un des hommes du clan d'Araglin. Racontez-m'en davantage sur ce peuple, père abbé.

— Leur histoire se résume à peu de chose. Ils vivent en communauté fermée dans les montagnes autour du *rath* de leur chef. À l'est, des terres fertiles s'étendent le long de la rivière Araglin qui coule dans la vallée. Les membres du clan se suffisent à eux-mêmes et n'apprécient guère les étrangers. La tâche qui vous attend sera ardue.

— En l'absence de brehon, je suppose qu'ils ont un prêtre ?

— Oui, le père Gormán, qui vit depuis vingt ans au *rath*, près de la chapelle de Cill Uird, « l'église du rituel ». Il a étudié ici, à Lios Mhór. Il vous sera d'un grand secours, bien que ses conceptions ne correspondent guère aux vôtres.

— Comment cela ? s'étonna Fidelma.

Cathal lui adressa un sourire malicieux.

— Je préfère vous laisser découvrir par vous-même l'étendue de vos différends. Ainsi, personne ne pourra m'accuser de vous avoir influencée.

— J'ai compris. Encore un adepte de Rome !

Cathal sourit.

— Vous êtes très perspicace, ma sœur. Oui, il estime que les préceptes de Rome devraient l'emporter sur nos coutumes locales. Et il n'est pas le seul, si l'on en juge par la chapelle romaine réputée pour son opulence qu'il a fait édifier à Ard Mór. Il semblerait que le père Gormán a des appuis haut placés.

— Et pourtant, Cill Uird est construite dans un endroit peu fréquenté. Cela ne vous paraît-il pas bizarre ?

— N'y voyez pas malice, l'admonesta gentiment Cathal. Le père Gormán est un homme d'Araglin qui tient à propager son interprétation de la foi, voilà tout.

Beccan s'amusa de l'attitude contrite de la jeune femme.

— Le problème avec vous, Fidelma de Kildare, c'est votre esprit trop aiguisé pour la profession que vous exercez. Savez-vous que votre sagesse est devenue proverbiale dans les cinq royaumes d'Éireann ?

— Cette pensée me contrarie, grommela Fidelma. Je sers la loi pour apporter la justice au peuple, non pour en tirer une gloire personnelle.

— Ne vous fâchez pas, mon enfant. Votre réputation vous a suivie dans le sillage de vos succès, acceptez-la de bonne grâce. Après tout, vous avez résolu des affaires difficiles qui alimentaient la controverse, et maintenant…

Il se tourna vers l'abbé.

— Il est temps que je me mette en route si je veux atteindre Ard Mór avant la nuit. *Vive valeque*[1], Cathal de Lios Mhór.

— *Vive, vale*, Beccan.

Et sur un bref sourire à Fidelma et un léger hochement de tête à l'adresse d'Eadulf, le vieil homme quitta la pièce.

Fidelma se tourna vers Eadulf avec un regard interrogateur.

— N'accompagnez-vous pas Beccan ?

Le moine au regard sombre, qui avait partagé bon nombre des aventures de Fidelma, prit un air détaché.

— Je pensais vous accompagner en Araglin, si vous n'y voyez pas d'objection, bien sûr. Je n'ai jamais visité cette région…

Fidelma se mordit la lèvre pour réprimer son envie de rire. La réponse très diplomatique d'Eadulf était à

---

1. Vis et porte-toi bien. (*N.d.T.*)

l'évidence destinée à détourner les soupçons que l'abbé aurait pu entretenir sur la nature de ses relations avec Fidelma.

Eadulf était un *gerefa*, ou magistrat héréditaire de son pays, le South Folk des Saxons. Converti à la foi chrétienne par Fursa, un missionnaire irlandais, il avait étudié dans les grands collèges d'Éireann pour y parfaire son éducation, d'abord au monastère de Durrow, puis au célèbre collège de médecine de Tuaim Brecain. Plus tard, il avait quitté l'Église de Colomba[1] pour celle de Rome. Le Saint-Siège l'avait alors nommé secrétaire du nouvel archevêque de Cantorbéry, Théodore, qui l'avait envoyé en mission auprès de Colgú de Cashel[2]. Eadulf était très à l'aise dans les cinq royaumes, dont il parlait couramment la langue.

— Je serai ravie que vous m'escortiez, dit Fidelma d'une voix douce. Avez-vous un cheval ?

— Votre frère a eu l'amabilité de me prêter une monture.

Peu de religieux possédaient un cheval. Fidelma devait le sien à son rang et à sa fonction de brehon des cours de justice.

— Parfait, dans ce cas, je vous propose de ne pas nous attarder plus longtemps.

— Ne préférez-vous pas attendre demain matin ? demanda l'abbé. Araglin est assez éloigné d'ici.

— Nous trouverons bien une hôtellerie en chemin, répliqua Fidelma avec une belle assurance. Si nous voulons empêcher les gens d'Eber de devancer la loi en prenant des mesures trop rapides contre l'accusé, mieux vaut gagner Araglin au plus vite.

Devant son impatience, Cathal céda à regret.

---

1. Nommée d'après saint Colomba (Colum-Cille), moine irlandais né en 529 après J.-C. Abbé d'Iona, il évangélisa l'Écosse. (*N.d.T.*)
2. Voir *Le Suaire de l'archevêque*, 10/18, n° 3631.

— Comme il vous plaira, Fidelma, mais je vais me faire du mauvais sang pendant que vous chevaucherez dans les montagnes la nuit. Veillez à vous trouver un abri sûr.

L'abbé ne parlait pas à une simple religieuse mais à la sœur du roi, dont il n'était pas autorisé à contester les décisions.

— Un de nos frères va vous préparer de l'eau et de la nourriture, et il veillera à ce que l'on prenne soin de vos chevaux avant de les seller, annonça Cathal.

Puis il quitta la pièce.

Dès que la porte se fut refermée, Fidelma s'avança d'un pas vif vers le moine saxon et lui prit les mains. Ses yeux bleu-vert débordaient de gaieté et, devant son visage frais et rieur, certains religieux n'auraient pas manqué de s'étonner qu'une jeune femme aussi séduisante ait choisi d'entrer dans les ordres. Son allure, sa silhouette élancée, semblaient exprimer le désir d'une vie plus active et joyeuse que celle que l'on mène derrière les murs des monastères retirés du monde.

— Eadulf ! On m'avait rapporté que vous étiez déjà en route pour le South Folk.

Devant l'enthousiasme de la jeune femme, le moine eut un sourire vaguement embarrassé.

— Quand j'ai appris que Beccan venait vous retrouver pour vous envoyer en mission à Araglin, j'ai déclaré à votre frère qu'il serait pour moi du plus haut intérêt d'assister à l'exercice de la justice dans cette région reculée. Cela me donnait une bonne excuse pour rester ici un peu plus longtemps.

— Je suis si heureuse, Eadulf ! En vérité, je m'ennuyais à Lios Mhór. Quel bonheur de partir avec vous pour les montagnes ! On dit qu'il y souffle un air sain et je me languis de renouer avec nos confrontations animées...

Eadulf éclata d'un rire franc et affectueux.

— Nos confrontations animées… j'imagine cela d'ici. Je vous connais, Fidelma.

La jeune femme rit elle aussi de bon cœur. Eadulf lui avait manqué. Lors de leurs joutes philosophiques, elle adorait le taquiner car il mordait aux hameçons qu'elle lui tendait avec une bonne humeur confondante. Mais leurs disputes n'allaient jamais jusqu'à l'inimitié. Tandis qu'ils argumentaient sur l'interprétation à donner aux préceptes des pères fondateurs de la foi, ils retiraient toujours quelque enseignement de leurs affrontements.

Eadulf, qui avait recouvré son sérieux, la contemplait maintenant d'un air grave.

— Nos débats m'ont également manqué, lui dit-il d'une voix contenue.

Ils se fixèrent en silence. Puis la porte s'ouvrit et l'abbé Cathal pénétra dans la pièce. Aussitôt ils se séparèrent d'un air gêné.

— Tout est prêt. Vous avez de la chance, car on m'a rapporté qu'un fermier d'Araglin s'apprêtait justement à retourner chez lui. Il pourra vous servir de guide.

— Un homme d'un certain âge ? s'enquit Fidelma qui se rembrunit.

L'abbé Cathal la regarda avec surprise.

— Non, un jeune homme accompagné de son amie. En quoi cela vous importe-t-il ?

— Eh bien, figurez-vous que je viens de prononcer un jugement en la défaveur d'un certain Muadnat qui n'aurait guère apprécié ma compagnie.

— Mais une sentence doit être acceptée de bonne grâce, s'étonna l'abbé Cathal qui semblait chagriné que l'on puisse éprouver du ressentiment devant une décision de justice.

— Certains le font de mauvaise grâce, père abbé, répliqua Fidelma.

Cathal était visiblement contrarié de les laisser partir.

— Peut-être nous voyons-nous pour la dernière fois, Fidelma, dit-il d'un ton solennel.

— Mais pourquoi donc ?

— La semaine prochaine, je partirai en pèlerinage pour la Terre sainte. Je mûris ce projet depuis fort longtemps. Frère Nemon me remplacera à l'abbaye.

— Quel beau voyage vous attend ! dit Fidelma d'un ton mélancolique. Moi aussi, j'espère le faire un jour, ce pèlerinage. Je vous souhaite beaucoup de joie, Cathal de Lios Mhór, et que Dieu vous accompagne sur votre route.

Elle tendit la main à l'abbé qui la serra dans la sienne.

— Et puisse-t-il continuer de vous inspirer dans vos jugements, ma chère enfant.

Il leur sourit et leva la main pour les bénir.

— Que la paix et la force soient avec vous jusqu'au bout du chemin.

CHAPITRE III

Dans la cour pavée de l'abbaye, ils retrouvèrent le jeune Archú et la jeune fille qui était avec lui lors du jugement. Assis à l'ombre du cloître, ils attendaient avec impatience l'instant du départ. Non loin de là, deux chevaux étaient déjà sellés. En voyant la *dálaigh*, Archú, toujours aussi agité et plein d'égards, s'avança vers elle.

— On m'a confié que vous auriez besoin d'un guide pour vous accompagner au pays d'Araglin, ma sœur, eh bien vous me voyez ravi d'offrir mes services à celle qui m'a rendu ma terre et mon honneur.

— Archú, vos remerciements sont superflus puisque, sur ces questions, la loi est le seul arbitre. Je vous assure que vous ne me devez rien.

Elle se tourna en souriant vers la blonde jeune fille qui s'approchait, les yeux baissés, timide et gracieuse. Fidelma estima qu'elle n'avait pas beaucoup plus de seize ans.

Archú lui prit la main et déclara avec un sérieux attendrissant :

— Je vous présente Scoth. Maintenant que j'ai une situation, nous allons nous marier. Je demanderai à notre prêtre, le père Gormán, de fixer dès que possible la date de la cérémonie.

La jeune fille rougit.

— Je t'aurais épousé même si tu avais perdu ton procès, le gronda-t-elle gentiment.

Puis elle se tourna vers Fidelma.

— Je vous jure que c'est la vérité.

— Cela ne doit pas vous empêcher de vous réjouir, dit Fidelma d'un air grave. Ne vaut-il pas mieux épouser un *óc-aire* qu'un homme sans fortune ?

Puis elle leur présenta frère Eadulf, et un des moines arriva en tirant par la bride les chevaux dont les sacs de selle avaient été remplis d'eau et de nourriture. Archú et Scoth portaient tous deux un balluchon et un gourdin d'épine.

— Je regrette, ma sœur, mais nous sommes venus à pied, expliqua Archú. Nous n'étions pas autorisés à emprunter des chevaux ou même des ânes à la ferme. Mon cousin Muadnat et son chef de troupeaux, Agdae, nous ont laissés nous débrouiller tout seuls.

— Ne vous inquiétez pas, les rassura Fidelma d'un ton enjoué, nos bêtes sont solides et vous ne pesez pas trop lourd. Scoth montera avec moi et vous, Archú, avec frère Eadulf.

L'après-midi était déjà bien avancé quand ils passèrent le grand portail en bois de l'abbaye et longèrent le fleuve en direction du nord, où se dressaient les montagnes.

— Araglin est situé tout là-haut, lança Archú grimpé derrière Eadulf. Nous y arriverons demain vers midi.

— Où aviez-vous l'intention de passer la nuit ? demanda Fidelma tandis qu'elle tirait sur les rênes de son étalon pour lui faire traverser un étroit pont de bois qui enjambait le cours d'eau.

— Je connais une taverne où nous devrions arriver avant la tombée de la nuit. Nous emprunterons la route de Cashel sur un mile et commencerons notre ascension vers Araglin en suivant le lit d'une petite rivière qui naît dans les montagnes arides puis traverse une forêt très dense.

— Demain, le voyage ne présentera pas de difficultés particulières, pépia la jeune Scoth, les bras passés autour de la taille de Fidelma. Nous ne serons qu'à quelques heures de la grande faille qui communique avec la vallée d'Araglin. De là, pour rejoindre le *rath* du chef, c'est tout droit.

Frère Eadulf tourna légèrement la tête vers son jeune compagnon.

— Savez-vous pourquoi nous nous rendons là-bas ?

Archú cligna des paupières.

— Oui, le père abbé nous a appris la nouvelle.

— Vous connaissiez Eber ? s'enquit Fidelma.

Le meurtre de son chef ne semblait pas émouvoir le garçon outre mesure, une attitude qui éveillait la curiosité de la *dálaigh*.

— J'ai entendu parler de lui, car il était un lointain cousin de ma mère, mais la plupart des habitants d'Araglin ont des liens de parenté. Notre ferme est située dans la vallée du Black Marsh, un endroit passablement isolé, à plusieurs miles du *rath* du chef où nous allions très rarement. Quant à Eber, il n'a jamais rendu visite à ma mère car lui aussi désapprouvait son mariage, mais le père Gormán venait nous voir de temps à autre.

— Et vous, Scoth, connaissiez-vous Eber ?

— Je suis orpheline. Je travaille à la ferme de Muadnat comme servante et on ne m'a jamais autorisée à me rendre au village, mais j'ai souvent vu Eber quand il venait chasser ou festoyer chez Muadnat. Il y a quelques années de cela, ils s'y sont retrouvés pour fomenter une bataille contre le clan des Uí Fidgente. Ces deux-là s'entendaient comme larrons en foire et ils se montraient souvent grossiers et injurieux, surtout quand ils avaient bu.

— Mon père, Artgal, a répondu à l'appel d'Eber et il est parti se battre contre les Uí Fidgente pour ne plus jamais revenir, ajouta Archú avec amertume.

— En somme, ce que vous savez sur Eber se résume à peu de chose.

— Qu'est-ce donc qui vous intéresse tant chez lui ?

— Je cherche à me faire une idée de sa personnalité. Malgré ses manières peu délicates et son goût pour la boisson, était-il considéré comme un bon chef ?

— La plupart des gens l'aimaient bien, concéda Archú. Mais quand j'ai demandé l'avis du père Gormán au sujet de mon affaire, il m'a conseillé de me rendre à Lios Mhór plutôt que d'en appeler directement à Eber.

Fidelma estima qu'il s'agissait là d'une étrange recommandation. Après tout, solliciter dans un premier temps l'arbitrage du chef d'un clan, même s'il s'agissait d'un clan de peu d'importance, semblait assez naturel puisque ses attributions lui permettaient de prononcer un premier jugement. Puis elle se rappela que Beccan avait précisé qu'aucun brehon n'était attaché à Araglin, auquel cas la recommandation du père Gormán relevait peut-être du simple bon sens.

— Le père Gormán s'est-il justifié d'une quelconque manière quand il vous a adressé directement à Lios Mhór ?

— Du tout.

— N'est-il point curieux qu'une personne ayant grandi sur le territoire d'un même clan ne soit pas certaine de reconnaître son chef avec certitude ? s'étonna Eadulf.

Archú éclata d'un rire désarmant.

— Araglin est une contrée très étendue. On peut aisément se perdre dans les montagnes et passer toute une vie sans jamais rencontrer le voisin de l'autre côté de la colline. Ma ferme…

Le garçon marqua une pause pleine de fierté.

— Ma ferme est située dans une vallée isolée qui ne compte qu'une seule autre propriété, celle de Muadnat.

Scoth poussa un profond soupir.

— J'espère que maintenant ma vie va changer. Jusqu'à présent, mon horizon s'est limité à la cuisine de Muadnat et je connais tout juste la campagne alentour.

— Vous ne vous êtes pas sauvée ? dit Fidelma.

— Si. À peine atteint l'âge du choix[1], je me suis enfuie. Mais où pouvais-je aller ? On m'a rattrapée et ramenée chez Muadnat.

Fidelma était choquée.

— A-t-on utilisé la force ? Pourtant vous n'apparteniez pas à la classe des personnes « non libres » ?

— J'ignorais qu'il existait des esclaves dans les cinq royaumes ! s'exclama Eadulf.

— Je parlais de ceux qui n'ont aucun droit à l'intérieur du clan, répliqua aussitôt Fidelma.

— Voilà une magnifique définition des esclaves.

— Vous vous trompez. Il s'agit de prisonniers de guerre, d'otages et de pleutres qui n'ont pas répondu à l'appel du clan quand il était menacé. Et j'oubliais ceux qui ont été condamnés par la justice et n'ont pas payé les amendes exigées. Ils sont alors privés de leurs droits civiques, mais non pas exclus de la société. On utilise leur force de travail afin qu'ils contribuent au bien commun, mais il leur est interdit de porter des armes et ils sont inéligibles pour les charges officielles.

Eadulf fit la grimace.

— Difficile de les distinguer des esclaves.

Fidelma montra des signes d'agacement.

— La classe « non libre » est divisée en deux groupes. Ceux qui peuvent louer leurs services, cultiver la terre et payer des impôts, et ceux qui sont déloyaux et en constante rébellion. Tous peuvent se racheter par leur labeur jusqu'à ce qu'ils aient payé leurs amendes.

---

1. Quatorze ans pour les filles. (*N.d.T.*)

— Et s'ils n'y parviennent pas ?

— Alors ils demeurent ainsi, privés de leurs droits civiques jusqu'à leur mort.

— Et leurs enfants deviennent des esclaves ?

— Le terme d'esclave est inapproprié ! s'insurgea à nouveau Fidelma. Et d'après la loi, quand une personne meurt, ses dettes s'éteignent avec elle. Ses enfants jouissent de tous leurs droits.

Elle surprit un sourire amusé sur les lèvres d'Eadulf. Ne jouait-il pas à l'avocat du diable afin de la provoquer ? Elle-même avait plus d'une fois usé de ce stratagème pour le contredire et le défier dans ses croyances. À son contact, aurait-il acquis un sens de l'humour plus subtil ? Alors qu'elle s'apprêtait à poursuivre leur joute verbale, la jeune Scoth les ramena à l'origine de la discussion.

— Je n'appartenais pas à la classe « non libre ». Muadnat était mon tuteur légal et je lui avais été confiée jusqu'à ce que j'atteigne l'âge du choix. Malheureusement, à ma majorité, même si en théorie il n'avait plus aucun droit sur moi, je n'avais nulle part où aller. J'ai quitté la ferme mais, comme j'étais dans l'impossibilité de subvenir à mes besoins, j'ai été obligée de retourner chez lui.

— Maintenant, les choses ont changé, dit Archú en arborant un petit air satisfait.

Fidelma le mit en garde.

— Méfiez-vous de Muadnat. Il m'est apparu comme un homme rancunier.

— Oh, oui ! Je ne le connais que trop bien, et soyez assurée que je serai vigilant.

Les chevaux avaient maintenant commencé l'ascension des collines, s'éloignant de la rivière au cours tranquille. Ils grimpaient vers les cimes qui dominaient la forêt. La route que l'on empruntait depuis des siècles était largement dégagée et une charrette y passait facilement par temps sec.

Le vent était tombé. On n'entendait plus que le souffle rauque des chevaux. De temps à autre, le jappement d'un chien sauvage ou le hurlement d'un loup, surpris par cette intrusion dans leur territoire, brisaient le silence.

Le soleil commençait déjà à descendre derrière les montagnes et les ombres s'allongeaient. L'air s'était rafraîchi. Fidelma se rappela que le lendemain serait jour de fête, en souvenir de Conláed le bienheureux, un ferronnier de Kildare qui avait forgé les vases sacrés du monastère de Brigitte. Comme chaque année, elle allumerait un cierge en mémoire de Conláed. L'été irlandais commençait, et il s'achèverait avec la fête de Lughnasa, un des festivals païens populaires que la nouvelle foi n'était pas parvenue à abolir. Les chevaux grimpaient sans se presser, et Eadulf jetait des coups d'œil inquiets aux dernières lueurs flamboyantes du soleil, derrière eux.

— Il va bientôt faire nuit, fit-il observer.

— Nous ne sommes plus très loin, le rassura Archú. Vous voyez ce virage vers la droite ? Là, nous emprunterons le sentier qui grimpe dans la montagne en longeant le ruisseau qui coupe notre route.

Ils progressaient en silence, puis les chevaux s'engagèrent l'un derrière l'autre dans la forêt d'ifs et de chênes, peinant sur une piste caillouteuse visiblement peu fréquentée.

Une heure s'écoula.

— Êtes-vous certain que nous sommes sur la bonne voie ? demanda Eadulf pour la troisième fois. Je ne vois point d'auberge à l'horizon.

Archú pointa le doigt.

— Elle va nous apparaître au bout de cette courbe.

Le chemin se perdait entre les arbres. Malgré le ciel dégagé, la forêt obscurcissait leur vision et, en levant la tête, ils distinguaient à peine quelques étoiles qui scintillaient entre les branches. Fidelma repéra celle du soir, à l'éclat plus soutenu. L'atmosphère se fit plus oppressante. Ils n'avaient rencontré personne depuis qu'ils avaient quitté la grand-route. Fidelma se demandait s'il ne vaudrait pas mieux s'arrêter pour bivouaquer en attendant l'aube quand le chemin s'élargit, et elle vit une lanterne accrochée à un grand poteau en bordure d'une *faitche*, une pelouse qui s'étendait devant une bâtisse en pierre.

— Nous y sommes, annonça Archú d'un ton joyeux.

Ils arrêtèrent leurs chevaux près du poteau. Sur une planche en bois, clouée sous la lanterne, Fidelma déchiffra *Bruden na Réaltaí*, l'hôtellerie des Étoiles, gravé en caractères latins. Et effectivement, ce soir-là, des myriades d'entre elles scintillaient dans les cieux. L'auberge portait bien son nom.

À cet instant, un vieil homme en ouvrit la porte et s'avança pour les accueillir.

— Bienvenue, voyageurs ! s'exclama le vieillard d'une voix enrouée. Entrez vite vous réchauffer pendant que je m'occupe de vos chevaux.

À l'intérieur, un grand feu flambait dans la cheminée. Dans un chaudron accroché au-dessus des flammes mijotait une soupe d'où s'échappait un fumet délicieux. L'endroit était confortable et chaleureux. Les lumières des lanternes se reflétaient sur les lambris de chêne et de sapin rouge. Sur une table à un bout de la pièce, Fidelma remarqua un assemblage de cailloux disposés de façon ornementale. Intriguée, elle en prit un qui pesait dans sa main aussi lourd que du métal.

Perplexe, Fidelma fronça les sourcils puis retourna près du feu mais ne s'assit pas. Après la chevauchée, elle avait besoin de se dérouiller les jambes.

Quand Archú la rejoignit, il avait l'air nerveux.

— Excusez-moi, ma sœur, j'aurais dû vous prévenir avant notre départ, mais Scoth et moi n'avons pas d'argent. D'ailleurs, nous avions prévu de dormir dans les bois. Le temps est sec et contrairement à ce que prétend l'hôtelier, il ne fait pas très froid.

Fidelma secoua la tête.

— Vous oubliez que vous êtes un *óc-aire*. Vous avez gagné votre procès et j'aurais mauvaise grâce à ne pas vous avancer le prix de la nourriture et du logement pour la nuit.

— Mais…

— Le problème est réglé, Archú. Un lit vaut mieux que la terre humide et le potage qui mitonne dans cette marmite vous met l'eau à la bouche.

Elle jeta un coup d'œil curieux à l'hôtellerie déserte.

— Il semblerait que nous sommes les seuls voyageurs sur cette route, ce soir, lança Eadulf en s'asseyant sur une chaise près du foyer.

— Elle est peu fréquentée, mais il n'y a que ce chemin pour aller dans le pays d'Araglin, expliqua Archú.

— Dans ce cas, et s'il s'agit de l'unique auberge, je m'étonne que votre cousin Muadnat ne s'y soit pas arrêté.

— J'en remercie Dieu, murmura Scoth en prenant place à la table.

— Pourtant, lui et son compagnon…

— Agdae, son neveu et son chef de troupeaux, précisa Scoth.

— Eh bien, Muadnat et Agdae ont quitté Lios Mhór avant nous et…

— Pourquoi se soucier de Muadnat ? dit Eadulf en bâillant, les yeux fixés sur le chaudron.

— Je n'aime pas les mystères non résolus.

La porte s'ouvrit et l'aubergiste au visage rond et rougeaud couronné de cheveux gris réapparut. Ses manières étaient plaisantes et chaleureuses, et un large sourire illuminait sa face.

— Je suis très heureux de vous accueillir chez moi. Je me suis occupé de vos chevaux et les ai menés à l'écurie. Je m'appelle Bressal et ma maison est la vôtre.

— Nous aimerions dormir ici cette nuit, lui annonça Fidelma.

— Mais certainement, ma sœur.

— Et aussi assouvir notre faim, ajouta Eadulf, décidément très intéressé par ce qui mijotait.

— Et vous ne refuserez pas de l'hydromel pour étancher votre soif ? dit l'hôtelier d'un ton jovial. Mon hydromel est le meilleur de la région.

— Parfait ! s'exclama Eadulf avec enthousiasme. Servez-nous donc le repas.

— Nous devons d'abord nous purifier de la poussière du voyage, intervint Fidelma.

Les coutumes irlandaises voulaient que l'on se lave chaque soir avant le principal repas de la journée. Ne pas se baigner avant le dîner était considéré comme un manque d'éducation mais, ce rituel n'ayant pas cours dans le pays saxon, Eadulf avait du mal à s'y soumettre.

— Je vais faire chauffer de l'eau pour vos ablutions, ce qui me prendra un peu de temps, car je n'ai personne ici pour m'aider, s'excusa le vieil homme.

— Je m'accommoderai très bien d'un bain froid, dit aussitôt Eadulf. Et vous, Archú ?

Le jeune homme acquiesça après un instant d'hésitation, et Fidelma fit une moue désapprobatrice.

Elle croyait au rituel de la purification accompli selon les règles.

— Faites comme bon vous semble pendant que Scoth et moi aidons Bressal à porter les seaux.

Bressal ouvrit les mains d'un air gêné.

— Je regrette d'être obligé de vous mettre à contribution, ma sœur. Venez, je vais vous montrer la maison des bains. Quant à vous, mon frère, il y a un ruisseau tout près d'ici. Tenez, prenez cette lanterne.

Archú prit la lanterne à regret et Eadulf lui donna une bourrade.

— Oubliez les baquets, mon garçon, une baignade à cette saison n'a jamais tué personne.

Une bonne heure s'écoula avant qu'ils se retrouvent autour de la table. La soupe d'avoine et de poireaux

aux herbes fut suivie d'un plat de truites pêchées dans un cours d'eau voisin et servies avec du pain frais et de l'hydromel doux. Ses hôtes félicitèrent Bressal pour ses talents de cuisinier.

Tandis qu'il les servait, il leur fit la conversation et les entretint des menus événements agitant la contrée. Comme il vivait dans un certain isolement, il n'était pas encore informé du meurtre du chef d'Araglin et Archú, qui depuis le jugement avait acquis une certaine assurance, lui conta l'histoire sur le ton qui convenait à sa nouvelle situation d'*ócaire* en Araglin.

Puis Fidelma demanda :

— Sommes-nous les uniques voyageurs que vous ayez reçus ce soir ?

Bressal fit la grimace.

— Vous êtes mes seuls clients en une semaine. Cette route n'est malheureusement pas très fréquentée.

— Je suppose qu'il existe d'autres voies menant en Araglin ?

— Une seule, qui part de l'est de la vallée, et permet de rejoindre Lios Mhór, Ard Mór et Dún Garbháin. Vous avez emprunté celle qui relie Cashel à Lios Mhór, au sud. Pourquoi me posez-vous cette question ?

Archú fronça les sourcils.

— On m'avait pourtant affirmé que c'était l'unique itinéraire conduisant à Lios Mhór.

— Qui donc vous a renseigné ?

— Le père Gormán d'Araglin.

— Je ne comprends pas, la route à l'est permet d'atteindre plus rapidement Lios Mhór, s'étonna Bressal. Je m'étonne que le père Gormán connaisse aussi mal la région.

Fidelma détourna son attention en désignant l'assortiment de cailloux sur la petite table à l'autre extrémité de la pièce.

— Vous avez là un arrangement décoratif des plus intéressants.

— C'est l'œuvre de mon frère Morna, expliqua Bressal. Il travaille dans les mines situées à l'ouest, dans la plaine des Minéraux. Il m'a confié ces pierres et je les garde pour lui.

Très intéressée, Fidelma en prit quelques-unes qu'elle tourna et retourna dans sa main.

— Morna les collectionne depuis des années. Mais il y a un jour ou deux, il m'a rendu visite et m'a annoncé qu'il avait fait une découverte qui ferait de lui un homme riche. Il avait apporté un nouvel éclat de roche et semblait très excité. Comment pensait-il s'enrichir avec ça, je l'ignore. Il a passé la nuit ici et il est reparti le lendemain.

— De quelle pierre s'agit-il ?

Bressal se gratta la tête.

— Je ne me souviens pas très bien.

Il en choisit une et la lui tendit.

— Celle-là, je crois.

Fidelma l'examina attentivement. Pour un œil non exercé, le caillou ressemblait à un morceau de granit ordinaire qu'elle rendit à l'hôtelier qui le remit en place.

— Désirez-vous quelque service particulier avant de vous retirer pour la nuit ? demanda alors l'aubergiste.

Archú et Scoth décidèrent d'aller se coucher tandis qu'Eadulf se servait un autre gobelet d'hydromel et annonçait qu'il resterait un moment au coin du feu. Quant à Fidelma, elle rapprocha sa chaise de celle de Bressal. Elle avait dans l'idée de le faire parler, car les hôteliers représentaient toujours une bonne source d'information. Bressal n'avait vu Eber que cinq ou six fois, sur la route de Cashel, et, d'après lui, les opinions sur le chef étaient très partagées. Certains le décrivaient comme un tyran tandis que d'autres le louaient pour sa gentillesse et sa générosité.

Quand Fidelma se retira pour la nuit, il était encore tôt. Le premier étage consistait en une seule grande pièce divisée en alcôves par des tentures, car, dans les petites hôtelleries de ce genre, il était rare de trouver des chambres séparées pour y loger les voyageurs. Fidelma alla s'étendre sur la paillasse qui lui avait été allouée, et ramena sur elle l'épaisse couverture de laine. L'endroit était propre, chaud et confortable, et elle poussa un soupir de contentement avant de sombrer dans le sommeil.

Elle se réveilla en sursaut alors qu'il lui semblait qu'elle venait à peine de poser sa tête sur l'oreiller. En sentant une main qui lui serrait doucement le bras, elle cligna des yeux et voulut se débattre quand la voix d'Eadulf lui murmura :

— Chut, c'est moi. J'ai repéré des hommes armés à l'extérieur de l'auberge.

Une lumière grise filtrait de la fenêtre sans rideaux et Fidelma aperçut une ou deux étoiles pâlissantes annonciatrices de l'aube.

— Qu'est-ce qui vous inquiète, concernant ces hommes ? chuchota Fidelma.

— Il y a environ un quart d'heure, j'ai entendu des chevaux. En regardant dehors, j'ai aperçu les ombres de cinq ou six cavaliers qui chevauchaient en silence. Ensuite, ils ont caché leurs montures dans les bois et ont grimpé dans les arbres qui sont face à la porte de l'auberge.

Fidelma se redressa brusquement.

— Des bandits ?

— Peut-être. En tout cas, ils portaient des arcs.

— Avez-vous alerté Bressal ?

— C'est lui que j'ai averti le premier. Il est en train de barricader les portes.

— A-t-il été attaqué auparavant ?

— Jamais. De riches hôtelleries sur la route principale reliant Lios Mhór à Cashel ont parfois été pillées par des bandes de hors-la-loi, mais je ne comprends pas l'intérêt de s'en prendre à cette pauvre auberge.

— Les jeunes gens sont debout ?

— Non, pas encore…

Fidelma entendit un sifflement assourdi et crut sentir une odeur de fumée. Au deuxième sifflement, une flèche dont la pointe était garnie de paille enflammée traversa la fenêtre et alla se ficher dans le mur derrière elle, tandis qu'ils entendaient distinctement un homme donner des ordres à l'extérieur.

Fidelma bondit de sa paillasse.

— Réveillez Archú et Scoth !

À cet instant arriva une autre flèche qui se planta dans le plancher. Fidelma se précipita pour l'arracher et la jeta par la fenêtre, et fit de même avec la première. Puis elle rabattit son capuchon sur sa tête et entreprit de faire tomber les tentures, de crainte qu'elles ne prennent feu. Archú, secoué de sa torpeur par Eadulf, se précipita pour l'aider.

— Allongez-vous et restez ici, lui ordonna Fidelma. Si d'autres flèches pénètrent dans cette pièce, éteignez les flammes avec les couvertures.

Et sans attendre sa réponse, elle dévala les marches de l'escalier.

Dans la pièce principale, Bressal tentait maladroitement de bander un arc.

Quand il releva la tête, son visage était plissé par la colère.

— Des bandits ! grommela-t-il. C'est bien la première fois qu'ils s'aventurent jusqu'ici. Je dois défendre ma maison.

À son tour, Eadulf descendit les marches quatre à quatre.

— Vous avez bien dit que vous estimiez le nombre de ces hommes à cinq ou six ? lui demanda Fidelma.

— Oui. Bressal, avez-vous d'autres armes ?

L'hôtelier, qui ne comprenait pas qu'un homme d'Église lui pose cette question, fixait Eadulf d'un air ahuri.

— Vite ! s'écria ce dernier.

L'autre sursauta.

— Je ne possède que deux épées et cet arc.

Autant qu'Eadulf pouvait en juger, l'arc d'if, souple et solide, était en bon état de fonctionnement.

— Savez-vous vous en servir ?

— Pas vraiment, confessa l'aubergiste.

— Alors donnez-le-moi.

— Mais… vous êtes un moine !

Fidelma tapa du pied.

— Ne discutez pas !

Eadulf lui arracha l'arc des mains et le banda avec une aisance née d'une longue expérience.

— Moi, je prendrai une des épées, annonça Fidelma.

Elle n'avait pas le temps d'expliquer à l'hôtelier stupéfait qu'en tant que fille de Failbe Flann, roi de Cashel, son apprentissage des armes avait précédé celui de la lecture et de l'écriture.

Eadulf se saisit de la poignée de flèches posées sur la table.

— Y a-t-il une autre issue ?

Bressal fit un geste en direction de l'arrière de la maison et Fidelma consulta Eadulf du regard.

— Je vais essayer de les prendre à revers, expliqua Eadulf.

— Je vous accompagne.

Eadulf n'avait pas le temps de l'en dissuader.

Fidelma se tourna alors vers Bressal.

— Nos jeunes compagnons à l'étage éteindront les flèches enflammées qui tombent dans la pièce. Vous, restez ici, mais bâclez bien la porte dès que nous serons sortis.

Les événements se succédaient à un rythme trop rapide pour Bressal qui resta muet.

Les deux religieux s'avancèrent vers la porte de derrière. Bressal en ôta la barre, jeta un rapide coup d'œil à l'extérieur et leur fit signe que la voie était libre. Eadulf rejoignit en courant les arbres de l'autre côté de la cour, suivi par Fidelma quelques secondes plus tard. Ils remercièrent le ciel que leurs attaquants n'aient pas eu la présence d'esprit d'encercler l'hôtellerie.

En contournant la maison ils constatèrent que des flèches avaient été tirées sur la façade. Une ou deux avaient atterri sur le toit de chaume et, si l'assaut n'était pas rapidement repoussé, bientôt l'auberge serait réduite en cendres.

Le jour commençait à se lever.

Fidelma, qui se tenait à couvert, aperçut des silhouettes dans le sous-bois en face d'eux. Elle comprit tout de suite qu'il ne s'agissait pas de guerriers professionnels car les assaillants se déplaçaient et s'interpellaient bruyamment pour signaler leurs positions. À l'évidence, ils ne s'attendaient à aucune résistance de la part de l'aubergiste et de ses hôtes. Fidelma s'étonna cependant qu'ils n'aient pas choisi de pénétrer en force dans la maison pour y dépouiller ses occupants. Apparemment, ils n'avaient pas d'autre but que de brûler l'hôtellerie.

Eadulf, qui avait bandé son arc, attendait le bon moment pour intervenir.

Quand un des hommes qui tiraient des flèches enflammées se redressa, Fidelma plissa les paupières. Sa silhouette qui se détachait dans la lumière du petit matin faisait une merveilleuse cible. Fidelma posa la main sur le bras d'Eadulf qui regarda dans la direction qu'elle lui indiquait. Il leva son arc, visa avec soin, et blessa l'homme à l'épaule droite. Fidelma, qui aurait été contrariée qu'il fût tué, se dit qu'elle n'aurait pas fait mieux. L'assaillant poussa un cri, laissa échapper son arc, et porta la main à son épaule, plié en deux.

Le silence se fit.

Puis quelqu'un courut vers le blessé et des voix rauques s'élevèrent. Ce vacarme aurait fait honte à d'authentiques guerriers. Eadulf, qui avait de nouveau bandé son arc, croisa le regard de Fidelma. Elle hocha la tête.

Eadulf décocha sa flèche et toucha à l'épaule l'archer qui se tenait près de son acolyte.

L'homme hurla et se mit à jurer comme un charretier.

— Nous sommes attaqués, fuyons ! s'écria une voix affolée.

Une clameur et des hennissements s'ensuivirent, et les deux éclopés prirent leurs jambes à leur cou, trébuchant entre les arbres.

Eadulf se saisit d'une troisième flèche.

Des bois en face d'eux sortirent six cavaliers, galopant vers le chemin sans demander leur reste. Les deux blessés, couchés sur le cou de leurs montures, semblaient en piteux état. La petite bande passa près de l'endroit où se tenait Eadulf qui s'apprêtait à les suivre quand Fidelma le retint par la manche.

— Ne forçons pas le destin, lui dit-elle d'un ton apaisant.

Ils avaient eu de la chance d'avoir affaire à des amateurs facilement mis en déroute et elle murmura une courte prière d'action de grâces.

Tandis qu'elle regardait les attaquants s'éloigner, elle avisa le dernier homme du groupe, un grand gaillard assez laid avec une tignasse et une barbe rousses. Eadulf le visa puis abaissa son arc. L'individu se déplaçait à une trop grande vitesse.

Quand les bandits eurent disparu dans la forêt, le moine se tourna vers Fidelma.

— Pourquoi les a-t-on laissés s'échapper ? lui demanda-t-il d'un air faussement naïf.

Fidelma sourit.

— Si vous acculez un lâche, il réagit comme un animal terrorisé et se bat furieusement pour sa liberté. Et puis on a besoin de nous à l'auberge. Le feu couve sous le chaume et les flammes commencent à s'élever.

Elle se dépêcha de rejoindre l'hôtellerie et cria à Bressal qu'ils avaient mis les bandits en déroute. Il sortit pour évaluer les dégâts, amena une échelle et ils eurent tôt fait de former une chaîne pour arroser le toit.

Finalement, l'incendie fut maîtrisé, le chaume humide ne fumait plus et Bressal, transpirant et reconnaissant, sortit un flacon d'hydromel qu'il versa dans des gobelets avant de les distribuer à la ronde.

— Trinquons ! Je vous remercie de tout mon cœur d'avoir sauvé mon auberge des assauts de ces coquins.

— Les avez-vous vus de près, ma sœur ? s'enquit le jeune Archú.

— Je les ai juste entr'aperçus.

— Deux d'entre eux vont souffrir de l'épaule, ajouta Eadulf d'un air grave.

— Que diable venaient-ils faire ici, un des endroits les plus pauvres de la région ? s'étonna Archú.

Fidelma haussa les sourcils.

— À mon avis, leur but était de brûler cette maison et non de nous voler.

Eadulf hocha la tête.

— Sinon, ils auraient fait irruption à l'intérieur pour nous détrousser.

— Et s'ils avaient agi sous l'emprise d'une impulsion subite alors qu'ils passaient ici par hasard ? avança Bressal d'un ton peu convaincu.

Moue dubitative d'Eadulf.

— Vous avez dit vous-même que l'endroit était isolé et que la route ne menait qu'à Araglin.

Bressal ouvrit les mains d'un air désemparé.

— Avez-vous des ennemis ? lui demanda Eadulf. Connaissez-vous quelqu'un qui souhaiterait vous bannir de ces lieux ?

— Personne, affirma aussitôt Bressal. Nul ne profiterait de la destruction de cette auberge. J'ai vécu et travaillé ici toute ma vie.

— Dans ce cas…

Fidelma coupa brutalement son compagnon.

— Sans doute s'agissait-il d'une bande de brigands intéressés par des rapines faciles. Mais nous leur avons donné une bonne leçon.

Eadulf allait poursuivre quand il croisa le regard de Fidelma qui le fixait avec intensité et il referma la bouche.

— J'ai été sauvé grâce à vous, dit Bressal qui n'avait rien remarqué. Tout seul, je n'aurais jamais pu les repousser.

— Et maintenant, je crois qu'il est temps que nous rompions le jeûne de la nuit avant de repartir, jugea Fidelma.

Après qu'ils se furent restaurés, Archú annonça que lui et Scoth se rendraient directement à la ferme d'Archú sans passer par le *rath* d'Araglin. Ils proposèrent à Bressal de passer une heure ou deux avec lui pour l'aider à nettoyer l'auberge et réparer le chaume, tandis que les deux religieux poursuivraient leur chemin.

Bressal leur offrit alors de garder les armes qu'ils avaient empruntées.

— Comme vous l'avez constaté vous-mêmes, elles ne me sont pas d'une grande utilité car je ne sais pas m'en servir. Et comme ces bandits ont pris le chemin d'Araglin, je serais fort contrarié que vous vous retrouviez désarmés s'ils vous cherchaient à nouveau querelle.

Sans l'intervention de Fidelma, Eadulf aurait volontiers accepté le présent de Bressal.

— Nous ne vivons pas selon l'épée, déclara-t-elle avec solennité. D'après le bienheureux Matthieu, le Christ a dit à Pierre : « Tous ceux qui prennent le glaive périront par le glaive[1]. » Mieux vaut avancer mains nues dans le monde.

Bressal fit la grimace.

— Si vous voulez mon avis, face à ceux qui vivent par l'épée, mieux vaut être capable de se défendre.

Quelques instants plus tard sur le chemin d'Araglin, Eadulf interrogea Fidelma sur son attitude.

— Pourquoi diable m'avez-vous empêché de dire ce qui tombait sous le sens ?

— À savoir que ces bandits venaient d'Araglin ?

— Oui, et vous aussi vous suspectez Muadnat.

Fidelma nia avec énergie.

— Pas du tout, et soulever cette question aurait pu effrayer Archú et Scoth, alors que de nombreuses hypothèses s'offrent à nous. Devons-nous croire Bressal quand il affirme qu'il n'a pas d'ennemis ? Et il n'a pas forcément tort quand il se demande s'il ne s'agit pas d'une attaque improvisée. À moins que cette regrettable échauffourée ne soit liée à la mort d'Eber.

Eadulf parut sceptique.

— Vous pensez vraiment qu'une personne impliquée dans l'assassinat d'Eber tenterait par de tels moyens de s'opposer à votre enquête ?

— Je ne faisais que suggérer d'autres possibilités et je ne prétends point détenir la vérité. Demeurons vigilants, Eadulf, car on est facilement égaré par des suppositions qui ne s'appuient pas sur des preuves tangibles.

---

1. Matthieu, 26, 52. Les citations bibliques sont celles de la Bible de Jérusalem (Éditions du Cerf, 1998). (*N.d.T.*)

CHAPITRE IV

Par une matinée ensoleillée, après avoir longtemps chevauché en silence, Fidelma et Eadulf émergèrent de la forêt pour se retrouver sur un chemin à flanc de colline d'où l'on avait une vue magnifique sur une vallée d'environ un mile de large, où coulait une rivière argentée. Cette vallée, dominée par des hauteurs dénudées, avait depuis longtemps été métamorphosée par la main de l'homme et les champs cultivés, délimités par des murets de pierres sèches, alternaient avec les vertes prairies et les ajoncs dorés.

Fidelma eut le soufflé coupé par la beauté du paysage. Au loin, elle distingua un cerf, des biches et des faons tachetés de blanc. Des troupeaux se déplaçaient lentement dans les riches pâturages. Quant à la rivière, elle regorgeait certainement de saumons et de truites.

Eadulf se pencha sur l'encolure de son cheval.

— Cet Araglin ressemble au paradis, murmura-t-il.

Fidelma pinça les lèvres.

— N'oubliez pas qu'un serpent s'y est glissé.

— Cette terre serait un motif de meurtre suffisant. Un chef à la tête de ces richesses est nécessairement vulnérable.

— Je croyais que vous connaissiez mieux nos coutumes, s'énerva Fidelma. À la mort d'un chef, le *derbfhine* de la famille se réunit pour confirmer la nomination du *tanist*, l'héritier présomptif qui est intronisé chef, puis il désigne un nouveau *tanist*. Seul l'héritier peut tirer un bénéfice direct du décès d'un chef, ce qui, en cas d'assassinat, ferait immédiatement porter les soupçons sur lui. Il est donc fort rare qu'un chef soit supprimé en raison de sa fonction.

— Le *derbfhine* ? En quoi consiste-t-il exactement ? Mes souvenirs sont assez vagues.

— Ce conseil est composé de la famille du chef, qui comprend trois générations de parents.

— Ne serait-il pas plus simple de transmettre le pouvoir au fils aîné, comme chez les Saxons ?

— Nous préférons choisir la personne la plus apte à exercer de hautes responsabilités plutôt qu'un imbécile, nommé seulement parce qu'il est le plus âgé des fils.

Puis Fidelma tendit le doigt vers un point de la vallée.

— Regardez, voici le *rath*.

Eadulf savait qu'un *rath* était une fortification, mais les bâtiments qu'il apercevait au loin, entourés d'ifs en fleur et de hêtres aux feuilles toutes neuves, ressemblaient davantage à un village. Au cours de ses pérégrinations dans les cinq royaumes, Eadulf avait rencontré des dignitaires vivant dans des forteresses, mais ce *rath* ne comportait que des fermes et des chaumières en bois. Il repéra cependant quelques bâtiments de pierre, dont la chapelle de Cill Uird, adjacente à une bâtisse ronde où siégeait sans doute la grande assemblée.

— Les gens d'Araglin, des paysans pour la plupart, expliqua Fidelma en constatant sa surprise, sont protégés par les montagnes. Cette petite communauté ne menace personne et elle n'a jamais vu la nécessité d'édifier des murailles pour se protéger de ses ennemis. Nous avons cependant pour habitude d'appeler *rath* le lieu de résidence d'un chef.

Elle enfonça ses talons dans les flancs de son cheval qui s'engagea sur la pente conduisant à la vallée. Bientôt, Eadulf arrêtait sa monture devant une grande croix de dix-huit pieds de haut qui se dressait au bord du sentier.

— Je n'avais jamais rien vu de tel auparavant, dit-il d'un ton admiratif.

Fidelma sourit. Le royaume comptait quelques croix spectaculaires. Les scènes évangéliques sculptées dans la pierre étaient peintes de couleurs vives. Eadulf reconnut la chute d'Adam, Moïse fendant le rocher, le Jugement dernier et la crucifixion. Le sommet de la croix évoquait une église au toit de bardeaux avec pignon à fleurons. Sur le socle était gravé *Oroit do Eoghan lasdernad inn Chros*, une prière pour Eoghan qui a conçu cette croix.

— Voilà une borne spectaculaire pour marquer la limite d'une aussi petite communauté, fit observer Eadulf.

— Petite mais riche, le corrigea Fidelma. Allons, venez.

Ils arrivèrent au *rath* vers midi. Quand ils passèrent devant un gardien de troupeau, ce dernier les dévisagea avec un intérêt non dissimulé. Un homme occupé à sarcler les mauvaises herbes dans son champ de céréales s'appuya sur sa houe, et leur lança un salut jovial. Fidelma le bénit en retour. Non loin de là, des chiens se mirent à aboyer et deux chiens de chasse vinrent à leur rencontre, jappant et agitant la queue.

Un pont de chêne d'une conception audacieuse, qui permettait d'accéder au *rath*, enjambait le cours d'eau bouillonnant. Eadulf remarqua qu'un large fossé, maintenant à moitié comblé et recouvert d'herbe et de broussailles, avait autrefois encerclé le village. On le distinguait à peine des champs verdoyants alentour. Des moutons paissaient dans cette dépression, seule trace d'une ancienne fortification. Une clôture d'osier entrelacé de branches de noisetier avait remplacé les murailles. Elle servait à maintenir les loups et les sangliers à distance, mais se serait révélée bien peu efficace contre d'éventuels agresseurs. Un portail grand ouvert, pratiqué dans cette haie, permettait de pénétrer à l'intérieur du hameau.

Tandis qu'ils franchissaient la rivière, les sabots des chevaux résonnèrent sur le pont de bois, puis ils grimpèrent le court chemin menant aux grilles.

Un homme apparut à l'entrée, armé d'une épée et d'un bouclier. C'était un solide gaillard dans la force de l'âge et dont la barbe noire, taillée avec soin, comptait quelques fils d'argent. Debout au milieu du chemin, il posa sur eux un regard curieux, dénué d'hostilité.

— Si vous venez ici en paix, soyez les bienvenus, les salua-t-il selon le rituel.

— Que Dieu bénisse ce village, répondit Fidelma. Nous sommes bien au *rath* du chef d'Araglin ?

— Vous y êtes.

— Alors nous aimerions voir le chef.

— Eber est mort.

— Nous en avons déjà été informés. Je voulais parler du *tanist* qui doit lui succéder.

Le guerrier hésita un instant.

— Suivez-moi, dit-il enfin. La *tanist* se trouve en ce moment même au siège de l'assemblée.

L'homme les mena vers l'imposant édifice rond conçu pour impressionner les étrangers. Il donnait sur le portail, cela afin qu'aucun visiteur ne puisse l'éviter. Près de la porte à double battant se dressait un chêne émondé de douze pieds de haut, dont le sommet avait été sculpté en forme de croix. Même Eadulf savait qu'il s'agissait là de l'ancien totem du clan, son *crann betha* ou arbre de vie, qui symbolisait le bien-être moral et matériel du peuple. On lui avait raconté qu'au cours d'un conflit, un clan pouvait organiser un raid pour couper ou brûler l'arbre sacré d'un clan adverse. Un tel acte, quand il était couronné de succès, démoralisait les gens et permettait à leurs assaillants de se déclarer victorieux.

Fidelma et Eadulf glissèrent de leurs selles et attachèrent leurs chevaux à un pieu non loin de là. En les voyant, plusieurs personnes qui vaquaient à leurs occupations s'étaient déjà arrêtées et étudiaient les deux religieux avec un intérêt évident.

— Les étrangers sont peu fréquents en Araglin, fit observer le guerrier. Notre communauté de paysans est rarement troublée par les événements du monde extérieur.

Fidelma ne fit aucun commentaire.

L'ensemble des constructions disposées en un large demi-cercle autour du siège de l'assemblée respirait la prospérité. Il y avait là des granges, des étables, un moulin et un pigeonnier. Au-delà s'égaillaient des chaumières et des cabanes en bois, ainsi que la maison du chef et de ses parents. Le tout occupait la surface d'un village de taille moyenne. Fidelma estima rapidement la population à quelques dizaines de familles. L'édifice le plus impressionnant demeurait la chapelle en pierre, de proportions harmonieuses, sise à côté du siège de l'assemblée. Fidelma l'identifia aussitôt comme Cill Uird, l'« église du rituel » du père Gormán.

Le guerrier, qui s'était avancé jusqu'à la porte en chêne, se saisit d'un maillet rangé dans une niche et frappa sur un rectangle en bois encastré dans un des battants. La coutume voulait qu'un chef mette un *bas-chrann* ou heurtoir à la disposition des visiteurs afin qu'ils signalent leur présence s'ils demandaient audience. Le guerrier entra et disparut.

Eadulf se tourna vers Fidelma.

— Je croyais qu'un tel rite ne s'appliquait qu'aux demeures privées des grands chefs, murmura-t-il.

— Chaque chef est grand à ses propres yeux, répliqua Fidelma avec philosophie.

Les portes se rouvrirent et le guerrier les fit pénétrer à l'intérieur. Ils se retrouvèrent dans une pièce de proportions imposantes, lambrissée de sapin et de chêne. Un peu partout étaient accrochés des boucliers en bronze brunis et incrustés de pierreries. Ici et là, des tapisseries apportaient des notes de couleur. Le plancher, les bancs et les tables étaient en chêne foncé. Face à l'entrée s'élevait une plate-forme haute d'un pied, où se dressait un magnifique fauteuil en bois incrusté de bronze et d'argent. Une peau d'ours avait été jetée sur un des bras.

Ce bâtiment sans fenêtres était éclairé par des lampes à huile qui pendaient des poutres, et un feu brûlait dans une énorme cheminée. Des lumières vacillantes dansaient dans toute la pièce, prêtant à cet endroit une atmosphère mystérieuse.

Le guerrier leur demanda d'attendre un instant et les laissa seuls dans ce cadre magnifique destiné à impressionner les visiteurs.

Eadulf était très admiratif et Fidelma elle-même dut reconnaître que cette salle n'aurait pas déparé dans le château de son frère, à Cashel.

Bientôt, une jeune femme surgit de derrière une tapisserie et vint se placer devant le fauteuil sculpté. Malgré l'atmosphère enfumée, Fidelma vit qu'elle n'avait pas vingt ans et qu'elle était séduisante, avec de longues tresses blondes et des yeux bleu pâle. Mais il se dégageait de sa personne une certaine sévérité, due à son regard glacial et à ses lèvres dédaigneuses.

Elle portait une robe de soie bleue et un châle en laine de la même teinte attaché par une broche en or de grande valeur. Les mains croisées devant elle, elle posa sur les visiteurs un regard distant.

— Je suis Crón, *tanist* d'Araglin. On m'a rapporté que vous désiriez me voir.

Sa voix claire et bien timbrée était dénuée de toute chaleur.

Fidelma dissimula son étonnement. Comment une fille aussi jeune pouvait-elle représenter un clan ? Les communautés rurales étaient plutôt conservatrices quant au choix de leurs chefs.

— Vous m'attendiez, il me semble, répliqua Fidelma d'un ton neutre.

La jeune fille demeura impassible.

— Nous n'attendons aucun religieux. Le père Gormán subvient à nos besoins spirituels et il s'acquitte très bien de cette tâche.

Fidelma poussa un soupir agacé.

— Je suis *dálaigh* des cours de justice et on m'a demandé de venir en ces lieux pour mener une enquête sur la mort d'Eber, votre ancien chef.

Le visage de Crón trahit une expression de surprise vite effacée.

— Eber était mon père, dit-elle. Il a été assassiné. C'est sans mon approbation que ma mère a envoyé un messager à Cashel pour requérir un *dálaigh*. En ce qui concerne cette affaire, j'estime être en mesure de conduire ma propre enquête. Cependant, je m'étonne que le roi de Cashel réponde à notre requête en nous envoyant une personne aussi jeune que vous, et sans doute assez peu informée des choses de ce monde. Je suppose que vous vivez confinée dans un cloître ?

Frère Eadulf, qui se tenait juste derrière Fidelma, vit ses épaules se crisper. Mais alors qu'il s'attendait à un éclat de colère, elle demeura très calme.

— Mon frère Colgú, roi de Cashel…

Là, elle marqua une pause.

— … m'a priée de me charger personnellement de cette affaire. Vous vous trompez en vous imaginant que je manque d'expérience. On m'a élevée à la fonction d'*anruth*, et je serais tentée de croire que ma pratique des choses de ce monde, comme vous dites, dépasse de loin la vôtre, *tanist* d'Araglin.

La qualification d'*anruth* venait juste avant la plus haute dignité accordée par les collèges séculiers et ecclésiastiques d'Irlande.

Les deux femmes s'affrontèrent en silence, évaluant rapidement leurs forces et leurs faiblesses, yeux bleus contre yeux verts dans des visages fermés.

— Je vois, murmura Crón d'une voix douce.

Puis elle revint à sa manière hautaine.

— Et quel est votre nom, sœur de Colgú ?

— Fidelma.

— Votre compagnon… semble étranger en ce pays.

— Je vous présente frère Eadulf.

— Un Saxon ? s'étonna Crón.

— Il est l'émissaire de l'archevêque de Cantorbéry à la cour de Cashel. Il a étudié dans nos collèges, connaît bien les cinq royaumes et a exprimé le désir de voir comment nous appliquions la loi dans les campagnes.

Il s'agissait d'une vérité tronquée, mais Fidelma estima qu'elle suffisait pour l'instant.

La jeune femme toisa Eadulf, inclina la tête et retourna à Fidelma sans prendre la peine de demander à ses hôtes s'ils désiraient s'asseoir.

— L'affaire qui nous occupe, et que j'aurais très bien pu résoudre moi-même, se résume en quelques mots. Mon père a été poignardé jusqu'à ce que mort s'ensuive. Móen, le meurtrier, a été découvert près du corps. Ses mains, qui tenaient un poignard, et ses vêtements étaient couverts de sang.

— On m'a parlé du cadavre d'une deuxième personne.

— Ma tante Teafa, retrouvée plus tard, a été tuée de la même manière. Elle avait élevé Móen qui vivait dans sa maison.

— Je vous remercie. En attendant que j'entreprenne mes investigations, peut-être pourriez-vous donner des instructions pour que l'on nous conduise à l'hôtellerie des invités ? Après ce voyage, un bain et de la nourriture nous seraient fort agréables car il est midi passé. Quand nous nous serons restaurés, nous interrogerons les personnes impliquées dans ce drame.

Crón s'empourpra. Si la religieuse n'avait été une personne d'un rang supérieur au sien, la *tanist* aurait considéré la façon dont Fidelma l'avait rappelée à ses devoirs d'hôtesse comme une insulte. Ses yeux bleus brillèrent d'un éclat métallique et, pendant un court instant, Eadulf se demanda si elle n'allait pas leur refuser l'hospitalité. Puis elle haussa les épaules, prit une clochette en argent sur une petite table et l'agita vigoureusement.

Ils attendirent dans un silence pesant qu'une vieille femme légèrement voûtée apparaisse à une porte latérale. Elle avait un visage de paysanne aux joues creusées, des cheveux gris, une peau tannée plissée par les rides et des yeux délavés, mais vifs et soupçonneux comme ceux d'un chat sauvage. Malgré son âge, elle dégageait une impression de force et ses mains calleuses témoignaient d'une vie de durs labeurs. Elle s'avança d'un air anxieux vers Crón.

— Dignait, veillez à ce que nos invités ne manquent de rien. Sœur Fidelma s'est déplacée jusqu'ici pour enquêter sur le meurtre de mon père.

Avant qu'elle ne baisse les paupières, Fidelma crut lire de la surprise et de la crainte dans le regard de la servante.

— Si vous voulez bien me suivre... dit Dignait avec raideur.

Sur ces entrefaites, Crón leur tourna le dos et se dirigea vers la tenture.

— Quand vous serez prêts, lança-t-elle avant de disparaître, je vous expliquerai les détails des tristes événements qui nous ont affligés.

Ils sortirent par la porte latérale et suivirent Dignait qui traversa une cour menant à l'hôtellerie, une maison en bois de plain-pied, située derrière le siège de l'assemblée. La chaumière consistait en un seul espace divisé en plusieurs alcôves par des panneaux en bois de sapin. Chaque alcôve était pourvue d'une paillasse, d'un drap de lin et de couvertures en laine, ainsi que d'une bûche polie creusée en son milieu pour y poser la tête. Les invités prenaient leurs repas à une extrémité de la pièce, meublée d'une table et de deux bancs. Dignait proposa d'allumer un feu dans la cheminée mais Fidelma lui répondit que ce ne serait pas nécessaire car le temps était clément. La salle des bains et les cabinets étaient dissimulés derrière une porte à laquelle était accrochée une petite croix en fer. Fidelma supposa qu'il s'agissait là de l'œuvre du père Gormán, car certains religieux appelaient les toilettes le *fialtech* ou « maison voilée », une conception qui leur venait de Rome. Les Romains croyaient que le démon se tenait caché en embuscade dans les toilettes, et la coutume voulait maintenant que l'on fasse le signe de croix avant d'y entrer.

Quand Fidelma s'inquiéta pour leurs chevaux, Dignait lui dit que Menma, le chef des troupeaux, se chargerait de les panser et de les nourrir.

Fidelma déclara alors que le logement et les commodités lui convenaient tout à fait mais quand Dignait fit mine de partir, elle la retint, et la servante obtempéra avec réticence.

— Je suppose que vous servez depuis de longues années chez vos maîtres ? s'enquit Fidelma.

La vieille femme, les paupières mi-closes, sembla redoubler de méfiance.

— Je suis entrée au service de la mère de Crón il y a plus de vingt ans.

— Vous connaissez Móen ?

La lueur de crainte réapparut dans les yeux de la servante.

— Tout le monde ici connaît Móen. Nous comptons une douzaine de familles, qui entretiennent de nombreux liens de parenté.

— Qui sont les plus proches parents de Móen ?

La vieille servante frissonna et fit une génuflexion.

— C'est un enfant trouvé et Dieu seul sait de quel ventre fécondé par une semence maudite il est sorti. Teafa, paix à son âme égarée, l'a recueilli alors qu'il n'était qu'un nourrisson. Un jour de malheur pour cette gentille dame.

— Sait-on pour quelle raison Móen a tué Eber et Teafa ?

— Il faudrait interroger le Seigneur en personne. Et maintenant excusez-moi mais j'ai du travail qui attend. Pendant que vous prendrez votre bain, Menma s'occupera de vos chevaux et je veillerai à ce que l'on vous fasse porter un repas.

Fidelma fixa la porte qui venait de se refermer sur la vieille domestique.

— Quelque chose vous a troublée ? s'enquit Eadulf.

— Cette femme est hantée par la peur, murmura Fidelma en s'asseyant.

CHAPITRE V

Quand ils se furent lavés et restaurés, ils allèrent retrouver Crón qui avait été prévenue qu'ils désiraient lui parler. Elle les attendait, trônant dans le fauteuil réservé au chef.

À leur entrée, Crón se leva avec des gestes lents qui manquaient d'empressement mais marquaient le respect que la *tanist* devait à la sœur du roi.

— Vous êtes-vous rafraîchis ? demanda-t-elle en leur indiquant des sièges disposés à leur intention devant l'estrade.

— Oui, je vous remercie, répondit Fidelma.

Les deux jeunes femmes s'assirent d'un même mouvement, Fidelma irritée d'être placée dans une position qui l'obligeait à lever la tête vers Crón. Sa charge de *dálaigh* et d'*anruth* l'autorisait à se situer sur le même plan que les rois. Dans l'exercice de ses fonctions, le haut roi de Tara lui-même l'appelait parfois à se placer à sa hauteur pour discuter librement avec elle. Fidelma se montrait très jalouse de ses prérogatives, mais seulement en présence de ceux qui se glorifiaient de leur position. Cependant, si dans la situation présente elle affirmait son rang, elle déclencherait des hostilités ouvertes, ce qui l'empêcherait d'obtenir les informations qu'elle désirait. Elle choisit donc de céder.

Eadulf, qui avait pris place à ses côtés, leva un regard intéressé vers la *tanist*.

— Et maintenant, dit Fidelma en s'appuyant au dossier de sa chaise, je vous écoute. Rapportez-moi les faits concernant la mort de votre père.

Les mains croisées sur ses genoux et le regard fixé au loin, Crón inclina légèrement le buste.

— Les faits se résument en une seule phrase, déclarat-elle d'un ton d'ennui. Móen a tué mon père.

— Vous en avez été le témoin ?

Crón fronça les sourcils et lui adressa un rapide coup d'œil.

— Bien sûr que non. Vous me demandez les faits, je vous les donne.

Les lèvres de Fidelma s'étirèrent en un bref sourire.

— Dans l'intérêt de la justice, je vous demande de me raconter les événements de votre point de vue personnel.

— Je ne suis pas sûre de comprendre.

Fidelma fit un effort pour dominer son impatience.

— Quand avez-vous appris qu'Eber avait été assassiné ?

— J'ai été réveillée au cours de la nuit.

— Il y a combien de jours ?

— Il y a six nuits. Juste avant l'aube pour être plus précise.

Fidelma ignora l'ironie qui perçait dans la voix de la jeune femme.

— En l'occurrence, la précision est une qualité indispensable et elle sert l'intérêt de tous, répliquat-elle avec une politesse glaciale. Par qui avez-vous été réveillée ?

Crón battit des paupières en comprenant que Fidelma ne se laisserait pas intimider. Puis elle haussa les épaules d'un air dédaigneux.

— Par Dubán, le commandant des gardes de mon père. Il avait…

— Contentez-vous de me rapporter ses propos.

— Il s'est écrié qu'il s'était passé quelque chose de terrible et qu'Eber avait été assassiné par Móen, reprit Crón, les traits crispés par la colère.

— Ce sont les termes exacts qu'il a employés ? ne put s'empêcher de demander Eadulf.

Crón le dévisagea et, sans même daigner lui répondre, s'adressa à nouveau à Fidelma.

— Je l'ai prié de me raconter les événements plus en détail. Il m'a alors appris que Móen avait poignardé mon père et qu'il avait été pris sur le fait.

— Comment avez-vous réagi ?

— Je me suis levée et me suis inquiétée du sort de Móen. Il m'a dit qu'il avait été emmené dans une écurie d'où il n'a pas bougé depuis.

— Ensuite ?

— J'ai prié Dubán d'aller chercher ma tante Teafa.

— Et pourquoi donc ?

— Elle est… elle était la seule personne capable de calmer Móen quand il se mettait en fureur.

— Vous confirmez qu'elle l'avait élevé ?

— Oui, depuis sa plus tendre enfance.

— Et aujourd'hui, quel âge a-t-il ? s'enquit Eadulf.

Crón s'apprêtait à passer outre à la question du moine quand Fidelma haussa le ton.

— C'est une question valide, Crón.

— Il a vingt et un ans.

Cette réponse surprit Fidelma. D'après la façon dont Crón et Dignait parlaient de Móen, elle aurait juré qu'il n'était qu'un enfant.

— C'est un garçon difficile ?

— Vous en jugerez par vous-même, répliqua Crón d'un ton aigre.

Fidelma hocha la tête. La *tanist* avait marqué un point.

— Je vous l'accorde. Nous en étions à Teafa, la seule personne en mesure de calmer Móen. Et alors ?

— Dubán a découvert…

Crón se reprit pour mieux formuler sa phrase.

— Quelques instants plus tard, Dubán a réapparu, il venait de découvrir le corps de Teafa. Elle aussi avait été poignardée et il est évident que Móen l'avait assassinée en premier puisque...

Fidelma leva la main.

— Pas de spéculations. Nous devons procéder selon les termes de la loi.

Crón renifla avec agacement.

— Mes prétendues spéculations sont exactes.

— Nous verrons cela plus tard. Qu'est-il arrivé ensuite ?

— Je suis allée prévenir ma mère.

— Votre mère était la femme d'Eber ?

— Bien sûr.

— Donc à cette heure-là, elle ignorait la mort de son époux ?

— Je viens de vous le dire.

— Elle ne se trouvait pas auprès de son mari ?

— Non, elle dormait dans sa chambre.

Fidelma préféra ne pas insister.

— Ensuite ?

Crón haussa les épaules d'un air indifférent.

— On a enfermé Móen et, sans m'en avertir, ma mère a envoyé un jeune guerrier du nom de Crítán à Cashel, pour informer le roi de la tragédie. Sans doute a-t-elle pensé qu'il valait mieux qu'un brehon mène l'enquête plutôt que de laisser sa fille exercer ses pouvoirs en tant que *tanist*. Ma mère ne souhaitait pas que je sois élue *tanist*.

L'amertume de la jeune femme était flagrante.

— Crítán est rentré il y a deux jours en annonçant que le roi enverrait quelqu'un. Comme la coutume l'exige, nous avons donc enterré mon père et Teafa dans le tumulus des chefs. En accord avec la loi, j'ai alors pris la relève de mon père. Et j'aurais été en mesure de dispenser la justice sans complications inutiles.

— Vous oubliez, répliqua Fidelma, que le *derbfhine* doit d'abord se réunir avant de vous confirmer dans vos fonctions. En de telles circonstances, il est indispensable qu'un brehon qualifié assume la charge de l'enquête.

La jeune *tanist* resta muette.

— Très bien, dit Fidelma. Les faits tels que vous me les avez présentés me semblent assez clairs. Dubán a-t-il lui-même découvert le corps de votre père ?

Crón secoua la tête.

— C'est Menma qui a entendu ses cris d'agonie et s'est précipité dans sa chambre pour surprendre Móen en train de commettre son forfait.

— Qui est Menma ?

Il semblait à Fidelma qu'elle avait déjà entendu ce nom.

— Il est en charge des étables de mon père…

Elle se corrigea.

— De mes étables.

Fidelma se rappela soudain que Dignait avait fait allusion à Menma.

— Vous ne voyez aucune zone d'ombre dans les événements tels qu'ils vous ont été rapportés ? reprit Fidelma après un instant de réflexion. Rien ne vous a troublée ou déconcertée ?

— Où voyez-vous des mystères ?

— Comment expliquez-vous que Móen ait tué Eber et Teafa ?

— Il n'existe pas de motivation logique, répondit la jeune femme avec assurance. Mais la logique ne fait pas partie du monde de Móen.

Le ton désabusé de la jeune femme surprit Fidelma qui tenta de percer la raison de cette attitude.

— Si Teafa a élevé Móen, ne lui en était-il pas reconnaissant ? Il doit bien y avoir un mobile quelque part.

— Qui peut deviner ce qui se passe dans l'esprit dormant et enténébré d'une personne telle que Móen ? répliqua la *tanist*.

Le choix des termes utilisés par Crón était des plus étranges et Fidelma faillit la presser de s'expliquer. Puis elle songea que cela influerait sur le regard qu'elle-même porterait sur Móen lors de leur première confrontation, et elle préféra s'en tenir là.

— Il est temps que j'interroge Menma, qui a été le témoin du meurtre, annonça-t-elle.

— Ne vous donnez pas cette peine ! s'écria Crón avec vivacité. Je connais tous les détails de la scène qui m'a été rapportée par Dubán.

— Une *dálaigh* ne procède point ainsi. Les témoignages de première main lui sont indispensables.

— L'important c'est que vous décidiez au plus vite du châtiment de Móen.

— Donc il ne fait aucun doute dans votre esprit que Móen est coupable ?

— Bien sûr, puisque Menma l'a surpris en pleine action.

— Sans doute.

La religieuse se leva, imitée par Eadulf.

— Quel sort réservez-vous à Móen ? insista Crón, déconcertée par l'attitude de Fidelma, car elle n'était pas habituée à ce que des visiteurs prennent congé avant qu'elle les ait congédiés.

— Pour l'instant, je l'ignore. Nous devons tout d'abord nous entretenir avec les différents témoins. Puis nous tiendrons une audience qui permettra à Móen de plaider pour sa défense.

À leur grand étonnement, Crón éclata d'un rire hystérique.

Fidelma attendit patiemment que la *tanist* se calme et demanda :

— Où se trouve Menma, à cette heure ?

— Dans l'écurie, derrière l'hôtellerie des invités, répondit Crón entre deux gloussements.

Ils se dirigeaient vers la sortie quand Crón recouvra son sérieux et les interpella.

— Il vaudrait mieux régler cette affaire au plus vite. Mon père, un homme bon et généreux, était aimé de ses sujets. Nombreux sont ceux de mon peuple qui jugent les vieilles lois de compensation inadaptées à ce crime. Ils préfèrent le châtiment prôné par la nouvelle foi : œil pour œil, dent pour dent, brûlure pour brûlure. Si vous ne tranchez pas rapidement, d'autres se chargeront de faire justice.

Fidelma, qui allait ouvrir la porte, se retourna.

— Je suppose que vous voulez parler de la justice exercée par une foule aveugle ? En tant que chef élu de ce clan – supposons pour l'instant que vous serez confirmée dans cette fonction par votre *derbfhine* – je vous charge de faire circuler l'information suivante : Toute personne qui posera la main sur Móen avant qu'il soit jugé conformément à la loi sera jugée à son tour. Peu importe la position qu'elle occupe en ces lieux.

Crón déglutit avec difficulté et les deux jeunes femmes s'affrontèrent du regard.

— Encore une chose, *tanist*. Qui a prêché la loi du talion au nom de la foi ?

La jeune femme releva le menton.

— Je vous ai déjà avertie qu'ici une seule personne suffisait aux besoins spirituels de notre communauté.

— Le père Gormán ? suggéra Eadulf.

— Le père Gormán, confirma Crón.

— Ce religieux semble très éloigné des conceptions du droit telles qu'elles nous sont enseignées dans les cinq royaumes, lâcha Fidelma d'un ton glacial. Et où se trouve cet aimable avocat de la foi chrétienne ? Dans son église ?

— Il est parti en visite dans quelques fermes éloignées et rentrera demain.

— Je suis impatiente de le rencontrer.

Sur ces mots, Fidelma sortit de l'édifice, suivie d'Eadulf.

Menma était un homme laid, robuste, avec une barbe rousse en broussaille. Assis sur une souche devant les étables, il aiguisait une serpette avec une pierre. À leur approche, il s'immobilisa et se mit lentement sur son séant.

Eadulf entendit Fidelma reprendre bruyamment sa respiration et il lui jeta un coup d'œil surpris. Elle étudiait avec attention la tête de fouine de Menma, qui exprimait la ruse et la fourberie. Quand il s'arrêta devant lui, Eadulf fronça le nez. L'homme dégageait une terrible puanteur et le moine fit un pas de côté pour tenter de se protéger de ces effluves nauséabonds.

Menma tira sur sa barbe.

— Savez-vous que je suis une avocate des cours de justice, chargée par le roi de Cashel d'enquêter sur le meurtre d'Eber ? lança Fidelma.

Menma hocha la tête.

— La nouvelle de votre arrivée a eu tôt fait de se répandre dans le village.

— C'est donc vous qui avez découvert le corps d'Eber ?

Il cligna des paupières.

— C'est exact.

— Et en quoi consiste votre tâche au *rath* d'Araglin ?

— Je suis en charge des étables.

— Vous travaillez ici depuis longtemps ?

— Crón sera le quatrième chef d'Araglin que je sers. J'ai commencé avec Eoghan, dont le passage dans ce monde est marqué par la grande croix qui délimite les terres du clan, sur la route qui descend de la montagne.

— Nous l'avons vue, dit Eadulf.

— Puis il y eut Erc, le fils d'Eoghan mort à la guerre contre les Uí Fidgente. Et maintenant qu'Eber est passé dans l'autre monde, je vais servir sous les ordres de sa fille Crón.

— Racontez-moi dans quelles circonstances vous avez découvert Eber.

Les pâles yeux bleus de Menma se fixèrent sur Fidelma d'un air étonné.

— Les circonstances, dites-vous ?

Fidelma se demanda si l'homme n'était pas un peu idiot.

— Oui. Où et quand avez-vous trouvé le corps ?

— Quand ?

Son front se plissa.

— Ben, la nuit où Eber a été tué.

Frère Eadulf se mordit la lèvre pour ne pas éclater de rire. Avait-il l'esprit embrumé ou faisait-il exprès de ne pas comprendre ?

— Et c'était quand ? reprit Fidelma d'une voix douce.

— Oh, il y a six nuits.

— À quelle heure ?

— Juste avant l'aube.

— Que faisiez-vous dans la maison privée du chef juste avant l'aube ?

Menma leva une grosse main noueuse et la passa dans sa tignasse cuivrée.

— J'allais mettre les chevaux à la pâture et surveiller la traite. Il me revient aussi de tuer les bêtes pour la table du maître. En me dirigeant vers les étables, je suis passé près de la demeure d'Eber…

Fidelma se pencha en avant.

— Donc le chemin qui va de votre chaumière aux étables passe par le logis d'Eber ?

Menma la contempla d'un air ahuri.

— Tout le monde sait ça.

Fidelma se força à lui sourire.

— Il vous faudra être patient avec moi, Menma, car je suis une étrangère ici et j'ignore la géographie des lieux. Pouvez-vous m'indiquer où se situent les appartements d'Eber ?

Il indiqua la direction avec la lame de sa serpette.

— Eh bien, allons-y.

Menma se mit en branle en traînant les pieds. Ils passèrent derrière l'hôtellerie des invités, longèrent le mur de granit du siège de l'assemblée, puis rejoignirent des édifices en bois construits entre le siège et la chapelle. Menma désigna l'un d'eux.

— Eber vivait ici. Je suis entré par cette porte mais il y en a une autre qui communique avec le siège de l'assemblée.

— Et où se trouve votre maison ?

Il orienta à nouveau la lame de son outil, et Fidelma constata que Menma était bien obligé de passer devant les appartements du chef, près de l'église, pour se rendre à son travail.

— Qui s'occupe de la traite ? demanda-t-elle tandis qu'ils rebroussaient chemin.

Elle se demanda si Eadulf savait que cette tâche incombait aux femmes. Dans la plupart des communautés, sitôt levés, les hommes allaient mener les chevaux au pré et les femmes trayaient les vaches.

— Les femmes, bien sûr, répondit Menma.

— Comment se fait-il que vous, le gardien des troupeaux, ayez l'obligation de les surveiller ?

— Cela remonte à quelques semaines. Du bétail a été volé dans la vallée et Eber m'a ordonné de compter les bêtes chaque matin.

— De tels méfaits sont-ils fréquents ? Des voleurs ont-ils été surpris ?

Menma se frotta le menton d'un air pensif.

— C'est la première fois qu'on cherche à dépouiller le clan d'Araglin. Nous sommes une communauté isolée. Dubán a poursuivi les brigands pendant des journées entières mais il a perdu leur trace dans les hauts pâturages.

— Pourquoi donc ?

— Là-haut, les animaux sont nombreux et ils brouillent les pistes.

Fidelma était fatiguée d'arracher les informations à ce rustre.

— Bien. Nous sommes juste avant l'aube, vous passez devant la demeure d'Eber et que se passe-t-il alors ?

— J'ai entendu un gémissement. J'ai cru qu'Eber était malade et je l'ai appelé pour savoir s'il avait besoin d'aide.

— Et alors ?

— Personne n'a répondu, mais les gémissements ont continué.

— Qu'avez-vous fait ?

— Je suis entré chez Eber et je l'ai trouvé sur son lit, dans sa chambre.

— Les plaintes sortaient de sa bouche ?

— Non, de celle de son assassin, Móen.

— Vous avez tout de suite vu le corps d'Eber ?

— Non, d'abord Móen agenouillé près du lit, un couteau à la main.

— Comment pouviez-vous distinguer quelque chose s'il faisait encore nuit ?

— Une lampe était allumée et j'ai très bien reconnu Móen. Il était accroupi près du lit, brandissant un poignard.

Menma fit une grimace de dégoût en se rappelant la scène.

— La lame était tachée de sang. Et aussi la figure et les vêtements de Móen. Et c'est à ce moment-là que j'ai vu le cadavre du chef.

— Móen vous a-t-il parlé ?

Menma émit un reniflement.

— Pour dire quoi ?

— Vous l'avez accusé du meurtre ?

— Quel intérêt ? Je suis tout de suite parti à la recherche de Dubán.

— Où l'avez-vous trouvé ?

— Au siège de l'assemblée. Il m'a renvoyé à mon travail, les chevaux et les vaches ne peuvent pas

81

attendre et ils ne doivent pas souffrir des caprices des hommes.

— Móen a été laissé seul ?

— Oui.

— Vous ne craigniez pas qu'il se sauve ?

— Pour aller où ?

— Évidemment. Ensuite ?

— J'allais mener les chevaux au pré quand Dubán et Crítán sont arrivés avec Móen.

— Crítán n'est-il pas l'homme qui a été envoyé à Cashel ?

— Oui, c'est un des guerriers de Dubán. Ils ont conduit Móen à l'écurie où il a été enchaîné. Nous n'avons pas de prison en Araglin.

— Móen a-t-il avoué son crime et tenté d'expliquer son geste ?

Menma parut perplexe.

— Il ne pouvait rien dire. Et puis c'était clair pour tout le monde.

Fidelma échangea un regard surpris avec Eadulf.

— A-t-il présenté une quelconque résistance ?

— Il s'est débattu en geignant pendant que Crítán l'entravait. Et puis Dubán est allé réveiller Crón.

— Avez-vous eu des contacts avec Móen depuis qu'il est enfermé ?

Menma haussa les épaules.

— Je l'aperçois quand je me rends aux étables. Mais c'est Crítán qui s'en occupe. Avec Dubán.

Fidelma hocha la tête d'un air pensif.

— Merci, Menma. Il est possible que j'aie d'autres questions à vous poser mais, pour l'instant, j'aimerais m'entretenir avec Dubán.

Menma fit un geste en direction de l'entrée des écuries, où le guerrier qui les avait accueillis discutait avec un jeune homme.

— Voici Dubán et Crítán.

Il allait partir quand Fidelma le retint.

— Une dernière chose. Vous vous levez toujours avant l'aube pour vous occuper des chevaux ?

— Toujours. La plupart des gens ici sont debout avant le lever du soleil.

— Et ce matin ?

Menma fronça les sourcils.

— Comment cela ?

— Avez-vous mené les chevaux au pré ce matin ? répéta-t-elle d'une voix coupante.

— Ben oui.

— À quelle heure vous êtes-vous couché hier au soir ?

Menma secoua la tête.

— Tard, je crois.

— Vous croyez ?

— J'avais pas mal bu.

— Avec quelqu'un de votre connaissance ?

L'homme massif secoua la tête.

Quand il eut disparu, Fidelma se tourna vers Eadulf qui semblait perplexe.

— En quoi les occupations de Menma ce matin concernent-elles les meurtres de la semaine dernière ?

— Vous ne l'avez pas reconnu ?

Eadulf ouvrit de grands yeux.

— Qui cela ? Menma ?

— Qui d'autre ? répondit la religieuse, irritée par la lenteur d'Eadulf.

— Non, je vous assure.

— Il appartenait à la bande de brigands qui ont attaqué l'auberge ce matin.

Eadulf en resta la bouche ouverte. Il se retint de lui demander « En êtes-vous sûre ? », car Fidelma pesait toujours ses paroles et détestait que l'on mette ses affirmations en doute.

— Alors il mentait ?

— Exactement. Quand nos assaillants sont passés près de nous, l'un d'eux m'a particulièrement frappée par sa laideur et sa barbe rousse. Je ne pense pas qu'il ait vu mes traits mais, moi, je ne risquais pas de l'oublier.

— Autre chose m'intrigue. Il semblerait que tout le monde tienne la culpabilité de Móen pour acquise, sans chercher à expliquer pourquoi il a assassiné Eber et Teafa.

Fidelma acquiesça.

— Allons voir comment le récit de Menma s'accorde avec celui de Móen.

Ils s'avancèrent vers les deux guerriers. Le plus jeune, à peine sorti de l'adolescence, était peu soigné, ses cheveux d'un blond sale tombaient sur son visage aux traits assez grossiers. Appuyé au montant de la porte, un bouclier pendant de son épaule et une épée de belle facture accrochée à sa ceinture, il ne fit aucun effort pour se redresser en voyant les deux visiteurs s'avancer vers lui.

— Vous êtes vraiment le brehon ? demanda-t-il d'une voix nasillarde.

Fidelma l'ignora et se tourna vers le guerrier plus âgé.

— On m'a dit que Dubán était votre nom et que vous commandiez les gardes du chef.

Le solide guerrier se balança d'un pied sur l'autre d'un air gêné.

— Je suis Dubán et voici Crítán qui est…

— Le champion d'Araglin ! lança le jeune garçon d'un air fanfaron.

— Vraiment ? Et dans quelle discipline ? dit Fidelma d'un ton indifférent qui ne sembla pas affecter Crítán.

— L'épée, l'arc ou la lance ! s'écria-t-il. C'est moi qu'on a envoyé à Cashel prévenir le roi. Je crois que je l'ai impressionné. J'ai d'ailleurs l'intention de rejoindre ses gardes.

— Le roi a-t-il été informé de vos ambitions ?

Impossible de savoir par l'expression de son visage si elle était amusée ou fâchée par l'impertinence du garçon. Eadulf se décida pour le mépris.

Crítán, lui, ne perçut pas l'ironie de sa réflexion.

— Je ne lui ai rien dit pour l'instant mais dès qu'il connaîtra ma réputation, il acceptera mes services avec gratitude.

Devant la gêne de Dubán, Fidelma planta là le jeune vantard qui se renfrogna et prit le guerrier à part.

— Vous n'ignorez pas que je suis avocate des cours de justice ?

— J'en ai été informé, reconnut Dubán. La nouvelle de votre venue a rapidement fait le tour du *rath*.

— Bien. J'aimerais maintenant voir Móen.

— Il est là-dedans, dit l'autre avec un geste du pouce.

— Après notre entrevue, je vous poserai quelques questions. Móen a-t-il fait des déclarations depuis que vous le retenez prisonnier ?

Dubán parut troublé.

— Mais non, voyons.

Fidelma faillit lui répondre, puis changea d'avis.

— Ouvrez cette porte.

Sur un signe de Dubán, le jeune garçon exécuta l'ordre de la *dálaigh*.

L'écurie, sombre et humide, dégageait une odeur fétide.

— Je vais aller chercher une lampe, dit Dubán sur un ton d'excuse. Nous avons laissé les chevaux dans les prés pour convertir cet endroit en geôle.

Fidelma scruta l'obscurité.

— N'avez-vous pas de meilleur endroit pour y retenir le prisonnier ? Les ténèbres ajoutées à cette puanteur peuvent être assimilées à de mauvais traitements. Pourquoi ne lui avez-vous pas laissé de la lumière ?

Crítán, qui se tenait derrière elle, éclata de rire.

— Vous ne manquez pas d'esprit !

D'un ton sec, Dubán renvoya le garçon monter la garde à l'entrée puis il s'enfonça dans l'obscurité. Bientôt, les deux religieux l'entendirent frotter deux

85

pierres de silex et une étincelle mit le feu à la mèche d'une lampe à huile que le guerrier brandit au-dessus de sa tête avant de se tourner vers eux.

— Venez par ici.

Fidelma s'avança. Dans un coin, elle distingua ce qui ressemblait à un paquet de vêtements grossiers. Le tas informe bougea et elle entendit un cliquetis de chaînes. Fidelma avala sa salive avec difficulté en comprenant qu'un homme, là, était attaché par le pied gauche à un des piliers qui soutenaient le toit du bâtiment. Puis une tête échevelée se redressa d'un geste brusque, se tourna dans sa direction et se pencha sur le côté, comme si la créature écoutait, avant de laisser échapper une étrange plainte.

— Je vous présente Móen, dit la voix de Dubán.

CHAPITRE VI

Fidelma frissonna.

— Au nom du ciel, qu'est-ce que cela signifie ? Jamais je ne garderais un animal dans de telles conditions, encore moins un homme, même s'il est soupçonné de meurtre.

Elle s'avança, toucha la forme grotesque tassée sur elle-même. Elle n'était pas préparée à ce qui allait suivre.

La créature sursauta avec un hurlement angoissé et Fidelma la vit s'éloigner à toute vitesse, à quatre pattes, jusqu'à ce que la chaîne, tendue à son maximum, la précipite à terre où elle tomba en portant les mains à sa tête pour la protéger. Puis elle se redressa pour faire face, fixant les religieux de ses yeux blancs dont les pupilles étaient à peine visibles.

— *Retro Satana !* murmura Eadulf en faisant le signe de croix.

— Il s'agit bien de Satan, mon frère, acquiesça Dubán d'une voix grave.

L'homme, car il s'agissait d'un homme couvert de saletés et d'excréments, avait une chevelure abondante et tellement emmêlée qu'elle lui cachait le visage dont on ne distinguait pas les traits. La bouche baveuse et grande ouverte laissait échapper un gémissement continu et les globes blanchâtres de ses yeux roulaient dans leurs orbites.

— Voici donc Móen, accusé des meurtres d'Eber et Teafa, chuchota Fidelma, atterrée.

— Móen... ce nom ne veut-il pas dire simple d'esprit ? s'enquit Eadulf.

— Vous avez raison, mon frère, acquiesça Dubán. Et il a toujours été ainsi.

— Il est aveugle ? demanda Fidelma, remplie de pitié pour la malheureuse créature.

— Aveugle et sourd-muet.

— Et on accuse ce malheureux d'avoir tué deux adultes en bonne santé ? s'étonna Fidelma.

— Pourquoi personne ne nous a-t-il informés de la condition de l'accusé ?

Eadulf paraissait choqué et Dubán manifesta sa surprise.

— Tout le monde connaît Móen et il ne m'est pas venu à l'esprit...

Fidelma leva la main.

— Vous n'y êtes pour rien. Et maintenant...

Elle se tut car la créature s'avançait lentement vers eux, la tête relevée, humant l'air comme un animal.

— Reculez-vous, ma sœur, la prévint Dubán, même s'il ne peut ni les voir ni les entendre, il sent les gens.

Trop tard. Une main froide et noire de crasse venait d'attraper la cheville de Fidelma qui se dégagea et recula, effrayée.

Móen s'immobilisa brusquement.

Dubán s'avança vers lui, et, levant sa lanterne, s'apprêta à abattre son poing, mais Fidelma l'arrêta.

— Ne frappez pas celui qui ne peut voir venir le coup, l'adjura-t-elle avec fermeté.

Móen s'était assis et agitait les mains dans l'air, le visage tourné vers le plafond.

Fidelma secoua la tête avec tristesse.

— N'y prêtez pas attention, grommela Dubán. Il a été maudit par Dieu.

— Ne pourriez-vous au moins le laver ? demanda Fidelma.

Dubán parut stupéfait.

— Pour quoi faire ?

— C'est un être humain.

Le guerrier fit la grimace.

— Franchement, je n'en suis pas persuadé, dit-il d'un ton sarcastique.

— Dubán, d'après la loi, c'est une offense de se moquer d'un infirme.

Et, sans laisser au guerrier le temps de protester, elle ajouta :

— Avant ma prochaine entrevue avec lui, je vous prierai de lui faire prendre un bain et de le nourrir correctement. Quels que soient les chefs d'accusation qui pèsent sur lui, c'est une créature de Dieu.

Puis elle tourna les talons devant un Eadulf médusé et troublé par le visage amer du guerrier.

Une fois dehors, où Eadulf la rejoignit, elle prit de profondes inspirations pour contrôler sa colère. Crítán avait disparu et ils se dirigèrent à pas lents vers les appartements d'Eber.

— Difficile de blâmer Dubán, dit Eadulf, s'efforçant de jouer le rôle de conciliateur. Rappelez-vous que ce pauvre hère a tué son chef.

Il tressaillit en croisant le regard de Fidelma dont les yeux verts lançaient des éclairs.

— La culpabilité de Móen n'est pas prouvée. En tant qu'être humain, il jouit des mêmes droits que n'importe qui, rien ne justifie qu'il soit traité plus bas qu'un animal.

— Vous avez raison, concéda Eadulf, ce comportement…

— Et lors de son procès, il doit être défendu.

— Mais vous oubliez qu'il est sourd, muet et aveugle par-dessus le marché. Comment communiquer avec un être tel que lui ? Et sur quoi appuyer une plaidoirie ?

— Je vais y travailler. En tant que *dálaigh*, j'ai prêté un serment et je jure de le respecter.

Ils restèrent un instant silencieux, puis Eadulf demanda :

— Y a-t-il vraiment une loi qui punit ceux qui se moquent des infirmes ?

— Ce n'est pas moi qui rédige les lois, répondit Fidelma d'un ton sec. De lourdes amendes peuvent être exigées de ceux qui persécutent les infirmes, qu'ils soient épileptiques ou qu'ils présentent des difformités physiques ou mentales.

— C'est difficile à croire. J'ai beau avoir étudié dans votre pays, je demeure prisonnier de ma propre culture. Dans notre société, nous reconnaissons que l'homme est une créature cruelle, souvent destinée par Dieu à une existence courte et brutale. N'est-ce pas dans l'ordre des choses et de la nature que l'homme suive parfois un chemin tourmenté ?

Fidelma ouvrit de grands yeux.

— Je suis heureuse que vous vous frottiez à d'autres philosophies que celle des Saxons, Eadulf.

— Toute philosophie est transitoire et la vie sujette à de brusques changements de cap. Partout les guerres, les querelles, la maladie, la faim et l'oppression nous guettent. Et nous nous inclinons devant la volonté de notre Père, dans les cieux, dont la volonté est insondable.

Fidelma secoua la tête.

— Nos lois et la façon dont nous conduisons nos vies ne plaident-elles pas pour la lutte contre la misère et ses diverses manifestations que vous acceptez sans vous révolter dans votre pays ? Mais remettons nos querelles théoriques à plus tard, Eadulf, car nous avons bien des problèmes à résoudre et votre soutien m'est indispensable. S'il s'avère, après une enquête approfondie, que Móen est coupable, je ne pourrai le tenir pour responsable de ses actes et devrai me retourner contre son tuteur légal, dont j'ignore l'identité. Encore une chose à tirer au clair. Ah…

Elle porta la main à son front.

— Il faut que je me rappelle précisément le premier chapitre du *Do Brethaib Gaire*…

— De quoi s'agit-il ?

— D'un traité sur l'obligation de la parentèle à veiller sur ses membres infirmes. La première partie traite justement des sourds-muets aveugles.

Les lois de compensation du droit irlandais pour les victimes et leurs familles, qui s'appliquaient même dans les affaires de meurtres, ne cessaient d'étonner Eadulf. Chez lui, dans le South Folk, la peine de mort était de rigueur non seulement pour les assassins mais aussi pour les voleurs et ceux qui les avaient hébergés ou protégés. Les traîtres, les sorcières, les esclaves en fuite, les hors-la-loi et ceux qui ne les avaient pas dénoncés pouvaient être pendus, décapités, lapidés, brûlés ou noyés. Pour les délits mineurs, on coupait les mains, les pieds, le nez, les oreilles, la lèvre supérieure ou la langue, on pouvait même castrer, aveugler, scalper, marquer et écorcher. Les évêques saxons préféraient la mutilation à la mort, car cela donnait le temps au pécheur de se repentir. Quant à ces Irlandais, qui refusaient la notion pourtant très satisfaisante de la vengeance et parlaient de dédommager une victime en obligeant le malfaiteur à travailler à son bénéfice… Eadulf admirait leur générosité mais se demandait si on ne s'écartait pas de la justice.

Alors qu'ils longeaient le mur de granit du siège de l'assemblée, Dubán les rappela en courant derrière eux.

— J'ai donné des ordres à Crítán, ma sœur. Móen sera rendu présentable afin de…

Il chercha le mot juste.

— … afin de ne pas heurter votre sensibilité.

— Je n'ai jamais douté de votre bonne volonté, Dubán, répondit Fidelma d'une voix douce.

Le guerrier, qui semblait encore un peu contrarié, fronça les sourcils, car il craignait que ces paroles ne recèlent un sens caché. Bien que vexé par les critiques de Fidelma, on l'avait apparemment convaincu de suivre ses instructions.

— Crón m'a chargé de vous assister pendant votre séjour et de satisfaire à toutes vos exigences.

— Je vous remercie. Nous nous rendions dans les appartements d'Eber pour voir où Menma avait découvert le corps et où se tenait Móen.

— Permettez que je vous serve de guide, dit Dubán en les conduisant jusqu'à une maison de plain-pied, comme la plupart des demeures alentour.

Ils pénétrèrent dans une salle de réception où le chef prenait ses repas et recevait des invités en privé. Elle communiquait avec le siège de l'assemblée grâce à une porte dérobée à la vue par une des tapisseries. Une table et des chaises étaient disposées devant la cheminée où un chaudron trônait sur un trépied. Aux murs étaient accrochés les armes d'Eber avec ses trophées de chasse. Partout, des tapis étouffaient les pas. Une porte pratiquée dans un mur lambrissé donnait sur la chambre à coucher où une paillasse reposait sur d'épais tapis tachés de sang.

Fidelma avisa la lampe sur la table de chevet.

— Je suppose qu'il s'agit de la lanterne qui était allumée quand Menma est entré ?

— Oui, confirma Dubán. On n'a pas touché à cette pièce depuis la tragédie. Quand je suis venu ici avec Menma, la lanterne brûlait encore. Et Móen était agenouillé près du lit.

— A-t-il tenté de s'enfuir ?

— Vous oubliez que c'est un sourd-muet aveugle ! fit observer Dubán dans un bref éclat de rire.

— Justement, puisque vous connaissez son état, peut-être pourrez-vous m'expliquer comment il est parvenu à se glisser jusqu'ici pour tuer Eber, dit Fidelma en examinant attentivement les lieux.

Avant qu'il ait pu répondre, elle ajouta :

— Racontez-moi comment vous avez vécu les événements.

— Cette nuit-là, j'étais de garde.

— Votre *rath* est isolé. Pourquoi aviez-vous jugé bon de monter la garde alors que vous êtes protégés par les montagnes ?

— Il y a quelques semaines, on nous a volé du bétail dans la vallée et Eber prenait ses précautions.

— Ah oui, j'avais oublié. Donc vous vous teniez à l'entrée du *rath*.

L'homme baissa la tête d'un air confus.

— Pour tout vous avouer, à l'approche de l'aube je m'étais endormi sur une chaise dans l'entrée du siège de l'assemblée. Menma m'a réveillé pour m'annoncer qu'il avait découvert Eber sans vie et que Móen était l'assassin. Je me suis précipité ici et le cadavre d'Eber gisait en travers de la paillasse, exactement comme me l'avait décrit Menma. Il baignait dans son sang et Móen en était tout éclaboussé. Il se tenait là, accroupi, et tenait fermement un couteau à la lame vermeille.

— Que faisait-il ?

— Il se balançait d'avant en arrière en gémissant doucement.

— Ensuite ? l'encouragea Fidelma.

— J'ai ordonné à Menma de retourner à son travail et je partais chercher Crítán quand il est arrivé pour prendre son tour de garde. Nous avons emmené Móen aux étables et je suis allé porter la nouvelle à Crón.

— Et pourquoi pas à l'épouse d'Eber ?

— Crón est la *tanist*, l'héritière présomptive d'Araglin, et le protocole exige qu'elle soit la première informée.

Fidelma hocha la tête.

— Quand on a voulu enchaîner Móen, il s'est mis à hurler et à se débattre. Crón m'a alors conseillé d'aller chercher Teafa.

— Et vous l'avez trouvée morte ?

— Oui.

— D'après mes renseignements, Teafa, la sœur d'Eber, était la seule personne du *rath* capable de calmer Móen.

— Oui, car elle s'en était occupée depuis qu'il était bébé.

— Móen n'était pas son fils ?

— Non et personne ne sait d'où il vient. Mais il n'était pas né de Teafa car elle n'était pas enceinte au cours des semaines qui ont précédé la naissance de Móen. Nous vivons dans une très petite communauté.

— Justement, comment se fait-il que l'on ignore l'identité de la mère ?

— Cet enfant n'a pas été mis au monde par une femme de la vallée.

— Qui l'a trouvé et pourquoi Teafa l'a-t-elle adopté ?

Dubán se frotta le nez.

— Teafa est partie seule à la chasse dans les montagnes et elle est revenue quelques jours plus tard avec l'enfant, je n'en sais pas plus.

— A-t-elle expliqué où elle l'avait découvert ?

— Dans les bois. J'ai quitté Araglin peu de temps après cet événement pour aller m'enrôler dans l'armée du roi de Cashel, et je suis rentré il y a environ trois ans. Quand Móen a grandi, on s'est rendu compte qu'il souffrait d'infirmités, mais Teafa a toujours refusé de l'abandonner. Elle ne s'est jamais mariée. C'était une femme au cœur généreux. Elle communiquait avec Móen d'une curieuse façon. Comment exactement, je l'ignore.

— Combien de temps vous êtes-vous absenté d'Araglin ?

— Dix-sept ans, puis je suis revenu servir Eber.

— Qui, dans le *rath*, en saurait plus que vous sur Móen ?

Dubán haussa les épaules.

— Le père Gormán, je suppose. Maintenant que Teafa est décédée, peut-être pourra-t-il vous en apprendre davantage mais il ne rentrera que dans un jour ou deux.

— Et la veuve d'Eber ?

— Lady Cranat ?

Dubán fit la moue.

— Elle a épousé Eber un an après que Teafa se fût chargée de Móen. À mon retour, j'ai constaté que Cranat et Teafa entretenaient des relations distantes, peu compatibles avec leur degré de parenté.

Eadulf dressa l'oreille.

— Insinuez-vous que Cranat n'appréciait guère Teafa ?

Dubán parut peiné.

— Vous autres Saxons, vous vous exprimez avec trop de brutalité. Il me semble pourtant que j'ai été suffisamment clair.

— Absolument, intervint Fidelma. Cranat et Teafa s'entendaient donc assez mal.

— Voilà.

— Et à quand remonte cette inimitié, selon vous ?

— À une époque où Crón avait environ treize ans. Elles se sont querellées, après quoi elles ne se sont pratiquement plus adressé la parole. Et il y a environ trois semaines, j'ai assisté à une violente dispute.

— À quel sujet ?

— Ce n'est pas vraiment à moi de vous le dire.

Dubán n'appréciait pas les commérages et répugnait à colporter des médisances.

— Vous en avez trop dit ou pas assez. Expliquez-vous.

— Teafa criait après Cranat qui était en pleurs.

— Vous avez bien une vague idée de ce qui a provoqué cet accès de colère ?

— Du tout. Elles ont mentionné Móen et aussi Eber. Teafa a prononcé le mot de divorce.

— Elle demandait à Cranat de divorcer de son frère ?

— Peut-être. Cranat a alors couru jusqu'à la chapelle pour chercher consolation auprès du père Gormán.

Fidelma ne fit pas d'autre commentaire, examina attentivement la chambre, et retourna dans la salle de réception qu'elle étudia avec la même minutie.

— Pour un sourd-muet aveugle, Móen semble avoir le don de se déplacer avec une grande facilité dans ce *rath*, dit-elle à Eadulf. Il a fallu qu'il entre, se fraye un chemin jusqu'au lit, prenne son couteau, trouve sa cible et la tue avant qu'Eber ait remarqué sa présence. Chez un individu normal, ce n'est déjà pas évident, mais chez un infirme comme lui…

Dubán, qui les avait rejoints, afficha un visage désapprobateur.

— Niez-vous les faits ?

— Je cherche seulement à les vérifier.

— C'est pourtant simple, Móen a été surpris en pleine action.

— Pas exactement, le corrigea Fidelma. On l'a retrouvé auprès du corps d'Eber. Personne ne l'a surpris en train de tuer le chef.

Dubán rejeta la tête en arrière avec un rire rauque.

— Est-ce là la logique d'un brehon, ma sœur ? Si je trouve un loup avec du sang sur le museau près de la carcasse d'un mouton fraîchement égorgé, n'est-il pas naturel que je blâme le loup ?

— Je vous le concède. Mais il ne s'agit pas d'une preuve positive.

Dubán secoua la tête avec incrédulité.

— Prétendez-vous que…

— J'essaye de découvrir la vérité, le coupa Fidelma. Je n'ai pas d'autre but.

— Dans ce cas, apprenez que Móen était capable de se mouvoir sans difficultés excessives dans certaines parties du *rath*.

— Comment est-ce possible ? demanda Eadulf, très intrigué.

— Je suppose qu'il possède une mémoire, et il a aussi un excellent odorat qui lui permet de trouver son chemin.

— Simplement par l'odeur ?

Eadulf semblait sceptique.

— Vous avez bien vu, dans l'écurie, comment il reniflait pour identifier les étrangers qu'il ne connaissait pas. Il a développé un odorat très sensible, comme les animaux.

— Donc vous n'êtes pas surpris qu'il se soit glissé jusqu'ici ?

— Pas du tout.

Eadulf haussa les épaules.

— Dans ce cas, il n'y a plus de mystère.

Fidelma n'était pas convaincue.

— Où est le couteau que Móen a utilisé pour poignarder Eber ?

— C'est moi qui l'ai.

— A-t-il été identifié ?

— Comment cela ? demanda Dubán d'un air ahuri.

Fidelma s'arma de patience.

— Connaît-on le nom de son propriétaire ?

— Je crois bien qu'il s'agit d'un des couteaux de chasse d'Eber.

Il désigna un mur où était accrochée une collection d'épées et de couteaux, près d'un bouclier. Un des fourreaux était vide.

— J'ai vu qu'il manquait un poignard, sans doute celui que Móen a pris.

Depuis la porte principale, Fidelma se dirigea vers le fourreau vide tout en contournant divers obstacles avant d'atteindre le râtelier. Puis elle fit le tour de la table, évita un banc et rejoignit la porte de la chambre.

Là, elle s'arrêta et réfléchit un instant.

— Il faut que j'examine rapidement l'arme du crime, conclut-elle.

Dubán hocha la tête.

— Très bien.

— Et maintenant, allons voir où Teafa a été découverte et de quelle façon.

CHAPITRE VII

Ils revinrent sur leurs pas en passant derrière les étables où le chemin contournait des réserves situées près d'un four à sécher le blé. Ils traversèrent une cour avec un puits, passèrent un petit portail et arrivèrent devant une chaumière en pisé.

— Teafa avait emménagé loin de sa famille, expliqua Dubán.

— Pour la sœur célibataire d'un chef, n'est-ce pas inhabituel de vivre en dehors du cercle immédiat des demeures familiales ? fit observer Eadulf.

— Pourquoi donc ? Elle n'avait pas quitté le *rath*, répondit Dubán, ne comprenant pas trop où il voulait en venir.

Dans le South Folk, les femmes étaient considérées jusqu'à leur mariage comme la propriété du chef de famille, qui était toujours un homme. Et même dans un village, on ne les aurait pas autorisées à s'éloigner. Eadulf comprit que cette conception n'avait pas cours dans les cinq royaumes.

— Frère Eadulf s'étonne que, vu son rang, elle n'ait pas logé dans une maison plus confortable et plus proche du siège de l'assemblée, dit Fidelma.

Dubán haussa les épaules.

— Elle préférait cette solution. Je me rappelle qu'elle avait choisi cette chaumière juste après l'adoption de Móen.

Contrairement aux apparences, la maisonnette était assez spacieuse et comptait trois pièces. Celle où Teafa et celui dont elle s'occupait faisaient la cuisine, mangeaient et se tenaient la plus grande partie du temps s'appelait la *tech immácallamae* ou « pièce de la conversation ». Deux portes donnaient accès aux chambres. Celle de Móen n'avait pas de fenêtre et ne contenait qu'une paillasse.

Fidelma allait s'éloigner quand quelque chose attira son attention, derrière la porte.

— Voyez-vous une bougie ou une lampe ? demanda-t-elle.

À l'aide d'amadou et d'une pierre de silex posés dans un coin, Dubán alluma une chandelle dont la mèche crépita.

Fidelma la prit et pénétra dans la chambre. Derrière la porte, un œil non exercé n'aurait vu qu'un entassement de fagots, liés par des lanières en cuir.

— Eadulf, venez voir.

— Drôle d'endroit pour amasser du petit bois, dit Dubán en regardant par-dessus son épaule.

Eadulf se saisit d'un lot de branches. Les baguettes, pour la plupart de coudrier et quelques-unes d'if, mesuraient toutes dix-huit pouces environ. Eadulf défit le lien et les examina avec attention avant de se tourner vers Fidelma.

— Il est rare de découvrir d'aussi beaux spécimens en dehors des grandes bibliothèques, s'extasia-t-il d'un air réjoui.

Dubán les fixait d'un air idiot.

— Je ne comprends rien.

Fidelma jeta un regard de connivence à Eadulf.

— Ce petit bois, comme vous dites, s'appelle en réalité des « bâtons de poète ». Ce sont de très vieux livres. Examinez-les de plus près et vous y verrez des encoches, qui correspondent aux lettres de l'ogam, l'ancien alphabet.

Dubán se pencha avec révérence. Apparemment, il n'avait jamais entendu parler de cette antique forme d'écriture.

— Teafa était-elle une érudite ? s'interrogea Eadulf.

Le guerrier secoua la tête.

— Elle n'a jamais eu cette prétention, mais je crois néanmoins qu'elle était versée dans les arts et la poésie. Je ne m'étonne donc point qu'elle se soit initiée au vieil alphabet.

— Tout de même, murmura Fidelma, je n'ai jamais vu de collection aussi précieuse en dehors d'une bibliothèque d'abbaye.

Eadulf renoua avec soin le lien autour du lot de baguettes qu'il remit en place, tandis que Fidelma se rendait dans la chambre de Teafa, richement meublée comme il sied à la fille et à la sœur d'un chef. Il y faisait clair et Fidelma souffla la chandelle avant de se tourner vers Dubán.

— Donc, quand Crón vous a demandé d'aller chercher Teafa pour calmer Móen, vous êtes venu directement ici ?

— Oui, et en arrivant, j'ai vu que la porte était mal fermée. J'ai tout de suite su que quelque chose n'allait pas.

— Une porte mal close n'a rien de particulièrement inquiétant.

— Teafa ne laissait jamais la sienne entrouverte.

— Pour garder Móen enfermé ? hasarda Eadulf.

— Non, non, Móen se déplaçait librement, mais Teafa craignait qu'il ne tombe si la porte s'ouvrait par inadvertance. J'ai donc poussé le battant et je suis resté un instant sur le seuil. L'aube se levait et dans le demi-jour, j'ai distingué un monticule de vêtements sur le sol. En y regardant de plus près, j'ai compris qu'il s'agissait du corps de Teafa.

— Montrez-moi où vous l'avez découverte, dit Fidelma.

Dubán pointa du doigt le foyer rempli de cendres grises et froides. Dès qu'elle était entrée dans la maison, Fidelma avait été frappée par la puissante odeur de feu de bois.

— J'ai allumé une chandelle, celle-là même que vous teniez tout à l'heure. Teafa gisait devant la cheminée, ses vêtements ensanglantés : elle avait été sauvagement frappée à la poitrine, autour du cœur.

Fidelma s'accroupit. Du sang séché maculait le sol, mais son attention fut attirée par une zone plus sombre, là où une partie du plancher avait brûlé, et elle comprit que c'était cette petite superficie qui dégageait de puissants effluves. Juste à côté, elle tomba sur une tache plus brillante. Aussitôt, elle y frotta son doigt qu'elle renifla.

— Y avait-il un objet posé à cet endroit ?

— Une lampe à huile brisée, se rappela Dubán après un temps de silence. Je suppose qu'on l'a jetée.

— Pensez-vous que Teafa la tenait à la main quand on l'a agressée ?

— Je n'y avais pas réfléchi mais maintenant que vous le mentionnez, il semblerait en effet qu'elle tenait une lanterne. Elle l'a laissée tomber quand on l'a attaquée et le feu a pris mais Dieu merci, il s'est éteint. Sans doute de lui-même.

Fidelma fixait pensivement les lames de parquet calcinées.

— La maison a bien failli s'embraser. Et juste là, il y a encore de l'huile.

Elle montra son index graisseux.

— À votre avis, pour quelle raison ce début d'incendie aurait-il été étouffé ?

— Je l'ignore mais, quand je suis arrivé, il était déjà éteint.

Fidelma allait se relever quand elle avisa dans la cheminée un bout de coudrier noirci, entaillé d'encoches. Il mesurait environ trois pouces. Elle le prit et l'examina avec attention.

— Qu'est-ce que c'est ? demanda Eadulf.

— Ce qui reste d'une baguette d'ogam.

Elle déchiffra quelques lettres, « ER VEUT », qui ne voulaient pas dire grand-chose. Pourquoi Teafa tenait-elle tellement à détruire ce texte ? Fidelma glissa le bout de bois dans son *marsupium* – la poche de cuir qu'elle transportait toujours avec elle, accrochée à sa ceinture –, se redressa et contempla la chambre parfaitement ordonnée, tout comme celle d'Eber. À l'évidence, le mobile des crimes n'était pas le vol.

— Dubán, vous avez mentionné que l'épouse d'Eber ne s'entendait pas avec Teafa, mais Teafa entretenait-elle des relations étroites avec son frère ?

— Forcément, puisque nous vivons dans une petite communauté.

— Auriez-vous été le témoin de frictions ou d'une animosité marquée entre eux ?

Dubán ouvrit les mains, comme s'il cédait à des forces qui le dépassaient.

— Comment vous expliquer, ils étaient séparés par une… distance. Moi, j'ai une sœur, je vais souvent manger chez elle et son mari, j'emmène ses enfants à la chasse… mais Teafa n'a jamais entretenu de relations chaleureuses avec Eber. Cela remonte-t-il au jour de l'adoption de Móen ? Je l'ignore.

— Je crois qu'il serait temps que nous parlions à lady Cranat, murmura Fidelma.

— Et comment décririez-vous les relations entre Teafa et Crón ? intervint Eadulf.

— Courtoises, sans plus.

— Et d'une manière générale, comment Móen était-il perçu dans cette communauté ?

— La plupart des gens le traitaient avec une certaine tolérance, ils avaient pitié de lui. Ils le connaissaient depuis toujours et lady Teafa était très respectée. Eber passait du temps avec lui, contrairement à Crón qui le fuyait et lui manifestait une grande indifférence. Et le père Gormán lui interdisait l'entrée de sa chapelle.

— Dans une communauté saxonne, il aurait été tué à la naissance, ne put s'empêcher de commenter Eadulf.

— Et vous appelez cela une attitude chrétienne ?

Eadulf rougit et Fidelma regretta la vivacité de sa réponse, car elle se doutait bien que le moine n'aurait jamais pris part à un acte aussi barbare.

— Eadulf, ici, les gens qui souffrent d'infirmités ne sont pas éligibles à des postes de premier plan, comme roi ou chef, mais ils n'en appartiennent pas moins à la communauté et ils jouissent des mêmes droits que les autres. Et leur responsabilité devant la loi dépend de l'importance de leur infirmité. Par exemple, un épileptique, s'il est sain d'esprit, devra répondre de ses actes. Par contre, un sourd-muet n'est pas condamnable et le plaignant devra se retourner contre son tuteur légal.

— Donc Móen n'était pas maintenu dans une position inférieure ?

— Du tout. Et si quelqu'un s'était avisé de se moquer, Teafa aurait été autorisée à porter l'affaire devant un tribunal, car celui qui dénigre l'infirmité d'un individu est soumis à une amende sévère, que sa victime soit épileptique, boiteuse, aveugle, sourde-muette ou atteinte de la lèpre.

— Il semblerait que je vienne de prendre une leçon de droit irlandais, dit Eadulf d'un air contrit.

— Le père Gormán le récuse, intervint Dubán, impassible.

Fidelma se tourna vers lui.

— Expliquez-nous cela.

— Il prêche la règle de Rome, qu'il appelle le pénitentiel.

Effectivement, les nouvelles conceptions en provenance de Rome s'infiltraient peu à peu dans les cinq royaumes, certains prêtres de la faction proromaine tentaient même de les substituer au système juridique des royaumes. Parallèlement au droit criminel et civil en vigueur, un nouveau corpus de lois ecclésiastiques était en train de s'élaborer.

Fidelma se rappela l'avertissement de l'abbé Cathal de Lios Mhór : le père Gormán soutenait avec ardeur les coutumes romaines et, grâce à l'argent levé par les tenants de la faction dont il était un membre actif, il avait même construit une autre chapelle à Ard Mór. Le conflit entre les ecclésiastiques des églises des cinq royaumes s'envenimait. Le concile de Witebia, dans le royaume d'Oswy, où Fidelma avait rencontré Eadulf deux ans auparavant[1], n'avait fait qu'aggraver les divergences. On y avait débattu des disparités entre les philosophies de l'Église de Rome et de celle des cinq royaumes. Malgré des échanges passionnants, Oswy s'était décidé en faveur de Rome. Les ecclésiastiques qui souhaitaient que le Saint-Siège établisse son autorité sur les cinq royaumes avaient marqué des points. Ultán, archevêque d'Ard Macha, primat des cinq royaumes, s'était lui aussi déclaré en faveur de Rome. Mais tout le monde n'acceptait pas l'autorité d'Ultán. Différentes coteries s'affrontaient pour interpréter la nouvelle foi.

— Iriez-vous jusqu'à prétendre que le père Gormán désapprouvait l'adoption de Móen par Teafa ?

— Oui.

— Vous disiez que Teafa était capable de communiquer avec l'enfant. Quelqu'un d'autre était-il en mesure de le faire ?

Dubán secoua la tête.

— Personne n'avait de rapports avec lui en dehors de Teafa.

— Expliquez-nous comment elle s'y prenait.

— Franchement, ma sœur, je n'en ai aucune idée.

---

1. Voir *Absolution par le meurtre*, 10/18, n° 3630.

— Vous n'êtes pas très nombreux et quelqu'un a bien dû assister à leurs échanges.

Dubán haussa les épaules.

Brusquement, il vint à Fidelma une idée qui la remplit d'effroi.

— Mais alors… Móen ignore pourquoi il est détenu ?

Dubán la fixa un instant et se mit à rire.

— Il sait bien qu'il a tué Teafa et Eber !

— Mais s'il n'est pas le meurtrier, il se perd en conjectures sur les raisons d'un tel traitement. Dans la mesure où vous êtes incapables de communiquer avec lui, comment saurait-il ce dont on l'accuse ? A-t-il essayé d'établir un contact avec vous ?

Dubán souriait, sans parvenir à la prendre au sérieux.

— Sans doute, à la façon d'un animal.

— Comment cela ?

— Il nous prend les mains et fait des gestes pour attirer notre attention. Mais il doit bien savoir que seule Teafa pouvait le comprendre.

— Et il ne vous est pas venu à l'esprit qu'il voulait que vous alliez chercher Teafa dont il ignore le décès ?

Dubán se renfrogna.

— Quoi que vous en pensiez, ma sœur, il a tué Teafa.

— Dubán, vous êtes un homme obstiné.

— Et si nous tentions de communiquer avec cette créature ? proposa Eadulf.

— Excellente suggestion, Eadulf, déclara Fidelma en sortant de la chaumière.

Un coin de l'écurie avait été nettoyé, une paillasse propre était posée sur le sol, ainsi qu'une cruche d'eau et une chaise percée. Móen, bien qu'enchaîné par une cheville, était assis en tailleur sur la paillasse.

Fidelma constata qu'on avait exécuté ses instructions. Móen avait été lavé, ses cheveux coupés et sa barbe taillée. Maintenant, seuls ses yeux blancs écarquillés et l'angle de son cou et de sa tête le signalaient comme un être à part. En réalité, songea Fidelma avec tristesse, le jeune homme était assez beau.

À leur entrée, ses narines frémirent et il tourna la tête dans leur direction. On aurait juré qu'il les voyait.

— Et maintenant, s'exclama Dubán avec une pointe de cynisme, montrez-nous un peu comment vous allez vous y prendre pour établir un contact avec lui, ma sœur !

Fidelma l'ignora, fit signe à Eadulf de ne pas bouger et se dirigea vers Móen.

Elle s'arrêta juste devant lui.

Il recula, leva un bras pour se protéger la tête et Fidelma se tourna d'un air courroucé vers Dubán.

— Cela en dit long sur la façon dont ce malheureux a été traité.

Dubán rougit.

— Ce n'est pas moi ! protesta-t-il. Et puis vous oubliez que cette créature a tué à deux reprises.

— Ce n'est pas une excuse pour le brutaliser. Oseriez-vous tourmenter un animal parce qu'il est privé de la parole ?

Elle se tourna vers Móen, lui prit la main qu'il tenait au-dessus de sa tête et la ramena doucement le long de son corps.

Le jeune homme se redressa et fixa le vide avec une grande intensité, narines frémissantes pour capter l'odeur de Fidelma qui s'assit auprès de lui.

Dubán fit un pas en avant, la main sur la poignée de son épée, mais Eadulf le retint avec une fermeté qui surprit le guerrier.

— Attendez, lui ordonna Eadulf à mi-voix.

Maintenant, Móen explorait le visage de Fidelma du bout des doigts. Fidelma le laissait faire sans broncher. Puis elle prit son crucifix et le plaça dans les mains du garçon dont le visage s'illumina d'un grand sourire.

— Il comprend que je suis une religieuse, dit Fidelma à l'adresse des deux hommes.

Dubán ricana d'un air entendu.

— N'importe quelle bête apprécie la douceur.

Móen prit les mains de Fidelma qui fronça les sourcils.

— Que fait-il ? demanda Eadulf.

— Il me donne de petites tapes, comme des signaux... ou plutôt des symboles. Il essaye de me transmettre un message. Oui, mais lequel ?

Avec un soupir d'exaspération devant son impuissance, elle se saisit de la main de Móen et y traça des mots en latin.

Móen poussa un grognement, ôta sa main tout en retenant celle de la religieuse et il recommença son manège, tambourinant sur sa paume, y traçant des signes et la caressant.

— Voilà la manière dont lui et Teafa communiquaient, soupira Fidelma, au comble de la frustration. Mais moi, je n'y comprends rien.

— Peut-être s'agit-il d'un code que seuls Móen et Teafa connaissaient ? s'interrogea Eadulf.

— C'est possible mais pas certain.

Fidelma repoussa doucement les doigts de Móen qui comprit que sa quête était inutile et laissa retomber ses mains sur ses genoux. Son visage exprimait un profond désespoir et il poussa un soupir poignant.

Submergée par la tristesse, Fidelma lui effleura la joue et elle s'aperçut qu'il pleurait.

— Comme je comprends ta déception, Móen ! dit-elle d'une voix brisée par l'émotion. Si seulement tu pouvais parler et me dire ce qui s'est passé la nuit du drame.

Elle serra la main de Móen dans la sienne et il inclina la tête, comme s'il percevait sa sympathie et l'en remerciait.

Puis Fidelma se leva d'un mouvement lent avant de rejoindre Eadulf et Dubán.

Le guerrier contemplait avec stupeur l'infirme qui semblait plongé dans ses réflexions.

— Seule Teafa était capable de le calmer ainsi.

Fidelma s'éloigna de la stalle, suivie de ses deux compagnons.

— Si vous le traitiez comme un être humain, peut-être obtiendriez-vous les mêmes résultats, déclara-t-elle, luttant contre la colère.

Sur le seuil de la porte, ils tombèrent sur Crítán.

Le jeune vantard sale et dégingandé les accueillit avec un sourire moqueur.

— Maintenant qu'il est tout beau tout propre, vous pouvez aller le présenter à la cour de Cashel, dit-il en indiquant Móen.

Fidelma le toisa et se détourna de lui.

Alors qu'elle s'éloignait, le guerrier ajouta d'un ton méprisant :

— Ainsi arrangée, cette créature fera meilleur effet quand elle pendra au bout d'une corde.

Fidelma pivota sur ses talons.

— Et même s'il était coupable, qui vous dit qu'il devrait être puni par la peine de mort ?

— Le père Gormán, bien sûr. « Œil pour œil, dent pour dent », voilà ce qu'il nous enseigne.

— Comme l'a écrit Plaute dans sa *Comédie de l'âne* : *Lupus est homo homini*[1] !

La figure de Crítán s'allongea.

— Je ne comprends ni le latin ni le grec.

— Même si l'on accepte votre philosophie de la vengeance, êtes-vous certain que dans l'affaire qui nous occupe, c'est la vie de Móen qui doit être sacrifiée ?

Crítán la regarda d'un air niais, puis il se ressaisit.

— Je suis sûr que Móen est l'assassin.

— D'où tenez-vous pareille certitude ?

— Je l'ai vu.

1. « L'homme est un loup pour l'homme. » (*N.d.T.*)

Le coup était rude et Fidelma cligna des paupières tandis qu'Eadulf se penchait vers lui.

— Vous confirmez que vous avez été le témoin du crime ?

Crítán sourit d'un air entendu.

— Pas exactement, mais c'est tout comme.

— Assez de mystères, l'admonesta Fidelma. N'est indubitable que le témoignage direct.

Ravi d'avoir capté son attention, Crítán faisait durer le plaisir.

— J'ai vu Móen pénétrer dans les appartements d'Eber.

Ni Menma ni Dubán n'avaient indiqué que Crítán se trouvait à proximité de la demeure d'Eber avant la découverte du corps.

— Venez-en aux faits, je vous écoute ! s'écria Fidelma.

— Ça se passait le matin où Menma a tout découvert, environ une demi-heure avant que j'aille prendre mon tour de garde.

Fidelma consulta Dubán du regard. Ébahi, le guerrier semblait entendre cette histoire pour la première fois.

— Que faisiez-vous donc en pleine nuit devant chez Eber ? demanda Fidelma d'une voix douce.

Le jeune homme hésita.

— Si vous voulez le savoir…

Il s'empourpra.

— … je me suis rendu dans un certain endroit.

— Un certain endroit ?

Dubán éclata d'un rire graveleux.

— Je parierais qu'il a rendu une petite visite au bordel de Clídna, situé à quelques miles d'ici en suivant la rivière.

L'air mortifié de Crítán ressemblait fort à un aveu.

— Quand je suis passé devant le siège de l'assemblée, Dubán ronflait sur un banc, dans l'entrée.

Dubán rougit à son tour.

— Et j'ai aussi aperçu cette créature qui se glissait dans l'ombre. Bien sûr, Móen ignorait ma présence.

— Était-il seul ?

Crítán bomba le torse.

— Oui. Tout le monde sait qu'il peut se mouvoir librement, bien qu'il soit aveugle et sourd-muet. Un genre d'instinct.

— Et il a pénétré dans la maison d'Eber ?

— Je le jure.

— Comment ?

Crítán battit des cils.

— Je ne comprends pas.

— Si vous vous trouviez à l'entrée du siège de l'assemblée, il vous aurait fallu vous éloigner de trente pieds environ pour distinguer la porte d'Eber au lever du jour, alors dans l'obscurité…

— Quand je l'ai vu se faufiler dans l'ombre, je me suis demandé où il se rendait. J'ai donc attendu qu'il passe près de moi et je l'ai suivi.

— De quelle façon a-t-il pénétré dans les appartements ?

— Par la porte, répondit l'autre avec ingénuité.

— J'entends bien, mais aviez-vous l'impression qu'il se cachait ou bien a-t-il annoncé sa présence en frappant à cette porte ?

— Difficile à dire, il faisait sombre…

— … mais vous l'avez vu entrer, ce dont je vous félicite. Comment avez-vous réagi ?

— J'étais pressé de retourner à l'hôtellerie des gardes pour me laver avant de prendre la relève. J'ai donc continué mon chemin et n'ai rien dit quand Teafa…

Il s'arrêta et son regard vacilla.

— Quand Teafa ? insista Fidelma.

— Eh bien, j'avais dépassé les étables et je me dirigeais vers l'hôtellerie, près du moulin, quand Teafa est sortie de chez elle une lampe à la main. Elle s'est penchée pour ramasser une branche près de sa porte, sans doute pour faire du feu, puis elle a remarqué ma présence et m'a demandé si j'avais croisé Móen.

Fidelma parut songeuse.

— L'avez-vous informée ?

— Non, car je n'avais pas le temps de l'aider à le chercher. Je lui ai donc dit que je ne l'avais pas vu. Puis je me suis lavé, j'ai changé de vêtements et je suis parti rejoindre Dubán. C'est lui qui m'a appris ce qui s'était passé.

À cet instant de son récit, le visage de Crítán s'éclaira d'un sourire triomphant.

— Vous comprenez maintenant pourquoi il est impossible que Móen n'ait pas tué Eber et Teafa ?

Eadulf hocha la tête.

— Cela semble assez convaincant.

— Résumons votre témoignage, dit Fidelma. Plongé dans l'obscurité la plus complète puisque le jour ne s'est pas encore levé, vous voyez Móen entrer chez Eber. Comment expliquez-vous cela ?

— Mes yeux étaient habitués à l'obscurité car je venais de chevaucher dans la campagne en revenant de chez Clídna.

— Je m'étonne que vous ne vous soyez pas manifesté quand vous avez eu connaissance des crimes.

— Pour quoi faire puisqu'il y avait d'autres témoins ?

— Quand avez-vous appris que Teafa avait elle aussi été tuée ?

— Après que Dubán fut allé la chercher pour calmer Móen.

— Merci, Crítán, vous m'avez été d'un grand secours.

Perdue dans ses pensées, Fidelma se dirigea vers l'hôtellerie des invités, suivie par Eadulf.

— Avez-vous encore besoin de moi ? cria Dubán.

Fidelma se retourna d'un air absent.

— Pouvez-vous aller quérir le couteau de chasse qu'aurait utilisé Móen pour accomplir ce forfait ?

— Je m'en occupe sur l'heure.

En chemin, Eadulf attendit patiemment les commentaires de Fidelma.

— Les preuves sont assez claires, dit-il après quelques instants. Des témoignages oculaires, la découverte de Móen tenant le couteau… que désirer de plus ? Certes, Móen est digne de pitié mais il n'en demeure pas moins coupable.

Les yeux verts de Fidelma plongèrent dans les yeux bruns d'Eadulf.

— Au contraire, mon ami, je crois que ces « preuves » concourent à démontrer l'innocence de Móen, affirma la religieuse avec une assurance déconcertante.

CHAPITRE VIII

Dubán lui ayant fait savoir que Fidelma lui demandait audience, Cranat, la veuve d'Eber, répondit qu'elle acceptait de rencontrer la religieuse et son compagnon au siège de l'assemblée.

À leur arrivée, Crón était installée dans le fauteuil symbolisant sa fonction mais, cette fois-ci, un autre siège était placé à côté du sien et les mêmes chaises, en bas de l'estrade, attendaient les visiteurs. Fidelma et Eadulf avaient à peine rejoint leurs places que Cranat fit son entrée.

Pour une personne approchant la cinquantaine, Cranat était encore très séduisante, et ses gestes gracieux et aristocratiques. Elle avait le teint clair, un joli visage ovale aux traits fins, et sa chevelure blonde sans le moindre cheveu blanc flottait sur ses épaules. Les ongles de ses longues mains soignées étaient teintés de pourpre et ses sourcils redessinés avec un jus de baies noir. Une infusion de l'écorce et du fruit d'un arbre très ancien, le *ruam*, rehaussait ses pommettes d'un soupçon de rouge. Et Cranat n'avait pas lésiné sur le parfum car elle dégageait une entêtante odeur de roses.

Elle portait une robe de soie rouge avec un liseré doré, des bracelets d'argent et de bronze blanc cliquetaient à ses poignets et un collier d'or lui enserrait le cou. Cranat était une femme riche et son comportement trahissait un statut supérieur à celui de l'épouse d'un chef d'Araglin.

Fidelma attendit qu'elle daigne lui prêter quelque attention, mais ce fut Crón qui brisa le silence sans se lever de son fauteuil.

— Mère, je vous présente Fidelma, l'avocate qui s'est déplacée jusqu'ici pour juger Móen.

Cranat daigna enfin lever la tête et Fidelma croisa le même regard bleu que celui de Crón.

— Ma mère, poursuivit Crón, Cranat des Déisi.

Fidelma ne broncha pas. Maintenant, elle s'expliquait mieux le comportement de Cranat. La légende disait que pendant le règne du haut roi Corman mac Airt, le clan des Déisi avait été banni de sa terre ancestrale, autour de Tara. Certains s'étaient réfugiés à l'étranger, sur la terre des Bretons, d'autres dans le royaume de Muman où ils s'étaient divisés en deux clans, les Déisi du Nord et ceux du Sud. En conférant à sa mère le titre « des Déisi », Crón signifiait aux visiteurs que Cranat était la fille d'un prince de son peuple. Cela n'excusait en rien la façon dont elle avait accueilli Fidelma qui rougit sous l'affront. Elle avait une première fois laissé insulter son rang et sa position sans protester, mais cette fois-ci, et pour le bénéfice de son enquête, elle ne pouvait rester sans réagir.

Elle monta aussitôt sur l'estrade, se situant ainsi à la même hauteur que Crón et Cranat.

Les deux femmes la regardèrent d'un air effaré et Eadulf se mordit la lèvre pour réprimer son amusement, car il avait déjà assisté aux esclandres de Fidelma pour faire appliquer les règles du protocole quand elle voulait remettre les gens à leur place. Il se saisit d'une chaise et la posa sur l'estrade, à l'endroit que Fidelma lui avait indiqué.

— Ma sœur, vous vous oubliez ! s'écria Cranat, dont c'étaient les premiers mots.

Fidelma s'assit et considéra la veuve du chef d'un air pensif.

— Qu'aurais-je donc oublié, selon vous, Cranat d'Araglin ?

Elle avait choisi à dessein le titre actuel de la dame. Pétrifiée, Cranat se gratta la gorge.

— Ma mère est… commença Crón, puis elle se reprit quand Fidelma la fixa d'un air mauvais.

— Mère, j'avais négligé de vous préciser que Fidelma de Kildare est non seulement avocate mais aussi sœur de Colgú de Cashel.

— Mettons de côté mon lignage et le rang de mon frère, susurra Fidelma d'un ton aimable alors qu'elle venait de réduire à néant les prétentions royales de Cranat. J'ai été honorée du rang d'*anruth*, ce qui m'autorise à m'asseoir en présence du haut roi des cinq royaumes et à discuter d'égal à égal avec lui.

Cranat pinça les lèvres et détourna ses yeux de glace pour fixer un point éloigné.

— Et maintenant, lança Fidelma avec un grand sourire, oublions ces détails sans intérêt et venons-en à la tragédie qui nous préoccupe.

La mère et la fille, doublement mortifiées dans leur orgueil, demeurèrent silencieuses.

— Cranat, j'aurais quelques questions à vous poser.

— Dans ce cas, je suis certaine que rien ne vous retiendra de le faire, répliqua Cranat sans changer de position.

— On m'a rapporté que c'était vous qui aviez envoyé un messager à mon frère à Cashel pour requérir la présence d'un brehon. Vous avez agi sans l'assentiment de votre fille, qui est pourtant *tanist*. Pour quelles raisons, je vous prie ?

— Ma fille est jeune. Elle manque d'expérience dans les domaines politique et juridique. Il me semblait que cette affaire devait être traitée selon les règles les plus strictes afin qu'aucune tache ne vienne souiller la réputation de la famille d'Araglin.

— Que craigniez-vous ?

— La condition de celui qui a commis les crimes, par ailleurs fils adoptif de lady Teafa, aurait pu provoquer des commentaires désagréables sur la famille d'Araglin.

Fidelma jugea cette explication raisonnable.

— Revenons au matin où vous avez appris la mort de votre mari, Eber.

— J'ai déjà expliqué ce qui s'était passé, intervint Crón.

Fidelma fit claquer sa langue avec irritation.

— Vous m'avez donné votre version. Maintenant, c'est le témoignage de votre mère qui m'intéresse.

— Il n'y a pas grand-chose à raconter, soupira Cranat. J'ai été réveillée par ma fille.

— À quelle heure ?

— Juste quand le soleil se levait.

— Et alors ?

— Elle m'a informée qu'Eber avait été assassiné et que Móen était le meurtrier. Je me suis habillée et nous nous sommes retrouvées ici, au siège de l'assemblée. Puis Dubán est arrivé pour annoncer que Teafa avait elle aussi été poignardée.

— Vous êtes allée voir le corps d'Eber ?

Cranat secoua la tête.

— Vous n'avez pas songé à aller faire vos adieux à votre défunt mari ?

— Ma mère était bouleversée, intervint Crón sur la défensive.

Fidelma tint le regard d'un bleu transparent de Cranat sous le sien.

— J'étais bouleversée, dit Cranat en écho.

À l'évidence, elle s'était saisie de l'excuse proposée par sa fille.

— Comment se fait-il que vous ne partagiez point la couche de votre époux ?

Crón laissa échapper une exclamation étouffée.

— Comment osez-vous ? Quelle impertinence !...

— Ma fonction m'autorise à poser toutes les questions qui peuvent servir la vérité et il me semble, Crón d'Araglin, que vous avez encore beaucoup à apprendre concernant les devoirs et la sagesse d'un chef. Votre mère avait raison d'envoyer quérir un brehon à Cashel.

Le temps que Crón cherche une réponse cinglante à cette remontrance, Fidelma s'était déjà retournée vers Cranat.

— Je vous écoute.

Cranat la toisa avec hostilité, mais les yeux verts de Fidelma jetaient des éclairs et elle comprit que la *dálaigh* ne se laisserait pas impressionner.

— Cela faisait des années que je ne dormais plus avec lui, dit-elle d'un ton détaché.

— Pourquoi donc ?

— Eh bien... disons que, dans ce domaine, nous nous étions éloignés.

— Vous en souffriez ?

— Non.

— Et Eber ?

— Où voulez-vous en venir ?

— Vous connaissez les lois du mariage aussi bien que moi. Les défaillances sexuelles de l'une ou l'autre partie sont un motif suffisant pour demander le divorce.

Cranat rougit et Crón baissa les yeux sur Eadulf en contrebas.

— Est-il bien utile que le Saxon assiste à cet entretien ?

Gêné, Eadulf fit mine de se lever mais Fidelma le retint.

— Il s'est déplacé jusqu'ici pour assister à la mise en application de la justice dans notre pays, et rien de ce qui est du ressort de la loi ne doit être considéré comme gênant ou immoral.

— Nous avions passé un accord à l'amiable, reprit Cranat, résignée devant la détermination de Fidelma, et n'avions pas estimé nécessaire de nous séparer.

— Pourtant, si l'un de vous deux répugnait aux relations sexuelles, il pouvait facilement obtenir le divorce. La stérilité et l'impuissance sont également des motifs recevables.

— Ma mère connaît la loi, intervint Crón, outrée. En l'occurrence, mes parents préféraient dormir dans des chambres séparées.

— Très bien, concéda Fidelma. Cependant, j'aurais préféré connaître la raison d'une telle attitude.

— Ma fille vient de vous dire que nous préférions dormir seuls, dit Cranat en haussant le ton.

— Mais pour le reste, vous meniez la vie de tous les conjoints ?

— Oui.

— Et votre époux n'a jamais songé à prendre une concubine ?

— C'est interdit, lâcha Crón d'un ton sec.

— Interdit ? releva Fidelma d'un ton surpris. D'après le *Cáin Lánamna*, la polygamie est tout à fait légale. Un homme peut avoir une épouse et une concubine, qui, bien que d'un statut inférieur devant la loi, est dotée de la moitié des avantages de la première femme.

— En tant que sœur de la foi, comment pouvez-vous approuver de tels usages ? s'énerva Crón.

— Qui dit que je les approuve ? Je ne fais qu'énoncer les règlements des cinq royaumes tels qu'ils sont appliqués. Et je m'étonne qu'on y trouve à redire dans une communauté rurale comme la vôtre, où les anciennes coutumes reçoivent généralement l'appui du peuple.

— Le père Gormán les condamne.

— Ah, le père Gormán ! Il semblerait que le bon père exerce une influence prépondérante en ces lieux. Il est vrai que les adeptes de la nouvelle foi sont nombreux à s'opposer à la polygamie, mais ils n'ont pas été suivis. En réalité, le *scriptor* des textes de loi, le *Bretha Crólige*, tente de justifier la polygamie en s'appuyant sur l'Ancien Testament. Le peuple élu de Dieu vivait dans la pluralité des unions et nous, les gentils, devrions nous conformer à ce livre sacré.

Cranat poussa une exclamation de dépit.

— Vous aurez tout le loisir de discuter théologie avec le père Gormán quand il reviendra. Quant à Eber, il n'a jamais envisagé de divorcer ni de prendre une concubine. Nous vivons ici en bonne entente et mes relations avec Eber ne vous concernent en rien puisque son assassin a été clairement identifié.

— Bien sûr, murmura Fidelma comme si elle s'était laissé distraire. Revenons à ce qui nous préoccupe…

— Je ne sais rien de plus que ce que je vous ai conté. Je n'ai été informée de la mort d'Eber que par des témoignages indirects.

— Et d'après votre fille, vous étiez bouleversée.

— Oui.

— Mais suffisamment lucide pour demander au jeune Crítán de chevaucher jusqu'à Cashel afin d'exiger l'assistance d'un brehon ?

— En tant que femme de chef, j'accomplissais mon devoir.

— Avez-vous été choquée quand on vous a dit que Móen était l'auteur du meurtre de votre mari ?

— Choquée ? non. Plutôt attristée. Il était inévitable qu'un jour ou l'autre cette bête sauvage se retourne contre quelqu'un.

— Vous n'aimiez pas Móen ?

La veuve d'Eber haussa les sourcils.

— Pour aimer une personne, encore faut-il la connaître.

— Bien sûr, il lui était impossible de communiquer ses pensées, ses espoirs et ses ambitions, mais entreteniez-vous des contacts réguliers avec lui ?

— Vous semblez accorder à cette créature la même sensibilité qu'à une personne normale ! s'esclaffa Crón.

— Être privé de la vue, de la parole et de l'audition n'entraîne pas nécessairement une absence de sensibilité, l'admonesta Fidelma, et Móen a grandi dans l'entourage de votre mère.

Cranat pinça les lèvres.

— Rien ne permet d'en déduire que j'ai noué des liens avec cette créature. J'ai vu des petits cochons se transformer en truies et ne les fréquente pas pour autant.

— Donc vous considérez Móen comme un animal et non comme un être humain ?

— Je vous laisse juge.

— J'essaye simplement de comprendre votre attitude vis-à-vis de Móen. Et maintenant, parlez-moi de Teafa. On m'a raconté qu'elle savait communiquer avec lui.

— Le berger communique-t-il avec ses moutons ?

— Et aussi que vous vous entendiez mal avec elle.

— Qui se permet de répandre de telles calomnies ?

— Vous le niez ?

Cranat hésita puis haussa les épaules.

— Au cours de ces dernières années, nous avons eu quelques différends.

— Pour quelles raisons ?

— Elle suggérait que je divorce d'Eber et perde mon statut d'épouse du chef. Elle me faisait pitié. Mais elle avait amené le malheur sur sa tête.

— Comment l'entendez-vous ?

— Dans sa frustration alors qu'elle n'était plus en âge de se marier, elle avait adopté Móen qui ne pouvait lui retourner son affection.

— Elle n'en demeurait pas moins la sœur de votre mari.

— Teafa appréciait la solitude. Elle participait parfois aux fêtes religieuses, mais ne s'accordait pas avec le père Gormán sur l'interprétation à donner aux textes de la foi. Bien que sa maison ne soit située qu'à quinze toises d'ici, elle vivait retirée.

— Pour quelles raisons Móen aurait-il tué Eber ?

Cranat écarta les bras.

— Comment voulez-vous que je sache ce qui est passé par la tête de cette bête sauvage ?

— Móen ne vous inspire aucun autre commentaire ?

— Aucun.

— Dois-je en déduire qu'il a été considéré comme une bête sauvage, ce sont vos propres termes, par la famille de Teafa au cours des années qu'il a vécu dans cette communauté ?

Une fois de plus, Crón s'interposa.

— Il était mieux traité que les animaux de ce *rath*, personne ne se montrait cruel avec lui, et je ne vois pas quel autre comportement nous aurions pu adopter à son égard.

— Après toutes ces années, vous attribuez donc les actes qui lui sont reprochés à son instinct bestial ?

— Absolument.

— Il faut beaucoup de ruse à un animal pour prendre un couteau, tuer la femme qui a toute sa vie pris soin de lui et trouver son chemin jusqu'à la couche d'Eber pour le poignarder à son tour.

— Qui a dit que les animaux n'étaient pas rusés ? riposta Crón.

Cranat grimaça un sourire approbateur.

— Il me semble, jeune dame, que vous vous efforcez par tous les moyens de disculper Móen. Pour quelles raisons, je vous prie ?

Fidelma se leva.

— Ma quête de la vérité n'implique en rien que je partage votre vision des choses, Cranat d'Araglin. Mais en tant qu'avocate des cinq royaumes, j'ai fait le serment d'évaluer le degré de responsabilité de ceux qui ont enfreint la loi et de rechercher les raisons qui les ont poussés à commettre ces infractions, cela dans le but de prononcer un jugement qui établira des compensations équitables. Et maintenant, je vous remercie de votre collaboration.

Si les regards avaient pu tuer, songea Eadulf, Fidelma sera tombée raide morte aux pieds des deux femmes. Au lieu de quoi elle descendit tranquillement de l'estrade et se dirigea vers la porte, escortée du moine.

— Vous ne semblez pas porter Cranat et sa fille dans votre cœur, fit observer Eadulf quand ils se retrouvèrent dehors.

Fidelma lui adressa un sourire taquin.

— Vous qui me connaissez bien savez que je ne suis guère tolérante envers certaines attitudes. Par exemple l'arrogance. Et j'ai la faiblesse de me battre sur le même terrain plutôt que de tendre l'autre joue comme nous y invitent les Évangiles, car je crains qu'un tel comportement ne pousse à de nouvelles offenses.

— Du moins reconnaissez-vous vos fautes, le plus grand péché étant de n'en reconnaître aucune.

Fidelma se mit à rire.

— Votre philosophie m'agrée, Eadulf de Seaxmund's Ham, et accordez-moi la grâce d'admettre que l'affrontement auquel vous venez d'assister nous a permis d'apprendre qu'on ne pouvait se fier à Cranat.

— Parce qu'elle n'est pas allée s'incliner devant la dépouille de son mari, mais a cependant eu la présence d'esprit d'envoyer un messager à Cashel car elle se défiait de sa fille ? Moi aussi j'ai trouvé cela un peu étrange.

Fidelma jeta un coup d'œil en direction de la chapelle dont la porte était ouverte.

— Le redoutable père Gormán serait-il de retour ? Venez, allons faire sa connaissance.

Prévoyant une nouvelle algarade, le moine la suivit en protestant un peu. D'après le portrait qu'on leur avait dressé du prêtre, il se doutait bien que lui et Fidelma s'entendraient comme chien et chat.

Des cierges brillaient dans la chapelle lambrissée de sapin et une forte odeur d'encens les accueillit. Fidelma examina avec curiosité la débauche de luxe qui les entourait. Des statues en or se dressaient sur leurs socles et une croix incrustée de pierreries surmontait l'autel où était posé un calice en argent. Il n'y avait pas de sièges, car les fidèles demeuraient debout pendant l'office. Les cierges dégageaient des parfums d'épices tellement puissants qu'Eadulf et Fidelma eurent du mal à reprendre leur respiration. À l'évidence, le père Gormán était à la tête d'une congrégation prospère.

Devant eux, le prêtre était abîmé dans ses dévotions. Il se retourna en percevant une présence, termina ses prières, fit une génuflexion devant l'autel et vint accueillir les visiteurs.

La silhouette du père Gormán, grande et mince, était un peu efféminée, mais il présentait un visage large et hâlé aux lèvres rouges, couronné de cheveux gris peu fournis autrefois de la même teinte que ses yeux noirs. S'il gardait les traces d'un physique avantageux, il donnait maintenant l'impression d'un homme d'un certain âge aux mœurs dissolues. Cela surprit Fidelma qui s'attendait à un prêtre romain de fort tempérament. Cependant, il les accueillit d'une voix grave et tonitruante qui n'avait certainement aucun mal à promettre les feux de l'enfer à ses fidèles. En tant que partisan de Rome, il avait adopté la *corona spina* sur le haut du crâne et non la tonsure en demi-couronne, à l'avant de la tête, du clergé irlandais. Fidelma remarqua également qu'il portait des gants de cuir grossiers.

En voyant la tonsure romaine d'Eadulf, son regard s'adoucit.

— Bienvenue, mon frère, lança-t-il de sa voix de stentor. Je suis heureux d'accueillir un homme qui a choisi la voie de la sagesse.

Cet enthousiasme plongea Eadulf dans l'embarras.

— Je suis Eadulf de Seaxmund's Ham. Jamais je ne me serais attendu, dans ces montagnes, à tomber sur une chapelle aussi richement dotée.

Le père Gormán éclata de rire, visiblement ravi.

— La terre est généreuse, mon frère, pour les partisans de la vraie foi.

— Et moi je suis Fidelma de Kildare, s'interposa aussitôt Fidelma.

Les yeux noirs lui jetèrent un regard approbateur.

— Ah, oui. Dubán m'a parlé de vous, ma sœur. Bienvenue dans ma petite chapelle. Cill Uird, comme je l'appelle, « l'église du rituel », car c'est grâce à la liturgie que nous vivons dans le Christ. Que le Seigneur vous bénisse pendant votre séjour et vous accorde la paix de l'âme quand vous nous quitterez.

Fidelma inclina la tête.

— Si vous pouviez nous accorder un peu de votre temps, mon père… On vous a certainement informé du but de notre visite ?

— Oui, bien sûr. Suivez-moi.

Il les conduisit dans la sacristie, repoussa une cape bicolore posée sur un banc où il leur fit signe de s'asseoir tandis qu'il s'installait sur une chaise. Puis il ôta ses gants.

— Je viens de rentrer et je porte toujours des gants pour chevaucher dans la région, expliqua-t-il.

— Il est rare qu'un prêtre possède un cheval, fit observer Eadulf.

Le père Gormán gloussa.

— De riches fidèles m'en ont offert un afin que je puisse veiller sur mon troupeau plus à mon aise. Vu l'étendue de ma paroisse, je n'ose imaginer ce que serait ma vie si je devais me déplacer à pied. Et maintenant, parlons un peu de vous. Je vous ai vus tous les deux à l'abbaye d'Hilda, pendant le concile.

— Vous étiez à Witebia ?

Eadulf était stupéfait.

— Oui, mais je doute que vous vous souveniez de moi. Je revenais, avec Colmán, d'une mission d'évangélisation et je me suis arrêté à Streoneshalh pour assister au synode, en tant que simple auditeur et non comme délégué. J'ai beaucoup apprécié les débats passionnants entre les Églises de Colomba et de Rome.

— Donc vous étiez présent quand nous avons résolu le mystère de la mort de l'abbesse Étain, s'exclama Eadulf, et…

— J'étais là, l'interrompit le père Gormán en haussant le ton, quand le roi Oswy, dans sa sagesse, s'est prononcé en faveur de Rome et a jugé que les adeptes de Colomba étaient dans l'erreur.

— Nous avions compris qu'en ce qui vous concerne vous suiviez les ordres de Rome, lança Fidelma d'un ton sec.

— Et qui aurait eu le front de contredire la décision d'Oswy après avoir entendu les arguments des uns et des autres ? rétorqua le prêtre. Depuis ce jour béni, je m'efforce de guider Araglin sur la voie de la vérité.

— Bien des voies mènent à Dieu.

— Sottises ! Seuls ceux qui suivent la voie unique trouveront le Seigneur.

— Vous ignorez le doute ?

— Oui, car je suis fermement ancré dans mes convictions.

— Je vous envie, père Gormán.

— Tant que vous douterez, vous ne connaîtrez pas la liberté.

— Il me semble pourtant que même le Christ, à la fin de sa vie, a traversé des moments d'égarement, répliqua Fidelma d'un air innocent.

Le père Gormán parut scandalisé.

— Seulement pour nous démontrer que nous devons rester fidèles à nos croyances.

— Je ne partage pas les vôtres. Mon mentor, Morann de Tara, m'a enseigné que la vérité craint davantage les certitudes que les mensonges.

Le père Gormán s'apprêtait à répliquer vertement quand Fidelma leva la main.

— Mais je ne suis pas venue ici pour débattre de théologie avec vous, Gormán de Cill Uird. Remettons nos différends à plus tard, quand l'affaire qui m'a amenée ici sera résolue car j'ai été appelée en ces lieux en tant qu'avocate des cours de justice.

— Il s'agit du meurtre d'Eber, ajouta Eadulf, craignant que le prêtre ne s'obstine à poursuivre la controverse.

Le père Gormán se calma brusquement.

— Alors je ne vous serai d'aucun secours car j'ignore tout de ces événements, dit-il d'un ton sans réplique.

— Mais d'après mes renseignements, vous dormez dans votre église et personne n'est plus proche que vous des appartements d'Eber. Vous confirmez cependant n'avoir rien entendu ?

— Je dors dans cette pièce, dit le père Gormán en désignant une petite porte derrière eux, mais je puis vous assurer que j'ignorais tout du meurtre. C'est le tapage à l'extérieur de la maison d'Eber qui m'a réveillé.

— À quelle heure ?

— Après le lever du soleil. En apprenant la nouvelle, des gens s'étaient rassemblés devant la demeure du chef. Je suis alors sorti pour comprendre la raison de cette agitation.

— Je croyais que Rome avait établi des règles très strictes quant à l'heure du réveil, glissa Eadulf d'un air narquois.

Le père Gormán le toisa avec une animosité non dissimulée.

— Vous devriez savoir que ce qui est bon pour un pays méridional n'est pas nécessairement souhaitable sous nos climats plus rudes. L'heure indiquée par Rome correspond au lever du jour et je ne vois pas l'intérêt de s'agiter dans le froid et l'obscurité pour imiter nos frères romains.

Un large sourire illumina le visage de Fidelma.

— Vous conviendrez donc que tout n'est pas mauvais dans les règles édictées par l'Église de Colomba ?

Le prêtre tressaillit sous la pique.

— Plaisantez tant que vous voudrez, ma sœur, il n'en demeure pas moins qu'en ce qui concerne la théologie et l'enseignement, les règles prônées par Rome ont été consacrées par le Christ. Les seules différences sont dues à la géographie.

— Restons-en là pour l'instant. La nuit du crime, êtes-vous bien sûr que rien n'est venu perturber votre sommeil ?

— J'ai célébré l'Angélus de minuit avant de me retirer dans ma chambre et non, rien n'a troublé mon repos.

— Pas de cris ni d'appels au secours ?

126

— Non, vous dis-je.

— Lorsqu'un homme est attaqué et poignardé, il semblerait qu'il doive pousser des hurlements.

— Ayant été agressé quand il dormait, sans doute n'en a-t-il pas eu le loisir.

— Un sourd-muet aveugle pénètre dans une pièce sans déranger personne, murmura Fidelma comme si elle se parlait à elle-même. Et il prend un couteau qu'il plonge à plusieurs reprises dans la poitrine d'Eber alors que le chef se trouve dans une pièce éclairée. N'est-ce pas étrange ?

— Sans doute mais qu'y puis-je ? ironisa le père Gormán.

— N'avez-vous pas été surpris d'apprendre que Móen se tenait près du corps d'Eber et que, selon des témoins, tout l'accusait ?

Le prêtre réfléchit un instant.

— Non, je n'ai pas été étonné. Un animal sauvage autorisé à rôder à sa guise dans une maison se retournera tôt ou tard contre ceux qui y vivent.

— C'est ainsi que vous voyez Móen ? Un animal sauvage ?

— Oui. Cet enfant de l'inceste que je n'ai jamais autorisé à entrer dans cette chapelle est maudit de Dieu.

— Pour un chrétien, n'est-ce pas une étrange manière de traiter un affligé ? s'étonna Fidelma.

— Qui suis-je pour demander des comptes à Dieu sur la punition de Sa créature ? S'Il l'a privée de ce qui nous constitue en tant qu'êtres humains, Il avait ses raisons. Le Christ n'a-t-il pas dit : « Le Fils de l'homme enverra ses anges, qui ramasseront de son Royaume tous les scandales et tous les fauteurs d'iniquité et les jetteront dans la fournaise ardente : là seront les pleurs et les grincements de dents[1] » ? Dieu nous sanctionne autant qu'Il nous récompense.

1. Matthieu, 13, 41. (*N.d.T.*)

— Êtes-vous sûr que Dieu a créé Móen pour le châtier et non pour éprouver l'ardeur de notre foi ?

— Voilà une intolérable impertinence.

— Ce que vous qualifiez ainsi n'est que l'argument ultime des gens qui refusent de répondre à l'une de mes questions. Pauvre Móen, il semblerait qu'on l'ait bien mal toléré en ces lieux.

— Remettriez-vous en question mon éthique chrétienne ?

Le prêtre s'était fait subtilement menaçant.

— Dieu m'en garde, répondit Fidelma avec une fausse humilité.

— Et qu'Il vous entende, répliqua le père Gormán d'un ton sec, se méprenant sur le sens de ses paroles.

— Donc la culpabilité de Móen ne suscite en vous aucune interrogation ? hasarda Eadulf.

Le père Gormán secoua la tête.

— De quoi parlez-vous ? Il y a eu des témoins.

— Vous ne vous êtes jamais demandé pourquoi Móen aurait accompli un acte pareil ?

— Cette créature est coupée de nous et ses raisonnements nous échappent. Il vit dans un monde à part. Qui peut mesurer l'amertume et la haine qu'il nourrit pour les gens normaux ?

— Vous lui accordez donc des sentiments humains, s'empressa de remarquer Fidelma.

— Les émotions que je lui accorde, je les prête aussi aux animaux. Si vous rudoyez un chien, il peut très bien vous mordre.

Fidelma se pencha vers lui et le fixa avec intensité.

— Eber aurait-il maltraité Móen ?

— Je vous donnais des raisons d'ordre général et ne parlais pas en particulier.

— Est-ce que Teafa brutalisait Móen ?

Il secoua la tête.

— Non, elle l'adorait. Toute la famille du chef d'Araglin est perverse.

— Incluez-vous Eber dans ce jugement ?

— Surtout lui. Prions le Seigneur que Crón tienne de sa mère et non de son père.

Fidelma plissa les paupières.

— Pourtant, selon de nombreux témoignages, Eber était la générosité même et tout le monde le respectait en Araglin. M'aurait-on menti ?

Le père Gormán grimaça un sourire.

— La générosité d'Eber était bien la seule vertu que je lui reconnaissais car il accumulait les vices. Pourquoi pensez-vous que sa femme ait déserté sa couche ?

— Elle affirme qu'il s'agissait d'un accord mutuel.

Le père Gormán émit un reniflement méprisant.

— J'ai essayé de la persuader de divorcer. Mais c'est une femme fière, comme il convient à une princesse de son peuple.

— Pourquoi l'avoir poussée à une telle résolution ?

— Les liens du mariage ne convenaient pas à cet homme.

— Ce n'est pas l'avis de Cranat. Pourriez-vous être plus explicite ?

— Eh bien, Eber…

Il frissonna d'un air dégoûté.

— … souffrait de dérèglements sexuels.

— De quelle manière l'entendez-vous ?

— Préférait-il les garçons ? intervint Eadulf, entrevoyant soudain une raison qui aurait pu fournir un motif d'assassinat à Móen.

— Oh, non ! Il appréciait trop les femmes !

— Je vois. Et Cranat était-elle informée de ses écarts ? reprit Fidelma.

— Tout le monde savait sauf elle. Ses frasques ont commencé dès l'âge de la puberté et ses sœurs en étaient informées. Teafa a fini par en instruire Cranat qui m'a tout raconté quand elle a décidé de déserter le lit conjugal.

— Pourquoi Cranat ne l'a-t-elle pas quitté ?

— À cause du scandale et de sa fille, Crón. Et puis Cranat, malgré son rang de princesse, ne possédait ni terre ni argent. Elle avait épousé Eber pour ses richesses et lui l'avait prise pour femme à cause de son lignage et de ses relations. Sans doute n'était-ce pas une base très solide pour une union durable.

— Mais si Cranat avait divorcé en invoquant les motifs que vous m'avez exposés, elle aurait pu récupérer ses biens personnels. Si elle n'en avait aucun, elle était néanmoins habilitée à s'approprier un neuvième de l'accroissement des richesses de son mari depuis le jour de leur mariage qui remontait à une vingtaine d'années. Cela représentait une coquette somme d'argent qui lui aurait permis de vivre à son aise.

Le père Gormán hocha la tête. Il semblait mélancolique.

— Je ne cessais de le lui répéter, mais elle avait choisi de rester.

Fidelma le contempla d'un air songeur.

— Vous appréciez beaucoup Cranat, n'est-ce pas ?

Il s'empourpra.

— Il n'y a rien de mal à vouloir redresser des torts.

— Rien, sauf que votre prise de position a certainement contrarié Eber. D'autre part, on m'a appris que vous étiez partisan d'ôter la vie à Móen pour le punir de son forfait.

— Les paroles de Dieu ne sont-elles pas explicites ? Œil pour œil, dent pour dent. Je crois dans la pleine mesure du châtiment prôné par Rome.

Fidelma secoua la tête.

— L'extrême justice est souvent injuste.

— Cela sent l'hérésie pélagienne, ricana le prêtre.

— Pélage était-il si hérétique que cela ?

Le père Gormán faillit s'en étouffer d'indignation.

— Vous en doutez ? Êtes-vous à ce point ignorante ?

— Je sais que le pape Zosime l'a déclaré innocent malgré les pressions exercées par Augustin d'Hippone qui persuada l'empereur Honorius de publier un décret impérial le condamnant.

Le père Gormán pinça les lèvres.

130

— Mais le pape Zosime a fini par le déclarer coupable d'hérésie.

— Forcé et contraint par l'empereur. J'ai du mal à considérer cela comme une décision d'ordre théologique. Et n'est-il point ironique qu'il ait été condamné à cause de l'auteur du traité *De libero arbitrio*, Sur le libre arbitre ?

— Donc vous soutenez un hérétique, comme la plupart des gens de votre espèce qui ont pris le parti de Colomba ?

— Nous refusons de fermer nos esprits à la raison, comme Rome le commande à ses adeptes. Après tout, que signifie exactement « hérésie » ? C'est le mot grec pour « choix », qui plus tard évoluera vers « préférence ». Comme il est dans notre nature de choisir librement, alors nous sommes tous des hérétiques.

— Pélage avait trop mangé de porridge irlandais ! Il a été condamné à juste titre pour avoir refusé de voir la vérité de la doctrine d'Augustin sur la chute de l'homme et le péché originel !

— J'aurais préféré qu'Augustin soit condamné pour son refus d'admettre la théorie de Pélage sur le libre arbitre.

— Votre insolence met votre âme en péril !

Le père Gormán était devenu rouge de colère tandis que Fidelma demeurait impassible.

— Reconsidérons les faits, dit-elle avec calme. La faute revenait à Adam et les descendants d'Adam ont été punis par Dieu pour son péché. Vous êtes d'accord ?

— Oui, une malédiction est tombée sur l'humanité tout entière en attendant que le Christ rachète le monde.

— Mais Adam a désobéi à Dieu ?

— Je vous l'accorde.

— Et pourtant, on nous enseigne que Dieu est tout puissant et qu'Il a créé Adam.

— L'homme a reçu le libre arbitre mais en défiant Dieu, Adam est tombé en disgrâce.

— Et Pélage pose la question suivante : avant la chute, Adam pouvait-il choisir entre le bien et le mal ?

— Pour se guider, il disposait des commandements de Dieu qui lui a expliqué ce qu'il devait faire. Mais la femme l'a induit en tentation.

— Ah, oui. *La femme.*

Frère Eadulf changea de position d'un air gêné. Fidelma jouait avec le feu mais il ne voyait aucun moyen de l'arrêter.

— Si Dieu tout-puissant a créé Adam et Ève, Sa volonté n'était-elle pas suffisante pour les guider ?

— L'homme était doté du libre arbitre.

— Donc la volonté d'Adam, et par là même celle de *la femme*, était plus forte que celle de Dieu ?

Visage outragé du père Gormán.

— Non, bien sûr. Dans Sa toute-puissance, Dieu a accordé la liberté à l'homme.

— Selon la logique, Dieu tout-puissant était en mesure de prévenir le péché mais Il s'y est refusé tout en prévoyant le comportement d'Adam. Selon la loi, Dieu était complice par instigation.

— Vous blasphémez, bégaya le père Gormán.

— Et si je vais au bout de mon raisonnement, Dieu acquiesçait au péché d'Adam.

— Sacrilège ! s'écria le prêtre au bord de l'apoplexie.

— Calmez-vous, c'est juste une question de bon sens. L'humanité a été maudite à cause du péché d'Adam, mais Dieu l'avait anticipé. D'où j'en déduis que les hommes ont été créés pour souffrir par millions.

— Vous et votre esprit limité n'avez pas accès au grand mystère de l'univers, la fustigea Gormán.

— Ce mystère restera à jamais obscur si nous élaborons des mythes qui empêchent d'y accéder. Voilà où nos chemins se séparent. Moi, je me tiens aux côtés de Pélage, qui était un homme de notre peuple. Voilà pourquoi Rome a toujours attaqué nos églises, ici et chez les Bretons et les Gaulois qui partagent notre philosophie. Nous sommes des gens curieux qui questionnons toute chose dans l'espoir de nous approcher du grand mystère, et il est de notre devoir de lutter pour la vérité, même contre le reste du monde.

Elle se leva d'un geste vif.

— Je vous remercie de nous avoir consacré un peu de votre temps, père Gormán.

Puis elle sortit d'un pas décidé, Eadulf sur les talons.

Une fois dehors, leurs regards se croisèrent.

— Eh bien, on dirait que le brouillard commence à se dissiper, lança-t-elle d'un air satisfait.

Eadulf, perplexe, fit la moue.

— Vous parlez de Pélage ?

Fidelma se mit à rire.

— Non, du père Gormán.

— Vous le suspectez ?

— A priori, je soupçonne tout le monde. Mais il est clair que Gormán est dévoué à Cranat jusqu'à la passion.

— À leur âge ? s'étonna Eadulf d'un ton réprobateur.

— Mais enfin, Eadulf de Seaxmund's Ham, l'amour peut frapper à tout âge !

— Quand même, un prêtre et une femme mûre…

— Aucune loi n'interdit à un prêtre de prendre une épouse, même Rome le tolère. Avec des réticences, je vous l'accorde.

— Insinuez-vous que le père Gormán avait ses raisons pour souhaiter la mort d'Eber ?

Fidelma s'absorba dans la contemplation d'une pierre à ses pieds.

— Les mobiles ne lui manquaient pas. Mais avait-il les moyens d'exaucer son souhait ou de s'arranger pour qu'on le réalise à sa place ?

CHAPITRE IX

Ce soir-là, ils prirent un bain, puis dînèrent seuls. Crón ne les avait pas conviés à dîner au siège de l'assemblée, comme l'aurait voulu le protocole, ce qui ne surprit pas Eadulf outre mesure. En dehors du pauvre Móen, et encore, rien n'était moins certain, Fidelma ne s'était pas fait beaucoup d'amis au cours de la journée.

Une jeune fille d'une quinzaine d'années leur apporta des plateaux chargés de nourriture. Elle avait de beaux cheveux bruns, un teint pâle et semblait nerveuse. Fidelma s'efforça de la rassurer.

— Comment vous appelez-vous ?

— Grella, ma sœur. Je travaille pour Dignait.

Fidelma lui sourit.

— Vous aimez votre travail, Grella ?

La jeune fille fronça les sourcils.

— J'ai été élevée dans les cuisines du chef et c'est la tâche qui m'a été assignée, voilà tout. Je suis orphe- line, ajouta-t-elle en guise d'explication.

— Vous avez dû être bien désolée d'apprendre la mort d'Eber d'Araglin, vous qui avez grandi dans sa maison.

À la surprise de Fidelma, la jeune fille secoua la tête avec véhémence.

— Non… non, mais j'ai été bien triste pour Teafa. C'était une gentille dame.

134

— Vous n'en diriez pas autant d'Eber ?

— Teafa s'est montrée très bonne pour moi, répliqua la petite d'un air anxieux. Lady Teafa était une bénédiction pour tout le monde.

À l'évidence, elle refusait de critiquer le chef disparu.

— Et Móen ? Vous aimez Móen ?

Grella parut interdite.

— Je n'étais pas très à l'aise quand il rôdait dans le coin. Seule Teafa pouvait le commander.

— Comment lui parlait-elle ? demanda aussitôt Fidelma.

— Elle parvenait à communiquer avec lui.

— Savez-vous comment ? intervint aussitôt Eadulf, piqué par la curiosité.

La jeune fille haussa les épaules.

— Pas vraiment. Ils se tapotaient sur les paumes des mains avec le bout des doigts.

— Vous avez assisté à ces conversations ? s'enquit Fidelma. Teafa vous a-t-elle initiée à ce langage ?

— Non, mais je les ai vus bien des fois. Peut-être que c'était juste un rituel pour calmer Móen.

La déception se peignit sur le visage de Fidelma.

Grella inclina la tête sur le côté, le regard vague. Puis un grand sourire illumina ses traits.

— Je me souviens. Elle disait que c'était Gadra qui lui avait appris l'art de pénétrer dans l'esprit de Móen.

Fidelma reprit espoir.

— Qui est Gadra ?

Grella frissonna et fit une génuflexion.

— Un croque-mitaine. On dit qu'il vole les âmes des enfants méchants. Et maintenant il faut que je retourne auprès de Dignait, sinon je vais me faire gronder.

Les deux religieux prirent leur repas dans un silence méditatif. Puis, rassemblant son courage, Eadulf se risqua à encourir le déplaisir de Fidelma en abordant un sujet qui le tourmentait depuis longtemps.

— Trouvez-vous sage, dit-il d'un air pénétré, de provoquer la colère de tous ceux que vous rencontrez ?

Fidelma releva la tête.

— Je crois percevoir une note de désapprobation dans cette remarque, dit-elle d'un ton solennel démenti par l'étincelle malicieuse qui brillait dans ses yeux.

Eadulf fit la grimace.

— Excusez-moi, mais il me semble que le tact et la discrétion vous conduiraient aux mêmes résultats.

— Donc vous estimez que je suis inutilement brutale ? soupira Fidelma qui paraissait sincèrement désolée.

Eadulf, davantage habitué à ses éclats de colère qu'à ses accès de modestie, fut troublé par cette réaction.

— Ma mère disait souvent qu'on ne défait pas un point de broderie avec une hache, grommela-t-il.

— C'est la première fois que vous me parlez de votre mère...

— Elle n'est plus de ce monde, mais j'admirais sa sagesse.

— Dont je n'ai aucune raison de douter. Cependant, quand vous vous trouvez devant une porte verrouillée, il est parfois nécessaire de recourir à une hache pour atteindre la personne qui s'est barricadée dans son orgueil. Les gens arrogants prennent souvent la courtoisie pour de la faiblesse, et même de la servilité.

— Et défoncer les portes vous permet vraiment de découvrir la vérité ?

— Disons que cela m'en rapproche, mais je vous concède que cela ne me permet pas d'y accéder.

— Parfait, et dans le cas qui nous préoccupe, quelle stratégie avez-vous élaborée ?

— Dès que nous aurons terminé ce repas, je voudrais voir Dubán. Peut-être découvrirons-nous que ce croque-mitaine existe vraiment. Et si le dénommé Gadra est en mesure de m'apprendre par quel moyen

Teafa communiquait avec Móen, alors nous aurons fait un grand pas en direction de la lumière. Imaginez que Móen nous raconte ce qu'il sait !

Eadulf parut sceptique.

— Un père fouettard qui vole les âmes des enfants… cela ressemble fort à un conte de fées.

— Les contes de fées recèlent toujours une part de vérité.

— En somme, si Gadra existe, s'il a vraiment appris à Teafa un code secret, et en admettant qu'un tel mode de communication ait jamais été conçu, car il suppose un esprit prisonnier de cette créature sourde, muette et aveugle… vous aurez bien avancé dans vos investigations. N'êtes-vous pas un peu présomptueuse ? Sans compter que vous vous êtes persuadée de l'innocence de Móen, ce qui reste à prouver !

Fidelma, qui avait fini de manger, se balança sur sa chaise.

— J'avoue que je ne le crois pas coupable. Une intuition que rien ne vient étayer me prévient en sa faveur, or quand un sixième sens me détourne d'une logique apparemment sans faille, je suis mon pressentiment.

— Les illusions les plus dangereuses ne sont-elles pas le fruit de notre imagination ?

— Vous pensez que je me trompe ?

— Ma logique personnelle suggère qu'au bout du compte, ce qui s'apparente à la cécité se révèle souvent être de l'aveuglement.

Fidelma pouffa de rire et posa la main sur le bras de son compagnon.

— Vous êtes la voix de ma conscience et savez comme personne tempérer mes excès d'enthousiasme. Et maintenant, je vais me renseigner sur Gadra le sorcier. Attendez-moi là.

Eadulf poussa un soupir résigné.

Crítán, qui montait la garde devant les étables, informa Fidelma que Dubán avait quitté le *rath*.

— Où donc est-il parti ?

— Il a rejoint les hauts pâturages avec des guerriers.

— Pourquoi cette chevauchée alors que la nuit descend ?

Crítán afficha un air maussade.

— Ne craignez rien, ma sœur, il y a suffisamment d'hommes pour garder le *rath*.

— Vous n'avez pas répondu à ma question.

— Une ferme isolée, de l'autre côté des montagnes, aurait été attaquée par des voleurs de bétail.

Aussitôt, Fidelma dressa l'oreille.

— Connaît-on les coupables ?

— Non, mais il s'agit sans doute des bandits qui ont fait une incursion dans la vallée il y a quelques semaines. Je voulais accompagner Dubán mais on m'a ordonné de rester ici pour veiller sur Móen. C'est pas juste.

Il ressemblait davantage à un enfant boudeur qu'à un adulte.

— Un guerrier, dit Fidelma en pesant ses mots, n'est jamais entravé par un devoir qu'il a librement accepté.

Crítán fit la moue.

— Je ne comprends pas.

— Justement.

Puis elle s'empressa de changer de sujet.

— Dites-moi, Crítán, le nom de Gadra vous rappelle-t-il quelque chose ?

Le garçon haussa les épaules.

— On se sert de lui pour faire peur aux enfants, on raconte qu'il est un croque-mitaine qui vole les âmes.

— Il existe vraiment ?

— Moi, je ne crois pas aux croque-mitaines mais une fois, j'ai interrogé Dubán à son propos.

— Qu'a-t-il répondu ?

— Eh bien, dans sa jeunesse, Gadra était un ermite qui s'était retiré dans les montagnes parce qu'il refusait la vraie foi.

— Il vit toujours ?

— Ça se passait il y a très longtemps. Il avait trouvé refuge dans une petite vallée, là-haut dans la forêt, mais je ne sais pas où exactement. Il faudra demander à Dubán.

Fidelma remercia le jeune homme et retourna à l'hôtellerie où l'attendait Eadulf.

— Et maintenant ? s'enquit celui-ci quand elle l'eut informé du résultat de ses investigations.

— Nous verrons ça demain.

À minuit passé, alors qu'Eadulf dormait à poings fermés dans l'alcôve près de la sienne, Fidelma entendit du bruit. Elle se leva, s'enveloppa dans son manteau et s'avança pieds nus vers la fenêtre.

Un homme descendait de cheval près du portail. À la lumière des torches, elle reconnut Menma, le chef des troupeaux. Elle s'apprêtait à retourner dans son lit quand une ombre se détacha pour venir accueillir le rouquin.

C'était le père Gormán, qui semblait très agité. Il parlait d'une voix irritée mais elle ne comprenait pas ce qu'il disait.

Menma lui répondit avec véhémence.

Le père Gormán fit un geste en direction de l'hôtellerie et Fidelma comprit qu'avec Eadulf, ils étaient au centre de la conversation. Oui, mais pour quelle raison ?

Menma tira sur les rênes de son cheval tandis que le père Gormán, les mains sur les hanches, le regardait s'éloigner en direction des écuries. Puis le prêtre rejoignit sa chapelle à grandes enjambées.

Songeuse, Fidelma retourna se coucher.

Quand elle rejoignit Eadulf pour le petit déjeuner servi par Grella, le soleil brillait par la fenêtre, réchauffant la pièce. Eadulf attendit que Fidelma ait fini de rompre son jeûne de la nuit puis lui demanda :

— Croyez-vous que Dubán soit rentré ?

— Je vais de ce pas l'interroger sur l'ermite et, pendant ce temps-là, je vous charge d'aller bavarder avec les habitants du *rath* pour tenter d'en tirer quelque information.

En passant devant le siège de l'assemblée, elle entendit des éclats de rire. Aussitôt, elle s'abrita dans un recoin et dirigea ses regards vers les bâtiments d'où provenaient les bruits. Un robuste cavalier de haute taille et aux habits couverts de poussière venait de sauter de son cheval. Fidelma reconnut aussitôt Muadnat, le fermier qui s'était présenté devant la cour qu'elle présidait à Lios Mhór. Et quand elle identifia la personne qui l'étreignait avec force et lui rendait ses baisers avec la passion d'une jeune fille, la respiration lui manqua. Cette grande femme au teint clair vêtue d'un manteau bicolore n'était autre que Cranat.

Quand elle s'écarta de son amant, Fidelma se rencogna dans l'ombre. Pour un homme venant de perdre sept *cumals* de terre, Muadnat semblait d'excellente humeur et son comportement avec la veuve du chef trahissait une intimité qui ne datait pas de la veille. Quand Muadnat éclata à nouveau d'un rire tonitruant, Cranat plaça un doigt sur ses lèvres et jeta un coup d'œil alarmé autour d'elle, puis, après que Muadnat eut attaché son cheval à une barrière, elle l'entraîna à l'intérieur de la maison juste derrière eux.

Fidelma poursuivit alors son chemin jusqu'aux portes du siège de l'assemblée qui étaient grandes ouvertes. Elle s'apprêtait à annoncer sa présence quand elle perçut des voix qui résonnaient à l'intérieur. En reconnaissant celle de Dubán, elle s'immobilisa.

— Je pense que vous devriez vous montrer plus aimable et lui témoigner davantage de respect, disait-il d'un ton grondeur. Du moins, je vous en prie, ne provoquez pas son inimitié.

— Quelle importance ? Elle ne va pas s'éterniser ici. Et il me semble qu'elle outrepasse les instructions qui lui ont été données.

Dubán s'entretenait avec Crón dans une pièce latérale dont la porte était entrouverte. Fidelma s'avança sur la pointe des pieds.

— La sœur de Colgú est une femme intelligente et rien n'échappe à ses yeux verts.

— Ah ! Vous avez remarqué la couleur de ses yeux ? répondit Crón d'une voix maussade.

Fidelma fronça les sourcils en reconnaissant l'accent indéniable de la jalousie.

Dubán éclata de rire.

— Avec ce genre de personne, mieux vaut ne pas essayer de jouer au plus fin, mon cœur.

Fidelma cligna des paupières en entendant le mot tendre prononcé avec désinvolture.

— Elle ne croit tout de même pas que Móen est innocent ? dit Crón d'un ton plus conciliant.

— Elle a des doutes. Le père Gormán est persuadé qu'elle fera tout pour le disculper. Il était passablement bouleversé quand elle l'a quitté, hier au soir.

— Je pensais que cette affaire serait vite résolue. Quel besoin avait ma mère d'envoyer chercher un brehon ?

— Rien n'est jamais simple, ma jolie. Et si ses soupçons se détournent de Móen, alors elle cherchera ailleurs. Voilà pourquoi je vous conseille vivement de vous en faire une amie.

Crón poussa un profond soupir.

— Vous craignez qu'elle n'apprenne à quel point je haïssais mon père ?

— Elle finira bien par découvrir que tout le monde le détestait. Quoi qu'il en soit, il faut que vous traitiez avec cet imbécile de Muadnat. Quand je pense qu'il a choisi ce moment précis pour venir nous embêter au *rath*. Ne pouvez-vous renvoyer ce procès à la semaine prochaine, quand tout sera terminé ?

— Mais mon ami, son manque de tact et de sensibilité l'empêchera d'accéder à ma requête et cela risque de nous causer des problèmes. Non, il faut que je règle cette affaire dans les plus brefs délais. Qu'il se présente ici à midi, transmettez-lui ma décision.

— Très bien mais je vous en prie, montrez-vous plus aimable avec la sœur.

— J'essaierai et maintenant partez, du travail nous attend.

Sans faire plus de bruit qu'une souris, Fidelma revint sur ses pas et frappa à la porte du siège de l'assemblée avec le maillet avant de pénétrer à l'intérieur. Quand Crón sortit de la pièce latérale, elle était seule et accueillit Fidelma avec une civilité distante.

— Je cherche Dubán, déclara Fidelma.

— Qu'est-ce qui vous fait penser qu'il pourrait être ici ? demanda la *tanist* sur la défensive.

— C'est un endroit comme un autre pour y rechercher le commandant de vos gardes, non ? lança Fidelma d'un air innocent.

Consciente de sa maladresse, Crón se força à sourire.

— Il est rentré tard cette nuit et je suppose qu'il dort encore.

Elle mentait avec une aisance déconcertante.

— Si je le vois, je lui dirai que vous désirez vous entretenir avec lui et maintenant excusez-moi, je dois me préparer.

Fidelma n'était pas du genre à se laisser congédier aussi facilement.

— Vous préparer pour quoi ?

— Même si ma mère estime que mes connaissances juridiques sont insuffisantes, je suis autorisée à expédier les affaires courantes, comme vous ne l'ignorez pas.

— De quel type de différend s'agit-il ?

— Rien qui vous concerne, répliqua Crón.

Puis elle se reprit.

— Excusez-moi, il s'agit de dommages causés par des animaux domestiques. Le requérant, qui est furieux, exige des compensations et une sentence immédiate.

Il arrivait assez régulièrement que des bêtes détruisent des clôtures ou ravagent des récoltes. Les fermiers dont les propriétés se touchaient avaient souvent recours aux « gages par anticipation », ou *tairgille,* pour couvrir les dégâts potentiels causés par les animaux.

Ce système de gages servait à s'assurer que les obligations légales seraient remplies. En tant que juge, Fidelma devait confier au brehon en chef du district un dépôt de cinq onces d'argent dans l'éventualité où son arbitrage serait contesté. Et si le brehon estimait sa sentence mal fondée, elle était alors contrainte de dédommager ceux qu'elle avait lésés. Le plaignant disposait d'un certain laps de temps pour se manifester et si le brehon principal estimait sa réclamation recevable, le dépôt du premier juge était confisqué. Un juge qui aurait refusé de donner les cinq onces d'argent se serait vu interdire l'exercice de sa profession sur le territoire des cinq royaumes.

En ce qui concernait le litige que Crón devait arbitrer, il ne présentait pas de difficultés particulières et Fidelma s'apprêtait à prendre congé quand une brusque intuition l'arrêta.

— Le requérant ne s'appelle-t-il pas Muadnat ?

Crón la regarda avec de grands yeux.

— Seriez-vous dotée de prescience, ma sœur ? Que savez-vous de Muadnat ?

À l'évidence, Crón ignorait que Fidelma avait siégé en tant que brehon à Lios Mhór. Cela expliquait que Muadnat se soit présenté au *rath* du chef.

— Saviez-vous qu'Archú, le cousin de Muadnat, lui avait intenté un procès ?

Crón fronça les sourcils, puis hocha la tête.

— Maintenant je me rappelle. On m'a rapporté que Muadnat avait été convoqué devant un brehon à Lios Mhór. Il aurait perdu une ferme qu'il avait indûment occupée.

— J'étais ce juge. Et c'est au cours de mon séjour à Lios Mhór que mon frère m'a envoyé un messager me demandant de me rendre ici.

La jeune femme semblait maintenant très intéressée.

— Qui est l'autre partie ? poursuivit Fidelma.

— Justement, Archú.

— Ah ! Pourriez-vous m'exposer brièvement sur quoi repose le conflit ?

Crón faillit refuser, puis changea d'avis.

— Cette fois-ci, c'est Muadnat qui réclame contre Archú, répondit-elle, sur la défensive.

— De quoi s'agit-il exactement ?

— Eh bien, depuis qu'Archú a récupéré sa ferme du Black Marsh, il est devenu le voisin de Muadnat dont les terres jouxtent les siennes. Muadnat affirme qu'Archú, par négligence ou par malice, a laissé ses cochons franchir les clôtures la nuit. Ils auraient causé des dommages à la propriété de Muadnat sans compter que les animaux auraient déféqué dans sa cour.

Fidelma réfléchit.

— En d'autres termes, si Muadnat dit la vérité, il sera en mesure d'exiger d'importantes compensations.

— Il le clame haut et fort.

— Donc il a déjà consulté les textes de loi ?

— Qu'entendez-vous par là ? lança la jeune *tanist* d'un ton sec.

— Qu'il est très prévoyant. Quand des animaux causent des dommages, la personne lésée peut effectivement se retourner contre leur propriétaire ; si ces déprédations se sont produites la nuit, cela double le montant de l'amende et si les animaux ont déféqué, elle s'en trouve encore augmentée. En d'autres termes, Archú devra payer des compensations très élevées.

Crón tomba d'accord avec elle.

— Sans doute la moitié ou plus de la valeur de sa propriété. Il perdra probablement sa ferme, à moins qu'il ne possède suffisamment de bétail.

— Et nous savons toutes deux qu'il est pauvre. Les visées de Muadnat sont évidentes.

— Mais il n'en demeure pas moins que la loi est la loi.

Fidelma retourna un instant le problème dans sa tête.

— Écoutez, en tant que chef élu, c'est votre prérogative de rendre seule la justice en l'absence d'un brehon.

— J'en suis tout à fait consciente, répliqua Crón d'un air soupçonneux.

— Surtout ne vous offensez pas, mais quel est votre niveau d'instruction ?

— Pendant trois ans, à Lios Mhór, j'ai étudié le *Bretha Comaithchesa*, le droit du voisinage, qui se révèle indispensable dans une communauté comme la nôtre. Mais je n'ai pas dépassé le niveau de *Freisneidhed*.

Cela correspondait à la qualification de la plupart des chefs des cinq royaumes, qui devaient obligatoirement passer par un collège car ils étaient confrontés à de multiples tâches dans le cadre de leurs fonctions. Devant l'hostilité à peine voilée de Crón, Fidelma décida d'utiliser la voie diplomatique comme Eadulf le lui avait conseillé, car ses relations avec la jeune femme demeuraient épineuses.

— Cela vous dérangerait-il que je siège à vos côtés pour vous servir de conseiller ?

Crón s'empourpra.

— Vous oubliez que pendant des années j'ai appris de mon père à rendre la justice en assistant à toutes les audiences.

— Loin de moi l'idée de mettre vos capacités en doute, Crón. Mais j'ai le sentiment que cette affaire va plus loin qu'un simple problème de clôture. Rappelez-vous que j'ai déjà vu Muadnat à l'œuvre quand il a essayé une première fois de déposséder Archú.

— Ne craignez-vous pas, dans ce cas, de manquer d'impartialité ? répliqua Crón d'un ton provocant.

— C'est possible et voilà pourquoi je vous suggère de mener les débats et de prononcer le jugement, tandis que je resterai à vos côtés pour préciser certains points qui pourraient vous échapper. Mon avis restera purement théorique.

Crón hésita un instant.

— Vous vous engagez à ne pas interférer avec ma conduite des débats ?

— Vous êtes l'élue des Araglin.

Crón savait pertinemment qu'en tant qu'*anruth*, Fidelma était en droit d'exiger de prendre sa place. Dans un lieu qui n'en comptait point, un brehon de haut rang pouvait automatiquement se substituer à un petit chef. Crón estima donc que Fidelma ne cherchait pas à remettre en cause son autorité.

— Quelles failles entrevoyez-vous dans l'allégation de Muadnat ?

— Je l'ignore, mais Muadnat était hors de lui quand le jugement a été prononcé à ses dépens.

— Vous croyez donc qu'il a forgé cette accusation de toutes pièces ?

— Je ne veux pas vous influencer, protesta aussitôt Fidelma. Je me contenterai d'énoncer les lois pendant que vous évaluerez la gravité des faits. Et je vous promets de ne jamais sortir de mon rôle.

— Alors je suis d'accord, dit Crón avec un grand sourire.

C'était sa première manifestation d'amitié à l'égard de Fidelma.

— À quelle heure Muadnat doit-il se présenter devant vous ?

— À midi.

— J'ai tout juste le temps d'aller prévenir Eadulf.

— Je le trouve assez intéressant, votre Saxon, fit observer Crón d'un air entendu.

— Eadulf n'appartient ni à moi ni à personne, répliqua vertement Fidelma.

— Vous paraissez cependant assez proches. J'espère que ce beau moine ne souscrit pas aux convictions du père Gormán qui adjure les serviteurs de Dieu, hommes et femmes, de demeurer dans le célibat.

Pour son plus grand déplaisir, Fidelma se sentit rougir.

Elle venait de réaliser que si elle avait débattu de tous les aspects des enseignements de Rome avec Eadulf, elle n'avait jamais abordé le problème du célibat et lui non plus. Or même si Rome n'avait pas pris de position définitive sur le sujet, un nombre croissant de membres du clergé considérait que les religieux ne devaient ni cohabiter ni se marier. Mais, selon Fidelma, une idée tellement contraire à la nature humaine ne pourrait jamais prévaloir.

Elle croisa le regard de Crón qui l'observait d'un air amusé et releva le menton.

— Mon amitié avec frère Eadulf remonte à notre rencontre au synode de Witebia, en Northumbrie. N'y voyez rien d'autre.

Crón ne se laissa pas impressionner par son assurance.

— C'est vraiment *merveilleux* d'avoir un tel ami.

— À ce propos, rétorqua Fidelma d'un air innocent, il faut que je m'entretienne avec Dubán.

— Pour quel motif urgent ?

— Avez-vous entendu parler de Gadra ?

Crón parut surprise.

— Bien sûr. Je l'ai connu pendant mon enfance mais je m'en souviens à peine. Il a vécu pendant quelque temps chez Teafa et puis il est reparti. C'est un ermite que de nos jours on présente comme un croque-mitaine. Comme il a disparu dans les montagnes, les adultes se servent de lui pour effrayer les enfants désobéissants.

— Savez-vous où je pourrais le trouver ?

Crón secoua la tête.

— Je ne suis même pas certaine qu'il soit encore en vie mais, en imaginant qu'il ait survécu, vous aurez du mal à le débusquer. Il a refusé de se soumettre à la nouvelle foi et a fait alliance avec le diable.

— Comment cela ?

Crón hocha la tête avec un sérieux confondant.

— Il a refusé d'abjurer la foi de nos ancêtres païens, et on prétend qu'il s'est retiré dans les montagnes lointaines.

À cet instant, Fidelma se retourna pour voir Dubán qui s'avançait dans la salle.

Le guerrier dans la force de l'âge feignit la surprise en présence des deux jeunes femmes, puis il leva la main pour saluer sa *tanist*. Son aisance dans le mensonge persuada Fidelma qu'elle devait se méfier de lui.

— Il semblerait que votre expédition n'ait pas été couronnée de succès, Dubán, lança Crón d'un ton sévère, comme si elle n'avait pas vu le guerrier de la matinée.

L'autre fit une grimace contrite.

— Ce n'est pourtant pas faute d'avoir cherché car nous avons parcouru des miles et des miles. Deux vaches ont été volées à la ferme de Díoma et ces bandits nous ont menés jusqu'à la lisière du Black Marsh. Ensuite, leurs traces se perdaient dans la forêt et ils nous ont échappé.

Crón parut très contrariée.

— Je n'ai pas souvenir que des brigands aient pu en toute impunité se livrer au vol de bétail dans notre vallée. Notre honneur est en jeu...

— Je m'en occuperai dès que j'aurai rassemblé une nouvelle troupe de guerriers, grommela Dubán.

— En attendant, nous avons cette audience à affronter et sœur Fidelma m'a proposé de siéger avec moi. J'ai accepté. Je lui ai également promis que vous l'aideriez à recueillir des informations sur Gadra.

Crón quitta la salle, laissant derrière elle un Dubán perplexe.

— Qu'est-ce qu'elle entend par là ? dit-il d'un air embarrassé. En quoi Gadra…

— Il paraît que vous connaissiez ce vieillard.

— Oui, mais il est mort.

Fidelma sentit le découragement la gagner.

— Vous en êtes sûr ?

Dubán se frotta le menton.

— Eh bien, mon chemin n'a pas croisé le sien depuis que j'ai quitté Araglin, et cela remonte à très longtemps.

Fidelma reprit espoir.

— Crón dit qu'autrefois, il a séjourné avec Teafa au *rath*. Où croyez-vous qu'on puisse le trouver ?

— Dans les montagnes, au sud, où il vivait dans une petite vallée.

— J'aimerais que vous m'y conduisiez, avec frère Eadulf.

Dubán parut déconcerté.

— Je crains que ce voyage ne soit inutile. Et puis il faut bien une bonne journée pour s'y rendre.

— Je m'en accommoderai.

— Vous oubliez mes obligations.

— Crón ne voyait pas d'objection à ce que vous nous conduisiez là-bas, insista Fidelma qui n'hésita pas à déformer un peu la vérité.

— Je ne comprends pas ce que vous voulez à cet ermite. Que sait-il donc qui pourrait faire avancer vos investigations ?

— Cela me regarde.

Dubán finit par accepter à contrecœur la mission qui lui était proposée.

— Quand partons-nous ? demanda-t-il.

— En début d'après-midi, dès que nous en aurons terminé avec ce procès.

Dubán tira sur sa barbe d'un air pensif.

— Donc il nous faudra dormir en route.

— Ne craignez rien, je suis une voyageuse aguerrie.

Dubán ouvrit alors les bras en un geste résigné.

— Très bien. Mais nous devrons respecter la retraite de Gadra et, dans l'éventualité où il serait toujours de ce monde, nous ne partirons qu'à trois pour ne pas le déranger.

Fidelma le rassura et sortit à son tour du siège de l'assemblée.

Dehors, elle tomba sur la fiancée d'Archú, Scoth, dont le visage s'illumina à la vue de la religieuse.

— Oh, ma sœur, s'écria-t-elle en lui prenant les mains, j'ai prié pour que vous ne soyez pas repartie ! Nous avons grand besoin de votre aide.

— Je sais. Où est Archú ?

— Il est en quête d'un logement pour la nuit, dit Scoth, au bord des larmes.

Fidelma la prit par le bras et la conduisit à l'hôtellerie des invités.

La jeune fille lui adressa un sourire douloureux.

— Muadnat est comme un corbeau charognard survolant un champ de bataille. Il attend le bon moment pour fondre sur ses proies et nous n'avons que vous pour nous défendre.

— Détendez-vous, je suis là.

— Il est si pressé de reprendre la ferme qu'il n'a même pas envisagé votre présence au *rath*. Je remercie Dieu que vous présidiez la cour.

Fidelma secoua la tête.

— Ce n'est pas mon jugement qu'il devra affronter mais celui de Crón, votre *tanist* et chef élu.

Scoth pâlit.

— Vous ne pouvez pas abandonner Archú, gémit-elle. Crón soutient les siens !

— Je ne vous abandonne pas, Scoth. Dois-je déduire de vos discours que Muadnat a inventé cette accusation de dommages causés par des animaux domestiques ?

— Non, il est dans le vrai, dit une voix masculine.

Fidelma se retourna vers Archú qui se tenait derrière elle.

— Je suis désolée que vous vous retrouviez dans cette triste situation.

— Ne pouvez-vous intervenir pour le débouter ? insista Scoth avec les accents du désespoir.

— Scoth ! intervint Archú d'un ton indigné. Tu oublies que sœur Fidelma a prêté serment !

Ils étaient maintenant arrivés devant l'hôtellerie, Fidelma les entraîna à l'intérieur et Eadulf vint à leur rencontre. Fidelma lui raconta les nouvelles puis s'adressa à Archú.

— Vous me confirmez que Muadnat n'a pas inventé les charges qui pèsent sur vous ?

— Il est bien trop rusé pour forger ces accusations !

Archú paraissait très agité et Fidelma demeura un instant silencieuse.

— Vous réalisez ce que cela signifie ? soupira-t-elle.

— Cela signifie, dit Archú avec amertume, que mon cher cousin Muadnat va récupérer ma ferme dont j'ai eu très provisoirement la jouissance, il va à nouveau occuper la maison de ma mère et je me retrouverai sans rien.

CHAPITRE X

Par-dessus sa robe de soie bleue, Crón avait revêtu une longue cape bicolore attachée par une broche en or finement ouvragée. Fidelma se retint de sourire en constatant qu'elle portait aussi des gants pareillement désassortis. Dans de nombreux clans, c'était la coutume chez les chefs de porter des capes et des gants de couleurs distinctes qui signalaient leur fonction quand ils rendaient la justice. Crón s'était préparée avec soin pour remplir sa charge, elle s'était même parfumée à la lavande, une odeur fraîche et agréable, et tout indiquait qu'elle prenait son rôle très au sérieux.

Crón s'installa sur son fauteuil sculpté. Une chaise placée juste derrière la *tanist* attendait Fidelma. En tant que commandant des gardes, Dubán se tenait en bas de la plate-forme, un peu à l'écart, tandis que les acteurs du procès avaient pris place sur des bancs en bois amenés pour l'occasion. Muadnat et l'homme au visage émacié qui l'avait déjà accompagné à Lios Mhór étaient assis à droite, Archú, Scoth et Eadulf à gauche. Les guerriers de la garde de Dubán avaient pris position à l'arrière de la salle. Quand elle pénétra dans le siège de l'assemblée, Fidelma remarqua le père Gormán, qui s'était installé sur le dernier banc.

À peine Fidelma avait-elle rejoint sa place que Muadnat reconnut la religieuse. Aussitôt, il bondit sur ses pieds et hurla :

— Je proteste !

Crón se carra dans son fauteuil et le fixa d'un air imperturbable.

— Vous protestez déjà ? Et à quel propos, je vous prie ?

Muadnat pointa un doigt vers Fidelma. Ses yeux jetaient des éclairs.

— Je refuse que cette femme se prononce sur ma requête.

Crón pinça les lèvres.

— Cette femme ? À qui vous référez-vous ?

— À Fidelma de Kildare, lança-t-il d'un air mauvais.

— C'est sur mes instances que sœur Fidelma siège à mes côtés, car elle est une *dálaigh* des cours de justice des cinq royaumes, connue pour son érudition en matière de droit. Pour quelles raisons vous opposez-vous à sa présence, Muadnat ?

— À cause de… de… sa partialité ! Elle a déjà tranché en faveur de l'accusé lors d'une précédente affaire, quand il a réclamé une propriété qui m'appartenait et qu'elle lui a attribuée. Je la récuse !

— Vous n'en avez nul besoin car c'est moi et moi seule qui prononcerai la sentence pour le présent litige. Sœur Fidelma m'assiste en tant que conseillère juridique. Et maintenant je vous écoute, Muadnat.

Sœur Fidelma se pencha vers Crón, lui parla à l'oreille et la *tanist* hocha la tête.

— Je regrette, mais je ne puis laisser passer vos insultes à l'égard d'un brehon. Ce délit est considéré avec le plus grand sérieux et l'outrage requiert le paiement du prix de l'honneur de l'offensée.

Muadnat serra les dents.

— Comme vous avez parlé dans l'ignorance des faits, reprit Crón après lui avoir laissé le temps de la réflexion, sœur Fidelma accepte de renoncer à cette amende. Cependant, elle ne peut ignorer l'insulte car en agissant ainsi, elle se rend coupable de la tolérer et perd ainsi son prix de l'honneur. Il nous faudra donc trouver un compromis. Nous y reviendrons en temps utile, quand j'aurai statué sur les charges que vous désirez me soumettre.

L'homme hésita, se balançant d'un pied sur l'autre comme s'il avait reçu un coup en pleine poitrine.

— Très bien, articula-t-il enfin d'une voix monocorde en regardant droit devant lui. Les faits sont simples et j'ai un témoin pour ce que j'avance – mon neveu et chef de troupeaux Agdae, ici présent.

— Venons-en aux faits.

Une ondulation parcourut les tapisseries derrière les deux jeunes femmes et Cranat apparut, vêtue avec recherche, comme à l'accoutumée. En voyant Fidelma siéger à la place qu'elle considérait à l'évidence être la sienne, elle fronça les sourcils d'un air contrarié. Crón devança ses observations.

— Bienvenue, mère. Vous ne m'aviez pas dit que vous désiriez assister à cette audience.

Cranat jeta un coup d'œil en direction de Muadnat. Le robuste fermier lui avait-il fait un signe d'avertissement ? Toujours est-il que Cranat se contenta de prendre un air réprobateur.

— Je me contenterai de vous observer, ma fille, lança-t-elle avant de se retirer sur un banc inoccupé.

Elle arrangea sa robe et articula distinctement :

— Du vivant d'Eber, je n'avais pas à demander la permission d'assister aux audiences.

— Sœur Fidelma n'est ici que pour me conseiller au cas où j'aurais besoin de préciser certains points de droit, expliqua Crón avec courtoisie.

Puis elle se tourna à nouveau vers Muadnat.

— Poursuivez, je vous prie.

— Eh bien, ma propriété jouxte celle d'Archú et il y a deux nuits de cela, ses cochons ont piétiné les clôtures et ils ont endommagé mes récoltes. De plus, un de ses verrats s'est battu avec un des miens, et les porcs ont déféqué dans ma cour. N'est-il pas vrai, Agdae ?

L'homme à la longue figure hocha la tête avec gravité.

— En tant que fermier de ce pays, je connais la loi, reprit Muadnat, et j'exige les compensations qui me sont dues.

Sur ces mots, il se rassit et Crón se tourna vers Agdae.

— Vous portez-vous garant, sans peur ni partialité, des faits rapportés par Muadnat dont vous êtes le parent et le serviteur obligé ?

— Les choses se sont passées très exactement de la façon dont mon oncle les a décrites.

Crón se tourna alors vers Archú.

— Vous avez entendu les charges qui pèsent sur vous. Qu'avez-vous à dire pour votre défense, Archú ? Contestez-vous les faits ?

Le jeune homme se leva, le visage las et résigné. Scoth lui tenait la main pour l'encourager.

— C'est vrai, lâcha-t-il d'une voix éteinte. Les cochons se sont sauvés et ont provoqué les dégâts qui leur sont imputés.

La large figure de Muadnat se plissa en un sourire matois.

— Il le reconnaît ! s'écria-t-il en jetant à la ronde un regard triomphant.

Crón l'ignora.

— N'avez-vous rien à ajouter, Archú ? Réfléchissez bien.

— J'avais construit un enclos temporaire pour les cochons et j'ai découvert que les piquets avaient été arrachés. Ça ne pouvait pas être l'œuvre des bêtes, tout de même.

Crón inclina le buste vers lui.

— Alléguez-vous que la clôture a été délibérément enlevée ?

— Oui.

Muadnat émit un hennissement.

— Le désespoir pousse ce garçon à mentir !

— Pouvez-vous mettre un nom sur la personne responsable de cet acte ?

Archú adressa un regard plein de haine à Muadnat.

— Comment porter plainte ? Je n'ai aucun témoin pour appuyer mes dires et je n'ai pas vu celui qui a ouvert l'enclos.

— Les faits sont clairs, intervint Muadnat avec une impatience mal contrôlée. Le garçon les a reconnus. Accordez-moi la pleine mesure des compensations qui me reviennent.

— Jugez-moi comme vous le semblez bon, conclut Archú d'un ton résigné avant de se rasseoir.

Fidelma posa alors la main sur le bras de Crón.

— M'autorisez-vous à poser quelques questions pour éclaircir certains points ?

Crón hocha la tête.

— Je vous en prie.

— Archú, quand êtes-vous rentré en possession de votre ferme ?

Archú battit des cils.

— Mais vous le savez !

— Répondez à ma question, le tança Fidelma d'un ton agacé.

— Dès l'instant où vous avez rendu votre jugement à Lios Mhór, il y a quatre jours, balbutia Archú, désarçonné.

— Oui, la ferme est maintenant à lui et aussi les cochons et la responsabilité, gloussa Muadnat tandis qu'Agdae acquiesçait bruyamment.

— Et donc auparavant, cette ferme vous appartenait, n'est-ce pas, Muadnat ? reprit Fidelma.

L'ombre d'un doute traversa l'esprit du fermier.

— Vous le savez très bien, répliqua-t-il d'un air bravache.

— Cultiviez-vous la terre d'Archú séparément de la vôtre ou bien alors comme s'il s'agissait d'une surface d'un seul tenant ?

Muadnat, flairant le piège, hésita, puis se tourna vers Crón.

— *Tanist* d'Araglin, je ne comprends pas où cette femme veut en venir.

— Répondez à la question, insista Fidelma. Votre ignorance de ce qu'implique ma requête n'excuse pas le refus de répondre à une *dálaigh*. Et n'oubliez pas que vous avez déjà été reconnu coupable d'insulte à ma fonction.

Muadnat cligna des paupières et avala sa salive. Puis il jeta un regard implorant à Crón qui le pressa de répondre d'un geste de la main.

— Je les cultivais ensemble, reconnut-il d'un ton bourru.

— Or la loi à laquelle vous vous référez pour réclamer des dommages et intérêts énonce que les clôtures séparant deux propriétés doivent être entretenues. N'ai-je pas raison ?

Muadnat resta muet.

— Êtes-vous sourd ?

— La ferme d'Archú a été mienne et les clôtures n'étaient alors nullement nécessaires.

— La ferme d'Archú n'était pas la vôtre, vous l'exploitiez en tant que gardien légal des intérêts de votre parent.

Quand elle comprit où Fidelma voulait en venir, Crón la regarda avec une admiration non dissimulée. Malgré ses réticences, elle ne pouvait s'empêcher d'apprécier l'esprit aiguisé et la parfaite maîtrise de la religieuse.

— Pourquoi laisser des clôtures entre des terres qui m'appartenaient ? s'énerva Muadnat qui perdait pied.

Un bref sourire passa sur les lèvres de Fidelma.

— Donc vous ne niez pas ?

— Il n'y a rien à démentir.

Fidelma se tourna alors vers Crón.

— Si vous le souhaitez, et à moins que vous n'ayez d'autres questions à poser, je suis maintenant en mesure de vous conseiller sur un aspect précis de la législation.

Désirez-vous que je vous expose mon point de vue en public ou en privé ?

— Je crois que les parties en présence ont le droit d'entendre l'énoncé de la loi, répliqua Crón avec solennité.

— Très bien. Archú, qui était propriétaire *de jure*, c'est-à-dire de droit, l'est devenu *de facto* il y a quatre jours seulement. Auparavant, Muadnat, qui exploitait la ferme d'Archú pour son propre bénéfice, a admis avoir retiré les barrières entre les deux domaines. Il s'agit d'un acte illégal, dont nous ne tiendrons pas rigueur à Muadnat qui était de bonne foi.

Muadnat bondit sur ses pieds.

— Taisez-vous pendant que la *dálaigh* me porte conseil, lança Crón d'un ton sans réplique.

Cranat, qui jusqu'alors semblait pétrifiée, changea de position et croisa nerveusement les doigts.

— Ma fille, est-il nécessaire de vous adresser avec tant de dureté à l'un de vos parents qui a fidèlement servi votre père ? protesta-t-elle. Vous nous couvrez de honte devant des étrangers.

Crón la toisa d'un air impassible.

— Mère, je suis *tanist*. Une *tanist* doit siéger dans une atmosphère recueillie que même vous n'êtes pas autorisée à troubler.

Cranat écarquilla des yeux scandalisés mais garda le silence.

— Poursuivez, sœur Fidelma, reprit Crón.

— Et donc si nous considérons qu'Archú n'a repris l'exploitation que depuis quatre jours, on est en droit de supposer qu'il n'a pas encore eu le temps de veiller au rétablissement des clôtures.

— La loi est claire, s'écria Muadnat, et le temps ne fait rien à l'affaire !

— C'est inexact, dit Fidelma qui s'adressait toujours à Crón. Le temps est pris en compte. Le *Bretha Comaithchesa* est sans ambiguïté sur ce point. Deux paysans qui ont des fermes adjacentes sont responsables à parts égales des barrières, considérées alors comme une propriété commune.

Elle se tourna vers celui qui était devenu son ennemi.

— Muadnat, qu'avez-vous fait pour rétablir les palissades que vous aviez détruites ?

Cramoisi, l'autre n'arrivait plus à parler.

— Rien, si j'en juge par votre silence. Et revenons aux délais qui vous ont échappé : quand une personne entre en possession d'une ferme, trois jours lui sont accordés pour marquer le périmètre de sa propriété, et dix pour édifier la clôture. En l'absence de clôture, aucune amende n'est prévue. Par contre, il y a contrainte indirecte, dans l'éventualité d'un procès, pour dommages causés par des hommes ou des animaux.

Fidelma marqua une pause et se tourna vers Crón.

— Et maintenant, c'est à vous de juger, Crón, en accord avec la loi.

— Eh bien, il semble évident que Muadnat n'était pas fondé de présenter un recours par voie judiciaire pour le motif qu'il a invoqué, puisque Archú n'avait pas disposé du temps prévu par la loi pour édifier des barrières.

Muadnat, qui tremblait de rage, se leva avec difficulté.

— Puisque je vous dis qu'il a poussé ses cochons à commettre des dégâts par malice et négligence !

— La négligence ne peut être retenue. Quant à la malice, inutile d'épiloguer. Muadnat, je vous rappelle que vous êtes responsable à part égale de l'édification des clôtures. Quant à sœur Fidelma, elle a interprété la loi en votre faveur quand elle suggère que vous êtes absous de toute responsabilité pour les avoir détruites. Personnellement, je ne suis pas certaine que je me serais montrée si généreuse. Et maintenant, assurez-vous que ces clôtures seront rétablies dans le laps de temps qui vous a été imparti.

Muadnat dévisageait Fidelma avec haine. Il s'apprêtait à parler quand Agdae, son neveu, l'attrapa par le bras.

— Je n'ai pas terminé, dit Crón. Pour avoir intenté un procès sans vous être suffisamment renseigné sur les textes, je vous condamne à me payer un *séd*, et un autre à sœur Fidelma pour ses conseils avisés. Vous pouvez vous acquitter de votre dette en monnaie ou en nature, à savoir deux vaches à lait, que vous remettrez à mon régisseur à la fin de cette semaine.

Muadnat s'apprêtait à partir quand Crón le rappela.

— Il nous reste la question de l'insulte à *dálaigh* dans l'exercice de ses fonctions.

Elle se tourna vers Fidelma avec un regard interrogateur.

— En gage de cette insulte, qui devrait normalement correspondre à mon prix de l'honneur, Muadnat donnera la valeur d'une vache à lait à l'église locale, ou son équivalent en heures de travail pour les réparations qu'il choisira en accord avec le prêtre.

— Me croyez-vous aveugle à vos manigances, *tanist* ? explosa Muadnat. *Tanist* par subornation et corruption, oui ! Vous n'êtes pas une vraie…

Le père Gormán s'avança d'un pas vif.

— Muadnat ! Vous vous oubliez !

Et avec Agdae, ils le traînèrent dehors où il continua de hurler. Quant à Cranat, elle ne tarda pas à le rejoindre avec une hâte qui frisait l'indécence.

Crón contemplait rêveusement le charmant tableau que formaient Archú et Scoth, qui se tenaient embrassés.

— Muadnat a été débouté, Archú, mais prenez bien garde…

Archú lui fit face tout en remettant de l'ordre dans sa tenue et en arborant une contenance respectueuse.

— … vous avez un ennemi irréconciliable en la personne de Muadnat.

Archú hocha la tête et, après un grand sourire à Fidelma, il prit la main de Scoth et ils s'éclipsèrent.

Crón se renversa alors sur son siège et adressa un regard admiratif à Fidelma.

— D'un labyrinthe de textes vous parvenez à faire une promenade d'agrément, ma sœur. J'aimerais bien avoir vos connaissances et votre talent.

— J'ai été formée à ce métier depuis mon plus jeune âge, répondit Fidelma avec indifférence.

— Mon avertissement à Archú vaut aussi pour vous. Muadnat est rancunier. C'est un cousin éloigné du côté de mon père dont il était très proche. Peut-être n'aurais-je pas dû me montrer si dure avec lui ? J'ai bien senti qu'aujourd'hui je n'avais pas l'approbation de ma mère.

— À l'évidence, votre mère considère elle aussi Muadnat comme un ami intime.

— Dans l'exercice de sa fonction, un chef doit oublier les relations privilégiées.

— Tout comme moi, vous devez vous en tenir à ce que la loi et votre devoir vous dictent.

— Vous avez raison mais ici, en Araglin, Muadnat a exercé une certaine influence. Et le père Gormán l'apprécie.

Cette remarque suscita l'intérêt de Fidelma.

— Et Muadnat et votre père…

— Ont grandi ensemble et sont partis tous deux se battre contre les Uí Fidgente.

Fidelma réfléchit, puis se détendit. Muadnat ne pouvait pas être concerné par la mort d'Eber puisqu'il se trouvait à Lios Mhór au moment du meurtre. Elle se leva et jeta un coup d'œil à Dubán qui attendait.

— Et si nous partions à la recherche de Gadra ?

Crón se leva à son tour, toute rose d'excitation. Pour la première fois depuis qu'elle était arrivée au *rath*, Fidelma la découvrait vive et bienveillante. En dépit de ses déclarations, elle avait à l'évidence pris beaucoup de plaisir à contrecarrer Muadnat.

— Fidelma, j'ai beaucoup apprécié votre efficacité, je vous fais pleinement confiance pour découvrir la vérité quant au meurtre de mon père et…

Elle marqua un moment d'hésitation.

— Je veux que vous sachiez que je mettrai tout en œuvre pour vous aider dans votre enquête.

Fidelma haussa les sourcils.

— Pensez-vous plus précisément à des événements que j'ignore et qui pourraient éclairer ma lanterne ?

Elle crut voir une lueur d'angoisse dans les yeux clairs de la *tanist*.

— Du tout. Je voulais simplement m'excuser pour mon comportement désinvolte quand vous vous êtes présentée ici. La courtoisie ne coûte rien et je me suis montrée arrogante.

— Souvenez-vous-en et vous serez appréciée de votre peuple, répliqua Fidelma avec gravité. Et c'est plus important que la pelisse qui proclame votre rang.

Crón joua d'un air gêné avec la broche en or sur son épaule qui fermait sa cape, puis elle sourit.

— Ici, en Araglin, c'est la coutume que les chefs et leurs épouses portent le manteau et les gants bicolores dans l'exercice de leurs fonctions.

— C'est une grande responsabilité que d'être élevée à une telle position. S'ajuster aux circonstances demande du temps.

— Cela n'excuse en rien la suffisance. Vous avez mentionné Gadra, ce qui m'a rappelé un de ses enseignements, dispensé au *rath* quand j'étais petite fille. Les orgueilleux, disait-il, se placent à distance des autres et, les observant de loin, les jugent insignifiants. Ils oublient que cette même distance les réduit d'autant au regard des autres.

Fidelma hocha la tête en souriant.

— Gadra est un homme sage. Si on ne lève pas les yeux, on s'imagine toujours que l'on domine le monde. Venez, Dubán, allons retrouver ce saint homme.

— S'il est encore en vie, grommela Dubán qui n'y croyait pas trop.

CHAPITRE XI

Dubán et Fidelma chevauchaient de front sur le chemin étroit serpentant au milieu des grands chênes des gorges montagneuses. Frère Eadulf venait derrière eux. Dans des endroits aussi sinistres et peu fréquentés, ils pouvaient sans s'en rendre compte passer à quelques toises d'une bande de brigands. Dans cette forêt impénétrable où le soleil ne filtrait pas à travers les arbres, il faisait froid, les fleurs étaient rares et les plantes qui appréciaient l'humidité obscure avaient envahi les sous-bois, ce qui rendait la progression pénible, l'atmosphère étouffante. L'œil aux aguets, Eadulf laissait sa monture avancer au rythme des chevaux de tête.

La tranquillité du lieu était oppressante. Les pépiements d'oiseaux isolés résonnaient étrangement. De temps à autre, on percevait des bruissements de feuilles et la fuite précipitée d'un animal dérangé par leur intrusion.

— Voilà un endroit bien lugubre pour y élire domicile ! clama Eadulf, brisant le silence qu'ils observaient depuis qu'ils avaient pénétré dans ces bois.

Dubán lui adressa un bref sourire.

— C'est dans la nature des ermites de s'installer dans des lieux qui rebutent le commun des mortels, Saxon.

— J'en ai connu de plus salubres. Quel intérêt de se retirer loin du monde si c'est pour y laisser sa santé ?

— Ça se discute, Saxon. On raconte qu'aujourd'hui, Gadra compterait plus de quatre fois vingt ans. On aura de la chance s'il est encore parmi nous.

— Dites-nous-en davantage sur l'ermite Gadra et ses enseignements remplis de sagesse, intervint Fidelma.

— Pour moi, Gadra est sans âge et éternellement le même.

— Mais d'où vient-il ?

Dubán haussa les épaules.

— Il serait un religieux du temps jadis, je n'en sais pas plus.

— Un druide ? s'exclama Fidelma.

Dans les cinq royaumes, ceux qui adoraient les dieux païens se faisaient rares. Fidelma en avait tout de même rencontré quelques-uns qui s'accrochaient aux croyances et aux coutumes anciennes. Elle avait toujours admiré leur philosophie, que la nouvelle foi dans le Christ n'avait pas encore totalement effacée.

— Sans doute. Quand j'étais petit, on nous recommandait de nous tenir éloignés de lui. Le prêtre prétendait qu'il se livrait à des sacrifices humains dans cette forêt désolée aux chênes centenaires.

Fidelma poussa une exclamation indignée.

— Quand on ne comprend pas une autre religion que la sienne ou qu'on désire l'éliminer, on a toujours recours à cet ultime mensonge des sacrifices humains. Brigitte au nom béni, fondatrice de mon ordre à Kildare, était druidesse et fille d'un druide, un homme très honorable. Pour en revenir à Gadra, sait-on quand il est arrivé ici ?

— Du temps, je crois, où le père d'Eber était enfant. Il avait des dons de guérisseur et on l'admirait pour sa clairvoyance.

— Comment aurait-il pu guérir s'il ne croyait pas dans la vraie foi ? protesta Eadulf.

Fidelma sourit à son compagnon.

— Comment réfuter une telle logique ? répondit-elle avec malice.

— Propose-t-il ses traitements au nom du Christ roi ? s'obstina Eadulf d'un air fâché.

— Il traite les affligés en son nom personnel, répliqua Dubán. Bien sûr, le père Gormán s'empressait de dénoncer les malheureux qui étaient allés chercher du secours auprès de Gadra, dont cela fait maintenant plusieurs années que je n'ai pas entendu parler. À mon avis, il est mort et nous perdons notre temps.

Eadulf s'apprêtait à répondre quand Dubán leva la main.

— Nous approchons de la clairière où il avait élu domicile.

Ils tirèrent sur la bride de leurs chevaux et Fidelma examina les alentours avec curiosité.

— Restez ici, leur ordonna Dubán. S'il est encore de ce monde, je pense qu'il me reconnaîtra.

Il enfonça ses talons dans les flancs de sa monture et s'avança sur le chemin caillouteux vers la petite clairière lumineuse, devant eux, où l'on entendait le murmure d'un ruisseau. Fidelma crut distinguer une chaumière en lisière de la forêt.

— Gadra ! Gadra !

La voix du guerrier, dont les rochers alentour se faisaient l'écho, résonna au loin.

— C'est Dubán d'Araglin ! Êtes-vous toujours vivant ?

Le silence se fit, puis une voix forte et grave, enrouée par l'âge, s'éleva :

— Si je suis mort, Dubán d'Araglin, alors c'est sûrement un spectre qui te répond.

Puis plus rien. Après quelques instants, Dubán héla ses compagnons qui le rejoignirent.

Sur un terrain plat, près d'un cours d'eau qui dévalait la montagne, s'élevait une solide maisonnette en bois au toit de chaume, entourée d'un potager et d'arbres fruitiers. Dubán sauta de son cheval qu'il attacha à un buisson. Il se tenait à quelques pieds d'un petit vieillard avec une masse de cheveux blancs, appuyé à un bâton d'épine poli. À première vue, il semblait assez frêle, mais cette apparence était trompeuse. Sec et musclé, revêtu d'une robe safran, un cercle d'or enserrait son cou, gravé de symboles inconnus de Fidelma.

Elle sauta de son étalon qu'elle confia à Eadulf.

— Soyez béni, Gadra, dit-elle en inclinant la tête.

Des yeux perçants d'un gris bleuté brillaient dans le visage hâlé par la vie en plein air qui lui faisait face. La chevelure blanche du vieil homme lui tombait jusqu'aux épaules et sa barbe soyeuse, coupée court, laissait apparaître le collier resplendissant sur sa poitrine. À l'évidence, Gadra avait atteint un âge canonique que laissaient deviner ses épaules voûtées, mais, à la grande surprise de Fidelma, son visage était resté jeune et lisse.

— Bienvenue en ces lieux, fille de Failbe Flann.

Elle tressaillit.

— Mais comment… ?

Le vieil homme éclata de rire.

— Qu'avez-vous appris d'autre de Dubán ? ajouta aussitôt la religieuse d'un air contrit.

Gadra hocha la tête.

— Vous avez l'esprit vif.

Il jeta un coup d'œil au moine qui s'occupait des chevaux.

— Venez par ici, Eadulf de Seaxmund's Ham, et discutons un peu.

Fidelma s'assit spontanément en tailleur devant l'ermite, la position de la novice devant le maître qui était la sienne quand elle suivait l'enseignement de Morann de Tara. Eadulf préféra se percher sur une grosse pierre ronde et Dubán l'imita, pensant sans doute que sa dignité souffrirait de se retrouver le derrière dans l'herbe. Gadra, qui malgré son grand âge ne manquait pas de souplesse, adopta la même posture que la jeune femme.

— Avant de commencer notre entretien…

Gadra posa la main sur le croissant d'or à son cou.

— … ceci vous dérange-t-il ?

— Du tout, pourquoi ?

Gadra pointa son crucifix du doigt.

— Certains pensent qu'ils sont incompatibles.

— Pendant des siècles, votre croissant a pour notre peuple représenté un symbole de lumière et de connaissance, pourquoi le craindrais-je ?

— Ceux qui se sont tournés vers le Christ s'en offensent souvent.

Eadulf changea de position sur sa pierre. Se retrouver en compagnie d'une personne qui arborait un emblème païen le dérangeait.

— Vous n'avez pas embrassé la vraie foi ? demanda-t-il d'un ton de reproche.

Gadra lui adressa un sourire amusé.

— Je suis un vieil homme, frère saxon. En moi, les dieux et les déesses refusent de s'éteindre. Mais je ne m'oppose point à vos nouvelles coutumes, vos pensées novatrices et vos récents espoirs. Le passé se désagrège pour laisser la place à une vie nouvelle, ce qui est une bénédiction et dans la nature des choses, mais aussi un danger pour les enfants de Danu, la déesse-mère. Les cycles se succèdent à l'infini. Les anciens dieux meurent pour céder la place à d'autres, et le temps viendra où eux aussi disparaîtront.

Eadulf faillit s'étrangler d'indignation.

— Nous sommes les prisonniers de notre époque, se hâta d'ajouter Fidelma.

Gadra gloussa de plaisir.

— Vous avez une bonne perception des choses, Fidelma. Pouvez-vous me dire ce qui est plus rapide que le vent ?

— La pensée, répliqua aussitôt Fidelma, car elle connaissait le jeu auquel jouait le vieil homme.

— Et ce qui est plus blanc que la neige ?

— La vérité.

— Et plus aigu que l'épée ?

— La connaissance.

— Alors nous sommes faits pour nous entendre, ma fille. Je suis le dépositaire d'un savoir qui s'évanouira quand je mourrai. Ainsi soit-il. Et voilà pourquoi je suis venu finir mes jours dans la forêt.

Fidelma resta un instant silencieuse, puis demanda :

— Dubán vous a-t-il donné des nouvelles d'Araglin ?

— Non. Mais je suppose que vous n'avez pas fait ce voyage dans le seul but de me saluer.

— Eber a été assassiné.

Gadra ne parut pas autrement surpris.

— De mon temps, on aurait célébré la mort d'une âme ici-bas, car cela signifiait qu'une âme était née dans l'autre monde. Et nous pleurions une naissance car une âme avait trépassé dans l'au-delà.

— La mort d'Eber me concerne de plus près, Gadra, car je suis avocate des cours de justice des cinq royaumes.

— Excusez-moi si j'ai parlé en philosophe. Bien sûr, la façon dont il est passé de vie à trépas ne m'est pas indifférente. Je suppose que Muadnat a été élu chef ?

Fidelma le fixa d'un air ébahi.

— Crón est *tanist* et sera chef quand le *derbfhine* de sa famille confirmera son élection.

Gadra détourna le regard.

— Donc Eber a été supprimé et vous, mon enfant, êtes chargée de mener l'enquête ?

— C'est exact.

— En quoi puis-je vous aider ?

— Móen a été retrouvé auprès du corps d'Eber, un couteau sanglant à la main.

Une expression de stupeur vite dissipée se peignit sur le visage serein de l'ermite.

— Móen serait-il soupçonné d'avoir poignardé Eber ?

— En effet.

— Si je n'avais vécu suffisamment longtemps pour être le témoin d'événements inconcevables, j'affirmerais que ce garçon est incapable d'un tel acte.

Fidelma fronça les sourcils.

— Mais vous acceptez qu'il ait pu le commettre ?

— Dans des circonstances déterminées, le plus docile des êtres humains peut tuer.

Fidelma fit la grimace.

— Docile n'est pas le mot que j'emploierais pour Móen.

Gadra soupira.

— Croyez-moi, je connais ce garçon sensible qui est d'une nature pacifique. Teafa et moi lui avons appris tout ce qu'il sait et je l'ai regardé grandir.

— Comment cela, vous lui avez *appris* ?

— Il s'agit du terme exact. Que répond le garçon à ces accusations ?

— Móen étant sourd, muet et aveugle, comment s'exprimerait-il ?

Gadra poussa une exclamation d'impatience.

— Grâce à Teafa, bien sûr. Il communique par son intermédiaire. Alors ?

— Eh bien…

Gadra la fixa avec intensité.

— Il est arrivé quelque chose à Teafa ?

— Elle est morte.

Gadra se redressa, les yeux perdus au loin.

— Je prierai pour qu'elle ait une belle renaissance dans l'autre monde, murmura-t-il. C'était une femme bonne et dotée d'une âme noble. Elle a été tuée par Eber ? Le garçon l'a défendue contre lui ?

Fidelma secoua la tête, troublée par la réaction du vieil homme.

— Móen est accusé d'avoir poignardé Teafa avant de se rendre chez Eber qu'il aurait tué de la même façon.

— Est-ce possible ?

Gadra, malgré ses longues années d'autodiscipline pour contrôler ses émotions, semblait profondément bouleversé.

— Je suis venue pour vérifier les faits.

— Ils sont faux, affirma Gadra d'un ton péremptoire. Si Eber l'avait provoqué avec une grande cruauté, je vous concède que Móen aurait pu se retourner contre lui, mais il n'aurait jamais frappé Teafa, sa mère nourricière.

— Des fils ont déjà tué leur mère, intervint Eadulf.

Gadra l'ignora.

— Quelqu'un a-t-il été en mesure d'établir un contact avec Móen depuis la mort de Teafa ?

Fidelma secoua la tête.

— D'après mes renseignements, seule Teafa possédait ce don. Un sourd-muet aveugle…

Gadra parut très attristé.

— Il existe diverses formes d'échanges. Le garçon peut toucher, sentir les odeurs et les vibrations. Quand certains sens nous sont refusés par le destin, nous en développons d'autres. Il s'est donc muré dans le silence ?

— Oui, ce qui explique ma venue ici.

— Il faut que je retourne avec vous au *rath* pour parler avec lui, lança l'ermite avec fermeté.

Fidelma était abasourdie. Elle était venue lui demander conseil, mais n'aurait jamais imaginé qu'il insisterait pour les raccompagner au village.

— Si je suis le témoin de vos échanges, alors je croirai aux miracles.

— Pauvre Móen, murmura Gadra, ignorant les événements qui ont conduit à son enfermement et en proie à une terreur sans nom…

— S'il est innocent, il traverse une terrible épreuve, intervint Eadulf. Mais je m'étonne que personne au *rath*, à part Teafa, n'ait été en mesure de communiquer avec lui.

Gadra leva un regard las vers Eadulf.

— Vous avez l'esprit pratique, Saxon. Seule Teafa a eu la patience d'apprendre la méthode permettant d'avoir accès à l'esprit de Móen. À son tour, elle aurait pu l'enseigner à quelqu'un. Mais je crois qu'elle y a renoncé parce qu'elle estimait que cela valait mieux ainsi.

— Pourquoi donc ?

— Elle a emporté son secret dans la tombe.

Gadra se leva, imitée par Fidelma.

— Je n'ai pas de cheval, annonça le vieil homme.

— Préférez-vous monter avec Dubán ou avec frère Eadulf ?

— Je choisis le second.

Le moine alla chercher les chevaux.

— Votre Eadulf parle très bien notre langue, murmura Gadra à l'adresse de Fidelma qui s'empourpra.

— Il visite notre pays et a été formé dans nos collèges. Et il n'est pas *mon* Eadulf.

— Pourtant, quand vous parlez de ce Saxon, votre voix est chargée d'une vibration particulière, la taquina l'ermite.

— Il n'est qu'un excellent ami ! répliqua Fidelma, les joues en feu.

— Ne reniez pas vos sentiments, mon enfant, et arrêtez de vous mentir, lui glissa le vieil homme à l'oreille, puis il tourna les talons et disparut dans sa maisonnette.

Fidelma sourit. Païen ou pas, elle appréciait l'ermite, sa sincérité et sa sagesse. Elle croisa le regard de Dubán qui l'observait d'un air inquisiteur.

— Bien que vos croyances diffèrent, je vois que vous estimez Gadra, ma sœur.

— Vous savez, une fois que l'on a dépouillé les choses de leur nom, les différences sont bien minces. Nous avons tous les mêmes ancêtres.

— Peut-être.

L'ermite réapparut avec un manteau de voyage et un *sacculus*, une besace avec une lanière qu'il passa à son épaule et qui contenait quelques effets et des objets personnels.

— Dites-moi, frère saxon, dit-il tandis que le moine l'aidait à se hisser sur son cheval, je suppose que mon vieil adversaire Gormán vit toujours au *rath* ?

— Le père Gormán est le prêtre d'Araglin.

— Mais il n'est pas mon père, grommela Gadra. Je ne vois aucune objection à appeler mes semblables mon frère ou ma sœur, mais ils sont peu nombreux sur cette terre que je saluerais du nom de père. Et celui dont l'âme est rongée par le chancre de l'intolérance ne doit pas y compter.

Eadulf se mordit la lèvre, mais l'amusement du Saxon ne trouva aucun écho chez Fidelma, qui demeura de marbre.

— Ne vous souciez pas de Gormán, lança-t-elle en sautant sur son étalon. Au *rath* d'Araglin, vous serez placé sous mon autorité.

Gadra se mit à rire.

— Chaque personne est placée sous sa propre autorité, Fidelma.

Sur le chemin du retour, ils restèrent silencieux. L'atmosphère de ces bois sombres étonnamment tranquilles semblait favoriser la méditation mélancolique.

Fidelma réfléchissait au mode de communication que Gadra prétendait avoir inventé avec Teafa pour établir des contacts avec un infirme aussi atteint que Móen. Après tout, pourquoi douter de sa sincérité ?

Elle jeta un coup d'œil à Eadulf qui devait se sentir bien mal à l'aise en présence d'une personne qui rejetait la nouvelle foi et suivait les anciens rites. Gadra l'avait bien défini, cela résumait tout à fait Eadulf, si terre à terre. Il acceptait ce qu'on lui enseignait puis s'y tenait sans jamais dévier de son chemin, tel un navire fendant les océans. En comparaison, elle-même n'était qu'une barque légère et capricieuse avançant au gré des vagues. Elle se rappela soudain une maxime d'Hésiode. Admirez la frêle embarcation mais mettez vos marchandises dans le navire.

Elle soupira et se concentra à nouveau sur la tâche qui l'attendait. Mais tant que Gadra n'aurait pas interrogé Móen, elle se perdrait en vaines conjectures. Et maintenant, elle bouillait d'impatience de retourner au *rath* pour en savoir davantage. L'impétuosité, elle le savait, était son principal défaut, et Eadulf l'avait déjà plusieurs fois sermonnée à ce sujet. Mais elle se consolait en se disant qu'un esprit agité apportait au moins la preuve qu'on était bien vivant.

À cet instant de ses réflexions, Dubán tira brusquement sur les rênes de sa monture et leva la main. Ils s'immobilisèrent tandis que le guerrier écoutait, la tête très droite.

Puis il leur fit signe de sauter à terre.

— Que se passe-t-il ? murmura Fidelma.

— Des chevaux approchent et leurs cavaliers ne se préoccupent pas de dissimuler leur présence.

Fidelma perçut au loin des voix fortes qui s'interpellaient.

— Vite, lança Dubán, par ici, il y a des rochers derrière lesquels nous pourrons nous abriter.

Fidelma exécuta ses ordres sans discuter. Quand un guerrier donnait de tels conseils, mieux valait remettre les questions à plus tard.

Ils le suivirent en silence dans le sous-bois. Eadulf s'éloigna avec les chevaux, escorté de Gadra, tandis que Dubán et Fidelma allaient se cacher pour surveiller le chemin depuis leur poste d'observation.

Maintenant, des rires et des beuglements résonnaient dans la forêt. Fidelma adressa un regard en coin à Dubán. Le guerrier fronçait les sourcils, visiblement anxieux.

— Qu'est-ce qui vous inquiète ? chuchota-t-elle. Vous commandez la garde du chef en Araglin. Pourquoi nous cachons-nous ?

— Un guerrier ne prend jamais la température de l'eau avec les deux pieds. Écoutez.

— Je n'entends que des cavaliers…

— Et moi le bruit de harnachements de guerre, des épées tapant sur des boucliers, le pas de montures lourdement chargées. Et quand je vois un chien de meute rentrer dans un parc à moutons, je m'inquiète de ses intentions.

Il posa un doigt sur ses lèvres.

À travers les arbres, ils virent défiler une douzaine de cavaliers, dont certains portaient des capes légères, et des boucliers à l'épaule. D'autres brandissaient des lances.

À la fin de la colonne, des hommes surveillaient six ânes chargés de paniers de bât. Ils riaient, s'interpellaient, et l'un d'eux raconta une histoire grivoise tandis que les autres s'esclaffaient.

Quand Fidelma aperçut celui qui chevauchait en queue du cortège, elle plissa les paupières. Il ne portait pas de manteau, un arc était accroché à son épaule gauche et il portait le bras droit en écharpe.

Puis la petite troupe s'éloigna, Dubán et Fidelma se redressèrent et allèrent retrouver Eadulf et Gadra qui les attendaient près des bêtes.

— À quoi rime cette comédie ? s'exclama aussitôt Eadulf.

Dubán tira distraitement sur sa barbe noire aux fils d'argent.

— Je parierais que ce sont les voleurs de bétail qui s'en sont pris aux fermes d'Araglin.

— Comment le savez-vous ? s'étonna Fidelma.

— Je n'ai jamais rencontré cette troupe d'étrangers en armes auparavant. À ma place, qu'en déduiriez-vous ?

— Votre raisonnement est assez logique, concéda Eadulf.

— Oui, mais s'ils sont des voleurs de bétail, à quoi riment ces ânes lourdement chargés ? Et où se rendent-ils ? demanda Fidelma.

— Cette route mène vers le sud. En traversant les vallées, vous rejoignez la côte en peu de temps, Lios Mhór et Ard Mór ne sont pas très loin.

— Cette voie est donc plus rapide que celle qui passe par l'hôtellerie de Bressal ? s'enquit Fidelma.

— Elle vous permet de gagner une bonne demi-journée, précisa l'ermite.

— Mais pourquoi nous méfier de ces gens ? s'obstina Eadulf. Je suis peut-être un étranger dans ce pays mais je sais qu'en Irlande, ceux qui portent l'insigne et les vêtements de la foi sont respectés.

— Frère saxon, dit Gadra en posant sa main frêle sur le bras du moine, les coutumes les plus ancrées ne résistent pas à une motivation suffisamment puissante. Pour votre salut, appuyez-vous sur votre bon sens plutôt que sur les vêtements que vous portez.

— Excellent conseil, renchérit Fidelma. Surtout que nous avons déjà rencontré un de ces individus auparavant.

Eadulf écarquilla les yeux.

— Ah bon ?

— Où ça ? s'enquit Dubán.

— Celui qui porte le bras en écharpe. Eadulf lui a décoché une flèche, il y a près de deux jours, lors d'une attaque de l'auberge de Bressal.

Gadra fixa le moine d'un air ébahi, puis il se mit à glousser.

— Eadulf a tiré une flèche sur ce bandit ?

— Comme vous pouvez le constater, il m'arrive parfois de me fier à d'autres moyens de défense que mes vêtements, fit observer Eadulf, très pince-sans-rire.

Gadra lui donna une petite tape dans le dos.

— Vous me plaisez, frère saxon. Il m'arrive parfois d'oublier les charmes de l'esprit pratique, or une barque privée de rames ne permet pas d'avancer sur l'eau.

Eadulf, qui ne savait pas trop comment interpréter la remarque du vieil homme, décida qu'il s'agissait d'un compliment.

Quant à Dubán, il semblait soucieux.

— Donc d'après vous, cette clique aurait attaqué l'auberge de Bressal ?

Fidelma hocha la tête.

— Je suis prête à en témoigner.

— Et Menma ? intervint Eadulf qui s'arrêta net en voyant Fidelma le foudroyer du regard.

Dubán se tourna vers lui d'un air inquisiteur.

— Qu'est-ce que Menma vient faire là-dedans ?

— Eadulf pensait à la nécessité de protéger le *rath* d'un raid de ces bandits, s'empressa de répondre Fidelma.

Dubán haussa les épaules.

— Menma ne nous serait pas d'un grand secours, mon frère. Le jeune Crítán et certains autres de mes guerriers se chargent de veiller sur le *rath*, et donc vous vous inquiétez pour rien.

Eadulf se demandait pourquoi Fidelma tenait tant à ce que Dubán ignore la présence de Menma lors de l'assaut de ces brigands contre l'hôtellerie de Bressal. Puis il croisa le regard amusé de Gadra.

Se détournant d'un air irrité, il ramena sa jument sur le chemin.

Cette fois, Dubán les mena à un train plus rapide, lançant son cheval au trot dès que les étroits défilés le permettaient.

À un moment donné, Gadra, en croupe derrière Eadulf, glissa à l'oreille du moine :

— Tournez plusieurs fois votre langue dans votre bouche, frère saxon, et vos paroles n'en seront que plus sages.

Eadulf poussa un grognement agacé et maudit en silence l'intuition du vieil homme.

CHAPITRE XII

Crítán amena Móen à l'hôtellerie des invités, que Fidelma avait jugée plus propice que les étables à son interrogatoire. À part Fidelma et Eadulf, seul Gadra était présent. Dubán était parti s'entretenir des voleurs de bétail avec Crón.

Le silence se fit quand le jeune guerrier, toujours aussi insouciant et arrogant, traîna l'infortuné Móen dans la pièce. Fidelma constata cependant que Móen était propre et ne semblait pas avoir été maltraité. Mais son visage exprimait une peur et un désarroi pitoyables, car il ne comprenait toujours pas l'hostilité dont il était l'objet.

Crítán l'obligea à s'asseoir sur une chaise où il s'affala, la tête penchée sur le côté. Puis le jeune guerrier se tourna vers eux avec un sourire mauvais.

— Le voilà. Et maintenant, quels tours allez-vous lui faire exécuter ?

Gadra s'avança, la respiration sifflante de colère, et pendant un instant Fidelma crut qu'il allait frapper le jeune insolent.

Puis il se passa une chose curieuse.

Móen releva la tête et huma l'air. Pour la première fois, Fidelma vit une expression d'espoir se peindre sur ses traits et il commença à émettre de petits gémissements.

Gadra alla aussitôt s'asseoir auprès de lui.

En voyant le visage de l'infirme s'illuminer d'une joie et d'un espoir insensés, Fidelma resta pétrifiée. Gadra avait pris la main gauche que Móen lui tendait, paume ouverte, et il y traça très rapidement des signes et des circonvolutions. Fidelma comprit que c'était là le contact que Móen avait tenté d'établir avec elle dans l'écurie. Et maintenant, n'importe qui aurait pu témoigner qu'il s'était engagé une conversation entre l'infirme et l'ermite, dont les doigts et les mains s'agitaient en un manège incessant.

Soudain, Móen poussa un cri étranglé, puis il se mit à se balancer d'avant en arrière, comme s'il souffrait le martyre. Gadra passa un bras autour des épaules du garçon et leva la tête vers Fidelma. Ses yeux étaient noyés de tristesse.

— Je viens de lui apprendre la disparition de Teafa.

— Comment a-t-il pris la mort d'Eber ?

— Sans surprise, car je pense qu'il en était déjà informé. Je lui ai rapporté ce qui s'était passé et de quoi il était accusé.

— Vous lui avez parlé ? s'exclama Crítán avec un rire cynique. Allons, vieux fou, je goûte la plaisanterie mais...

— Taisez-vous et sortez d'ici ! le rabroua Fidelma. Vous reviendrez quand on vous rappellera.

— Ce prisonnier a été placé sous ma responsabilité, éructa le jeune homme qui s'était empourpré. C'est mon devoir...

— ... d'obéir à mes ordres sans discussion. Et maintenant vous allez dire à Dubán que je ne veux plus jamais vous revoir auprès du captif. Dehors !

— Vous ne pouvez pas...

Eadulf se leva, enserra le bras du guerrier d'une poigne de fer, l'escorta jusqu'à la porte et le jeta dehors avec autant de ménagement qu'il en avait montré à l'égard de Móen.

Quand il revint dans la pièce, il croisa le regard de Gadra qui l'observait en souriant.

— Je reconnais bien là votre sens pratique, une qualité que j'apprécie, frère saxon.

Fidelma, qui était penchée sur Móen, se tourna vers Gadra.

— Pendant qu'il se remet du choc de la terrible nouvelle que vous venez de lui annoncer, j'aimerais connaître la méthode que vous utilisez pour vérifier qu'elle est authentique.

Le vieil homme poussa une exclamation agacée.

— Vous me décevez, mon enfant. Vous pensez vraiment que j'ai inventé tout ça ?

— Pas du tout, s'empressa de rectifier Fidelma, mais, pour présenter cette affaire devant une cour de justice, j'ai besoin de comprendre comment vous vous y prenez.

Gadra hocha la tête d'un air dubitatif.

— En tant qu'avocate, je suppose que vous connaissez l'ancien alphabet ?

Fidelma écarquilla les yeux.

— Voilà donc le moyen que vous utilisez ?

L'ogam était la forme d'écriture la plus ancienne chez les peuples des cinq royaumes. On retranscrivait les vingt caractères de cet alphabet grâce à des encoches horizontales ou verticales tracées en fonction d'une ligne de base. La mythologie disait que le dieu Ogma, patron de la connaissance et de l'apprentissage venu du sud-ouest de Muman, lieu de toutes les initiations, avait appris aux sages l'usage des caractères afin qu'ils puissent voyager et enseigner l'écriture. En Éireann et au-delà des mers. Des textes étaient retranscris sur des baguettes de coudrier ou de tremble et de nombreuses pierres tombales portaient des inscriptions en ogam. Avec l'introduction de l'enseignement du latin dans les royaumes, l'ogam était tombé en désuétude. Fidelma l'avait cependant étudié car de nombreux textes n'existaient que sous cette forme archaïque.

Gadra s'amusa de la stupéfaction de Fidelma tandis qu'elle saisissait la simplicité de sa méthode.

— Voulez-vous essayer ? lui demanda-t-il.

Fidelma hocha la tête avec enthousiasme.

Gadra échangea quelques informations avec Móen, puis il s'adressa à la religieuse.

— Vous prenez la paume de la main de Móen, et vous utilisez comme ligne de base celle qui va de la première phalange du majeur à la pliure du poignet. Maintenant, présentez-vous en inscrivant votre nom.

Fidelma traça maladroitement trois traits au-dessus de la ligne pour *f*, cinq points sur la ligne pour *i*, deux traits au-dessous pour *d*, quatre points au-dessus pour *e*, deux traits au-dessous pour *l*, un trait en travers pour *m*, et un seul point pour *a*.

Puis elle attendit la réponse.

Le jeune homme sourit et prit la main gauche qu'elle lui offrait. Une diagonale pour *m*, deux points sur la ligne pour *o*, une courte pause puis quatre points pour *e* et quatre traits vers la droite pour *n*. Móen.

Fidelma était en admiration devant la simplicité de cet agencement, et scandalisée que ce jeune homme fin et sensible ait été traité plus bas que terre.

Elle commença à épeler lentement les mots sur la paume de Móen.

— Je suis une avocate des cours de justice venue enquêter sur les meurtres d'Eber et Teafa. Vous me comprenez ?

— Oui. Je ne les ai pas tués.

— Racontez-moi ce qui s'est passé.

Aussitôt le jeune homme entama son récit, mais ses doigts bougeaient avec une telle rapidité que Fidelma dut l'interrompre.

— Vous allez trop vite. Je ne suis pas habituée à ce mode de communication. Gadra va nous servir d'intermédiaire.

— Très bien.

Fidelma se redressa, expliqua à Gadra ce qu'elle attendait de lui et il la relaya aussitôt. Puis la porte s'ouvrit sur Dubán qui les regarda d'un air ébahi tandis que Fidelma se tournait vers lui d'un air impatient. Gêné, il se balança d'un pied sur l'autre.

— Crítán s'est plaint que…

— Je suis parfaitement consciente de ce que Crítán a pu vous raconter.

Dubán changea aussitôt de tactique.

— Je comprends que le comportement de ce garçon vous agace, dit-il, et je veillerai à ce qu'il ne s'occupe plus de Móen puisque c'est ce que vous désirez.

Il jeta un coup d'œil à Gadra et Móen.

— C'est donc vrai ce qu'on raconte ? Ils communiquent entre eux ?

— Oui, je m'y suis même essayée avec Móen et ça fonctionne très bien. Cela vous dérangerait-il d'attendre dehors ? Lors de cet interrogatoire, nous devons accorder à Móen les mêmes protections qu'à n'importe lequel d'entre nous dans le cadre de la loi.

Le commandant des gardes se retira d'un air déçu.

Fidelma et Eadulf se concentrèrent à nouveau sur Móen qui traçait avec une étonnante virtuosité des signes sur la paume de Gadra. De temps à autre, l'ermite arrêtait le jeune homme et lui posait une question pour clarifier ses déclarations. Puis il entreprit de servir d'interprète entre Fidelma et Móen.

— Móen, avez-vous tué Eber et Teafa ? commença Fidelma

— Non.

Une pause.

— J'aimais Teafa. Elle m'a élevé comme son fils.

— Dites-nous ce qui s'est passé la nuit où vous avez été fait prisonnier.

— Je vais essayer.

— Prenez votre temps et donnez-nous tous les détails dont vous vous souviendrez.

— Bien. J'ai parfois des difficultés à trouver le sommeil et il m'arrive d'aller me promener.

— Pendant la nuit ?

— La nuit ou le jour, pour moi cela ne fait aucune différence.

Móen sourit à sa propre plaisanterie.

— Et donc cette nuit-là vous êtes allé marcher ?

— Oui.

— Savez-vous quelle heure il était ?

— Hélas non. Pour moi, le temps n'a pas le même sens que pour vous, mais je distingue le froid et le chaud et je perçois les odeurs. Je peux donc vous préciser qu'il faisait froid et humide mais je ne sentais pas les fleurs. Je me suis levé et j'ai ouvert la porte. Je me déplace sans bruit.

— Vous retrouvez facilement votre chemin dans le village ?

— Oui, mais il m'arrive de buter sur un objet qu'on a laissé traîner au milieu du chemin. Parfois je tombe, je réveille les chiens et les gens sont furieux. Mais d'habitude, je me débrouille assez bien.

— Où êtes-vous allé cette nuit-là ?

— Difficile à dire mais je peux vous montrer.

— Plus tard. Qu'avez-vous fait au cours de votre promenade ?

— Rien de spécial. Je me suis assis au bord de l'eau pour respirer les senteurs de la terre qui apaisent l'âme et le corps. Mais à cette heure, les exhalaisons sont plus faibles.

— Vous êtes allé au bord de la rivière ?

— Oui, l'eau qui court.

— Cela vous arrive souvent ?

— Oui. Je m'assieds là et je réfléchis, c'est un de mes grands plaisirs dans la vie, surtout en été.

Fidelma s'extasia en silence sur l'intelligence et la sensibilité du jeune homme.

— Ensuite ?

— J'ai voulu rentrer.

— Chez Teafa ?

— Oui. Mais en arrivant devant la porte, quelqu'un m'a attrapé par le bras et m'a glissé un morceau de bois dans la main. Puis, de l'autre main, il m'a fait caresser la baguette pour être sûr que je comprenne ce qui était écrit dessus, avec l'alphabet que nous utilisons maintenant.

— Qui était-ce ?

— Je l'ignore. Je ne connaissais pas son odeur.

— Que disaient les symboles ?

— Eber veut te voir.

— Qu'avez-vous fait ?

— J'ai obéi.

— Vous n'avez pas pensé à réveiller Teafa ?

— Elle n'aurait pas approuvé ma visite à Eber.

— Pourquoi donc ?

— Elle pensait que c'était un méchant homme.

— Et vous ?

— Eber s'est toujours montré gentil avec moi. Il me donnait des bonnes choses à manger, je sentais sa main sur ma tête et mon visage, mais il ne possédait pas les connaissances suffisantes pour communiquer avec moi. J'ai demandé à Teafa de lui apprendre mais elle ne voulait pas.

— Elle vous a expliqué pourquoi ?

— Elle s'y est toujours refusée.

— Donc quand vous avez reçu ce message, vous avez pensé qu'il avait découvert le moyen d'entrer en contact avec vous ?

— Oui. Si Eber était en mesure de maîtriser l'écriture, il pouvait me parler.

Le raisonnement était logique.

— Qu'avez-vous fait avec la baguette ?

Móen marqua une pause.

— Je crois que je l'ai laissée tomber. Non, j'ai heurté quelque chose, elle m'a échappé des mains et je n'ai pas pris la peine de la ramasser. J'étais impatient de rejoindre Eber.

— Vous avez trouvé votre chemin jusque chez lui ?

— Ce n'était pas difficile.

— Ensuite ?

— J'ai frappé à la porte, comme Teafa me l'a appris. Puis j'ai soulevé la clenche et je suis entré. Personne n'a approché. Je suis resté là un moment et j'ai pensé qu'il y avait sans doute une autre pièce. En longeant les murs, j'ai trouvé une deuxième porte, j'ai encore frappé, puis je l'ai ouverte.

— Et alors ?

— Rien. J'attendais qu'Eber vienne à ma rencontre. J'ai alors songé à une troisième pièce et en cherchant mon chemin je suis tombé sur un objet chaud. Une lampe qui vous sert à voir dans le noir.

Fidelma hocha la tête, puis réalisa que son mouvement était inutile.

— Oui, une lampe était allumée sur une table, confirma-t-elle.

— J'ai fait le tour de la table et mes pieds ont rencontré l'extrémité d'une paillasse. J'ai décidé de passer par-dessus pour poursuivre ma progression en utilisant le mur comme guide. J'étais obnubilé par la troisième porte. Quand je me suis retrouvé à quatre pattes sur la paillasse…

Le mouvement des doigts s'arrêta… puis reprit.

— J'ai compris qu'un homme était étendu là. Je l'ai touché et il était mouillé et collant. Quand j'ai porté un doigt à ma bouche, le goût salé m'a rendu malade. J'ai voulu explorer les traits de son visage mais ma main est tombée sur un objet froid et mouillé lui aussi, avec une lame très aiguisée. C'était un couteau.

Le jeune homme frissonna.

— Je me suis agenouillé, complètement perdu. J'ai tout de suite reconnu l'odeur d'Eber mais la vie l'avait quitté. J'ai voulu ressortir pour aller prévenir Teafa quand des mains brutales m'ont attrapé. J'ai eu très peur et je me suis débattu, alors on m'a frappé, on m'a entravé, et on m'a traîné jusqu'à un endroit puant. Personne ne s'approchait plus de moi. J'ai fini par comprendre qu'Eber avait été tué avec le couteau dont je m'étais saisi et j'ai passé une éternité dans un purgatoire. Mes geôliers ne pouvaient être que les assassins d'Eber ou des gens qui pensaient que je l'avais tué.

« J'ai essayé de trouver un morceau de bois pour graver un message à l'intention de Teafa. Je ne comprenais pas pourquoi elle m'avait abandonné. De temps à autre, on me jetait des bouts de nourriture et on me tendait un seau d'eau. Parfois j'arrivais à boire et à manger mais souvent je ne retrouvais pas les aliments par terre et personne ne m'aidait. Personne.

Il demeura un instant silencieux.

— Je ne sais pas combien de temps ça a duré. Finalement j'ai senti une odeur, la vôtre, Fidelma. Après ça, des mains rêches et dures m'ont lavé et m'ont correctement nourri. J'étais toujours enchaîné mais on m'a fourni une paillasse confortable et l'endroit sentait moins mauvais. Mais c'est seulement maintenant que je peux m'exprimer et comprendre ce qui s'est passé.

Fidelma poussa un profond soupir tandis que Gadra finissait de traduire les signes tracés par le jeune homme.

— Móen, vous avez été la victime d'une grande injustice, dit-elle enfin.

Gadra retranscrivit ses paroles.

— Même si vous aviez été coupable, rien ne justifiait que vous soyez traité comme un animal. Pour cela, je dois vous demander pardon.

— Vous n'avez rien à vous faire pardonner, Fidelma, car c'est vous qui m'avez tiré de cet enfer.

— Malheureusement, vous n'êtes pas encore sauvé, car il nous faut d'abord prouver votre innocence et identifier le coupable.

— Je comprends. Comment puis-je vous aider ?

— Grâce à vous, nous avons déjà beaucoup avancé et, plus tard, je m'entretiendrai à nouveau avec vous. En attendant, vous retournerez vivre dans la maison de Teafa, qui vous est familière. Si Gadra n'y voit pas d'objection, il prendra soin de vous jusqu'à ce que nos investigations soient terminées. Pour votre sécurité, je vous demanderai de ne pas sortir de chez vous, à moins que vous ne soyez accompagné.

— Je comprends. Merci, sœur Fidelma.

— Encore un détail, ajouta-t-elle.

— Quoi donc ?

— Vous avez dit que vous aviez senti mon odeur.

— Oui, je me suis retrouvé dans l'obligation de développer les sens que Dieu m'a laissés. Le toucher, le goût et l'odorat. Je peux aussi percevoir les vibrations, l'approche d'un cheval ou d'un petit animal, le courant de la rivière... ce qui me donne une bonne idée de ce qui se passe autour de moi.

Il sourit en direction de frère Eadulf.

— Par exemple, je sais que vous avez un compagnon, Fidelma.

Gêné, Eadulf changea de position.

— Je te présente frère Eadulf, intervint Gadra en s'activant sur la paume de Móen.

Puis il se tourna vers Eadulf.

— Si vous ne connaissez pas l'ogam, venez serrer la main de Móen.

Eadulf s'avança et s'exécuta d'un geste maladroit. Une pression répondit à sa poignée de main.

— Dieu vous bénisse, frère Eadulf, traduisit Gadra quand Móen recommença à écrire sur la paume du vieil homme.

— Revenons à votre sens de l'odorat, reprit Fidelma. Móen, essayez de vous souvenir de l'instant où une personne a saisi votre main pour y placer la baguette avec les inscriptions en ogam vous demandant de vous rendre auprès d'Eber. Vous m'avez confié ne pas avoir reconnu l'odeur de cette personne, mais confirmez-vous avoir perçu un effluve spécifique ?

Móen réfléchit un instant.

— Oui, et maintenant que j'y pense, c'était une fragrance de fleurs.

— Comment cela ? Selon votre témoignage, il faisait froid. Le jour ne s'était pas encore levé et les fleurs qui sentent la nuit sont peu nombreuses.

— Il s'agissait d'un parfum. J'ai d'abord cru que la personne qui me tendait la baguette était une femme mais les mains qui ont touché les miennes étaient rudes et calleuses. Celles d'un homme, sans aucun doute. Le toucher ne ment pas.

— De quel genre de parfum s'agissait-il ?

— Je sais identifier les odeurs mais je ne peux pas leur donner un nom, comme vous. Cependant, je suis formel, les mains appartenaient à un homme.

Fidelma se renversa sur sa chaise.

— Très bien. Gadra, je vous confie la garde de Móen. Pour l'instant, veillez à ce qu'il ne quitte pas la maison.

Gadra lui adressa un regard anxieux.

— Croyez-vous que le garçon soit innocent des crimes dont on l'accuse ?

Fidelma détourna la tête.

— Croire et prouver sont deux étapes distinctes, Gadra. Faites de votre mieux pour le bien-être de Móen et je vous tiendrai informé.

L'ermite conduisit Móen vers la porte gardée par Dubán. Après que Fidelma lui eut communiqué ses instructions, le guerrier s'écarta pour laisser passer les deux hommes.

— Certaines personnes dans le *rath* n'apprécieront guère cette décision, grommela-t-il.

Les yeux de Fidelma jetèrent des éclairs.

— Je suis ravie d'apprendre que les coupables seront mécontents.

Dubán cligna des paupières.

— J'en informerai Crón. D'autre part, j'ai à vous annoncer une nouvelle qui devrait retenir votre attention.

— Quelle est-elle ?

— Un cavalier vient d'arriver au *rath*. Une ferme isolée a été attaquée tôt ce matin et je pars sur-le-champ avec des hommes pour porter assistance aux paysans. Je crois que cela vous intéressera d'apprendre de quelle ferme il s'agit.

— Venons-en aux faits, Dubán.

— Des bandits ont donné l'assaut à la propriété d'Archú.

Eadulf émit un sifflement.

— Quelqu'un a-t-il été blessé ?

— Un berger des environs est venu nous prévenir. Il a vu du bétail s'enfuir, une grange en feu et il pense que quelqu'un a été tué.

— Qui ? s'écria Fidelma.

— Il l'ignore.

— Où est-il ?

— Il a quitté le *rath* pour retourner veiller sur son troupeau.

Eadulf se tourna vers Fidelma :

— Voilà qui est plutôt curieux. Archú nous avait affirmé qu'il était seul avec Scoth dans cette vallée.

— Dubán, nous allons vous accompagner. Je me suis attachée à ces jeunes gens et leur sort ne m'est pas indifférent. Je soupçonne Muadnat d'avoir organisé ce raid et d'en faire porter la responsabilité aux voleurs de bétail.

— Je n'aime pas beaucoup Muadnat, mais je l'imagine mal se livrant à une manœuvre aussi stupide. Vous le jugez mal. De plus, nous avons vu les bandits de nos propres yeux.

Eadulf se mordit la lèvre.

— Il a raison, Fidelma, vous ne pouvez nier la présence de ces brigands.

Fidelma lui jeta un regard agacé et revint à Dubán.

— Nous avons, en effet, croisé des cavaliers, mais ils se dirigeaient vers le sud et emmenaient des ânes chargés de paniers de bât. Où avez-vous vu des vaches ? Je crois qu'il est temps de se mettre en route pour la ferme d'Archú.

CHAPITRE XIII

Dubán avait rassemblé six cavaliers, tous armés. Fidelma fut soulagée que l'arrogant jeune Crítán ne soit pas parmi eux. Fidelma remarqua que ni Crón ni sa mère Cranat n'étaient venues les saluer à leur départ du *rath*. Deux par deux, Fidelma et Eadulf fermant la marche, ils passèrent le portail et prirent la direction de l'est au petit trot de leurs montures en longeant la rivière, traversant la vallée fertile d'Araglin avec ses champs de céréales et ses troupeaux de vaches dans les prés. Dubán les menait à une allure tranquille mais régulière.

Ils n'avaient pas parcouru quelques miles qu'en suivant une courbe de la rivière formant un méandre ils tombèrent sur un havre de tranquillité, protégé sur trois côtés par le cours d'eau. Il était planté d'arbres, les fleurs y poussaient en abondance et une charmante maisonnette en rondins y avait été construite, entourée d'un jardin où s'affairait une femme qui se redressa à leur approche. Elle était petite et potelée, mais ils passèrent trop loin d'elle pour que Fidelma distingue ses traits.

Elle les suivit du regard tandis qu'ils s'éloignaient, sans pour autant les saluer ou leur faire un signe de la main. Fidelma nota avec curiosité que deux des hommes de Dubán échangeaient des regards entendus en riant.

Fidelma remonta la colonne de cavaliers jusqu'à Dubán.

— Qui est-ce ? demanda-t-elle.

— Personne qui puisse vous intéresser, répondit le guerrier d'un ton bourru.

— Pourtant, elle m'a semblé éveiller l'attention de certains de vos hommes.

Dubán parut mal à l'aise.

— Il s'agit de Clídna, une femme de chair.

Cette expression était une métaphore pour signifier une prostituée.

— Je vois.

Fidelma immobilisa sa monture en attendant qu'Eadulf la rejoigne et lui transmit l'information. Il soupira et secoua la tête avec tristesse.

— Tant de péché dans un endroit si charmant.

Fidelma ne répondit rien.

Au bout de la vallée, ils s'engagèrent dans la forêt et commencèrent l'ascension d'un chemin assez large pour y laisser passer une charrette, qui allait les mener dans une seconde vallée située à une plus haute altitude. À un moment donné, Fidelma désigna du doigt une colonne de fumée qui s'élevait derrière une colline.

Dubán se retourna sur sa selle, vit que Fidelma avait déjà repéré le signe éloquent d'un incendie et lui fit signe de le rejoindre.

— La vallée du Black Marsh ! lui lança-t-il. Cette fumée vient de la ferme d'Archú et ces terres, à votre gauche, appartiennent à Muadnat.

Les champs cultivés, les riches pâturages et les troupeaux de vaches et de cervidés faisaient partie d'une propriété qui valait bien plus de sept *cumals*. Fidelma l'évalua à cinq fois le coût de la ferme d'Archú.

La route, bordée d'arbres et d'arbustes ou s'ouvrant sur des espaces non clôturés, courait en lisière du domaine qu'elle surplombait à flanc de colline. Au-dessous d'eux, la ferme semblait déserte. Personne ne s'affairait alentour.

— Sans doute les paysans attachés à Muadnat sont-ils partis porter secours à Archú, dit Dubán.

Les lèvres de Fidelma s'étirèrent en un petit sourire incrédule.

Dubán accéléra l'allure et la file des chevaux s'élança sur le chemin qui serpentait à flanc de coteau.

La combe où demeurait Archú, dont les terres étaient en grande partie cachées depuis le sentier qu'ils avaient emprunté, formait un angle de quarante-cinq degrés environ avec l'aire du Black Marsh où régnait Muadnat. Bientôt, le chemin devint tellement escarpé qu'ils durent avancer au pas.

— Vous connaissez bien la région, Dubán ? demanda Fidelma.

— Assez bien, répondit le guerrier.

— Existe-t-il une autre voie pour accéder à ce vallon ?

— Celle-ci est la plus fréquentée mais, à pied ou à cheval, des hommes pourraient se frayer un chemin en passant par les cimes.

Fidelma leva les yeux vers les sommets.

— Seulement poussés par le désespoir, lui fit-elle observer.

Eadulf inclina le buste vers elle.

— À quoi pensez-vous ?

— La bande de cavaliers se dirigeant vers la ferme d'Archú a forcément traversé les terres de Muadnat et elle n'a pu passer inaperçue.

Ils atteignirent bientôt la ferme et les bâtiments qui la composaient : une maison d'habitation, un four pour y sécher le blé, une porcherie, une grange et, un peu à l'écart, une autre grange qui avait brûlé et d'où s'élevait une colonne de fumée.

Dans un enclos étaient parquées quelques bêtes, dont une vache qui meuglait.

Dubán se dirigea vers la maison.

— N'approchez pas si vous tenez à la vie ! s'écria une voix haut perchée.

La petite troupe s'arrêta net.

— Nous sommes armés, reprit la voix, et suffisamment nombreux. Repartez d'où vous venez, sinon…

— Archú ! s'écria Fidelma en faisant avancer son étalon. C'est moi, Fidelma. Nous sommes venus vous porter assistance.

Aussitôt la porte s'ouvrit et Archú apparut, les yeux exorbités, une vieille épée rouillée à la main. La jeune Scoth, qui s'était abritée derrière lui, jetait des regards craintifs par-dessus son épaule.

— Sœur Fidelma, Dieu soit loué ! Nous pensions que les voleurs étaient de retour, déclara Archú en clignant des paupières devant les cavaliers.

Fidelma sauta à terre, suivie d'Eadulf et de Dubán. Les autres restèrent en selle, jetant des regards suspicieux autour d'eux.

— Un berger a chevauché jusqu'au *rath* pour nous prévenir que des bandits vous avaient attaqués.

Scoth fit quelques pas en avant.

— C'est Librén. Nous dormions encore quand ils sont arrivés. On a été réveillés par des hurlements et par le meuglement des bêtes. Quand on a compris de quoi il retournait, nous nous sommes barricadés dans la maison. Mais ils n'ont pas donné l'assaut. Ils sont partis avec du bétail et ils ont mis le feu à une des granges. Le jour s'était à peine levé et on ne distinguait pas grand-chose.

— Vous ne les avez pas reconnus ?

Archú secoua la tête.

— Il faisait trop sombre.

— Ils étaient combien ?

— À mon avis, moins d'une douzaine.

— Pourquoi ont-ils décampé ? intervint Dubán.

Archú fronça les sourcils.

— Pourquoi ont-ils…

— Ils se sont contentés de brûler une grange, vous avez des vaches, des moutons et des cochons à l'enclos, et vous êtes sains et saufs dans votre maison. Cela ne vous semble pas bizarre ?

— Justement, dit Scoth, je me suis demandé pourquoi ils s'étaient enfuis aussi rapidement sans tenter de forcer la porte de chez nous ou même d'incendier la ferme. À mon avis, ils cherchaient à nous effrayer.

— Peut-être que nous avons été sauvés par Librén ? suggéra Archú. Quand il a vu les flammes qui s'élevaient de la grange, il a sonné de son cor de berger et il a dévalé la colline pour nous prévenir.

— Un brave homme, murmura Eadulf.

— Un idiot, oui, le corrigea Dubán.

— Un idiot courageux, s'obstina Eadulf.

— C'est grâce à lui qu'ils n'ont emporté que deux vaches, fit remarquer Scoth.

— Et tout ça parce qu'un berger arrive en courant pour vous porter secours ? ironisa Dubán.

— C'est pourtant vrai, protesta Archú. Quand Librén a sonné du cor, ils ont juste pris deux vaches et se sont enfuis.

— Quelle direction ont-ils empruntée ? demanda Eadulf.

Scoth pointa du doigt les terres de Muadnat.

— Librén affirme qu'ils ont disparu de ce côté.

— C'est la route qui mène au marais du Black Marsh et elle s'arrête aux terres de Muadnat, expliqua Dubán, mal à l'aise.

— Où est passé Librén ? s'enquit Fidelma.

Scoth se tourna vers le sud.

— Librén s'occupe de son troupeau, là-haut. Il est resté ici jusqu'à l'aube, au cas où les bandits reviendraient. Puis il a emprunté un de nos chevaux, car Archú refusait de me laisser seule ici, et il est parti vous avertir. Il a réapparu il y a environ une demi-heure pour nous annoncer votre venue.

— Pourquoi n'a-t-il pas attendu ?

— Ses bêtes avaient besoin de lui, intervint Archú. Et puis à quoi cela aurait-il servi ?

Fidelma regarda autour d'elle.

— Ce Librén a raconté que quelqu'un avait été tué. Où est le corps ?

Dubán se frappa le front.

— Quel idiot je fais ! J'avais oublié.

Il interpella Archú.

— De qui s'agit-il ?

— Le corps est par là, dit Archú d'un air malheureux. Près des ruines. Personne n'a compris comment c'était arrivé. C'est seulement quand on a essayé d'éteindre les flammes qu'on est tombé sur ce cadavre.

— Un homme est tué sur votre terre pendant une attaque et vous ne savez rien de lui ? lâcha Dubán d'un ton cynique. Allons, mon garçon, s'il s'agit d'un des attaquants, vous n'avez rien à craindre. Vous étiez en état de légitime défense.

— Je vous jure bien que je n'ai tué personne. Nous n'avons pas d'armes et nous nous sommes barricadés pendant l'assaut. Nous n'avons rien vu. Librén était lui aussi très surpris que nous ne le connaissions pas.

— Assez perdu de temps, allons examiner le corps, s'énerva Fidelma.

Un des hommes de Dubán qui l'avait déjà repéré le désigna sans un mot quand ils s'approchèrent de la grange.

Il s'agissait d'un homme d'environ trente-cinq ans, assez laid, avec un visage qui portait des cicatrices et un nez bulbeux et aplati, sans doute par un coup qu'il avait reçu. Ses vêtements, recouverts d'une fine poussière blanche, étaient tachés de sang. Les yeux noirs fixaient le vide. Il avait eu la gorge tranchée et la tête était à moitié séparée du corps. C'est ainsi qu'on égorgeait les bêtes. En tout cas, une chose était certaine, il n'avait pas été tué dans une échauffourée mais délibérément assassiné. Les poignets portaient les marques de liens qui avaient irrité la chair. Fidelma se tourna vers Dubán.

— Je n'ai jamais vu cet homme en Araglin auparavant, dit-il aussitôt. C'est un étranger.

Fidelma se passa la main sur le front d'un air pensif.

— Cette histoire devient de plus en plus embrouillée. Les bandits ont tué un prisonnier ou alors un des leurs. Puis ils sont repartis sans pratiquement rien emmener. Pourquoi ?

— Si ce sont des hommes de Muadnat qui ont fait le coup, l'explication coule de source, déclara Scoth d'une voix pleine de ressentiment.

— Pourquoi pensez-vous qu'il s'agit d'un prisonnier ou d'un des brigands ? demanda Dubán à Fidelma.

— Il a récemment eu les mains attachées derrière le dos, ce qui expliquerait qu'il ait été égorgé sans se débattre, car je ne distingue aucune autre blessure. Et puis il était bien avec les autres, sinon d'où voulez-vous qu'il sorte ?

Elle se pencha et l'examina plus attentivement.

— Cet homme travaillait avec ses mains, qui portent des cals et des cicatrices. Et il a les ongles noirs.

Puis, en observant son visage, elle tressaillit.

— Ne vous rappelle-t-il pas quelqu'un que nous avons rencontré récemment ? demanda-t-elle au moine.

Eadulf étudia la figure du cadavre et secoua la tête.

— Non, je ne vois pas.

Fidelma jeta un coup d'œil à Archú.

— Il n'a pas plu depuis hier, n'est-ce pas ?

Le jeune homme hocha la tête d'un air surpris.

Fidelma passa un doigt sur les vêtements poudreux de l'inconnu, puis elle se releva.

— Décidément, Araglin est le pays des mystères, murmura-t-elle. Et maintenant je pense que nous devrions aller à la ferme de Muadnat.

— Le soupçonnez-vous ? se récria Dubán en fronçant les sourcils.

— Après ce que nous venons de constater, j'estime qu'il serait logique de l'interroger.

— Sans doute, admit Dubán à regret, car cela semble étrange, en supposant que nous ayons affaire à des voleurs, qu'ils s'en soient pris à la ferme d'Archú et non à celle de Muadnat, plus accessible et plus riche en bétail.

Dubán ordonna à un de ses hommes de rester avec Archú pour enterrer le corps. Le reste de la troupe se remit en selle et reprit la route. Fidelma et Eadulf venaient en dernier.

— Croyez-vous qu'il soit raisonnable de s'impliquer dans cette histoire ? demanda-t-il.

— Il est un peu tard pour faire marche arrière.

— On vous a envoyée ici pour enquêter sur la mort d'Eber, et non pour vous mêler d'une querelle entre Archú et son oncle.

— Les choses me semblent plus compliquées que cela, Eadulf. Dubán et Crón dissimulent leurs relations amoureuses. Officiellement on affirme qu'Eber était un chef aimé et respecté, mais on chuchote qu'il était haï de tous. Où se trouve la vérité ? Muadnat déteste son jeune cousin... cette vallée aurait-elle été contaminée par la haine ? À moins qu'une toile d'araignée, tissée par une force maléfique, ne relie tous ces éléments disparates ?

Eadulf réprima un soupir.

— Je ne suis qu'un étranger dans ce pays et aussi un homme simple dépassé par ces subtilités.

Tout en parlant, il comprit qu'il se cherchait des excuses faciles pour éviter de proposer des actions positives. Fidelma, qui avait fait la même analyse, ne répondit rien.

Quand ils eurent franchi les contreforts montagneux et traversé les champs cultivés, ils virent des paysans qui couraient vers les bâtiments de la ferme pour prévenir de leur arrivée. Puis une silhouette familière apparut : le chef des troupeaux de Muadnat, Agdae, qui se tenait en travers du chemin, les jambes écartées et les mains sur les hanches, entouré de quelques hommes armés.

— Est-ce là une façon d'accueillir des visiteurs ? s'écria Dubán en se dirigeant vers lui.

— Vous arrivez avec des guerriers, répliqua Agdae, impassible. Vous présentez-vous ici en amis ou en ennemis ? Autant s'en assurer avant de poser nos armes et de vous accueillir en frères.

Dubán arrêta son cheval devant Agdae.

— Je vous laisse juge.

Agdae adressa un sourire froid à Dubán et fit signe aux paysans de se disperser.

— Que cherchez-vous en ces lieux ?

— Où est votre oncle ?

— Aucune idée. Mais c'est moi qui le remplace quand il est absent. Que lui voulez-vous ?

— La ferme d'Archú a été attaquée.

Le regard d'Agdae vacilla, puis il reprit aussitôt son attitude agressive.

— Et vous voudriez que je sois désolé pour lui alors qu'il a escroqué sa propriété à Muadmat ?

Fidelma s'apprêtait à intervenir quand Dubán leva la main.

— Voyez-vous cette colonne de fumée derrière la colline ?

— Oui, et alors ?

— Alors je constate que vous n'avez pas éprouvé le besoin de voler à son secours. Depuis quand les hommes de la petite communauté d'Araglin refusent-ils de s'entraider ?

Agdae haussa les épaules.

— Comment aurais-je pu deviner que ce garçon était en danger ?

— La fumée ne vous suffisait pas ? intervint Fidelma.

— Hélas, je ne suis pas comme vous capable de divination, *dálaigh*. Archú pouvait aussi bien brûler les chaumes de ses champs. Si je partais bride abattue pour découvrir ce qui se passe à chaque fois que j'aperçois de la fumée, je n'en aurais jamais fini. De plus, Archú a des amis haut placés dans les cours de justice et si je lui avais rendu visite, je me serais peut-être retrouvé avec des compensations à payer pour attentions inopportunes.

— Prenez garde, une langue trop bien pendue mène souvent à un faux pas, répliqua Fidelma. Mais maintenant que vous êtes informé de la situation, peut-être pousserez-vous l'obligeance jusqu'à nous confier où se trouve Muadnat.

Agdae la fixa avec un sourire narquois et Dubán répéta la question sur un ton menaçant.

— Que voulez-vous que je vous dise ? persifla Agdae. Muadnat est parti à la chasse hier et il reviendra quand ça lui chante.

— Et où chasse-t-il ? insista Dubán.

— Qui peut prévoir dans quelle direction vole un faucon pour fondre sur sa proie ?

— Très drôle, dit Fidelma. Il ne nous reste plus qu'à espérer que le faucon ne croisera pas des aigles en route.

Agdae cligna des paupières.

— Muadnat est parfaitement capable de veiller sur sa personne.

— Je n'en doute pas. Aucun de vos paysans ne s'est absenté ?

— Aucun. Pourquoi me posez-vous cette question ?

— Quelqu'un a été tué par les brigands à la ferme d'Archú, et nous n'avons pas été en mesure de l'identifier.

Dubán décrivit l'homme et Agdae secoua la tête.

— Tous nos journaliers sont ici.

— Rassemblez vos gens devant moi.

À l'appel d'Agdae, une douzaine d'hommes apeurés se réunit sous le regard scrutateur du guerrier. La plupart étaient âgés et suffisamment musclés pour la charrue et la faucille, mais peu préparés à la rude vie de voleur de bétail. Dubán se tourna vers Fidelma.

— Ces laboureurs sont hors de cause. Désirez-vous que nous fouillions les bâtiments ?

Fidelma secoua la tête.

— Ne vaudrait-il pas mieux suivre la piste qu'Archú nous a indiquée ? suggéra-t-elle.

Dubán se mit à rire.

— En dehors de celle qui mène ici, les autres s'enfoncent dans les marais du Black Marsh. Je ne vous les conseille pas.

Frère Eadulf se pencha vers Agdae.

— J'ai une question pour vous, dit-il d'une voix douce.

— Posez toujours, Saxon.

— Derrière votre propriété, un sentier semble mener vers les collines du Nord, dans la direction opposée au chemin qui nous ramènera au *rath* d'Araglin. Or je croyais qu'il n'y avait qu'un seul itinéraire pour atteindre cette vallée.

— Et alors ?

Fidelma leva les yeux vers l'endroit indiqué par Eadulf. Il avait raison. Un chemin s'élevait le long des hauts pâturages et rejoignait la lisière de la forêt.

— Où cela mène-t-il ? demanda Eadulf.

— Nulle part, répliqua Agdae d'un ton sec.

— Les voleurs sont pourtant partis vers votre ferme. Comme leur présence vous a échappé, la seule possibilité est qu'ils ont suivi cette piste, enchaîna aussitôt Dubán.

— Elle se perd dans les collines.

— Je n'en doute pas, car si les brigands l'avaient empruntée, quelqu'un n'aurait pas manqué de les voir, n'est-ce pas, Agdae ? s'interposa Eadulf.

L'homme parut un instant déconcerté, puis il se rasséréna.

— Vous avez raison, Saxon, nous les aurions repérés.

Eadulf demeura silencieux et Fidelma se demanda pourquoi il ne suggérait pas à Dubán d'aller explorer ce sentier avec ses hommes. Elle en déduisit qu'il avait ses raisons.

— Je vais envoyer deux de mes guerriers vérifier que les bandits ne sont pas cachés là-haut, décida Dubán. S'ils ne trouvent rien, nous poursuivrons notre route.

Agdae poussa une exclamation agacée.

— Vous perdez votre temps.

Sur un signe de Dubán, deux hommes disparurent au trot de leur cheval en direction des collines.

Agdae jeta un regard mauvais à Fidelma.

— Il semblerait que vous soyez déterminée à brosser un portrait fort déplaisant de mon oncle, *dálaigh*.

— Muadnat est parfaitement capable de brosser lui-même son portrait, répliqua Fidelma d'un air détaché.

— Dubán, un cavalier vient par ici ! s'écria un des gardes.

Tous se tournèrent dans la direction du *rath*. Et ils reconnurent bientôt la silhouette du père Gormán.

— Que se passe-t-il ? demanda le prêtre quand il arriva à leur hauteur.

— Vous nous avez effrayés, déclara Dubán. On aurait cru que vous surgissiez de nulle part.

Il jeta un coup d'œil à la tenue du prêtre et ajouta :

— Il fait bien froid pour se promener sans cape.

Le père Gormán haussa les épaules.

— Ce matin quand je suis parti, le temps était superbe. Mais qu'est-ce qui vous amène ici ?

— La ferme d'Archú a été attaquée. Ce qui explique notre nervosité quant aux cavaliers.

Le prêtre parut mal à l'aise.

— Ces voleurs de bétail empoisonnent le pays. Justement, je me rendais chez Archú, mais peut-être vaudrait-il mieux que je renonce à mon projet pour rester en votre compagnie.

— Les voleurs se sont éclipsés depuis longtemps et puis votre foi vous gardera des mauvaises rencontres, ironisa Fidelma. D'ailleurs, vous serez bien accueilli là-bas : il y a un cadavre qui attend votre bénédiction.

Le père Gormán tressaillit.

— De qui s'agit-il ?

— Nul ne le sait, confessa Dubán qui se redressa sur sa selle en voyant revenir ses hommes.

— Nous avons examiné le chemin sur un mile. Il est beaucoup trop caillouteux pour retenir des empreintes de pas ou de sabots, dit l'un d'eux.

Dubán était déçu.

— Inutile de perdre notre temps dans des battues infructueuses, conclut-il. Agdae, je n'ai pas d'autre solution que de vous croire. Mais quand votre oncle rentrera, dites-lui que je désire le voir. Et maintenant je pense que nous en avons terminé.

Il chercha le regard de Fidelma qui hocha la tête en signe d'approbation.

Ils laissèrent le père Gormán en discussion avec Agdae et prirent la route du *rath*. Alors qu'ils sortaient de la vallée, Fidelma se tourna vers Eadulf pour lui demander pourquoi il avait soulevé le problème de cette piste tout en étant prêt à accepter sans discuter l'explication qu'Agdae leur proposait.

— Je voulais juger de sa réaction car j'ai vu quelqu'un sur ce chemin alors que nous nous dirigions vers la ferme de Muadnat. Tout le monde était concentré sur Agdae et personne n'a repéré cette silhouette à part moi.

— J'avoue que je n'y ai pas prêté attention.

— La personne est passée rapidement à cheval et s'est évanouie dans les arbres, derrière la ferme.

— Qui était-ce ? Muadnat ?

Eadulf secoua la tête.

— Non, j'ai distinctement reconnu la silhouette d'une femme dans le soleil.

Fidelma réprima son exaspération. Elle ne supportait pas les effets dramatiques d'Eadulf, une habitude dont il était coutumier.

— L'avez-vous identifiée ? demanda-t-elle d'une voix posée.

— Je pense que c'était Crón.

CHAPITRE XIV

En regardant par la fenêtre de l'hôtellerie des invités, Fidelma aperçut un cheval qui passait au galop les grilles du *rath*. Elle terminait le premier repas du jour avec Eadulf. Ils étaient rentrés tard. Dubán avait décidé d'envoyer un deuxième homme pour veiller sur la ferme d'Archú, mais il n'en demeurait pas moins convaincu que l'attaque était à mettre sur le compte des bandits.

Eadulf et Fidelma venaient de commencer de manger quand Dubán et un groupe de guerriers s'étaient mis en route pour une battue dans la campagne, c'est du moins ce que les religieux en avaient déduit. Sur l'insistance de Fidelma, ils avaient gardé pour eux l'apparition de la mystérieuse cavalière. En fait, Eadulf n'appuyait son identification que sur le manteau bicolore qu'elle portait, semblable à celui de Crón pendant l'audience, mais il n'avait pas distingué ses traits.

Quand un tonnerre de sabots avait résonné sur le pont de bois, Fidelma avait juste eu le temps d'entrevoir un cavalier pénétrant au galop dans le *rath*. Lorsqu'il sauta à terre et courut vers le siège de l'assemblée, elle reconnut Agdae.

— Quoi encore ? grommela Eadulf d'un ton fâché.

Fidelma se rassit et termina tranquillement son repas.

— J'ai le sentiment que la réponse à votre question ne va pas tarder à nous être communiquée.

Et effectivement, quelques instants plus tard, Dignait vint leur demander de rejoindre Crón au siège de l'assemblée. La jeune *tanist* était très préoccupée.

— C'est au sujet de Muadnat, annonça-t-elle quand ils pénétrèrent dans la grande salle.

Fidelma poussa un soupir.

— Je suppose que notre ami enclin à la chicane accuse maintenant le jeune Archú d'avoir brûlé sa propre grange ?

— Il se pourrait bien qu'Archú soit accusé d'un crime autrement plus sérieux, Fidelma. Mais cette fois-ci, ce n'est pas Muadnat qui portera l'affaire devant une cour de justice. On a découvert son corps pendu à la haute croix d'Eoghan, qui marque l'entrée sur le territoire d'Araglin.

Fidelma ouvrit de grands yeux.

— Si ma mémoire est bonne, cette croix n'est pas située sur la route qui conduit à la ferme de Muadnat mais sur celle qui communique avec la vallée dans la direction opposée. Qui a découvert le corps ?

— Agdae. Le haut pâturage au-delà de la croix lui appartient. Il affirme que Muadnat a quitté la ferme hier après-midi. Tôt ce matin, comme il n'était pas rentré, Agdae est parti à sa recherche et c'est alors qu'il a fait cette macabre découverte. Muadnat allait souvent chasser dans ces collines. Agdae est venu jusqu'ici pour demander du secours et il est retourné sur le lieu du crime avec quelques hommes.

Fidelma fit la grimace.

— Je suppose que Dubán vous a informée de notre visite à la ferme de Muadnat, hier ?

Crón hocha la tête.

— Il semblerait qu'Agdae n'ait pas cru bon de nous indiquer les terres où il savait que Muadnat s'était rendu.

203

— C'est important ?

— Je l'ignore. Mais hier, Agdae a prétendu ne pas savoir où était passé son oncle. Et ce matin, inquiet de son absence, il se dirige tout droit vers son cadavre.

— Agdae accuse déjà Archú de meurtre.

— Pour quelles raisons ?

— Parce qu'il était le seul ennemi de Muadnat en Araglin. Il prétend qu'Archú, par votre intermédiaire, a fait porter le blâme de l'attaque sur Muadnat, hier.

— Ce n'est pas tout à fait exact.

Fidelma se tourna vers Eadulf.

— Nous ferions bien de nous rendre sur place.

Eadulf hocha la tête puis se tourna vers la *tanist*.

— Dans combien de temps Dubán sera-t-il de retour ? Nous pourrions avoir besoin de ses services pour protéger Archú des accusations non fondées d'Agdae.

Crón parut ennuyée.

— Tout cela ne concerne en rien les meurtres de mon père et de ma tante. Ne devriez-vous pas vous consacrer à découvrir leur assassin, puisque vous affirmez maintenant qu'il ne s'agit pas de Móen ? Même si à mon avis vous aurez un long chemin à parcourir avant de persuader le peuple d'Araglin de son innocence.

Bien qu'il lui en coûtât, Fidelma demeura impassible.

— Quand on mène une enquête, Crón, mieux vaut garder un esprit ouvert. Les secrets en Araglin se multiplient. On m'a raconté des mensonges. Et qui me dit que la mort de Muadnat n'est pas reliée aux meurtres d'Eber et Teafa ? Si vous détenez des informations que vous ne m'avez pas encore communiquées, peut-être serait-il temps de réparer cet oubli.

Fidelma eut la satisfaction de lire l'incertitude et la peur sur le visage de la jeune femme.

— Mes observations étaient dictées par la logique, n'allez pas en déduire que je vous cache quelque chose,

répondit-elle d'un air faussement détaché. Si vous estimez de votre devoir de vous rendre à la grande croix,
très bien, mais il me semble que vos investigations traî-
nent en longueur.

— Mes investigations prendront le temps qu'il faut,
les gens doivent se montrer patients.

— Justement, Agdae pourrait bien refuser de patien-
ter. Il a juré de retrouver Archú et de se venger.

Fidelma lui adressa un regard aiguisé.

— Je ne saurais trop vous conseiller d'envoyer
Dubán contenir la colère d'Agdae. Peut-être même
qu'on devrait amener Archú et Scoth au *rath* pour assurer leur protection.

— Agdae était un parent de Muadnat, tout comme
moi. Il ne laissera pas son meurtrier échapper à la justice, lança Crón d'un ton glacial.

— J'entends bien, mais rassurez-vous, nous retrou-
verons son assassin, quels que soient son sexe et son
identité.

Sur ces mots, Fidelma tourna les talons et sortit à
grands pas de la salle, Eadulf à ses côtés. Bientôt, ils
chevauchaient à vive allure vers la scène du drame.

Le jeune guerrier Crítan était déjà là en compagnie
de deux hommes robustes, des paysans si on en jugeait
par leur physionomie. Ils s'apprêtaient à décrocher le
corps de Muadnat, pendu par une corde passée à
l'intersection des deux barres de la croix, pour le charger sur un âne. Les pieds de Muadnat pendaient à
quelques pouces du sol et Fidelma remarqua aussitôt
sa chemise trempée de sang.

Un des laboureurs s'apprêtait à dresser une échelle
contre la croix quand il aperçut Fidelma et Eadulf.
S'interrompant dans son travail, il grommela quelque
chose à l'intention de ses compagnons qui se retour-
nèrent et firent face aux deux religieux.

— Vous n'êtes pas les bienvenus ici, déclara le jeune
Crítan avec arrogance.

Sans s'émouvoir, Fidelma sauta à terre.

— Cela n'a aucune importance, lança-t-elle avec calme.

À son tour, Eadulf glissa de sa monture, prit les rênes de l'étalon de Fidelma et alla attacher les chevaux à l'écart.

Crítán se tenait les mains sur les hanches et fixait Fidelma avec ressentiment. À l'évidence, il ne lui avait pas pardonné de l'avoir humilié.

— Partez d'ici, femme. Vous avez par deux fois donné raison à Archú dans ses querelles avec Muadnat. Maintenant, vous voyez où cela nous a menés. Cette fois, Archú ne s'en sortira pas comme ça. Pas plus que cette créature du diable avec laquelle vous conspirez pour ne pas lui faire porter les meurtres d'Eber et de Teafa.

Fidelma se tenait au milieu du chemin, les mains sagement croisées devant elle. Elle souriait.

— Je suis une avocate des cours de justice des cinq royaumes, Crítán, dit-elle d'un ton aimable. Dois-je comprendre que vous me menacez ?

L'arrogance alliée à l'inexpérience eut raison de l'esprit rusé du jeune homme qui releva le menton.

— Vous êtes en Araglin. Ici, vous ne jouissez pas de la protection de votre église ou des guerriers de votre frère.

Quel ne fut pas son trouble lorsqu'il vit le sourire de Fidelma s'élargir !

— Je n'ai nul besoin qu'ils appuient mon autorité en ces lieux, susurra-t-elle.

Jusqu'à présent, les deux paysans, qui hésitaient sur la conduite à suivre, avaient laissé Crítán s'exprimer en leur nom. Mais celui qui tenait l'échelle, estimant que le jeune guerrier était allé trop loin dans ses menaces, s'avança de quelques pas.

— Il est vrai que votre présence nous dérange, ma sœur, dit-il d'une voix respectueuse. Notre parent…

Il désigna le cadavre d'un geste du pouce.

— ... a été assassiné et nous savons qui doit payer pour ce forfait. Mieux vaut que vous restiez à l'écart de tout cela.

— Vous avez décidé de l'identité du meurtrier de Muadnat et résolu de le châtier avant même de savoir s'il est coupable ou non, intervint Eadulf. Pourquoi ne pas attendre d'avoir trouver le vrai coupable ?

— Vous, Saxon, on ne vous a rien demandé ! glapit Crítán. Et maintenant déguerpissez. C'est un avertissement que je ne répéterai pas.

Fidelma le contempla d'un air rêveur. Un mauvais signe pour ceux qui la connaissaient bien, comme Eadulf. Elle avait remarqué le visage enflammé, les yeux brillants, les gestes dramatiques et l'élocution trop précise du jeune homme qui ce matin-là avait bu pour se donner du courage.

— Je veux bien vous pardonner vos manières grossières pour cette fois, Crítán. Je les mettrai sur le compte de la jeunesse et de l'inexpérience. Je vais examiner le corps de Muadnat, comme ma fonction m'en donne le droit.

Crítán, déconcerté par l'attitude de Fidelma que ses gesticulations n'avaient pas intimidée, jeta un coup d'œil à ses acolytes qui semblaient embarrassés. Pour la seconde fois, il se sentit humilié.

— Ces hommes sont des parents de Muadnat, s'obstina-t-il. Et nous vous empêcherons d'infléchir la loi pour permettre à Archú d'échapper à notre justice.

— Sont-ils les témoins de ce meurtre ?

Elle se retourna vers l'homme à l'échelle.

— Vous, dit-elle en pointant un doigt sur lui, avez-vous vu Archú assassiner Muadnat ?

L'homme rougit.

— Non, bien sûr que non, mais...

— Et vous ? dit Fidelma en se tournant vers l'autre laboureur.

— Qui d'autre, à part Archú, aurait pu commettre cet acte ? répliqua-t-il d'un ton hargneux.

207

— Voilà ce que la loi doit éclaircir avant que vous ne passiez votre colère sur un garçon qui est peut-être innocent.

Crítán éclata d'un rire cynique.

— Vous êtes très douée pour jouer sur les mots, femme. Mais on vous a assez entendue. Fichez le camp d'ici avant que je vous y oblige.

Il porta la main à son épée.

Eadulf s'avançait quand Fidelma le retint avec fermeté par le bras.

— Oseriez-vous menacer une dame ? gronda Eadulf. Qui plus est une religieuse ?

Le jeune homme brandit son épée, le visage cramoisi et les yeux étincelants de colère.

— Reculez, Eadulf, le prévint Fidelma.

Le paysan à l'échelle paraissait très nerveux. Des intimidations verbales ne prêtaient pas trop à conséquence, mais des menaces physiques contre une religieuse et une avocate des cours de justice ne présageaient rien de bon.

— Peut-être ferions-nous mieux de la laisser examiner le corps ? proposa-t-il d'un air anxieux.

À l'idée de perdre la face devant Fidelma, le garçon redoubla d'insolence.

— Ici, c'est moi qui donne les ordres !

— Crítán, intervint le second paysan, non seulement elle appartient à un monastère mais…

— Elle est celle dont la langue de serpent a permis à Archú d'usurper ce qui revenait de droit à Muadnat. Et elle est aussi responsable de sa mort !

— Crítán ! s'écria Fidelma d'une voix claire. Abaissez votre épée et allez dormir au *rath* où vous purgerez les effets de l'alcool. Vous êtes ivre. Mais je suis prête une fois de plus à ne pas vous en tenir rigueur.

Le jeune homme se mit à trembler de rage.

— Si vous étiez un guerrier !… hurla-t-il.

Fidelma plissa les paupières.

— Si vous désirez vraiment m'affronter, je ne laisserai pas ma condition de femme vous en empêcher.

— Crítán ! s'écria l'homme à l'échelle tandis que le garçon levait son épée et avançait de quelques pas vers Fidelma, qui leva la main pour le faire taire et fit signe aux autres de ne pas bouger.

Elle se tenait jambes écartées et bras détendus. Quand elle parla, sa voix était douce et sifflante.

— Vous avez dépassé les bornes, mon garçon. La jeunesse et la boisson ne sont plus une excuse. Si vous voulez utiliser votre épée, allez-y. Même une vieille courbée par les ans l'emporterait sur un gamin de votre espèce.

Ces paroles, destinées à exaspérer Crítán, atteignirent leur but.

Il poussa un hurlement de fureur et chargea. Tenté de s'élancer pour défendre Fidelma, Eadulf se força à ne pas intervenir, présumant ce qui allait arriver. À Rome, il avait déjà été témoin de ses talents dans la discipline du *troid-sciathagid*, le combat par la défense. Elle lui avait raconté que lorsque les religieux irlandais partaient pour des contrées lointaines afin d'y prêcher la bonne parole, ils se retrouvaient souvent seuls et vulnérables ; comme ils refusaient de porter des armes, ils avaient élaboré une forme de défense à mains nues.

La cause fut entendue en moins de temps qu'il ne faut pour le dire.

Le garçon bondit, l'épée levée, et un instant plus tard il gisait sur le dos dans la poussière, tandis que Fidelma posait un pied ferme sur le poignet de la main qui avait tenu l'arme. Crítán avait volé par-dessus l'épaule de la religieuse qui avait à peine bougé. Le principe de cette science consistait à utiliser la force de son adversaire pour le déstabiliser. Assommé, le garçon luttait pour reprendre sa respiration tandis que les deux paysans contemplaient leur compagnon d'un air ébahi.

Eadulf ramassa l'arme. Crítán sentait l'hydromel à plein nez et le moine secoua la tête d'un air entendu.

— *Plures crapula quam gladius*. Et comme vous ne comprenez pas le latin, je vais traduire pour vous. L'ivresse tue davantage que l'épée.

Fidelma se tourna vers un des laboureurs.

— Vous, je vous charge de ramener ce garçon au *rath*. Quand il aura recouvré ses esprits, informez-le que ses prétentions à la fonction de guerrier sont réduites à néant. Faites part de ma décision à votre *tanist*. Il pourra travailler la terre ou garder les troupeaux, mais il lui sera interdit de porter une arme dans le royaume de Muman.

Le paysan remit le jeune homme éméché sur ses pieds, puis il voulut récupérer l'épée que tenait Eadulf mais Fidelma s'interposa.

— Les couteaux tranchants ne sont pas des jouets pour les enfants.

Derrière elle, l'homme à l'échelle regarda son acolyte qui traînait Crítán sur le chemin et il murmura :

— Ne m'associez pas à la folie de ce garçon, ma sœur. Je ne recherche que la vérité.

Sans répondre, Fidelma lui fit signe de l'aider à poser l'échelle contre la croix, et elle y grimpa pendant qu'Eadulf la maintenait en place.

La gorge de Muadnat avait été tranchée d'un geste adroit et la tête à moitié séparée du corps, selon la méthode utilisée pour tuer un animal. L'épanchement de sang indiquait que la corde avait été passée au cou du supplicié après, puis qu'on avait accroché le cadavre à la croix. Le couteau ayant servi à infliger la blessure fatale avait disparu.

— Vous pouvez disposer de la dépouille, dit Fidelma en redescendant.

Eadulf aida le paysan à décrocher le corps, qui pesait son poids, pendant que Fidelma tournait autour du calvaire, les yeux fixés sur le sol.

— Eadulf ! s'écria-t-elle soudain.

Le moine la rejoignit. Elle lui montra des brins d'herbe éclaboussés de sang, et il s'agenouilla près d'une plante aux larges feuilles qu'il examina plus attentivement.

— Vous croyez qu'on l'a tué ici même ? demanda-t-il.

— Cela me semble une supposition raisonnable. Vous ne remarquez rien d'autre ?

Eadulf, qui s'apprêtait à se relever, marqua une pause et poussa un cri de surprise.

— Alors ?

— J'ai trouvé une touffe de cheveux roux.

Il la posa dans le creux de sa main.

— Vous croyez qu'elle est liée au meurtre ?

— En tout cas, elle a été arrachée à un cuir chevelu, on voit les racines.

Fidelma prit la touffe et la rangea avec soin dans son *marsupium*.

— Et maintenant, nous ferions bien de rentrer au *rath*. Il faut que je questionne Agdae.

Elle pinça les lèvres.

— À ce propos, pourquoi n'est-il pas ici ?

Elle se tourna vers le paysan qui attachait le corps de Muadnat sur le dos de l'âne.

— Agdae est-il revenu après qu'il fut parti chercher de l'aide au *rath* ?

— Non, ma sœur. Il nous a chargés de ramener la dépouille de Muadnat chez lui. Je crois qu'il s'est lancé à la poursuite d'Archú.

Fidelma leva les mains au ciel.

— Vous m'avez bien dit que vous étiez un parent de Muadnat ?

L'homme hocha la tête.

— Oui, mais la plupart des gens ici sont apparentés, et cela vaut aussi pour la *tanist*.

— Pourquoi Muadnat avait-il une aussi piètre opinion d'Archú, son cousin germain ?

— Il détestait son père, un étranger, répondit aussitôt le paysan. Muadnat estimait qu'Artgal avait usurpé l'affection de sa parente, Suanach.

— Usurpé l'affection de Suanach, dites-vous ? Voilà une expression des plus étranges, qui suppose qu'on a détourné cette femme de quelqu'un. Aurait-on forcé sa volonté quant au choix de son époux ?

L'homme parut mal à l'aise.

— Muadnat avait arrangé son mariage avec Agdae, mais Suanach l'a éconduit car elle était très éprise d'Artgal.

— Donc il faut chercher la raison de la querelle dans la vision déformée qu'avait Muadnat de cette relation ?

— Sans doute. Mais ce n'est pas bien de dire du mal des morts.

— Dans ce cas, concentrons-nous sur les vivants et efforçons-nous de les protéger de l'injustice.

— À vous en croire, Archú pâtirait des sentiments hostiles que Muadnat portait à son père, s'étonna Eadulf. Voilà une attitude des plus mal fondées.

Le paysan parut gêné.

— Sans doute, mais cela ne justifie pas qu'Archú ait tué Muadnat, s'obstina-t-il.

— Et vous êtes toujours convaincu qu'il a commis ce crime ?

— Agdae l'affirme.

— Cela rend-il pour autant son hypothèse valide ? D'après ce que vous nous avez raconté, Agdae a autant de raisons que Muadnat de détester Archú, sinon plus.

— Agdae, qui est non seulement le neveu de Muadnat mais aussi son fils adoptif, ne connaît-il pas la vérité mieux que personne ?

— Son fils adoptif ? s'exclama Fidelma. Donc Muadnat n'a pas d'enfants à lui ?

— Pas que je sache. Il a élevé Agdae depuis l'enfance.

— C'est donc Agdae qui va hériter de sa ferme ?

— Sans doute.

Fidelma s'avança vers son cheval.

— Je vous charge de ramener le corps à la maison de Muadnat. Si vous voyez Agdae avant moi, prévenez-le de ne pas se livrer à des actes qui amèneraient sur lui les foudres de la loi. Cet avertissement vaut également pour vous.

Eadulf monta en selle et la rejoignit.

— Et maintenant, où allons-nous ? demanda-t-il alors qu'ils redescendaient la colline.

— Chez Archú, bien sûr.

— Mais vous croyez que ce décès est lié à celui d'Eber ou de Teafa ?

— Ne vous semble-t-il pas bizarre que cette riante vallée d'Araglin, qui n'a connu aucune mort suspecte depuis des années, soit soudain le théâtre d'autant de drames ? Des fermes autrefois bien protégées sont attaquées, les voleurs ne s'emparent que de quelques têtes de bétail à chaque fois, puis surviennent les morts violentes d'Eber, de Teafa, de Muadnat et d'un quatrième homme non identifié. Je ne crois pas aux coïncidences, Eadulf.

Elle enfonça les talons dans les flancs de son cheval qui partit au trot.

— Allons vite rejoindre Archú, cria-t-elle à son compagnon, au cas où Agdae mettrait ses menaces à exécution !

Le moine peinait à maintenir l'allure imposée par Fidelma, qui était une cavalière émérite. Ils longèrent la rivière jusqu'à la maison de la prostituée Clídna, puis entreprirent l'ascension des collines escarpées jusqu'à la vallée du Black Marsh en forme de L, le domaine de Muadnat.

Aussi loin que remontaient ses souvenirs, Fidelma avait pratiqué l'équitation. Son cheval répondait à la moindre pression qu'elle exerçait sur lui, comme si elle le dirigeait par la pensée. Fidelma adorait chevaucher en liberté, parcourir la campagne, et les sentiers abrupts lui avaient toujours procuré une saine excitation. Penchée sur l'encolure de son étalon, la brise soufflant dans ses cheveux, le bruit des sabots répondant aux rythmes de son corps, elle se laissa bercer dans un état méditatif des plus agréables.

Enfin elle respirait, loin du monde mesquin de la vindicte humaine, comme si elle ne faisait plus qu'un avec la nature et la douceur de ce début d'été, humant les odeurs des bois et des champs, le visage offert au soleil. Elle ferma brièvement les yeux, envahie par un pur plaisir sensuel.

Puis elle se reprit avec un curieux sentiment de culpabilité.

Des gens étaient morts et elle était investie du devoir de découvrir leurs assassins.

C'est alors qu'elle distingua deux cavaliers qui venaient à leur rencontre. Dubán et un de ses hommes.

Elle tira sur les rênes de sa monture et Eadulf la rejoignit. Elle allait interpeller Dubán quand il la prit de court.

— J'ai déjà été informé de la nouvelle, ma sœur. Crón m'a envoyé un messager et j'ai laissé deux de mes gardes avec Archú et Scoth. Ils refusent de quitter leur ferme, mais ils sont en sécurité.

— Vous n'auriez pas croisé Agdae, par hasard ?

— Non, mais cela m'étonnerait qu'il tente de nuire à Archú sachant que mes hommes sont avec lui. Sa colère lui passera, il reviendra à la raison et comprendra que ce garçon n'est pas responsable de la mort de Muadnat.

Fidelma parut perplexe.

— Vous paraissez bien sûr de vous. De mon point de vue, il est impensable qu'Archú soit coupable de ce crime.

— Je sais qu'il est innocent, déclara Dubán d'un ton solennel.

Fidelma haussa les sourcils.

— D'où tenez-vous pareille certitude ?

— N'y voyez pas mystère. Souvenez-vous qu'hier, j'ai laissé deux de mes hommes avec Archú et Scoth, et ils se portent garants qu'ils n'ont à aucun moment quitté la ferme.

Fidelma eut un sourire contrit.

— Je suis bien sotte de l'avoir oublié ! Voilà qui nous épargnera la peine d'avoir à prouver l'innocence d'Archú. Il ne nous reste plus qu'à découvrir le vrai coupable.

— Je retourne au *rath*, annonça Dubán. Je suis surpris que Crítán ne vous ait point escortés. Ce matin, je lui avais confié la responsabilité des gardes.

Fidelma lui raconta ce qui s'était passé et Dubán ne parut pas étonné outre mesure.

— Il est rongé par l'ambition et ignore le dévouement. Au fond de moi-même, je me doutais que ce garçon n'avait pas l'étoffe d'un guerrier.

— Il en possède les aptitudes sans en avoir la moralité. Il me fait penser à une flèche dont on ne contrôle pas la trajectoire.

— Mon expérience m'avait déjà soufflé qu'il tournait mal. J'en discuterai avec Crón.

— Je ne doute pas qu'elle vous écoute et suive vos conseils.

Dubán plissa les paupières et étudia le visage énigmatique de Fidelma.

— Je ne suis pas idiote, dit-elle enfin.

— Je ne vous ai jamais considérée comme telle, protesta Dubán.

— Alors à l'avenir, souvenez-vous-en. Et dites à Crón que parler vrai est encore le plus simple. Mieux vaut la vérité qu'une demi-vérité ou un authentique mensonge.

Puis elle fit un geste à Eadulf et poursuivit sa route.

— Maintenant qu'ils ont disparu, dit plus tard Eadulf, expliquez-moi quelle est la signification à donner à cet échange.

215

Fidelma arrêta son étalon.

— Je plantais une graine, admit-elle d'un ton enjoué. Il serait temps que les fausses pistes et les déclarations mensongères le cèdent à la réalité.

— Mais ce faisant, n'avez-vous pas averti Crón et Dubán que vous les soupçonniez d'être impliqués dans ces manipulations ?

— Parfois, pour faire sortir le renard, vous devez enfumer son terrier.

— Donc vous attendez leur réaction ?

— Oui, je le reconnais.

Eadulf émit un reniflement désapprobateur.

— Cette pratique peut se révéler dangereuse car quand un renard est acculé, il lui arrive d'attaquer les chasseurs. Et puis où allons-nous, Fidelma ? Archú ne peut rien nous apprendre que nous ne sachions déjà.

— Pour tout vous avouer, j'aimerais beaucoup voir où mène la piste que vous avez repérée hier.

Eadulf parut inquiet.

— Ne vaudrait-il pas mieux être accompagnés ? Et si ce sentier menait au repaire des voleurs de bétail ?

Fidelma lui sourit.

— Ne craignez rien, Eadulf, je n'ai nulle intention d'aller me jeter dans la gueule du loup.

— Ce ne sont pas vos actions délibérées que je crains, mais votre impétuosité incontrôlée, grommela Eadulf.

Pour la première fois depuis longtemps, elle éclata d'un rire joyeux. Ils étaient maintenant arrivés sur la partie du sentier qui dominait les terres de Muadnat et Fidelma examina le paysage avec attention.

— Je ne voudrais pas que l'on nous observe, expliqua-t-elle.

— Difficile alors qu'il nous faut passer entre les bâtiments de la ferme, fit observer Eadulf.

Fidelma pointa un doigt.

— Au-delà de ces champs, une petite dépression traverse la vallée. Je crois qu'il s'agit d'un ruisseau ou d'un fossé de drainage. Ici et là, on aperçoit les buissons qui marquent son parcours. Si nous parvenons jusque-là, nous éviterons d'éveiller l'attention des curieux, et rejoindrons le sentier de l'autre côté de la combe.

Eadulf montra un enthousiasme modéré pour ce projet mais, comprenant que Fidelma était déterminée, il insista pour prendre les devants, et laissa son cheval trouver sa voie dans la pente caillouteuse. Ils longèrent des champs cultivés et se dirigèrent vers les fourrés et les bouquets d'arbres. Fidelma avait raison, la dépression dissimulait un torrent, qui à certains endroits ne dépassait pas six pieds de large. Ils le suivirent, dissimulés aux regards, remontèrent vers la lumière et se glissèrent derrière les bâtiments. Au-dessous d'eux, il n'y avait personne dans les champs ou autour des granges. Puis ils abordèrent la deuxième piste et commencèrent leur ascension des collines au nord.

— Avec toutes ces traces de sabots d'ânes et de chevaux, comment peut-on affirmer que ce sentier n'est pas fréquenté ? dit Fidelma après quelques instants. On distingue même les empreintes de roues de charrette. En bas, c'est assez caillouteux mais ici, la terre est plus abondante.

Le religieux saxon parut inquiet.

— Ne vaudrait-il pas mieux revenir visiter cet endroit avec des guerriers de Dubán ?

Pour toute réponse, Fidelma le foudroya du regard.

Le chemin qui montait en lacet les amena bientôt de l'autre côté de la colline.

— Avez-vous remarqué la position du soleil ? dit Eadulf.

— Oui, voilà un sentier très tortueux et nous tournons maintenant le dos à la ferme de Muadnat.

Beaucoup plus intéressant, le sentier avait été nivelé et il ne grimpait plus. Ils continuèrent à progresser vers l'est, puis virèrent brusquement vers le sud et se retrouvèrent sur un haut plateau.

— On dirait que nous avons parcouru un cercle, s'étonna Fidelma.

Eadulf sourit.

— Ce chemin que nous avons pris est situé parallèlement à la partie de la vallée où vit Archú et si nous grimpions cette élévation à droite, nous dominerions ses terres. On apercevrait même sa maison.

Ils avaient parcouru un demi-mile quand ils pénétrèrent dans une zone boisée qui s'étendait jusqu'au sommet des collines. Ils s'arrêtèrent en lisière de la forêt où la route s'élargissait. Des ornières marquaient le passage de roues de charrette.

— Mieux vaut retourner au *rath*, grommela Eadulf, sinon nous allons nous laisser surprendre par la nuit.

— Juste encore un peu, l'adjura Fidelma. Il me semble…

Elle s'arrêta brusquement et sauta à bas de son étalon.

— Vite, il faut cacher les montures et nous continuerons à pied.

Eadulf céda à ses instances et, une fois les chevaux à l'abri, ils suivirent un chemin parallèle à la piste.

Avant peu, ils arrivaient en vue d'un espace dégagé et un bruit sourd les fit sursauter. Quelqu'un coupait du bois. Ils s'arrêtèrent au bord d'une clairière à flanc de coteau.

Quelques rochers granitiques affleuraient çà et là et le vent soufflait dans les hautes herbes. Des chevaux et des ânes, de petits animaux robustes, broutaient dans un enclos improvisé, délimité par des cordes. Non loin, près d'un chariot, un feu avait été allumé. Un morceau de viande y cuisait à la broche, et la graisse qui en tombait crépitait dans les flammes. Des hommes déambulaient, chacun occupé à quelque tâche. Fidelma les examina avec attention.

218

Elle posa une main sur le bras d'Eadulf et désigna un autre enclos, un peu plus loin, qui retenait des vaches ruminant paisiblement, indifférentes au sort réservé à celle qui allait être dévorée à belles dents.

En hauteur, on entrevoyait l'entrée d'une caverne, suffisamment haute pour permettre le passage d'un homme, et protégée par une avancée de roches grises et vertes, en forme de dôme, qui en obscurcissait l'accès.

La mystérieuse piste n'allait pas plus loin. Ils avaient découvert le repaire des voleurs de bétail.

Fidelma et Eadulf se regardèrent. Eadulf semblait perplexe mais Fidelma, qui avait observé certains des outils déposés près du chariot, commençait à y voir plus clair. Ils s'apprêtaient à battre en retraite quand un solide gaillard émergea de la caverne, bâilla et s'étira longuement.

Il avait une barbe et une chevelure rousses.

Les deux religieux n'eurent aucun mal à reconnaître l'affreux Menma, chef des troupeaux du *rath* d'Araglin.

CHAPITRE XV

Ils chevauchaient en silence, Fidelma absorbée dans ses pensées. Eadulf garda pour lui les innombrables questions qui le taraudaient jusqu'à ce qu'ils sortent de la forêt. Puis, n'y tenant plus, il demanda :

— Que pensez-vous que soit ce camp retranché ?

— Si je le savais, tous les mystères seraient résolus, soupira Fidelma. Mais il y a de fortes chances que nous ayons découvert le repaire des bandits qui attaquent les fermes d'Araglin pour leur dérober du bétail.

— Mais pourquoi Menma s'est-il associé à ces hors-la-loi et que fabriquent-ils dans cette caverne ?

Fidelma grimaça un sourire.

— Ce ne sont pas des voleurs de bétail et je ne pense pas qu'ils se cachent.

— Alors ?

— N'avez-vous pas remarqué les outils épars près du chariot ?

— Non, j'étais trop occupé à observer les hommes.

Fidelma claqua la langue en signe de réprobation.

— Dans la recherche de la vérité, il ne faut jamais oublier l'observation et l'analyse de celle-ci. Ces outils sont la preuve que nous sommes en présence d'une mine.

— Une mine ?

— Quoi d'étonnant à cela ? Si en quittant Lios Mhór nous avions cheminé vers l'ouest, le long de l'Abhainn

Mór, nous serions tombés sur Magh Méine, la plaine des Minéraux, d'où l'on extrait le cuivre, le plomb et le fer.

— J'ai déjà entendu parler de cet endroit.

— Souvenez-vous, Bressal a mentionné que son frère y travaillait.

— Mais bien sûr ! s'exclama Eadulf. Et comment interprétez-vous la présence de Menma ?

— À nous de le découvrir.

— Et pourquoi…

— À quoi bon jouer aux devinettes si nous ne disposons pas des éléments d'information nous permettant d'échafauder des hypothèses ?

— Peut-être aurions-nous dû nous présenter et exiger des explications ? Après tout, vous êtes un personnage officiel de ce royaume.

Fidelma éclata de rire.

— Vous croyez vraiment que ces hommes respectent ma fonction ?

— Nous aurions pu les surprendre et les désarmer.

— *Vis consili expers mole ruit sua*, dit Horace dans ses *Odes*.

Eadulf hocha la tête.

— « La force privée de bon sens s'effondre sous son propre poids. »

Fidelma mit sa main en visière devant ses yeux et regarda la position du soleil.

— D'après vos calculs, si nous escaladons ce sommet, nous devrions nous retrouver au-dessus de la ferme d'Archú, non ?

Eadulf fronça les sourcils.

— Effectivement.

— Et si nous allions vérifier ?

— Vous plaisantez, j'espère ? Les pentes sont bien trop abruptes pour des chevaux.

Fidelma pointa un doigt en silence et Eadulf suivit la direction qu'elle indiquait.

Il mit un certain temps à distinguer la robuste silhouette d'un cerf, accompagné d'une biche, qui se profilait au loin.

Fidelma lui sourit.

— Là où ces animaux peuvent passer, un cheval et son cavalier aussi. Tenez-vous le pari ?

Eadulf leva les bras et les laissa retomber d'un air résigné.

— Regardez, il y a un sentier juste au-dessus de nous qui franchit la colline, la biche s'y est engagée.

Eadulf distingua une vague piste au milieu des fougères et des ajoncs.

— On ne peut pas grimper par là, protesta-t-il.

— Nous conduirons nos chevaux par la bride.

Elle glissa de sa selle et entreprit de se frayer un chemin au milieu des buissons.

Eadulf émit un grognement de lassitude et la suivit. En vérité, il n'appréciait guère les endroits escarpés et il ne quitta pas le sol des yeux.

— Est-il indispensable d'utiliser ce raccourci pour nous rendre chez Archú ? se plaignit-il.

— Nous irons plus vite et puis cela nous évitera d'éveiller les soupçons de quiconque, à la ferme de Muadnat, serait en relation avec les mineurs de la clairière.

— Mais en quoi cela concerne-t-il le meurtre d'Eber ?

Fidelma garda le silence.

Maintenant, le vent soufflait en rafales, ce qui rendait les chevaux nerveux. Fidelma repéra un troupeau de cervidés qui broutaient sur le chemin. Le vent ne les troublait guère et, de temps à autre, le cerf qui les conduisait relevait la tête, se détachant sur le ciel telle une statue avec sa magnifique ramure. Il surveillait la progression des deux intrus. Puis il se mit à pousser de curieux bramements pour obliger les siens à accélérer le pas. Les animaux bondissaient vers les hauteurs avant de s'arrêter à nouveau pour plonger le museau dans l'herbe tendre.

Eadulf avançait tête baissée, pour se protéger du vent et éviter de se confronter aux grands espaces. Il priait pour que son cheval ne s'affole pas car il doutait de ses capacités à le maîtriser.

Soudain, Fidelma s'arrêta.

— Que se passe-t-il ?

— Regardez par vous-même.

Eadulf jeta autour de lui un regard fébrile.

La vallée en forme de L s'étendait à leurs pieds mais il baissa aussitôt les yeux.

— Seriez-vous sujet au vertige, Eadulf ? lui demanda Fidelma, brusquement inquiète.

Le moine se mordit la lèvre.

— Je crains les endroits élevés et exposés, avoua-t-il. Ce n'est pas tant que j'aie peur de tomber en bas, mais plutôt dans le vide, enfin, si vous comprenez ce que je veux dire. Mes paroles doivent vous sembler confuses, non ?

Fidelma secoua la tête.

— Pourquoi ne m'avez-vous pas prévenue ?

— Je répugne à confesser cette... faiblesse.

— Mon mentor, Morann de Tara, disait qu'une souris ne peut pas boire plus que sa mesure.

Eadulf était perplexe.

— Voilà une philosophie bien obscure, grommela-t-il.

— J'ai cru comprendre, mais mon interprétation n'est pas nécessairement la bonne, que nous devons reconnaître nos insuffisances et nos points forts. Nos faiblesses nous renseignent sur nos qualités et nos qualités sur nos faiblesses.

— Donc, j'aurais dû accepter ma peur et vous en parler.

— La connaissance de l'autre ne permet-elle pas de mieux réagir aux événements ?

Eadulf poussa un soupir d'impatience.

— Croyez-vous que ce soit l'endroit pour discuter de cela ?

— Excusez-moi si mes pensées sont un peu embrouillées, murmura Fidelma.

La contrition convenait mal à son caractère mais elle était sincère.

— Et maintenant, il ne nous reste plus qu'à redescendre sur la ferme d'Archú. Vous aviez raison, nous surplombons ses terres.

— Alors allons-y, ronchonna Eadulf. Plus tôt nous amorcerons la descente, plus vite nous serons en bas.

Fidelma se remit en marche. Le troupeau de cervidés s'était égaillé dans la montagne, les laissant seuls. La pente très raide les obligeait à s'arrêter régulièrement pour calmer les chevaux et avancer avec précaution dans les parties les plus tortueuses. Une ou deux fois, ils suivirent des détours qui les amenèrent à revenir sur leurs pas, puis ils atteignirent des versants plus doux où la bruyère, les hêtres et les églantiers signalaient une terre moins aride.

Alors qu'ils arrivaient enfin sur le plat, ils tombèrent sur deux cavaliers qui les attendaient, arcs bandés.

— Sœur Fidelma ! s'écria Archú en les reconnaissant.

Aussitôt, il abaissa son arc et le guerrier qui l'accompagnait fit de même.

— Nous vous avions repérés de loin et nous nous demandions qui vous étiez, s'excusa Archú.

— Quelle idée d'aller vous perdre dans ces taillis ! s'étonna le guerrier.

— Je ne vous le fais pas dire, soupira Eadulf en s'épongeant le front.

— Cela fait une bonne heure que moi et mon compagnon vous observons. Pourquoi avez-vous emprunté ce sentier ? Il n'est fréquenté que par les bêtes.

— C'est une longue histoire, Archú, répondit Fidelma. Et si Scoth nous offre des rafraîchissements, je me ferai une joie de vous la conter.

— Avec grand plaisir, ma sœur. Allons vite à la ferme.

Le guerrier leva le nez vers les montagnes d'un air suspicieux.

— Personne ne vous a suivis, ma sœur ?

— Pas que je sache. Vous avez vu quelqu'un ?

— Non, mais nous devons rester vigilants. Savez-vous que Muadnat a été tué ?

— Nous avons appris la nouvelle par Crón. Dubán, rencontré en route, nous a confié qu'il vous avait chargé, avec un autre de ses hommes, de tenir compagnie au jeune Archú dans l'éventualité où Agdae serait tenté par un acte inconsidéré.

Archú se tourna vers son compagnon.

— Pourquoi ne restez-vous pas ici pour monter la garde quelques instants pendant que j'escorte sœur Fidelma et frère Eadulf jusque chez moi ?

Le guerrier opina du chef sans autre commentaire et les autres prirent le chemin de la ferme.

— Me voilà plongé dans une sale affaire, ma sœur, soupira Archú. Heureusement que les hommes de Dubán peuvent témoigner que je n'ai pas bougé d'ici, sinon je n'ose penser au sort qui m'attendait. Je connaissais Muadnat depuis toujours et il me haïssait, mais sa mort ne m'a pas laissé indifférent. C'était mon cousin. Que son âme repose en paix.

— Amen, dit Eadulf qui s'était remis de ses frayeurs et avait recouvré son entrain.

— Et comment vous entendez-vous avec Agdae ? Saviez-vous qu'il était le fils adoptif de Muadnat ?

Archú fit la grimace.

— Oui, bien sûr. Et lui aussi est mon cousin. Ses parents sont morts de la peste il y a bien longtemps. Agdae a survécu et Muadnat l'a ramené chez lui. Ma mère m'a raconté que Muadnat voulait qu'elle l'épouse mais elle a préféré mon père. Je vous confesse sans détour que nous nous évitons. Il a été élevé dans l'intolérance et m'a toujours manifesté une hostilité déclarée.

— Et vous ?

— Je ne l'apprécie guère. Ce n'est pas une personne avenante.

— À votre avis, qui a tué votre cousin ? demanda brusquement Fidelma.

Archú demeura un instant silencieux. Eadulf crut même qu'il refusait de répondre à la question. Puis il poussa un profond soupir.

— Je l'ignore. Pour moi, tout cela n'a aucun sens. Je ne connaissais pas Eber et Teafa, mais l'assassinat de Muadnat m'a bouleversé. Et je n'y comprends rien.

Arrivés à la ferme, Scoth ouvrit la porte pour les accueillir et le second guerrier vint s'occuper de leurs chevaux. Archú les conduisit à l'intérieur.

— Je vais vous servir du cidre, dit Scoth en allant chercher un pichet.

Eadulf sourit avec reconnaissance.

— Soyez bénie, j'ai la gorge complètement desséchée.

Ils s'assirent autour de la table tandis que Scoth versait la boisson et leur offrait une coupe de fruits.

Eadulf vida son gobelet d'un trait et poussa un soupir de satisfaction tandis que Fidelma buvait à petites gorgées d'un air gourmand.

— Méfiez-vous, Eadulf, admonesta-t-elle gentiment son compagnon qui avait laissé Scoth le resservir, ce breuvage soûle facilement.

Archú fit la grimace.

— Muadnat avait eu la bonté de nous en laisser quelques barils.

— Tu oublies de préciser que je l'avais confectionné de mes propres mains, intervint Scoth. Goûter le fruit de mon labeur me procure de grandes satisfactions et je suis bien heureuse que Muadnat en ait été privé.

Fidelma se tourna vers Archú.

— Vous avez passé toute votre vie dans cette vallée ?

— Oui. Je suis né dans cette ferme. Quand Muadnat l'a occupée après la mort de ma mère, il m'a envoyé dormir à l'étable avec les animaux jusqu'à ce que j'atteigne l'âge du choix et que j'aille présenter mes doléances à Lios Mhór. C'était la première fois que je quittais cette vallée.

— Cette colline dont nous sommes descendus tout à l'heure, à qui appartient-elle ?

— À moi.

— Je croyais que cette ferme comprenait sept *cumals* de terres ?

— Il y en a seulement quatre dans la vallée elle-même. Les terres sont divisées en terre arable, en terre des trois racines…

Eadulf releva la tête de son gobelet.

— Qu'est-ce que c'est que ça ?

— Vous découvrirez dans nos textes de loi que d'après l'ancienne classification, le sol le plus riche se reconnaît à la présence de trois plantes aux larges racines : le chardon, le séneçon et la carotte sauvage. Cette terre vaut alors très cher, car on sait qu'on pourra y pratiquer toutes sortes de cultures.

Malgré l'intérêt d'Eadulf, Fidelma revint rapidement au sujet qui l'intéressait.

— Et donc ces coteaux sont à vous ?

— Oui, il s'agit d'une terre de la hache. Pour la faire fructifier, il faudrait la débroussailler et la déboiser, ce qui représenterait beaucoup de travail. Même Muadnat ne s'y est pas risqué.

— Avez-vous déjà exploré cette friche ?

Archú la fixa d'un air surpris.

— Pour quoi faire ?

— Par curiosité.

— Je viens à peine de reprendre la ferme, ma sœur. Alors vous pensez bien que je n'ai guère eu le temps d'aller prospecter dans cet endroit aride.

— Et quand vous étiez enfant ?

— Ce n'est guère un lieu de promenade.

— Que savez-vous des cavernes qui s'y trouvent ?

Archú haussa les épaules.

— J'ai entendu parler de grottes, situées au nord. Il y a celle du Mouton gris. Ma mère m'a raconté qu'une fois une agnelle grise sortit de la grotte. Un fermier du coin la recueillit. L'agnelle devint une brebis qui mit bas des petits. Et puis un beau jour, le fermier décida d'abattre un des agneaux pour le manger. La brebis réunit alors ses petits et disparut avec eux dans la grotte. On ne les a jamais revus.

— Vous n'avez jamais entendu parler de mines ? s'impatienta Fidelma.

Archú réfléchit.

— S'il y en a, j'ignore leur emplacement. Mais pourquoi ces questions ?

— Nous avons trouvé… commença Eadulf.

Il tressaillit en recevant un coup de pied sous la table.

Archú et Scoth le regardaient, suspendus à ses lèvres.

— Nous avons élucidé quelques points qui nous intriguaient concernant la géographie de cette région, dit Fidelma avant d'ajouter à l'adresse d'Eadulf : Vous êtes sûr que ça va ? Je vous avais pourtant prévenu que cette boisson a des effets inattendus.

Eadulf fit la grimace.

— Ce n'est rien, grommela-t-il, juste une crampe. Je suis fatigué d'avoir trop marché.

— La journée a été longue et nous devons retourner au *rath*.

— Mais il faut que vous mangiez quelque chose avant de partir, protesta Scoth.

Fidelma secoua la tête à regret.

— Hélas, nous n'avons pas de temps à perdre si nous voulons arriver là-bas avant la nuit.

Joignant l'acte à la parole, elle se leva. Eadulf l'imita et ils firent leurs adieux.

Quelques instants plus tard, alors qu'ils chevauchaient sur la route, Eadulf se plaignit du comportement de Fidelma.

— Inutile de me donner un coup de pied aussi violent. Vous m'avez fait mal. Si vous désiriez passer sous silence ce que nous avions découvert, il suffisait de me prévenir.

— Je suis désolée. Mais il est clair que quelqu'un voulait garder le secret sur ces mines. À mon avis, comme elles sont situées sur les terres d'Archú, Muadnat les exploitait en secret. Aurions-nous découvert la vraie raison de l'attachement de Muadnat à la propriété de son cousin ?

Eadulf émit un sifflement admiratif.

— Voilà qui est parfaitement logique.

Il marqua une pause.

— Néanmoins, cela ne nous avance guère pour résoudre le mystère des meurtres d'Eber et de Teafa.

— Peut-être. Mais la présence de Menma...

Elle s'arrêta si brusquement qu'Eadulf crut qu'elle avait repéré un nouveau danger et il fouilla du regard la campagne environnante.

— Que se passe-t-il ?

— Non mais, quelle idiote je fais !

Eadulf attendait.

— Menma. Vous vous souvenez que c'est lui qui menait l'attaque contre l'auberge de Bressal ?

— Oui.

— Et maintenant il apparaît à la mine.

— Et alors ?

— Vous ne voyez pas le rapport ?

Eadulf réfléchit pendant que Fidelma bouillait d'impatience devant sa lenteur.

— Bressal avait un frère, non ?

La mémoire revint à Eadulf.

— Morna ! Un mineur qui possédait une collection de pierres...

— Et avait rendu récemment visite à son frère pour l'informer d'une découverte qui ferait de lui un homme riche. Il lui avait même ramené un caillou.

Eadulf se frotta le menton.

— Je ne suis pas sûr de vous suivre.

— Il venait de la caverne. Morna avait découvert qu'elle recelait de l'or et il pensait faire fortune. Et Menma a attaqué l'auberge de Bressal afin de récupérer ce caillou.

— Pourquoi donc ?

— Parce que cette découverte devait rester secrète.

— Menma serait responsable de l'exploitation de ce gisement ? Je ne le pense pas suffisamment intelligent.

— Sur ce point, vous avez raison. Il y a quelqu'un d'autre derrière cette affaire. Ce qui nous ramène à Muadnat. Menma a reçu l'ordre de faire disparaître ce que Morna avait rapporté à son frère Bressal. Et nous nous trouvions par hasard à l'hôtellerie cette nuit-là.

Eadulf hocha la tête.

— Moi, je croyais que cette attaque avait été fomentée par Muadnat qui désirait se débarrasser d'Archú et pensait qu'il dormirait à l'auberge.

— Je partageais la même opinion que vous mais Archú et Scoth cheminaient à pied et, cette nuit-là, ils n'auraient pas dû atteindre l'hôtellerie ni y passer la nuit puisqu'ils n'avaient pas d'argent. Non, il fallait chercher la motivation ailleurs et nous l'avons découverte.

— Mais quand avez-vous acquis cette certitude ?

— Rappelez-vous le corps de l'inconnu à la ferme d'Archú, un homme qui n'était ni fermier ni guerrier. Ses mains calleuses et la poussière de roche sur ses vêtements m'ont alors suggéré…

Eadulf ouvrit de grands yeux.

— Vous aviez deviné qu'il était mineur ?

— Je vous ai également demandé s'il ne vous rappelait pas quelqu'un.

— Il ne me rappelait personne.

— Vous n'êtes pas assez observateur, Eadulf. Il ressemblait de façon frappante à Bressal. Ce cadavre était celui de l'infortuné Morna, le frère du tenancier de l'auberge.

Fidelma tomba alors dans un silence méditatif tandis qu'ils poursuivaient leur chemin dans la vallée d'Araglin.

Quand ils arrivèrent au *rath*, Crón, debout sur le seuil du siège de l'assemblée, semblait les attendre avec impatience.

CHAPITRE XVI

Crón les héla. Fidelma et Eadulf sautèrent à bas de leurs montures que le moine conduisit aux écuries tandis que la religieuse rejoignait la *tanist*. La vieille servante Dignait était en train de laver le sol de la salle à grande eau.

— Laissez-nous, Dignait, lui ordonna Crón.

Avant de disparaître par une porte latérale, la vieille femme jeta un regard suspicieux à Fidelma qui s'assit sur un banc. Après un temps d'hésitation, la *tanist* prit place à ses côtés.

Elles demeurèrent un instant silencieuses.

— Vous vouliez me parler ? demanda Fidelma.

Crón leva sur elle ses yeux d'un bleu de glace puis les baissa.

— Oui.

— Je suppose que vous avez vu Dubán ?

Crón rougit et hocha la tête.

— Je me suis permis de lui faire remarquer que je n'étais pas une idiote. Pensez-vous que je me contenterais longtemps de demi-vérités ? Je sais que vous haïssiez votre père et maintenant, si vous m'expliquiez pourquoi ?

— C'est un sujet douloureux.

— Mieux vaut aérer les secrets plutôt que de les laisser pourrir à force de suspicion et de fausses accusations.

— Teafa, elle aussi, détestait mon père.

— Pour quelle raison ?

— Il avait abusé de ses sœurs.

Fidelma s'attendait à cette réponse car, lors de son altercation avec le père Gormán, ce dernier avait déjà fait allusion à une famille incestueuse.

— Il les a abusées physiquement ? demanda-t-elle pour formuler le chef d'accusation avec plus de précision.

— Si par là vous entendez qu'il a couché avec elles, en effet.

— C'est Teafa qui vous en a informée ?

— Oui, il y a quelques années de cela. Mais je ne détestais pas mon père au point de vouloir le tuer. Et en vérité, vos investigations sur les meurtres d'Eber et Teafa n'avancent guère.

— Vous vous trompez car ce que vous m'avez confié signifie...

— Je vous dérange ?

Une voix masculine et doucereuse interrompit Fidelma à l'instant où elle se penchait vers sa voisine en baissant la voix.

Le père Gormán se tenait sur le seuil du siège de l'assemblée.

Fidelma comprit au regard appuyé de Crón qu'il valait mieux remettre cette conversation à plus tard. Contrariée, elle se leva.

— Vous ne nous dérangez pas car j'allais partir. J'ai eu une journée longue et fatigante. Crón, nous reparlerons de tout cela demain, lorsque j'aurai l'esprit plus clair.

Quand Fidelma émergea de la salle des bains, le repas du matin était servi et Eadulf avait commencé à manger. Fidelma alla s'asseoir, dit ses grâces en silence et attaqua avec appétit le pain et la viande froide.

— Je suppose que nous allons retourner à la mine avec des hommes de Dubán ? dit Eadulf. Je brûle de résoudre tous ces mystères.

Fidelma, plongée dans ses pensées, contemplait les champignons dans son écuelle. Leur peau était d'un brun-jaune pâle, leurs chapeaux couverts d'alvéoles spongieux. Quelque chose la dérangeait. Elle avait souvent dégusté ces *miotóg bhuí*, une espèce comestible qui poussait dans les prés, non loin des cours d'eau, au début de l'été. On les pochait à l'eau bouillante, pour leur ôter leur amertume, et ils étaient alors considérés comme un mets délicat. Pourquoi ceux-ci étaient-ils crus ?

En les examinant de plus près, une brusque appréhension la saisit. Ce n'était pas des champignons un peu passés, dont la tête jaunâtre avait foncé avec le temps. Elle avait toujours été brune. Elle releva les yeux sur Eadulf qui portait sa cuillère à sa bouche et lui tapa sur la main.

Il lâcha son couvert avec un petit cri de surprise.

— Vous en avez mangé beaucoup ? lui demanda Fidelma d'un ton pressant.

Il la fixa sans comprendre.

— La quasi-totalité de ce qui se trouvait dans mon assiette. Qu'avez-vous ? Ce sont des morilles, qui poussent également dans le South Folk.

— *Dia ár sábháil !* hurla Fidelma en sautant sur ses pieds.

Eadulf pâlit.

La fausse morille, qui ressemblait à s'y méprendre à la vraie, était un poison mortel quand on la consommait crue.

— Il n'y a pas de temps à perdre, vite, allez vous faire vomir.

Eadulf, qui avait étudié dans le grand collège de médecine de Tuaim Brecain, connaissait très bien le processus d'empoisonnement par les champignons vénéneux.

Il bondit vers le *fialtech*, oubliant, dans sa hâte, de faire une génuflexion avant d'y entrer afin de repousser les tentations du Malin, qui avait la réputation de s'y livrer à ses travaux les plus noirs.

— Buvez beaucoup d'eau ! cria Fidelma.

Il ne répondit rien.

Fidelma examina les écuelles. Aucune erreur. Quelqu'un avait délibérément tenté de les empoisonner. Pourquoi ? Ils s'approchaient de la résolution des énigmes d'Araglin et on cherchait à les éliminer. Furieuse, elle prit les écuelles et les jeta devant la porte de l'auberge. Le pichet et les gobelets d'hydromel suivirent.

Elle entendit Eadulf qui vomissait dans les toilettes.

Pinçant les lèvres, elle se dirigea à grands pas vers les cuisines, désertes. Au siège de l'assemblée, elle découvrit Grella qui faisait le ménage.

Quand Fidelma s'avança vers elle, la jeune fille parut nerveuse.

— Qui nous a servi notre repas à l'hôtellerie des invités ce matin ?

— Dignait, je suppose. Elle supervise tout.

— Vous l'avez vue accommoder les aliments ?

— Non. Quand je suis arrivée ici, Dignait parlait avec lady Cranat. Elle m'a demandé d'aller vous porter le plateau que je trouverais à la cuisine.

— Selon vous, c'est Dignait qui a tout préparé ?

— Oui, mais vous m'effrayez, ma sœur...

— Vous rappelez-vous quels mets étaient disposés dans les écuelles ?

— Pourquoi, vous ne les avez pas mangés ?

— Vous n'avez pas répondu à ma question.

— De la viande froide, du pain... des champignons, et à côté des pommes et un pichet d'hydromel.

— Les champignons, des fausses morilles, sont vénéneux.

La jeune fille pâlit. Son visage reflétait un choc dénué de toute culpabilité.

235

— Je l'ignorais, dit-elle d'un air horrifié.

— Où est Dignait ?

— Je crois qu'elle s'est rendue chez elle. Voulez-vous que je vous y conduise ?

Fidelma acquiesça et Grella l'emmena jusqu'à de vieilles maisons de bois ne comportant qu'une seule grande pièce, à la lisière du village. Elle s'arrêta devant une porte et Fidelma y frappa. Pas de réponse. Elle appela sans plus de succès puis pénétra à l'intérieur.

Un grand désordre l'attendait. Les couvertures du lit, des vêtements, des objets étaient éparpillés un peu partout.

Grella poussa une exclamation de surprise.

Fidelma examina rapidement les lieux. Était-ce Dignait ou un étranger qui avait procédé à une fouille de son logement ? Et où était passée cette femme ? Soudain, elle plissa les yeux en découvrant une petite trace rouge sur la table. En l'étudiant plus attentivement elle acquit la certitude que c'était du sang.

Elle se tourna vers Grella qui s'était mise à trembler.

— Vous feriez bien de retourner à votre travail, Grella. Quand vous en aurez terminé, allez rejoindre le frère saxon. Il s'est purgé mais, plus tard, il peut avoir besoin de votre aide.

La jeune fille plia le genou en signe d'acquiescement.

— Moi, je vais partir à la recherche de Dignait et je vous retrouverai à l'hôtellerie des invités.

Grella hocha la tête et partit en courant.

Fidelma retourna à l'hôtellerie où Eadulf l'attendait, le visage blême, tout en buvant régulièrement de l'eau.

— Comment vous sentez-vous ? lui demanda-t-elle avec angoisse.

Eadulf haussa les épaules d'un air sombre.

— Demandez-le-moi d'ici quelques heures, c'est alors que le poison fera effet. J'ai rendu la plus grande partie des champignons mais certainement pas la totalité.

236

— Dignait a disparu. Sa chambre a été fouillée et il y a une tache de sang sur sa table.

— Dieu du ciel, vous croyez que Dignait…

— C'est la première personne que je dois interroger. Grella viendra s'occuper de vous pendant mon absence.

— Je veux venir avec vous, protesta Eadulf.

Fidelma lui jeta un regard attendri et refusa catégoriquement.

— Mon ami, restez ici et continuez de vous purger.

Eadulf allait la contredire mais la lueur inflexible dans les yeux de Fidelma l'en dissuada.

Elle trouva Crón très abattue au siège de l'assemblée. La *tanist* se redressa en la voyant.

— Je viens de parler avec Grella.

— Avez-vous une idée de l'endroit où Dignait pourrait se trouver ?

Crón secoua la tête.

— Grella m'a dit que vous aviez déjà visité sa maison.

— L'endroit est désert, les affaires de Dignait sont bouleversées et j'ai repéré une tache de sang sur la table.

— Je vais demander que l'on organise immédiatement une fouille du *rath*.

— Où est votre mère ? On m'a rapporté qu'elle connaît Dignait mieux que personne et qu'elle s'est entretenue avec elle très tôt ce matin.

— Elle est partie pour sa chevauchée quotidienne avec le père Gormán.

— Faites-moi savoir quand elle reviendra.

Puis Fidelma se rendit chez Teafa.

Quand Gadra ouvrit la porte, il comprit à l'expression désolée de la religieuse qu'il s'était passé quelque chose de grave et s'effaça pour la laisser entrer.

— Vous vous êtes levée de bonne heure, Fidelma, et votre visage semble marqué par de graves préoccupations.

— Comment se porte celui dont vous avez la charge ?

— Móen ? Il dort encore. Nous nous sommes couchés tard car nous avons longuement discuté de sujets théologiques.

— Vraiment ? s'étonna Fidelma.

— Móen a une compréhension étonnante de la théologie, lui confirma Gadra. Et nous avons aussi envisagé son avenir.

— Je suppose qu'il ne désire pas rester ici ?

Gadra eut un petit rire triste.

— Après la façon dont on l'a traité ? Non, certainement pas.

— Je le comprends.

— Je lui ai suggéré un sanctuaire où il serait protégé des maux de ce monde, par exemple une abbaye comme Lios Mhór. Il aurait beaucoup à gagner à une existence bien réglée chez des religieux qui seraient en mesure de communiquer avec lui, car la plupart d'entre eux connaissent l'ogam. Ils s'adapteront rapidement à ma méthode qui n'est pas très compliquée, comme vous avez pu le constater par vous-même.

— Voilà une idée fort raisonnable. Mais elle s'accorde mal à votre philosophie.

— J'appartiens à un monde agonisant et Móen doit s'adapter à celui-ci.

Il fronça les sourcils.

— Mais vous semblez très préoccupée et je doute que cela concerne Móen. Je vous écoute, mon enfant.

— Je crains pour la vie de mon compagnon, Eadulf, dit d'un trait Fidelma. Quelqu'un a tenté de nous empoisonner ce matin.

Gadra demeura interdit.

— Mais par quel procédé ?

— Des champignons vénéneux. De fausses morilles.

— Crus, ils sont toxiques, mais on les consomme rarement en l'état.

— C'est justement parce qu'on nous a servi ces *miotóg bhuí* crus que j'y ai regardé à deux fois. Je n'y ai pas touché, mais frère Eadulf en avait ingéré une assez grande quantité avant que je l'arrête.

Gadra parut très alarmé.

— Il faut qu'il se purge immédiatement.

— Il ne cesse de boire de l'eau afin de vomir le plus possible.

— Sait-on qui est responsable de cette tentative d'assassinat ?

— Probablement Dignait. Mais elle a disparu du *rath*. Sa maison est dans un désordre indescriptible et j'ai découvert une trace de sang sur sa table.

Gadra haussa les sourcils.

— Votre devoir exige que vous me posiez une question à laquelle je vais répondre sans plus attendre. Ni moi ni Móen n'avons quitté notre logement ce matin.

— Je ne vous ai pas soupçonné un seul instant, Gadra.

L'ermite se saisit de son *sacculus*, posé sur un siège, et en tira une petite fiole.

— Je ne me déplace jamais sans mes remèdes. Voilà une infusion, un mélange d'armoise et de lierre terrestre. Dites à votre ami saxon d'en boire la totalité mélangée à un peu d'eau. Cela l'aidera à vider son estomac.

Fidelma prit la bouteille d'un air hésitant.

— Prenez-la, insista le druide.

Et il ajouta avec un sourire :

— À moins que vous ne me soupçonniez de vouloir attenter à ses jours.

— Je vous suis très reconnaissante, Gadra, répondit Fidelma d'un air contrit.

— Et maintenant filez, et donnez-moi des nouvelles de votre ami.

Fidelma retourna à l'hôtellerie où Eadulf semblait très mal en point. Des cernes violacés étaient apparus autour de ses yeux et de sa bouche.

— Gadra vous envoie ceci, à prendre immédiatement.

— Qu'est-ce ?

— Un mélange d'armoise et de lierre terrestre.

— Une mixture destinée à nettoyer l'estomac, je suppose.

Il ôta le bouchon de la bouteille qu'il renifla avec une grimace de dégoût. Puis il en versa le contenu dans un gobelet, y ajouta de l'eau, fixa le remède d'un air dubitatif et l'avala d'un trait.

Il fut alors pris d'une terrible quinte de toux.

— Eh bien, balbutia-t-il quand il retrouva la parole, si le poison ne me tue pas, il est sûr que cette potion va m'achever.

— Comment vous sentez-vous ? lui demanda Fidelma au comble de l'inquiétude.

— Mal. Mais il faut au moins une heure avant que le poison ne fasse son effet et...

— Que se passe-t-il ? cria Fidelma devant ses yeux exorbités.

Il porta la main à sa bouche et courut vers le *fialtech*.

— Je peux vous aider, Eadulf ? gémit-elle quand elle le vit réapparaître un instant plus tard.

— Non, je le crains. Si je retrouve Dignait et si c'est elle qui... oh mon Dieu !

Et il se précipita à nouveau vers les toilettes.

À cet instant, on frappa à la porte et Crón entra.

— Dignait a disparu du *rath*, annonça-t-elle. Cela semble confirmer sa culpabilité.

Fidelma considéra la *tanist* d'un air morose.

— Je m'y attendais.

— J'ai envoyé un homme prévenir Dubán.

— Où se trouve-t-il en ce moment ?

— Dans la vallée du Black Marsh où il enquête sur la mort de Muadnat.

Elle poussa un profond soupir.

— J'ai du mal à croire que Dignait ait tenté de vous assassiner.

— Ne tirons aucune conclusion hâtive, répondit Fidelma, nous connaîtrons la part qu'elle a prise à ce forfait quand nous l'aurons dûment interrogée.

— Elle s'est toujours montrée une excellente servante pour notre famille.

— Oui, elle jouit d'une très bonne réputation.

En émergeant du *fialtech*, Eadulf se força à arborer une contenance détachée, mais Crón l'étudiait déjà avec une grimace de dégoût.

— Vous êtes malade, Saxon, lui lança la *tanist*.

— Votre perspicacité vous honore, Crón, répliqua Eadulf avec humour.

— Euh… s'il y a quelque chose que je… que nous…

Eadulf s'assit.

— Nous ne pouvons qu'attendre et je préférerais le faire seul.

Fidelma lui sourit.

— Vous avez raison, mon ami, nous vous avons déjà assez ennuyé. Reposez-vous, la jeune Grella viendra prendre de vos nouvelles.

Elle entraîna Crón hors de la pièce.

— À propos d'autre chose, où est passé Crítán ? demanda-t-elle quand elles se retrouvèrent dehors. S'est-il calmé depuis hier ?

— Il n'était pas suffisamment ivre pour ne pas se rappeler ce qui s'est passé. Vous l'avez humilié et il ne vous le pardonnera jamais.

— Il s'est mortifié tout seul, rectifia Fidelma.

— Après avoir tempêté en ma présence hier au soir, juste avant que vous ne rentriez au *rath*, il est parti à cheval en hurlant qu'il vendrait ses services à un chef capable d'apprécier ses talents.

— Figurez-vous que je m'en doutais. Malheureusement, il est surtout très doué pour l'arrogance et l'intimidation, et il trouvera toujours des hommes peu scrupuleux capables d'exploiter ce type de disposition.

Crón ouvrit de grands yeux.

— Vous ne pensez tout de même pas qu'il a conspiré avec Dignait pour…

— Je perds rarement mon temps en spéculations inutiles.

Une idée lui vint à l'esprit, puis elle fut distraite par Menma, le chef des troupeaux, qui sortait du *rath* monté sur une robuste jument. Il tirait derrière lui un âne chargé d'un lourd panier de bât.

— Où s'en va-t-il ? s'enquit Fidelma.

— Je lui ai demandé de se rendre dans les hautes terres du Sud pour y rattraper quelques chevaux égarés. Avez-vous besoin de ses services ? Désirez-vous que je le rappelle ?

— Non, je vous remercie.

Pour l'instant, Fidelma répugnait à se laisser distraire du cours de ses pensées, et elle releva la tête avec irritation en entendant des chevaux traverser le pont de bois. Cranat et le père Gormán croisèrent Menma sans le saluer.

Crón s'avança aussitôt vers sa mère pour lui annoncer les dernières nouvelles. Fidelma se tint en retrait afin d'observer l'attitude des deux femmes. Il semblait qu'une curieuse distance s'était établie entre elles.

Le père Gormán, qui avait écouté, descendit de son cheval dont il tendit la bride à un garçon d'écurie et s'approcha de Fidelma.

— Frère Eadulf est un adepte de la doctrine romaine, lança-t-il avec un empressement déplacé. Sa vie est en danger et je dois pourvoir à ses besoins.

— Ses besoins sont très bien pourvus, père Gormán.

— Je voulais parler d'une assistance spirituelle, de la confession et des rites de notre Église.

— Il n'est pas encore prêt à trépasser. *Dum vita est spes est.* Tant qu'il y a de la vie il y a de l'espoir, lança Fidelma avec mordant, puis elle s'avança vers Cranat : Il faut que je vous parle.

Celle-ci la dévisagea d'un air hautain.

— La coutume veut que vous demandiez audience.

— Frère Eadulf est entre la vie et la mort et je n'ai pas de temps à perdre avec l'étiquette. Ce matin, vous vous êtes entretenue avec Dignait. L'auriez-vous par hasard vue préparer les repas pour l'hôtellerie des invités ?

— Je ne me rends jamais dans les cuisines, répliqua Cranat avec une moue dégoûtée. Dignait est venue me trouver pour me parler de sujets domestiques. À un moment donné, Grella est arrivée et Dignait lui a ordonné d'aller vous apporter le plateau qui vous était destiné.

— Dignait a disparu. Avez-vous une idée de l'endroit où elle pourrait se cacher ?

Cranat toisa Fidelma avec dédain.

— Non, car la vie privée des serviteurs ne me concerne en rien. Et maintenant, avec votre permission...

Elle se détourna sans laisser à Fidelma le temps de poursuivre.

Quant au père Gormán, il n'avait pas bougé d'un pouce.

— J'insiste, ma sœur, pour voir le frère saxon agonisant. Vous portez en partie la faute de son malheur car vous avez relâché ce suppôt de Satan tout en sachant qu'il pouvait attenter à nos vies.

— Êtes-vous certain d'être un avocat de la doctrine chrétienne ?

Le père Gormán rougit.

— Davantage que vous, ce qui n'est pas difficile. Le Christ a dit : « Et si ta main est pour toi une occasion de péché, coupe-la : mieux vaut pour toi entrer manchot dans la Vie que de t'en aller avec tes deux mains dans la géhenne, dans le feu qui ne s'éteint pas[1]. » Il est grand temps que nous tranchions. Détruisez le démon afin qu'il soit expulsé de notre communauté.

— Frère Eadulf n'aura jamais besoin de votre bénédiction, Gormán de Cill Uird, répliqua Fidelma d'une voix très calme. Il ne mourra pas.

1. Marc, 9, 43, 44. (*N.d.T.*)

— Êtes-vous Dieu pour décider de ces choses ? ricana le prêtre.

— Non, mais ma volonté est aussi forte que celle d'Adam.

Le père Gormán, comprenant qu'il serait malséant de poursuivre la polémique, serra les dents et partit à grands pas vers sa chapelle dont il claqua la porte avec force.

Crón le suivit des yeux d'un air stupéfait.

— Si jamais vous avez besoin de mes services, vous savez où me trouver, dit-elle avant de s'éclipser.

Fidelma se dirigeait vers l'hôtellerie des invités quand Grella vint à sa rencontre en courant.

— Ma sœur, ma sœur…

Au visage de la jeune fille, Fidelma s'immobilisa et le cœur lui manqua.

— C'est frère Eadulf ?

— Venez vite, haleta Grella, mais Fidelma courait déjà.

Eadulf gisait sur sa paillasse, tremblant de tous ses membres, les yeux fermés et la sueur ruisselant sur son visage.

Fidelma tomba à genoux et prit la main chaude et moite du malade. Puis elle chercha son pouls qui battait irrégulièrement.

— Cela fait combien de temps qu'il est ainsi ? demanda-t-elle à Grella qui l'avait rejointe.

— Je l'ai trouvé dans cet état.

— Allez chercher Gadra, l'ermite.

Comme la jeune fille hésitait, elle s'écria :

— Dans la maison de Teafa, pressez-vous !

Eadulf ne la reconnaissait plus.

Elle se leva, alla chercher un pichet d'eau et un torchon, et s'employa à rafraîchir le visage congestionné de son ami.

Un instant plus tard, Gadra arrivait, suivi de Grella. D'un geste ferme il écarta Fidelma, se pencha sur le malade et se redressa.

— Soit sa fièvre le sauvera, soit elle l'emportera avec elle.

Fidelma se tordit les mains.

— N'y a-t-il rien que nous puissions entreprendre ?

— Le résidu de poison qu'il a ingéré va le tourmenter quelques heures encore. La température ne cesse de grimper. Si elle cède, nous aurons gagné. Sinon…

Il haussa les épaules.

Une rage impuissante s'empara de Fidelma tandis qu'elle contemplait le visage décomposé de son ami. Elle comprit à quel point sa vie serait affreuse si jamais Eadulf la quittait. Elle se rappela son trouble et sa tristesse quand elle l'avait laissé à Rome pour retourner en Irlande, les mois d'amère solitude qu'elle avait traversés. Dans son pays natal, une mélancolie insondable l'avait envahie, comme si un élément essentiel de son existence lui avait été arraché. Il lui avait fallu beaucoup de temps pour surmonter ces émotions contradictoires.

En réalité, il lui était difficile d'admettre un attachement sentimental. À dix-sept ans, elle était tombée amoureuse d'un jeune guerrier du nom de Cian. Il appartenait à la garde d'élite du haut roi de Tara. À l'époque, elle étudiait le droit avec le grand brehon Morann. Elle était jeune, insouciante et très éprise. Mais Cian l'avait abandonnée pour une autre. Elle avait alors perdu goût à la vie. Le temps passant, elle avait surmonté son chagrin, mais ne s'était jamais vraiment remise de cette douloureuse expérience. Si on y réfléchissait, se l'était-elle seulement autorisé ?

Eadulf de Seaxmund's Ham était le seul homme de son âge dont elle appréciait vraiment la compagnie. Avec lui, elle se sentait à l'aise et s'exprimait librement. Au début, elle lui lançait des défis sur des sujets théoriques et ces échanges formaient la base de leurs relations empreintes de gaieté et de bonne humeur. Leurs opinions et leurs philosophies divergentes, leurs débats sur des points de théologie et de culture étaient un moyen de se taquiner. Et même quand ils s'affrontaient un peu vivement, jamais l'inimitié ne s'en mêlait.

Pendant toute une année, Fidelma s'était languie d'Eadulf et en apprenant qu'il avait été envoyé comme émissaire auprès de Théodore, le nouvel archevêque de Cantorbéry représentant du Saint-Père dans les royaumes anglo-saxons, une grande joie l'avait envahie. Qu'il séjourne maintenant à la cour de son frère, Colgú de Cashel, ressemblait à un coup du destin.

Mais le destin pouvait-il se montrer assez cruel pour lui ravir Eadulf ?

— Laissez-moi veiller ce pauvre moine pendant que vous vous efforcerez de découvrir qui est responsable de cette ignominie, lui dit Gadra. Au moindre changement de son état, je vous ferai quérir.

Au bord des larmes, Fidelma fixa le visage douloureux de son ami.

— Merci, Gadra, murmura-t-elle d'une petite voix. Grella vous assistera. Vous le voulez bien, Grella ?

— Oh, ma sœur, croyez-vous que je serai punie ? dit la jeune fille en se frappant la poitrine. C'est moi qui vous ai apporté la nourriture !

Fidelma secoua la tête avec un sourire triste.

— Bien sûr que non. Mais si Gadra a besoin de votre aide, assurez-moi qu'il pourra compter sur vous.

— Je suis à son entière disposition, balbutia la jeune fille d'un air accablé.

Fidelma s'arracha à la contemplation d'Eadulf et sortit de l'hôtellerie. Là, elle réalisa que pour la première fois depuis longtemps, elle déambulait sans but précis, incapable de prendre une décision.

CHAPITRE XVII

Fidelma sauta de son cheval devant la maisonnette de plain-pied construite en rondins. Elle avait quitté le *rath* sur un coup de tête, sans savoir où elle se dirigeait. Depuis tout à l'heure, elle était obsédée par un vers de *L'Énéide* en relation avec Crítán. *Dux femina facti !* Et puis elle avait vu la chaumière nichée dans un méandre de la rivière.

Une femme se tenait dans le jardin, occupée à soigner ses plantes. Elle regarda Fidelma approcher avec intérêt. Plus très jeune mais bien faite, petite, blonde, avec un visage aux pommettes hautes, elle était habillée de vêtements aux couleurs criardes.

Fidelma attacha les rênes de son étalon à un pieu.

— Bienvenue en ma demeure, dit la femme. Mais... savez-vous où vous êtes, ma sœur ?

Fidelma lui sourit.

— On m'a dit que c'était la maison de Clídna. M'aurait-on mal renseignée ?

La jolie blonde secoua la tête.

— Je suis bien Clídna et je tiens un *meirdrech loc*.

— Vous faites commerce de vos faveurs ? Dans ce cas, on m'a bien informée.

— Les religieuses rendent rarement visite à une femme aux secrets, comme moi, à moins de vouloir me convertir à un nouveau mode de vie.

Fidelma se dit que cette métaphore de « femme aux secrets » convenait bien à celle qui l'accueillait.

— *Dux femina facti !* dit-elle à voix haute. Et tout commença avec une femme. C'est parce que vous êtes la dépositaire de tant de confidences que je tenais à vous rencontrer, Clídna.

La prostituée la regarda d'un air surpris.

— Donc, je ne vous offenserai pas en vous priant d'accepter mon hospitalité ?

— Pas du tout.

— Alors venez vous rafraîchir, mais je n'ai pas de grands vins ou d'hydromels raffinés à vous offrir.

Une fois à l'intérieur de la chaumière, elle indiqua un siège à Fidelma, prit une marmite qui cuisait sur le feu et la posa sur la table.

— Je viens de préparer une infusion.

— Que contient-elle ? demanda Fidelma en humant l'arôme forestier qu'elle dégageait.

— Eh bien, j'incise un bouleau pour en tirer de la sève que je fais chauffer avec des aiguilles de pin. Ensuite, je verse la mixture sur des feuilles de roseau afin de la filtrer.

Elle tendit un gobelet à Fidelma qui goûta la tisane dont le goût était original mais tout à fait plaisant.

— C'est excellent, jugea la religieuse.

— Rien de comparable à ce que vous buvez au palais de Cashel.

Fidelma haussa les sourcils.

— Donc vous savez qui je suis ?

— Vous oubliez ma fonction de femme aux secrets, répondit l'autre avec une lueur amusée dans ses yeux noisette. Je suis la dépositaire des murmures et des rumeurs.

— Parlez-moi de vous. Comment en êtes-vous arrivée à cette situation ?

— J'étais la fille d'Uí Fidgente, faits prisonniers après la bataille de Ford of Apples où Dicuil, fils de

Fergus, fut assassiné par les hommes de Cashel et retenus comme otages.

« Les otages n'avaient aucun droit dans cette société où on les exploitait jusqu'à ce qu'une rançon soit payée ou que la génération suivante soit automatiquement libérée.

« Étant née avant la capture de mes parents, on ne me reconnaissait aucun droit à l'intérieur du clan et voilà pourquoi je suis devenue une femme aux secrets, sans prix de l'honneur, sans statut, sans prix de mariage. Et sans propriété.

— À qui appartient votre maison ?

— Elle est située sur les terres d'Agdae.

— Agdae du Black Marsh ?

— Oui, je lui paye un loyer et je n'ai pas honte de l'existence que je mène.

— Je le comprends tout à fait.

— D'habitude, ceux de votre condition, par exemple le père Gormán, voudraient me faire flageller et me chasser de ce pays.

— Le père Gormán est un fanatique.

Clídna manifesta sa surprise.

— Ne me dites pas que vous m'approuvez ?

— Vous ou la profession que vous exercez ?

— Vous les distinguez ?

— Mon mentor, Morann de Tara, m'a enseigné de ne jamais prendre sur moi les mesures d'un manteau destiné à un autre. Cependant, je ne suis pas venue vous entretenir de votre vie, Clídna, mais vous demander de me fournir quelques informations.

La femme haussa les épaules.

— Je suis très au fait de ce qui se passe ici.

— Justement. *Dux femina facti !* Vous avez très bien pu recueillir certaines informations.

— Mais pas la solution du mystère qui vous tient en échec. Si beaucoup de gens détestaient Eber et souhaitaient sa mort, j'ignore combien étaient prêts à le tuer.

— Peut-être qu'Agdae avait des motifs suffisants ?

249

Clídna rosit et secoua la tête.

— Il était à Lios Mhór quand Eber a été assassiné.

— Il aurait pu louer les services d'hommes de main.

— Cela ne lui ressemble pas. C'est un homme impétueux, souvent aveuglé par sa loyauté envers son cousin Muadnat, mais il n'est pas violent.

— Il a proféré des menaces à l'encontre du jeune Archú et, pendant que nous parlons, il est peut-être en train de trouver un moyen de le tuer.

Clídna eut un gloussement de gorge.

— Vous êtes mal informée !

Fidelma haussa les sourcils.

— Vous en êtes certaine ?

Clídna se leva, ouvrit une porte qui communiquait avec une pièce plongée dans l'obscurité et fit signe à Fidelma de la suivre en posant un doigt sur ses lèvres.

La pièce mal aérée sentait l'alcool et un homme ronflait, étendu sur un lit en bois.

Clídna s'avança sur le parquet et alla repousser un volet. La lumière inonda la pièce, l'homme gémit et Fidelma n'eut aucun mal à reconnaître Agdae. Clídna referma le volet et les deux femmes regagnèrent la pièce principale.

— Depuis la mort de Muadnat, il n'a pas dessoûlé, expliqua Clídna. La mort de son cousin l'a beaucoup affecté mais c'est un homme doux, cela je peux vous l'assurer.

Fidelma buvait sa tisane d'un air pensif.

— Eber vous rendait-il visite ?

Clídna secoua la tête en riant. Elle semblait une femme plutôt gaie.

— Je n'étais pas à son goût car je ne suis pas une jeune fille ni une de ses parentes.

— Pourquoi les gens le haïssaient-ils ?

— Il se conduisait avec eux avec la rapacité d'un vautour.

— Dans ce cas, je m'explique mal sa réputation de gentillesse, de générosité et de courtoisie.

— À Cashel, Eber recherchait le pouvoir. Il se targuait d'être l'ami de tout le monde et il achetait les gens pour se gagner un siège à l'assemblée du roi.

— « Malheur, lorsque tous les hommes diront du bien de vous[1] ! » grommela Fidelma qui sourit devant la perplexité de Clídna. C'est une citation de l'Évangile de Luc, reprit-elle. En d'autres termes, un homme qui prétend avoir beaucoup d'amis n'en a aucun. Parlez-moi de ceux qui ne le portaient pas dans leur cœur.

— Par qui voulez-vous que je commence ?

— D'abord sa famille proche.

— Excellent début. Ils le haïssaient tous.

— Cranat ?

— Sans aucun doute. Elle considérait qu'elle s'était mariée au-dessous de sa condition de princesse des Déisi. Vivre en Araglin lui fait horreur et elle a épousé Eber pour son argent. Puisque vous aimez les citations latines, en voici une qu'un… ami m'a apprise.

Elle sourit.

— *Quaerenda pecunia primum est virtus post nummos.*

— Un vers des *Épîtres* d'Horace. Cherchez l'argent car la vertu vient après les richesses.

Clídna hocha la tête.

— Et Crón est la fille unique d'Eber ?

— Oui, dit-elle en appuyant sa joue sur sa main.

— Quand Cranat a-t-elle déserté la couche d'Eber ?

— Crón avait alors douze ou treize ans. On en a fait des gorges chaudes.

— Comment cela ?

— Eber préférait la compagnie de sa fille à celle de sa femme.

Fidelma se renversa sur son siège.

---

1. Luc, 6, 26. (*N.d.T.*)

— Encore un peu de tisane ? demanda Clídna d'un air détaché.

Fidelma lui tendit son gobelet.

— Et Crón, que ressentait-elle pour son père ?

— Ils entretenaient des relations étroites et elle travaillait avec lui. Elle a été élue *tanist* malgré son extrême jeunesse. Ici, nous sommes une communauté rurale, ma sœur, et les gens étaient furieux.

— Vraiment ?

— Une jeune fille nommée héritière présomptive du chef de la communauté !

— Cela s'est déjà vu. Dans les cinq royaumes, les femmes peuvent aspirer aux plus hautes fonctions.

— Mais chez les paysans, elles sont rarement élues. Sans compter que Crón prenait la place de Muadnat.

Fidelma tressaillit.

— En tant que cousin d'Eber, qui n'avait pas d'héritier mâle, Muadnat était *tanist* depuis longtemps. Puis Eber le déshérita en faveur de sa fille. On affirme qu'il a dépensé beaucoup d'argent pour soudoyer des membres du conseil.

Fidelma sauta sur ses pieds.

— Réveillez Agdae, je vous prie.

Clídna allait protester mais l'expression résolue de Fidelma l'en dissuada.

Il leur fallut de la patience pour amener Agdae à reprendre conscience. Assis sur le lit, il se frotta les yeux, l'esprit embrumé par la beuverie.

— Écoutez-moi attentivement, Agdae, lança Fidelma d'une voix coupante. Je veux que vous me disiez la vérité, sinon votre vie pourrait être menacée. Vous me comprenez ?

Agdae poussa un grognement.

— Quand Muadnat a-t-il été destitué par le *derbfhine* de la maison des chefs d'Araglin ?

Agdae la fixait d'un air vague.

— Je vous écoute.

— Quand ? soupira Agdae. Oh, il y a trois semaines.

— Et vous appartenez au *derbfhine* ?

Agdae se passa la main dans ses cheveux emmêlés et hocha la tête.

— Donnez-moi quelque chose à boire.

— Vous avez voté pour Muadnat ?

— Forcément, qu'est-ce…

— Qui d'autre a voté pour lui ?

Agdae laissa tomber sa tête sur sa poitrine et Fidelma le secoua.

— Arrêtez ! gémit-il. Juste Cranat, Teafa et moi, ah oui, et Menma. Personne d'autre.

— Menma est membre du *derbfhine* ?

— En tant que proche cousin d'Eber, il avait droit à une voix, intervint Clídna.

Abruti par la boisson, Agdae retomba dans sa torpeur. Fidelma s'attarda un instant puis rejoignit la pièce principale avec Clídna.

— Crón a été élue *tanist* il y a juste trois semaines et je sais qu'elle entretient une liaison avec Dubán. Comment décririez-vous les relations de Dubán et d'Eber ?

Clídna fit la grimace.

— Dubán détestait le chef.

— Pourtant, il était le commandant de ses gardes. Eber se doutait-il de son aversion à son égard ?

— Eber ne s'intéressait qu'à lui-même et assez peu à son entourage. Il était sensible à la flatterie et quand il se découvrait des ennemis, il les réduisait à sa merci en les achetant. Quand Dubán a réapparu après bien des années d'absence pour lui offrir ses services, Eber fut flatté qu'un guerrier rendu célèbre par les combats qu'il avait livrés aux Uí Fidgente vienne le solliciter.

— Je vois.

— Cependant, si vous soupçonnez Dubán d'avoir tué Eber, je vous engage à ne pas poursuivre dans cette voie. Dubán est un homme ambitieux et résolu, mais il suit un code de l'honneur. Il n'aurait pas hésité à tuer Eber en combat singulier mais il ne l'aurait jamais égorgé la nuit.

— J'ai vu des gens très honorables recourir à des moyens que l'on n'aurait jamais imaginés.

— De tous les habitants d'Araglin et malgré la répulsion que lui inspirait Eber, Dubán est le meurtrier le plus improbable.

— À quoi attribuez-vous son inimitié envers Eber ?

— C'est une histoire qui remonte à loin. Quand Dubán était jeune, un événement que j'ignore l'a poussé à chercher fortune dans les armées des rois de Cashel.

— Si vous étiez à ma place, sur qui porteraient vos soupçons ?

Clídna fit la moue.

— Vous ne vous offenserez pas de ma franchise ?

— Au contraire.

— Ce que je vais vous dire risque de vous déplaire.

— Aucune importance. Je place mes pas dans la voie de la justice, quel que soit l'endroit où elle me conduise. *Vincit omnia veritas*, la vérité triomphe de tout.

— Le père Gormán haïssait Eber. Ce fanatique passe son temps à menacer les gens des feux de l'enfer. Il a tenté d'intimider Eber et Teafa.

— De qui l'avez-vous appris ?

— De ce gamin arrogant qui prétend être un guerrier. Il m'a souvent rendu visite.

— Crítán ?

— Lui-même. Un soir qu'il était soûl, il est venu ici et il m'a raconté que le père Gormán avait prononcé de violentes diatribes contre Eber et Teafa. Il les a accusés de nombreux péchés, ajoutant que pour eux aucune fournaise ne serait assez brûlante pour les punir, ni l'éternité assez longue.

— Quand cela s'est-il passé ?

— D'après Crítán, il y a deux semaines. Eber fut tellement outragé qu'il frappa le père Gormán.

254

— Il a frappé un prêtre ? s'étonna Fidelma. Y avait-il des témoins ?

— Crítán, qui se trouvait dans le fenil, a assisté à la scène qui s'est déroulée dans les étables, mais ils ne l'ont pas remarqué.

— Sur quoi portait la dispute ?

— Il vous faudra interroger Crítán.

— Cela m'étonnerait qu'il se confie à moi. Mais ne vous inquiétez pas, si vous me rapportez ses paroles, vous ne serez impliquée dans aucune procédure. J'y veillerai personnellement.

— Crítán, qui s'était endormi, a été réveillé par des éclats de voix. Le prêtre, Eber et Teafa se querellaient. Il n'a pas entendu précisément de quoi il s'agissait mais le père Gormán réprimandait le chef et sa sœur pour leur manque de moralité. Móen a été mentionné. Et Eber a frappé le prêtre.

— Et alors ?

— Le père Gormán est tombé à terre en criant qu'Eber paierait ce geste de sa vie.

— Vous êtes sûre ?

— Crítán l'affirme.

— Vous souvenez-vous des termes exacts de l'échange… selon Crítán ?

— Le père Gormán se serait exclamé : « Vous serez foudroyé par le ciel pour avoir osé me toucher », ou quelque chose dans ce genre.

— Le ciel… il n'a pas dit qu'il s'en chargerait lui-même ?

Clídna secoua la tête.

— Et Agdae… est-il un propriétaire accommodant ?

— Ni pire ni meilleur qu'un autre.

— Mais il a votre préférence, non ?

— Rien n'interdit de rêver au-dessus de sa condition, admit Clídna en battant des cils.

— Et Muadnat, quelle opinion aviez-vous de lui ?

— Une tête brûlée. Il n'écoutait personne.

— Muadnat et Agdae fréquentaient tous les deux votre… maison ?

Clídna se mit à rire.

— Tout comme la moitié des hommes d'Araglin. Je n'en ai pas honte. C'est mon métier.

— Les auriez-vous, par hasard, entendus parler d'une mine ?

— En Araglin ?

— Oui. Par exemple au Black Marsh.

— Non, ni là ni ailleurs.

Fidelma était déçue.

— Remarquez… c'est peut-être sans intérêt mais… Menma a une fois signalé…

Fidelma attendait, vivement intéressée par cette brusque incursion du nom du rouquin dans la conversation.

— … Menma a mentionné un homme. Selon lui, il avait découvert un caillou qui ferait sa fortune.

— Vous êtes sûre ?

— Je n'y ai pas compris grand-chose. Menma vient souvent ici et il boit plus que de raison. Il y a quelques semaines, alors qu'il était ivre, il a commencé à discourir sur les richesses du sous-sol. Et puis il a parlé de cet homme qui connaissait le moyen de transformer les pierres en richesses qui surpasseraient celles d'Eber.

— A-t-il donné son nom ?

— Quelque chose comme Mór… Mór…

— Morna ?

— Il me semble, oui. Maintenant que j'y pense, ne peut-on extraire des métaux précieux des rochers ?

— Et Muadnat, a-t-il abordé le même sujet ?

— Non. Mais si cela peut vous aider, à cette époque, Menma et Muadnat semblaient très liés. Muadnat ne s'était jamais montré très amical avec le chef des troupeaux auparavant. Je le sais parce qu'Agdae s'est plaint que Muadnat et Menma allaient souvent chasser ensemble dans les collines et il se sentait exclu.

Fidelma se leva avec des gestes lents.

— Clídna, je vous remercie de votre hospitalité et j'ai apprécié votre aide, croyez-le.

Clídna parut sceptique.

— Si vous le dites.

— Je vous souhaite beaucoup de bonheur dans votre vie.

Fidelma sortit de la maisonnette, sauta sur son cheval et se dirigea vers la vallée du Black Marsh, absorbée dans ses pensées.

CHAPITRE XVIII

Elle avait d'abord songé à partir à la recherche de Dubán. Peut-être avait-il découvert où se cachait Dignait ? Même si Clídna lui assurait que le robuste guerrier n'était pas le premier sur la liste des suspects, Fidelma demeurait méfiante. Si Dubán détestait tant Eber, pourquoi était-il revenu en Araglin pour se mettre à son service ? Et s'il était sincèrement épris de Crón, la mort d'Eber leur bénéficiait à tous les deux. Le couple la troublait par sa facilité à mentir. Tout en réfléchissant, Fidelma prit la direction de la mine.

L'excursion fut pénible, car, pour éviter d'éventuelles rencontres, Fidelma emprunta des chemins détournés. Au plus profond d'elle-même, elle pressentait que les différents éléments de ses investigations trouvaient graduellement leur place dans l'entrelacs de la toile d'araignée. Maintenant, elle se rapprochait du centre, où l'image brouillée d'un grand manipulateur l'attendait, tissant les fils.

Elle pénétra dans la forêt qui menait à la clairière où Menma était apparu devant l'entrée d'une grotte. À chaque instant, elle craignait qu'on ne détecte sa présence et elle redoubla de prudence. Combien de mineurs creusaient cette galerie dont elle présageait qu'elle lui fournirait une des clés de cette énigme aux multiples ramifications ?

Au passage, elle remarqua les glands jaunes des chênes, l'éclosion des fleurs d'aubépine, blanches, rouges et roses, la fin de la floraison des ifs, les feuilles toutes neuves, brillantes et vernissées des hêtres. Ce cadre idyllique où la mort et le crime étaient embusqués lui serrait le cœur.

Soudain, son cheval fit un écart en entendant le glapissement haut perché d'un renard traquant sa proie.

Fidelma poussa un soupir. Ici, les hommes n'étaient pas les seuls à exercer leur cruauté. Des prédateurs y dévoraient leurs victimes sans défense.

Elle approchait du lieu où, avec Eadulf, ils avaient attaché leurs montures. Elle descendit de son étalon qu'elle laissa au même endroit et poursuivit à pied. À peine avait-elle parcouru quelques toises qu'elle entendit des bruits de sabots et se coucha à terre dans le sous-bois. Sur la route, un cheval arrivait du campement au galop, une silhouette féminine couchée sur son encolure, son manteau bicolore flottant au vent. Et c'est alors que Fidelma entendit un cri. Elle se redressa et s'avança avec précaution jusqu'à la clairière. Devant la grotte, deux chevaux sellés attendaient, de belles bêtes qui n'appartenaient certainement pas à des paysans. Elle s'abrita derrière des buissons.

La lourde charrette avait disparu, le feu n'était plus qu'un tas de cendres charbonneux, mais les outils n'avaient pas bougé de place. Seuls le souffle de la brise et le chant des oiseaux rompaient le silence.

Elle s'apprêtait à s'avancer en direction de la caverne quand, soudain, s'éleva un hurlement strident qui la figea sur place. Un homme hors d'haleine apparut, qui se mit à courir vers les chevaux.

C'était Menma, le rouquin. Le chef des troupeaux avait presque atteint sa monture quand une seconde silhouette sortit d'un pas tranquille de la grotte. Elle portait un arc.

— Menma !

La voix résonna dans les collines.

L'homme se retourna. Toute son attitude trahissait une terreur sans nom.

— Pour l'amour de Dieu, bafouilla-t-il, je peux vous payer ! Je peux…

Puis il attrapa l'épée qui pendait à sa selle et fit face pour affronter son poursuivant, fonçant sur lui en agitant son arme avec l'énergie du désespoir.

L'autre banda son arc, la flèche siffla, le vacher tomba à la renverse, la poitrine transpercée, son épée vola en l'air et il se tordit un instant sur le sol, puis il ne bougea plus.

Quand l'archer atteignit le corps inerte, il le considéra d'un air méprisant, enfonça la pointe de sa botte dans ses côtes, puis tira d'un coup sec sur la flèche qu'il remit dans son carquois. Du sang vermeil coula de la blessure mortelle. L'homme sauta sur sa monture et rejoignit la route en tirant le cheval de sa victime derrière lui.

Fidelma reconnut Dubán.

Accablée et transie, il lui fallut un certain temps pour reprendre ses esprits et se diriger à pas lents vers le cadavre de Menma. Là, elle fit une génuflexion et dit une prière pour le repos de son âme. Elle n'appréciait guère le chef de troupeaux à l'odeur nauséabonde, mais méritait-il une telle fin ? Quel motif avait poussé Dubán à abattre le rouquin de sang-froid ?

Son œil fut attiré par quelque chose qui dépassait de la ceinture du vacher et ne lui seyait guère. Elle se baissa et tira sur une feuille de vélin qui laissa échapper un petit crucifix de facture romaine qu'elle ramassa. Les reflets rouges signalaient de l'or mêlé de cuivre. Quant au parchemin, il portait une inscription en latin qu'elle traduisit facilement : « Si vous voulez connaître la réponse aux morts d'Araglin, regardez sous la ferme de l'usurpateur Archú. »

Elle fronça les sourcils. Le texte était correctement écrit, sans aucune faute de grammaire. Et le document glissé dans la ceinture de Menma avait échappé à

Dubán. Elle rangea les deux objets dans son *marsupium*.

— *Terra es, terram ibis*, murmura-t-elle.

Tu es poussière et tu retourneras à la poussière. N'était-ce pas la seule certitude en ce bas monde ?

Puis elle se détourna du corps. Maintenant que Dubán s'en était allé, il ne résonnait plus aucun bruit dans la grotte. C'est alors qu'elle avisa des outils, à l'entrée, et aussi une lampe à huile avec de l'amadou et des pierres de silex posés à côté. Sans hésiter, elle alluma la lanterne et pénétra à l'intérieur. À un endroit dégagé par les mineurs, elle remarqua une veine plus brillante, à hauteur d'homme, qui renvoyait des reflets jaune cuivré. Elle tendit la main pour toucher.

Une mine d'or.

Voilà en quoi résidait le mystère.

Elle examina le minerai avec attention. Elle s'y connaissait en métaux car des mines avaient été creusées dans différentes parties du royaume, par exemple à Kildare, siège de la célèbre maison religieuse fondée par Brigitte où elle-même avait passé la plus grande partie de sa vie de religieuse. On racontait que Tigernmas, le vingt-sixième haut roi régnant sur Éireann mille ans avant la naissance de Jésus, avait été le premier à fondre l'or. Vrai ou faux, ce métal avait failli remplacer le bétail pour acheter des biens, des services et sceller des engagements. À cause de sa qualité durable, il présentait de nombreux avantages comparé au système de troc traditionnel et de même que l'argent, le bronze ou le cuivre, on l'utilisait fréquemment comme monnaie d'échange. Quant aux propriétaires d'une mine d'or, ils s'enrichissaient à coup sûr.

Fidelma commençait à entrevoir le dessin de la toile, mais il lui manquait encore plusieurs éléments. Morna, le frère de Bressal, avait travaillé là et la mine avait été exploitée grâce à ses connaissances. Maintenant il était mort. Pour des raisons évidentes, Muadnat s'était désespérément accroché à ces terres. Mais il était mort. Quant

261

à Menma, qui travaillait pour Muadnat sans avoir les capacités de diriger seul cette mine, il avait connu le même sort.

Elle retourna à la lumière. Les oiseaux chantaient, le soleil brillait sur le corps sans vie du vacher... la scène semblait irréelle.

Quelle folie avait donc saisi la vallée d'Araglin ?

Fidelma traversa la clairière, s'enfonça dans la forêt et alla récupérer son cheval. Il fallait absolument qu'elle retourne chez Archú. Pour la seconde fois, elle entreprit à pied de descendre les collines qui dominaient la vallée en forme de L, tirant son étalon par la bride.

Elle arriva à la ferme en fin d'après-midi et Scoth vint en courant à sa rencontre.

— Quel bonheur de vous revoir si vite, ma sœur ! Frère Eadulf n'est pas avec vous ?

Fidelma lui raconta ce qui était arrivé à son compagnon. Elle s'efforçait de garder une attitude sereine, mais la tristesse voilant le visage de la religieuse n'échappa point à la jeune fille qui posa la main sur son bras.

— N'y a-t-il rien à faire ?

Fidelma tenta de chasser les mauvais pressentiments qui l'assaillaient.

— Non, il faut attendre que la fièvre tombe... si elle tombe. Où est Archú ?

— Dans un pâturage, là-haut, où il répare une clôture avec un des guerriers de Dubán. Un loup rôderait dans les parages.

— Vous ne devriez pas rester seule, dit Fidelma d'un ton anxieux. Un des guerriers ne vous tient-il pas compagnie ?

— Le second est à portée de voix, la rassura Scoth. Et puis ne craignez rien, d'où il se trouve, Archú a une vue plongeante sur les étrangers qui pénètrent dans la vallée.

— J'ai franchi la colline et il n'a apparemment rien remarqué.

— Il est venu me prévenir de votre arrivée il y a environ une demi-heure, répliqua gaiement Scoth. Ne vous inquiétez pas, il veille sur moi. Mais je suppose que vous êtes venue ici dans un but précis ?

— Rentrons un moment, suggéra Fidelma.

— Cela concerne Archú ? s'enquit la jeune fille d'un air angoissé.

Fidelma la guida vers la maison.

— C'est sans doute sans importance mais…

Elle fouilla dans son *marsupium* dont elle sortit la feuille de vélin.

— Lisez-vous le latin, Scoth ?

Celle-ci secoua la tête à regret.

— J'ai été élevée comme une servante. Archú m'a promis de m'apprendre à lire et à écrire dès que nous pourrons respirer. Sa mère lui a donné une bonne éducation.

— Eh bien, il s'agit d'un message en latin qui affirme que les réponses aux meurtres en Araglin se trouveraient ici.

Scoth s'empourpra.

— Voilà qui est méchant ! s'écria-t-elle avec colère. Qui donc… oh, je suppose que c'est encore un tour d'Agdae !

Fidelma secoua la tête.

— Une prose aussi élaborée ne lui ressemble guère.

— Une quoi ?

— Je veux dire… pourquoi écrirait-il en latin ?

— Je pense qu'il s'agit d'un nouveau plan pour nous expulser d'ici, dit Archú qui s'était encadré dans le chambranle de la porte en fronçant les sourcils.

« Je vous ai vue arriver, ma sœur. Je terminais de réparer une clôture dans un pâturage qui surplombe la vallée. Encore des soucis ?

— Quelqu'un a écrit à Fidelma pour l'avertir que nous étions responsables des morts en Araglin.

— Ce n'est pas exactement ce que j'ai dit, Scoth. Tenez, Archú. Savez-vous lire le latin ?

— Ma mère m'a appris à le déchiffrer, soupira Archú en prenant le document. Alors… Si vous voulez connaître la réponse aux meurtres en Araglin, regardez sous la ferme de l'usurpateur Archú.

Le jeune homme releva la tête d'un air ahuri.

— Qu'est-ce que cela signifie ?

— Je suis ici pour le découvrir. J'ai trouvé ce bout de parchemin sur le… cadavre de Menma.

— Mais Menma est passé ici ce matin pour nous transmettre un message !

Au tour de Fidelma de manifester sa surprise.

— En quoi consistait-il ?

— Dignait aurait disparu. Je devais avertir Dubán de partir à sa recherche.

— Quelqu'un veut salir notre nom pour nous obliger à quitter la ferme, gémit Scoth en se pendant au bras d'Archú.

— Je suppose qu'on m'a mise sur cette piste pour que je la suive.

— Si vous désirez fouiller la ferme, allez-y, dit Archú. Nous n'avons rien à cacher.

Fidelma récupéra le document qu'elle replaça dans sa besace.

— Qu'y a-t-il de particulier *sous* votre ferme, Archú ?

— Mais rien du tout !

— N'auriez-vous pas remarqué un bout de terrain dont la terre aurait été récemment remuée ?

Archú claqua soudain des doigts.

— Je crois que je sais à quoi ce message fait référence. Ma mère m'avait parlé d'une chambre souterraine. La maison a été construite sur un ancien site qui comportait des caves de ce type. Autrefois, on y conservait la nourriture pour faire face aux épreuves ou aux intempéries.

— Y êtes-vous déjà descendu ?

— Je ne m'en souviens pas. Ma mère disait qu'on l'avait fermée lorsque j'étais petit parce qu'un des enfants d'une servante y était tombé et était mort des suites de sa chute. Le père Gormán, qui nous avait rendu visite, avait organisé les recherches et il avait conseillé de sceller ce souterrain. À ma connaissance, nul ne l'a rouvert depuis. La mémoire est une chose curieuse car j'avais complètement oublié cet événement.

— Contrairement à l'auteur de cette missive. Il faut absolument retrouver l'entrée de ce cellier.

— Oui, mais par où commencer ?

— L'auteur du message est persuadé que la solution de cette énigme est à notre portée. Donc l'endroit a dû être utilisé récemment.

Un dallage de pierres recouvrait le sol de la ferme. Ils s'employèrent à le sonder mais sans résultat. Quand ils frappèrent sur les carreaux, aucun écho ne leur répondit et ils ne repérèrent aucun interstice fracturé.

Ensuite, ils arpentèrent les alentours de la maison, mais rien ne les incita à pousser plus loin leurs recherches.

— Et la grange ? demanda Fidelma en désignant celle qui n'avait pas brûlé.

— Elle n'a pas encore été nettoyée, dit Archú. On l'utilisait comme porcherie.

— Commençons par là.

L'endroit, sombre et humide malgré le soleil, dégageait une puanteur atroce. Debout sur le seuil, Fidelma eut un haut-le-cœur.

— J'ai décidé de loger les cochons ailleurs, expliqua Archú, parce que ce lieu est vraiment trop malsain.

— Il nous faudrait une lampe.

— Je vais en chercher une, dit Scoth.

Quelques instants plus tard, ils pénétraient dans la remise insalubre au sol pavé qui ne présentait là non plus aucune faille mais, dans un coin, Fidelma remarqua une petite plate-forme en bois, recouverte de paille. En ôtant la paille humide avec son pied, elle découvrit une trappe. Il leur fallut lutter pour la déverrouiller mais ils finirent par la soulever et, en l'appuyant au mur, Fidelma découvrit une volée de marches grossièrement taillées. Le passage, creusé de main d'homme, était tapissé de pierres jointes et surmonté de grands linteaux formant un toit.

Fidelma prit la lanterne des mains de Scoth et, sans un mot, elle descendit l'escalier. Elle arriva dans un couloir étroit qui obligeait à baisser la tête. Dans l'ancien temps, on l'appelait un *uaimh talamh*, un « chemin rampant » qui menait à différentes niches où l'on entreposait des provisions. L'endroit n'avait pas servi depuis fort longtemps.

Fidelma s'attendait à une découverte surprenante, mais elle n'était pas préparée à la vision que révéla la lumière de sa lanterne alors qu'elle avait à peine parcouru quelques toises.

Dignait reposait là, la gorge tranchée. De la blessure béante et encore rouge s'était échappé du sang maintenant coagulé. La servante, la tête pratiquement détachée du corps, était morte depuis plusieurs heures. Pour la troisième fois, Fidelma se retrouvait confrontée au cadavre d'une personne saignée comme un animal.

Archú l'aida à ramener le corps à l'air libre et Fidelma l'examina attentivement dans le jour déclinant sans trouver aucun indice qui puisse l'aider.

Il était évident que c'était Menma qui avait amené le corps de Dignait jusque-là. Elle se rappela que, tôt le matin, il était sorti du *rath* avec un cheval lourdement chargé d'un panier de bât.

— Menma est-il resté un instant seul quand il est venu ici ? demanda Fidelma.

— Après avoir transmis les instructions de Dubán aux hommes qui étaient avec moi dans le haut pâturage, il est revenu seul vers les bâtiments mais Scoth était présente.

— Je me trouvais dans la maison et Menma est juste passé me dire au revoir.

— Vous l'avez vu redescendre du pâturage ?

Scoth secoua la tête.

— Je faisais ma lessive et ne lui ai pas parlé avant qu'il frappe à la porte.

— Donc il a eu le temps de dissimuler le corps dans la cave.

Scoth parut horrifiée.

— Mais comment Menma a-t-il su où se trouvaient les chambres souterraines ?

— Menma était un cousin de Muadnat, qui connaissait les moindres recoins de cette ferme, intervint Archú.

Ils furent interrompus par le trot d'un cheval sur le chemin.

Archú se retourna avec nervosité puis se détendit.

— Ce n'est que Dubán. Ses hommes n'ont pas cru bon de nous avertir de son arrivée.

En voyant s'approcher le guerrier, Fidelma ressentit un malaise. Elle ignorait toujours les raisons qui l'avaient poussé à tuer Menma.

Dubán sauta à terre et leur adressa un large sourire. Puis il vit le corps à leurs pieds.

— Mais c'est Dignait ! s'écria-t-il.

— Nous l'avons trouvée dans une cave sous cette grange, annonça Archú.

Le guerrier s'accroupit un instant puis se redressa.

— Même si on ne peut s'en réjouir, voilà un problème de résolu, soupira-t-il. On m'a raconté que, ce matin, Dignait avait disparu après avoir servi des champignons vénéneux au moine saxon. Qu'est-ce que cela signifie, ma sœur ?

Fidelma s'efforça de paraître détendue.

— Je n'en sais pas plus que vous. Regardez, dit-elle en s'empressant de remettre la feuille de vélin au guerrier avant que l'un d'eux ne mentionne Menma.

À l'évidence, Dubán voyait ce parchemin pour la première fois.

— Je ne comprends pas comment la découverte du corps de Dignait expliquerait le mystère des morts en Araglin, conclut-il, perplexe.

Fidelma lui retira prestement le document des mains.

— Peut-être suis-je supposée déduire de ce message que c'est Dignait qui a commis tous ces crimes ?

— Impossible. Il est évident que la main qui a tué Muadnat a également assassiné Dignait. Les blessures au couteau sont identiques.

— Vous êtes très observateur, Dubán.

— La guerre et la mort sont mon métier, ma sœur. Mais quoi qu'il en soit, celui qui a rédigé ce texte nous a fourni un indice sans le vouloir.

— Comment cela ?

— Il est rédigé en latin, une langue dont la connaissance est peu répandue en Araglin.

— Vous n'avez pas tort. Et comme je le faisais remarquer à Scoth, Agdae ignorant le latin, il est innocenté. Et vous, Dubán, vous parlez le latin ?

— Bien sûr, répondit le guerrier sans la moindre hésitation. D'ailleurs, la plupart des gens cultivés en ont des rudiments, même Gadra, aussi païen soit-il.

Fidelma se tourna vers Archú.

— Je veux que vous et Scoth veniez au *rath* demain à midi. Non, ne protestez pas, les guerriers de Dubán vous escorteront.

Elle revint à Dubán.

— Donnez-leur des instructions pour qu'ils amènent également Agdae.

— Volontiers, si quelqu'un me dit où il se terre ! objecta Dubán.

— Vous le trouverez chez Clídna. Assurez-vous qu'il aura dessoûlé quand il arrivera au *rath* et priez Clídna de l'accompagner.

Dubán parut choqué.

— Vous rendez-vous compte de ce que vous exigez ?

— Tout à fait. Demain, je pense que nous serons en mesure de résoudre les énigmes qui hantent le clan d'Araglin.

Dubán ouvrit de grands yeux.

— Vraiment ?

— Obéirez-vous à mes ordres ? répliqua Fidelma avec un sourire froid.

Le guerrier marqua un temps d'hésitation, puis il hocha la tête avant de pivoter sur ses talons pour aller s'entretenir avec ses hommes.

Aussitôt, Fidelma se dirigea vers son cheval.

— Attendez, ma sœur ! s'écria Scoth. Ne préférez-vous pas dormir ici ? La nuit tombe et vous atteindrez le *rath* en pleine nuit.

— Ne vous inquiétez pas pour moi. Maintenant, je connais le chemin et il me reste du travail à accomplir. Rendez-vous demain à midi.

Elle sauta en selle et s'éloigna au trot de son étalon.

Elle n'avait pas parcouru un mile qu'elle entendit un cavalier galoper derrière elle. Cherchant un abri du regard, elle ne vit que la route rectiligne et les champs de céréales.

— Hé ho, ma sœur !

La voix de Dubán.

— Ce n'est pas raisonnable de chevaucher seule à cette heure, l'admonesta-t-il. Par les temps qui courent, la vallée n'est pas très sûre et puis, de toute façon, je dois regagner le *rath*.

Après la scène dont elle avait été le témoin à la ferme, Fidelma se méfiait de cet homme dont il lui était maintenant impossible de refuser la compagnie.

— Très bien, répondit-elle. Mais sachez que je peux affronter la plupart des prédateurs à deux pattes.

Dubán éclata de rire.

— C'est ce que j'ai cru comprendre. Cependant, vous oubliez les bêtes à quatre pattes. Archú m'a prévenu que des loups rôdaient dans les parages.

— Je ne me soucie guère des loups, par contre...

Leurs chevaux avançaient maintenant d'un pas tranquille.

— Ah, vous songiez à Agdae...

— Plutôt à Crítán ! J'ai humilié ce jeune homme et il est possible qu'il cherche à se venger.

— Vous n'avez rien à craindre de Crítán, dit le guerrier d'un ton qui manquait d'assurance. On m'a rapporté qu'il avait quitté Araglin pour se rendre à Cashel. Vous pensez vraiment que demain vous nous apporterez la clé des mystères qui empoisonnent l'atmosphère de la région ?

— Je ne parle jamais pour ne rien dire.

— Alors ce sera un soulagement pour Crón.

— Et aussi pour vous…

Elle fut interrompue par des bêlements plaintifs qui trahissaient la peur.

Dubán tira sur les rênes de sa monture, imité par Fidelma.

Dans la semi-obscurité, elle aperçut un troupeau de moutons qui s'agitaient sans relâche en poussant des cris pitoyables.

— Qu'est-ce que c'est ? demanda Fidelma à voix basse.

— Je l'ignore. En tout cas, quelque chose les a effrayés. Un animal, peut-être… je vais aller jeter un coup d'œil.

Dubán sauta à terre et disparut dans le crépuscule.

Il faisait froid et elle serra les pans de sa cape autour d'elle. Soudain, le cheval de Dubán hennit et tira sur sa bride, que Fidelma tenait d'une main ferme.

— Holà ! Tiens-toi tranquille !

Puis, sans prévenir, son étalon se cabra. Surprise, elle perdit l'équilibre et se retrouva projetée sur le sol. Heureusement, à cet endroit la terre était molle et humide. La respiration coupée, elle resta un instant sans bouger, puis elle s'assit en se frottant l'épaule et, chancelante, finit enfin par se remettre debout. La vexation succéda à la peur. Comment avait-elle pu, elle une cavalière aguerrie, se laisser surprendre de façon aussi stupide ?

— Hé !

Trop tard. Les deux destriers s'étaient échappés, l'abandonnant à son triste sort. Il ne manquait plus que ça !

Alors qu'elle faisait quelques pas hésitants dans leur direction, elle se sentit brusquement glacée en détectant un froissement d'herbes et de feuilles dans les broussailles, accompagné d'un grondement sourd.

Elle se figea.

Une grande bête noire surgit devant elle et s'arrêta. Ses yeux brillaient dans l'obscurité et ses babines découvraient des dents blanches et aiguisées.

Tandis qu'il la fixait, le grondement du loup s'amplifia.

Elle savait qu'au moindre mouvement de sa part, l'animal lui sauterait dessus, ses mâchoires cherchant sa gorge pour la broyer. Fidelma s'arrêta de respirer. Elle avait déjà vu des loups, mais aucun ne l'avait directement menacée. À cheval ou à pied, elle s'était toujours arrangée pour les éviter ou leur faire comprendre qu'elle avait les moyens de se défendre. Ces prédateurs très répandus dans les cinq royaumes descendaient rarement dans les vallées, ils n'attaquaient que les voyageurs isolés et désarmés dans des endroits déserts. D'une manière générale, ils préféraient les animaux sauvages ou domestiques et, s'ils s'en prenaient aux humains, c'était rarement pour les dévorer.

Fidelma, seule face à une bête agressive en quête d'une proie, fut envahie par une terreur sans nom mais son esprit continuait de fonctionner, et elle reconnut une louve affamée qui n'avait pas de temps à perdre car ses petits l'attendaient.

Il sembla à la religieuse qu'une éternité s'écoulait tandis qu'elle restait plantée là et, quand elle sentit qu'elle commençait à trembler, elle crut sa dernière heure arrivée.

C'est alors qu'un projectile frappa l'animal, lui arrachant un glapissement furieux tandis qu'il bondissait dans les fourrés et qu'une main la tirait en arrière.

Elle se retourna et se retrouva face à Dubán.

— Ça va ? demanda le guerrier d'une voix inquiète.

Elle éclata d'un rire nerveux.

— Je crois bien que je ne vais jamais m'en remettre.

Puis elle prit de profondes inspirations tout en se frottant le bras, là où Dubán l'avait empoignée.

— Pour un guerrier, vous avez des mains rugueuses, Dubán.

Il rit à son tour.

— Je porte des gants de cuir pour me protéger des cals. Et maintenant, partons vite à la recherche de nos chevaux, car cette bête pourrait bien revenir avec sa meute.

— Je suis désolée, dit Fidelma.

— Pourquoi donc ?

— Pour les avoir laissés s'échapper.

Dubán haussa les épaules.

— Même le meilleur des cavaliers ne peut prévoir tous les aléas d'un voyage, ma sœur. Le loup parcourait des cercles en se rapprochant du troupeau et sur son chemin il est tombé sur vous et a effrayé nos montures. Dieu merci, je lui ai envoyé un caillou bien placé et vous n'avez pas bougé d'un cil. Le moindre geste aurait pu vous être fatal.

Il marqua une pause.

— Vous ne vous êtes pas blessée en tombant, au moins ?

— Seule ma dignité a souffert, plaisanta Fidelma.

Et aussi ma confiance dans mon raisonnement et ma logique ajouta-t-elle en silence. Car si Dubán avait été la personne qu'elle supposait, il l'aurait laissée se faire égorger par cette bête féroce.

— Nous nous en sommes plutôt bien tirés, conclut Dubán tandis qu'ils se mettaient en marche.

— Vous croyez que la louve peut revenir ? s'inquiéta Fidelma.

— Oui, car elle est en quête de nourriture pour ses louveteaux.

— Ont-ils pour habitude de rôder autour des fermes ?

— Rarement à cette saison mais, en hiver, il leur est déjà arrivé de pénétrer dans le *rath* pour y voler des poules ou même un cochon.

Puis il poussa une exclamation de surprise.

— Regardez, nos chevaux nous attendent près de ce bouquet d'arbres. Ils ne sont pas allés bien loin !

Soulagée, Fidelma, que la perspective d'une promenade nocturne ne tentait guère, dit une prière silencieuse pour remercier la providence.

Les deux étalons semblaient ravis de les revoir et ils s'avancèrent vers eux en tendant le museau.

— Je vous remercie de m'avoir sauvé la vie, Dubán, dit Fidelma après quelques instants de chevauchée silencieuse.

Il haussa les épaules d'un air embarrassé.

— C'est bien normal. J'ai prononcé mon serment de guerrier devant Máenach, alors roi de Cashel, et juré de protéger les faibles et les opprimés.

Voilà qui piqua la curiosité de Fidelma. Dubán appartenait donc à l'ordre du Collier d'or ? On racontait qu'un millier d'années avant la naissance du Christ, un roi de Cashel, Muinheamhoin Mac Fiardea, régnait sur les cinq royaumes d'Éireann. C'était le huitième après Eber, fils de Mile, et le fondateur de l'ordre du Collier d'or, destiné à distinguer ses meilleurs soldats.

— J'ignorais que vous étiez un guerrier de l'ordre de Cashel.

— Je porte rarement la chaîne d'or de ma fonction, avoua Dubán. Je suis rentré en Araglin il y a trois années de cela, alors que je ne me sentais plus assez jeune ni assez viril pour servir les souverains. Et il se trouve qu'Eber avait besoin d'un homme expérimenté pour commander ses gardes.

Il soupira.

— Ce n'était pas une tâche très difficile. Mais tout compte fait, il aurait peut-être mieux valu que je reste à Cashel.

Fidelma fronça les sourcils.

— Si je comprends bien, vous n'aimiez pas beaucoup Eber ?

— Le bon, le noble, le généreux Eber ? ironisa Dubán avec amertume.

— Vous doutiez de ses qualités ?

— Allons, ma sœur, il serait temps que quelqu'un vous ouvre enfin les yeux.

— Pourquoi pas vous ?

— N'étant pas en mesure de prouver mes accusations, les révélations que je m'apprête à vous faire peuvent me coûter le peu de sécurité que je me suis assuré en Araglin pour mes vieux jours.

— Je n'ai nul désir de menacer votre perspective d'une tranquille vieillesse. Et puis en tant que roi de Cashel, mon frère ne tolérerait pas que vous ayez à pâtir de votre franchise. Pourquoi avez-vous tué Menma ?

Elle avait décoché sa question comme on lance une flèche, et elle entendit le guerrier reprendre sa respiration avec difficulté.

— Vous… vous le saviez ?

Il resta un instant silencieux, puis se résolut à poursuivre.

— Je cherchais Dignait quand je suis tombé sur Menma accompagné d'une bande d'hommes et d'une charrette lourdement chargée à la ferme de Muadnat. Aussitôt, je me suis caché. Nous avions déjà croisé certains de ces brigands au retour de notre expédition pour aller retrouver Gadra. Menma leur donna des instructions et ils rejoignirent seuls les collines.

— Ils progressaient vers le sud ?

— Oui. Quant à Menma, il s'était engagé sur la piste dont Agdae nous avait affirmé qu'elle ne menait nulle part, et bien sûr je l'ai suivi. Une personne l'attendait dans une caverne donnant sur une clairière.

— Qui était-ce ?

— Je l'ai seulement entendue discuter avec Menma. Elle lui ordonnait de tuer quelqu'un afin de le réduire au silence.

— Vous ne l'avez pas vue ?

— Non. Mais saisi d'une colère froide et oubliant que je n'avais que mon arc pour me défendre, j'ai pénétré dans la grotte et je les ai défiés. Menma s'est sauvagement battu tandis que son interlocuteur, qui n'était qu'une vague silhouette dans l'ombre, a réussi à s'enfuir. À un moment donné, Menma m'a échappé, il a couru vers son cheval et... vous avez vu ce qui s'est passé.

— J'étais effectivement présente, et je peux vous confirmer qu'un cavalier a traversé la clairière au galop avant de disparaître.

— Vous l'avez reconnu ?

— Non. Mais vous, vous l'avez entendu. Était-ce un homme ou une femme ?

— Je n'ai perçu qu'un bourdonnement de voix graves. Je me prononcerais plutôt pour un homme.

— Et maintenant, dites-moi pourquoi vous haïssiez Eber. La vérité, sur votre honneur.

Dubán porta la main à son cou, comme s'il s'attendait à y trouver la chaîne d'or de sa fonction.

— Vous faites bien de me rappeler à mon honneur, Fidelma. Peut-être qu'au cours de mon séjour en Araglin, ce mot a peu à peu perdu de sa signification.

— Parce que vous avez passé trop de temps à fréquenter de jeunes vauriens comme Crítán qui se prennent pour des guerriers ?

Devant eux, les lumières de la vallée apparurent.

— Voici le *rath*, murmura Dubán.

— Soulagez votre conscience avant qu'il ne soit trop tard.

— Vous savez, Eber n'était pas du tout ce que l'on croyait, mais un chef sans dignité.

— Soyez plus précis.

— D'un point de vue moral, il était profondément corrompu.

— Cela peut prendre bien des formes.

275

— Vous êtes-vous demandé pourquoi sa femme avait déserté sa couche ? Eber était comme un cerf en rut et il exigeait que les biches qu'il croisait sur son chemin se soumettent à sa volonté.

— Je vois…

— Non, vous ne voyez rien. Il entreprenait aussi les femmes de sa famille.

— Il a sexuellement abusé de membres de sa parentèle ? insista Fidelma qui tenait à avoir la version de Dubán des dérèglements d'Eber.

— Je ne peux rien prouver. Pas plus que je ne peux démontrer… qu'il était un assassin.

Cette assertion stupéfia Fidelma.

— Accordez-moi votre confiance, Dubán. Poursuivez, je vous en conjure.

— Très bien. Autrefois, j'étais amoureux de la jeune sœur d'Eber.

— Teafa ?

— Non, Tomnát, Teafa avait une année de plus que son frère. Eber terrorisait Tomnát. Quand j'ai essayé de la persuader de m'épouser et de m'accompagner à Cashel, elle m'a répondu que c'était impossible car la honte était tombée sur elle.

— Elle a donné ses raisons ?

— Non, et moi, à l'époque, je n'ai rien compris. Le lendemain, Tomnát avait disparu du *rath* et de la vallée d'Araglin. Nous n'en avons plus jamais entendu parler. Je suis convaincu qu'Eber l'a tuée pour l'empêcher de révéler ses perversions.

— Mais pour formuler une telle accusation…

— Je sais que la nuit précédant sa disparition, Tomnát et Eber ont eu une terrible dispute.

— Vous étiez présent ?

— J'ai entendu des éclats de voix alors que je montais la garde, mais mon devoir m'interdisait de pénétrer dans les appartements d'Eber. Au bout d'un moment, le silence retomba et, au matin, Tomnát s'était éva-

nouie dans la nature. J'adorais Tomnát. Elle était aussi
séduisante que Crón aujourd'hui.

— A-t-on lancé des recherches ?

— Pendant des mois, des battues ont été organisées
dans toute la vallée. Et puis, un beau jour, Teafa est
venue me trouver en m'adjurant d'oublier sa sœur.
Teafa était la seule à connaître l'étendue de mon amour
pour Tomnát. Elle m'a raconté que depuis qu'elle était
petite fille, Eber forçait Tomnát à partager son lit. On
ne l'a jamais retrouvée et je suis parti à Cashel proposer mes services au roi Máenach.

— Teafa a-t-elle accusé son frère d'avoir tué
Tomnát ?

— Non.

— Quand tout cela s'est-il passé ?

— Il y a plus de vingt ans. Plus précisément quelques mois avant que Teafa n'adopte Móen.

— Avez-vous dénoncé Eber pour le meurtre de sa
sœur ? En avez-vous parlé à d'autres ?

— Alors que je ne possédais pas la moindre preuve
de ce que j'avançais ? Allons donc !

— Et Teafa, qui vous avait informé de la conduite
d'Eber ?

— Elle ne pouvait ni trahir son frère, ni apporter la
honte sur sa famille. J'ai donc quitté Araglin. Plus
tard, je me suis rappelé ce que disaient les anciens
bardes – si vous détruisez votre vie dans un petit coin
du monde, elle ne pourra refleurir ailleurs. Alors que
je vieillissais au service de Cashel, j'ai compris que
jamais je n'étais parvenu à chasser le *rath* de mon
esprit. Je ne cessais de rêver que j'y retrouvais Tomnát. Et après vingt années d'absence, je suis rentré.

— Oui mais dans quel but, Dubán ?

— Vous l'avez déjà deviné : la vengeance.

— La vengeance est une entreprise risquée, ne vaut-
il pas mieux rechercher la justice ?

— Je voulais rassembler des preuves pour faire
éclater la vérité. Mais, en toute honnêteté, la vengeance

277

venait en premier. Œil pour œil, dent pour dent, brûlure pour brûlure, voilà ce que le père Gormán prêche
dans son église.

— Vous rendez-vous compte des conséquences
possibles de votre récit, Dubán ? Vous aviez un
mobile pour tuer Eber. Et comme vous étiez de garde
cette nuit-là, vous en aviez aussi l'occasion.

Le guerrier hocha gravement la tête.

— Et je souhaitais ardemment sa mort. Si je suis
revenu ici pour servir le chef d'Araglin, c'était dans
l'unique but de découvrir ce qui s'était passé et de
le punir si je le pouvais. Si cela me rend suspect à
vos yeux, tant pis. Traitez-moi comme vous l'enten-
drez. Mais je préférerais que vous découvriez le vrai
coupable.

— Vous niez avoir assassiné Eber ?

— Je n'ai pas versé de larmes quand j'ai appris son
décès, mais ma main n'est pas celle qui a poignardé
cet homme abominable. Et je n'avais aucune raison de
tuer Teafa que tout le monde respectait et moi aussi.

— Croyez-vous qu'Eber se soit repenti après la
mort de Tomnát ?

Dubán cracha sur le sol.

— Un loup reste un loup. Il ne peut changer sa
nature.

— Pourtant, la vôtre a évolué, lui fit remarquer
Fidelma.

— Je ne comprends pas.

— Vous avez transféré les sentiments que vous portiez à Tomnát sur Crón.

— Cela non plus je ne le nie pas, répliqua le guerrier
sur la défensive. Vivre avec un fantôme est épuisant.
Venu ici pour venger un amour perdu, j'en ai découvert
un autre.

— Ces vingt années auraient donc épuisé votre ressentiment pour Eber ?

— Non. Je vous disais simplement que Crón, dont je
n'ai pas tué le père, m'a apporté une certaine consola-

ion. Et si ce pauvre infirme, sourd, muet et aveugle n'y est pour rien lui non plus, alors qui ? L'assassin était certainement informé des mœurs d'Eber. Si vous découvrez la personne qui se dissimulait dans l'ombre de cette grotte avec Menma, alors vous tiendrez votre meurtrier.

Fidelma demeura un instant silencieuse.

— Vous avez peut-être raison, concéda-t-elle enfin. Eber a payé pour sa vie dissolue et puisse Dieu lui pardonner.

— Dieu, peut-être, mais moi, sûrement pas ! s'écria Dubán.

— Quand je vous ai rencontré, vous étiez vraiment convaincu que Móen était coupable ?

— Je n'avais aucune raison de supposer le contraire. Les voies de Dieu sont impénétrables, ma sœur. J'étais persuadé qu'Il avait utilisé cette infortunée créature comme instrument de Sa vengeance.

— Et Menma, pensez-vous que lui aussi était l'émissaire d'une personne qui le dominait ?

Dubán hocha aussitôt la tête.

— L'intelligence limitée de Menma s'accordait mal à son ambition, il n'était qu'un homme de main et la personne qui lui donnait des ordres dans la grotte est celle qui a écrit le message sur le parchemin. C'est elle qui a fait alliance avec le diable et sème le malheur dans cette vallée.

— Nous sommes d'accord. Surtout ne parlez à personne de notre conversation ni de la façon dont vous avez réglé son compte à Menma.

Ils arrivaient maintenant aux abords du *rath*. À leur approche, les chiens de garde se mirent à aboyer.

CHAPITRE XIX

Fidelma quitta Dubán aux écuries et, tandis qu'il veillait à ce qu'on prenne soin des chevaux, elle se dirigea à grands pas vers l'hôtellerie des invités.

Gadra attendait près de la porte, une expression solennelle peinte sur son visage, dont Fidelma ignorait si elle était de bon augure.

— Je crois que le pire est passé, mon enfant.

Fidelma tituba, recrue de fatigue et d'angoisse. Pendant son absence, elle s'était efforcée de ne pas penser à Eadulf de crainte de s'effondrer.

— Il dort et la fièvre est tombée, poursuivit Gadra. Je pense que votre Dieu vous a guidée vers moi afin que je puisse le soigner à une phase précoce de l'empoisonnement.

— Vous pensez qu'il se rétablira tout à fait ?

— J'en suis convaincu. Mais il faut qu'il se repose.

— Je peux le voir ?

— Ne le réveillez pas, surtout. Le sommeil est un grand guérisseur.

— Je vous le promets.

Tandis qu'elle pénétrait à l'intérieur de l'hôtellerie, Gadra resta sur le seuil de la porte. Eadulf reposait sur sa paillasse, paisible et détendu, mais son visage blême portait encore les marques de sa lutte avec la mort. Fidelma s'agenouilla auprès de lui et leva sa main menue pour la poser sur son front. Il était encore chaud. Elle ressentit une vague de tendresse pour le moine saxon, ferma les yeux et remercia le Seigneur.

Puis elle alla retrouver Gadra, qui était dans la pièce principale.

— Comment puis-je vous remercier ?

Le vieil homme leva vers elle ses prunelles délavées par l'âge.

— La jeune Grella m'a beaucoup aidé. Je viens juste de l'envoyer se coucher.

— Mais sans vous…

— Et si vous désirez me témoigner votre reconnaissance, innocentez Móen.

Fidelma inclina la tête.

— Une question pour éclairer mon jugement, Gadra. Tomnát était-elle sa mère ?

— Vous avez un esprit très vif, mon enfant.

— Alors votre souhait se réalisera, dit Fidelma en souriant au vieil homme.

Quand il fut parti, Fidelma se rendit au *fialtech* pour se laver et se préparer pour la nuit.

Le lendemain, la journée serait chargée.

Une terreur sans nom avait envahi Fidelma, seule dans la forêt.

Autour d'elle, des formes mystérieuses se glissaient entre les arbres et, dans l'obscurité, le sous-bois bruissait et frissonnait de mille frôlements.

Elle appelait à l'aide. Elle ne savait pas vraiment qui. Son père ? Oui, ce devait être son père. Il l'avait emmenée dans la forêt et puis il l'avait abandonnée. Maintenant, elle n'était plus qu'une petite fille perdue.

Mais au fond d'elle-même, elle savait que c'était impossible. Son père était mort quand elle était bébé. Pourquoi l'aurait-il amenée là pour l'égarer ?

Elle avançait en trébuchant, elle tombait et se relevait. Mais les arbres semblaient de plus en plus denses et, pour finir, elle se retrouva paralysée. Elle s'arrêta et leva la tête.

Bizarre comme les arbres ressemblaient à des pieds de champignons dont les chapeaux géants l'écrasaient.

Maintenant, les formes menaçaient de l'étouffer.

Elle cria un nom.

Elle comprit alors que ce n'était pas son père qui l'avait amenée là mais Eadulf.

Eadulf ?

Elle se remit en marche, tendit le bras devant elle, ouvrit les yeux... et poussa un gémissement, éblouie par les rayons du soleil.

Sa main pendait hors du lit.

Clignant des paupières, elle reprit conscience.

Le soleil était levé depuis longtemps et elle venait de se réveiller à l'hôtellerie des invités.

Puis elle entendit qu'on bougeait dans l'alcôve près de la sienne.

Elle sauta de sa paillasse et enfila sa robe de bure.

Dehors, elle trouva Gadra, assis sur les marches. Il lui sourit.

— Quelle belle journée, mon enfant !

— Vous êtes sûr ? demanda-t-elle en jetant un coup d'œil du côté de l'alcôve d'Eadulf.

Le vieil homme hocha la tête avec solennité.

— Oui.

Fidelma trouva son ami étendu, les yeux grands ouverts, le teint pâle et le visage encore crispé par les douleurs de la veille. Mais ses yeux sombres étaient paisibles et confiants.

— Fidelma ! murmura-t-il d'une voix enrouée par la fatigue. J'ai bien cru ne jamais revoir le jour.

Elle s'agenouilla près de lui avec un sourire affectueux.

— Vous aviez renoncé trop vite à la vie, Eadulf.

— Ce fut un sacré combat et je suis content qu'il soit derrière moi.

— Dignait est morte, lui annonça-t-elle.

Eadulf ferma un instant les yeux.

— Était-elle coupable ?

— Il semblerait qu'elle ait vu celui qui a préparé le plat de champignons.

— Mais alors, qui l'a tuée ?

— Je crois connaître la réponse. Il me reste juste un ou deux points à vérifier.

— Dignait avait disparu du *rath*. Où l'a-t-on retrouvée ?

— Dans une chambre souterraine, à la ferme d'Archú.

— Hein ? Je ne comprends pas.

— Je vais convoquer toutes les personnes concernées au siège de l'assemblée à midi, puis je révélerai le nom du coupable.

Eadulf fronça les sourcils.

— Je tiens absolument à assister à cette confrontation.

Elle secoua la tête.

— Non, vous resterez ici avec Grella jusqu'à ce que vous soyez rétabli.

Comme Eadulf ne protestait pas, elle en déduisit qu'il était encore très faible.

— Suggérez-vous qu'un seul meurtrier a commis tous ces crimes ? demanda-t-il.

— Je soupçonne une seule personne d'en être responsable.

— Qui ?

Fidelma eut un sourire énigmatique.

— Reposez-vous, Eadulf. Dès que mes soupçons auront été confirmés, je vous le ferai savoir.

Elle prit sa main et la serra dans la sienne.

Dans la salle, Gadra reniflait une potion à l'odeur âcre que Grella venait de lui apporter des cuisines. Fidelma adressa un sourire d'encouragement à la jeune fille et la remercia pour la peine qu'elle s'était donnée.

— Je vais tout de suite vous apporter votre repas, ma sœur, dit Grella, rougissant sous les compliments.

Le temps que Fidelma prenne un bain et se res-
taure, Gadra avait terminé de faire avaler son breuvage à un Eadulf récalcitrant. Ce n'était pas un malade
très docile et, quand Fidelma écarta la tenture, il protestait bruyamment contre le traitement qu'on lui
imposait.

— Honte sur vous, Eadulf. Si vous n'obéissez pas
aux injonctions de votre médecin, je ne vous dirai rien
des événements qui se dérouleront aujourd'hui à midi.

Gadra releva la tête en fronçant les sourcils.

— Que se passera-t-il à midi ?

— Toutes les personnes impliquées dans ce qui s'est
passé au *rath* doivent se réunir au siège de l'assemblée.
Bien sûr, votre présence est indispensable, Gadra, ainsi
que celle de Móen. À propos, comment va-t-il ?

— Vos bontés pour sa personne lui ont redonné
confiance. C'est un jeune homme sensible et intelligent, Fidelma, et il mérite qu'on lui donne une seconde
chance dans la vie. À midi, nous répondrons à votre
convocation.

Une demi-heure plus tard, Fidelma pénétrait dans
l'église de Cill Uird où le prêtre à genoux était en
contemplation devant l'autel.

— Père Gormán !

Le religieux sursauta.

— Vous avez interrompu mes prières, ma sœur,
lança-t-il d'un air outragé.

— Je dois m'entretenir avec vous de sujets urgents.

Le père Gormán fit le signe de croix et se releva
avec des gestes lents.

— De quoi s'agit-il ? demanda-t-il d'un air méfiant.

— Je pensais que vous voudriez être informé du
trépas de Dignait.

Le prêtre tressaillit mais ne sembla pas autrement
surpris.

— Tant de morts ! murmura-t-il.

— Déjà cinq dans cette vallée paradisiaque d'Araglin.

Gormán cligna des paupières.

— Cinq ?

— Oui. Et il est temps de mettre un terme à ce carnage. Nous devons collaborer dans ce but.

— Nous ? répéta le prêtre, interloqué.

— Je pense que vous pouvez m'aider.

— Je vous écoute.

— Vous étiez l'âme sœur de Muadnat, n'est-ce pas ?

— Je préfère le terme romain de confesseur. Je suis d'ailleurs le confesseur de la plupart des habitants d'Araglin.

— Peu importe le nom que l'on donne à la chose. J'aimerais juste savoir si Muadnat a mentionné en votre présence qu'il possédait de l'or.

— M'incitez-vous à rompre le secret de la confession ? tonna Gormán.

— Bien que je ne souscrive point à cette confidentialité, je respecte vos convictions, qui ne devraient cependant pas vous empêcher de répondre à quelques questions. Dignait servait ici depuis de longues années, n'est-ce pas ?

— Je croyais que vous désiriez me parler de Muadnat ?

— Concentrons-nous un instant sur Dignait. Elle est bien arrivée ici en même temps que Cranat quand elle a épousé Eber ?

— C'est exact.

— À qui allait sa loyauté ?

— À la maison d'Araglin !

— Pas à Cranat ?

Le père Gormán parut gêné.

— Dignait ne détestait-elle pas Eber ? reprit Fidelma.

Il secoua la tête.

— Si elle ne le respectait guère, il lui était assez indifférent. En réalité, elle était plus proche de Crón que de sa mère et aurait fait n'importe quoi pour elle.

— Vraiment ?

— Ce n'est pas un crime.

— Non, bien sûr. Vous n'aimez guère Dubán, n'est-ce pas ? demanda-t-elle brusquement.

— Je ne vois pas ce que mes préférences ou mes aversions viennent faire ici. C'est un intrigant dont l'ambition, selon moi, est de parvenir à la position de chef d'Araglin. Savez-vous pourquoi il cherche à enjôler la jeune Crón ?

— Le terme d'enjôler signifie à la fois séduire, ensorceler et tromper. Qu'en pensez-vous ?

Le père Gormán releva le menton.

— Observez cette relation par vous-même.

— Oh, mais je m'y suis employée !

— Je suis désolé pour Cranat, épouse d'un chef sans scrupules et mère d'une jeune femme innocente qui s'est entichée d'un homme de l'âge de son père.

— Oui, je me souviens que vous n'appréciiez guère Eber.

— Un pécheur devant Dieu et les hommes ne pouvait attendre aucun pardon du Seigneur ou de ses semblables !

— En tant que prêtre, n'éprouvez-vous aucune compassion ? Vous me semblez rempli de haine alors que c'est à vous de montrer le chemin du pardon. Dans son épître aux Éphésiens, Paul n'a-t-il pas écrit : « Montrez-vous bons et compatissants les uns pour les autres, vous pardonnant mutuellement, comme Dieu vous a pardonnés dans le Christ[1] » ? Si Dieu peut remettre les fautes, alors vous aussi, son serviteur.

Le père Gormán la fixa un instant puis grimaça de colère.

— Vous auriez dû lire plus loin cette épître. Paul a dit : « Car, sachez-le bien, ni le fornicateur, ni le débauché, ni le cupide – qui est un idolâtre – n'ont droit à l'héritage dans le Royaume du Christ et de

1. Épître aux Éphésiens, 4, 32. (*N.d.T.*)

Dieu[1]. » Eber n'aura pas d'héritage dans le royaume de Dieu.

— Parce qu'il a couché avec ses sœurs ? Ou pire encore ?

Le prêtre détourna les yeux.

— Ce monde se passe très bien d'Eber d'Araglin et plus tôt la vallée sera purgée du mal, mieux ce sera.

— Donc à vos yeux, elle n'est pas encore purifiée ? Vous n'ignorez pas que Muadnat possédait une mine d'or ?

Le père Gormán se mordit la lèvre.

— Que savez-vous à ce sujet ?

— Vous l'apprendrez bientôt. Soyez au siège de l'assemblée à midi.

Fidelma quitta la chapelle tandis que le prêtre la fixait sans ciller. Après son départ, il se précipita vers la sacristie.

Dehors, Fidelma rencontra Crón.

La jeune *tanist* l'accueillit avec un visage grave.

— Comment se porte frère Eadulf ?

— Bien, Dieu soit loué.

— J'ai parlé ce matin avec Dubán, poursuivit la *tanist*. Il dit que vous êtes sur le point de découvrir la personne qui a infligé tant de malheurs aux habitants de cette vallée.

— Justement, je voulais vous demander de pouvoir utiliser le siège de l'assemblée, à midi, aujourd'hui. Toutes les personnes concernées par les récents événements sont priées de s'y rendre, afin que je révèle les noms des responsables de ces terribles effusions de sang.

Crón semblait très éprouvée.

— Alors, vous savez qui a tué Eber et Teafa ?

— Je le crois, oui.

— Vous le croyez ? s'étonna la jeune femme.

1. Épître aux Éphésiens, 5, 5. (*N.d.T.*)

287

— Et je vous le démontrerai tout à l'heure, répliqua Fidelma d'un air serein. Soyez aimable de demander à votre mère de se joindre à nous. Je suis certaine qu'elle voudra entendre qui est responsable du meurtre de son époux.

— Très bien.

Fidelma s'éloigna sans prêter attention au trouble de Crón.

CHAPITRE XX

Tout le monde était là. À la demande de Fidelma, Crón trônait dans le fauteuil symbolisant sa fonction, car c'était son droit en tant que *tanist*. Pour l'occasion, elle portait sa cape bicolore et des gants de daim pareillement désassortis. Près d'elle siégeait sa mère, toujours aussi hautaine, le regard perdu dans les lointains. Au premier rang devant l'estrade se tenait Eadulf, pâle et les yeux cernés, s'appuyant d'un air souffrant au dossier de sa chaise. Malgré les protestations de Fidelma, il avait jugé que son état s'était suffisamment amélioré pour assister aux débats. Dubán avait pris place à ses côtés. Les coudes appuyés sur les genoux, il tenait son visage dans ses mains.

Derrière eux, sur des bancs, se tenaient Archú et Scoth, près de Gadra l'ermite dont les doigts tambourinaient sur la paume levée de Móen. Puis venaient Agdae, visiblement nerveux, et le père Gormán. Clídna s'était déplacée. Seule au fond de la salle, le menton relevé, la femme aux secrets semblait défier l'assistance. Grella, la jeune servante, se trouvait non loin d'elle.

Des hommes de Dubán gardaient les portes.

Fidelma traversa la salle, s'avança vers Crón et se plaça à sa gauche, au pied de l'estrade.

— Il me semble que tout le monde est là.

Crón inclina le buste vers elle.

— Êtes-vous prête à commencer ?

— Menma n'est pas là, dit Agdae. Or c'est lui qui a découvert le corps d'Eber et identifié Móen comme étant le meurtrier.

Crón parut déconcertée.

— Je l'ai envoyé hier rechercher du bétail égaré et je pensais qu'il était rentré. Devons-nous l'attendre ?

Fidelma lui adressa un large sourire.

— Poursuivons, *tanist* d'Araglin. Je me doutais de son absence.

— Plaît-il ? Accuseriez-vous Menma… commença Crón, oubliant son indifférence feinte.

Fidelma leva la main.

— Chaque chose en son temps. *Vincit qui patitur.* La victoire récompense la patience.

Tout le monde avait les yeux fixés sur la jeune femme élancée qui étudia les visages tendus vers elle avec attention avant d'initier la procédure.

— Je dois vous avouer qu'il s'agit là de l'investigation la plus pénible qu'il m'ait été donné de mener. D'habitude, je n'enquête que sur un meurtre à la fois et les circonstances tournent autour de ce seul crime. Là, j'ai dû affronter cinq assassinats qui au premier abord ne semblaient pas liés entre eux. Les événements se succédaient, indépendants les uns des autres en apparence, ce qui m'a entraînée sur de fausses pistes. En réalité, tout se tenait et se rassemblait autour d'un point central, comme dans une toile d'araignée géante au centre de laquelle attendrait une créature maléfique.

Un frémissement d'excitation parcourut la salle et elle marqua une pause avant de reprendre.

— Par où commencerai-je à dérouler le lacis soyeux de la fourberie qui a capturé tant de monde dans ses rets ? Je pourrais attaquer le centre de la toile, bondir sur l'araignée qui nous guette en ces lieux. En agissant ainsi, je risquerais de lui laisser l'opportunité de se glisser le long d'un fil qui lui permettrait à nouveau de s'échapper. Je vais donc opter pour la prudence et dérouler les filaments de l'extérieur, les détruisant un à un jusqu'à ce que l'araignée soit paralysée.

Crón se pencha vers elle d'un air sceptique.

— Tout cela est très poétique, ma sœur, mais êtes-vous certaine que votre rhétorique nous mène quelque part ?

Fidelma se tourna vers elle.

— Vous m'avez déjà vue à l'œuvre, Crón, vous avez même exprimé votre admiration pour ma méthode. Je ne prolongerai donc pas votre attente en défendant ma façon de plaider.

La jeune *tanist* rougit et se rejeta en arrière tandis que Fidelma s'adressait à nouveau à son auditoire.

— Le premier fil mène à Muadnat du Black Marsh.

— En quoi Muadnat est-il concerné par le meurtre de mon mari ? l'interrompit Cranat d'une voix dure. Il était son ami et, à une époque, son *tanist*.

— Avec de la patience, le *linum perenne* aux jolies fleurs bleues donne une chemise de lin, répliqua Fidelma avec humour, citant le proverbe favori de son mentor Morann de Tara. Mon implication dans cette affaire ayant débuté avec Muadnat, il convient qu'il soit le premier cité. Il y a quelque temps, Muadnat se retrouva à la tête d'une mine d'or, découverte sur la terre qu'il avait essayé de voler à son cousin Archú.

Le jeune fermier réagit aussitôt.

— Où se trouve-t-elle ? Je n'ai jamais entendu parler d'une mine d'or au Black Marsh.

— Elle est située au flanc de cette colline que vous considérez comme une « terre de hache ». Selon toute probabilité, elle avait été mise au jour par un mineur du nom de Morna, frère de Bressal qui tient une auberge sur la route à l'ouest reliant Lios Mhór à Cashel.

Le jeune fermier, qui n'en revenait pas, jeta un coup d'œil ébahi à Scoth.

— Vous voulez parler de l'hôtellerie où nous avons passé la nuit ?

— Celle-là même. Bressal nous a parlé de son frère Morna qui lui avait ramené un caillou dont il clamait qu'il ferait de lui un homme riche. Or cette pierre provenait d'une grotte recelant un gisement précieux, qui à ce moment-là était déjà en cours d'exploitation.

— C'est un mensonge ! s'écria Agdae. Muadnat n'a jamais mentionné ce gisement devant moi. Or j'étais son neveu et son fils adoptif.

— Muadnat désirait garder le secret, poursuivit Fidelma. Malheureusement, son cousin Archú revendiquait la propriété de la ferme de sa mère Suanach et il décida de porter l'affaire devant la justice. Muadnat se battit bec et ongles, mais s'il mettait tout en œuvre pour faire pencher les lois en sa faveur, il les respectait suffisamment pour ne pas les enfreindre tout à fait. Il a néanmoins eu de la chance qu'Archú ne fasse pas appel au jugement d'Eber mais préfère solliciter la cour de Lios Mhór. Eber, qui était un homme rusé, aurait pu poser des questions embarrassantes en s'avisant que Muadnat, un homme riche, tenait un peu trop à cette ferme.

Agdae arborait une mine lugubre.

— Pourquoi Muadnat ne m'a-t-il pas associé à son entreprise ?

— Vous n'étiez pas assez implacable ! intervint Clídna.

Fidelma, voyant que Crón s'apprêtait à remettre à sa place la femme aux secrets pour avoir osé élever la voix au siège de l'assemblée, s'empressa d'intervenir.

— Clídna a raison. Agdae n'est pas le genre de personne qui aurait accepté d'être mêlé à des fouilles illégales. Muadnat avait besoin de quelqu'un qui obéirait à ses ordres sans poser de questions. Il choisit donc son cousin Menma.

— Menma ?

Agdae allait de déception en déconvenue et Fidelma lui adressa un regard attristé.

— Menma dirigeait la mine, recrutait les mineurs, s'occupait de leur entretien, et veillait à ce que l'or soit transporté vers le Sud où il était entreposé dans un endroit sûr. Comment nourrir un groupe de mineurs affamés dans une vallée tranquille sans que les fermiers de la région s'en aperçoivent ? Pour le logement, ils pouvaient se débrouiller sur place, mais pour le ravitaillement ?

— Il suffisait d'organiser des expéditions pour voler du bétail, répondit Eadulf d'un air triomphant. Une vache ou deux par-ci par-là.

— Mais Muadnat était riche, objecta Crón. Il pouvait subvenir aux besoins des mineurs sans avoir recours à de tels subterfuges.

— Vous oubliez Agdae, chef des troupeaux de Muadnat. Il se serait forcément rendu compte que Muadnat faisait abattre plus de bétail que nécessaire pour les besoins de sa maison. Et Muadnat n'osait pas retirer sa charge à Agdae, son plus proche parent.

Agdae était mortifié.

— Quand avez-vous compris que les voleurs de bétail se livraient en réalité à d'autres occupations ? demanda Dubán.

— Eadulf m'avait fait remarquer qu'en temps normal, les brigands dérobaient des troupeaux entiers pour les revendre. Pourquoi ceux-là n'emmenaient-ils qu'une ou deux bêtes à la fois ? Pour manger. Mes soupçons se confirmèrent quand nous rencontrâmes certains des bandits, alors que nous revenions de l'ermitage de Gadra. Ils se dirigeaient vers le sud, avec des ânes portant des paniers de bât lourdement chargés. Ces paniers étaient remplis d'or.

— Menma les accompagnait ? demanda Dubán.

— Non, ni lui ni d'autres complices dont je vais bientôt révéler l'identité.

— Mais je ne vois pas le lien entre la mine de Muadnat et la mort d'Eber et Teafa, protesta Agdae.

— Continuons de dérouler le fil de l'araignée. Muadnat tenait absolument à poursuivre l'exploitation de la mine. Et il s'y est accroché, sans doute contre l'avis de son complice.

Le silence se fit.

— Muadnat n'aurait jamais pris l'avis de Menma sur quelque sujet que ce soit, rétorqua Agdae d'un air mauvais.

Fidelma l'ignora.

— Quand il s'est rendu à Lios Mhór, l'associé de Muadnat avait probablement décidé qu'il reprendrait la mine à son compte, pour la bonne raison que Muadnat attirait trop l'attention sur lui à cause de ses démêlés avec Archú. La mine devait rester secrète. Plus important, Muadnat était tombé en disgrâce auprès d'Eber.

« Jusqu'à il y a quelques semaines, Muadnat était le *tanist* d'Eber. À sa mort, il aurait dû devenir chef. Et il se trouva brusquement privé de son statut d'héritier présomptif. Eber avait persuadé le *derbfhine* de la famille de lui substituer sa fille Crón.

« L'attaque contre l'auberge de Bressal, par exemple, a probablement été conduite sans l'aval de Muadnat. Elle était dirigée par un homme que j'ai plus tard identifié comme étant Menma. On lui avait rapporté que Morna parlait trop. Il avait même donné un caillou avec des traces d'or à son frère en lui affirmant qu'il allait devenir riche, mais sans plus de précisions. Par chance, nous nous trouvions là quand l'attaque a été déclenchée.

— Qu'est-il arrivé à cet homme, Morna ? s'enquit Dubán.

— Il a été capturé, tué, et plus tard abandonné dans la cour de la ferme d'Archú. Les bandits espéraient qu'on le prendrait pour la victime d'un règlement de comptes. Quand je l'ai examiné, j'ai été frappé par sa ressemblance avec Bressal.

— Vous pensez donc que Muadnat ignorait l'attaque de l'auberge et l'assassinat du frère de Bressal ?
s'étonna Eadulf.

— Je ne vois toujours pas comment cette histoire
est liée au meurtre de mon père, s'énerva Crón.

Les lèvres de Fidelma s'étirèrent en un bref sourire.

— Je n'en suis qu'au premier fil de la toile. La mort
de Muadnat était maintenant devenue inévitable à cause
de deux vices coutumiers des humains – la peur et la
cupidité. Menma a égorgé Muadnat comme on saigne
un animal. De la même façon dont il a tué Morna. Cette
froide marque de métier, car c'est lui qui abattait le
bétail destiné à la table du chef, le désignait comme le
coupable. Cependant, je ne suis pas certaine que l'idée
d'accrocher Muadnat à la croix venait de lui. Sans
doute s'agissait-il d'égarer mes soupçons. Mais Menma
a commis une erreur. Avant de porter le coup fatal, il a
laissé Muadnat lui arracher une touffe de cheveux parfaitement reconnaissable que j'ai ramassée sur la scène
du crime.

— Mais qu'est-ce que cela rapportait à Menma
d'assassiner son associé ? demanda le père Gormán.
Cela n'a pas de sens puisque Agdae allait de toute
façon hériter des richesses de Muadnat.

— Oui, mais Agdae ignorait tout de la mine secrète.
Le complice pouvait donc continuer de récolter les
bénéfices de l'entreprise.

— Soutenez-vous que Menma est responsable de
tous les meurtres en Araglin ? s'étonna Dubán. J'ai du
mal à vous suivre.

— Menma n'était responsable que des morts de
Morna, Muadnat et Dignait, tous exécutés de la même
manière.

— Mais pourquoi Dignait ? dit brusquement le père
Gormán.

— Pour s'assurer qu'elle ne parlerait pas. Dignait
n'a pas préparé ce plat de champignons vénéneux
qui a failli mener frère Eadulf dans la tombe. Une

cuisinière connaît de bien meilleures façons pour empoisonner quelqu'un que de lui présenter un plat de fausses morilles facilement reconnaissables par tout un chacun.

— Mais pas par le Saxon, releva Crón avec ironie.

— Je sais que les morilles sont habituellement pochées. Je suis un étranger dans votre pays et pensais qu'il s'agissait d'une façon particulière de préparer ce plat, protesta Eadulf. Voilà pourquoi je n'ai pas prêté attention à ces champignons.

— Dignait a été assassinée pour la simple raison qu'elle avait vu l'assassin.

— S'agissait-il de Menma ? Ce matin-là, il circulait dans le *rath*, selon son habitude.

Grella avait trouvé le courage d'élever la voix.

— Je vous le dirai en temps utile. Revenons maintenant au meurtre d'Eber et Teafa. Voilà une affaire difficile vu que tout le monde ou presque avait une raison de tuer Eber. Il était haï, contrairement à Teafa que tout le monde tenait en haute estime. Il m'a donc semblé plus aisé de me pencher sur son cas. Si la même personne avait assassiné le frère et la sœur, cela me permettrait d'éliminer certains suspects.

Elle s'arrêta et haussa les épaules.

— Quand je suis arrivée ici, on m'avait juste informée que le chef d'Araglin avait été tué et son meurtrier arrêté.

« L'auteur du crime s'avéra être un sourd-muet aveugle, je veux bien sûr parler de Móen, également accusé d'avoir tué la femme qui l'avait élevé.

« Tout le monde concourait à me décrire Eber comme un homme gentil et généreux qui n'avait pas d'ennemis. Un parangon de vertu. Qui avait bien pu le poignarder sinon un animal privé de sa raison ? Car c'est ainsi que l'on me présenta Móen.

Móen laissa échapper un grondement de colère tandis que Gadra lui retranscrivait les propos de Fidelma.

— Remontons posément ce fil, armés de la logique. Il me fut peu à peu révélé qu'Eber, loin d'être irréprochable, était un homme étrange et pervers. Il buvait et pouvait se montrer verbalement agressif. Grâce à ses richesses, il s'achetait les faveurs de ceux qu'il avait offensés et, comme il était le chef, il ne payait jamais pour ses fautes. Mais lui et sa famille cachaient de noirs secrets... dont l'inceste.

Crón pâlit et reprit sa respiration avec difficulté. Cranat à ses côtés ne fit aucun effort pour la réconforter, gardant son attitude lointaine.

— L'inceste remontait à loin, Crón, dit Fidelma d'un ton plein de compassion. À l'époque où Eber et ses deux sœurs atteignaient l'âge de la puberté. Plusieurs personnes savaient, d'autres avaient des soupçons, et, au cours d'une conversation, quelqu'un laissa échapper que Móen était né de l'inceste.

Un silence de plomb s'était abattu sur la salle. Crón fixait Móen d'un air hagard.

— Vous voulez dire que... Teafa... sa mère ? Qu'Eber... ?

Elle frissonna sans parvenir à terminer sa phrase.

— Teafa, victime elle aussi des agressions d'Eber, poursuivit Fidelma sans se départir de son calme, avait une sœur du nom de Tomnát.

Dubán bondit sur ses pieds.

— Comment osez-vous prononcer son nom en ces lieux et suggérer qu'elle était la mère d'un... un...

— Gadra !

Ignorant l'interruption du guerrier, Fidelma s'était tournée vers le vieil ermite.

— Gadra, qui était la mère de Móen ?

Le vieil homme courba la tête.

— Vous connaissez déjà la réponse.

— Proclamez-la publiquement afin qu'éclate la vérité.

— Eh bien, l'année avant qu'Eber épouse Cranat, Tomnát est tombée enceinte d'Eber.

— Tomnát m'aimait ! s'écria Dubán d'une voix brisée par l'émotion.

Crón le fixait sans parvenir à en croire ses oreilles.

— Si c'était vrai, elle me l'aurait dit, poursuivit Dubán. Elle a disparu. Eber l'a tuée, j'en suis certain.

— C'est faux, répliqua Gadra avec tristesse. Tomnát n'avait partagé son secret qu'avec Teafa. Elle n'ignorait pas que si Eber ou le père Gormán étaient informés de sa grossesse, ils tueraient l'enfant, Eber pour cacher sa honte, et le père Gormán parce qu'il est animé d'une foi intolérante. Il approuvait la coutume qui sévit dans bien des terres chrétiennes et veut que l'on tue ces enfants du malheur au nom de la moralité. Si la pauvre Tomnát s'était tournée vers lui, il ne l'aurait certainement pas aidée.

— Pourquoi Tomnát ne s'est-elle pas adressée à Dubán puisqu'il affirme qu'ils s'aimaient ? l'interrogea Fidelma.

— Si vous voulez la vérité, Tomnát connaissait Dubán et ses ambitions. Il rêvait du collier d'or des guerriers de Cashel et malgré l'amour qu'il proclame, il n'aurait jamais accepté de mettre en danger son avenir pour l'enfant que portait Tomnát.

Dubán se couvrit le visage de ses mains.

— Donc elle s'est tournée vers vous ? demanda Fidelma.

— Avant que son état ne soit visible de tous, Tomnát quitta le *rath* et vint me rejoindre dans mon ermitage. Seule Teafa était informée du lieu de sa retraite.

— Mais pourquoi ne m'a-t-elle rien dit ? gémit Dubán. J'ai passé des semaines à parcourir la vallée en tous sens, persuadé qu'Eber l'avait tuée.

— Teafa respectait sa volonté. Et puis Tomnát mourut en couches. Teafa, qui l'avait assistée, décida d'adopter l'enfant. Par la suite, elle découvrit ses infirmités mais refusa de l'abandonner pour respecter la promesse faite à sa sœur.

Tous les yeux se tournèrent vers le jeune homme dont le visage était plissé par l'angoisse tandis que Gadra lui transcrivait la teneur des débats.

Fidelma tourna vers la salle un visage méprisant.

— Vous, une communauté de paysans, savez tout des accouplements consanguins. Dans la progéniture d'animaux à la filiation trop proche, certains traits de caractère ou certaines déficiences se retrouvent amplifiés. Les développements favorables peuvent mener à une plus grande intelligence – et les autres engendrer la surdité, la cécité ou l'incapacité de parler.

— Seriez-vous en train de dire, l'interrompit Crón d'un ton dégoûté, que nous devons reconnaître Móen comme le fils de mon père... qui serait aussi son oncle ? Et... et... comme mon demi-frère ?

— Tomnát est morte en donnant le jour à un enfant vivant, confirma Fidelma. Teafa, vous le savez, a prétendu qu'elle l'avait trouvé dans la forêt alors qu'elle y chassait. Tout d'abord, elle n'a pas vu qu'il était différent des autres. Mais quand elle comprit qu'il souffrait d'infirmités, elle envoya chercher Gadra, un homme sage et un guérisseur, qui réalisa d'où venait le problème. Il apprit alors à Teafa un moyen de communiquer avec Móen. En dehors de ses infirmités, l'enfant était d'une grande intelligence et Teafa a élevé un garçon plein de talents.

— Eber ignorait que Móen était son fils ? s'enquit Agdae.

— D'après tous les témoignages, il se montrait gentil avec Móen. Et parmi les personnes présentes, seul Móen aimait Eber.

Elle revint à Gadra.

— Demandez à Móen s'il savait qu'Eber était son père.

Gadra secoua la tête.

— Inutile, il a déjà trop souffert, et je confirme que Teafa n'en a jamais informé le garçon. Pour sa propre sécurité. Et Eber a lui aussi été tenu dans l'ignorance des origines de Móen.

— En réalité, Eber a fini par apprendre la vérité, le contredit Fidelma. Un jour, une dispute éclata dont le jeune Crítán a été le témoin. Nous y reviendrons plus tard.

— Pourquoi est-ce que la vie sexuelle de mon père…

Crón s'arrêta brusquement, luttant pour rassembler ses idées.

— Ces événements ne sont pas sans intérêt mais cela ne nous dit pas qui est responsable de la mort d'Eber et Teafa, s'obstina-t-elle.

— Oh, mais si !

— Alors expliquez-vous, l'invita la *tanist* d'un ton froid. Vous êtes-vous finalement persuadée que Móen était le coupable ? A-t-il découvert qui était son vrai père ? Le haïssait-il pour tout le mal qu'il avait fait à sa mère et à lui-même ?

Fidelma secoua la tête.

— Très tôt dans cette investigation, je n'ai pas retenu l'accusation portée contre Móen. Avant même de lui parler, je savais qu'il n'était pas le meurtrier.

— Vous pourriez peut-être nous expliquer pourquoi ? glapit le père Gormán. Pour moi, la chose est pourtant entendue.

— L'accusation première voulait que Móen ait tué Teafa avant de gagner les appartements d'Eber pour l'assassiner à son tour. Or certains éléments venaient contredire cette version des faits. Tout d'abord, j'ai appris de l'arrogant jeune Crítán qu'il avait vu Teafa vivante après que Móen se fut rendu chez Eber. S'il était l'auteur des deux meurtres, Móen aurait dû tuer Teafa avant le chef.

— Je ne vois toujours pas ce qui l'en aurait empêché, protesta Agdae.

— Parce que Menma a affirmé qu'il avait trouvé Móen penché sur le corps d'Eber, un couteau à la main. L'accusation établissait que Móen avait été surpris sur le fait.

L'assemblée reconnut en silence la justesse de cette remarque. Puis la voix de Crón s'éleva.

— Menma, que vous avez déjà condamné en tant que meurtrier, peut très bien avoir menti.

— Je vous l'accorde, lança Fidelma, impassible. Mais pas sur ce point car, pour lui, la découverte de Móen sur la scène du crime était un cadeau inespéré. Et Teafa était encore en vie quand Móen est entré chez Eber. Crítán, qui revenait de chez Clídna, a rencontré le garçon sur le chemin menant à la maison du chef, puis il a vu Teafa qui se tenait sur le seuil de sa chaumière, une lanterne à la main. Alors qu'il me racontait cet épisode, Crítán comprit l'incohérence de l'accusation portée contre Móen, mais, comme il désirait qu'il soit coupable, il passa outre.

« Móen, qui était parti se promener aux premières heures du matin, rentrait chez lui quand quelqu'un lui tendit une baguette gravée d'un texte en ogam. L'ogam est la méthode grâce à laquelle on peut communiquer avec Móen. Le garçon m'a raconté qu'une personne avec des mains calleuses mais dont il pensait, à cause du parfum qu'elle dégageait, qu'il s'agissait d'une femme, l'avait forcé à se saisir de l'objet. Le message disait qu'il devait se rendre sur-le-champ aux appartements d'Eber. Il obéit, buta sur le corps d'Eber et tomba à genoux. C'est là que Menma le découvrit. La personne qui lui a remis la baguette est celle qui voulait qu'il soit accusé et condamné.

— Quelle preuve avez-vous de l'existence de cette prétendue baguette priant Móen de se rendre chez Eber ? demanda le père Gormán.

— Je l'ai retrouvée, déclara Fidelma avec un large sourire. Voyez-vous, Móen l'avait laissé échapper avant de se précipiter à son rendez-vous. Reprenons. Le meurtrier fait tomber la baguette car il ne veut pas qu'on la découvre, mais, à l'instant où il s'apprête à la récupé-

301

rer, Teafa, réveillée par le bruit, s'aperçoit que Móen n'est pas là. Elle sort, une lampe à la main, avise la baguette d'ogam et la ramasse. C'est à cet instant que Crítán la voit. Elle lui demande s'il a croisé Móen. Il ment et poursuit son chemin. Le meurtrier, qui est resté dans l'ombre en attendant que Crítán s'en aille, a un sérieux problème. Comme Teafa est retournée dans sa maison pour lire le faux message en ogam, il se retrouve dans l'obligation de la tuer elle aussi. Au cours de la lutte qui va suivre, la lampe à huile que tient Teafa est renversée et met le feu à la chaumière. L'assassin s'empresse de l'éteindre, car il veut que Móen soit accusé d'un double meurtre. La baguette d'ogam est jetée au feu mais ne brûle pas complètement. Le texte, rapporté par Móen qui a une excellente mémoire, disait : « Eber veut te voir immédiatement. » Sur ce bout noirci, les lettres ER et VEUT sont encore lisibles.

Frère Eadulf souriait devant la simplicité de la reconstitution de Fidelma.

— D'autre part, lui fit-il remarquer, quand Menma a découvert Móen penché sur le corps, il a dit que c'était juste avant le lever du soleil. Or une lampe était allumée au chevet d'Eber.

— Je ne vois pas où est le problème, grommela Dubán, il fait nuit avant le lever du jour.

Eadulf rit.

— Oui, mais pourquoi Móen aurait-il allumé une lampe ? Cela réduit à néant la version qui voudrait qu'il soit entré furtivement pour poignarder Eber pendant son sommeil.

— Sauf à supposer qu'un aveugle a besoin d'une lampe pour s'éclairer, renchérit Fidelma.

— Eber a très bien pu allumer la lampe lui-même, objecta Agdae, afin de laisser entrer Móen et…

— Mais oui, bien sûr, ironisa Fidelma. Eber était réveillé, il a allumé la lampe et a laissé entrer Móen. Puis il est obligeamment retourné dans son lit et a attendu que Móen aille chercher un couteau de chasse, revienne à lui et le poignarde jusqu'à ce que mort s'ensuive. Non, je pense que la version de Móen est nettement plus convaincante. Quand il est entré dans la pièce, Eber avait déjà été assassiné. Le meurtrier s'est arrangé pour envoyer Móen chez Eber, puis s'est retrouvé dans l'obligation de supprimer Teafa. Quant à Eber, il a été tué par quelqu'un qu'il connaissait très bien, puisqu'il a laissé son visiteur entrer dans sa chambre après avoir allumé la lanterne.

— En qui Eber avait-il suffisamment confiance pour l'introduire dans sa chambre ? demanda Agdae. Sa femme ?

Crón poussa un petit cri.

— Accusez-vous ma mère ?

Fidelma observa pensivement Cranat. La veuve d'Eber la fixait d'un air dédaigneux.

— Je m'attendais à ce que vous me poursuiviez de vos allégations répugnantes, dit Cranat d'une voix sifflante. Sœur Fidelma, je vous rappelle que je suis princesse des Déisi. J'ai des amis puissants.

— Votre rang et vos amis ne m'impressionnent guère, Cranat. La loi s'applique à tous sans exception. Mais nous sommes enfin arrivés à l'araignée qui se cache au centre de cette toile aux multiples ramifications.

Crón regardait sa mère d'un air hagard.

— C'est impossible, vous vous fourvoyez !

— Cranat n'a jamais fait mystère de son désir de pouvoir et d'argent, ricana Agdae.

— Vous ne pouvez prouver que Cranat avait des raisons valables de tuer son propre mari, protesta le père Gormán.

— Essayons. Jusqu'à ce que Crón atteigne l'âge de treize ans, Cranat était prête à composer avec sa haine d'Eber en échange d'un train de vie enviable. Quand Teafa l'a informée des turpitudes d'Eber, elle s'est simplement refusée à lui mais a continué de vivre comme une épouse de chef – la richesse avant la vertu.

Eber semblait prêt à tolérer la situation. Peut-être désirait-il garder une épouse pour préserver les apparences ? Dubán m'a informée qu'il y a quelques semaines, une nouvelle querelle avait éclaté entre Teafa et Cranat quand Crón est devenue *tanist*. Au cours de la dispute, Móen a été évoqué. C'est à ce moment-là que Cranat a appris la vérité sur le fils de son mari. A-t-elle eu alors le désir de se venger ?

Fidelma marqua une pause. Plus personne ne soufflait mot.

— La vertu après la richesse. *Quaerenda pecunia primum est virtus poste nummos.* Cranat avait entamé une liaison avec Muadnat. Eber disparu, elle devenait la femme du nouveau chef.

Très excité, frère Eadulf se pencha en avant.

— Móen a dit que la personne qui lui avait donné la baguette d'ogam avait des mains calleuses, comme celles d'un homme. Mais il a senti un parfum de femme. Dignait avait des mains calleuses, elle était proche de Cranat parce qu'elle était des Déisi, et avait accompagné Cranat quand elle avait épousé Eber.

— Seules les femmes d'un certain rang se parfument, le corrigea Dubán.

Crón secouait la tête d'un air incrédule.

— Êtes-vous en train de dire que ma mère était l'associée de Muadnat dans la mine d'or et qu'elle a décidé de tuer mon père pour l'épouser ?

— Cranat avait des motifs de haïr Eber et Móen. Teafa l'avait informée de leur lien de parenté.

Elle marqua une pause.

— Vous lisez le latin, n'est-ce pas ?

— Oui, ma mère me l'a appris.

— C'est ce texte en latin écrit sur une feuille de vélin qui a permis aux derniers éléments de cette affaire de se mettre en place dans mon esprit. Menma, après avoir tué Dignait chez elle, reçut l'ordre d'aller cacher le corps dans une ancienne réserve à provisions souterraine, dans la ferme d'Archú. Puis il devait me donner le parchemin qui signalait où se trouvait le corps. Le texte était rédigé en excellent latin.

— Suis-je accusée à cause de l'excellence de mon latin ? ironisa Cranat.

— Votre ogam est-il aussi bon ? Rappelez-vous les mots de Térence : personne n'a jamais établi de plan où les événements n'aient introduit la nécessité de modifications. Dubán a suivi Menma à la mine, car il l'avait vu en compagnie des prétendus voleurs de bétail. En atteignant l'entrée de la caverne, il entendit le complice de Muadnat donner des instructions à Menma. Dubán entra. Menma bondit sur lui et permit à son chef de s'échapper. J'étais là également et j'ai aperçu sa silhouette fuyant à cheval sur le chemin.

— Et cette silhouette que vous avez entr'aperçue, ce serait donc moi ? ironisa Cranat.

— Elle était revêtue de la cape bicolore.

Crón grimaça un sourire.

— Moi aussi, je porte une telle cape.

— Et moi j'ai vu un cavalier portant un vêtement similaire grimper sur la piste menant à la mine le jour où nous étions à la ferme de Muadnat, intervint Eadulf.

— Accusez-vous Cranat ou sa fille ? tonna le père Gormán. Je n'y comprends plus rien.

— Il y a quelque temps, Crón m'a appris que ce manteau bicolore était porté par tous les chefs d'Araglin ainsi que leurs femmes. Vous en possédez un, n'est-ce pas, Cranat ? Et vous vous parfumez avec une essence de roses.

La veuve d'Eber la fixa d'un air outragé mais Fidelma fit un signe à Gadra.

— Gadra, amenez Móen jusqu'ici.

Puis elle se tourna vers les autres.

— Pour compenser ses déficiences, Móen a développé un odorat particulièrement sensible et il a une très bonne mémoire des odeurs qu'il respire.

Gadra obtempéra, et conduisit son protégé devant l'estrade.

— Père Gormán, venez, je vous prie. Je veux que vous soyez le témoin de cette procédure et témoigniez de la réaction de Móen.

Le prêtre s'avança, surmontant ses réticences. Fidelma se tourna alors vers Gadra.

— Demandez à Móen de sentir de la façon dont je l'instruirai. Dites-lui que je veux savoir s'il reconnaît l'effluve dégagé par la personne qui lui a remis la baguette d'ogam.

Elle tendit sa main que Móen renifla. Cranat avait bondi sur ses pieds.

— Je refuse que cet animal m'approche, protesta-t-elle en reculant d'un pas.

— Vous n'avez pas le choix, lança Fidelma en faisant signe à Dubán d'aller se placer derrière elle.

Móen avait secoué la tête devant le poignet de Fidelma qui, d'un geste, ordonna à Crón de tendre le sien. Móen recommença son manège, écrivit quelque chose sur la paume de Gadra qui secoua la tête.

Cranat cacha ses mains derrière son dos.

— Père Gormán, dit Fidelma, puisque Cranat répugne à se soumettre à cet examen, peut-être pourriez-vous l'aider ? Je suis sûre qu'elle n'opposera aucune objection à ce qu'un prêtre pose la main sur elle.

— Excusez-moi, lady, murmura le père Gormán en se saisissant du bras de la veuve.

Cranat se détourna d'un air dégoûté lorsque Móen huma son poignet.

Une onde d'excitation parcourut la salle tandis que Móen commençait à tracer à toute vitesse des signes sur la paume de Gadra. Le vieil homme parut choqué.

— C'est faux ! cria Cranat. Vous avez monté un complot contre moi pour me discréditer !

Mais le vieil homme ne regardait pas Cranat.

— Ce n'est pas le parfum de la femme qu'il a reconnu, dit Gadra en détachant ses mots tout en fixant le père Gormán d'un air hagard.

Le prêtre était devenu blême.

Le temps qu'il réagisse, Dubán s'était déjà saisi de lui. Mais il fronça les sourcils d'un air contrarié en contemplant les mains de celui qui se débattait en hurlant.

— Móen a dit que la personne à la porte de Teafa avait des mains calleuses. Celles-ci sont aussi douces que celles d'une dame.

Fidelma ne parut pas troublée.

— Vous ne portez pas vos gants de cuir, aujourd'hui, père Gormán ? Voyez-vous, Dubán, hier vous m'avez donné la réponse que je cherchais quand j'ai cru que vous aviez des mains calleuses. Or vous portiez simplement des gants.

Poussant un cri de rage, le père Gormán se libéra de l'étreinte de Dubán, sauta de l'estrade et voulut prendre la fuite mais il n'avait pas parcouru deux toises que des guerriers le maîtrisaient et le traînaient vers la sortie. Le visage déformé par la fureur, il se mit à hurler :

— Et le Christ a dit : « Serpents, engeance de vipères ! comment pourrez-vous échapper à la condamnation de la géhenne[1] ? »

— Un texte des plus appropriés, murmura Eadulf pour masquer sa stupéfaction.

Cranat se laissa retomber sur sa chaise, le visage cramoisi, luttant pour recouvrer sa respiration. Elle toisa Fidelma avec une animosité implacable.

— Vous devrez vous expliquer plus longuement avant que nous ajoutions foi à cette accusation extravagante, articula-t-elle d'une voix glaciale.

1. Matthieu, 23, 33. (*N.d.T.*)

CHAPITRE XXI

Fidelma, qui n'avait pas bougé de place devant l'estrade, les contemplait tous d'un air sombre.

— Il y a peu d'endroits dans les cinq royaumes où j'ai rencontré tant de haine, de fourberie et de tristesse, déclara-t-elle. L'atmosphère délétère qui régnait dans cette vallée a incité Gormán et Menma à commettre leurs forfaits et à trancher le cours de vies humaines.

« Eber était-il à l'origine de cette malignité ou lui aussi une victime ? Nous ne le saurons jamais. Tomnát était sans aucun doute à ranger dans la catégorie des souffre-douleur. L'aide de sa sœur et compagne d'infortune ne suffisait pas, elle aurait pu surmonter son malheur si elle s'était confiée à la seule personne capable de la sauver.

Elle fixa Dubán et le guerrier baissa les yeux sous le feu des yeux verts de la religieuse.

— Teafa aussi a été une victime, mais elle a recouvré sa dignité en sauvant le fils de sa sœur, victime navrante entre toutes.

— Et moi ? demanda Cranat d'une voix dure. Princesse des Déisi, j'ai pourtant été forcée d'épouser ce dépravé.

— Forcée ? Vous vous en êtes assez bien accommodée. Vous n'avez même pas réagi quand Teafa est venue vous avertir que votre mari avait renoué avec ses perversions et mis dans son lit votre propre fille alors âgée de douze ou treize ans !

— C'est faux ! s'écria Crón, le visage blême.

— Vraiment ? Vous en avez trop dit ou pas assez sur le sujet. Il est grand temps que les noirs secrets sortent à la lumière. Teafa a tout de suite compris de quelle façon Eber vous traitait, Crón. Vous deveniez une victime à votre tour. Elle est aussitôt allée prévenir Cranat, la suppliant de divorcer et de vous emmener avec elle. Mais Cranat s'est contentée de reprendre sa liberté et de continuer à vivre ici dans l'aisance et la sécurité. Elle a laissé sa fille se débattre seule dans ce piège. Ce n'est pas Cranat qui a rompu toute relation avec Teafa, mais Teafa avec Cranat.

Un silence pesant s'était abattu sur le siège de l'assemblée.

Fidelma posa alors sur Crón un regard plein de compassion.

— Oui, Crón, vous avez été abusée, mais d'une certaine façon, vous vous êtes rendue maîtresse de la situation. Vous avez utilisé les désirs lascifs de votre père pour acquérir du pouvoir. Il y a quelques semaines, vous vous êtes sentie suffisamment forte pour exiger d'Eber qu'il vous nomme *tanist* et use de son influence pour convaincre le *derbfhine* d'appuyer vos ambitions. Grâce à la corruption, Eber a convaincu tous les membres du conseil de vous soutenir sauf quatre : votre mère et Teafa, qui connaissaient le prix que vous deviez payer, Agdae, le neveu de Muadnat, et Menma, qui était lié à Muadnat en tant que parent, et associé à la gestion de la mine d'or. Je regrette, Crón, mais vous n'êtes pas digne de votre fonction.

Puis elle s'adressa à Dubán.

— Combien de temps votre amour pour Crón durera-t-il, Dubán, si votre amante est destituée de sa position de *tanist* ? Il y a vingt ans, Tomnát a reconnu chez vous une ambition démesurée qui l'a empêchée de vous confier son terrible secret. Maintenant que le

309

même secret, qui cette fois concerne Crón, est devenu public, lui demeurerez-vous fidèle ? Non !

Elle leva la main.

— Ne me répondez pas avant la réunion du *derbfhine* qui décidera si Crón deviendra chef d'Araglin.

Fidelma balaya l'assemblée d'un regard passionné.

— Selon Morann de Tara, le mal n'est jamais qu'une petite graine qui croît et prospère si l'on n'y prend garde, et finit par atteindre la taille d'un chêne. Ici, il a poussé une véritable forêt. C'est chez les jeunes gens comme Archú et Scoth qu'il faut chercher l'espoir d'Araglin.

Elle adressa un sourire soudain à Clídna.

— Et si un havre de moralité existe ici, on le trouvera chez cette femme.

Clídna rougit et baissa la tête tandis qu'Agdae se levait avec des gestes lents.

— Votre jugement sur Araglin est très dur, ma sœur, dit-il d'une voix blanche.

Puis, après avoir jeté un bref coup d'œil à Cranat et à sa fille, il ajouta :

— Mais vous avez bien parlé. Sans nous avoir révélé cependant comment vous en êtes venue à soupçonner le père Gormán, après avoir accumulé tant de griefs contre Cranat.

— En réalité, Cranat faisait une coupable peu crédible dans la mesure où elle avait envoyé un messager à Cashel demandant que mon frère détache un brehon pour mener une investigation officielle.

— Pourquoi a-t-elle agi ainsi ? demanda Eadulf.

— Avant toute chose, Cranat est une princesse des Déisi. Elle craignait que la suspicion entache la réputation de sa maison. Je crois qu'elle pensait sincèrement que Móen avait commis les crimes en apprenant la vérité sur sa naissance, et estimait que la présence d'un brehon prêterait une certaine respectabilité au jugement devant clore cette affaire.

« Et puis un point précis innocentait Cranat. Je l'ai
tu afin d'endormir les soupçons de Gormán et, Dieu
merci, personne ne l'a remarqué.

— En quoi consistait-il ? interrogea Agdae.

— Vous avez oublié que *summa sedes non capit
duos*, le siège le plus élevé ne se partage pas. Crón
devenue *tanist* à la place de Muadnat, l'assassinat
d'Eber ne pouvait servir Cranat, qui espérait devenir la
femme du nouveau chef.

— Mais comment avez-vous rassemblé les preuves
incriminant Gormán ? dit Gadra.

— Eh bien, à Lios Mhór, on m'a présenté Gormán
comme un avocat zélé de la cause de Rome. En réalité, l'objet de sa foi importe peu puisqu'il n'est fon-
damentalement qu'un fanatique intolérant. J'ai appris
qu'il avait fait construire une chapelle à Ard Mór, très
richement ornée et meublée. D'autre part, l'opulence
de la chapelle de Cill Uird frappe tous les visiteurs et,
contrairement à la plupart des prêtres, il avait les moyens
d'équiper et de monter un cheval.

— La prospérité n'est pas un signe de culpabilité,
protesta Cranat.

— Tout dépend de sa provenance. Gormán était
devenu le partenaire de Muadnat dans la mine d'or.
Pourquoi cette association ? Nous ne le saurons jamais
avec exactitude, mais sans doute Muadnat avait-il estimé
que, pour exploiter la mine sans payer de tribut à Eber,
le mieux était encore de passer par le père Gormán. En
tant que prêtre, il ne lui coûtait rien de prétendre qu'il
recevait des cadeaux de la part de ceux qui partageaient
ses convictions. L'or était ensuite échangé contre des
objets destinés aux chapelles d'Ard Mór et Cill Uird.
Mais Muadnat n'avait pas prévu la fièvre qui allait
s'emparer du prêtre car la cupidité n'épargne pas les
hommes de Dieu.

— Mais pourquoi a-t-il tué Eber et Teafa ? s'étonna
Crón, surmontant le ressentiment qu'elle nourrissait à

l'égard de Fidelma pour avoir révélé la teneur de sa relation avec son père.

— Mettez cela sur le compte de son fanatisme sectaire. Quand il apprit le nom du père de Móen, il fut transporté de fureur et jugea qu'Eber devait être expédié dans l'enfer tel qu'il le concevait et Móen, fruit de l'inceste, puni par une accusation de meurtre. En ce qui concerne Teafa, j'ai déjà expliqué qu'il l'avait tuée pour la réduire au silence.

— Mais comment a-t-il appris que Móen était le fils d'Eber alors que moi-même j'avais été tenue dans l'ignorance de cette filiation ?

Fidelma adressa à Cranat un regard empreint de dureté.

— Voilà une question dont votre mère connaît la réponse. Cranat, il y a deux semaines, Dubán vous a vue vous disputer avec Teafa. Puis vous vous êtes rendue directement à l'église. En découvrant que Crón avait utilisé sa relation avec son père pour devenir *tanist*, Teafa était venue vous trouver pour que vous mettiez un terme à ce scandale et, par la même occasion, elle vous a appris la vérité sur l'origine de Móen.

— En tant que prêtre, le père Gormán avait le droit de savoir, répliqua Cranat.

— Oui, mais Gormán est un fanatique. Saisi d'une terrible colère, il est allé trouver Eber et Teafa pour s'expliquer avec eux. Crítán a été le témoin de la confrontation et il a vu Eber frapper le prêtre. C'est alors que Gormán a décidé de le tuer.

— Que se serait-il passé si Móen n'avait pas reconnu le parfum d'encens ? réfléchit Eadulf. J'aurais pensé que cette senteur lui était familière et qu'il aurait immédiatement fait le rapprochement avec la chapelle.

Fidelma secoua la tête.

— Gormán nous a dit qu'il refusait l'entrée du lieu de culte à Móen et qu'il fuyait le garçon comme la peste.

Voilà pourquoi Móen n'a pas été capable de reconnaître cette odeur avant aujourd'hui.

— Mais pourquoi le père Gormán a-t-il voulu la mort de mon oncle ? s'étonna Agdae. Il était pourtant son associé dans la mine illégale.

— J'en ai brièvement mentionné la raison auparavant. Muadnat attirait l'attention sur lui à cause de son esprit procédurier et Gormán prit peur. Ce comportement pouvait mener à la découverte de la mine vu qu'un nombre croissant de personnes s'intéressait à cet endroit. Or Menma était l'homme de Gormán, non de Muadnat. Poussé par le lucre, le prêtre a donc ordonné au vacher de tuer Muadnat, puis Morna et Dignait.

— Comment avez-vous compris que Menma était aux ordres de Gormán ?

— Ils entretenaient des relations étroites, ce qui m'avait paru bizarre. Une fois, je les ai vus se quereller. Et quand Archú a prévenu Gormán qu'il désirait intenter un procès à Muadnat, le prêtre lui a conseillé de faire valoir ses droits à Lios Mhór. J'ai trouvé cela curieux, jusqu'à ce que je comprenne qu'en agissant ainsi, il empêchait Eber de s'intéresser de trop près à l'affaire. D'autre part, Gormán avait indiqué à Archú la route la plus longue pour se rendre à Lios Mhór. Certainement pour éviter qu'il ne tombe sur un convoi transportant de l'or à Ard Mór par un itinéraire plus court.

« Gormán découvrit alors que Morna, un des mineurs qu'il employait, avait apporté un caillou de la mine à son frère, Bressal. Menma reçut l'instruction de tuer Morna et de détruire l'auberge. L'excuse des hors-la-loi qui infestaient la région servirait de couverture.

« D'autres indices m'ont conduite à Gormán. À la ferme de Muadnat, Eadulf aperçoit une silhouette élancée vêtue d'une cape bicolore qui s'évanouit dans les collines. Quelques instants plus tard, Gormán apparaît sans cape. Or je savais que Gormán possédait une cape bicolore car j'en avais vu une dans sa sacristie. Et ses vêtements étaient imprégnés du lourd parfum de l'encens qu'il utilisait dans son église. D'autre part, il portait des gants. J'en tirai alors les conclusions que je vous ai exposées tout à l'heure.

« La nuit avant que le pauvre frère Eadulf ne mange les champignons vénéneux, Gormán m'entendit confier à Crón que je nommerais le nom du meurtrier le lendemain. Tôt le matin, il se glissa dans la cuisine et disposa de fausses morilles dans les écuelles. Surpris par Dignait, il comprit que quand la rumeur d'empoisonnement se répandrait, elle n'hésiterait pas à le mettre en cause pour dégager sa propre responsabilité. À moins qu'il n'ait prévu dès le début de lui faire porter le blâme. Toujours est-il que Menma fut chargé de la réduire au silence et Gormán donna également des instructions sur l'endroit où transporter le corps. Il était l'une des rares personnes connaissant l'existence de cette réserve à provisions creusée sous la grange d'Archú : Archú m'a rapporté qu'autrefois, il s'était produit un accident mortel et, à l'époque, Gormán avait conseillé de condamner l'entrée de cette cave. Autre indice : Gormán écrivait le latin et l'ogam. En ce qui me concerne, tout devenait clair.

Fidelma marqua une pause.

— Un facteur décisif confirma mes observations : Gormán avait appris que Móen était né d'une relation incestueuse d'Eber avec Tomnát. Et il laissa échapper une allusion sur ce sujet alors que nous discutions ensemble. Sa folie ne pouvait le tolérer, ce qui explique les assassinats d'Eber et Teafa, nullement liés à la mine d'or.

Trois jours plus tard, Fidelma et Eadulf s'arrêtaient à l'hôtellerie des Étoiles pour apprendre à Bressal la mort de son frère. L'aubergiste parut choqué mais résigné.

— Quand il n'a pas réapparu, je me suis bien douté qu'il était mort. Mon frère rêvait de devenir riche afin de passer le reste de sa vie dans l'oisiveté alors que l'inaction l'aurait rendu malheureux. Je regrette tellement qu'il n'ait pas pu le découvrir par lui-même !

Fidelma hocha la tête.

— *Auri sacra fames* – la soif de l'or détruit plus qu'elle ne crée. Le bienheureux Matthieu n'a-t-il pas écrit : « Ne vous amassez point de trésors sur la terre, où la mite et le ver consument, où les voleurs percent et cambriolent[1] » ?

Bressal eut un sourire triste.

— Priez pour le repos de Morna, ma sœur.

Leur mission terminée, les deux religieux prirent congé de l'hôtelier et chevauchèrent à travers bois pour rejoindre la route principale qui les mènerait à Cashel. Au cours des trois derniers jours passés au *rath* d'Araglin après les révélations de Fidelma, ils avaient appris que les mineurs avaient été retrouvés et la provision d'or de Gormán, cachée dans la chapelle d'Ard Mór, confisquée par le brehon local en attendant le résultat du procès de Gormán à Cashel. Mais pour finir, ce procès n'aurait pas lieu. Avec sa générosité coutumière, Fidelma avait donné son autorisation pour que le père Gormán soit emprisonné dans la sacristie de sa chapelle. Le jour suivant son incarcération, Gormán avait avalé une provision de fausses morilles et il était mort dans les quatre heures. Frère Eadulf, qui se sentait encore un peu fragile, estima qu'il s'agissait là d'une fin appropriée.

Après une réunion en urgence du *derbfhine* de la famille d'Eber, Agdae fut désigné *tanist* temporaire d'Araglin. Seule Crón protesta. À l'évidence, elle ne serait pas confirmée dans sa fonction de chef. Dubán n'avait pas attendu les résultats du conseil pour seller

---

1. Matthieu, 6, 19. *(N.d.T.)*

son cheval et disparaître dans les montagnes. Quant à Cranat, après avoir rassemblé quelques possessions, elle s'en était retournée au pays des Déisi.

Ce fut Eadulf qui eut le mot de la fin alors qu'ils cheminaient tranquillement au rythme de leurs chevaux.

— Je ne regretterai pas cet endroit. Après tous ces événements, j'ai grande envie de me baigner dans l'eau fraîche et pure d'une rivière.

Alors qu'ils arrivaient à la croisée des chemins, Fidelma aperçut deux silhouettes familières qui avançaient à pied sur la route de Lios Mhór : un vieillard aux épaules légèrement voûtées conduisant un jeune homme par la main.

— Gadra ! s'écria Fidelma.

Le vieil homme s'arrêta et ils virent ses doigts tambouriner sur la paume de Móen avant qu'il ne se tourne vers eux.

— Que votre voyage soit béni, mon enfant, dit-il en souriant à la jeune femme.

Puis il se tourna vers Eadulf.

— Ainsi que le vôtre, frère saxon.

Fidelma sauta à bas de son étalon.

— Nous nous demandions où vous étiez passé et regrettions de ne pas avoir eu l'occasion de vous saluer. Où donc vous dirigez-vous en compagnie de Móen ?

— À Lios Mhór.

— Au monastère ?

— Craignez-vous qu'un vieux païen dans mon genre ne soit pas le bienvenu dans une abbaye ?

— La maison du Christ est ouverte à tous. Mais je dois confesser que votre décision me surprend un peu.

— J'aurais préféré rejoindre mon ermitage dans les montagnes mais le garçon a besoin de moi.

— Ah, soupira Eadulf, j'admire votre sacrifice, mais pour Móen, un cloître offre une meilleure protection que la vie en pleine nature.

316

Gadra lui adressa un regard amusé.

— Il a surtout besoin de la compagnie de personnes capables de communiquer avec lui. Quand j'aurai enseigné ma méthode aux moines, j'aurai rempli mon devoir auprès de Teafa et Tomnát. Je pourrai alors suivre ma destinée et Móen la sienne.

— Voilà un geste généreux, dit Fidelma.

— Généreux ?

Gadra secoua la tête.

— En réalité, j'accomplis un devoir sacré envers l'intelligence remarquable de Móen. Ce garçon a démontré qu'il était doté d'un sens olfactif exceptionnel, et je suis certain que cette qualité peut être employée à des fins utiles.

— Dans quel sens l'entendez-vous ? demanda Eadulf, piqué par la curiosité.

— Eh bien, il peut rendre de grands services en composant des parfums et en identifiant les plantes qu'il mélangera dans les proportions requises pour fabriquer des remèdes.

— Donc vous vivrez avec Móen à Lios Mhór ?

— Pour l'instant.

— Et qui sait, peut-être que sous une influence aussi bénéfique vous deviendrez chrétien ? lança Fidelma d'un air malicieux.

— Cela m'étonnerait beaucoup, répondit Gadra en riant. J'ai vu à l'œuvre votre charité et votre amour chrétiens, et j'avoue qu'ils ne m'ont pas convaincu.

— Je suis certain que si vous écoutez les prêches des frères et des sœurs de Lios Mhór, vous aussi vous rejoindrez la parole de vérité, déclara Eadulf sur un ton solennel.

— Votre parole ou celle de Gormán ? lâcha Gadra d'un air faussement innocent.

— Ayez la foi ou la vérité vous échappera.

Gadra leva les yeux vers le ciel d'un bleu éclatant.

— Ne vous est-il jamais venu à l'esprit, frère saxon, que quand viendra le moment de passer dans

317

l'autre monde, les discussions véhémentes qui nous occupent en cet instant nous apparaîtront comme un grand malentendu ?

— Jamais ! s'écria Eadulf, outré.

Le vieil ermite l'observa un instant en silence.

— Alors votre foi est aveugle, conclut-il, et vous avez renoncé à votre libre arbitre, ce qui va à l'encontre de l'ordre spirituel de ce monde.

Fidelma posa la main sur le bras d'Eadulf pour le faire taire.

— Moi, je vous comprends, Gadra, car nous sommes issus des mêmes ancêtres. Avec le temps, les coutumes changent, nous avançons avec elles et il n'est point de retour en arrière possible. Mais je crois que nous partageons les mêmes convictions.

— Soyez bénie, ma sœur. Tous les chemins ne mènent-ils pas au centre des choses ?

C'est alors que Móen se manifesta.

— Il dit qu'il est désolé de ne pas avoir pris congé de vous avant de partir, traduisit Gadra. Mais il avait le sentiment d'avoir occupé le centre de votre attention pendant trop longtemps et ne voulait pas vous déranger davantage. Il pense que vous connaissez ses sentiments et se souvient qu'il vous doit la vie.

— Il ne me doit rien. Je suis une servante de la loi.

— Il imagine la loi comme une cage qui emprisonne ceux qui n'ont pas le pouvoir de s'acheter la clé.

— N'est-il pas mal placé pour émettre un tel jugement ? s'exclama Eadulf sur un ton indigné.

— Ce n'est pas la loi mais la juriste qui a donné la clé, interpréta Gadra.

— Le bienheureux Timothée a écrit dans les Écritures saintes que la loi est bénéfique si on ne la détourne pas de son but, répliqua Fidelma. Et un Grec érudit, Héraclite, a déclaré qu'un peuple devait lutter pour sa législation comme s'il construisait un mur pour se défendre contre une armée ennemie.

— Nous ne partageons pas le même point de vue car, pour moi, la loi ne peut pas édicter la moralité. Mais je vous remercie pour ce que vous avez fait. Adieu, Fidelma de Kildare. Adieu, frère saxon. Que la paix soit avec vous.

Le vieil homme s'éloigna avec Móen sur le chemin qui traversait la forêt, et Fidelma se sentit brusquement mélancolique.

— J'aurais aimé le convaincre que nos lois sont sacrées, le résultat de bien des siècles de sagesse humaine et d'expérience pour protéger et punir. Si je n'y croyais pas, je ne serais pas avocate.

Eadulf hocha la tête.

— Ce ne sont pas les lois qui sont corrompues mais ceux qui les appliquent.

Fidelma monta sur son étalon.

— D'après Eschyle, nous devons empêcher que le mal ne l'emporte par un excès de subtilités juridiques. Cela signifie qu'il faut soumettre la loi au bon sens et à son propre jugement. Saint Matthieu a très bien résumé ce dilemme en nous prévenant de ne pas juger si nous ne voulons pas être jugés.

Eadulf grimpa à son tour sur son cheval et ils prirent la route du nord qui menait à Cashel.

Impression réalisée sur Presse Offset par

BRODARD & TAUPIN

GROUPE CPI

La Flèche (Sarthe), 32713
N° d'édition : 3787
Dépôt légal : décembre 2005

Imprimé en France